W.I.T.C.H.

Will Irma Taranee Cornelia Hay Lin

Part II. Nerissa's Revenge
Volume 2

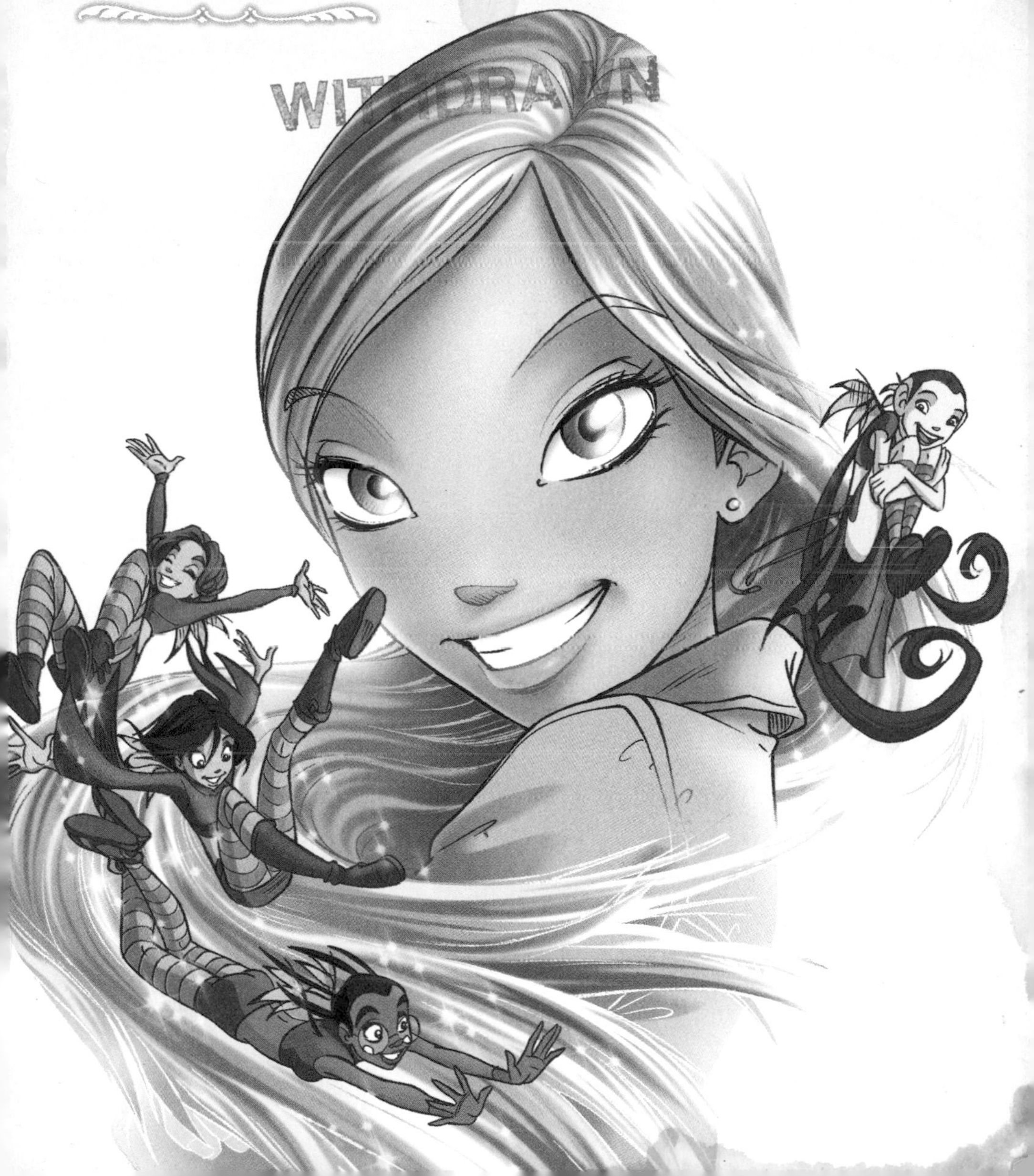

W.i.t.c.h.

Will   Irma   Taranee   Cornelia   Hay Lin

Part II. Nerissa's Revenge
Volume 2

CONTENTS

17

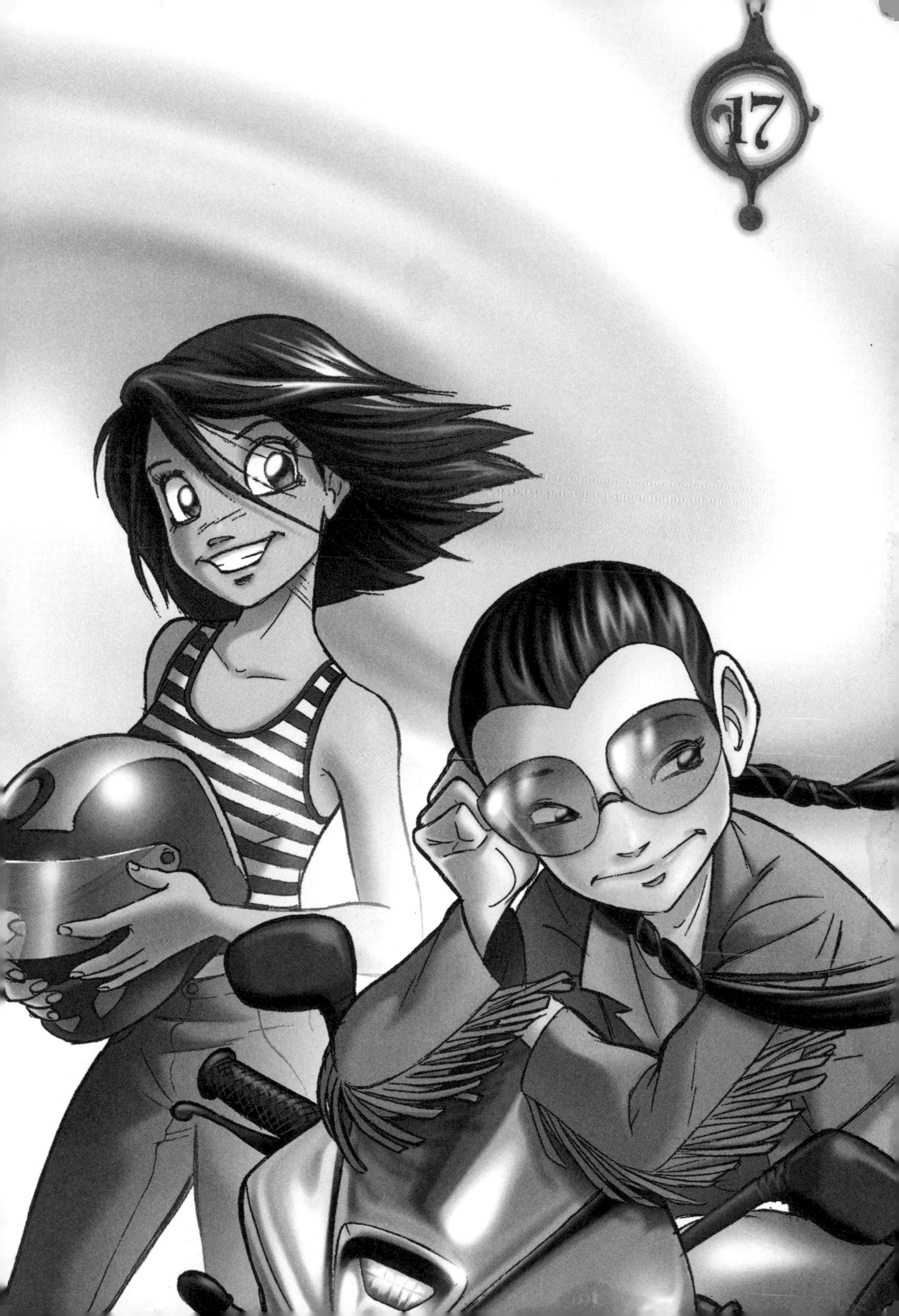

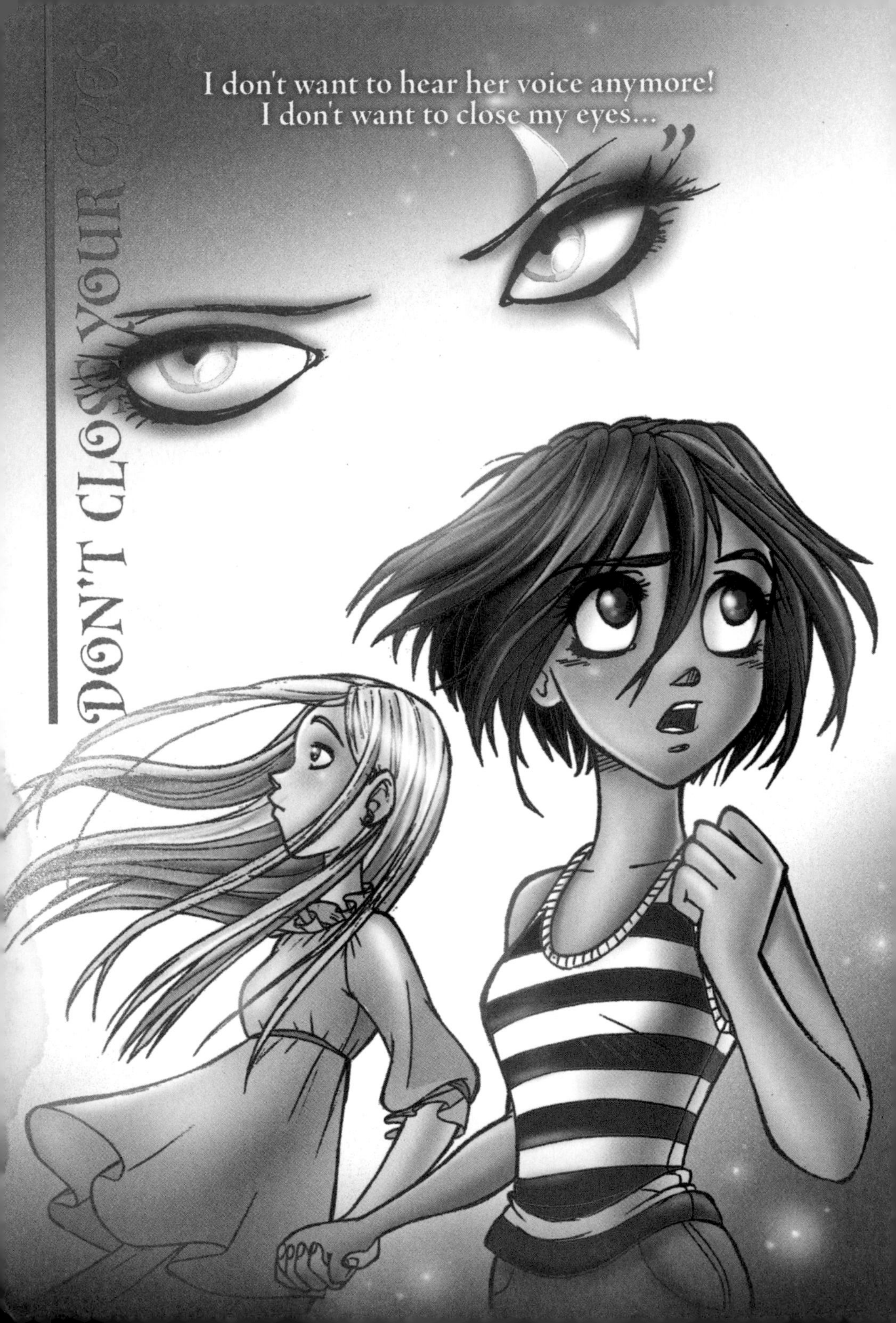
DON'T CLOSE YOUR EYES
I don't want to hear her voice anymore!
I don't want to close my eyes...

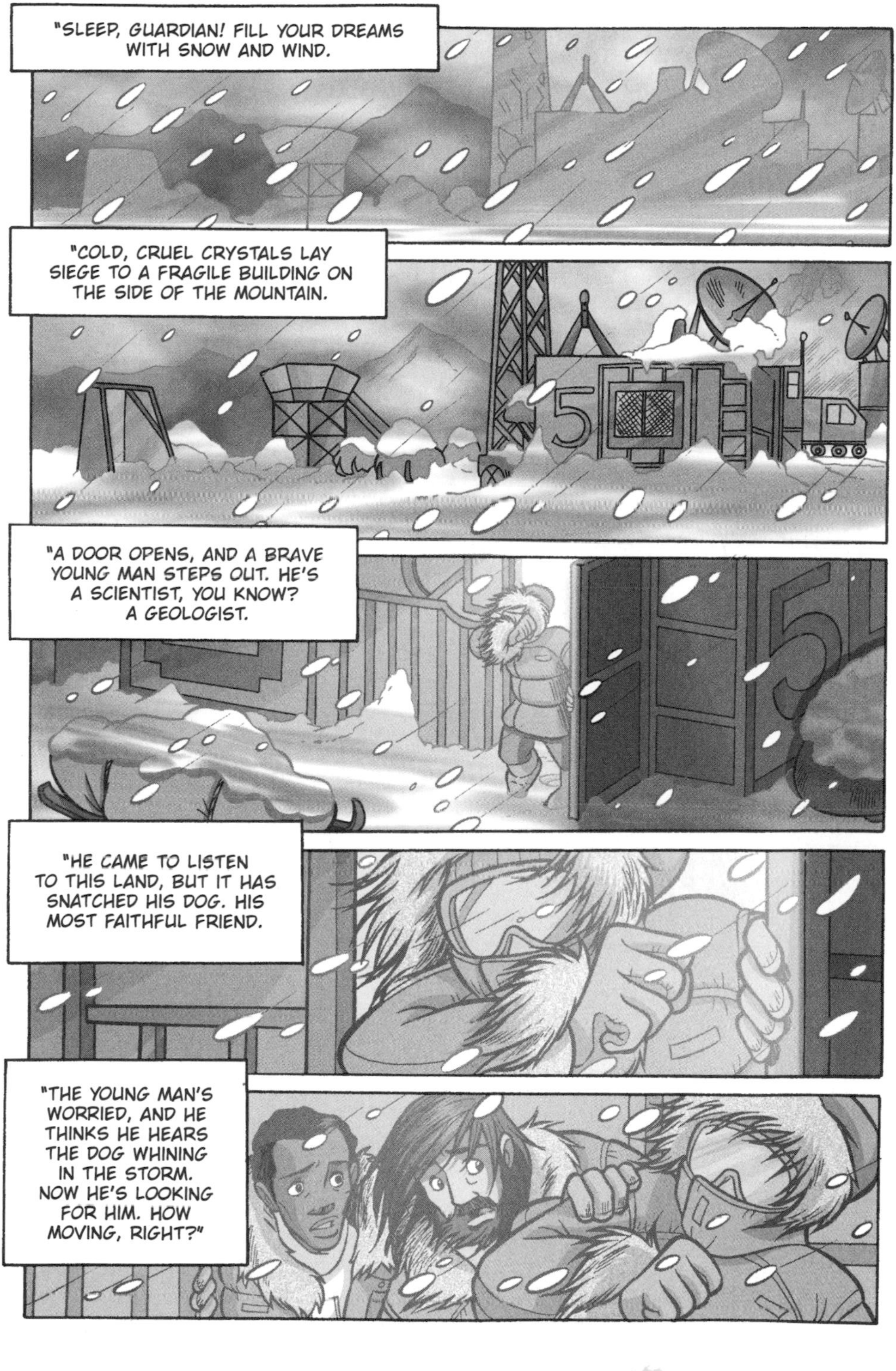
"SLEEP, GUARDIAN! FILL YOUR DREAMS WITH SNOW AND WIND.
"COLD, CRUEL CRYSTALS LAY SIEGE TO A FRAGILE BUILDING ON THE SIDE OF THE MOUNTAIN.
"A DOOR OPENS, AND A BRAVE YOUNG MAN STEPS OUT. HE'S A SCIENTIST, YOU KNOW? A GEOLOGIST.
"HE CAME TO LISTEN TO THIS LAND, BUT IT HAS SNATCHED HIS DOG. HIS MOST FAITHFUL FRIEND.
"THE YOUNG MAN'S WORRIED, AND HE THINKS HE HEARS THE DOG WHINING IN THE STORM. NOW HE'S LOOKING FOR HIM. HOW MOVING, RIGHT?"

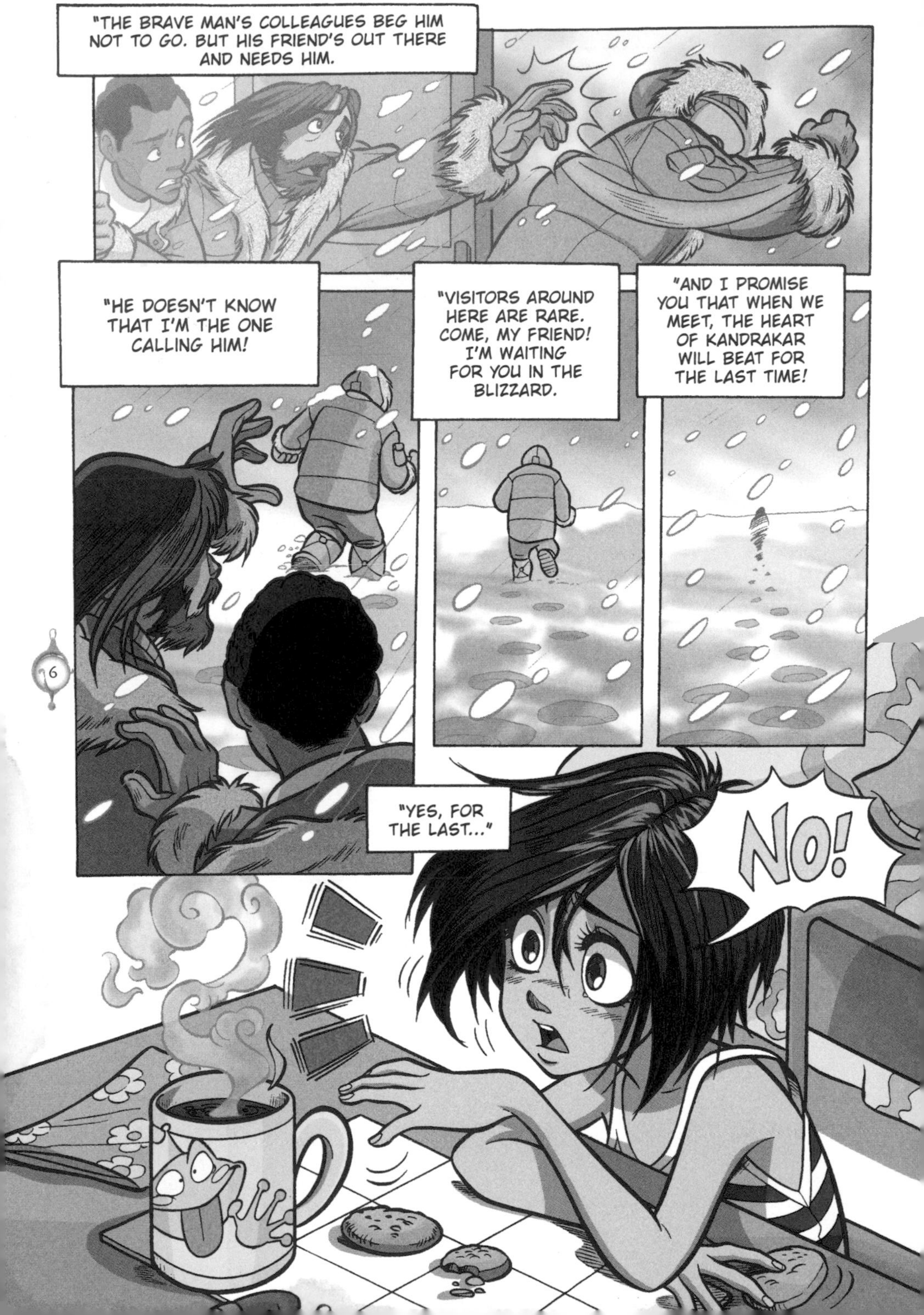
"THE BRAVE MAN'S COLLEAGUES BEG HIM NOT TO GO. BUT HIS FRIEND'S OUT THERE AND NEEDS HIM.
"HE DOESN'T KNOW THAT I'M THE ONE CALLING HIM!
"VISITORS AROUND HERE ARE RARE. COME, MY FRIEND! I'M WAITING FOR YOU IN THE BLIZZARD.
"AND I PROMISE YOU THAT WHEN WE MEET, THE HEART OF KANDRAKAR WILL BEAT FOR THE LAST TIME!
"YES, FOR THE LAST..."
NO!

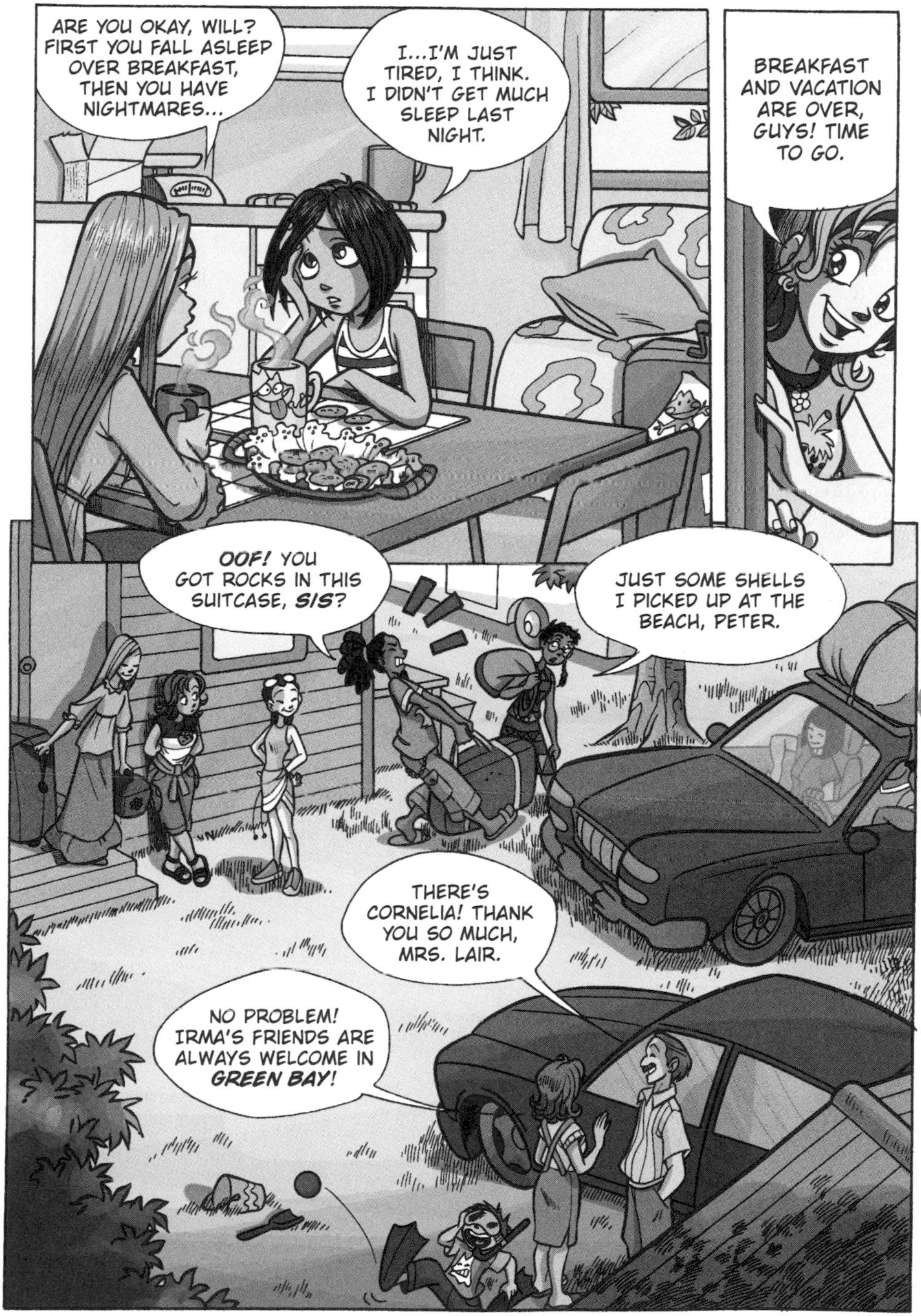
ARE YOU OKAY, WILL? FIRST YOU FALL ASLEEP OVER BREAKFAST, THEN YOU HAVE NIGHTMARES...
I...I'M JUST TIRED, I THINK. I DIDN'T GET MUCH SLEEP LAST NIGHT.
BREAKFAST AND VACATION ARE OVER, GUYS! TIME TO GO.
OOF! YOU GOT ROCKS IN THIS SUITCASE, SIS?
JUST SOME SHELLS I PICKED UP AT THE BEACH, PETER.
THERE'S CORNELIA! THANK YOU SO MUCH, MRS. LAIR.
NO PROBLEM! IRMA'S FRIENDS ARE ALWAYS WELCOME IN GREEN BAY!

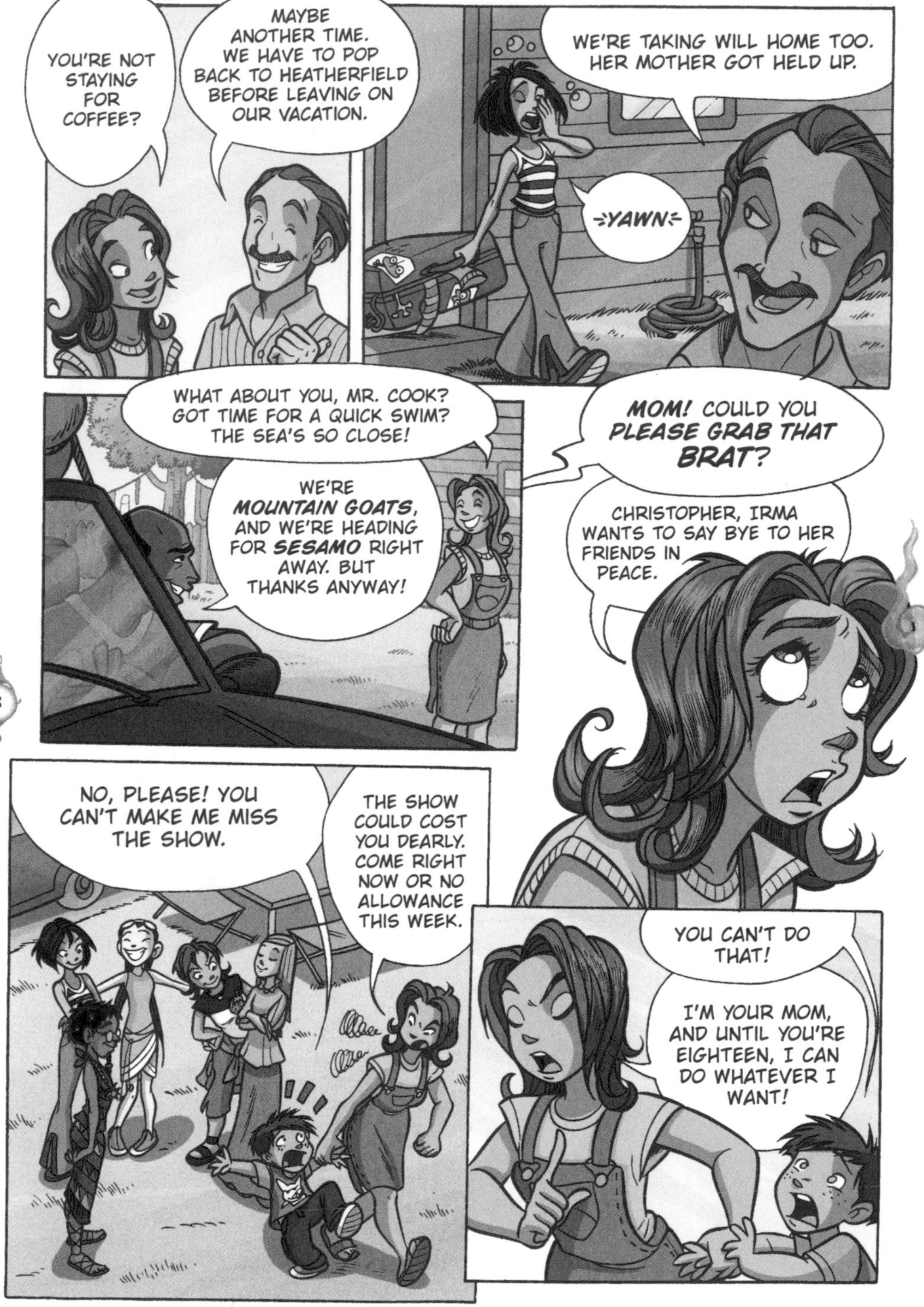
YOU'RE NOT STAYING FOR COFFEE?
MAYBE ANOTHER TIME. WE HAVE TO POP BACK TO HEATHERFIELD BEFORE LEAVING ON OUR VACATION.
WE'RE TAKING WILL HOME TOO. HER MOTHER GOT HELD UP.
YAWN
WHAT ABOUT YOU, MR. COOK? GOT TIME FOR A QUICK SWIM? THE SEA'S SO CLOSE!
WE'RE MOUNTAIN GOATS, AND WE'RE HEADING FOR SESAMO RIGHT AWAY. BUT THANKS ANYWAY!
MOM! COULD YOU PLEASE GRAB THAT BRAT?
CHRISTOPHER, IRMA WANTS TO SAY BYE TO HER FRIENDS IN PEACE.
NO, PLEASE! YOU CAN'T MAKE ME MISS THE SHOW.
THE SHOW COULD COST YOU DEARLY. COME RIGHT NOW OR NO ALLOWANCE THIS WEEK.
YOU CAN'T DO THAT!
I'M YOUR MOM, AND UNTIL YOU'RE EIGHTEEN, I CAN DO WHATEVER I WANT!

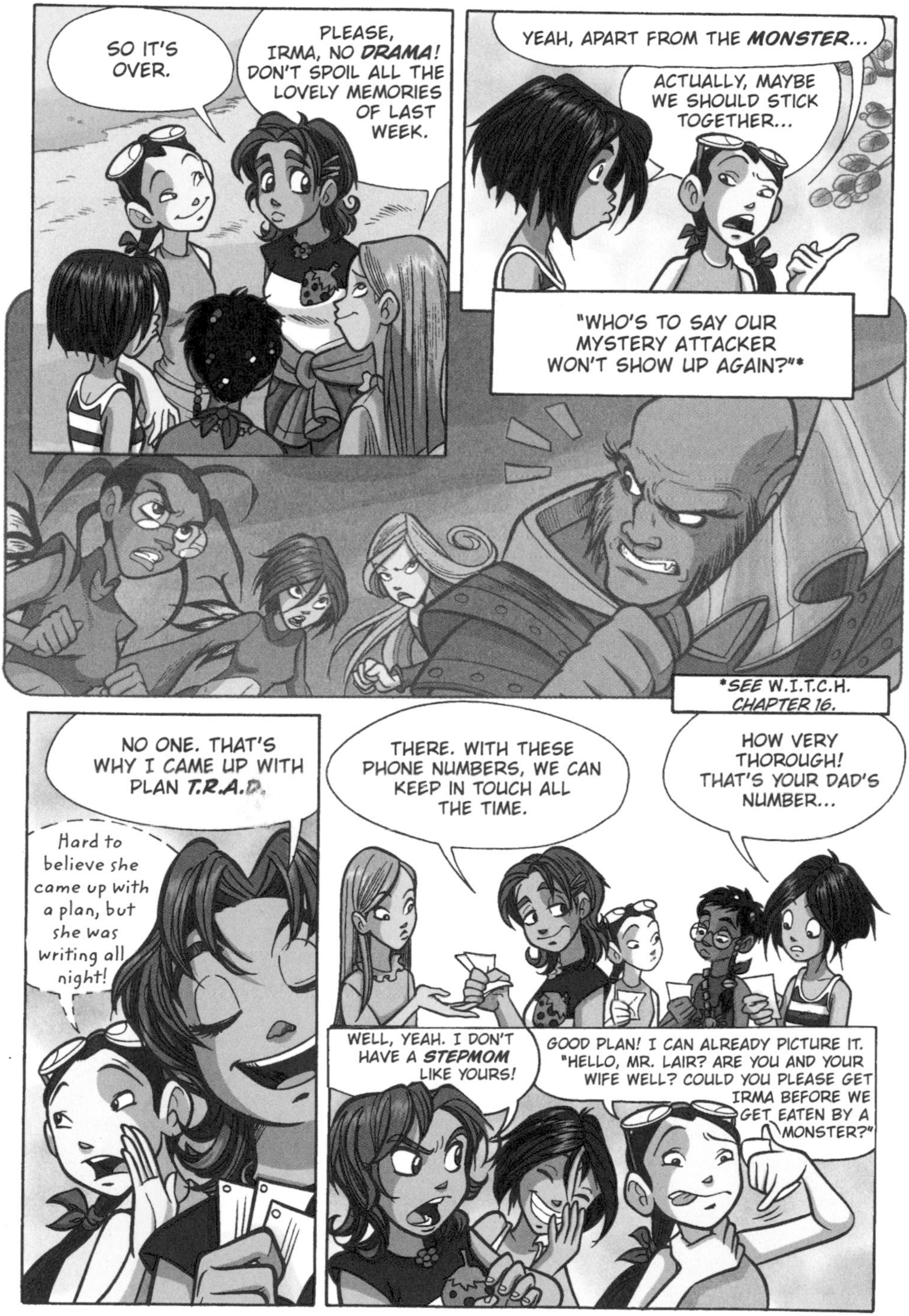

SO IT'S OVER.
PLEASE, IRMA, NO DRAMA! DON'T SPOIL ALL THE LOVELY MEMORIES OF LAST WEEK.
YEAH, APART FROM THE MONSTER...
ACTUALLY, MAYBE WE SHOULD STICK TOGETHER...
"WHO'S TO SAY OUR MYSTERY ATTACKER WON'T SHOW UP AGAIN?"*
*SEE W.I.T.C.H. CHAPTER 16.
NO ONE. THAT'S WHY I CAME UP WITH PLAN T.R.A.D.
Hard to believe she came up with a plan, but she was writing all night!
THERE. WITH THESE PHONE NUMBERS, WE CAN KEEP IN TOUCH ALL THE TIME.
HOW VERY THOROUGH! THAT'S YOUR DAD'S NUMBER...
WELL, YEAH. I DON'T HAVE A STEPMOM LIKE YOURS!
GOOD PLAN! I CAN ALREADY PICTURE IT. "HELLO, MR. LAIR? ARE YOU AND YOUR WIFE WELL? COULD YOU PLEASE GET IRMA BEFORE WE GET EATEN BY A MONSTER?"

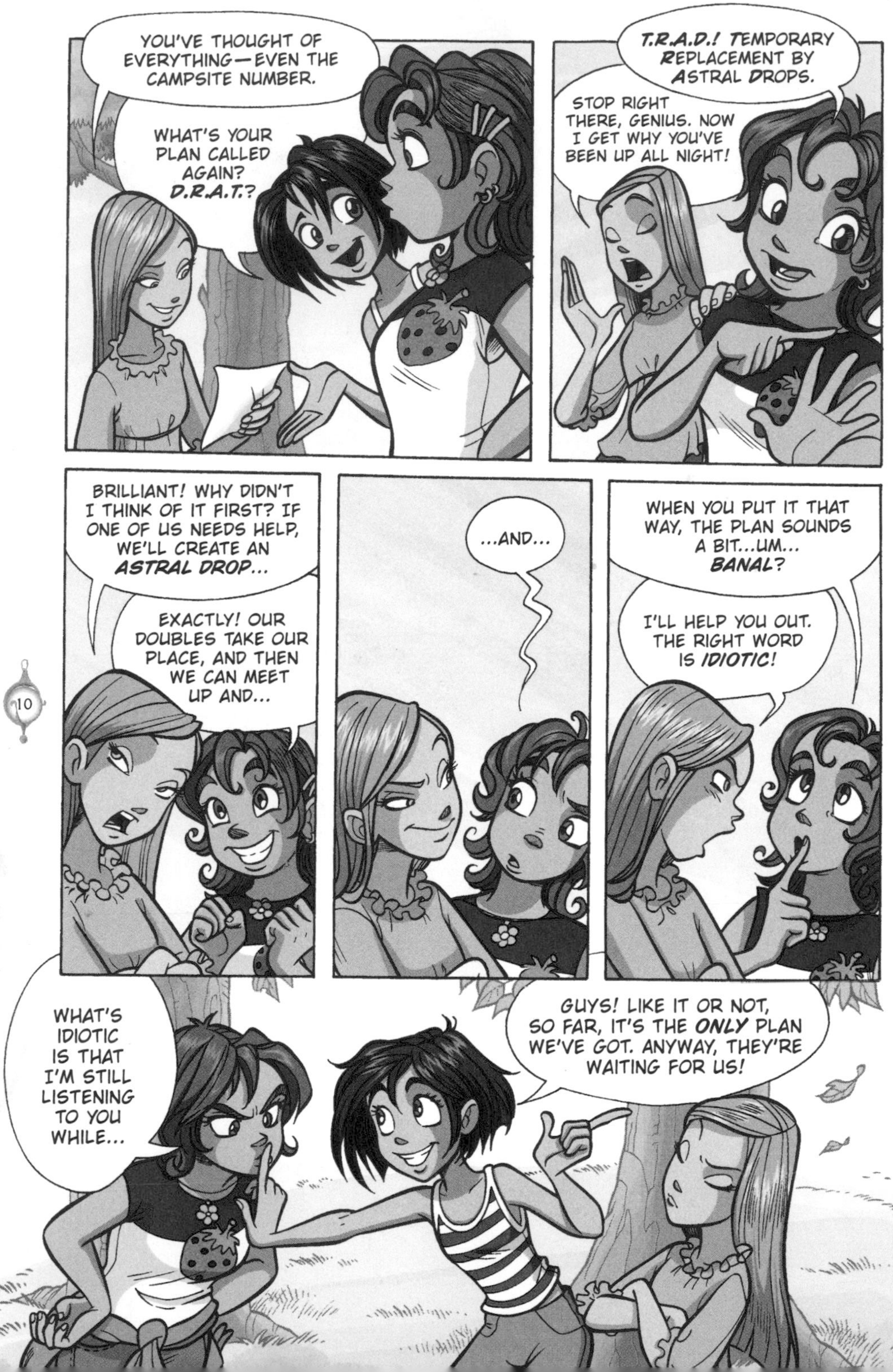

YOU'VE THOUGHT OF EVERYTHING—EVEN THE CAMPSITE NUMBER.
WHAT'S YOUR PLAN CALLED AGAIN? *D.R.A.T.*?
*T.R.A.D.! T*EMPORARY *R*EPLACEMENT BY *A*STRAL *D*ROPS.
STOP RIGHT THERE, GENIUS. NOW I GET WHY YOU'VE BEEN UP ALL NIGHT!
BRILLIANT! WHY DIDN'T I THINK OF IT FIRST? IF ONE OF US NEEDS HELP, WE'LL CREATE AN *ASTRAL DROP*...
EXACTLY! OUR DOUBLES TAKE OUR PLACE, AND THEN WE CAN MEET UP AND...
...AND...
WHEN YOU PUT IT THAT WAY, THE PLAN SOUNDS A BIT...UM... *BANAL*?
I'LL HELP YOU OUT. THE RIGHT WORD IS *IDIOTIC*!
WHAT'S IDIOTIC IS THAT I'M STILL LISTENING TO YOU WHILE...
GUYS! LIKE IT OR NOT, SO FAR, IT'S THE *ONLY* PLAN WE'VE GOT. ANYWAY, THEY'RE WAITING FOR US!

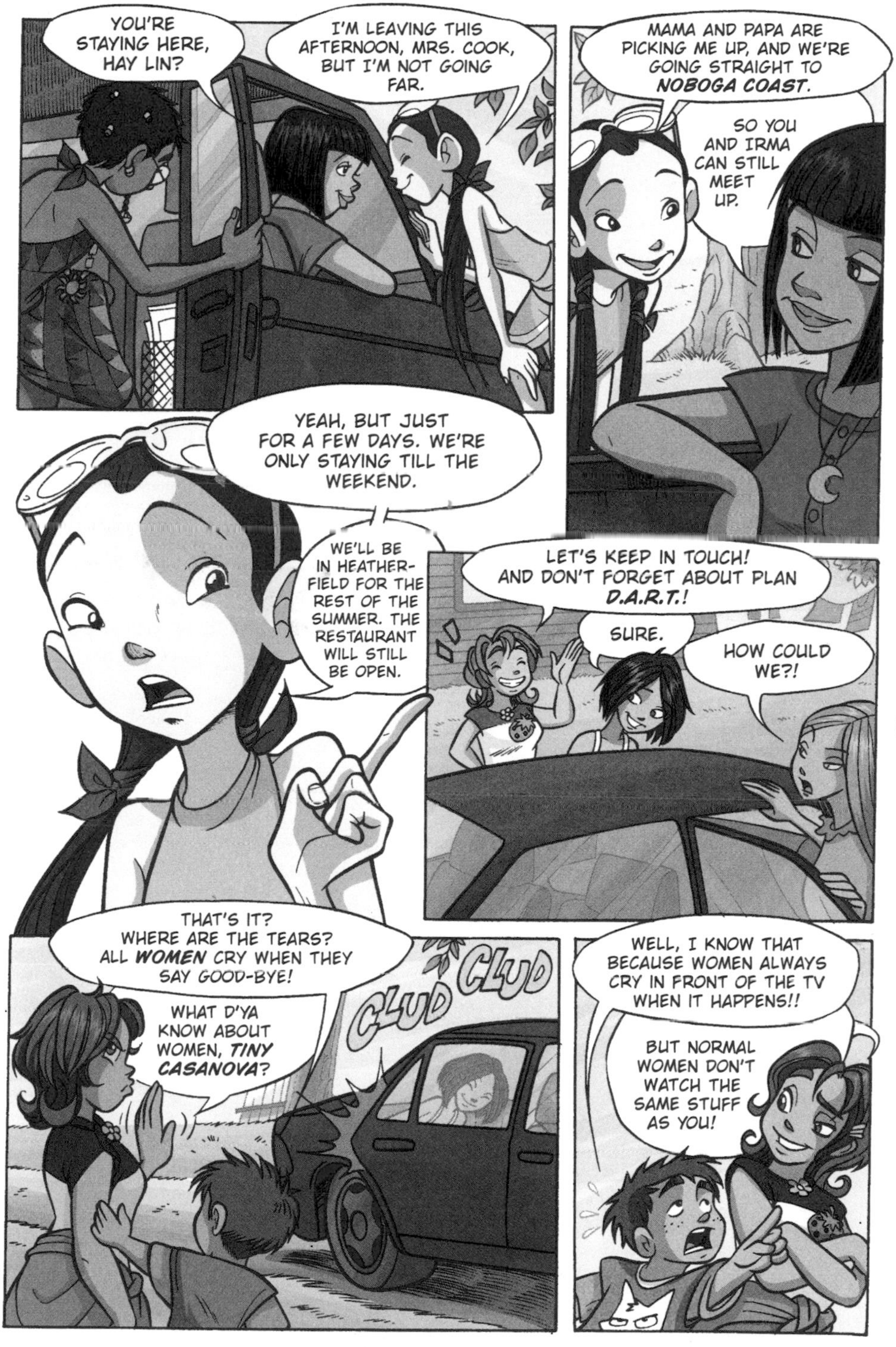
YOU'RE STAYING HERE, HAY LIN?
I'M LEAVING THIS AFTERNOON, MRS. COOK, BUT I'M NOT GOING FAR.
MAMA AND PAPA ARE PICKING ME UP, AND WE'RE GOING STRAIGHT TO NOBOGA COAST.
SO YOU AND IRMA CAN STILL MEET UP.
YEAH, BUT JUST FOR A FEW DAYS. WE'RE ONLY STAYING TILL THE WEEKEND.
WE'LL BE IN HEATHER-FIELD FOR THE REST OF THE SUMMER. THE RESTAURANT WILL STILL BE OPEN.
LET'S KEEP IN TOUCH! AND DON'T FORGET ABOUT PLAN D.A.R.T.!
SURE.
HOW COULD WE?!
THAT'S IT? WHERE ARE THE TEARS? ALL WOMEN CRY WHEN THEY SAY GOOD-BYE!
WHAT D'YA KNOW ABOUT WOMEN, TINY CASANOVA?
CLUD CLUD
WELL, I KNOW THAT BECAUSE WOMEN ALWAYS CRY IN FRONT OF THE TV WHEN IT HAPPENS!!
BUT NORMAL WOMEN DON'T WATCH THE SAME STUFF AS YOU!

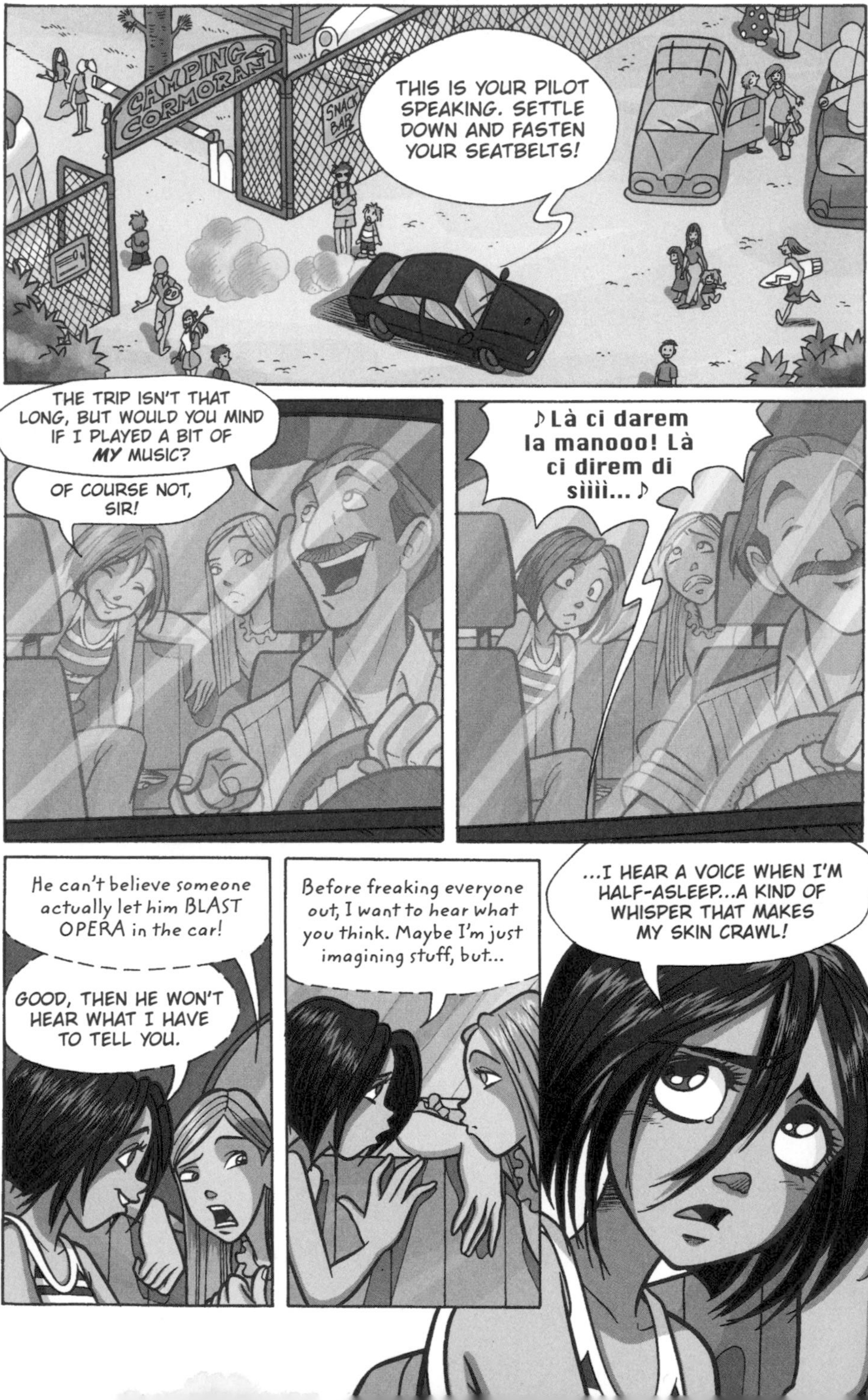
CAMPING CORMORANT
SNACK BAR
THIS IS YOUR PILOT SPEAKING. SETTLE DOWN AND FASTEN YOUR SEATBELTS!
THE TRIP ISN'T THAT LONG, BUT WOULD YOU MIND IF I PLAYED A BIT OF *MY* MUSIC?
OF COURSE NOT, SIR!
♪ Là ci darem la manooo! Là ci direm di sììì... ♪
He can't believe someone actually let him BLAST OPERA in the car!
GOOD, THEN HE WON'T HEAR WHAT I HAVE TO TELL YOU.
Before freaking everyone out, I want to hear what you think. Maybe I'm just imagining stuff, but...
...I HEAR A VOICE WHEN I'M HALF-ASLEEP...A KIND OF WHISPER THAT MAKES MY SKIN CRAWL!

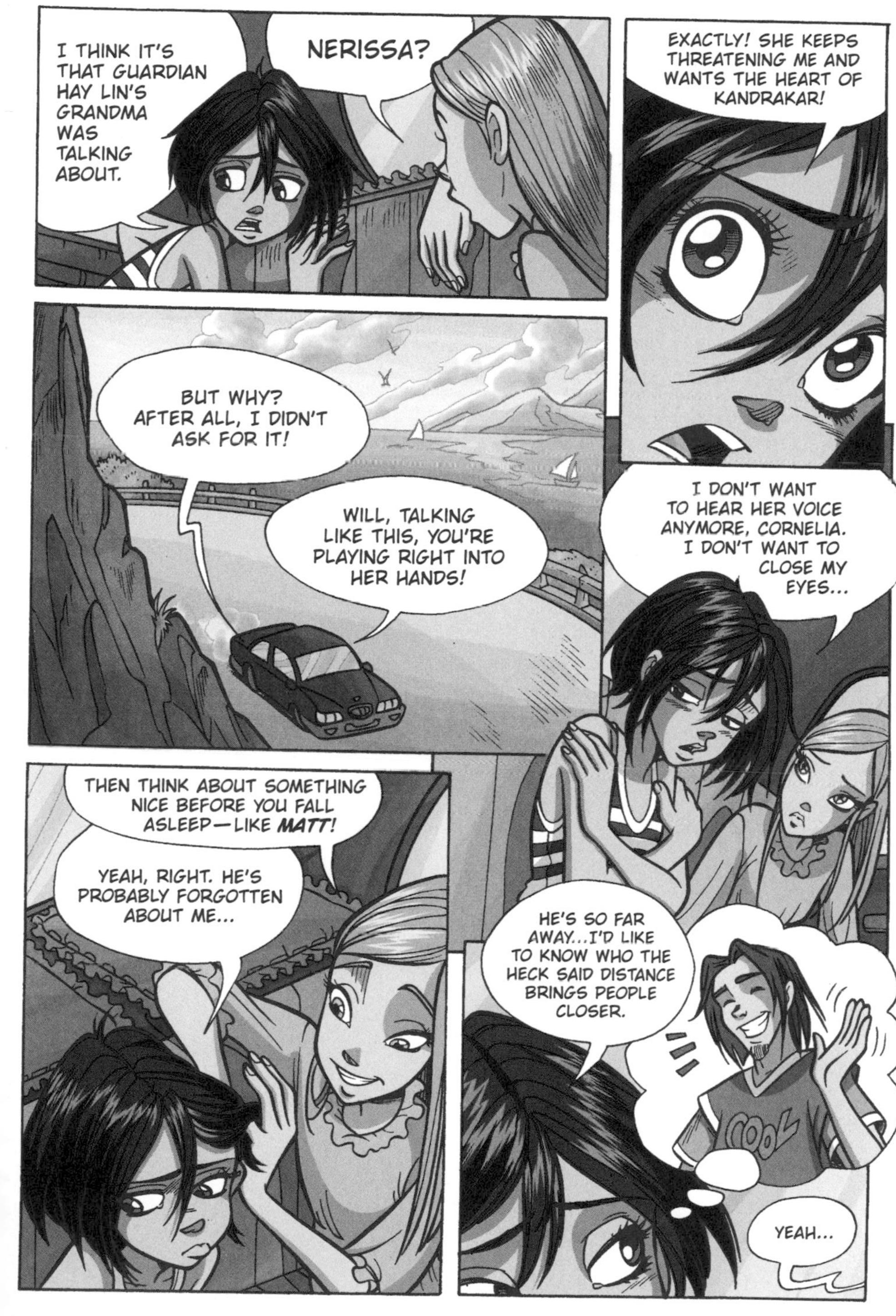

I THINK IT'S THAT GUARDIAN HAY LIN'S GRANDMA WAS TALKING ABOUT.
NERISSA?
EXACTLY! SHE KEEPS THREATENING ME AND WANTS THE HEART OF KANDRAKAR!
BUT WHY? AFTER ALL, I DIDN'T ASK FOR IT!
WILL, TALKING LIKE THIS, YOU'RE PLAYING RIGHT INTO HER HANDS!
I DON'T WANT TO HEAR HER VOICE ANYMORE, CORNELIA. I DON'T WANT TO CLOSE MY EYES...
THEN THINK ABOUT SOMETHING NICE BEFORE YOU FALL ASLEEP—LIKE *MATT*!
YEAH, RIGHT. HE'S PROBABLY FORGOTTEN ABOUT ME...
HE'S SO FAR AWAY...I'D LIKE TO KNOW WHO THE HECK SAID DISTANCE BRINGS PEOPLE CLOSER.
COOL
YEAH...

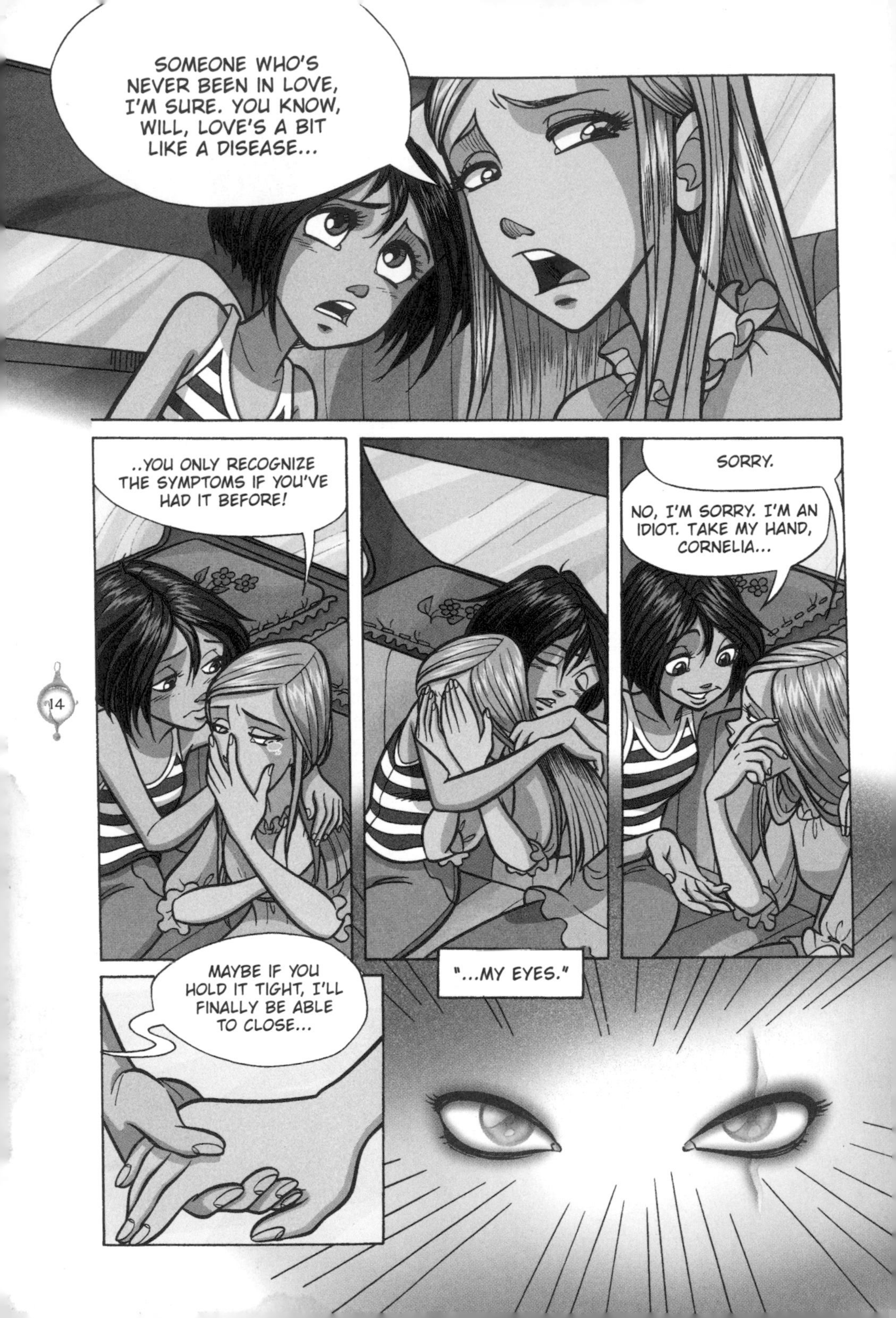
SOMEONE WHO'S NEVER BEEN IN LOVE, I'M SURE. YOU KNOW, WILL, LOVE'S A BIT LIKE A DISEASE...
..YOU ONLY RECOGNIZE THE SYMPTOMS IF YOU'VE HAD IT BEFORE!
SORRY.
NO, I'M SORRY. I'M AN IDIOT. TAKE MY HAND, CORNELIA...
MAYBE IF YOU HOLD IT TIGHT, I'LL FINALLY BE ABLE TO CLOSE...
"...MY EYES."

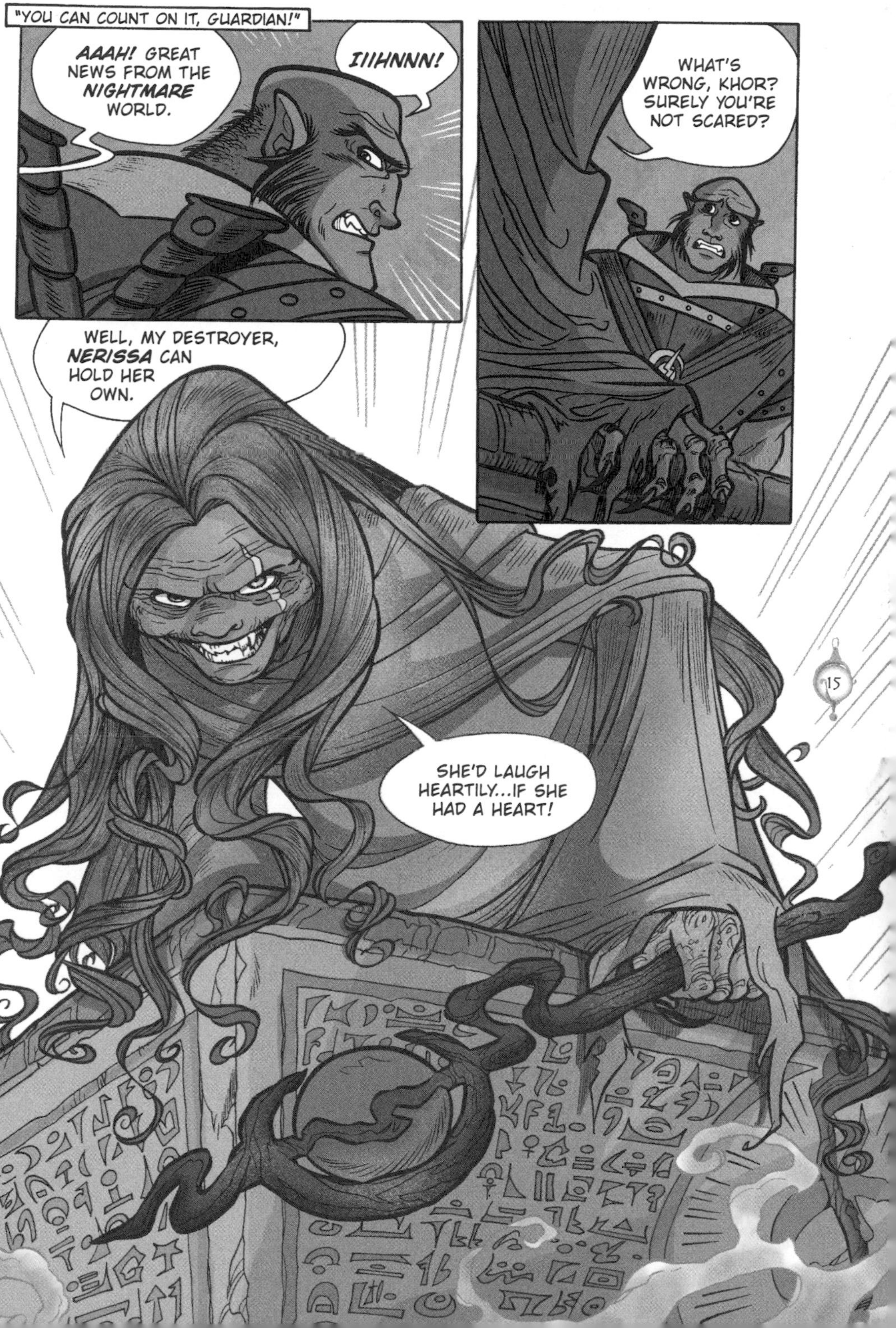
"YOU CAN COUNT ON IT, GUARDIAN!"
AAAH! GREAT NEWS FROM THE NIGHTMARE WORLD.
IIIHNNN!
WHAT'S WRONG, KHOR? SURELY YOU'RE NOT SCARED?
WELL, MY DESTROYER, NERISSA CAN HOLD HER OWN.
SHE'D LAUGH HEARTILY...IF SHE HAD A HEART!

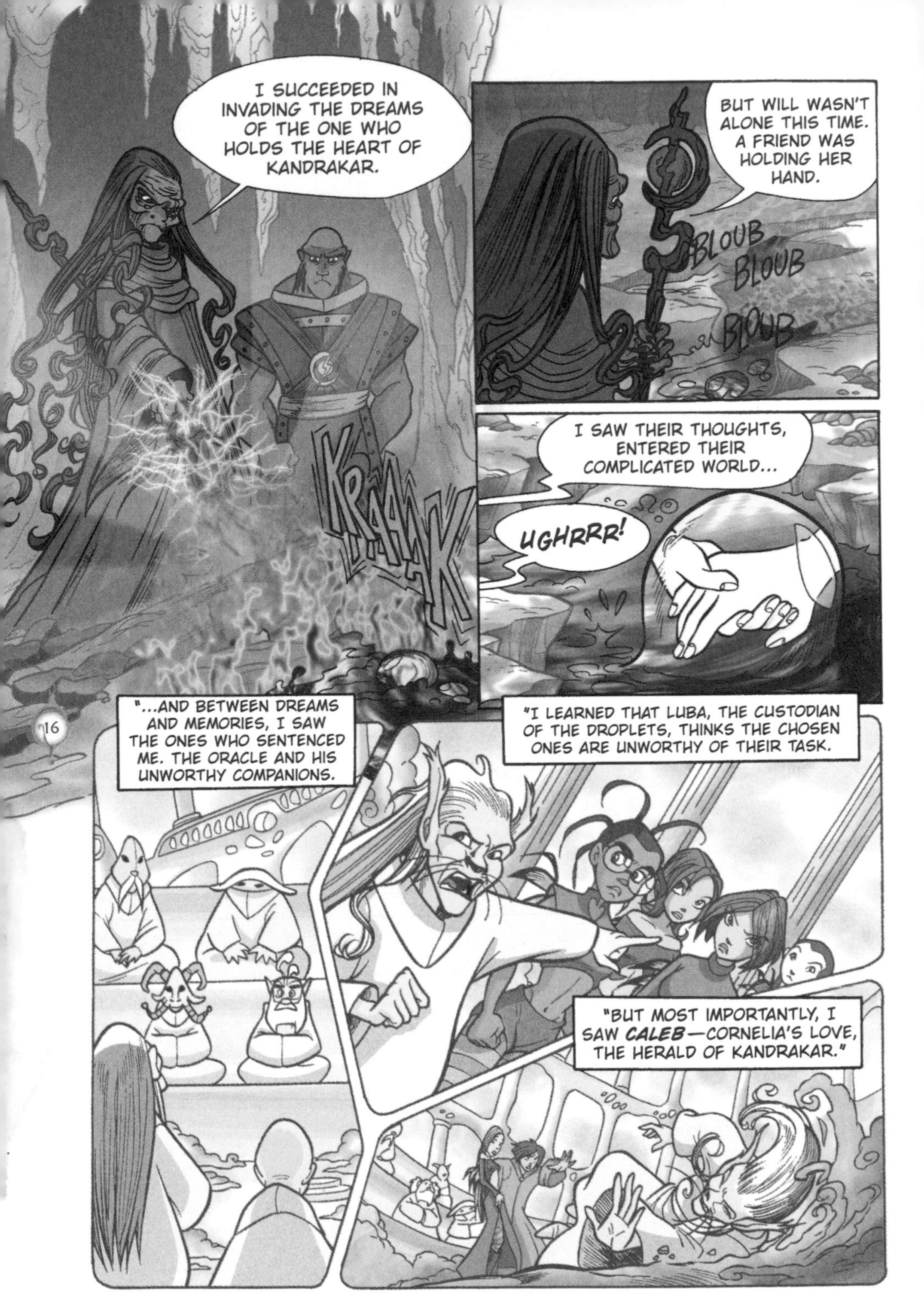

I SUCCEEDED IN INVADING THE DREAMS OF THE ONE WHO HOLDS THE HEART OF KANDRAKAR.
KRAAAK
BUT WILL WASN'T ALONE THIS TIME. A FRIEND WAS HOLDING HER HAND.
BLOUB
BLOUB
BLOUB
I SAW THEIR THOUGHTS, ENTERED THEIR COMPLICATED WORLD...
UGHRRR!
"...AND BETWEEN DREAMS AND MEMORIES, I SAW THE ONES WHO SENTENCED ME. THE ORACLE AND HIS UNWORTHY COMPANIONS.
"I LEARNED THAT LUBA, THE CUSTODIAN OF THE DROPLETS, THINKS THE CHOSEN ONES ARE UNWORTHY OF THEIR TASK.
"BUT MOST IMPORTANTLY, I SAW *CALEB*—CORNELIA'S LOVE, THE HERALD OF KANDRAKAR."

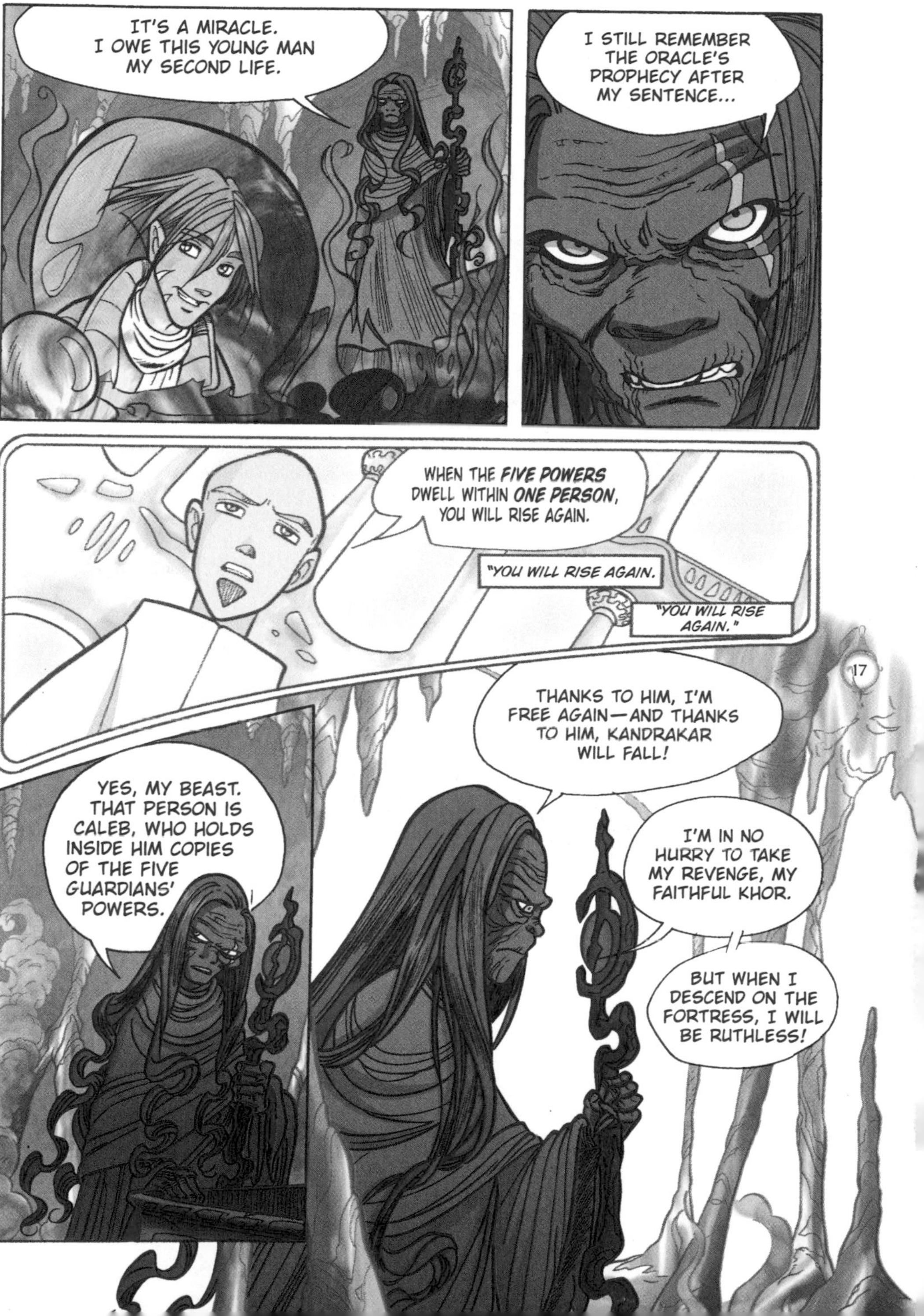

IT'S A MIRACLE. I OWE THIS YOUNG MAN MY SECOND LIFE.
I STILL REMEMBER THE ORACLE'S PROPHECY AFTER MY SENTENCE...
WHEN THE *FIVE POWERS* DWELL WITHIN *ONE PERSON*, YOU WILL RISE AGAIN.
"YOU WILL RISE AGAIN.
"YOU WILL RISE AGAIN."
THANKS TO HIM, I'M FREE AGAIN—AND THANKS TO HIM, KANDRAKAR WILL FALL!
YES, MY BEAST. THAT PERSON IS CALEB, WHO HOLDS INSIDE HIM COPIES OF THE FIVE GUARDIANS' POWERS.
I'M IN NO HURRY TO TAKE MY REVENGE, MY FAITHFUL KHOR.
BUT WHEN I DESCEND ON THE FORTRESS, I WILL BE RUTHLESS!

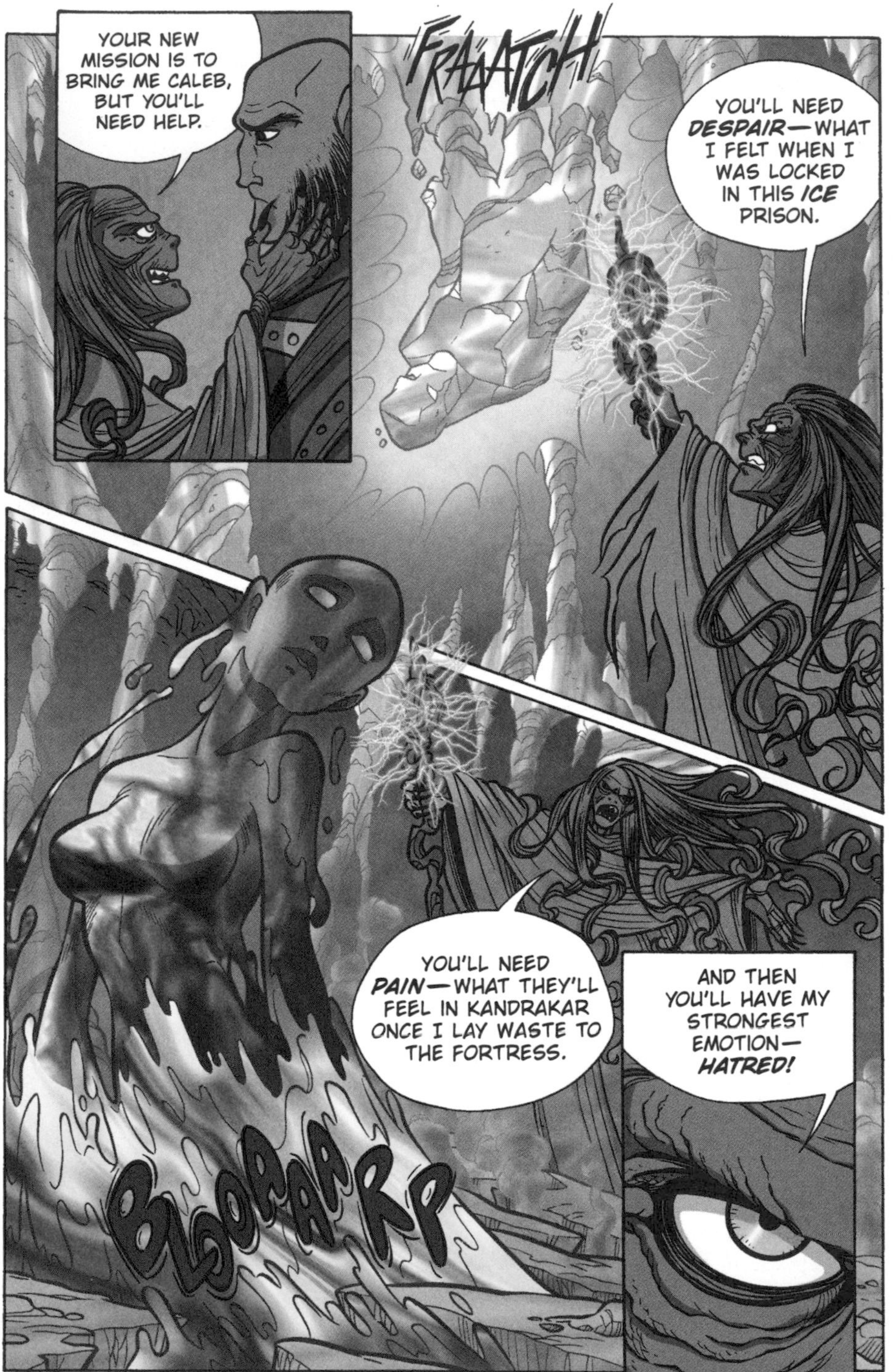

YOUR NEW MISSION IS TO BRING ME CALEB, BUT YOU'LL NEED HELP.
FRAAATCH
YOU'LL NEED DESPAIR—WHAT I FELT WHEN I WAS LOCKED IN THIS ICE PRISON.
YOU'LL NEED PAIN—WHAT THEY'LL FEEL IN KANDRAKAR ONCE I LAY WASTE TO THE FORTRESS.
AND THEN YOU'LL HAVE MY STRONGEST EMOTION—HATRED!
BLOOPAARP

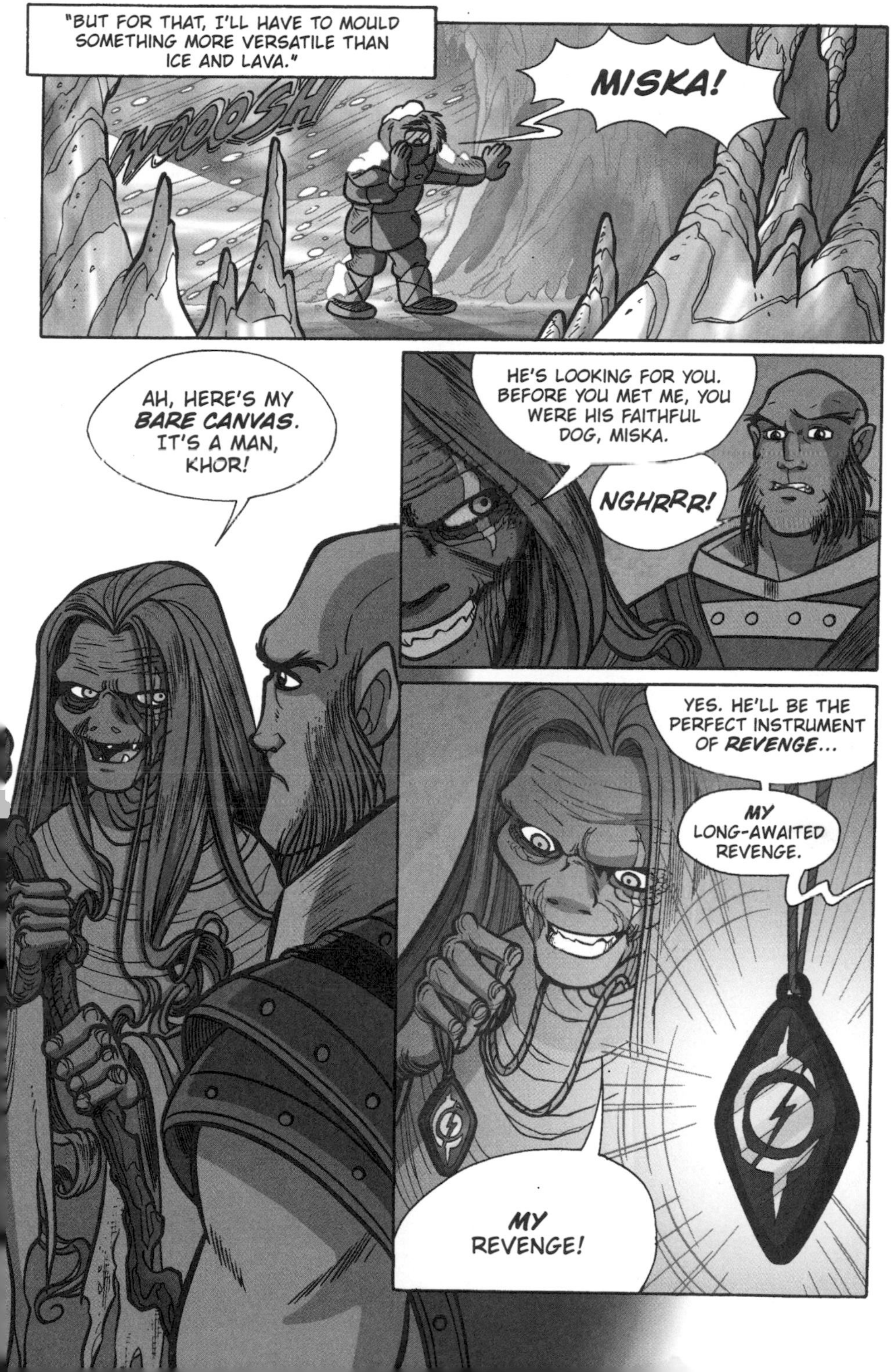

"BUT FOR THAT, I'LL HAVE TO MOULD SOMETHING MORE VERSATILE THAN ICE AND LAVA."
WOOOSH
MISKA!
AH, HERE'S MY BARE CANVAS. IT'S A MAN, KHOR!
HE'S LOOKING FOR YOU. BEFORE YOU MET ME, YOU WERE HIS FAITHFUL DOG, MISKA.
NGHRRR!
YES. HE'LL BE THE PERFECT INSTRUMENT OF REVENGE...
MY LONG-AWAITED REVENGE.
MY REVENGE!

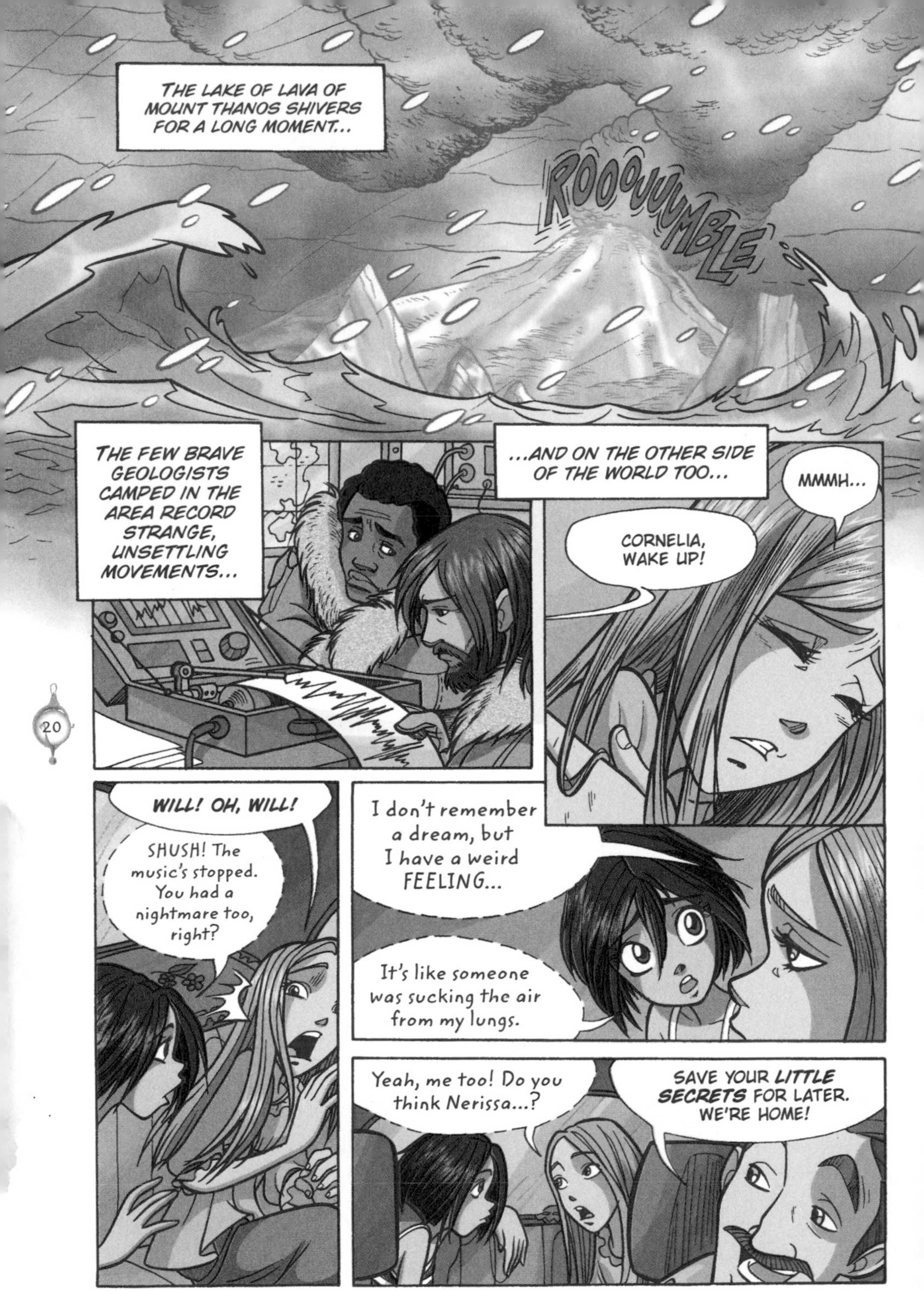
THE LAKE OF LAVA OF MOUNT THANOS SHIVERS FOR A LONG MOMENT...
ROOOUUUMBLE
THE FEW BRAVE GEOLOGISTS CAMPED IN THE AREA RECORD STRANGE, UNSETTLING MOVEMENTS...
...AND ON THE OTHER SIDE OF THE WORLD TOO...
MMMH...
CORNELIA, WAKE UP!
WILL! OH, WILL!
SHUSH! The music's stopped. You had a nightmare too, right?
I don't remember a dream, but I have a weird FEELING...
It's like someone was sucking the air from my lungs.
Yeah, me too! Do you think Nerissa...?
SAVE YOUR LITTLE SECRETS FOR LATER. WE'RE HOME!

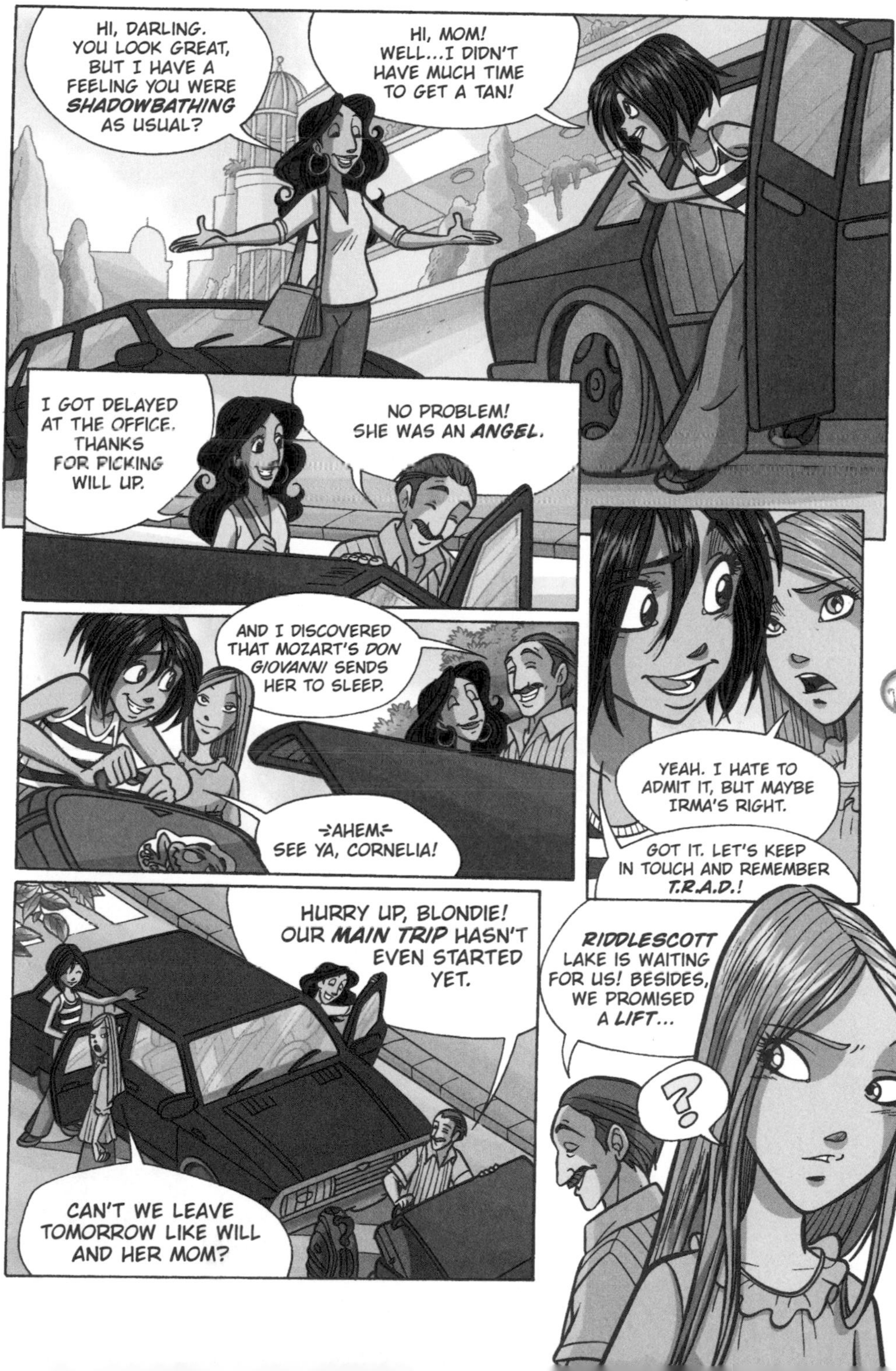

HI, DARLING. YOU LOOK GREAT, BUT I HAVE A FEELING YOU WERE SHADOWBATHING AS USUAL?
HI, MOM! WELL...I DIDN'T HAVE MUCH TIME TO GET A TAN!
I GOT DELAYED AT THE OFFICE. THANKS FOR PICKING WILL UP.
NO PROBLEM! SHE WAS AN ANGEL.
AND I DISCOVERED THAT MOZART'S DON GIOVANNI SENDS HER TO SLEEP.
AHEM
SEE YA, CORNELIA!
YEAH. I HATE TO ADMIT IT, BUT MAYBE IRMA'S RIGHT.
GOT IT. LET'S KEEP IN TOUCH AND REMEMBER T.R.A.D.!
HURRY UP, BLONDIE! OUR MAIN TRIP HASN'T EVEN STARTED YET.
CAN'T WE LEAVE TOMORROW LIKE WILL AND HER MOM?
RIDDLESCOTT LAKE IS WAITING FOR US! BESIDES, WE PROMISED A LIFT...
?

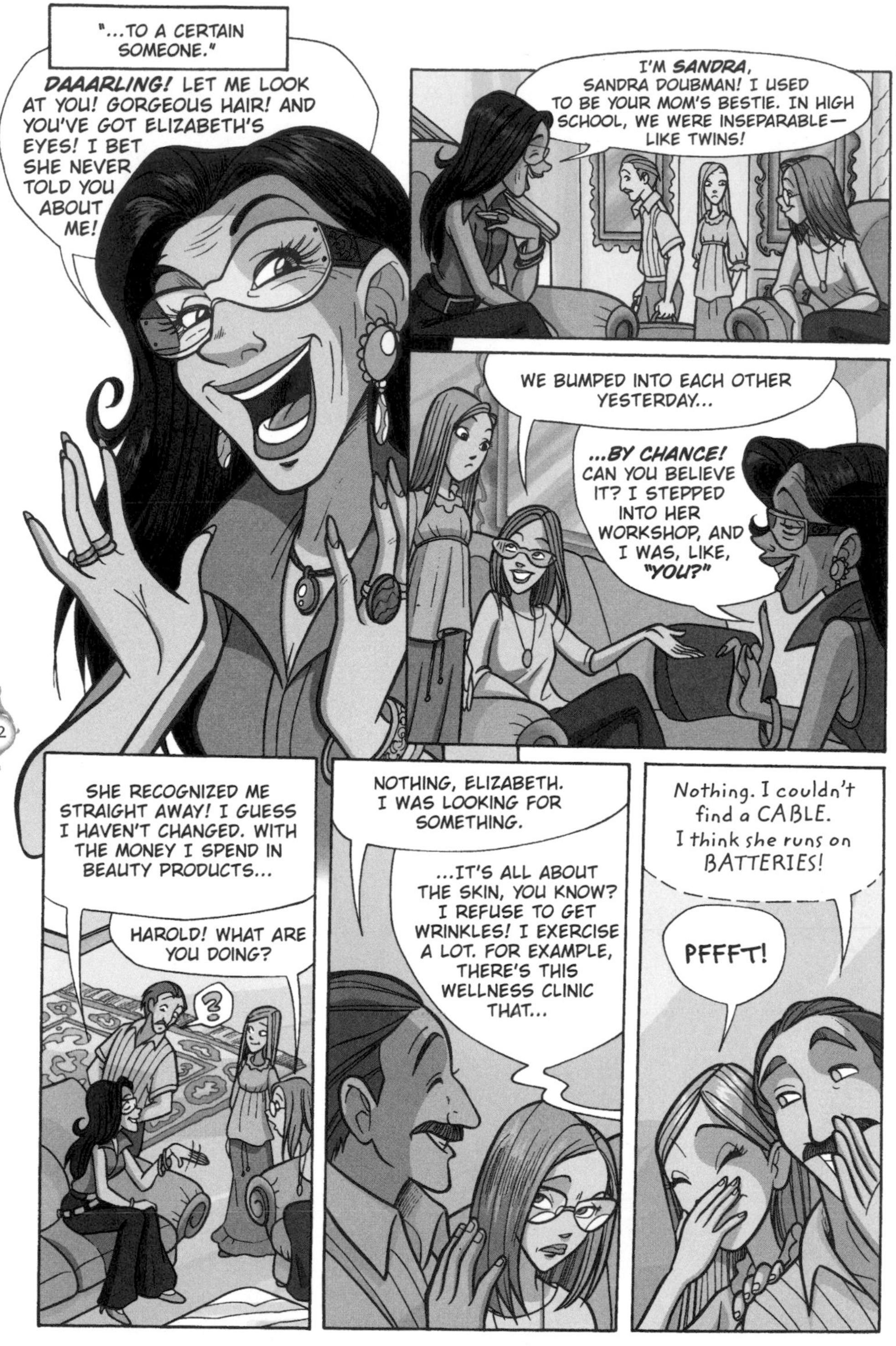

"...TO A CERTAIN SOMEONE."
DAAARLING! LET ME LOOK AT YOU! GORGEOUS HAIR! AND YOU'VE GOT ELIZABETH'S EYES! I BET SHE NEVER TOLD YOU ABOUT ME!
I'M SANDRA, SANDRA DOUBMAN! I USED TO BE YOUR MOM'S BESTIE. IN HIGH SCHOOL, WE WERE INSEPARABLE—LIKE TWINS!
WE BUMPED INTO EACH OTHER YESTERDAY...
...BY CHANCE! CAN YOU BELIEVE IT? I STEPPED INTO HER WORKSHOP, AND I WAS, LIKE, "YOU?"
SHE RECOGNIZED ME STRAIGHT AWAY! I GUESS I HAVEN'T CHANGED. WITH THE MONEY I SPEND IN BEAUTY PRODUCTS...
HAROLD! WHAT ARE YOU DOING?
?
NOTHING, ELIZABETH. I WAS LOOKING FOR SOMETHING.
...IT'S ALL ABOUT THE SKIN, YOU KNOW? I REFUSE TO GET WRINKLES! I EXERCISE A LOT. FOR EXAMPLE, THERE'S THIS WELLNESS CLINIC THAT...
Nothing. I couldn't find a CABLE. I think she runs on BATTERIES!
PFFFT!

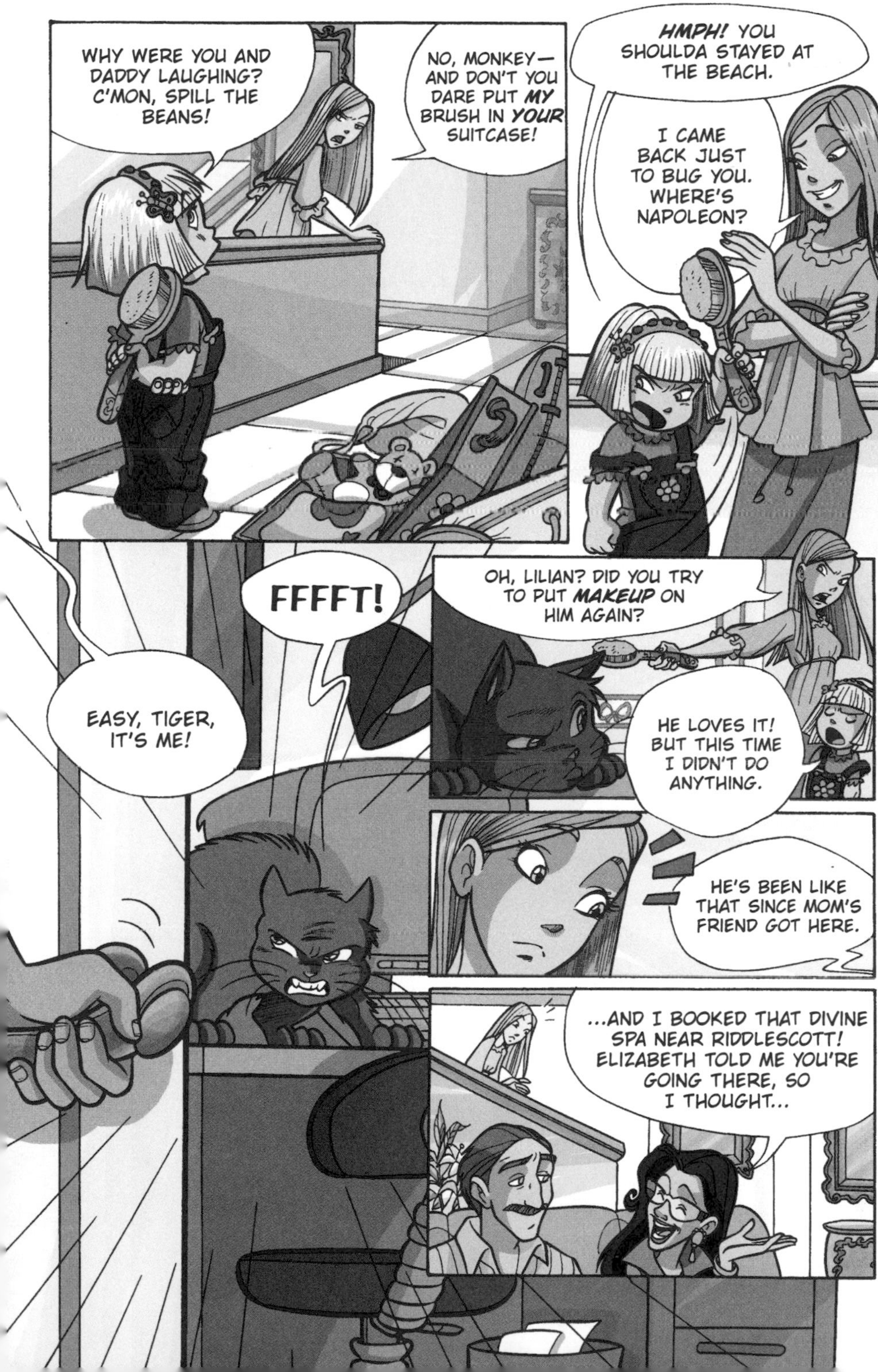
WHY WERE YOU AND DADDY LAUGHING? C'MON, SPILL THE BEANS!
NO, MONKEY—AND DON'T YOU DARE PUT *MY* BRUSH IN *YOUR* SUITCASE!
HMPH! YOU SHOULDA STAYED AT THE BEACH.
I CAME BACK JUST TO BUG YOU. WHERE'S NAPOLEON?
EASY, TIGER, IT'S ME!
FFFFT!
OH, LILIAN? DID YOU TRY TO PUT *MAKEUP* ON HIM AGAIN?
HE LOVES IT! BUT THIS TIME I DIDN'T DO ANYTHING.
HE'S BEEN LIKE THAT SINCE MOM'S FRIEND GOT HERE.
...AND I BOOKED THAT DIVINE SPA NEAR RIDDLESCOTT! ELIZABETH TOLD ME YOU'RE GOING THERE, SO I THOUGHT...

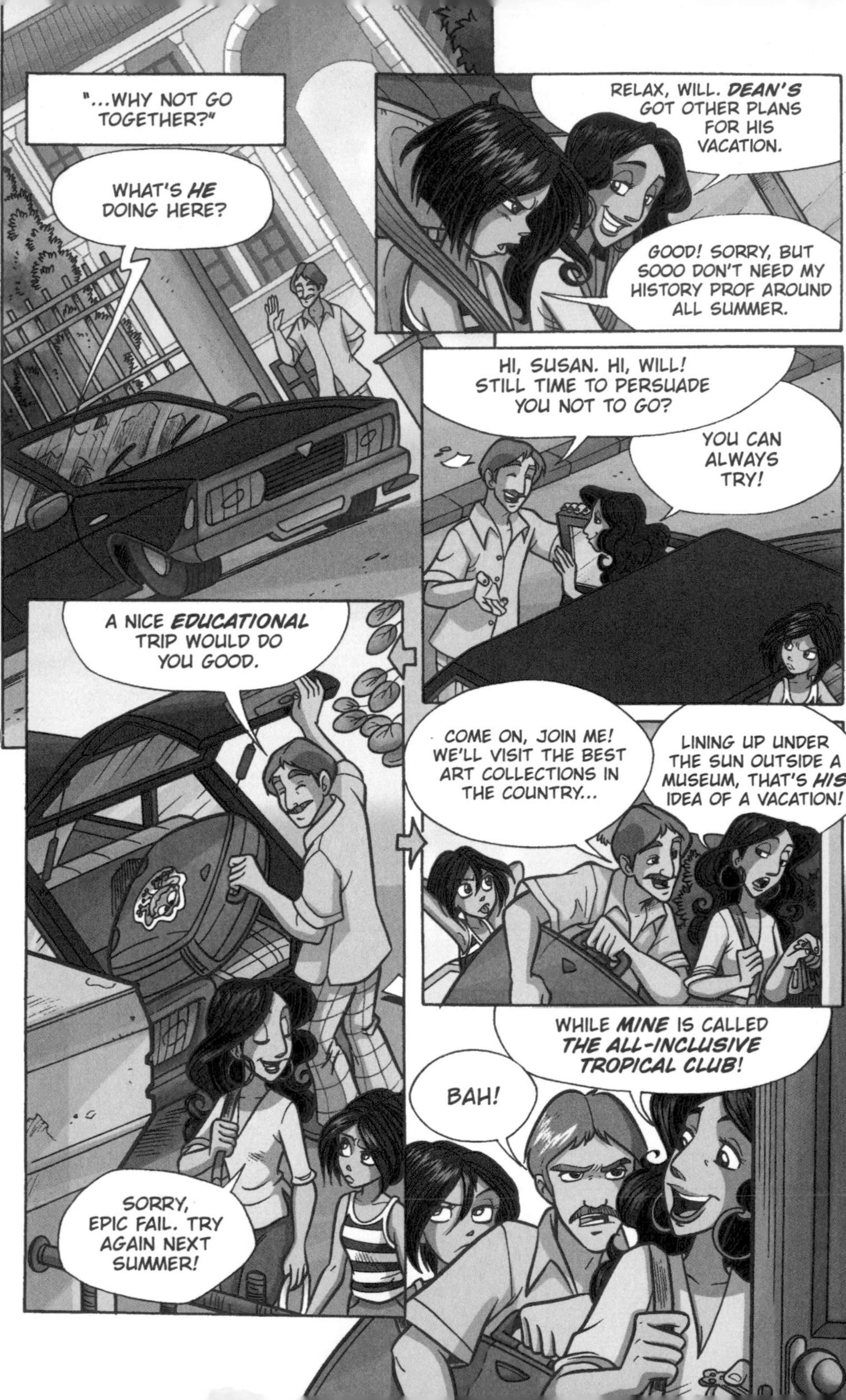
"...WHY NOT GO TOGETHER?"
WHAT'S HE DOING HERE?
RELAX, WILL. DEAN'S GOT OTHER PLANS FOR HIS VACATION.
GOOD! SORRY, BUT SOOO DON'T NEED MY HISTORY PROF AROUND ALL SUMMER.
HI, SUSAN. HI, WILL! STILL TIME TO PERSUADE YOU NOT TO GO?
YOU CAN ALWAYS TRY!
A NICE EDUCATIONAL TRIP WOULD DO YOU GOOD.
SORRY, EPIC FAIL. TRY AGAIN NEXT SUMMER!
COME ON, JOIN ME! WE'LL VISIT THE BEST ART COLLECTIONS IN THE COUNTRY...
LINING UP UNDER THE SUN OUTSIDE A MUSEUM, THAT'S HIS IDEA OF A VACATION!
WHILE MINE IS CALLED THE ALL-INCLUSIVE TROPICAL CLUB!
BAH!

24

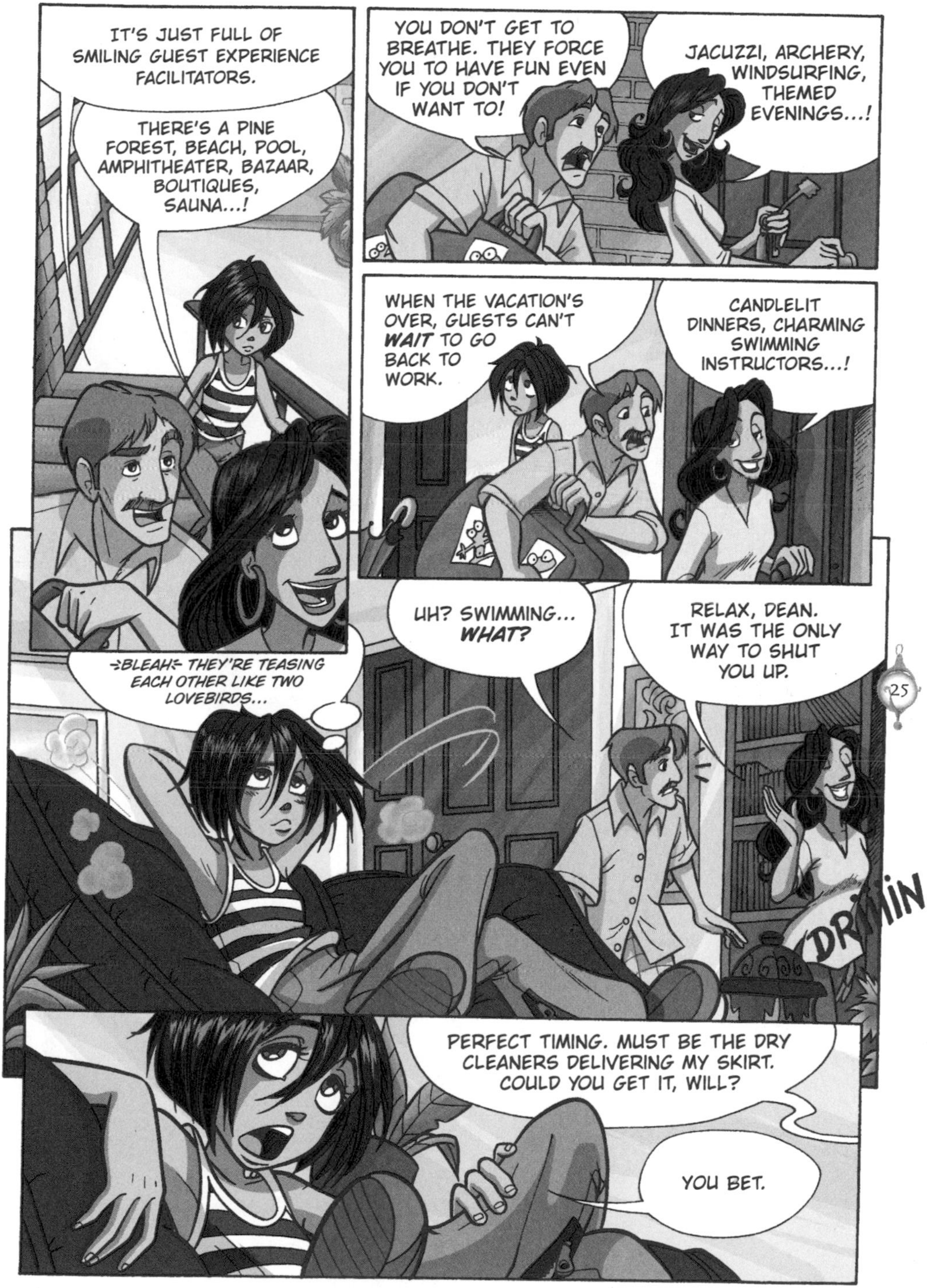
IT'S JUST FULL OF SMILING GUEST EXPERIENCE FACILITATORS.
THERE'S A PINE FOREST, BEACH, POOL, AMPHITHEATER, BAZAAR, BOUTIQUES, SAUNA...!
YOU DON'T GET TO BREATHE. THEY FORCE YOU TO HAVE FUN EVEN IF YOU DON'T WANT TO!
JACUZZI, ARCHERY, WINDSURFING, THEMED EVENINGS...!
WHEN THE VACATION'S OVER, GUESTS CAN'T WAIT TO GO BACK TO WORK.
CANDLELIT DINNERS, CHARMING SWIMMING INSTRUCTORS...!
BLEAH THEY'RE TEASING EACH OTHER LIKE TWO LOVEBIRDS...
UH? SWIMMING... WHAT?
RELAX, DEAN. IT WAS THE ONLY WAY TO SHUT YOU UP.
DRIIIN
PERFECT TIMING. MUST BE THE DRY CLEANERS DELIVERING MY SKIRT. COULD YOU GET IT, WILL?
YOU BET.

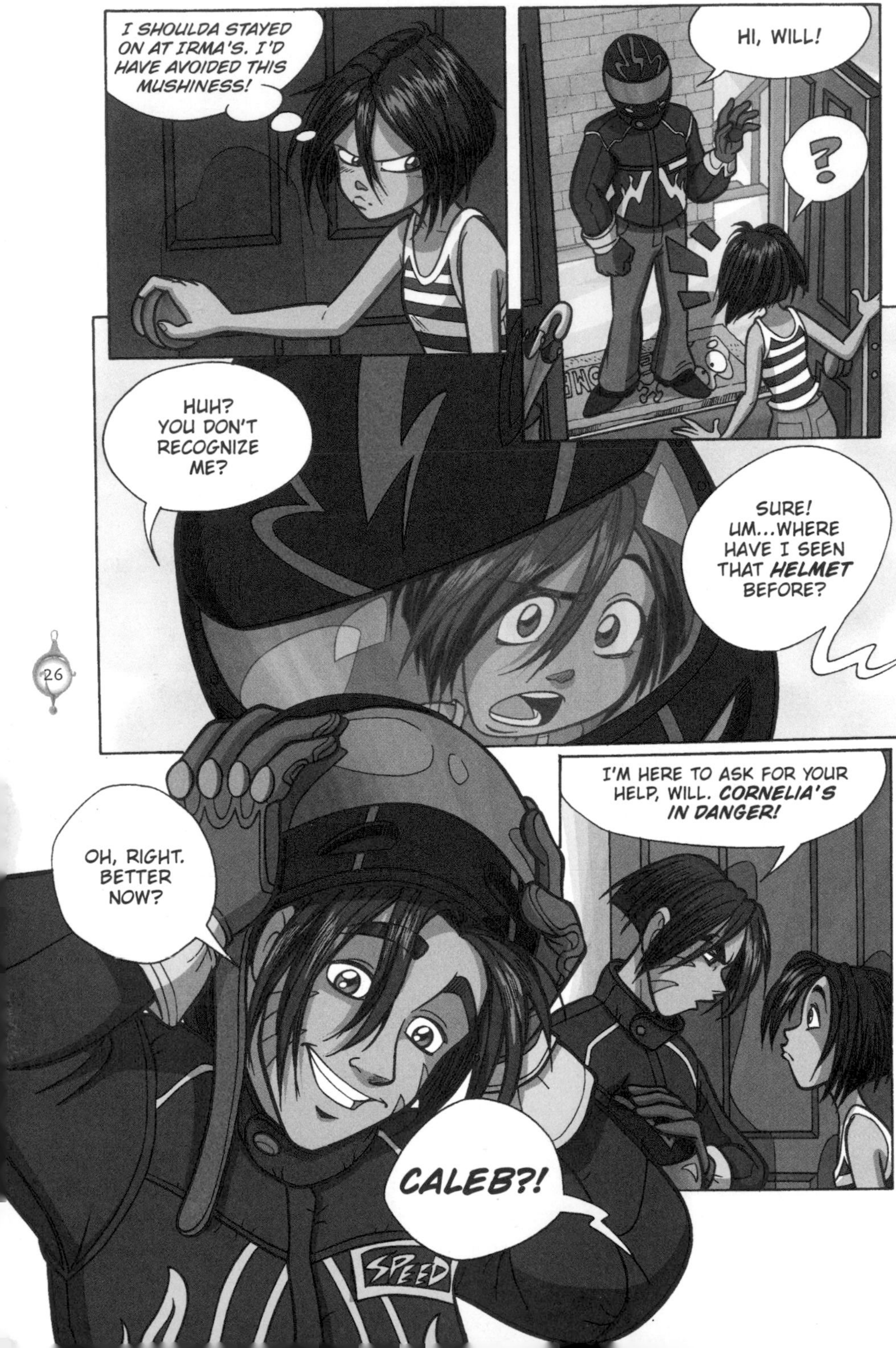
I SHOULDA STAYED ON AT IRMA'S. I'D HAVE AVOIDED THIS MUSHINESS!
HI, WILL!
?
HUH? YOU DON'T RECOGNIZE ME?
SURE! UM...WHERE HAVE I SEEN THAT HELMET BEFORE?
OH, RIGHT. BETTER NOW?
CALEB?!
I'M HERE TO ASK FOR YOUR HELP, WILL. CORNELIA'S IN DANGER!
SPEED

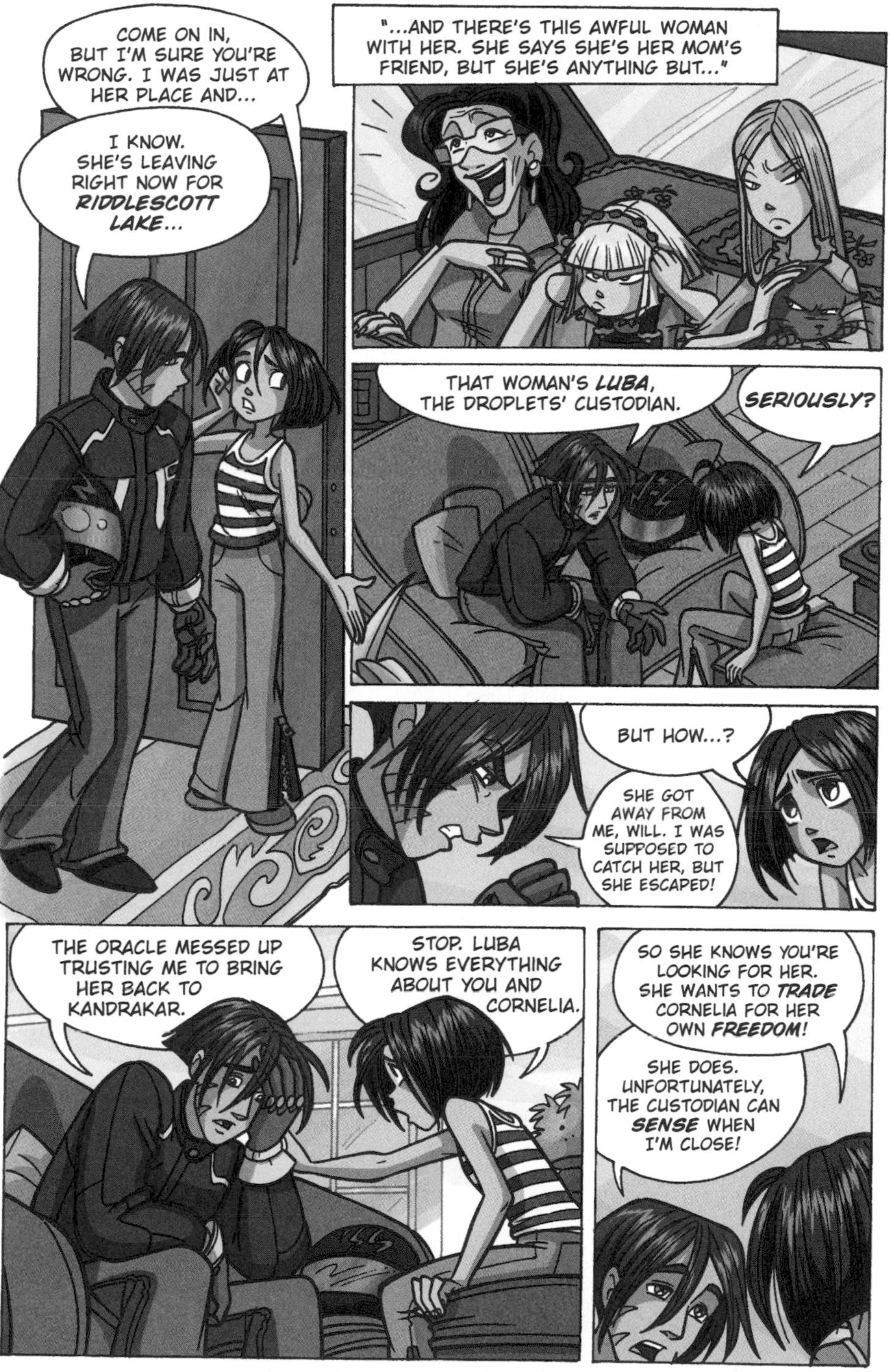
COME ON IN, BUT I'M SURE YOU'RE WRONG. I WAS JUST AT HER PLACE AND...
I KNOW. SHE'S LEAVING RIGHT NOW FOR RIDDLESCOTT LAKE...
"...AND THERE'S THIS AWFUL WOMAN WITH HER. SHE SAYS SHE'S HER MOM'S FRIEND, BUT SHE'S ANYTHING BUT..."
THAT WOMAN'S LUBA, THE DROPLETS' CUSTODIAN.
SERIOUSLY?
BUT HOW...?
SHE GOT AWAY FROM ME, WILL. I WAS SUPPOSED TO CATCH HER, BUT SHE ESCAPED!
THE ORACLE MESSED UP TRUSTING ME TO BRING HER BACK TO KANDRAKAR.
STOP. LUBA KNOWS EVERYTHING ABOUT YOU AND CORNELIA.
SO SHE KNOWS YOU'RE LOOKING FOR HER. SHE WANTS TO TRADE CORNELIA FOR HER OWN FREEDOM!
SHE DOES. UNFORTUNATELY, THE CUSTODIAN CAN SENSE WHEN I'M CLOSE!

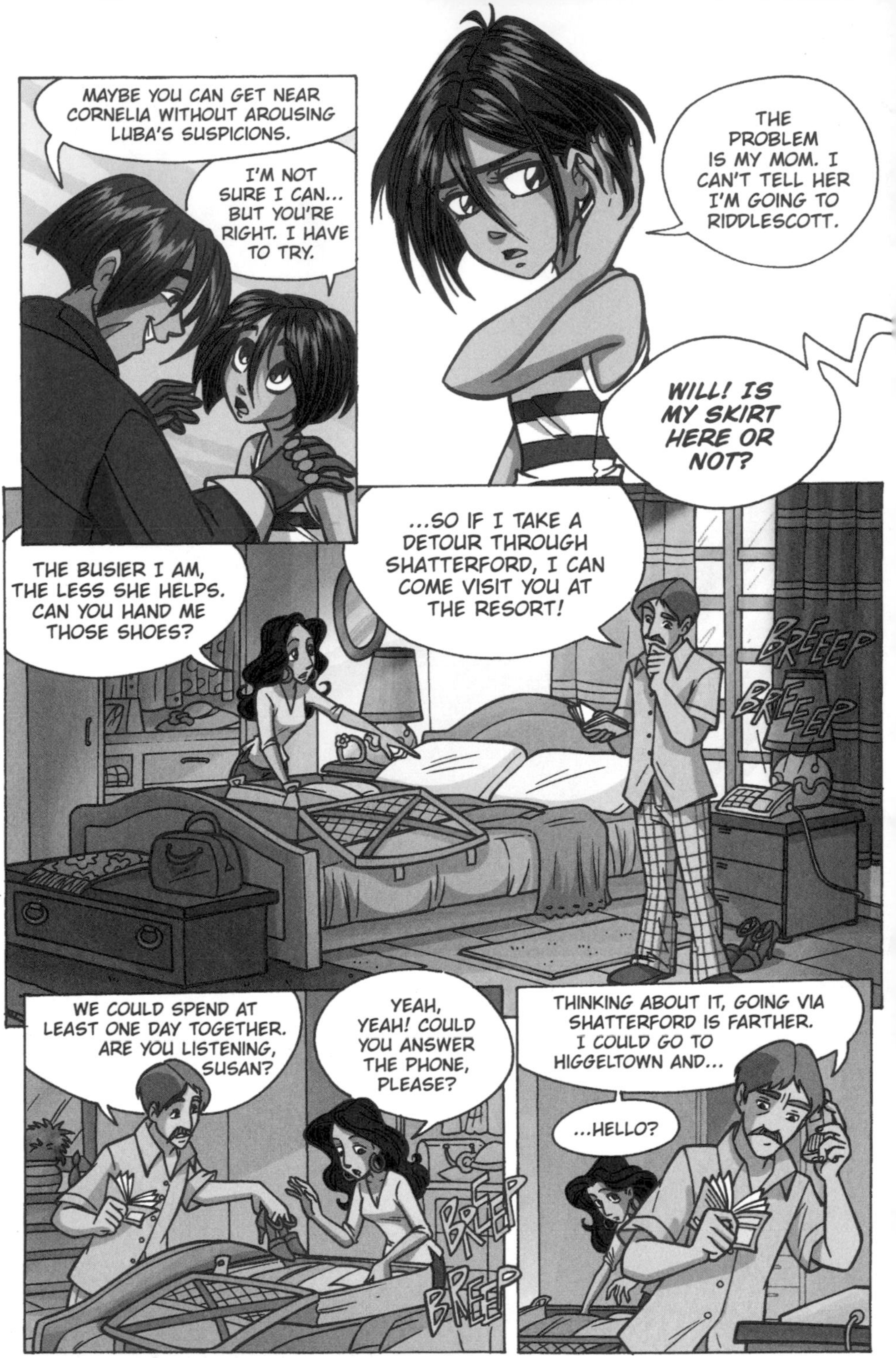
MAYBE YOU CAN GET NEAR CORNELIA WITHOUT AROUSING LUBA'S SUSPICIONS.
I'M NOT SURE I CAN... BUT YOU'RE RIGHT. I HAVE TO TRY.
THE PROBLEM IS MY MOM. I CAN'T TELL HER I'M GOING TO RIDDLESCOTT.
WILL! IS MY SKIRT HERE OR NOT?
THE BUSIER I AM, THE LESS SHE HELPS. CAN YOU HAND ME THOSE SHOES?
...SO IF I TAKE A DETOUR THROUGH SHATTERFORD, I CAN COME VISIT YOU AT THE RESORT!
BREEEP
BREEEP
WE COULD SPEND AT LEAST ONE DAY TOGETHER. ARE YOU LISTENING, SUSAN?
YEAH, YEAH! COULD YOU ANSWER THE PHONE, PLEASE?
BREEP
BREEP
THINKING ABOUT IT, GOING VIA SHATTERFORD IS FARTHER. I COULD GO TO HIGGELTOWN AND...
...HELLO?

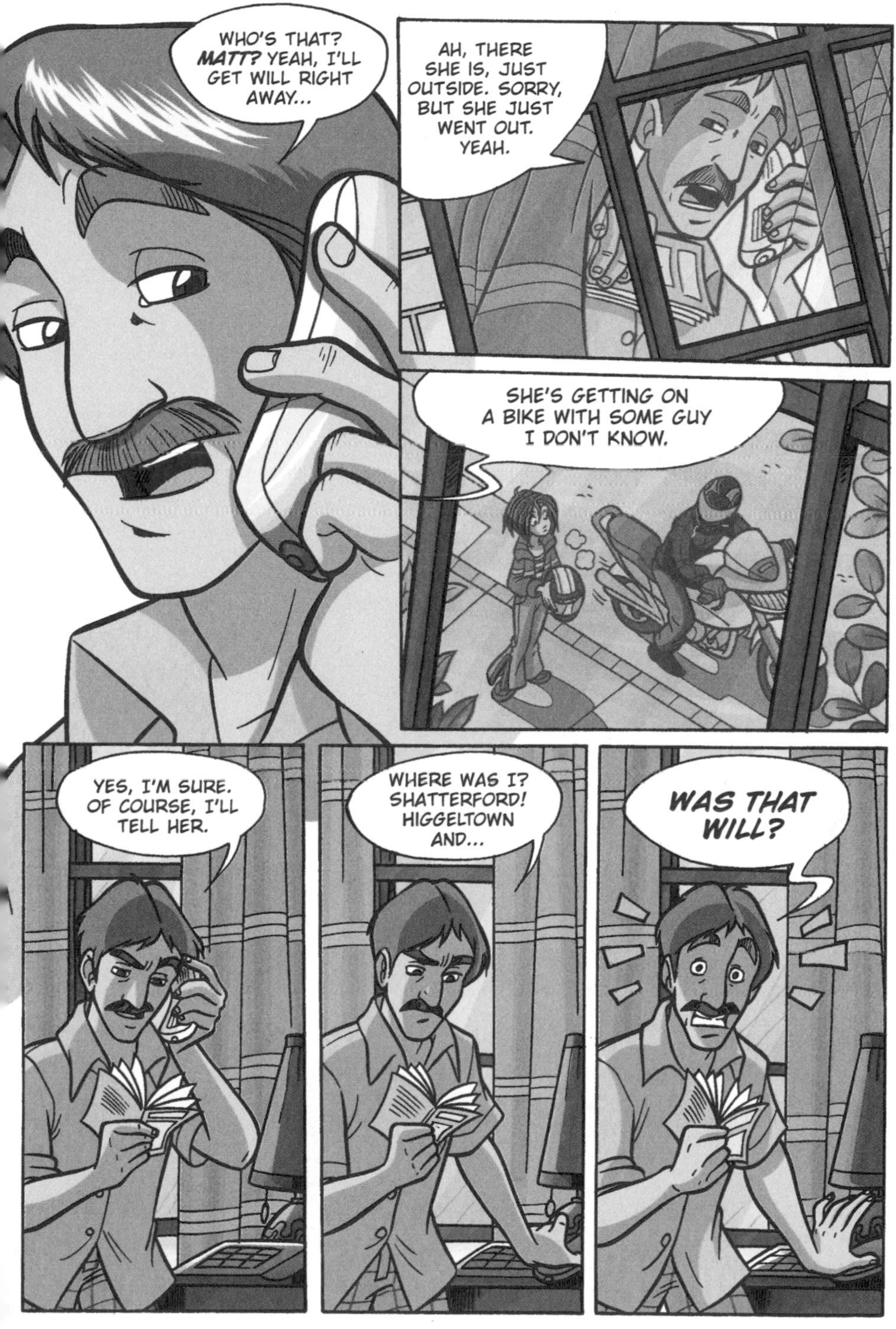
WHO'S THAT? *MATT?* YEAH, I'LL GET WILL RIGHT AWAY...
AH, THERE SHE IS, JUST OUTSIDE. SORRY, BUT SHE JUST WENT OUT. YEAH.
SHE'S GETTING ON A BIKE WITH SOME GUY I DON'T KNOW.
YES, I'M SURE. OF COURSE, I'LL TELL HER.
WHERE WAS I? SHATTERFORD! HIGGELTOWN AND...
WAS THAT WILL?

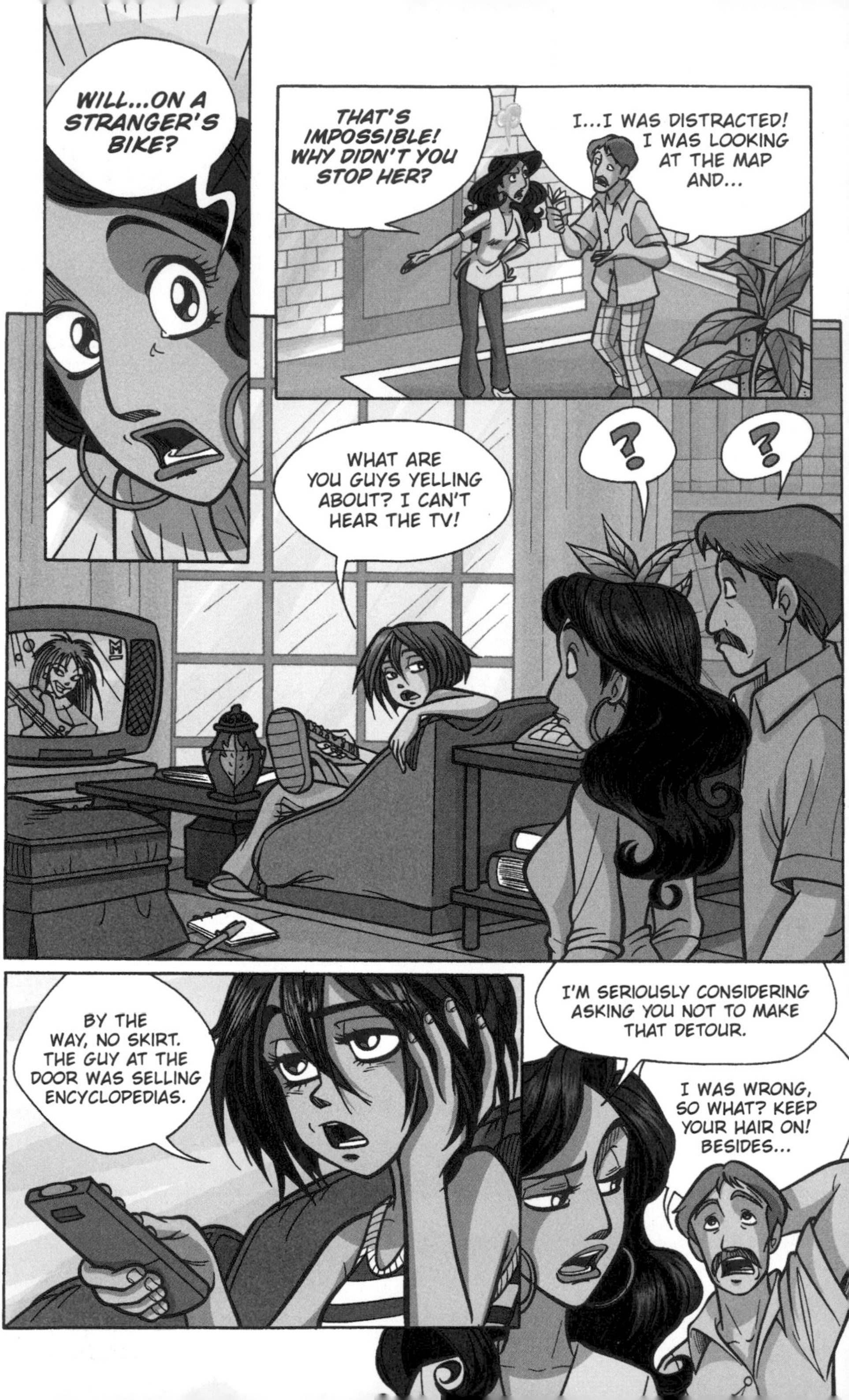
WILL...ON A STRANGER'S BIKE?
THAT'S IMPOSSIBLE! WHY DIDN'T YOU STOP HER?
I...I WAS DISTRACTED! I WAS LOOKING AT THE MAP AND...
WHAT ARE YOU GUYS YELLING ABOUT? I CAN'T HEAR THE TV!
?
?
BY THE WAY, NO SKIRT. THE GUY AT THE DOOR WAS SELLING ENCYCLOPEDIAS.
I'M SERIOUSLY CONSIDERING ASKING YOU NOT TO MAKE THAT DETOUR.
I WAS WRONG, SO WHAT? KEEP YOUR HAIR ON! BESIDES...

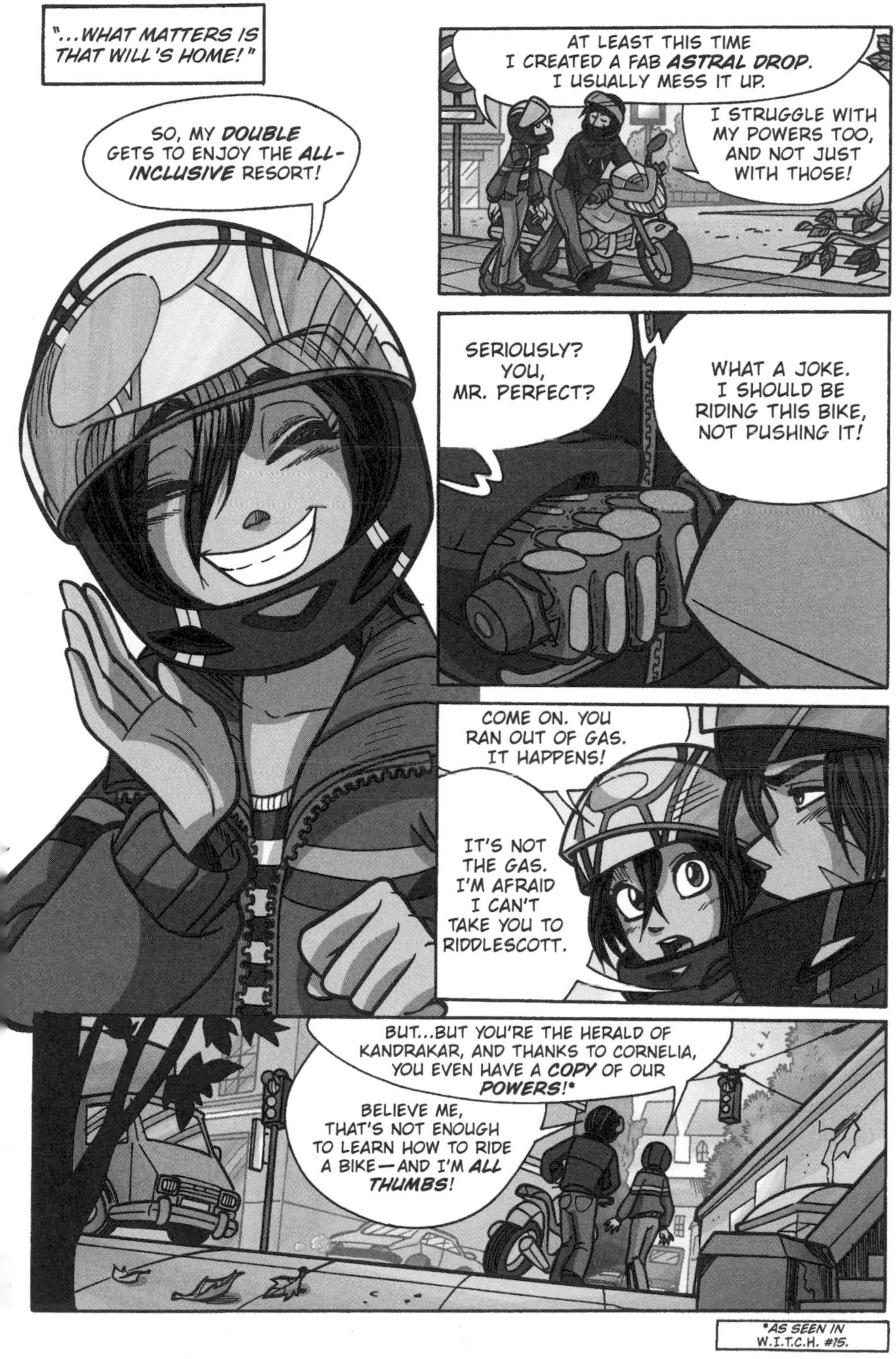
"...WHAT MATTERS IS THAT WILL'S HOME!"
SO, MY DOUBLE GETS TO ENJOY THE ALL-INCLUSIVE RESORT!
AT LEAST THIS TIME I CREATED A FAB ASTRAL DROP. I USUALLY MESS IT UP.
I STRUGGLE WITH MY POWERS TOO, AND NOT JUST WITH THOSE!
SERIOUSLY? YOU, MR. PERFECT?
WHAT A JOKE. I SHOULD BE RIDING THIS BIKE, NOT PUSHING IT!
COME ON. YOU RAN OUT OF GAS. IT HAPPENS!
IT'S NOT THE GAS. I'M AFRAID I CAN'T TAKE YOU TO RIDDLESCOTT.
BUT...BUT YOU'RE THE HERALD OF KANDRAKAR, AND THANKS TO CORNELIA, YOU EVEN HAVE A COPY OF OUR POWERS!*
BELIEVE ME, THAT'S NOT ENOUGH TO LEARN HOW TO RIDE A BIKE—AND I'M ALL THUMBS!

*AS SEEN IN W.I.T.C.H. #15.

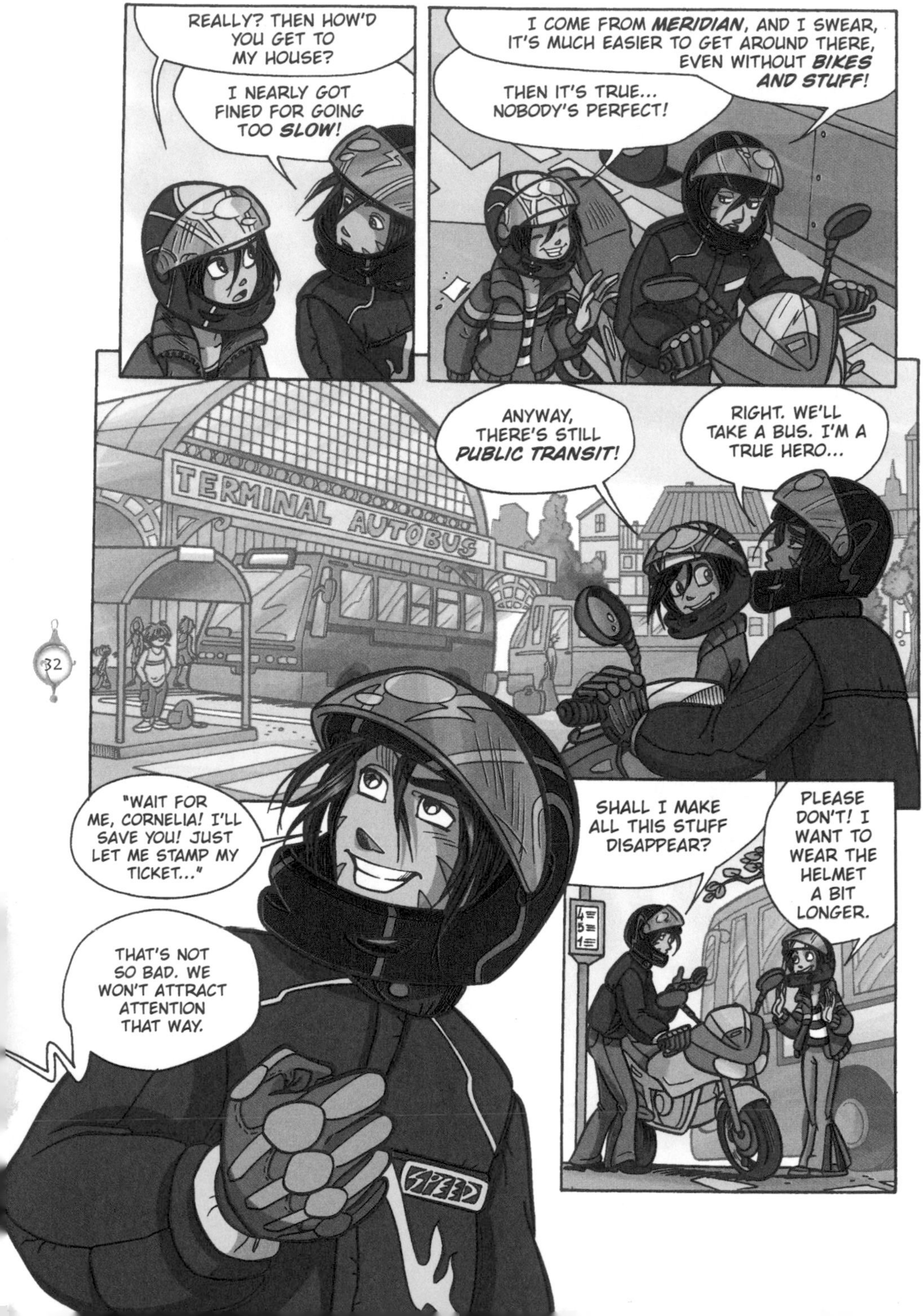
REALLY? THEN HOW'D YOU GET TO MY HOUSE?
I NEARLY GOT FINED FOR GOING TOO **SLOW**!
I COME FROM **MERIDIAN**, AND I SWEAR, IT'S MUCH EASIER TO GET AROUND THERE, EVEN WITHOUT **BIKES AND STUFF**!
THEN IT'S TRUE... NOBODY'S PERFECT!
TERMINAL AUTOBUS
ANYWAY, THERE'S STILL **PUBLIC TRANSIT**!
RIGHT. WE'LL TAKE A BUS. I'M A TRUE HERO...
"WAIT FOR ME, CORNELIA! I'LL SAVE YOU! JUST LET ME STAMP MY TICKET..."
THAT'S NOT SO BAD. WE WON'T ATTRACT ATTENTION THAT WAY.
SPEED
SHALL I MAKE ALL THIS STUFF DISAPPEAR?
PLEASE DON'T! I WANT TO WEAR THE HELMET A BIT LONGER.

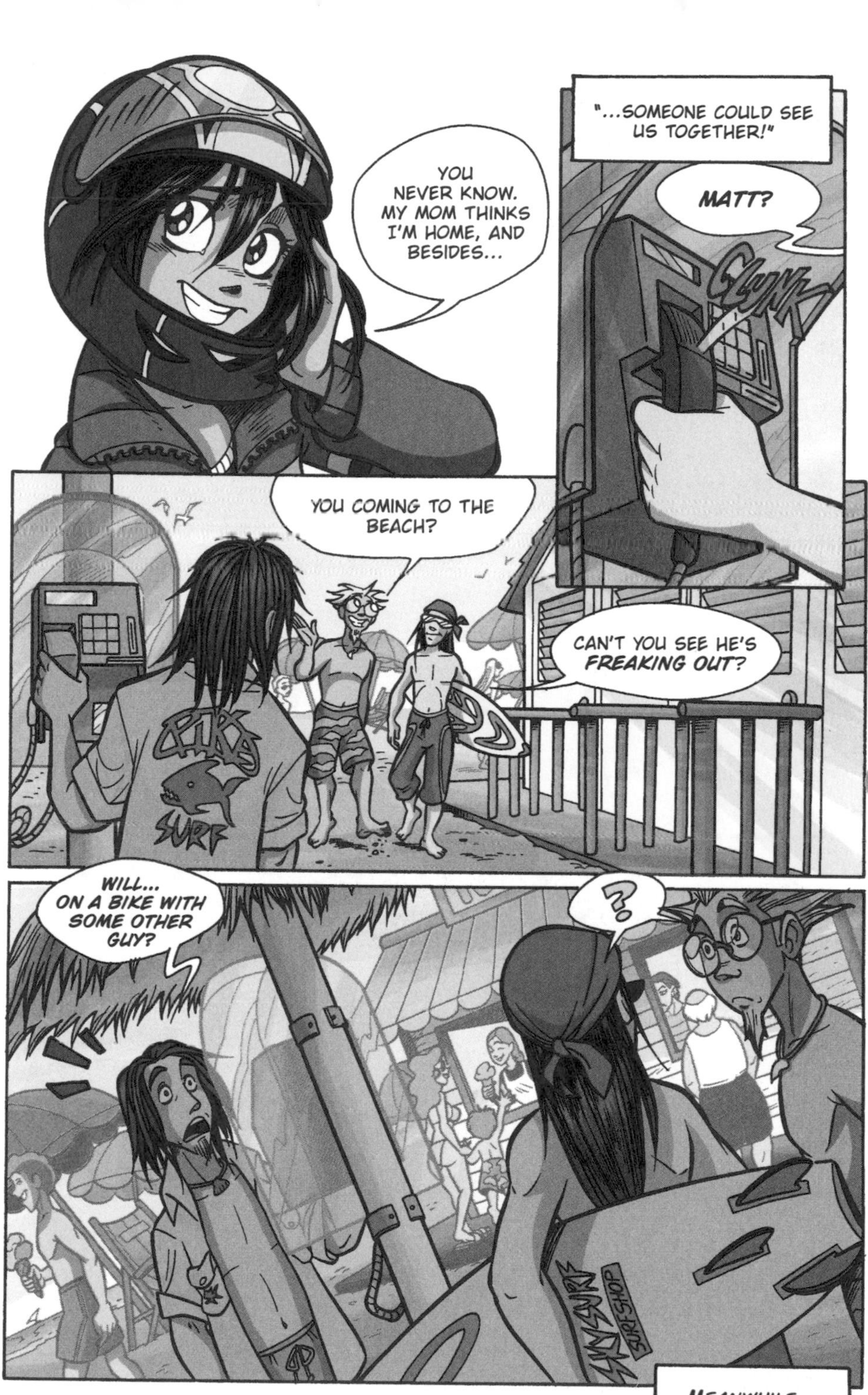

YOU NEVER KNOW. MY MOM THINKS I'M HOME, AND BESIDES...
"...SOMEONE COULD SEE US TOGETHER!"
MATT?
CLUNK
YOU COMING TO THE BEACH?
CAN'T YOU SEE HE'S FREAKING OUT?
WILL... ON A BIKE WITH SOME OTHER GUY?
?
MEANWHILE...

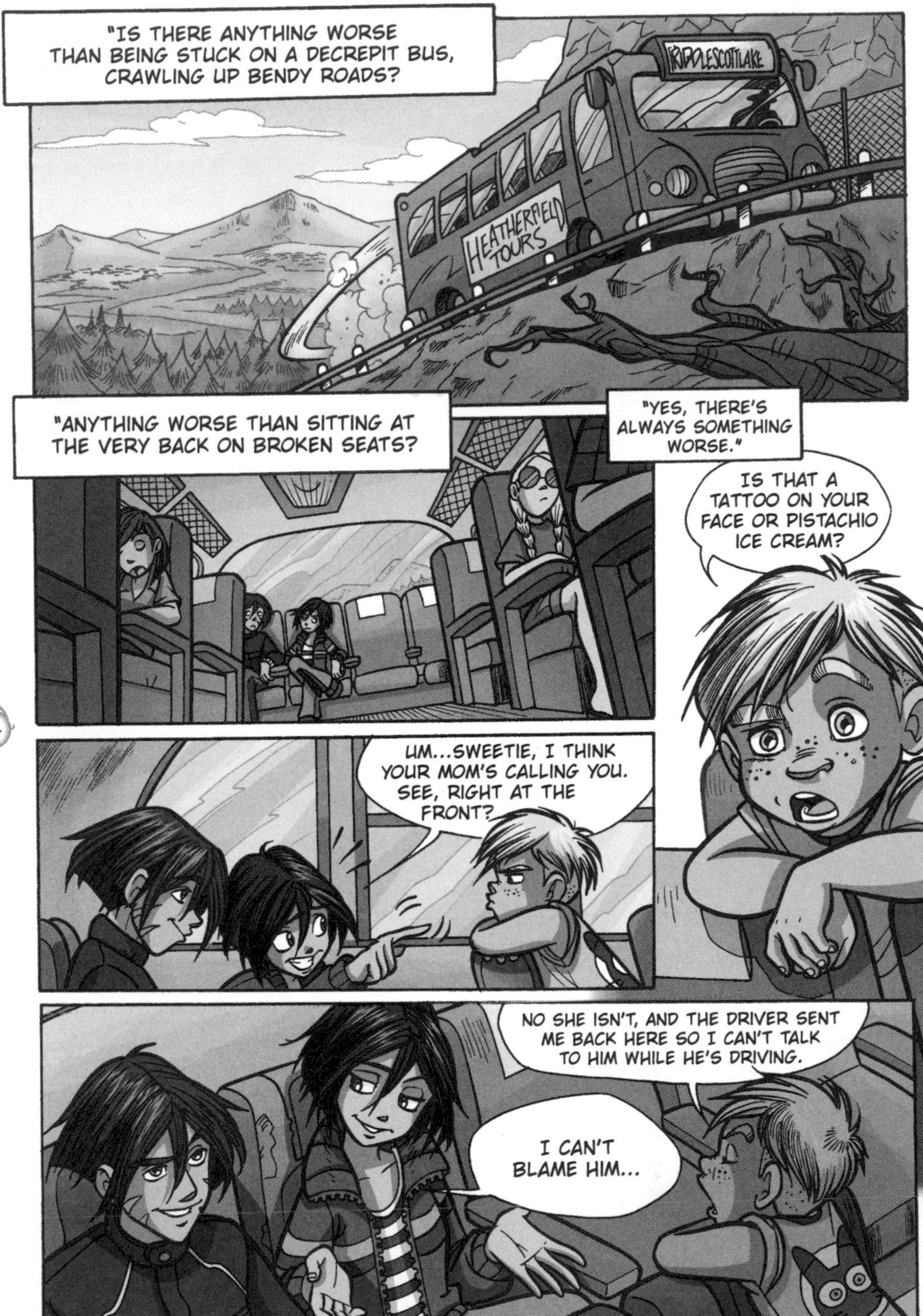

"IS THERE ANYTHING WORSE THAN BEING STUCK ON A DECREPIT BUS, CRAWLING UP BENDY ROADS?
HEATHERFIELD TOURS
"ANYTHING WORSE THAN SITTING AT THE VERY BACK ON BROKEN SEATS?
"YES, THERE'S ALWAYS SOMETHING WORSE."
IS THAT A TATTOO ON YOUR FACE OR PISTACHIO ICE CREAM?
UM...SWEETIE, I THINK YOUR MOM'S CALLING YOU. SEE, RIGHT AT THE FRONT?
NO SHE ISN'T, AND THE DRIVER SENT ME BACK HERE SO I CAN'T TALK TO HIM WHILE HE'S DRIVING.
I CAN'T BLAME HIM...

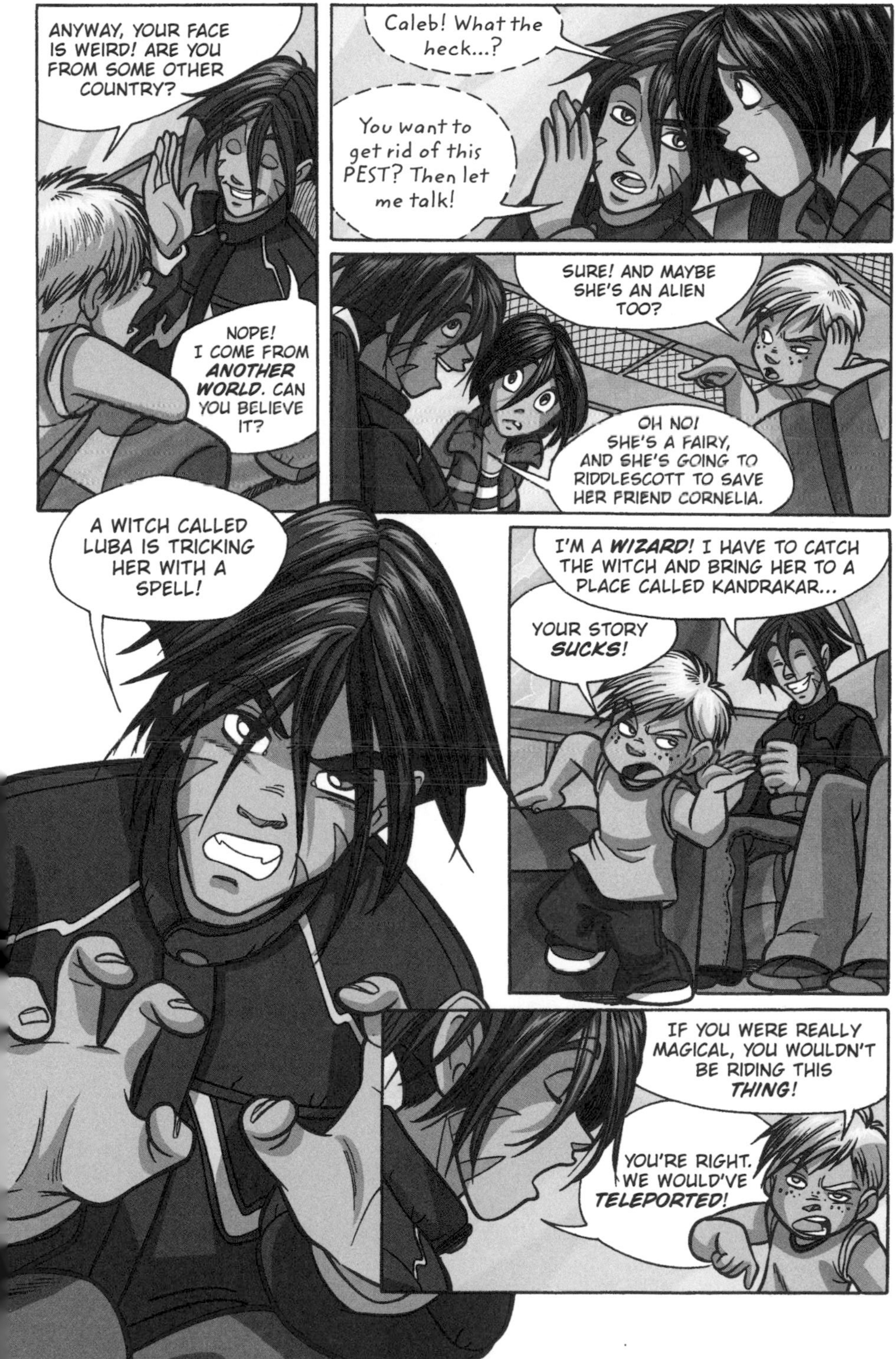
ANYWAY, YOUR FACE IS WEIRD! ARE YOU FROM SOME OTHER COUNTRY?
NOPE! I COME FROM ANOTHER WORLD. CAN YOU BELIEVE IT?
Caleb! What the heck...?
You want to get rid of this PEST? Then let me talk!
SURE! AND MAYBE SHE'S AN ALIEN TOO?
OH NO! SHE'S A FAIRY, AND SHE'S GOING TO RIDDLESCOTT TO SAVE HER FRIEND CORNELIA.
A WITCH CALLED LUBA IS TRICKING HER WITH A SPELL!
I'M A WIZARD! I HAVE TO CATCH THE WITCH AND BRING HER TO A PLACE CALLED KANDRAKAR...
YOUR STORY SUCKS!
IF YOU WERE REALLY MAGICAL, YOU WOULDN'T BE RIDING THIS THING!
YOU'RE RIGHT. WE WOULD'VE TELEPORTED!

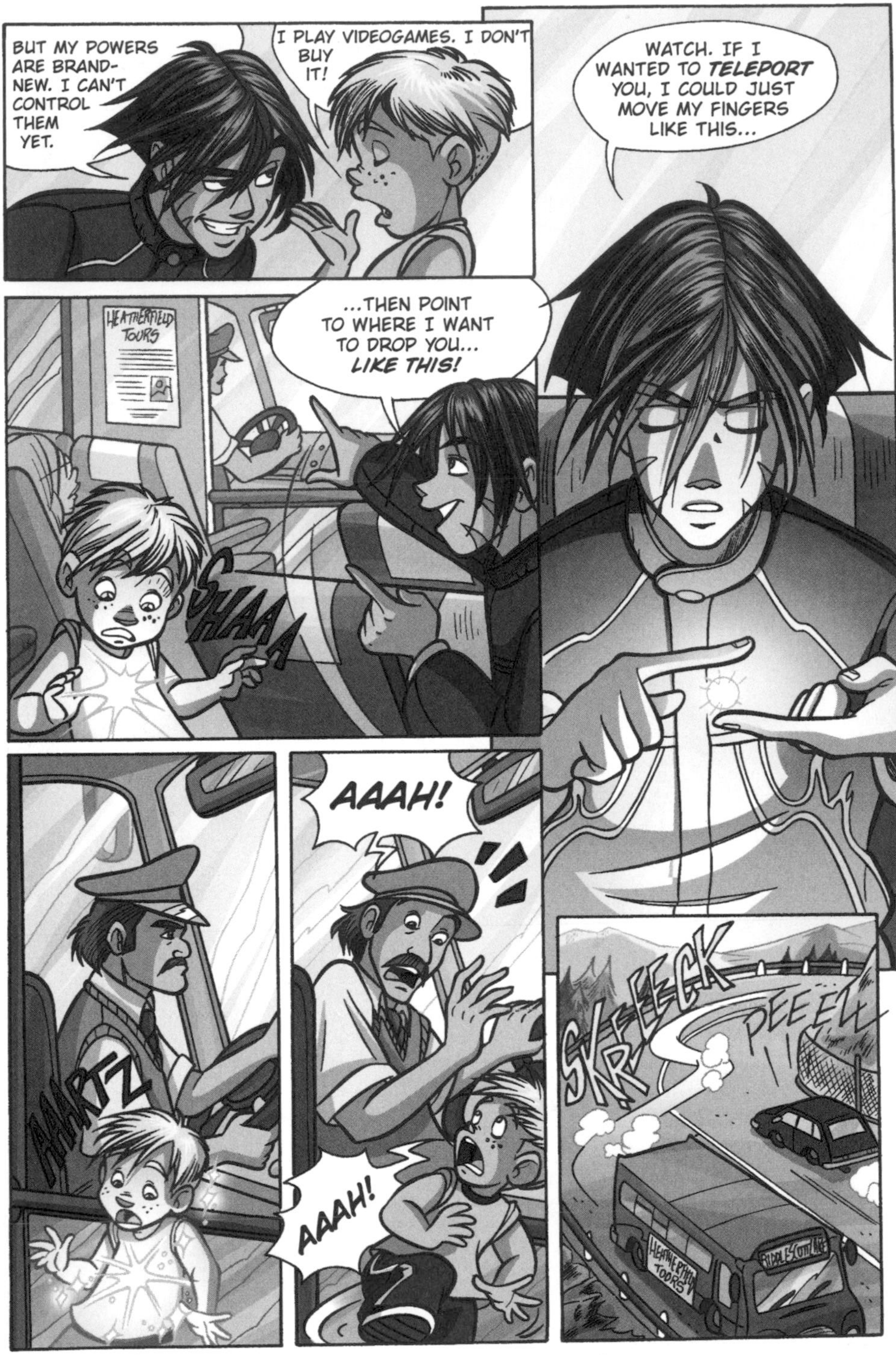
BUT MY POWERS ARE BRAND-NEW. I CAN'T CONTROL THEM YET.
I PLAY VIDEOGAMES. I DON'T BUY IT!
WATCH. IF I WANTED TO TELEPORT YOU, I COULD JUST MOVE MY FINGERS LIKE THIS...
HEATHERFIELD TOURS
...THEN POINT TO WHERE I WANT TO DROP YOU... LIKE THIS!
SHAAA
AAAH!
AAAH!
AAARTZ
SKREEECK
PEEEEE
HEATHERFIELD TOURS
RIDDLE'S CITY PARK

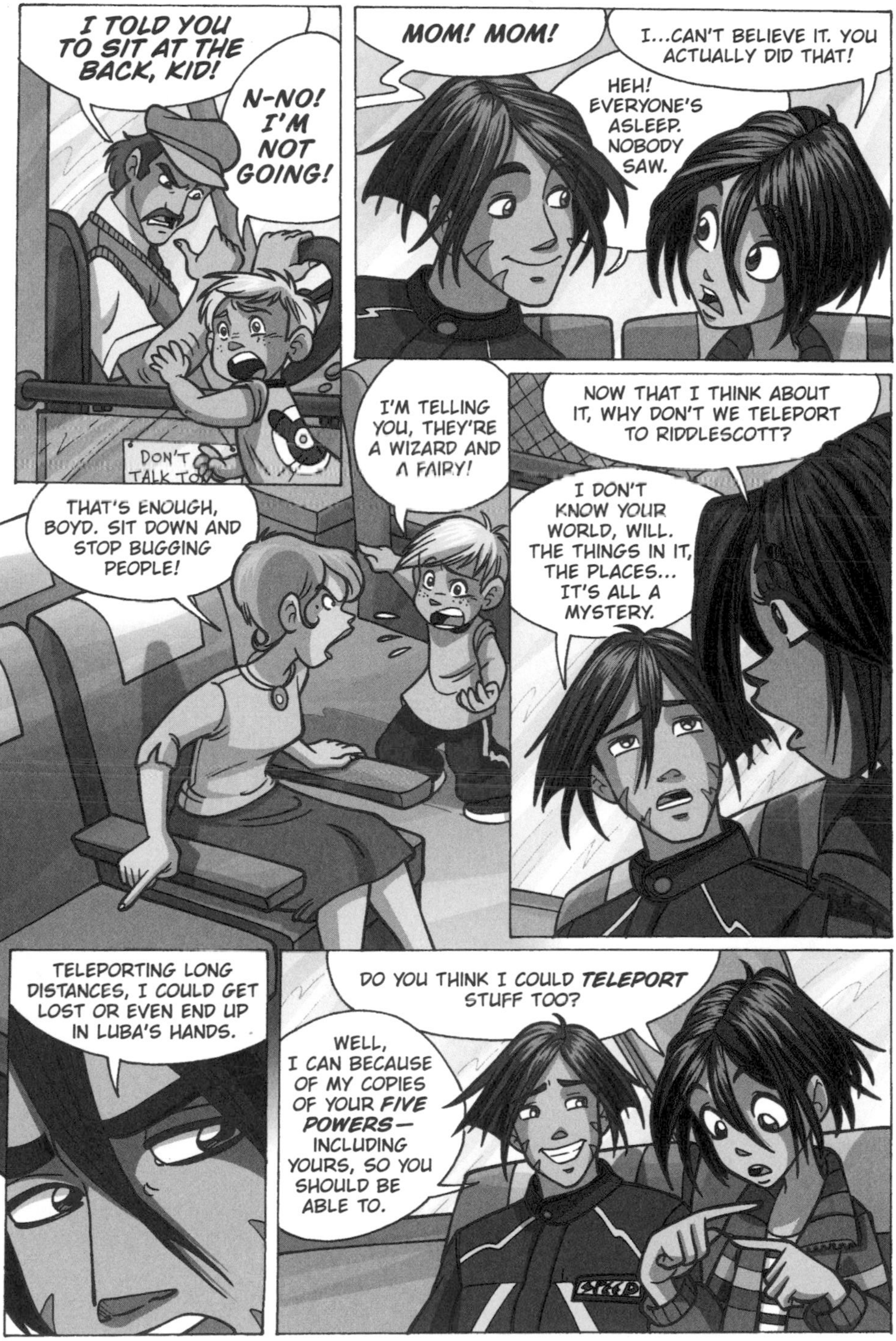

I TOLD YOU TO SIT AT THE BACK, KID!
N-NO! I'M NOT GOING!
DON'T TALK TO
MOM! MOM!
I...CAN'T BELIEVE IT. YOU ACTUALLY DID THAT!
HEH! EVERYONE'S ASLEEP. NOBODY SAW.
I'M TELLING YOU, THEY'RE A WIZARD AND A FAIRY!
THAT'S ENOUGH, BOYD. SIT DOWN AND STOP BUGGING PEOPLE!
NOW THAT I THINK ABOUT IT, WHY DON'T WE TELEPORT TO RIDDLESCOTT?
I DON'T KNOW YOUR WORLD, WILL. THE THINGS IN IT, THE PLACES... IT'S ALL A MYSTERY.
TELEPORTING LONG DISTANCES, I COULD GET LOST OR EVEN END UP IN LUBA'S HANDS.
DO YOU THINK I COULD TELEPORT STUFF TOO?
WELL, I CAN BECAUSE OF MY COPIES OF YOUR FIVE POWERS—INCLUDING YOURS, SO YOU SHOULD BE ABLE TO.
SPEED

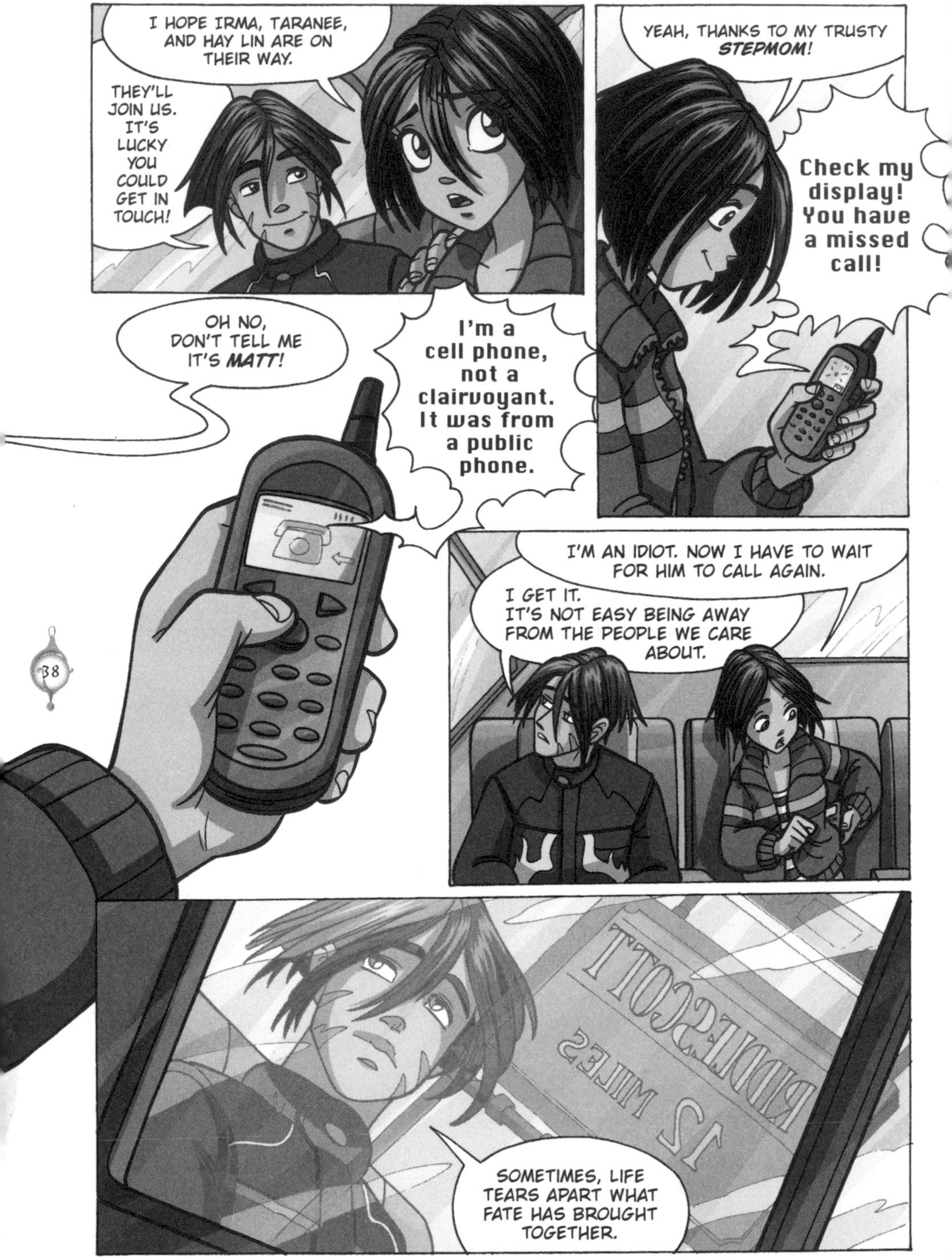
I HOPE IRMA, TARANEE, AND HAY LIN ARE ON THEIR WAY.
THEY'LL JOIN US. IT'S LUCKY YOU COULD GET IN TOUCH!
YEAH, THANKS TO MY TRUSTY STEPMOM!
Check my display! You have a missed call!
OH NO, DON'T TELL ME IT'S MATT!
I'm a cell phone, not a clairvoyant. It was from a public phone.
I'M AN IDIOT. NOW I HAVE TO WAIT FOR HIM TO CALL AGAIN.
I GET IT. IT'S NOT EASY BEING AWAY FROM THE PEOPLE WE CARE ABOUT.
RIDDLESCOTT 12 MILES
SOMETIMES, LIFE TEARS APART WHAT FATE HAS BROUGHT TOGETHER.

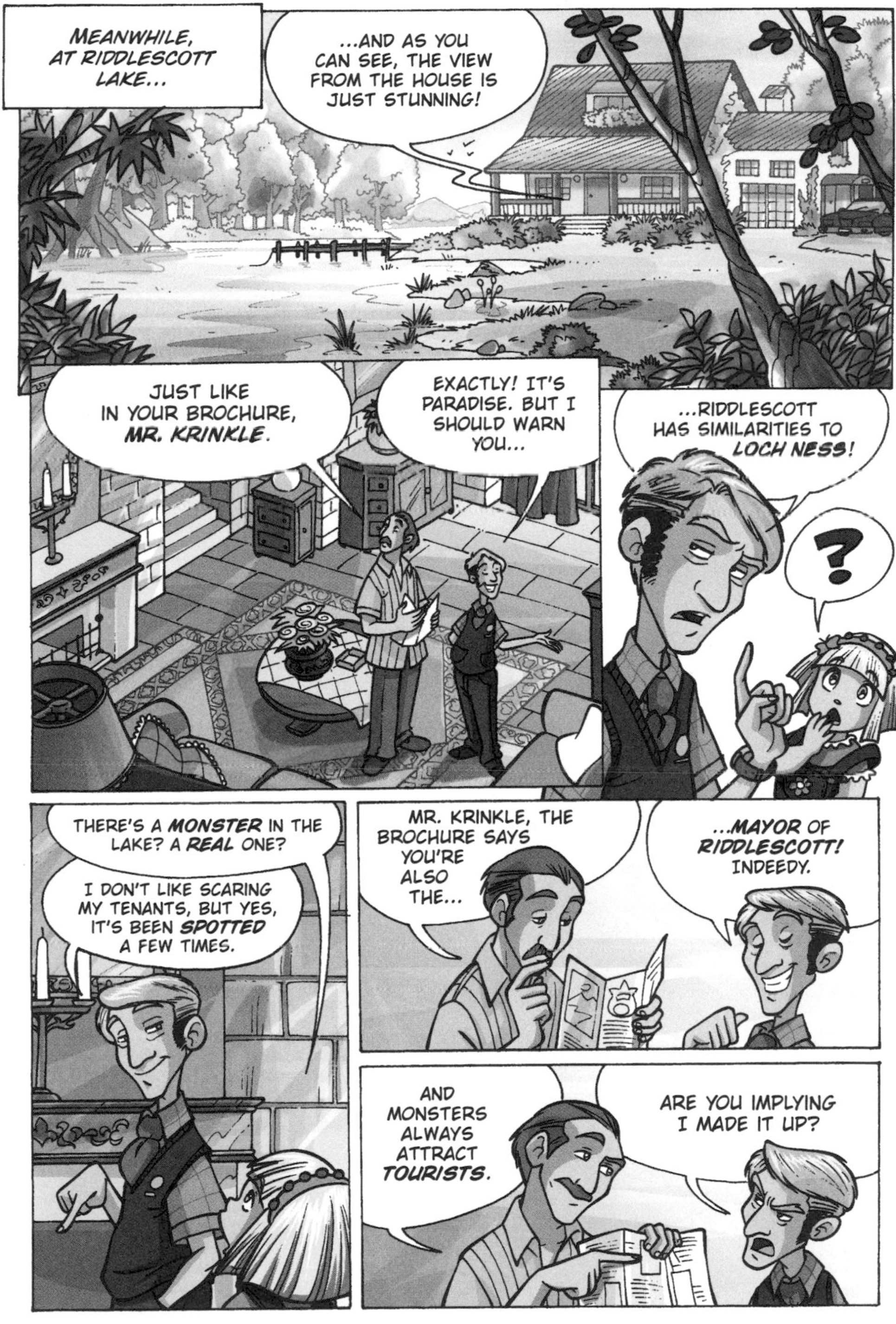
MEANWHILE, AT RIDDLESCOTT LAKE...
...AND AS YOU CAN SEE, THE VIEW FROM THE HOUSE IS JUST STUNNING!
JUST LIKE IN YOUR BROCHURE, MR. KRINKLE.
EXACTLY! IT'S PARADISE. BUT I SHOULD WARN YOU...
...RIDDLESCOTT HAS SIMILARITIES TO LOCH NESS!
?
THERE'S A MONSTER IN THE LAKE? A REAL ONE?
I DON'T LIKE SCARING MY TENANTS, BUT YES, IT'S BEEN SPOTTED A FEW TIMES.
MR. KRINKLE, THE BROCHURE SAYS YOU'RE ALSO THE...
...MAYOR OF RIDDLESCOTT! INDEEDY.
AND MONSTERS ALWAYS ATTRACT TOURISTS.
ARE YOU IMPLYING I MADE IT UP?

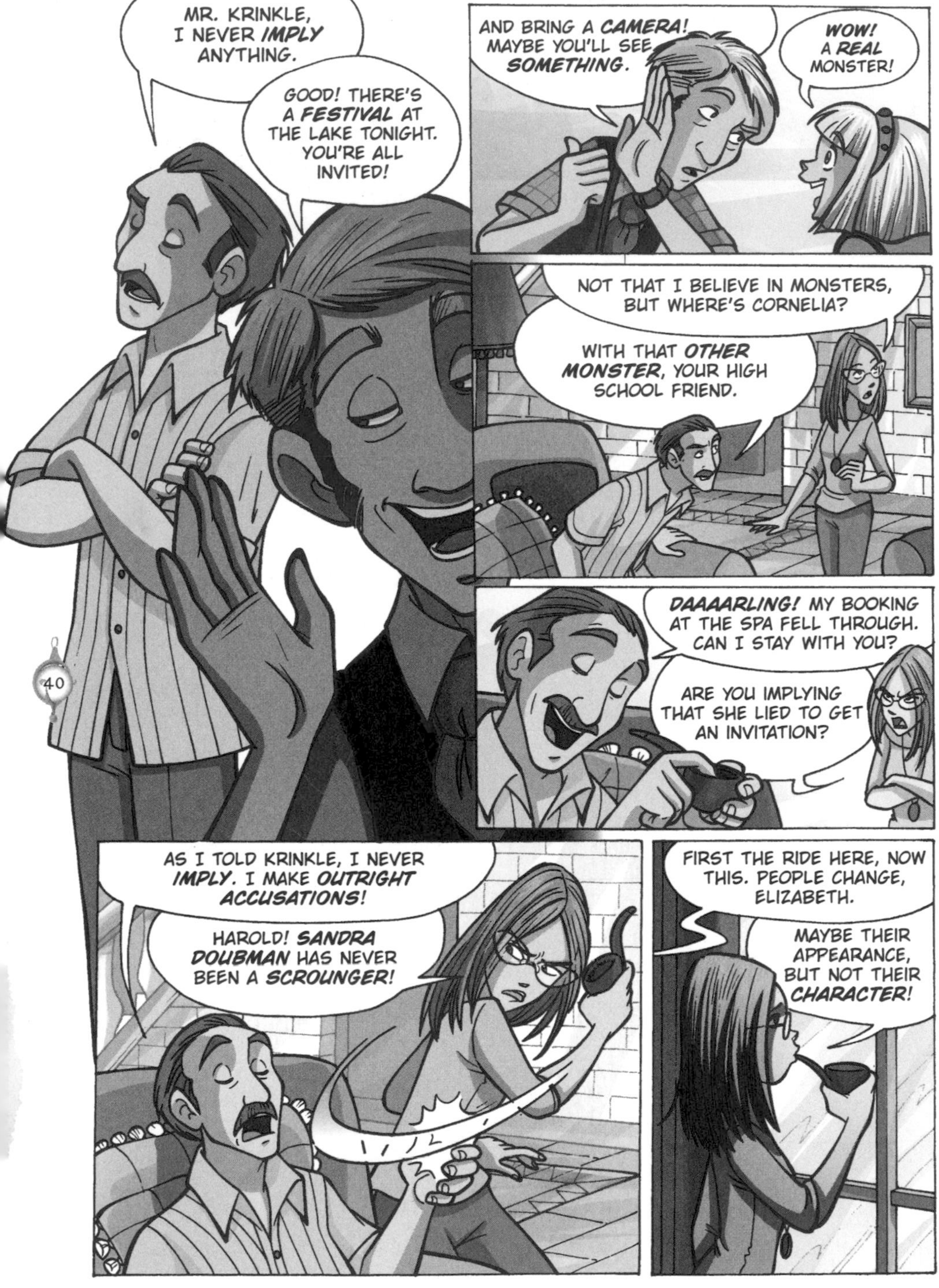

MR. KRINKLE, I NEVER *IMPLY* ANYTHING.
GOOD! THERE'S A *FESTIVAL* AT THE LAKE TONIGHT. YOU'RE ALL INVITED!
AND BRING A *CAMERA*! MAYBE YOU'LL SEE *SOMETHING*.
WOW! A *REAL* MONSTER!
NOT THAT I BELIEVE IN MONSTERS, BUT WHERE'S CORNELIA?
WITH THAT *OTHER MONSTER*, YOUR HIGH SCHOOL FRIEND.
DAAAARLING! MY BOOKING AT THE SPA FELL THROUGH. CAN I STAY WITH YOU?
ARE YOU IMPLYING THAT SHE LIED TO GET AN INVITATION?
AS I TOLD KRINKLE, I NEVER *IMPLY*. I MAKE *OUTRIGHT ACCUSATIONS*!
HAROLD! *SANDRA DOUBMAN* HAS NEVER BEEN A *SCROUNGER*!
FIRST THE RIDE HERE, NOW THIS. PEOPLE CHANGE, ELIZABETH.
MAYBE THEIR APPEARANCE, BUT NOT THEIR *CHARACTER*!

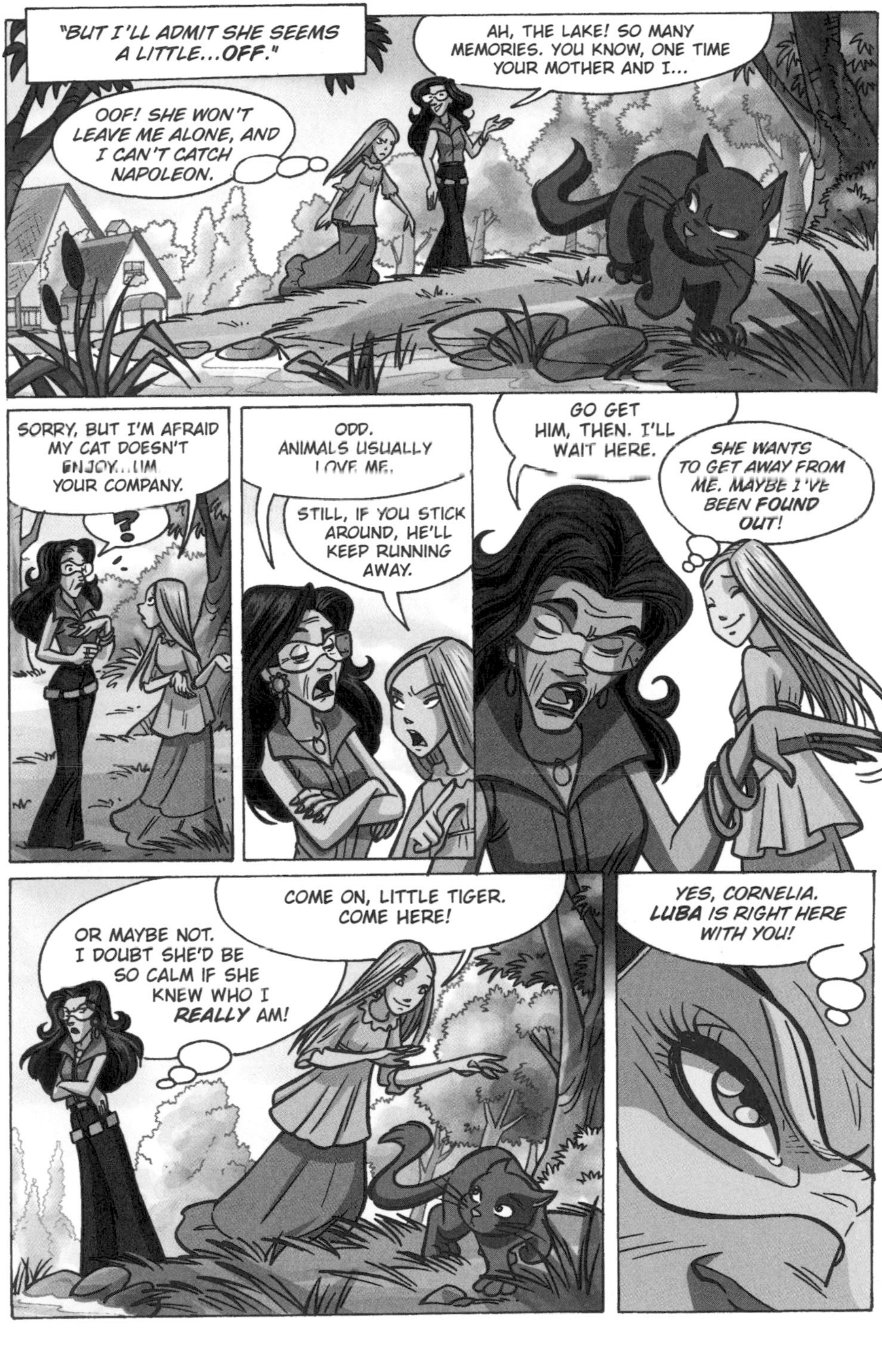
"BUT I'LL ADMIT SHE SEEMS A LITTLE...OFF."
AH, THE LAKE! SO MANY MEMORIES. YOU KNOW, ONE TIME YOUR MOTHER AND I...
OOF! SHE WON'T LEAVE ME ALONE, AND I CAN'T CATCH NAPOLEON.
SORRY, BUT I'M AFRAID MY CAT DOESN'T ENJOY...UM... YOUR COMPANY.
?
ODD. ANIMALS USUALLY LOVE ME.
STILL, IF YOU STICK AROUND, HE'LL KEEP RUNNING AWAY.
GO GET HIM, THEN. I'LL WAIT HERE.
SHE WANTS TO GET AWAY FROM ME. MAYBE I'VE BEEN FOUND OUT!
OR MAYBE NOT. I DOUBT SHE'D BE SO CALM IF SHE KNEW WHO I REALLY AM!
COME ON, LITTLE TIGER. COME HERE!
YES, CORNELIA. LUBA IS RIGHT HERE WITH YOU!

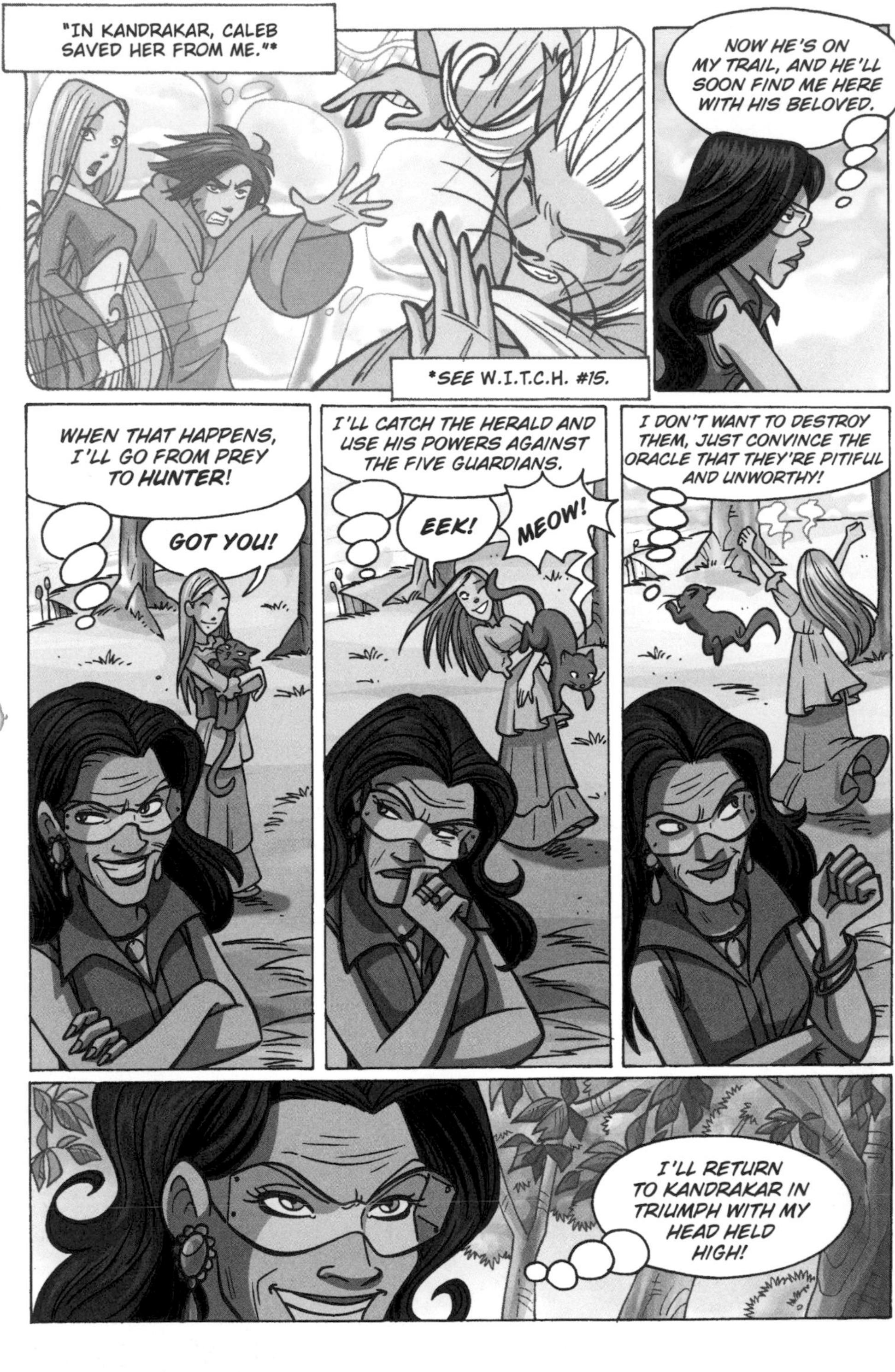
"IN KANDRAKAR, CALEB SAVED HER FROM ME."*
*SEE W.I.T.C.H. #15.
NOW HE'S ON MY TRAIL, AND HE'LL SOON FIND ME HERE WITH HIS BELOVED.
WHEN THAT HAPPENS, I'LL GO FROM PREY TO HUNTER!
GOT YOU!
I'LL CATCH THE HERALD AND USE HIS POWERS AGAINST THE FIVE GUARDIANS.
EEK!
MEOW!
I DON'T WANT TO DESTROY THEM, JUST CONVINCE THE ORACLE THAT THEY'RE PITIFUL AND UNWORTHY!
I'LL RETURN TO KANDRAKAR IN TRIUMPH WITH MY HEAD HELD HIGH!

RIDDLESCOTT, NAMED AFTER THE LAKE, IS A CHARMING TOWN OF 1,500 PEOPLE AND MAKES ITS LIVING FROM FISHING...

FISHING FOR *TOURISTS*, THAT IS.

PHOTOSCOTTY

EXCLUSIVE BLURRY PHOTOS OF SCOTTY

T-SHIRTS OF SCOTTY, THE LAKE MONSTER

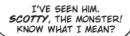

43

HUH? YOU TALKING TO US?

PSSSST! HEY, GUYS!

I'VE SEEN HIM. *SCOTTY*, THE MONSTER! KNOW WHAT I MEAN?

DO WE KNOW WHAT HE MEANS?

I THINK HE WANTS TO *SELL* US SOMETHING.

I KNOW THIS LAKE LIKE THE BACK OF MY HANDS. FOLLOW ME!

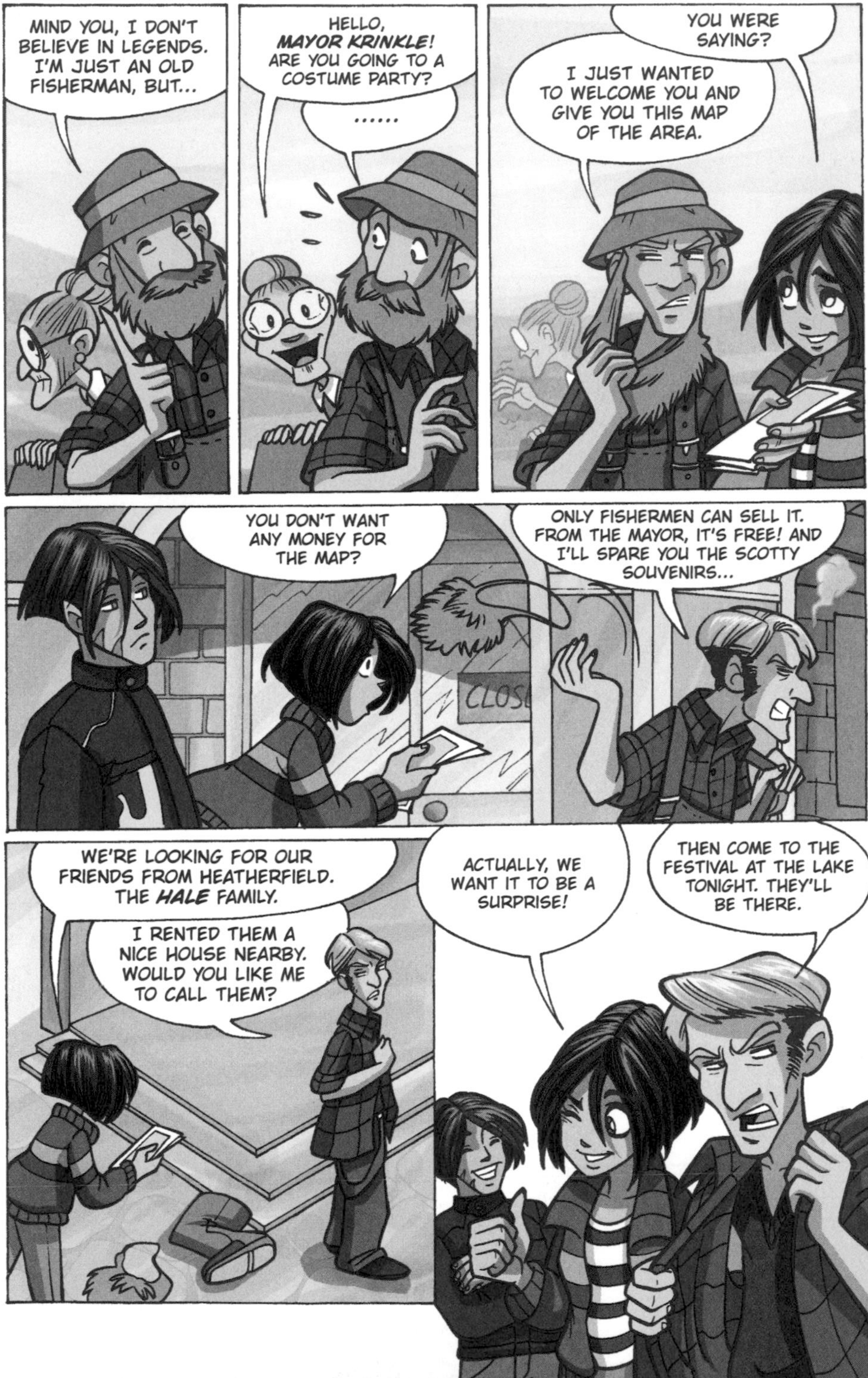

MIND YOU, I DON'T BELIEVE IN LEGENDS. I'M JUST AN OLD FISHERMAN, BUT...
HELLO, MAYOR KRINKLE! ARE YOU GOING TO A COSTUME PARTY?
......
YOU WERE SAYING?
I JUST WANTED TO WELCOME YOU AND GIVE YOU THIS MAP OF THE AREA.
YOU DON'T WANT ANY MONEY FOR THE MAP?
ONLY FISHERMEN CAN SELL IT. FROM THE MAYOR, IT'S FREE! AND I'LL SPARE YOU THE SCOTTY SOUVENIRS...
CLOS
WE'RE LOOKING FOR OUR FRIENDS FROM HEATHERFIELD. THE HALE FAMILY.
I RENTED THEM A NICE HOUSE NEARBY. WOULD YOU LIKE ME TO CALL THEM?
ACTUALLY, WE WANT IT TO BE A SURPRISE!
THEN COME TO THE FESTIVAL AT THE LAKE TONIGHT. THEY'LL BE THERE.

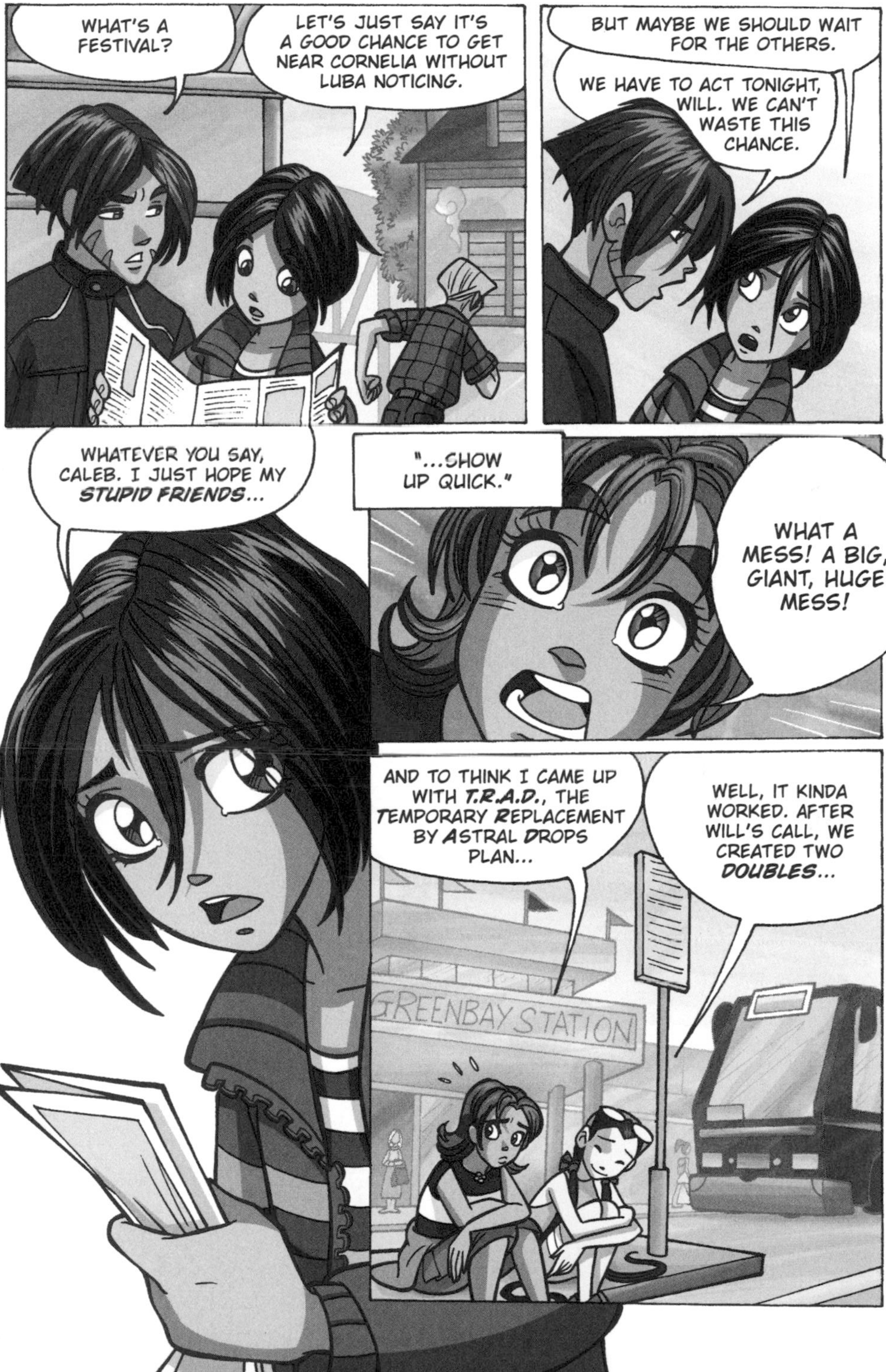
WHAT'S A FESTIVAL?
LET'S JUST SAY IT'S A GOOD CHANCE TO GET NEAR CORNELIA WITHOUT LUBA NOTICING.
BUT MAYBE WE SHOULD WAIT FOR THE OTHERS.
WE HAVE TO ACT TONIGHT, WILL. WE CAN'T WASTE THIS CHANCE.
WHATEVER YOU SAY, CALEB. I JUST HOPE MY STUPID FRIENDS...
"...SHOW UP QUICK."
WHAT A MESS! A BIG, GIANT, HUGE MESS!
AND TO THINK I CAME UP WITH T.R.A.D., THE TEMPORARY REPLACEMENT BY ASTRAL DROPS PLAN...
WELL, IT KINDA WORKED. AFTER WILL'S CALL, WE CREATED TWO DOUBLES...
GREENBAY STATION

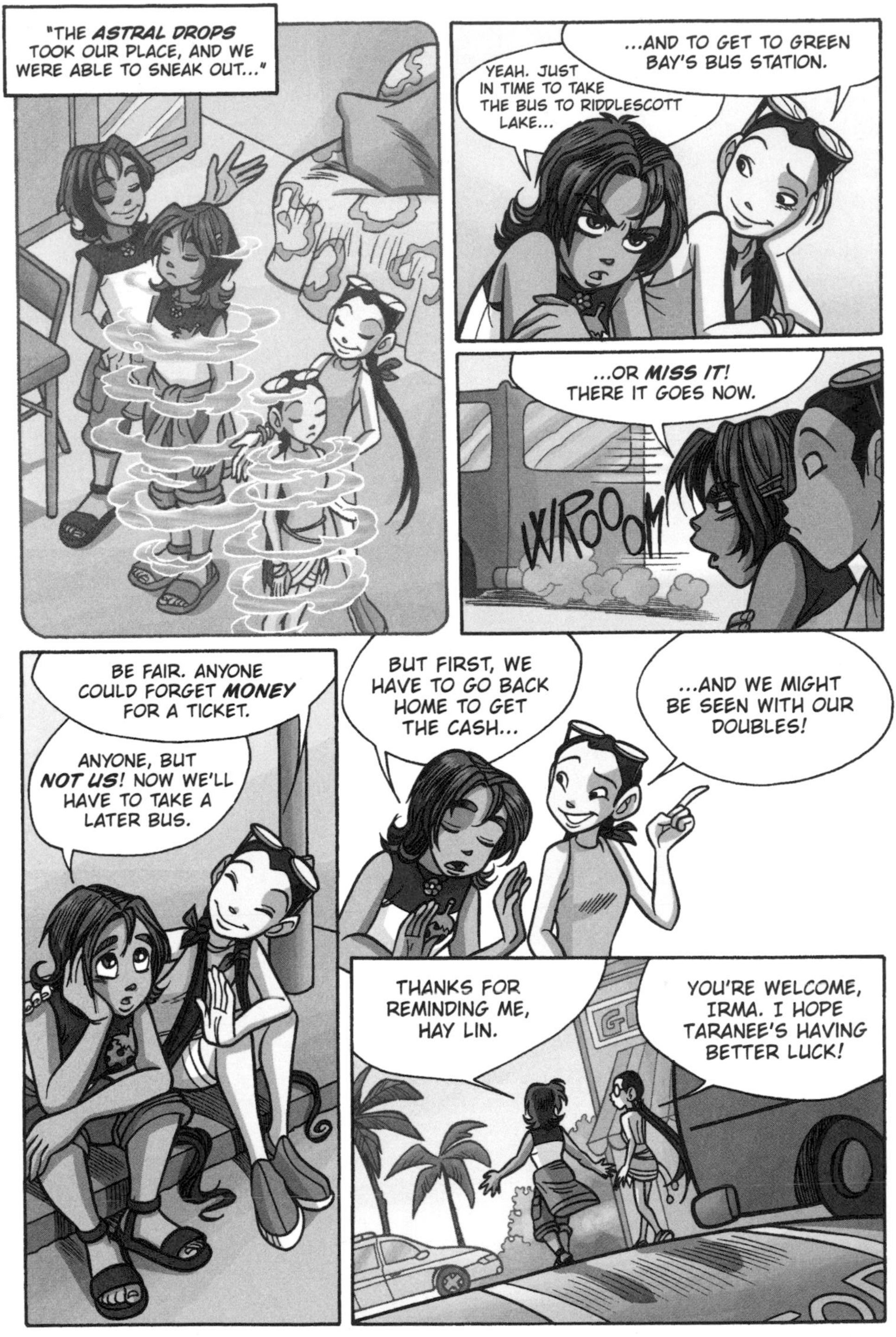
"THE *ASTRAL DROPS* TOOK OUR PLACE, AND WE WERE ABLE TO SNEAK OUT..."
YEAH. JUST IN TIME TO TAKE THE BUS TO RIDDLESCOTT LAKE...
...AND TO GET TO GREEN BAY'S BUS STATION.
...OR *MISS IT*! THERE IT GOES NOW.
WROOOM
BE FAIR. ANYONE COULD FORGET *MONEY* FOR A TICKET.
ANYONE, BUT *NOT US*! NOW WE'LL HAVE TO TAKE A LATER BUS.
BUT FIRST, WE HAVE TO GO BACK HOME TO GET THE CASH...
...AND WE MIGHT BE SEEN WITH OUR DOUBLES!
THANKS FOR REMINDING ME, HAY LIN.
YOU'RE WELCOME, IRMA. I HOPE TARANEE'S HAVING BETTER LUCK!

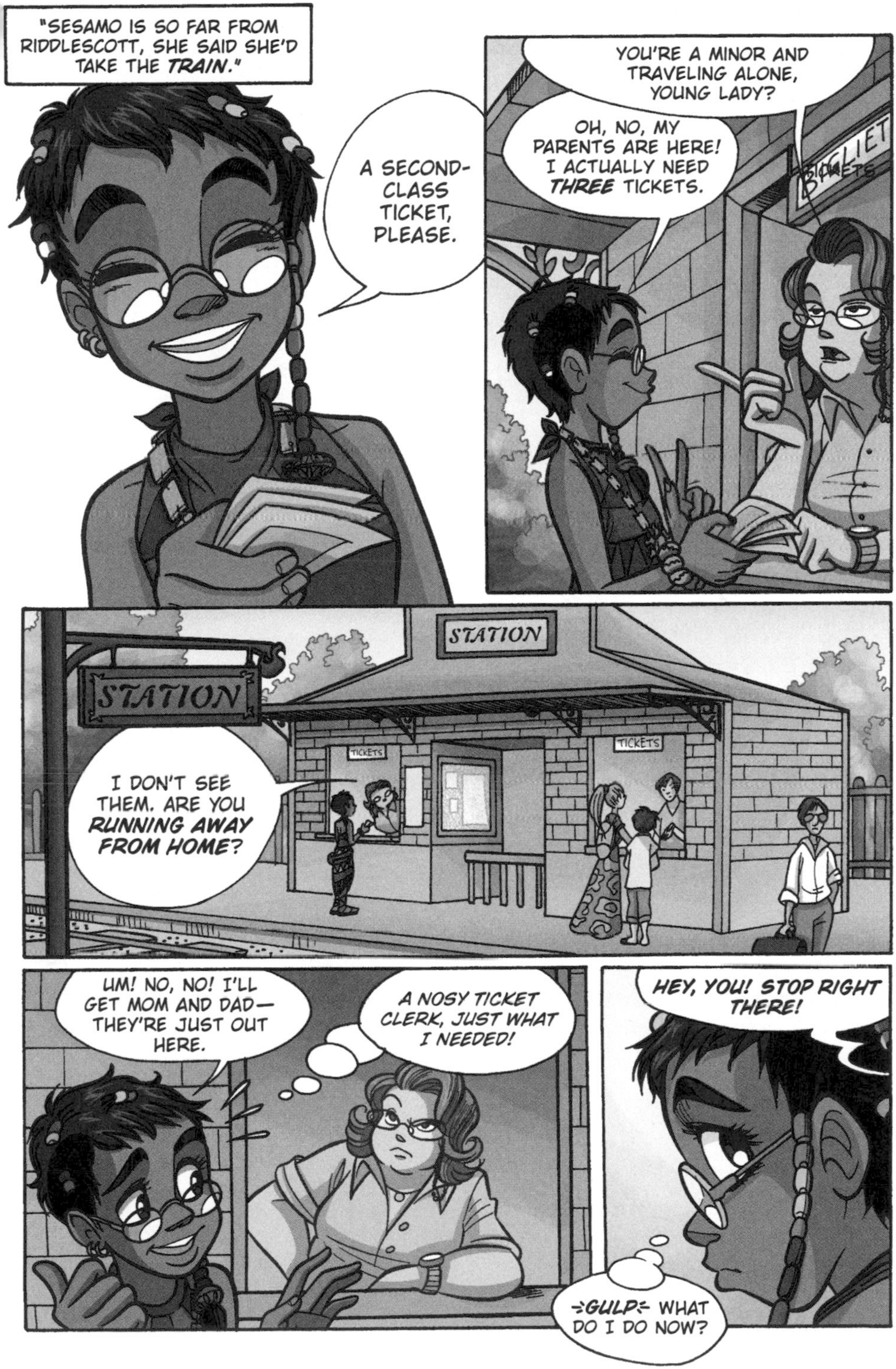
"SESAMO IS SO FAR FROM RIDDLESCOTT, SHE SAID SHE'D TAKE THE *TRAIN*."
A SECOND-CLASS TICKET, PLEASE.
YOU'RE A MINOR AND TRAVELING ALONE, YOUNG LADY?
OH, NO, MY PARENTS ARE HERE! I ACTUALLY NEED *THREE* TICKETS.
STATION
STATION
TICKETS
TICKETS
I DON'T SEE THEM. ARE YOU *RUNNING AWAY FROM HOME*?
UM! NO, NO! I'LL GET MOM AND DAD—THEY'RE JUST OUT HERE.
A NOSY TICKET CLERK, JUST WHAT I NEEDED!
HEY, YOU! STOP RIGHT THERE!
GULP WHAT DO I DO NOW?

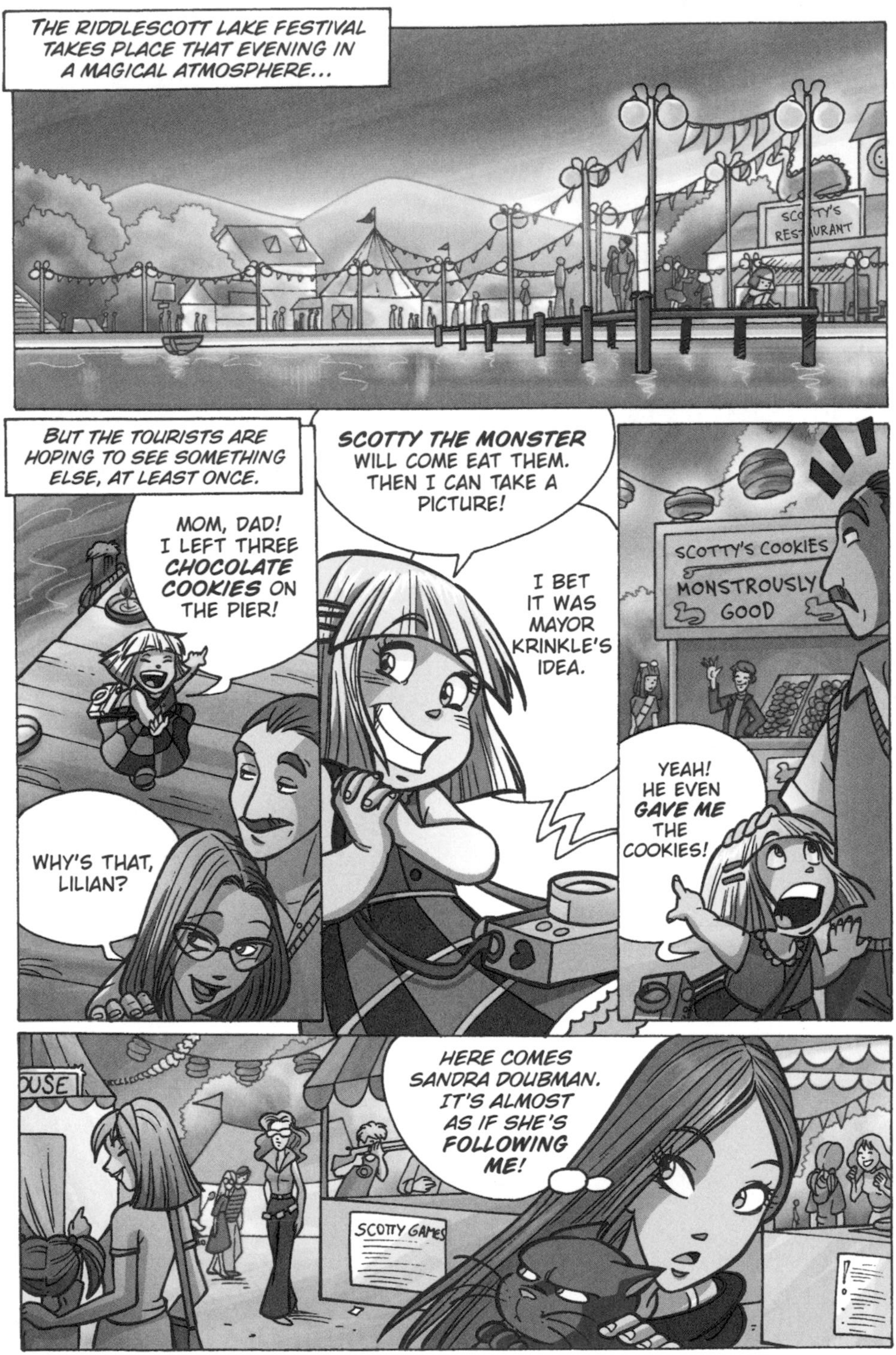
THE RIDDLESCOTT LAKE FESTIVAL TAKES PLACE THAT EVENING IN A MAGICAL ATMOSPHERE...
SCOTTY'S RESTAURANT
BUT THE TOURISTS ARE HOPING TO SEE SOMETHING ELSE, AT LEAST ONCE.
MOM, DAD! I LEFT THREE CHOCOLATE COOKIES ON THE PIER!
WHY'S THAT, LILIAN?
SCOTTY THE MONSTER WILL COME EAT THEM. THEN I CAN TAKE A PICTURE!
I BET IT WAS MAYOR KRINKLE'S IDEA.
SCOTTY'S COOKIES MONSTROUSLY GOOD
YEAH! HE EVEN GAVE ME THE COOKIES!
OUSE
SCOTTY GAMES
HERE COMES SANDRA DOUBMAN. IT'S ALMOST AS IF SHE'S FOLLOWING ME!

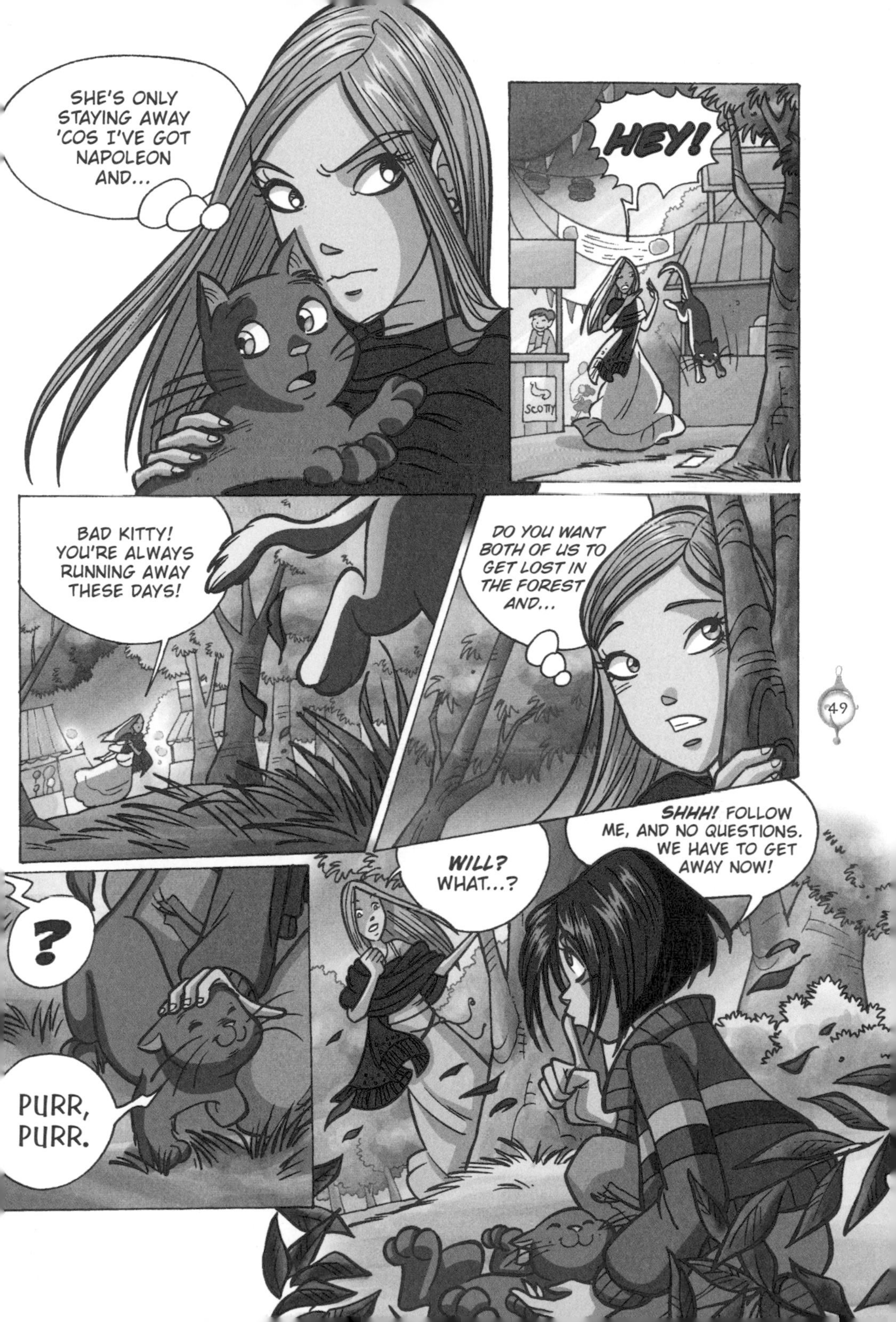
SHE'S ONLY STAYING AWAY 'COS I'VE GOT NAPOLEON AND...
HEY!
SCOTTY
BAD KITTY! YOU'RE ALWAYS RUNNING AWAY THESE DAYS!
DO YOU WANT BOTH OF US TO GET LOST IN THE FOREST AND...
?
PURR, PURR.
WILL? WHAT...?
SHHH! FOLLOW ME, AND NO QUESTIONS. WE HAVE TO GET AWAY NOW!

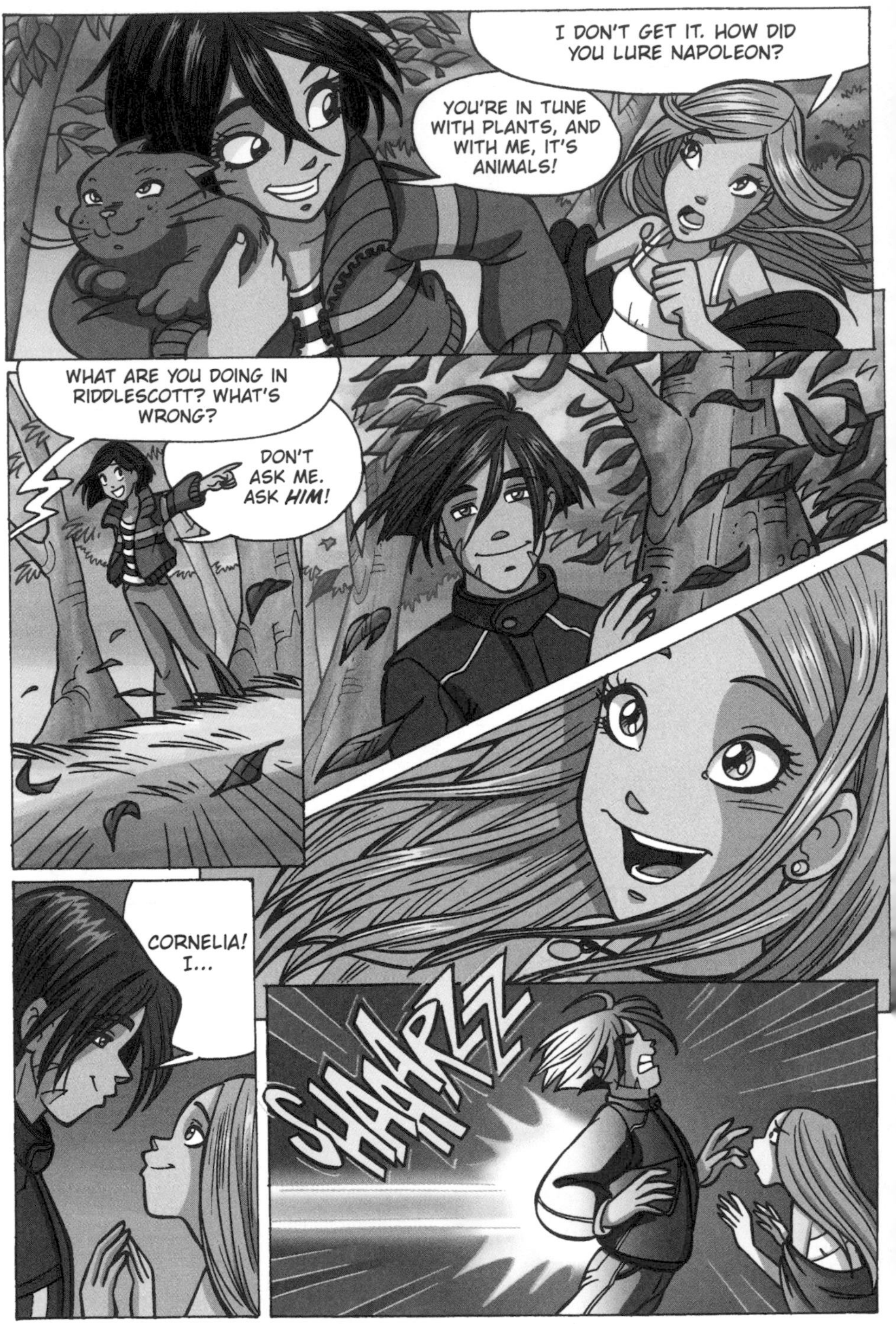
I DON'T GET IT. HOW DID YOU LURE NAPOLEON?
YOU'RE IN TUNE WITH PLANTS, AND WITH ME, IT'S ANIMALS!
WHAT ARE YOU DOING IN RIDDLESCOTT? WHAT'S WRONG?
DON'T ASK ME. ASK *HIM*!
CORNELIA! I...
SHAARZZ

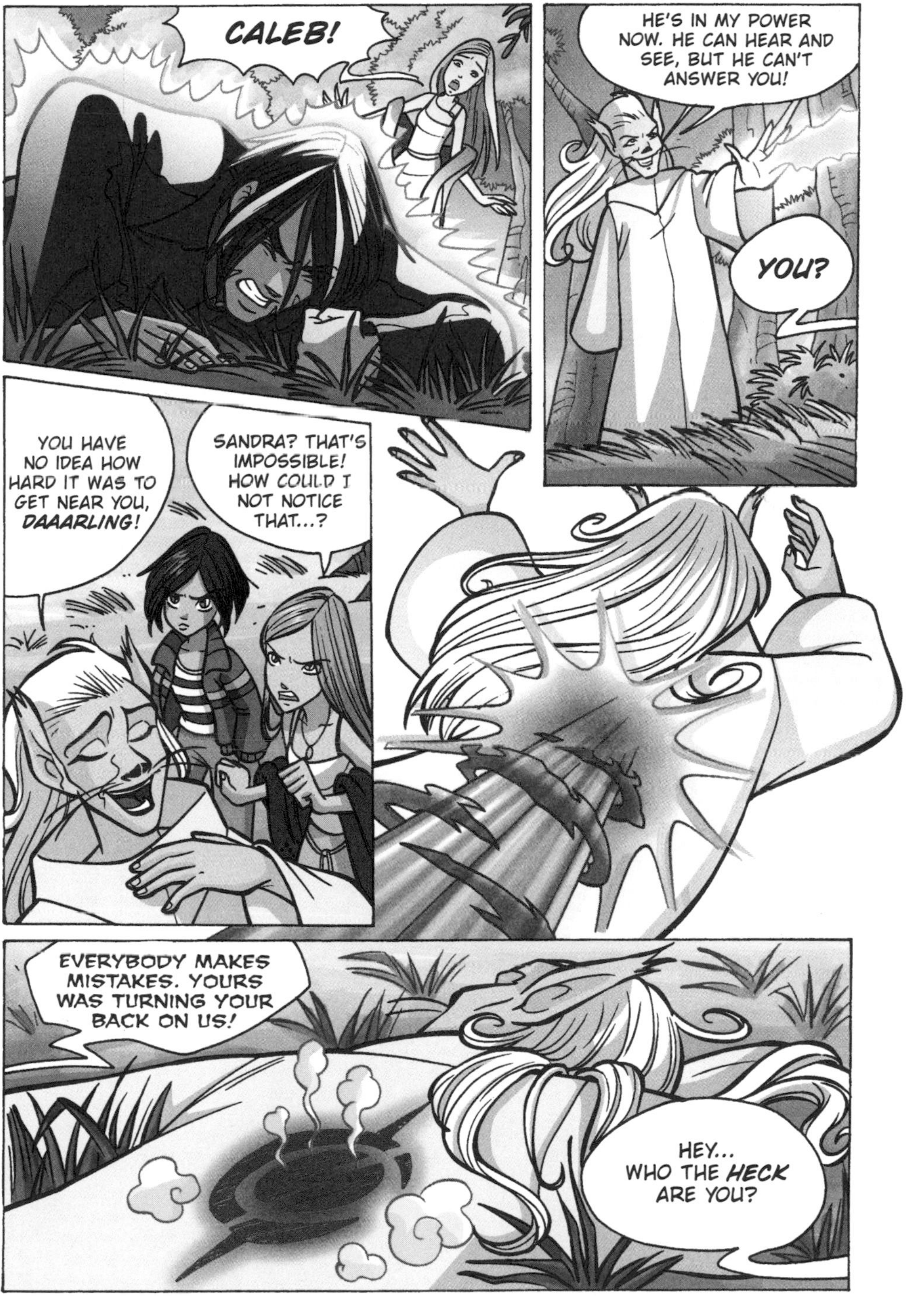
CALEB!
HE'S IN MY POWER NOW. HE CAN HEAR AND SEE, BUT HE CAN'T ANSWER YOU!
YOU?
YOU HAVE NO IDEA HOW HARD IT WAS TO GET NEAR YOU, DAAARLING!
SANDRA? THAT'S IMPOSSIBLE! HOW COULD I NOT NOTICE THAT...?
EVERYBODY MAKES MISTAKES. YOURS WAS TURNING YOUR BACK ON US!
HEY... WHO THE HECK ARE YOU?

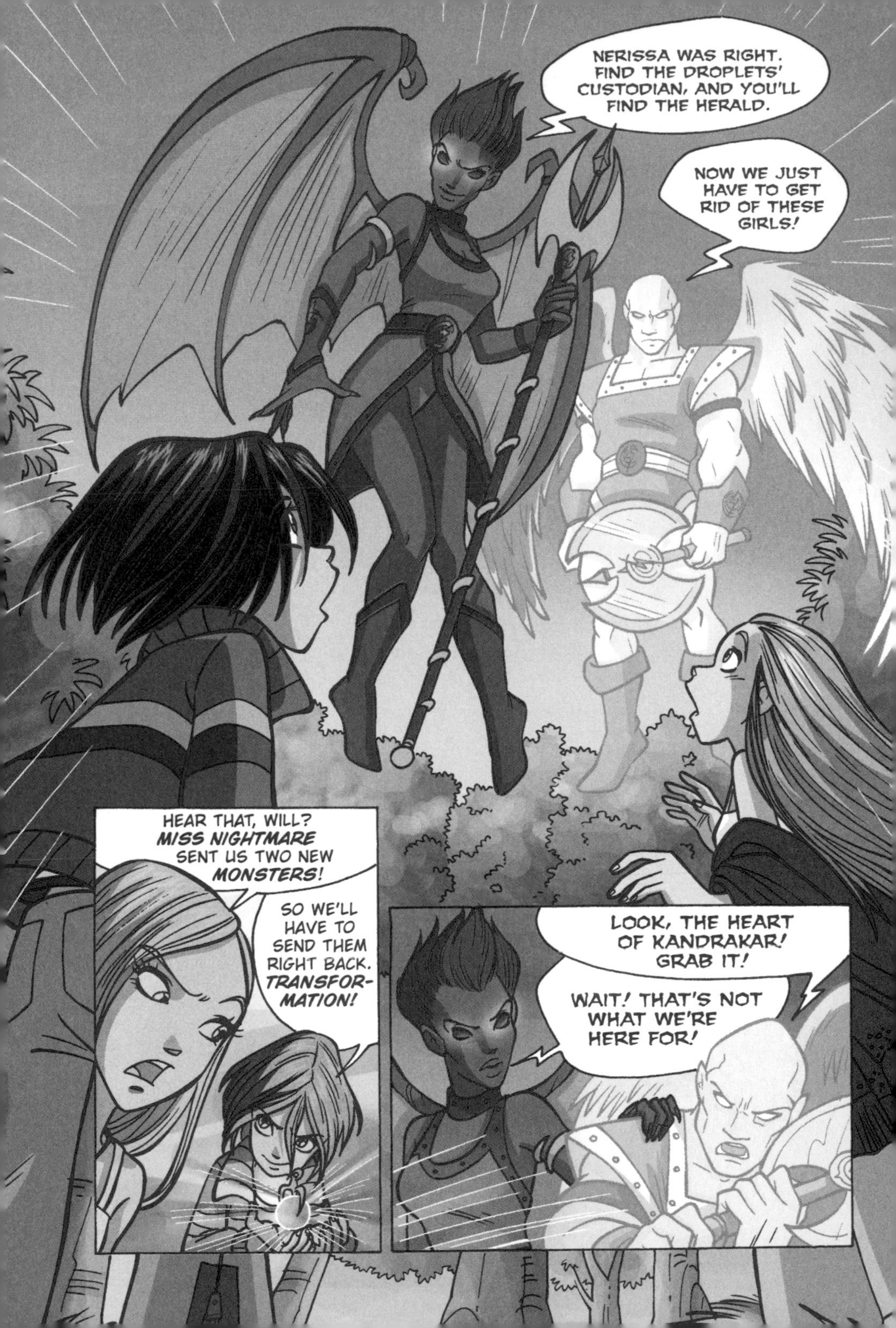
NERISSA WAS RIGHT. FIND THE DROPLETS' CUSTODIAN, AND YOU'LL FIND THE HERALD.
NOW WE JUST HAVE TO GET RID OF THESE GIRLS!
HEAR THAT, WILL? *MISS NIGHTMARE* SENT US TWO NEW *MONSTERS*!
SO WE'LL HAVE TO SEND THEM RIGHT BACK. *TRANSFORMATION*!
LOOK, THE HEART OF KANDRAKAR! GRAB IT!
WAIT! THAT'S NOT WHAT WE'RE HERE FOR!

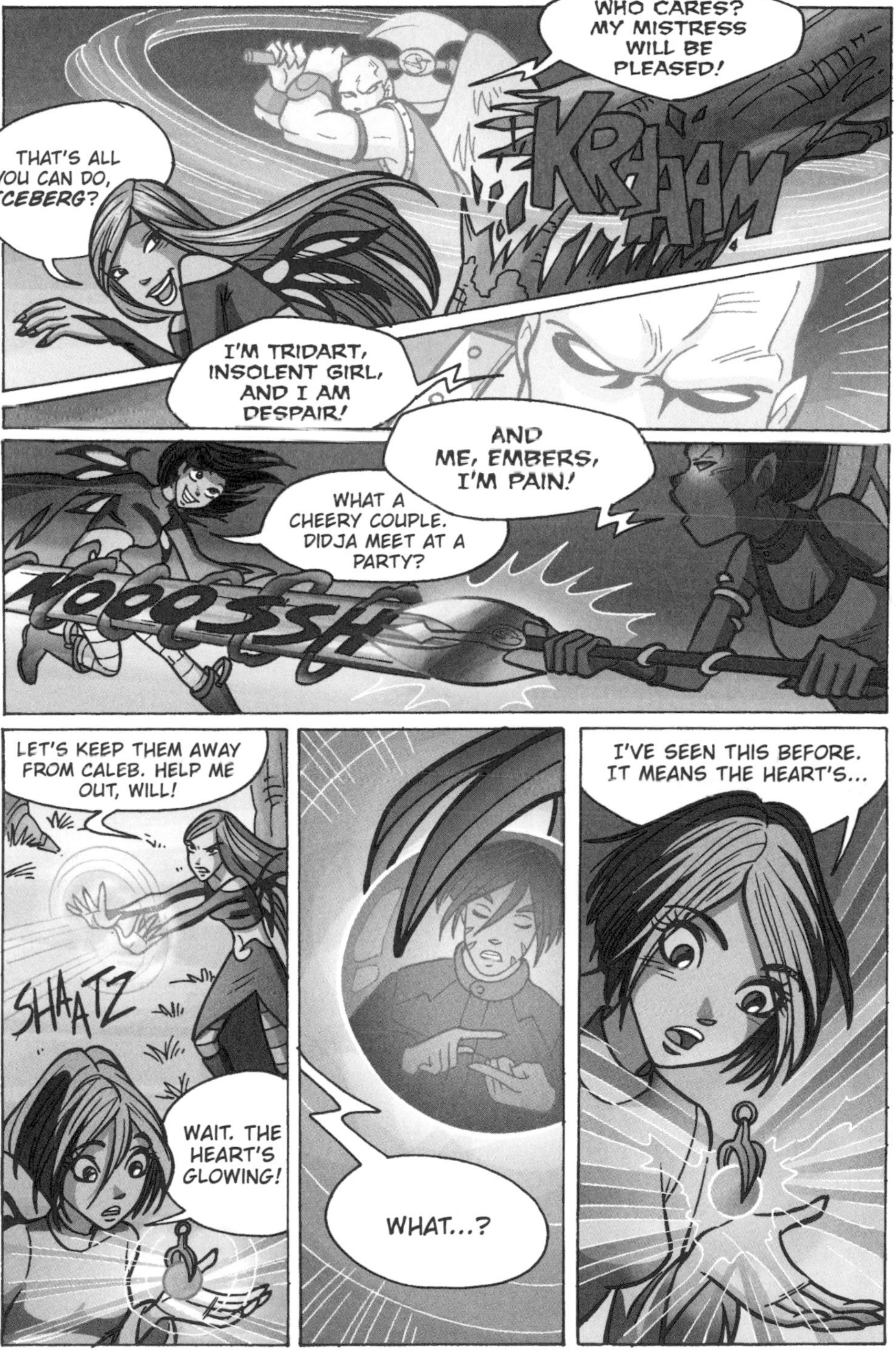
WHO CARES? MY MISTRESS WILL BE PLEASED!
KRAAAM
THAT'S ALL YOU CAN DO, *ICEBERG*?
I'M TRIDART, INSOLENT GIRL, AND I AM DESPAIR!
AND ME, EMBERS, I'M PAIN!
WHAT A CHEERY COUPLE. DIDJA MEET AT A PARTY?
WOOOSSH
LET'S KEEP THEM AWAY FROM CALEB. HELP ME OUT, WILL!
SHAATZ
WAIT. THE HEART'S GLOWING!
WHAT...?
I'VE SEEN THIS BEFORE. IT MEANS THE HEART'S...

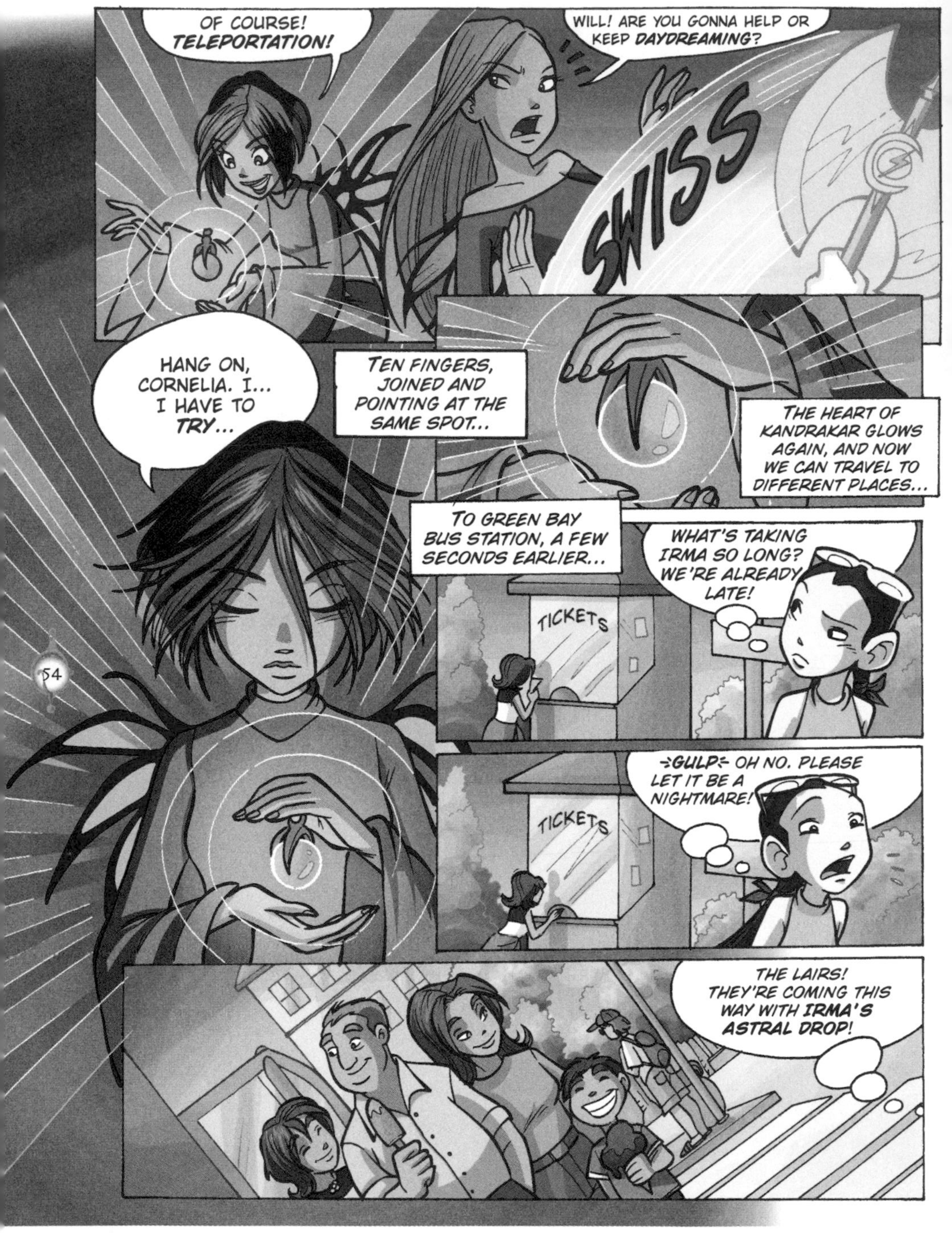
OF COURSE! TELEPORTATION!
WILL! ARE YOU GONNA HELP OR KEEP DAYDREAMING?
SWISS
HANG ON, CORNELIA. I... I HAVE TO TRY...
TEN FINGERS, JOINED AND POINTING AT THE SAME SPOT...
THE HEART OF KANDRAKAR GLOWS AGAIN, AND NOW WE CAN TRAVEL TO DIFFERENT PLACES...
TO GREEN BAY BUS STATION, A FEW SECONDS EARLIER...
WHAT'S TAKING IRMA SO LONG? WE'RE ALREADY LATE!
TICKETS
TICKETS
-GULP- OH NO. PLEASE LET IT BE A NIGHTMARE!
THE LAIRS! THEY'RE COMING THIS WAY WITH IRMA'S ASTRAL DROP!

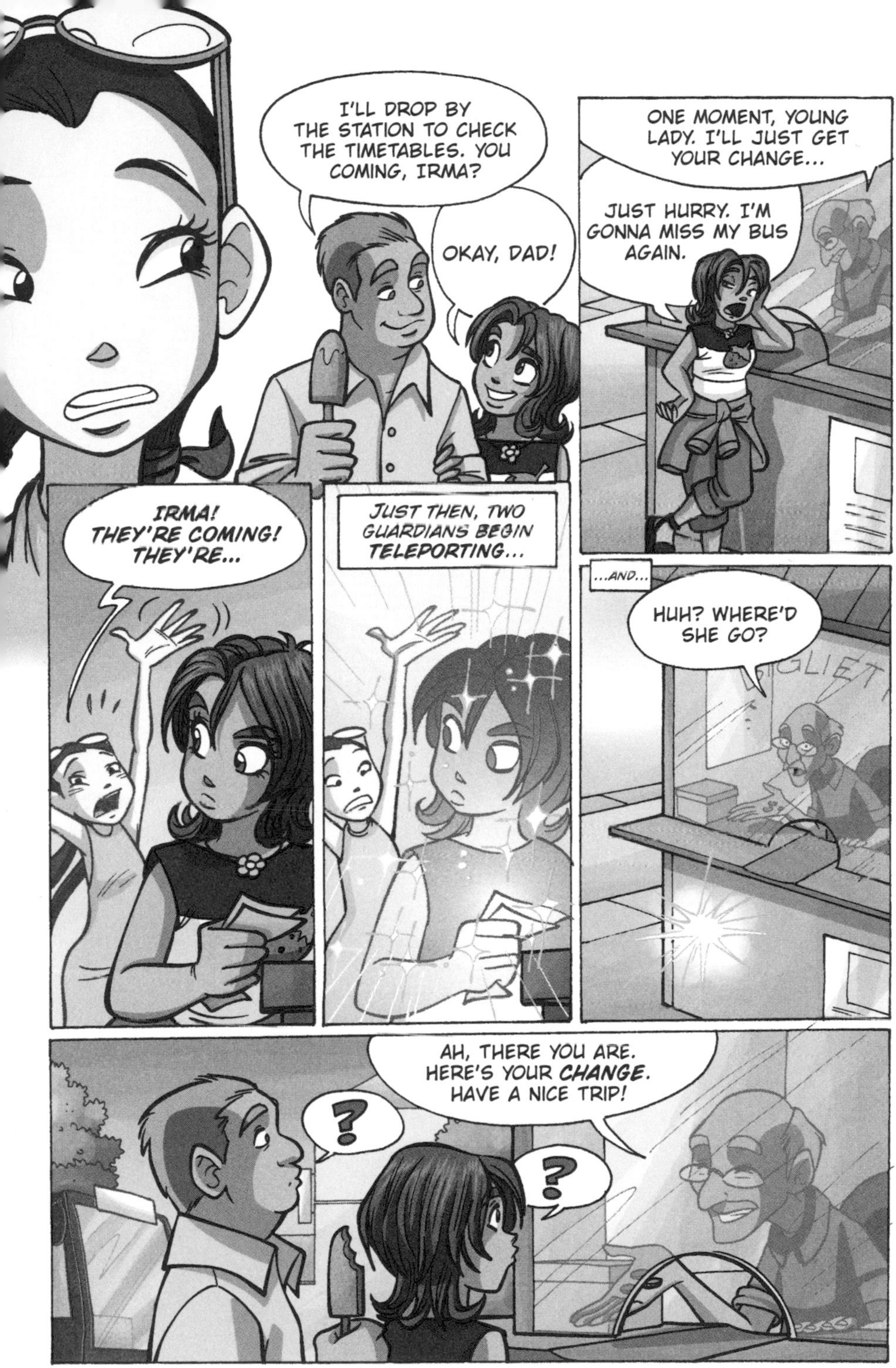
I'LL DROP BY THE STATION TO CHECK THE TIMETABLES. YOU COMING, IRMA?
OKAY, DAD!
ONE MOMENT, YOUNG LADY. I'LL JUST GET YOUR CHANGE...
JUST HURRY. I'M GONNA MISS MY BUS AGAIN.
IRMA! THEY'RE COMING! THEY'RE...
JUST THEN, TWO GUARDIANS BEGIN TELEPORTING...
...AND...
HUH? WHERE'D SHE GO?
AH, THERE YOU ARE. HERE'S YOUR CHANGE. HAVE A NICE TRIP!
?
?

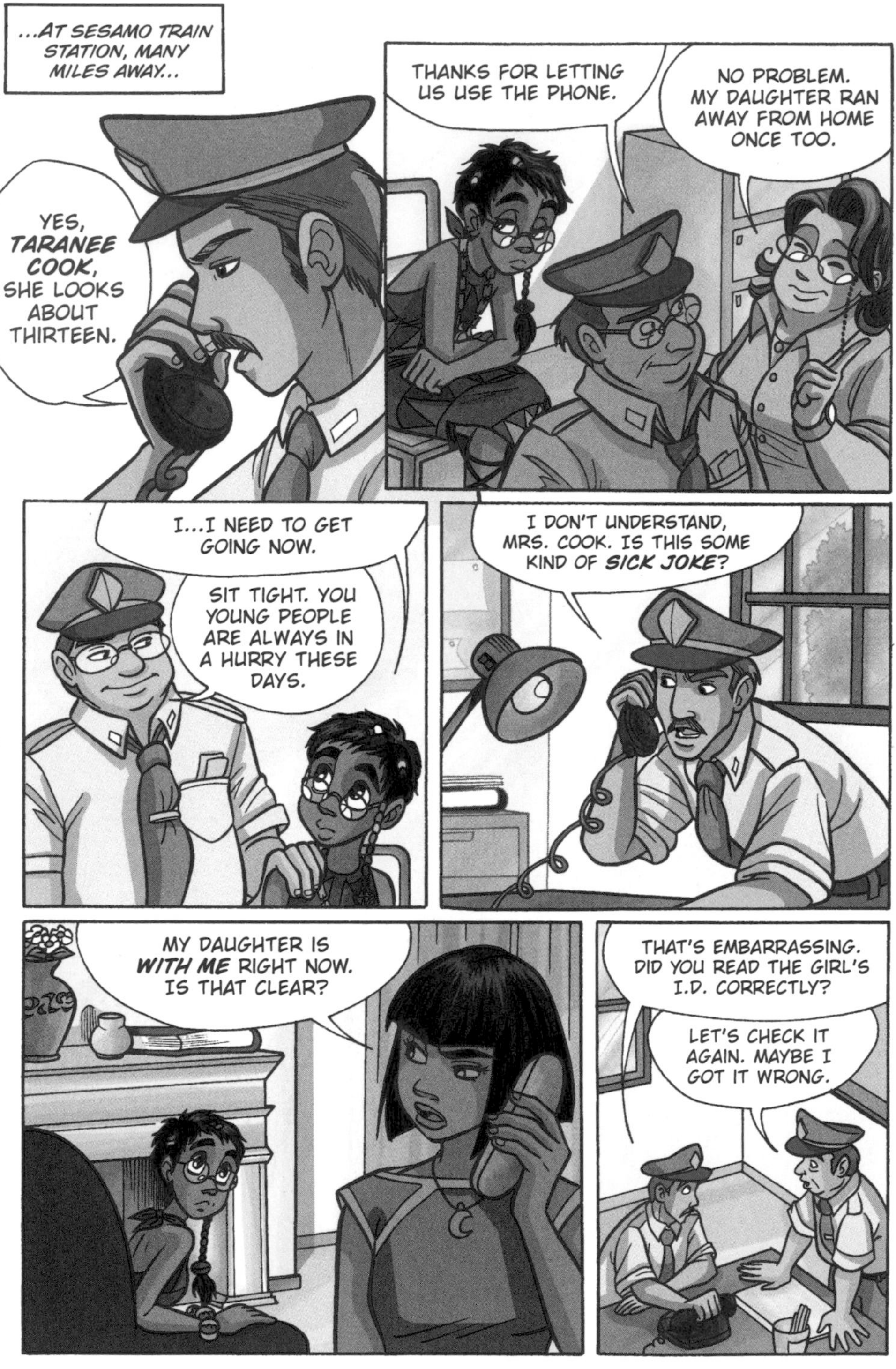
...AT SESAMO TRAIN STATION, MANY MILES AWAY...
YES, TARANEE COOK, SHE LOOKS ABOUT THIRTEEN.
THANKS FOR LETTING US USE THE PHONE.
NO PROBLEM. MY DAUGHTER RAN AWAY FROM HOME ONCE TOO.
I...I NEED TO GET GOING NOW.
SIT TIGHT. YOU YOUNG PEOPLE ARE ALWAYS IN A HURRY THESE DAYS.
I DON'T UNDERSTAND, MRS. COOK. IS THIS SOME KIND OF SICK JOKE?
MY DAUGHTER IS WITH ME RIGHT NOW. IS THAT CLEAR?
THAT'S EMBARRASSING. DID YOU READ THE GIRL'S I.D. CORRECTLY?
LET'S CHECK IT AGAIN. MAYBE I GOT IT WRONG.

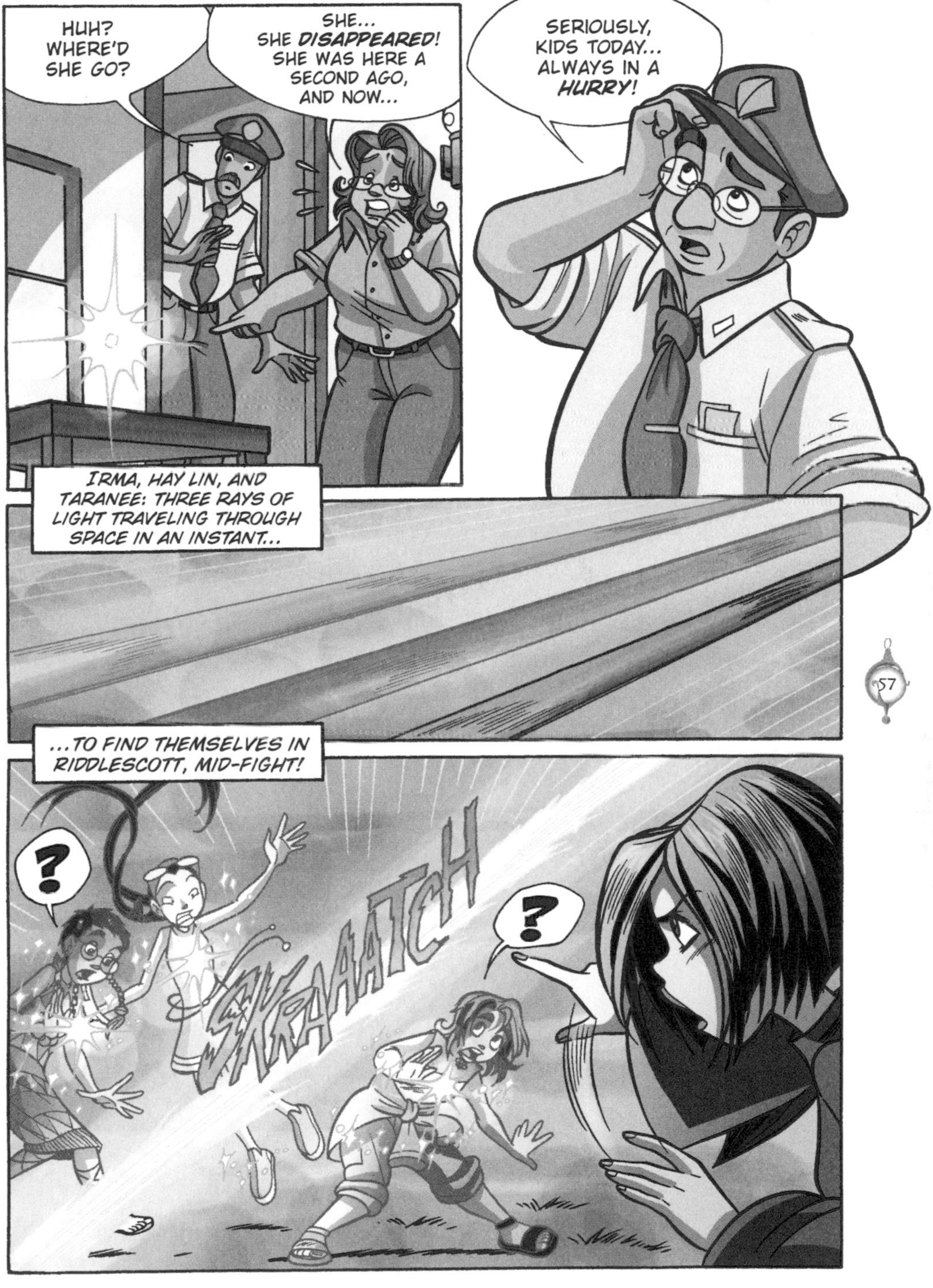
HUH? WHERE'D SHE GO?
SHE... SHE DISAPPEARED! SHE WAS HERE A SECOND AGO, AND NOW...
SERIOUSLY, KIDS TODAY... ALWAYS IN A HURRY!
IRMA, HAY LIN, AND TARANEE: THREE RAYS OF LIGHT TRAVELING THROUGH SPACE IN AN INSTANT...
...TO FIND THEMSELVES IN RIDDLESCOTT, MID-FIGHT!
?
SKRAAATCH
?

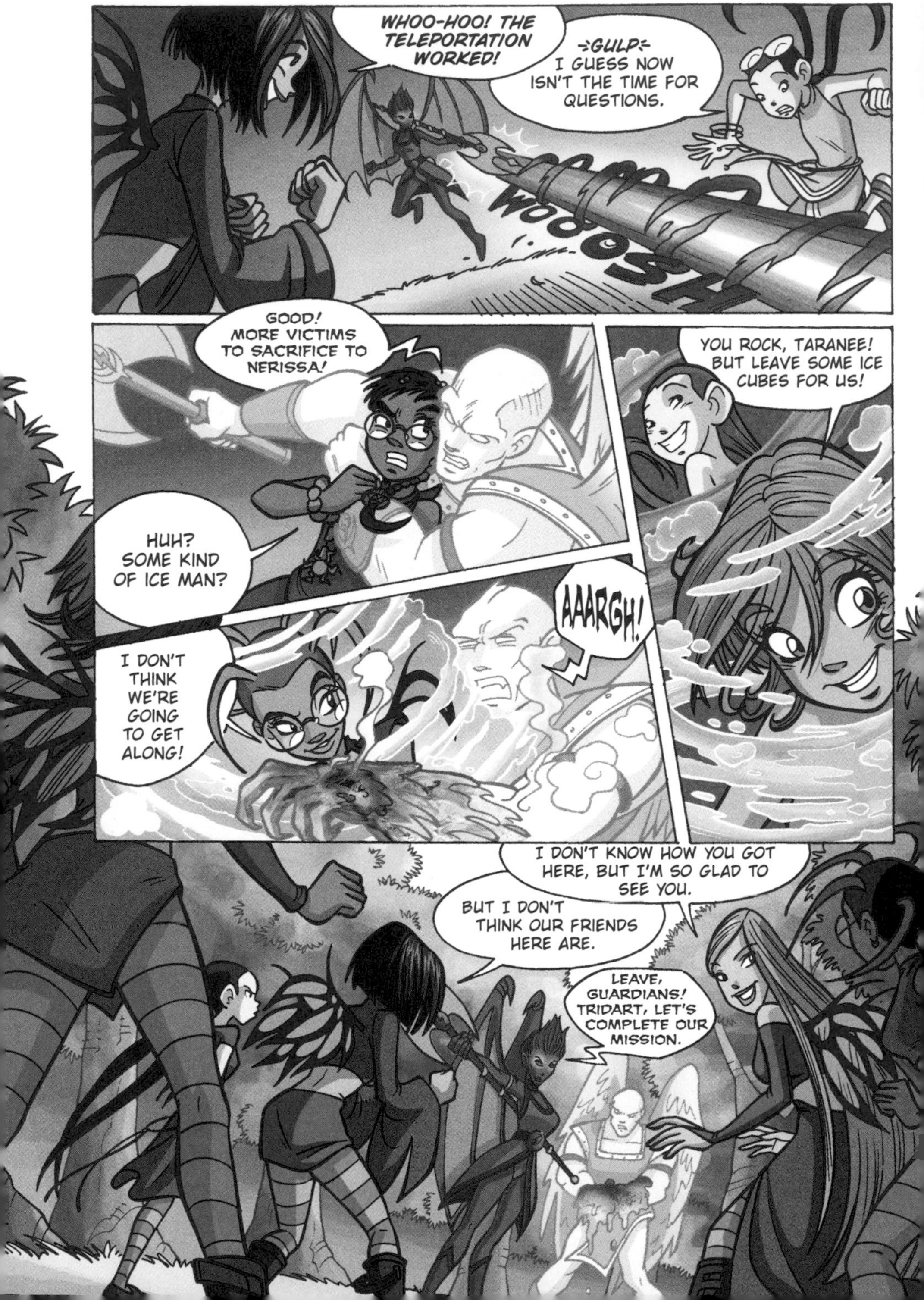
WHOO-HOO! THE TELEPORTATION WORKED!
GULP
I GUESS NOW ISN'T THE TIME FOR QUESTIONS.
WOOOSH
GOOD! MORE VICTIMS TO SACRIFICE TO NERISSA!
HUH? SOME KIND OF ICE MAN?
YOU ROCK, TARANEE! BUT LEAVE SOME ICE CUBES FOR US!
AAARGH!
I DON'T THINK WE'RE GOING TO GET ALONG!
I DON'T KNOW HOW YOU GOT HERE, BUT I'M SO GLAD TO SEE YOU.
BUT I DON'T THINK OUR FRIENDS HERE ARE.
LEAVE, GUARDIANS! TRIDART, LET'S COMPLETE OUR MISSION.

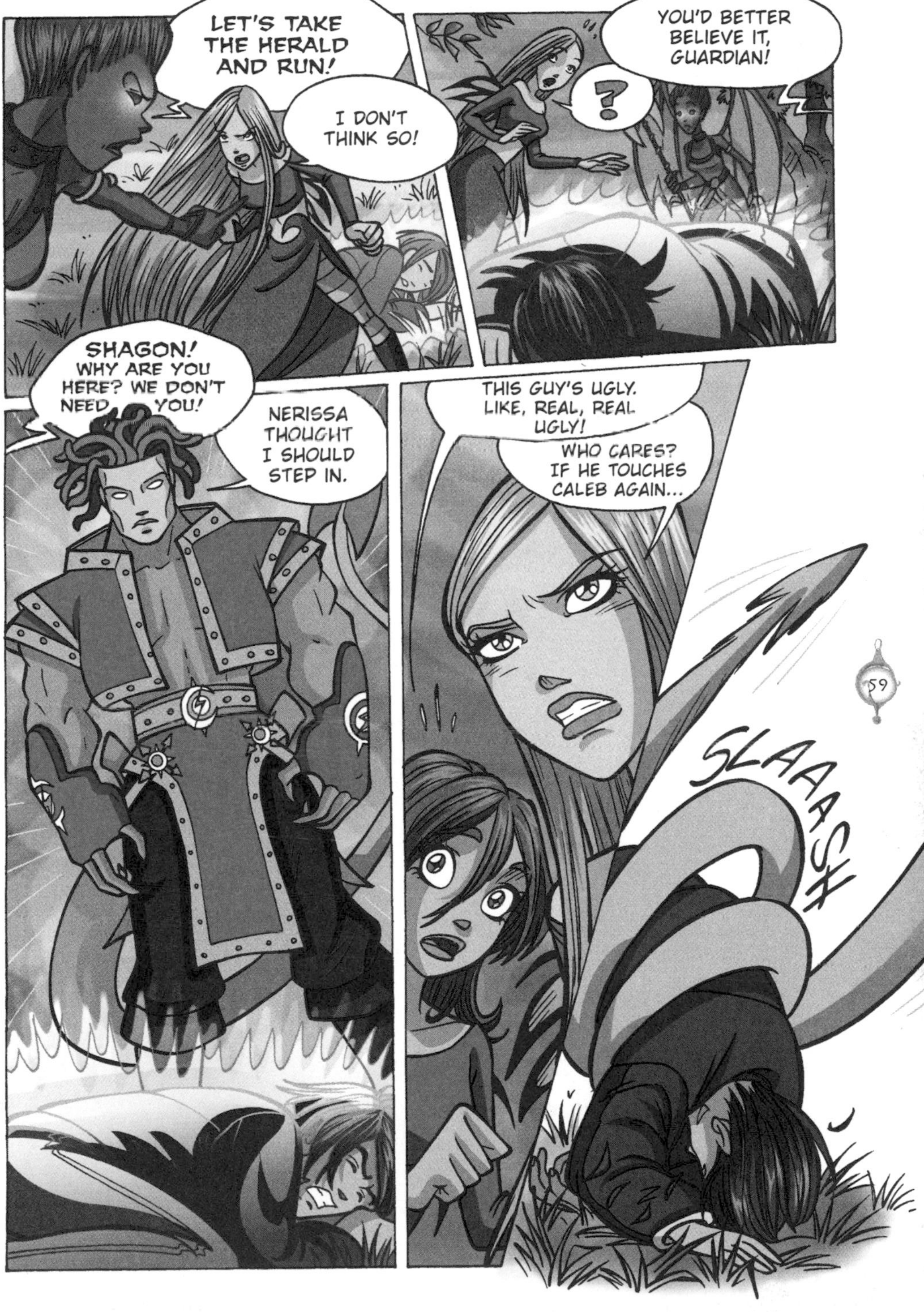
LET'S TAKE THE HERALD AND RUN!
I DON'T THINK SO!
?
YOU'D BETTER BELIEVE IT, GUARDIAN!
SHAGON! WHY ARE YOU HERE? WE DON'T NEED YOU!
NERISSA THOUGHT I SHOULD STEP IN.
THIS GUY'S UGLY. LIKE, REAL, REAL UGLY!
WHO CARES? IF HE TOUCHES CALEB AGAIN...
SLAAASH

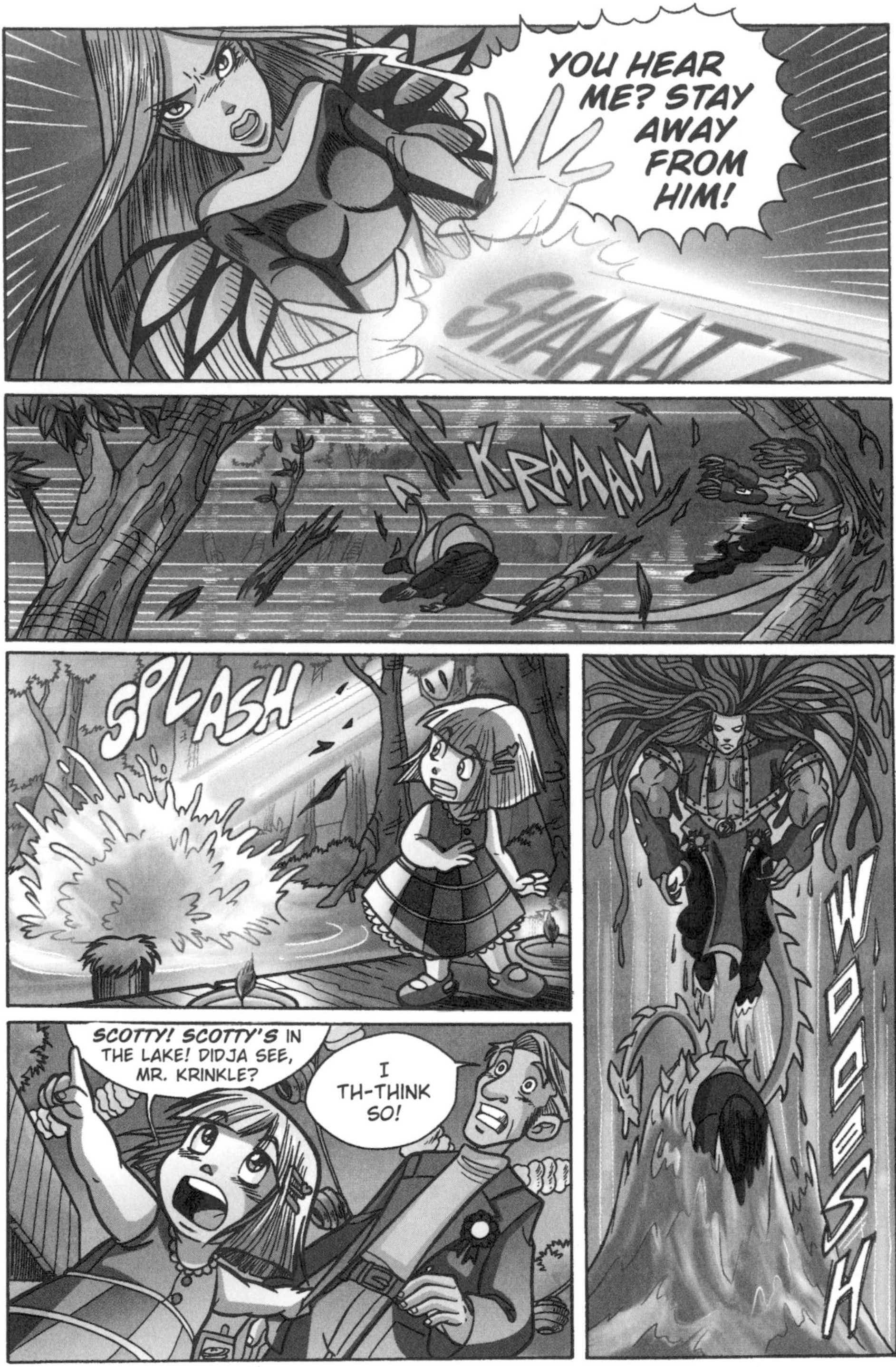
YOU HEAR ME? STAY AWAY FROM HIM!
SHAAATZ
KRAAAM
SPLASH
WOOOSH
SCOTTY! SCOTTY'S IN THE LAKE! DIDJA SEE, MR. KRINKLE?
I TH-THINK SO!

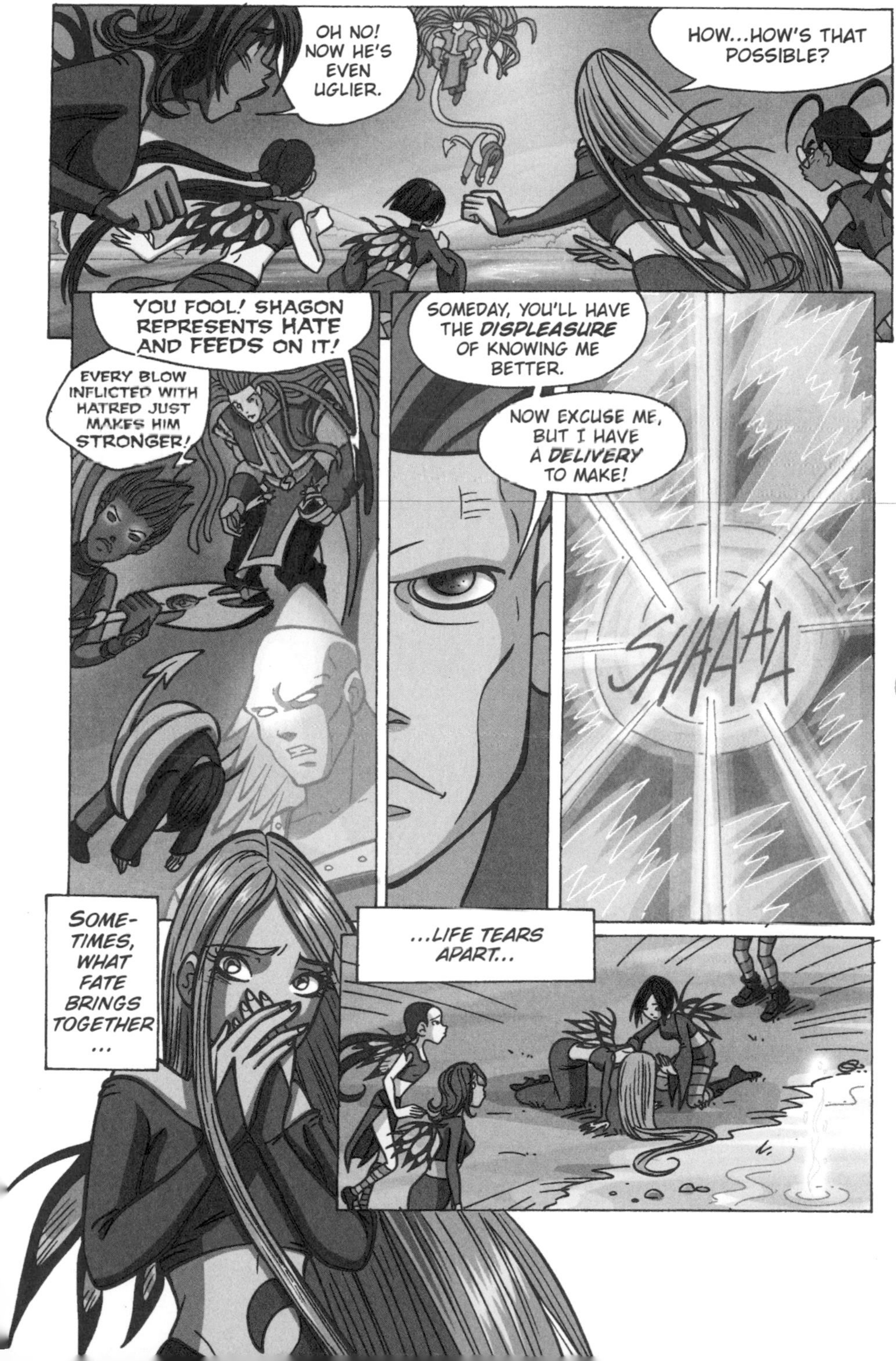
OH NO! NOW HE'S EVEN UGLIER.
HOW...HOW'S THAT POSSIBLE?
YOU FOOL! SHAGON REPRESENTS HATE AND FEEDS ON IT!
EVERY BLOW INFLICTED WITH HATRED JUST MAKES HIM STRONGER!
SOMEDAY, YOU'LL HAVE THE DISPLEASURE OF KNOWING ME BETTER.
NOW EXCUSE ME, BUT I HAVE A DELIVERY TO MAKE!
SHAAAA
SOMETIMES, WHAT FATE BRINGS TOGETHER...
...LIFE TEARS APART...

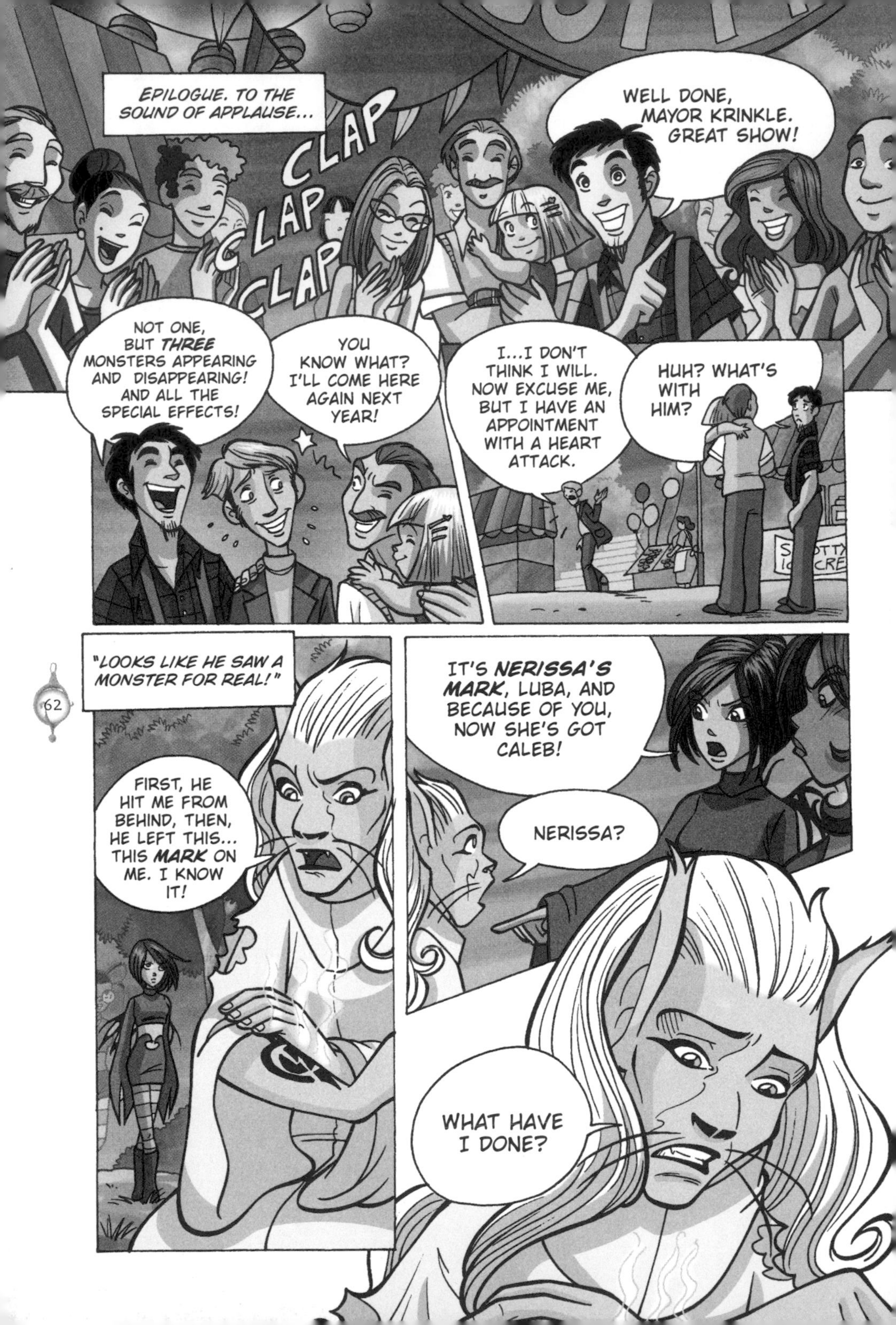

EPILOGUE. TO THE SOUND OF APPLAUSE...
CLAP CLAP CLAP
WELL DONE, MAYOR KRINKLE. GREAT SHOW!
NOT ONE, BUT THREE MONSTERS APPEARING AND DISAPPEARING! AND ALL THE SPECIAL EFFECTS!
YOU KNOW WHAT? I'LL COME HERE AGAIN NEXT YEAR!
I...I DON'T THINK I WILL. NOW EXCUSE ME, BUT I HAVE AN APPOINTMENT WITH A HEART ATTACK.
HUH? WHAT'S WITH HIM?
"LOOKS LIKE HE SAW A MONSTER FOR REAL!"
FIRST, HE HIT ME FROM BEHIND, THEN, HE LEFT THIS... THIS MARK ON ME. I KNOW IT!
IT'S NERISSA'S MARK, LUBA, AND BECAUSE OF YOU, NOW SHE'S GOT CALEB!
NERISSA?
WHAT HAVE I DONE?

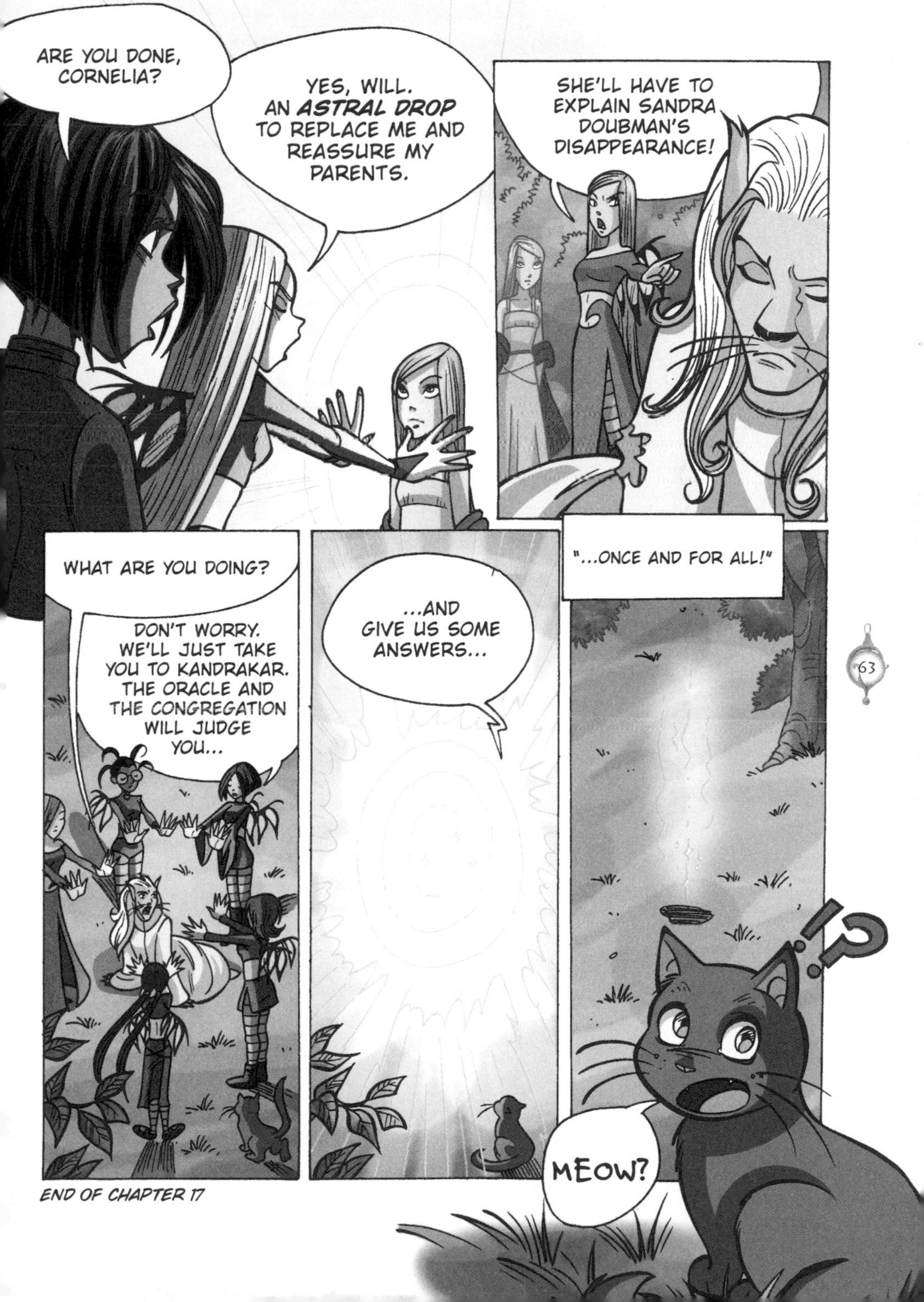
ARE YOU DONE, CORNELIA?
YES, WILL. AN ASTRAL DROP TO REPLACE ME AND REASSURE MY PARENTS.
SHE'LL HAVE TO EXPLAIN SANDRA DOUBMAN'S DISAPPEARANCE!
WHAT ARE YOU DOING?
DON'T WORRY. WE'LL JUST TAKE YOU TO KANDRAKAR. THE ORACLE AND THE CONGREGATION WILL JUDGE YOU...
...AND GIVE US SOME ANSWERS...
"...ONCE AND FOR ALL!"
!?
MEOW?

END OF CHAPTER 17

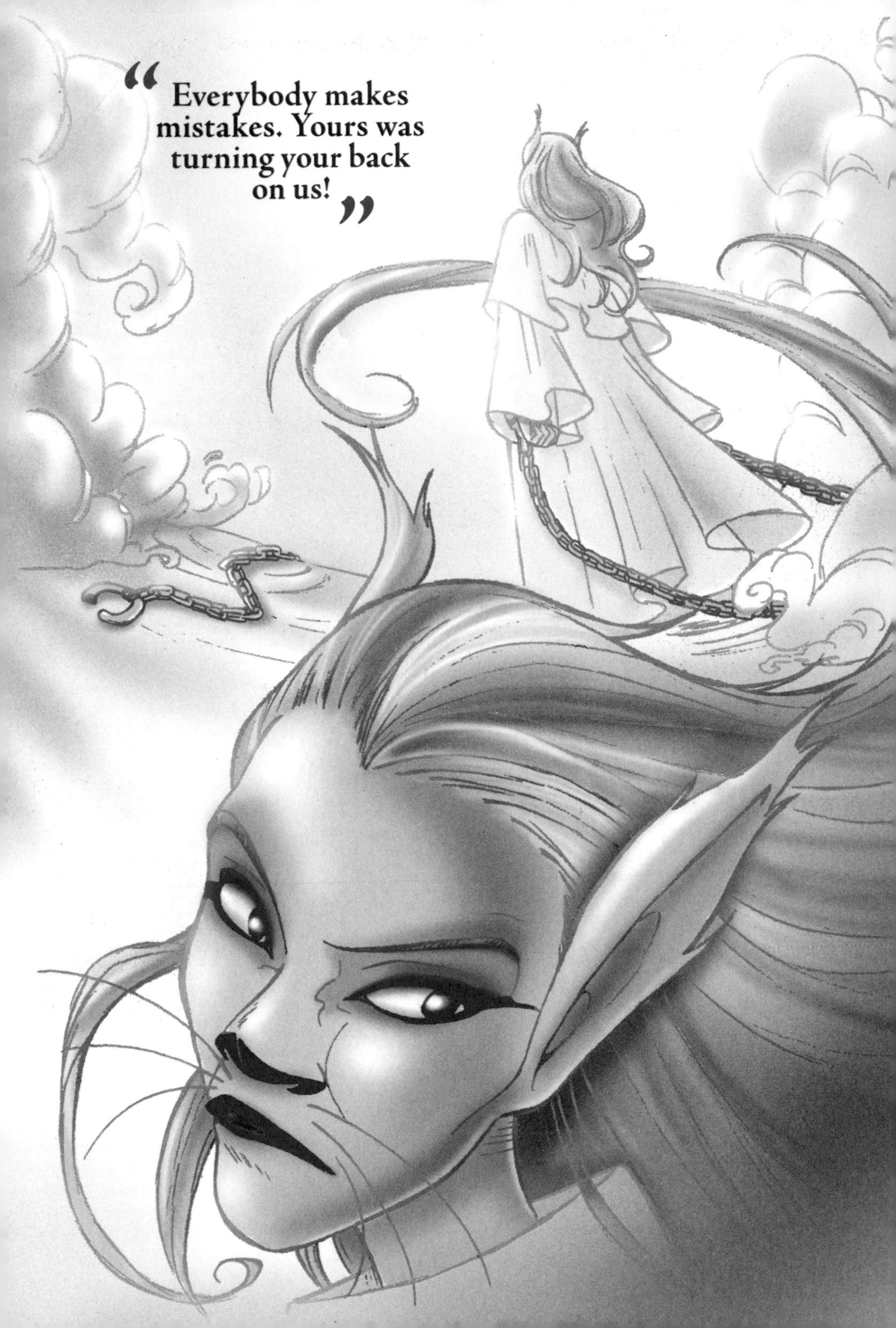
"Everybody makes mistakes. Yours was turning your back on us!"

18

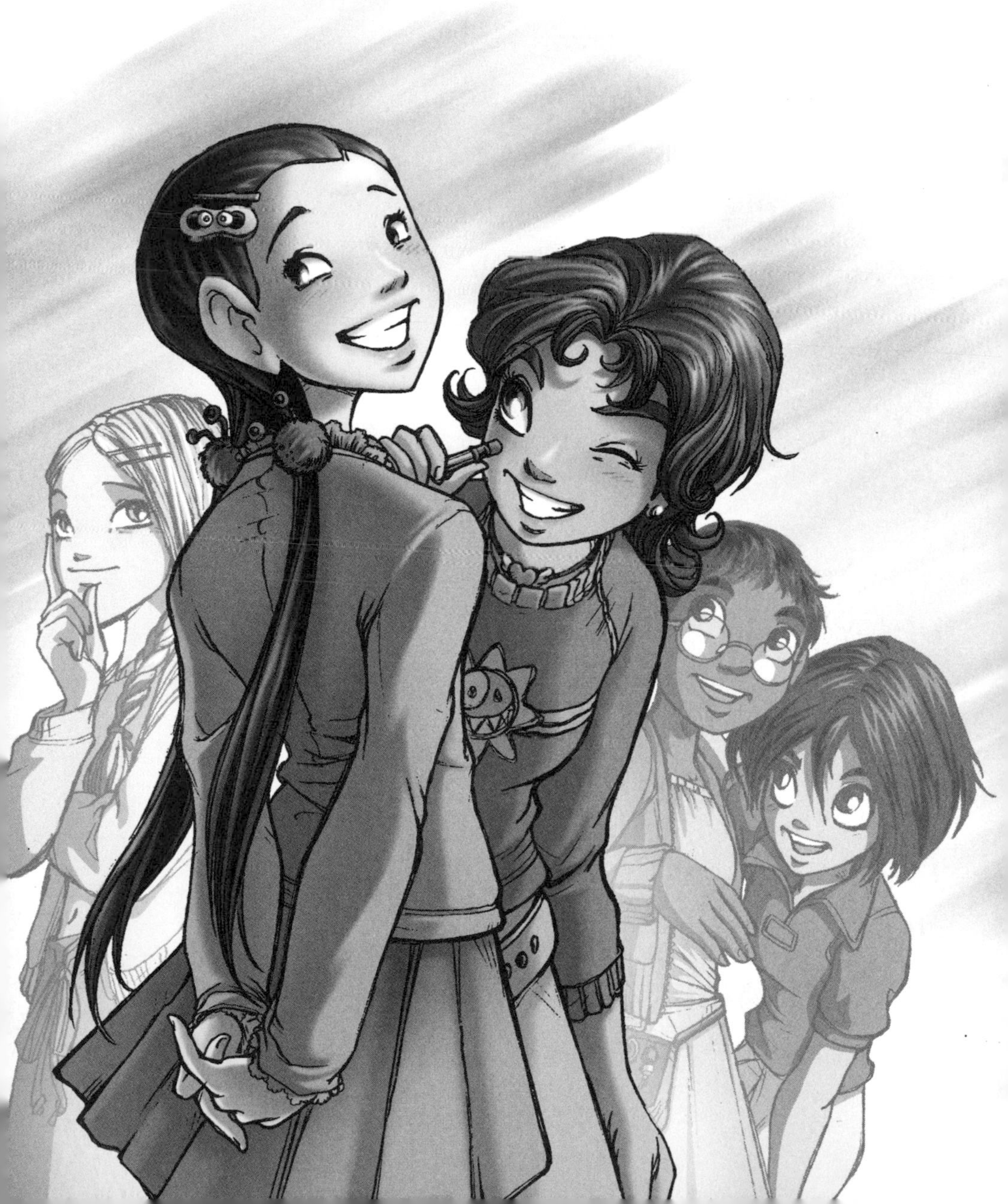

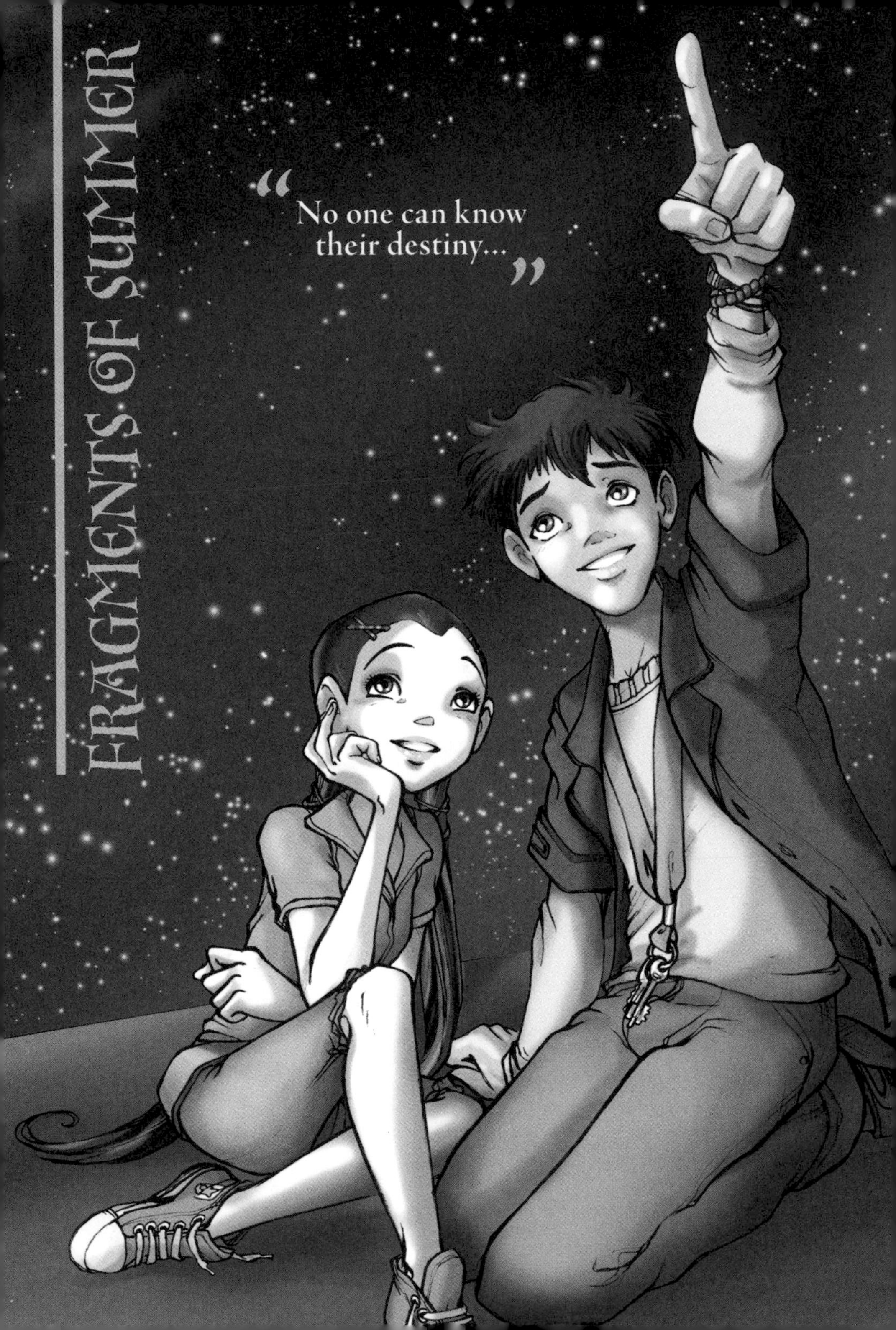
FRAGMENTS OF SUMMER
"No one can know their destiny..."

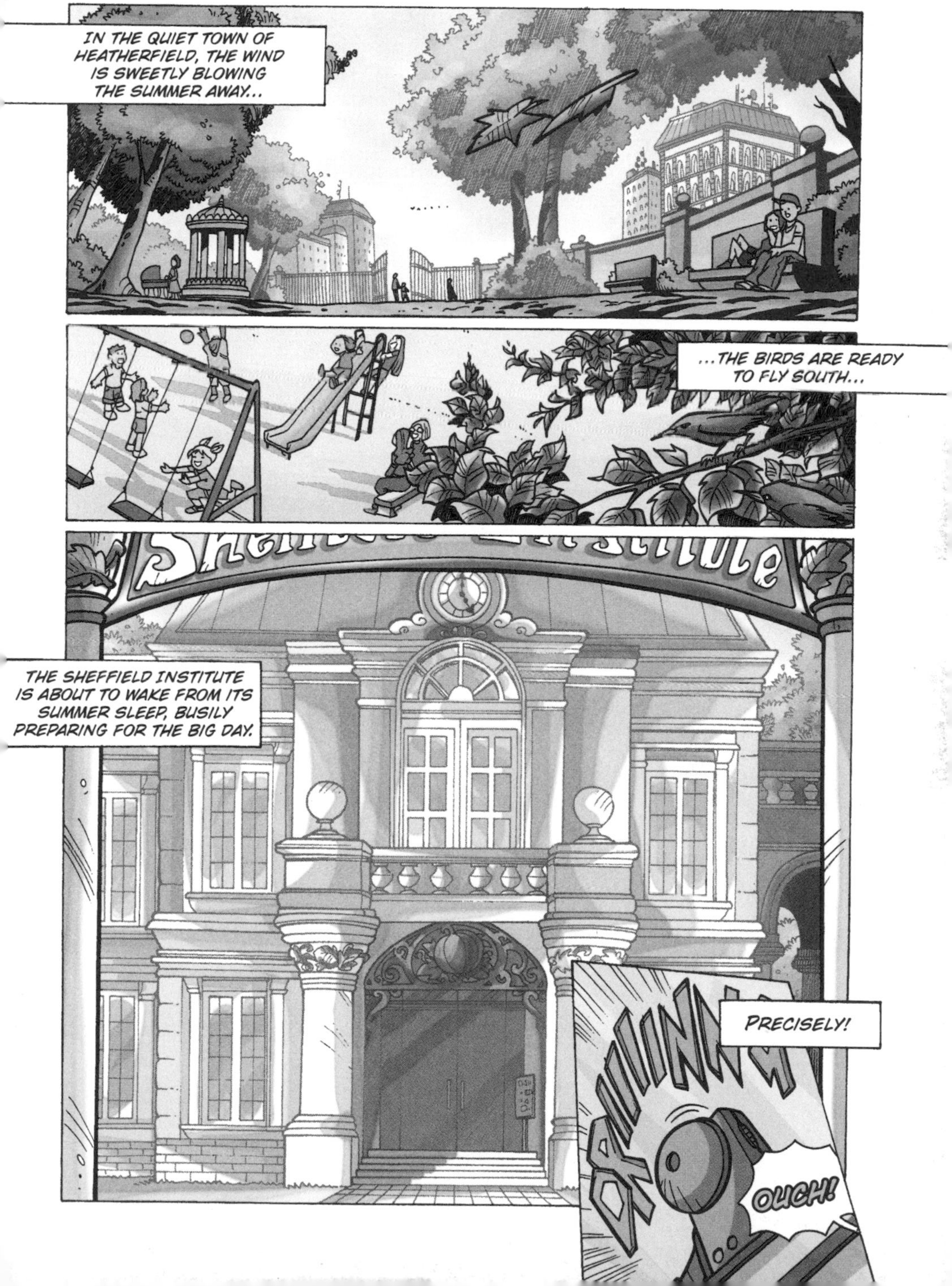

IN THE QUIET TOWN OF HEATHERFIELD, THE WIND IS SWEETLY BLOWING THE SUMMER AWAY...
...THE BIRDS ARE READY TO FLY SOUTH...
THE SHEFFIELD INSTITUTE IS ABOUT TO WAKE FROM ITS SUMMER SLEEP, BUSILY PREPARING FOR THE BIG DAY.
PRECISELY!
OUCH!

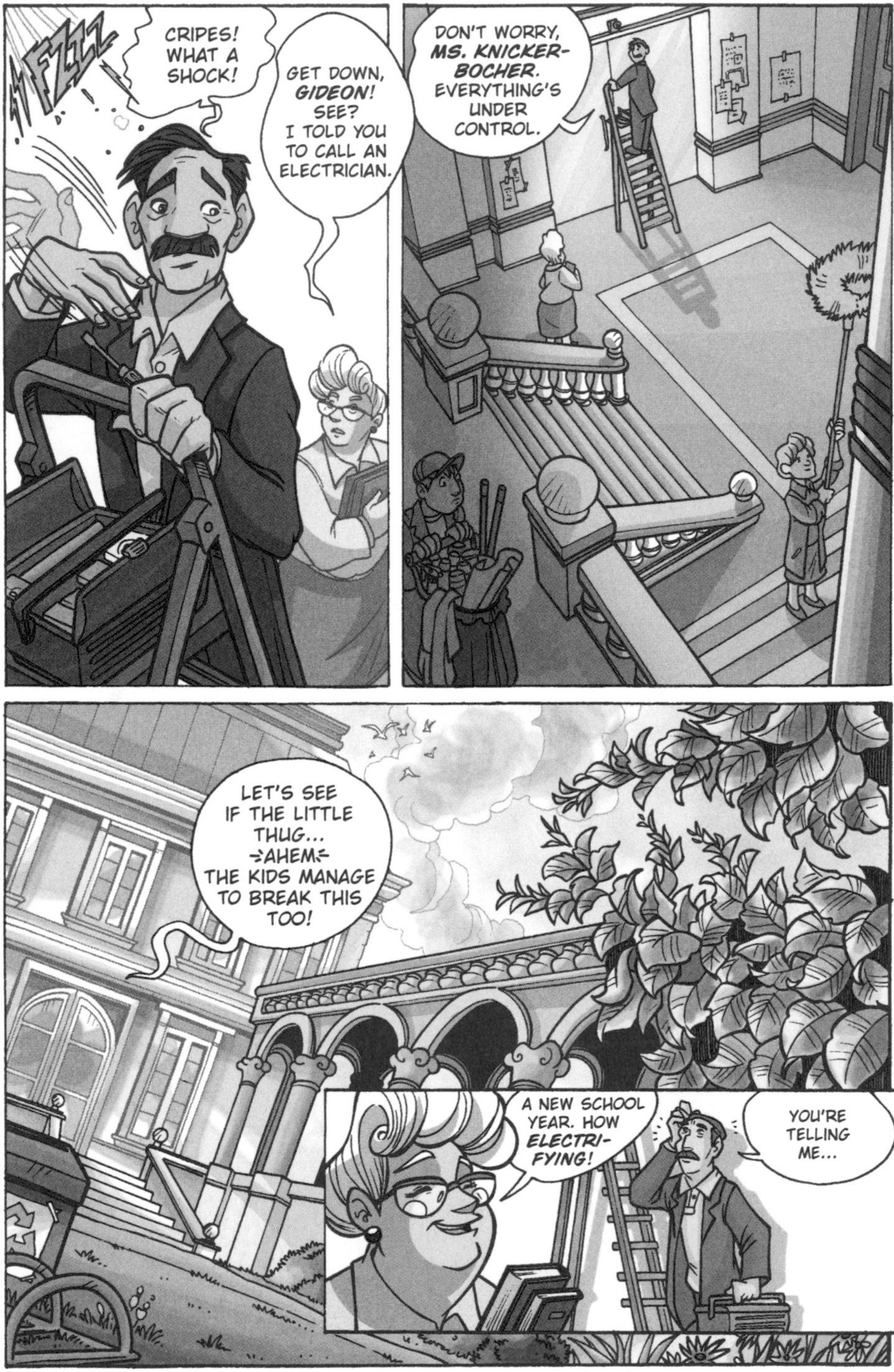
FZZZ
CRIPES! WHAT A SHOCK!
GET DOWN, **GIDEON!** SEE? I TOLD YOU TO CALL AN ELECTRICIAN.
DON'T WORRY, **MS. KNICKERBOCHER**. EVERYTHING'S UNDER CONTROL.
LET'S SEE IF THE LITTLE THUG... AHEM THE KIDS MANAGE TO BREAK THIS TOO!
A NEW SCHOOL YEAR. HOW **ELECTRIFYING!**
YOU'RE TELLING ME...

FINALLY! I THOUGHT YOU'D LEFT HEATHERFIELD FOREVER!

HI, HAY LIN!

WE MISSED YOU!

COME DOWNSTAIRS.

YEAH! A YEAR OF TESTS AND EXAMS AWAITS. WHOO-HOO!

THE FIRST DAY OF SCHOOL FOR A GROUP OF FRIENDS WE KNOW WELL...

69

Did she leave town at all?

I don't think so. The Silver Dragon stayed open the whole summer.

I MET A GUY!

MAN... MUST HAVE BEEN SOOO BORING!

NOPE! I RECKON I HAD MORE FUN THAN YOU DID.

OMPH!

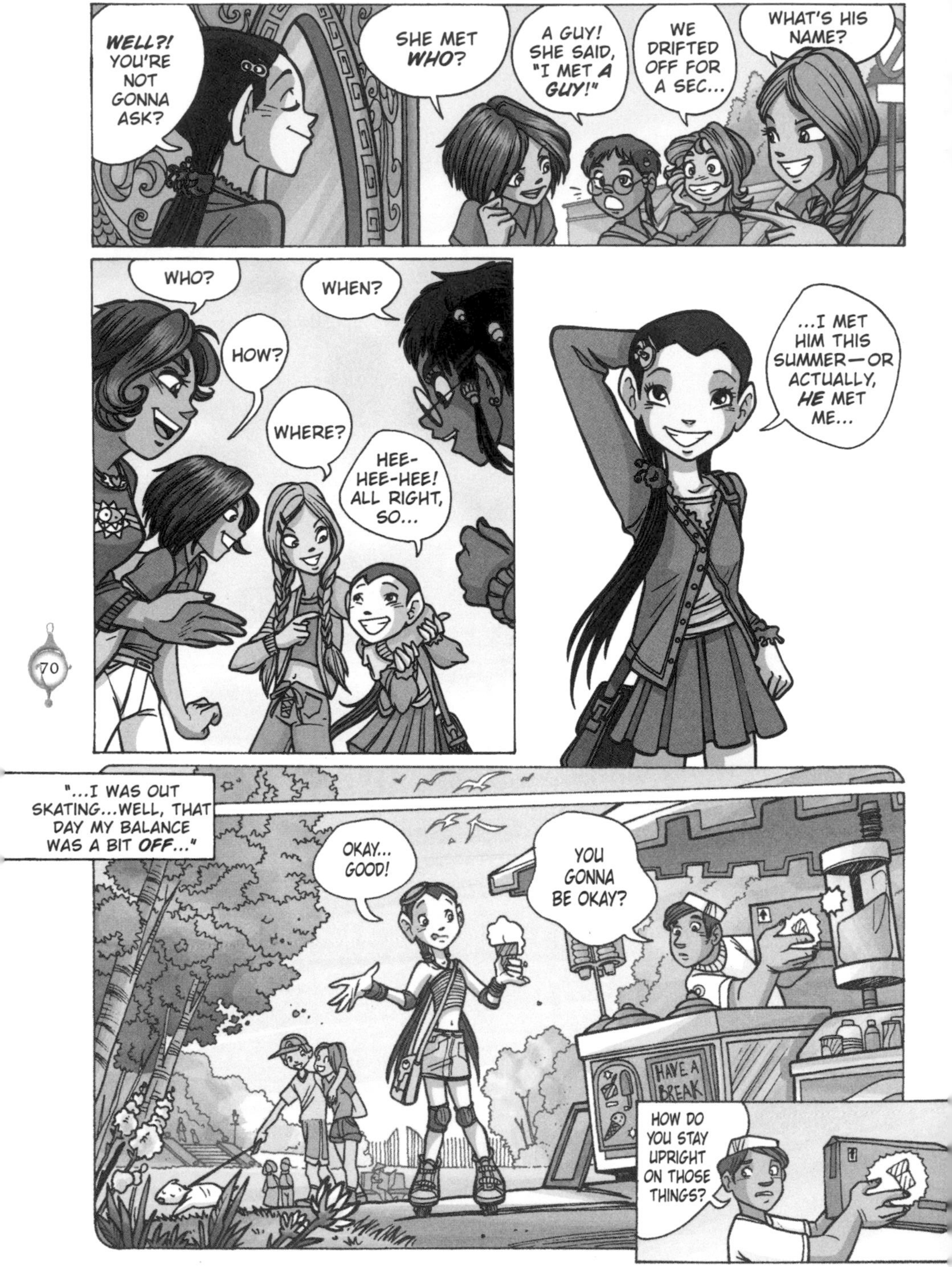
WELL?! YOU'RE NOT GONNA ASK?
SHE MET WHO?
A GUY! SHE SAID, "I MET A GUY!"
WE DRIFTED OFF FOR A SEC...
WHAT'S HIS NAME?
WHO?
WHEN?
HOW?
WHERE?
HEE-HEE-HEE! ALL RIGHT, SO...
...I MET HIM THIS SUMMER—OR ACTUALLY, HE MET ME...
"...I WAS OUT SKATING...WELL, THAT DAY MY BALANCE WAS A BIT OFF..."
OKAY... GOOD!
YOU GONNA BE OKAY?
HAVE A BREAK
HOW DO YOU STAY UPRIGHT ON THOSE THINGS?

OOOOOOOOH...

HEY... WHAT'S SHE...?

EEK!

TUMP

WHEN FATE BARGES IN...

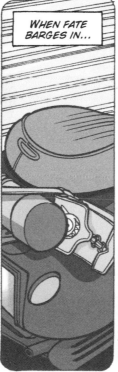

STOOOOOOOP!

THANK GOODNESS, I MISSED HER!

WROOM

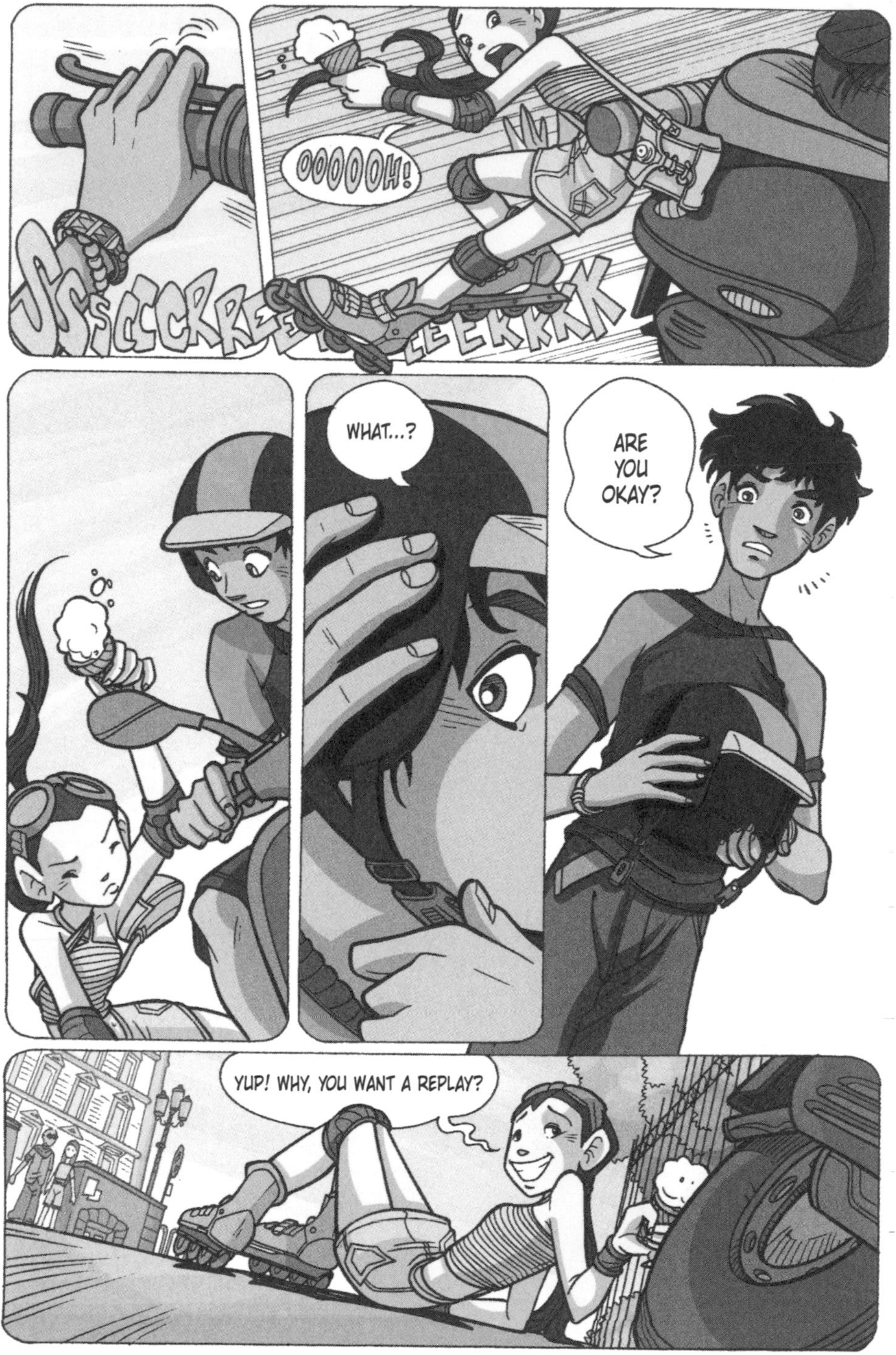
SSSCCCRREEEEEKKKK
OOOOOH!
WHAT...?
ARE YOU OKAY?
YUP! WHY, YOU WANT A REPLAY?

72

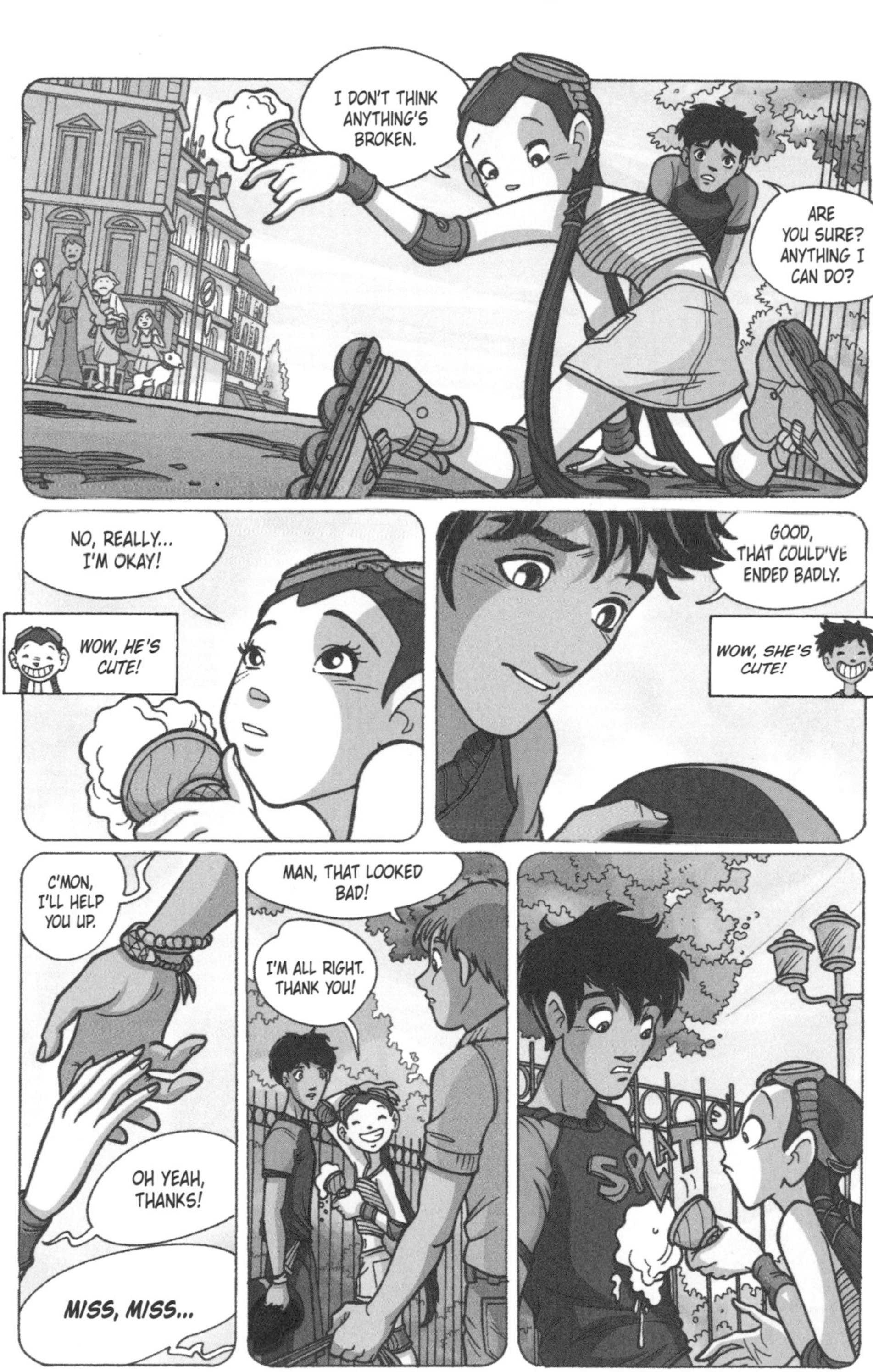
I DON'T THINK ANYTHING'S BROKEN.
ARE YOU SURE? ANYTHING I CAN DO?
NO, REALLY... I'M OKAY!
WOW, HE'S CUTE!
GOOD, THAT COULD'VE ENDED BADLY.
WOW, SHE'S CUTE!
C'MON, I'LL HELP YOU UP.
OH YEAH, THANKS!
MISS, MISS...
MAN, THAT LOOKED BAD!
I'M ALL RIGHT. THANK YOU!
SPLAT

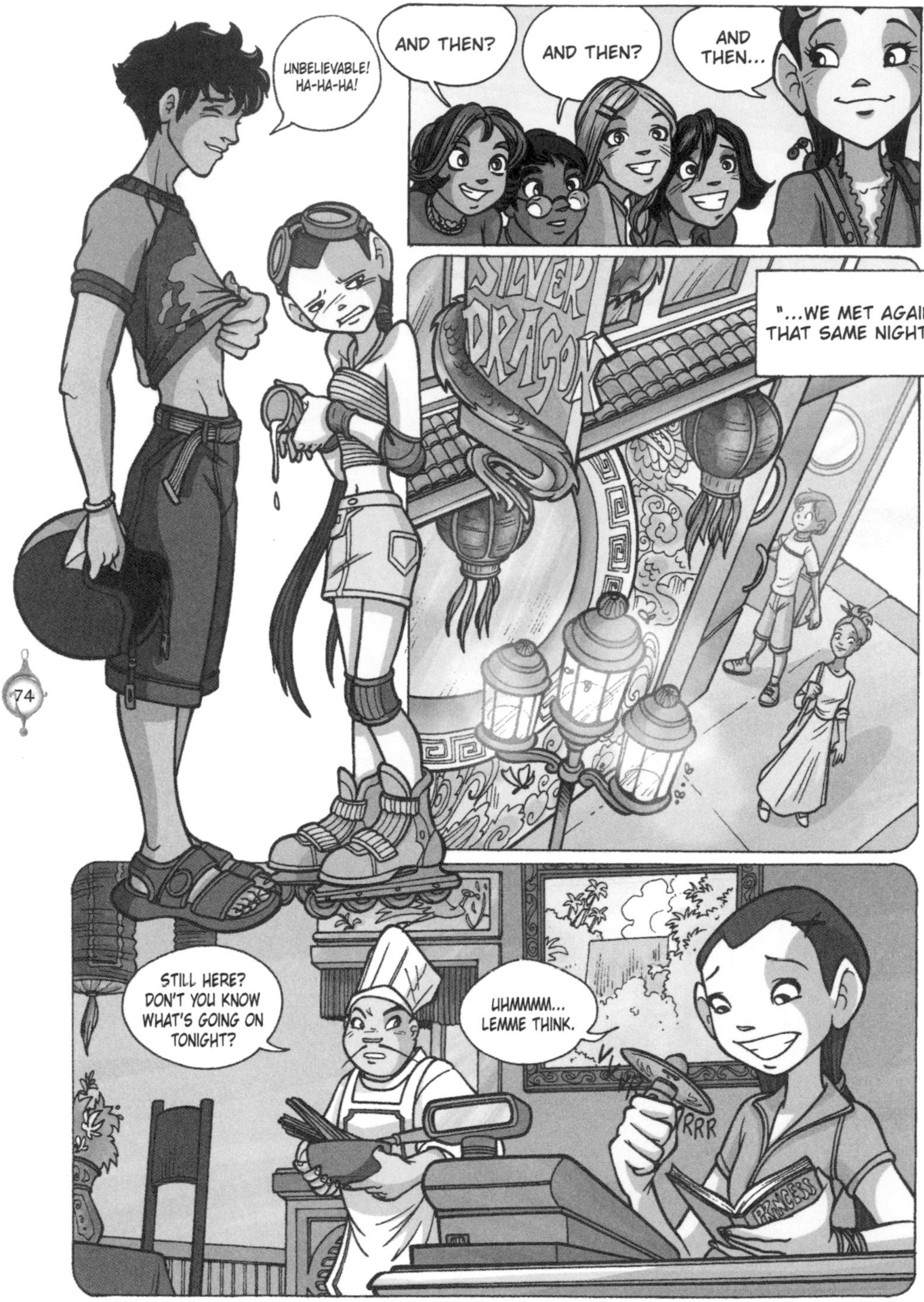
UNBELIEVABLE! HA-HA-HA!
AND THEN?
AND THEN?
AND THEN...
"...WE MET AGAIN THAT SAME NIGHT!"
SILVER DRAGON
STILL HERE? DON'T YOU KNOW WHAT'S GOING ON TONIGHT?
UHMMMM... LEMME THINK.
RRR
PRINCESS

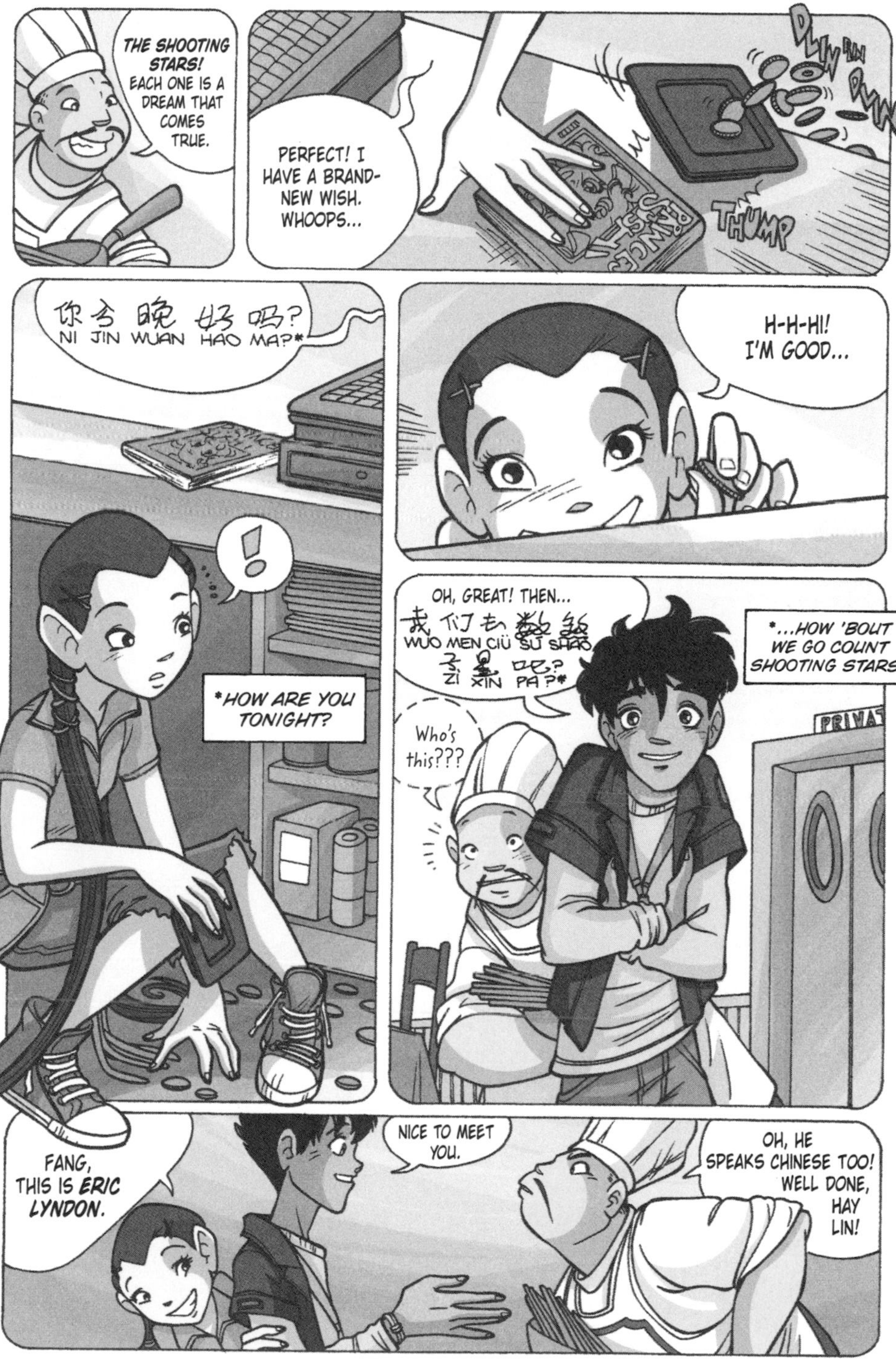

THE SHOOTING STARS! EACH ONE IS A DREAM THAT COMES TRUE.
PERFECT! I HAVE A BRAND-NEW WISH. WHOOPS...
DWIN DIN DWIN
THUMP
你今晚好吗?
NI JIN WUAN HAO MA?*
*HOW ARE YOU TONIGHT?
H-H-HI! I'M GOOD...
OH, GREAT! THEN...
WUO MEN CIÜ SU SHAO
ZI XIN PA?*
*...HOW 'BOUT WE GO COUNT SHOOTING STARS?
Who's this???
FANG, THIS IS ERIC LYNDON.
NICE TO MEET YOU.
OH, HE SPEAKS CHINESE TOO! WELL DONE, HAY LIN!

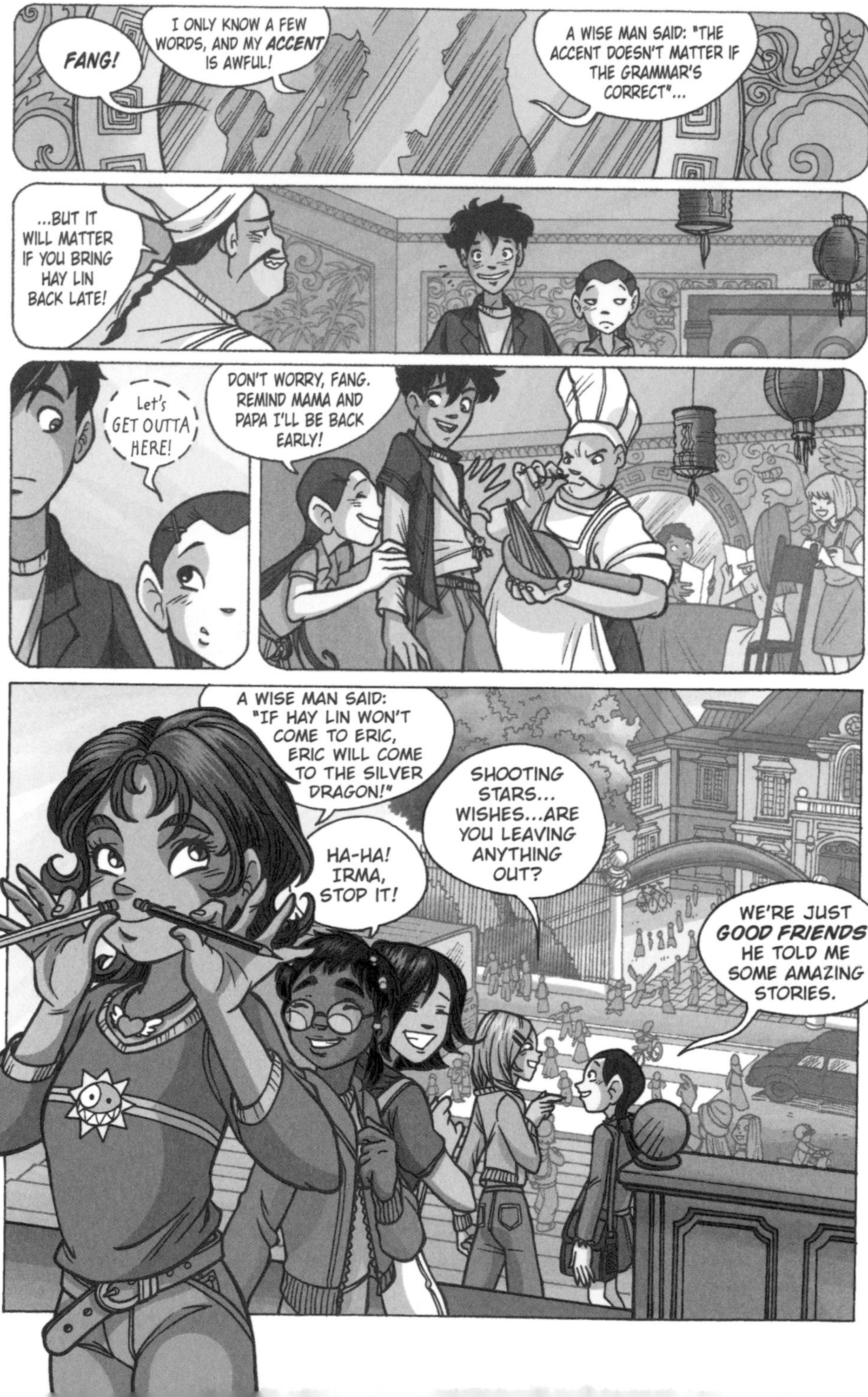
FANG!
I ONLY KNOW A FEW WORDS, AND MY *ACCENT* IS AWFUL!
A WISE MAN SAID: "THE ACCENT DOESN'T MATTER IF THE GRAMMAR'S CORRECT"...
...BUT IT WILL MATTER IF YOU BRING HAY LIN BACK LATE!
Let's GET OUTTA HERE!
DON'T WORRY, FANG. REMIND MAMA AND PAPA I'LL BE BACK EARLY!
A WISE MAN SAID: "IF HAY LIN WON'T COME TO ERIC, ERIC WILL COME TO THE SILVER DRAGON!"
HA-HA! IRMA, STOP IT!
SHOOTING STARS... WISHES...ARE YOU LEAVING ANYTHING OUT?
WE'RE JUST *GOOD FRIENDS*! HE TOLD ME SOME AMAZING STORIES.

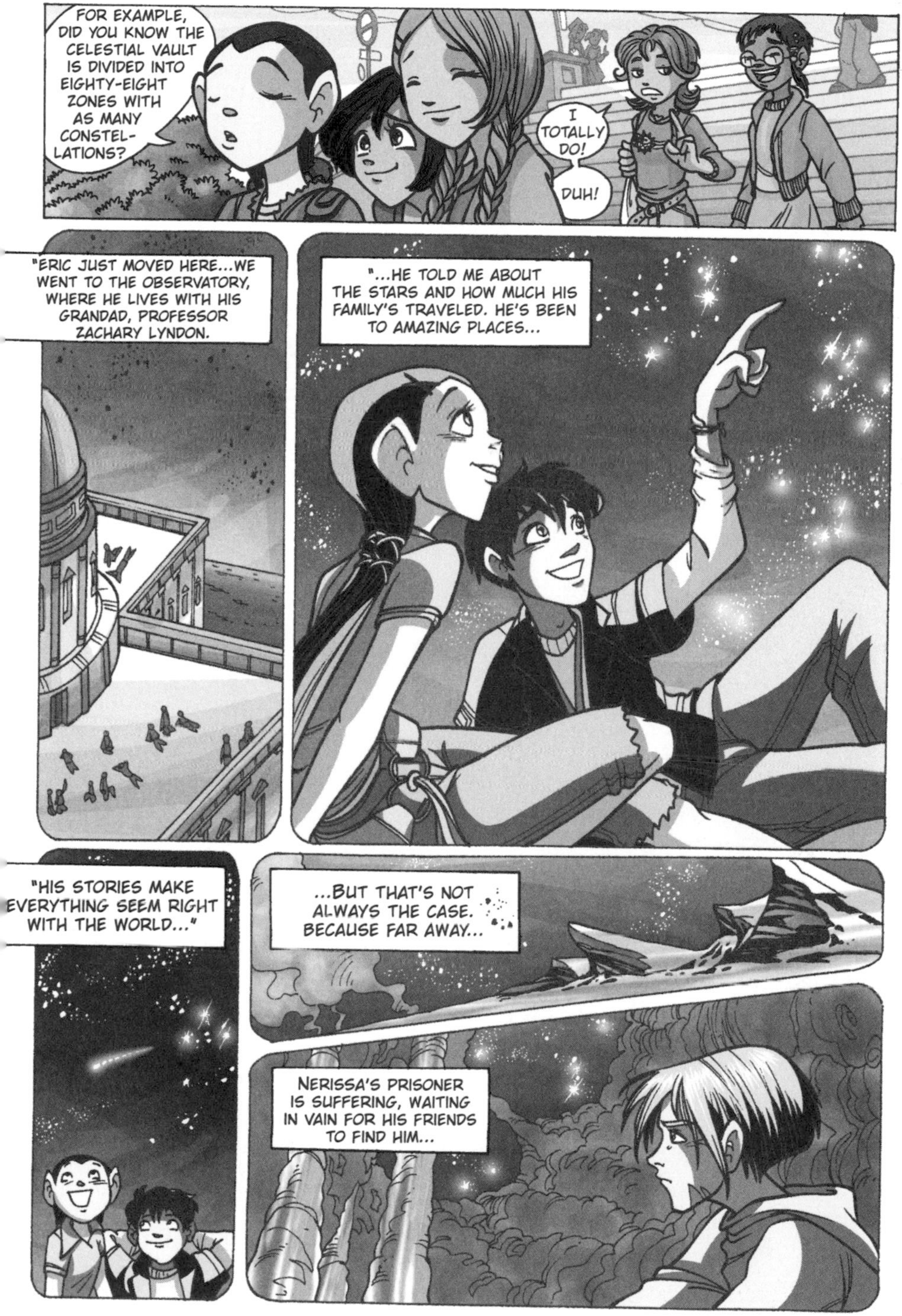
FOR EXAMPLE, DID YOU KNOW THE CELESTIAL VAULT IS DIVIDED INTO EIGHTY-EIGHT ZONES WITH AS MANY CONSTEL-LATIONS?
I TOTALLY DO!
DUH!
"ERIC JUST MOVED HERE...WE WENT TO THE OBSERVATORY, WHERE HE LIVES WITH HIS GRANDAD, PROFESSOR ZACHARY LYNDON.
"...HE TOLD ME ABOUT THE STARS AND HOW MUCH HIS FAMILY'S TRAVELED. HE'S BEEN TO AMAZING PLACES...
"HIS STORIES MAKE EVERYTHING SEEM RIGHT WITH THE WORLD..."
...BUT THAT'S NOT ALWAYS THE CASE. BECAUSE FAR AWAY...
NERISSA'S PRISONER IS SUFFERING, WAITING IN VAIN FOR HIS FRIENDS TO FIND HIM...

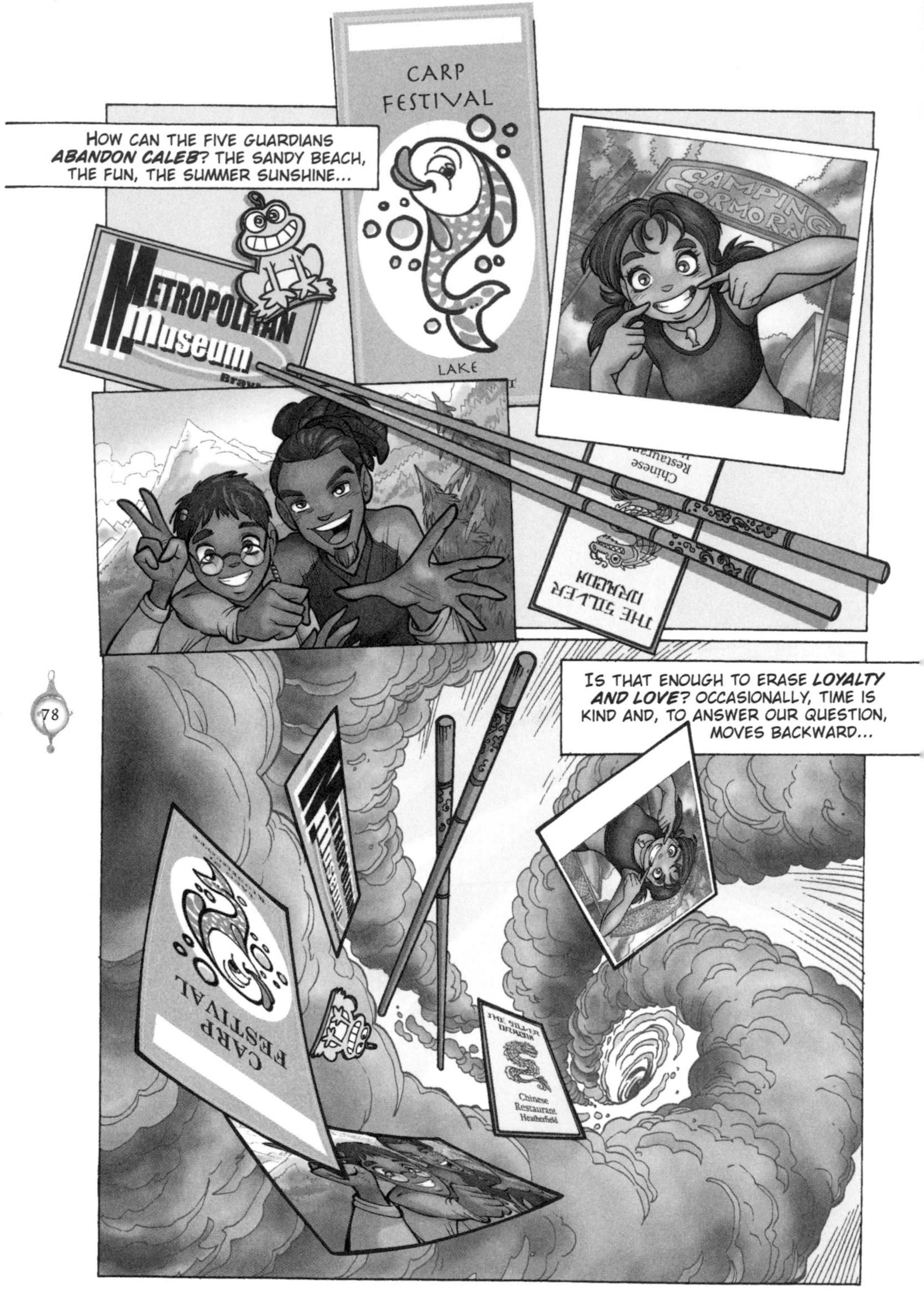
HOW CAN THE FIVE GUARDIANS ABANDON CALEB? THE SANDY BEACH, THE FUN, THE SUMMER SUNSHINE...
CARP FESTIVAL
LAKE
METROPOLITAN Museum
CAMPING
THE SILVER DRAGON
Chinese Restaurant
IS THAT ENOUGH TO ERASE LOYALTY AND LOVE? OCCASIONALLY, TIME IS KIND AND, TO ANSWER OUR QUESTION, MOVES BACKWARD...
CARP FESTIVAL
THE SILVER DRAGON
Chinese Restaurant Heatherfield

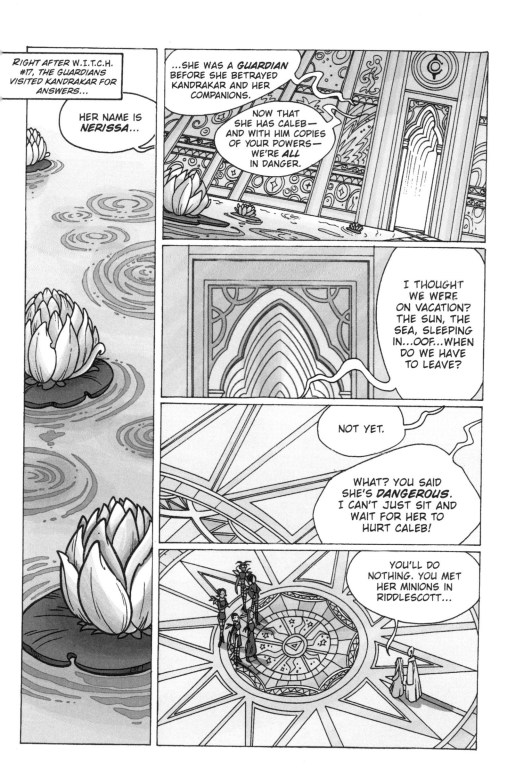

RIGHT AFTER W.I.T.C.H. #17, THE GUARDIANS VISITED KANDRAKAR FOR ANSWERS...

HER NAME IS **NERISSA**...

...SHE WAS A **GUARDIAN** BEFORE SHE BETRAYED KANDRAKAR AND HER COMPANIONS.

NOW THAT SHE HAS CALEB— AND WITH HIM COPIES OF YOUR POWERS— WE'RE **ALL** IN DANGER.

I THOUGHT WE WERE ON VACATION? THE SUN, THE SEA, SLEEPING IN...OOF...WHEN DO WE HAVE TO LEAVE?

NOT YET.

WHAT? YOU SAID SHE'S **DANGEROUS.** I CAN'T JUST SIT AND WAIT FOR HER TO HURT CALEB!

YOU'LL DO NOTHING. YOU MET HER MINIONS IN RIDDLESCOTT...

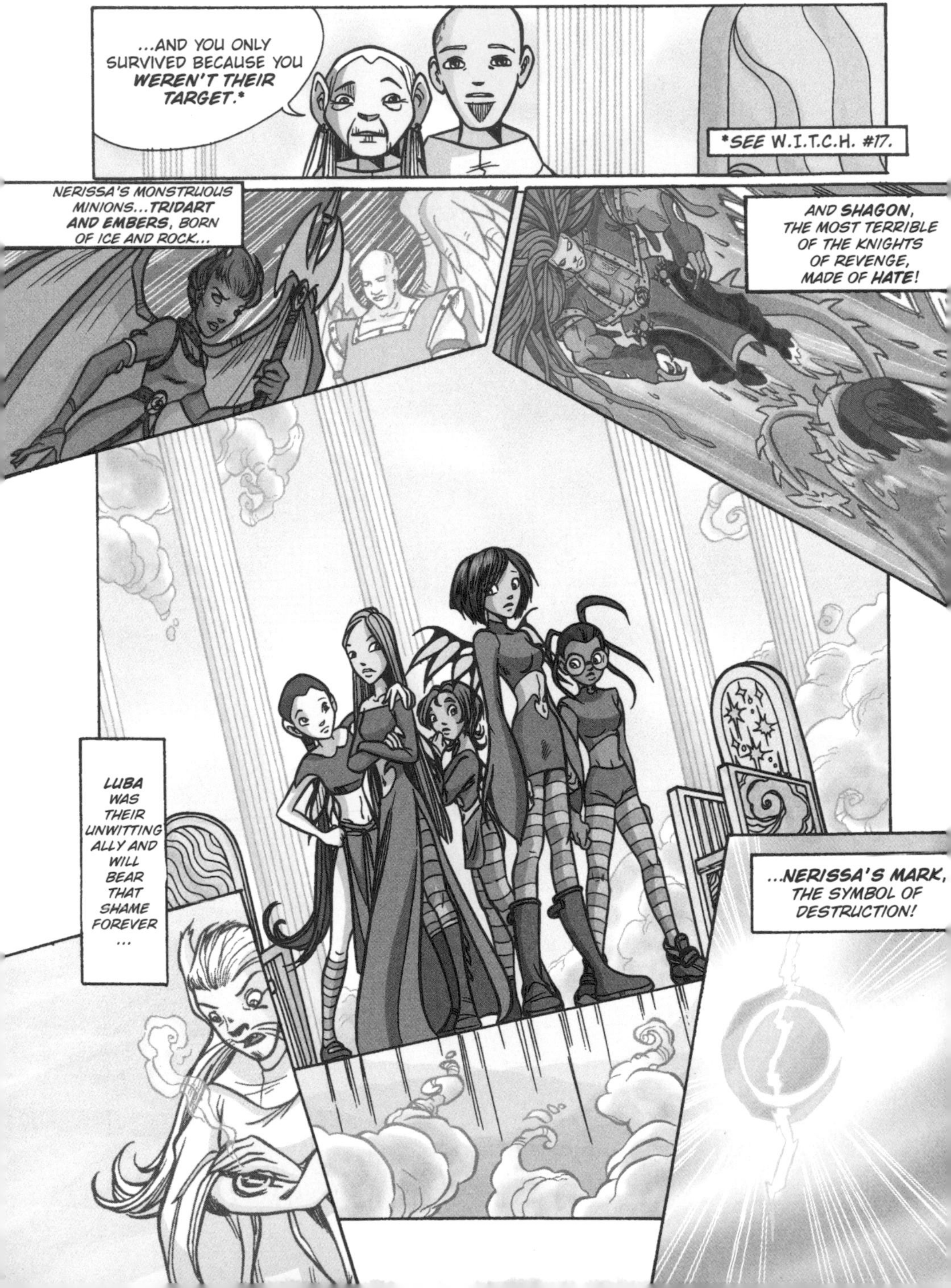

...AND YOU ONLY SURVIVED BECAUSE YOU WEREN'T THEIR TARGET.*
*SEE W.I.T.C.H. #17.
NERISSA'S MONSTRUOUS MINIONS...TRIDART AND EMBERS, BORN OF ICE AND ROCK...
AND SHAGON, THE MOST TERRIBLE OF THE KNIGHTS OF REVENGE, MADE OF HATE!
LUBA WAS THEIR UNWITTING ALLY AND WILL BEAR THAT SHAME FOREVER ...
...NERISSA'S MARK, THE SYMBOL OF DESTRUCTION!

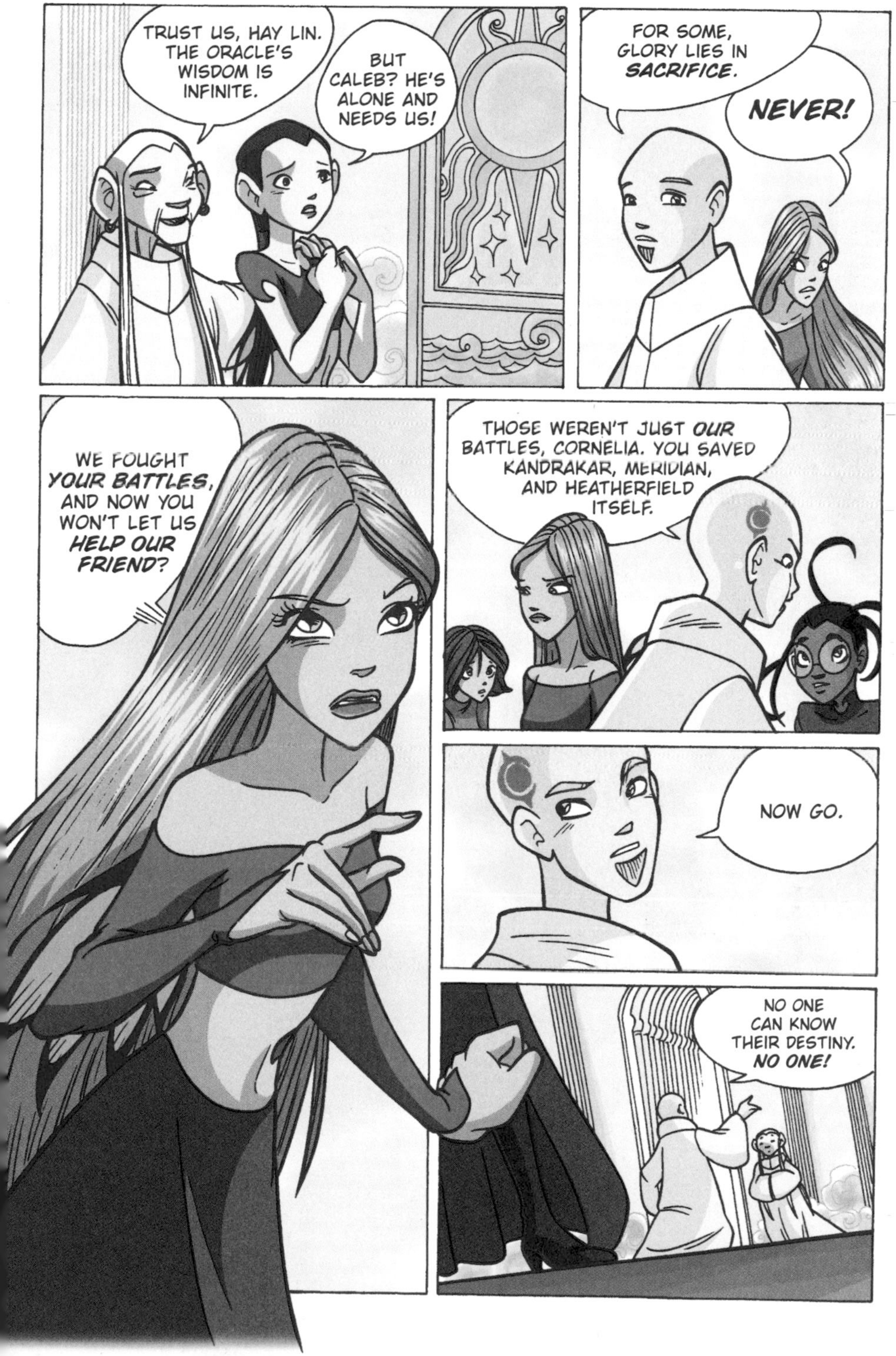
TRUST US, HAY LIN. THE ORACLE'S WISDOM IS INFINITE.
BUT CALEB? HE'S ALONE AND NEEDS US!
FOR SOME, GLORY LIES IN SACRIFICE.
NEVER!
WE FOUGHT YOUR BATTLES, AND NOW YOU WON'T LET US HELP OUR FRIEND?
THOSE WEREN'T JUST OUR BATTLES, CORNELIA. YOU SAVED KANDRAKAR, MERIDIAN, AND HEATHERFIELD ITSELF.
NOW GO.
NO ONE CAN KNOW THEIR DESTINY. NO ONE!

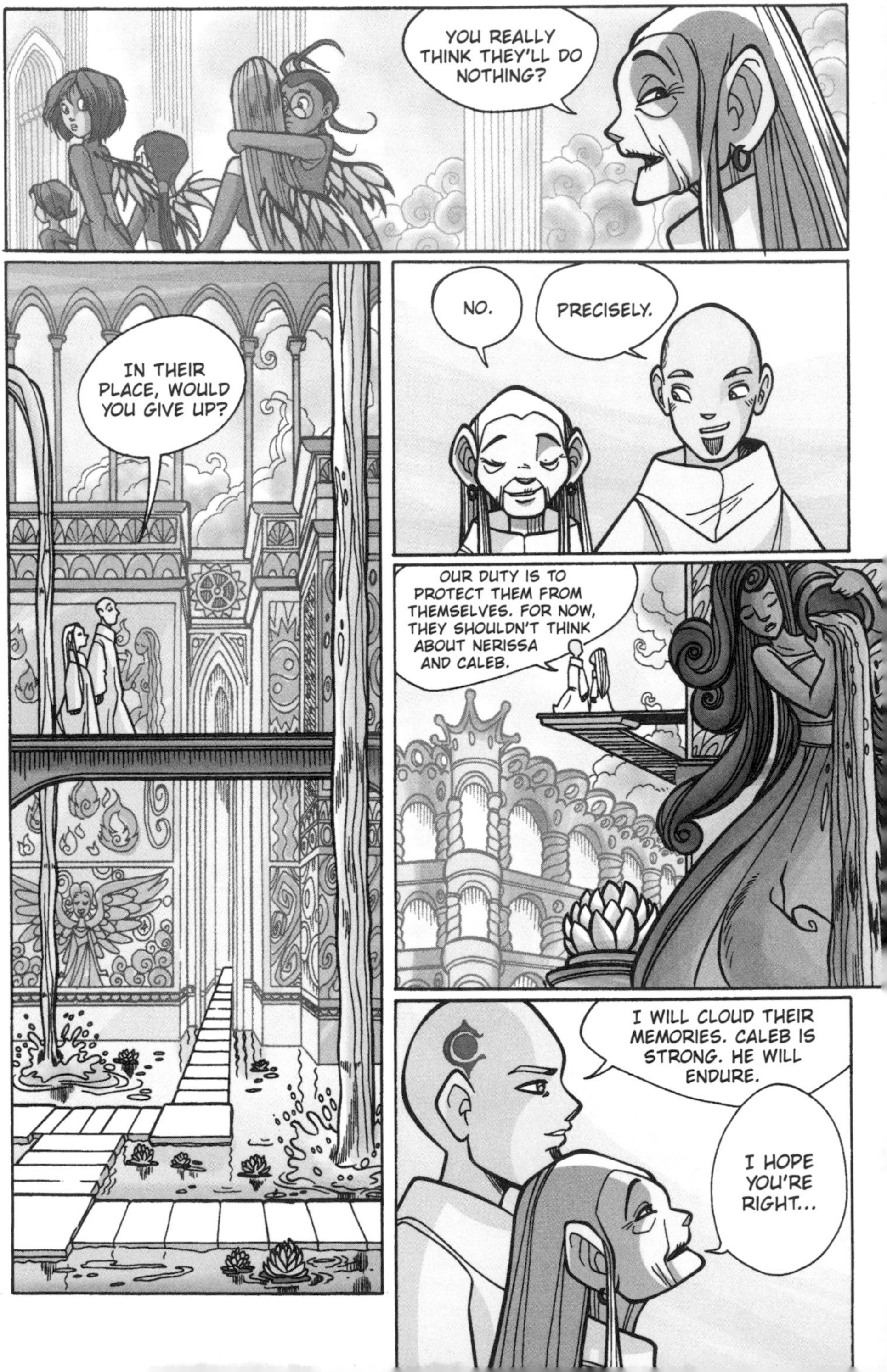
YOU REALLY THINK THEY'LL DO NOTHING?
IN THEIR PLACE, WOULD YOU GIVE UP?
NO.
PRECISELY.
OUR DUTY IS TO PROTECT THEM FROM THEMSELVES. FOR NOW, THEY SHOULDN'T THINK ABOUT NERISSA AND CALEB.
I WILL CLOUD THEIR MEMORIES. CALEB IS STRONG. HE WILL ENDURE.
I HOPE YOU'RE RIGHT...

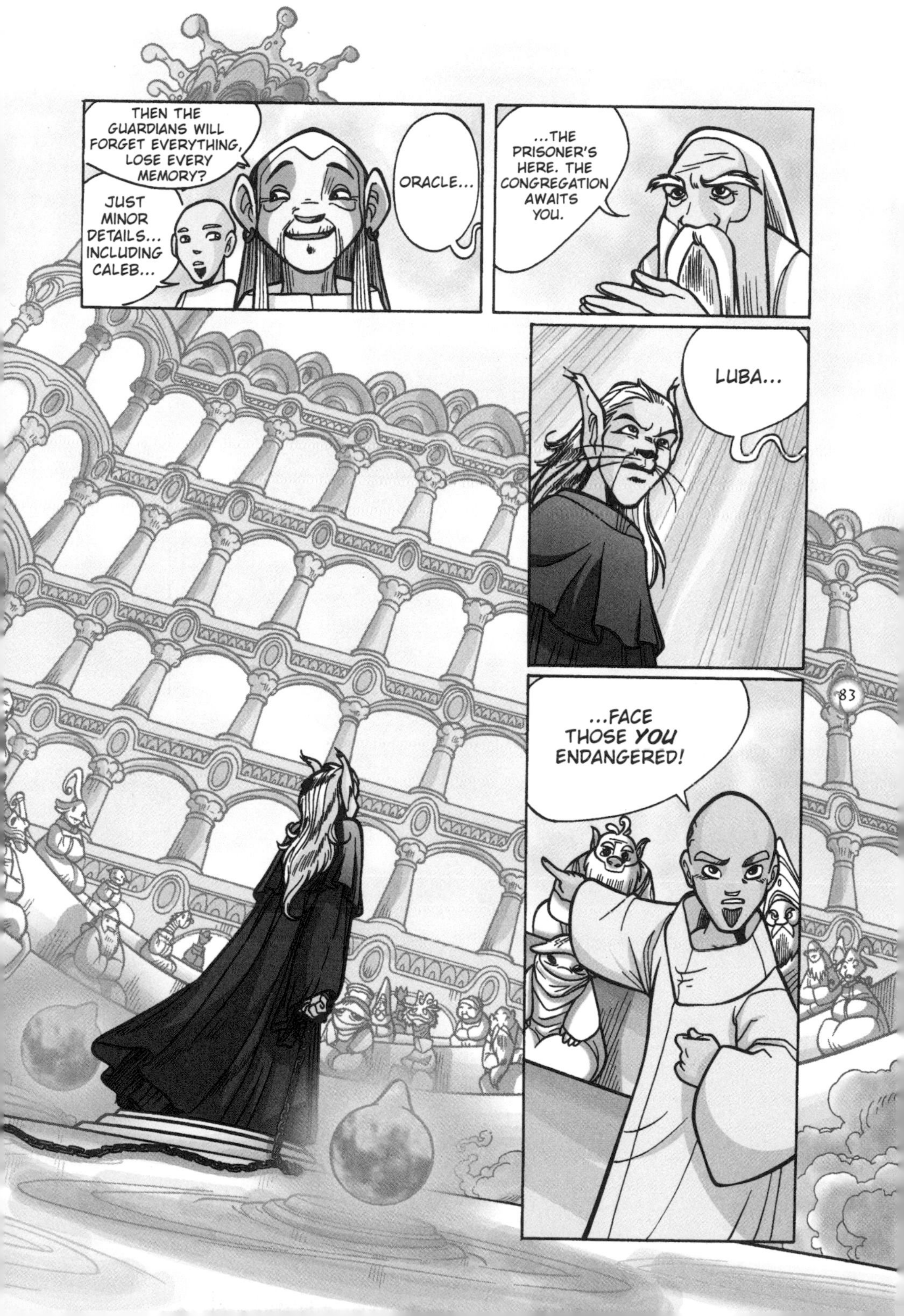
THEN THE GUARDIANS WILL FORGET EVERYTHING, LOSE EVERY MEMORY?
JUST MINOR DETAILS... INCLUDING CALEB...
ORACLE...
...THE PRISONER'S HERE. THE CONGREGATION AWAITS YOU.
LUBA...
...FACE THOSE *YOU* ENDANGERED!

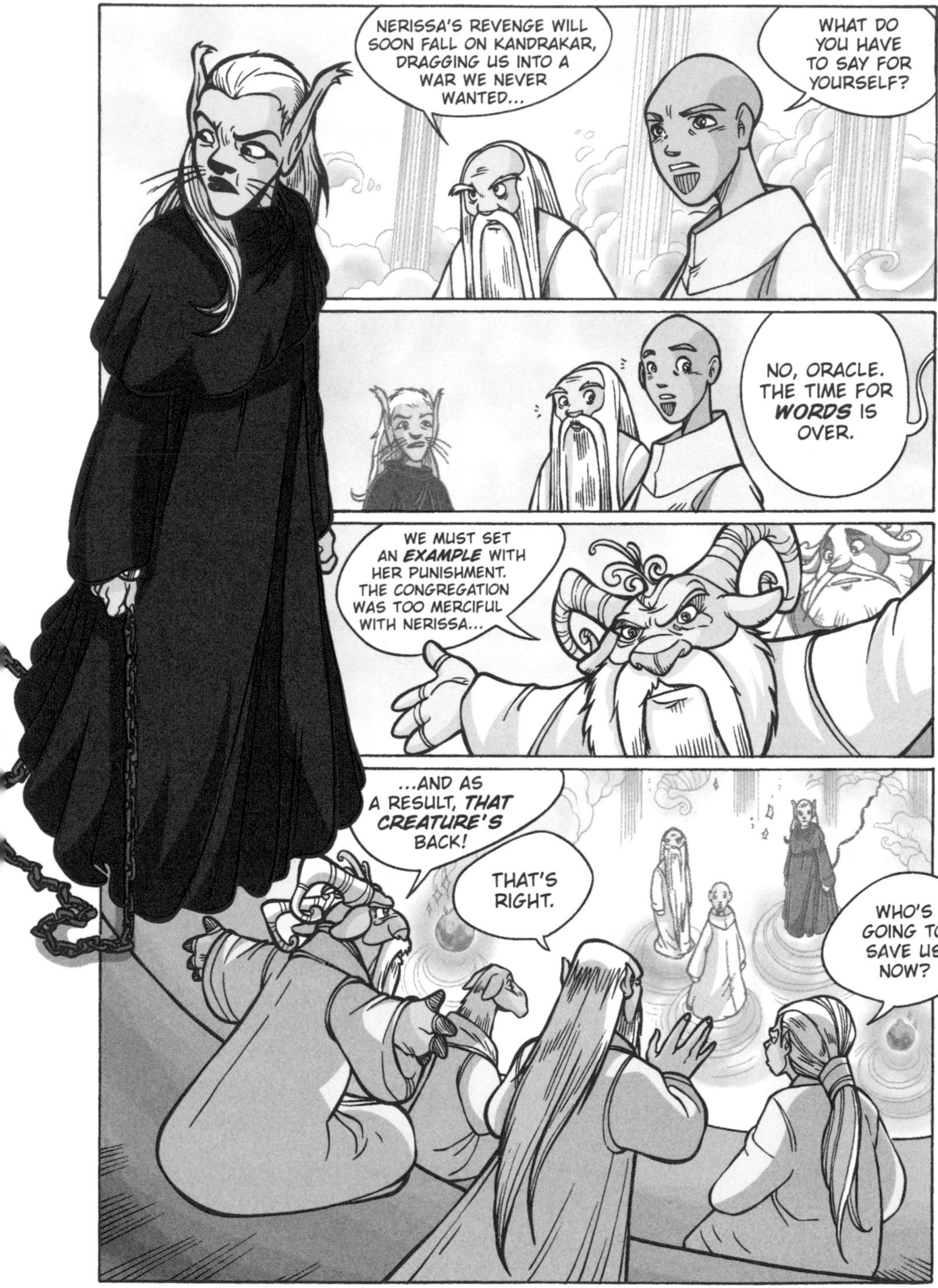
NERISSA'S REVENGE WILL SOON FALL ON KANDRAKAR, DRAGGING US INTO A WAR WE NEVER WANTED...
WHAT DO YOU HAVE TO SAY FOR YOURSELF?
NO, ORACLE. THE TIME FOR WORDS IS OVER.
WE MUST SET AN EXAMPLE WITH HER PUNISHMENT. THE CONGREGATION WAS TOO MERCIFUL WITH NERISSA...
...AND AS A RESULT, THAT CREATURE'S BACK!
THAT'S RIGHT.
WHO'S GOING TO SAVE US NOW?

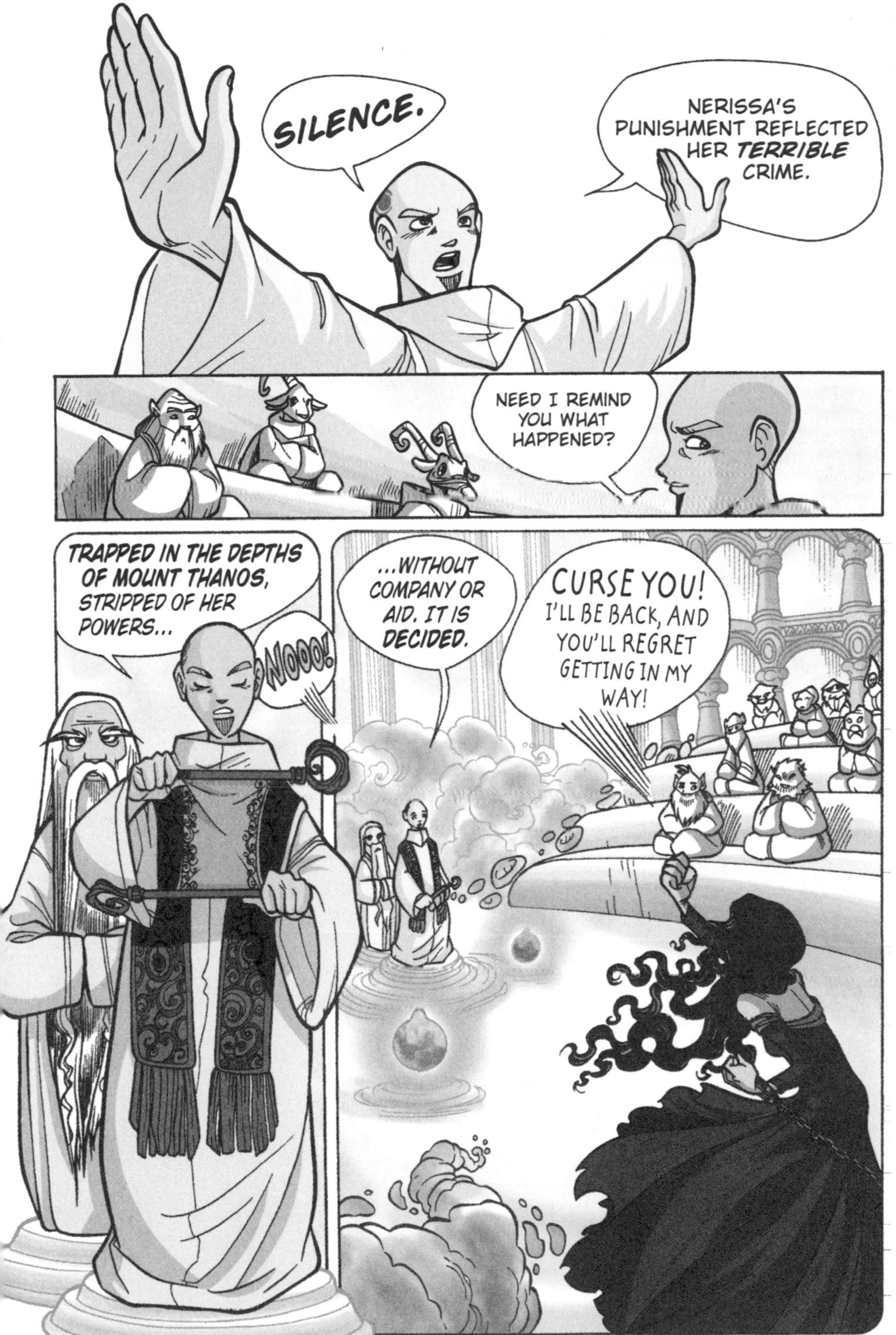
SILENCE.
NERISSA'S PUNISHMENT REFLECTED HER TERRIBLE CRIME.
NEED I REMIND YOU WHAT HAPPENED?
TRAPPED IN THE DEPTHS OF MOUNT THANOS, STRIPPED OF HER POWERS...
NOOO!
...WITHOUT COMPANY OR AID. IT IS DECIDED.
CURSE YOU! I'LL BE BACK, AND YOU'LL REGRET GETTING IN MY WAY!

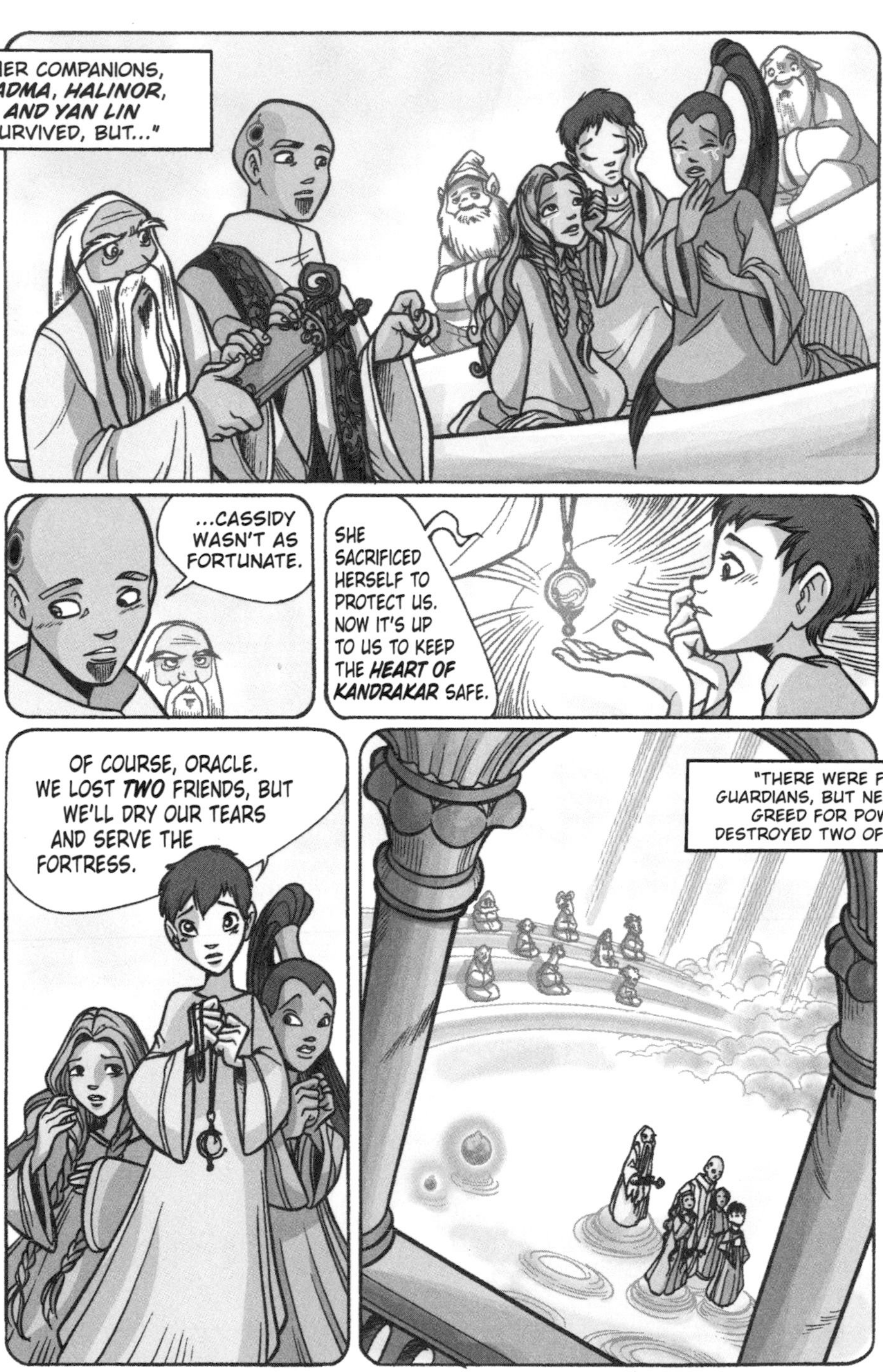
"HER COMPANIONS, KADMA, HALINOR, AND YAN LIN SURVIVED, BUT..."
...CASSIDY WASN'T AS FORTUNATE.
SHE SACRIFICED HERSELF TO PROTECT US. NOW IT'S UP TO US TO KEEP THE HEART OF KANDRAKAR SAFE.
OF COURSE, ORACLE. WE LOST TWO FRIENDS, BUT WE'LL DRY OUR TEARS AND SERVE THE FORTRESS.
"THERE WERE FIVE GUARDIANS, BUT NERISSA'S GREED FOR POWER DESTROYED TWO OF THEM."

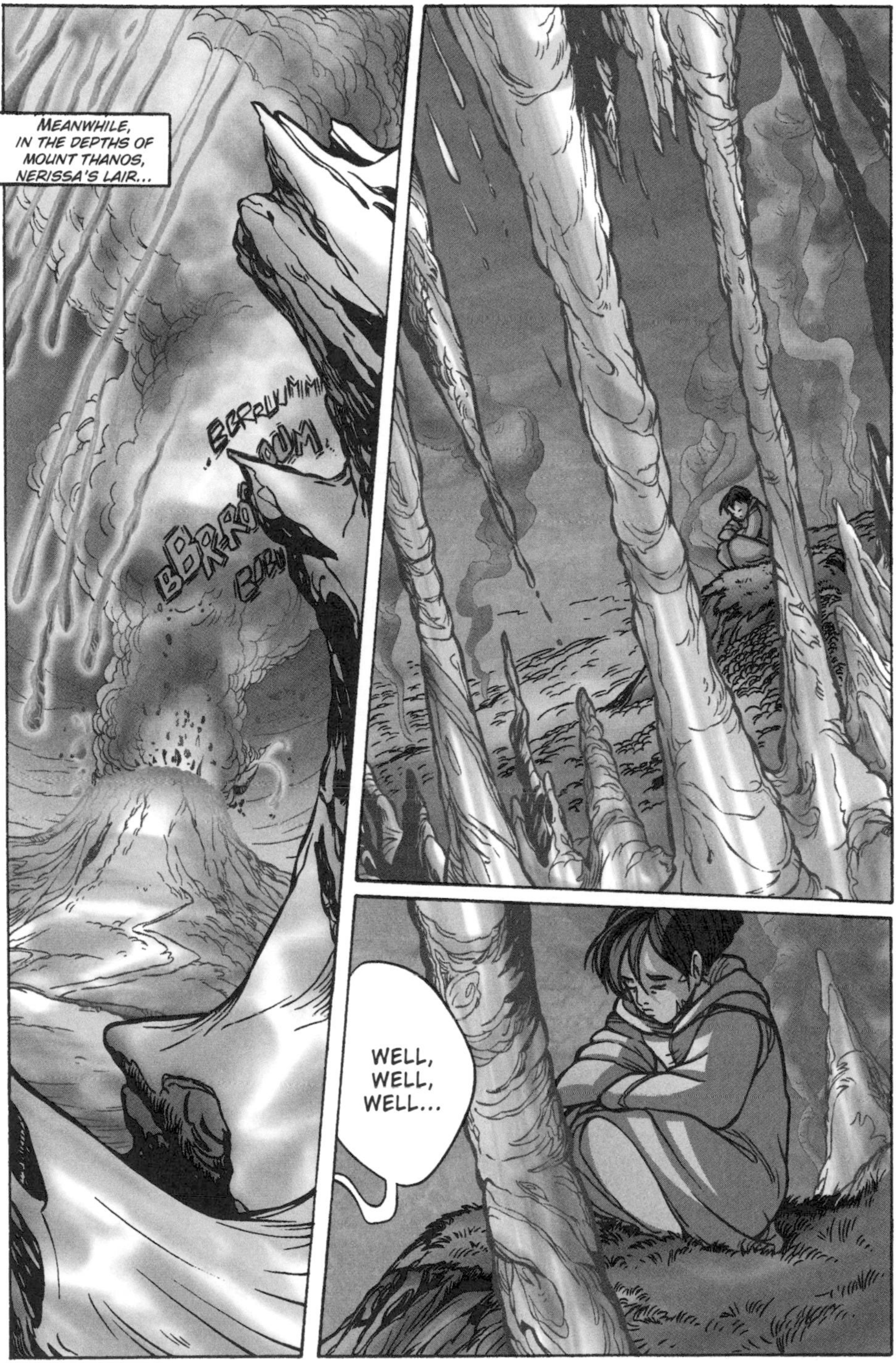
MEANWHILE, IN THE DEPTHS OF MOUNT THANOS, NERISSA'S LAIR...
BBRRUUMMM
BBRRROOOM
WELL, WELL, WELL...

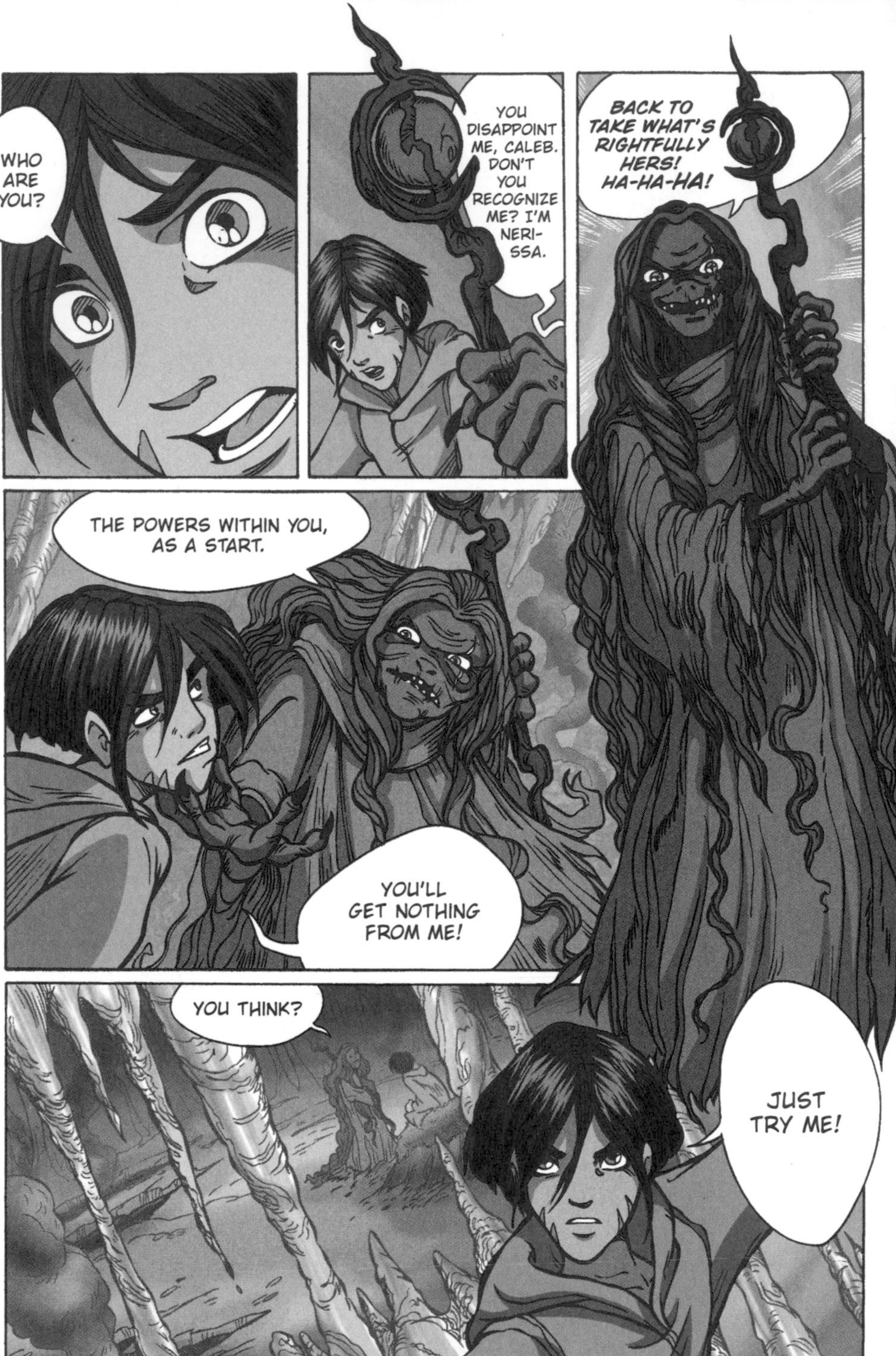
WHO ARE YOU?
YOU DISAPPOINT ME, CALEB. DON'T YOU RECOGNIZE ME? I'M NERI-SSA.
BACK TO TAKE WHAT'S RIGHTFULLY HERS! HA-HA-HA!
THE POWERS WITHIN YOU, AS A START.
YOU'LL GET NOTHING FROM ME!
YOU THINK?
JUST TRY ME!

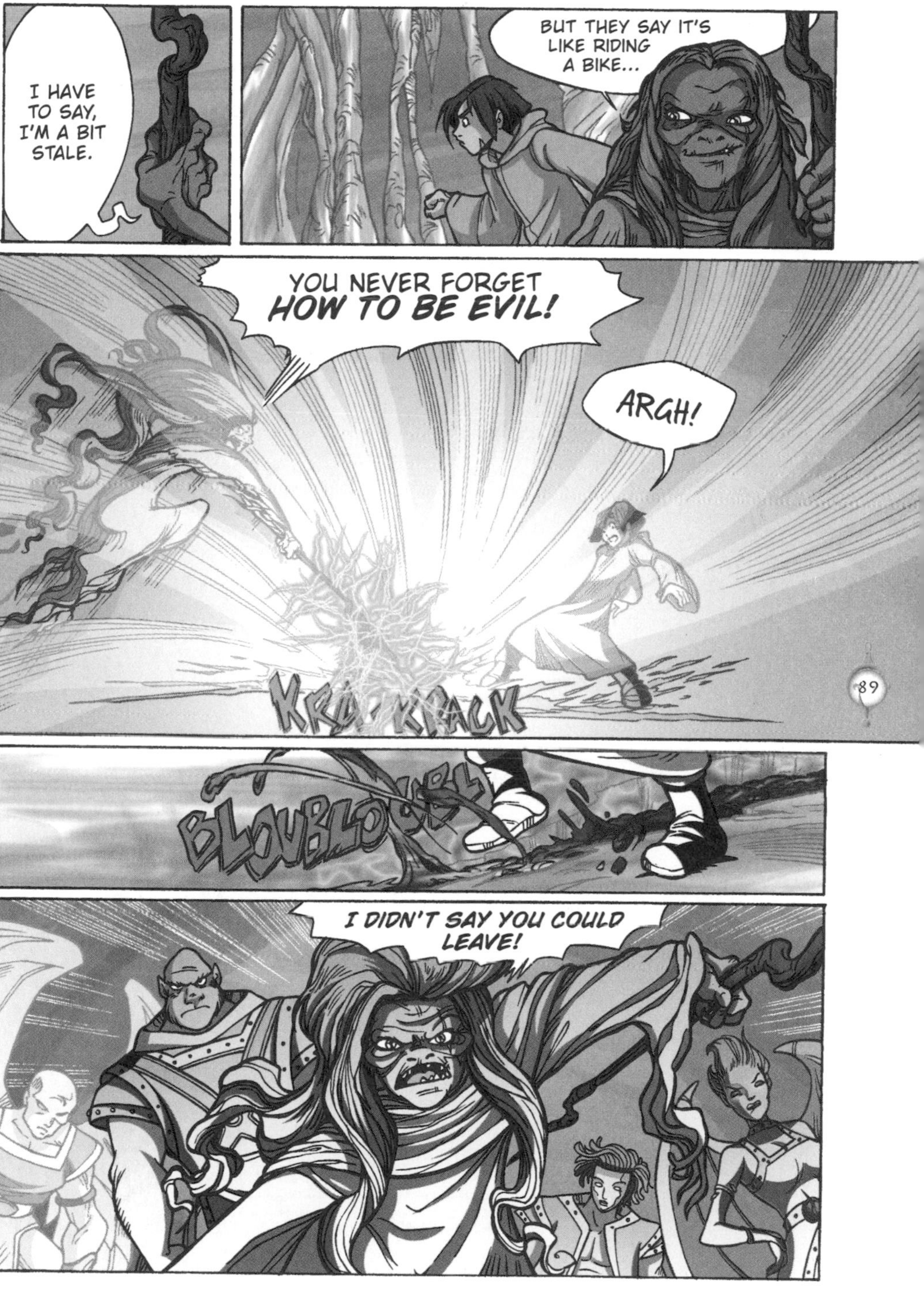
I HAVE TO SAY, I'M A BIT STALE.
BUT THEY SAY IT'S LIKE RIDING A BIKE...
YOU NEVER FORGET **HOW TO BE EVIL!**
ARGH!
KRACK
BLOUBLOUBL
I DIDN'T SAY YOU COULD LEAVE!

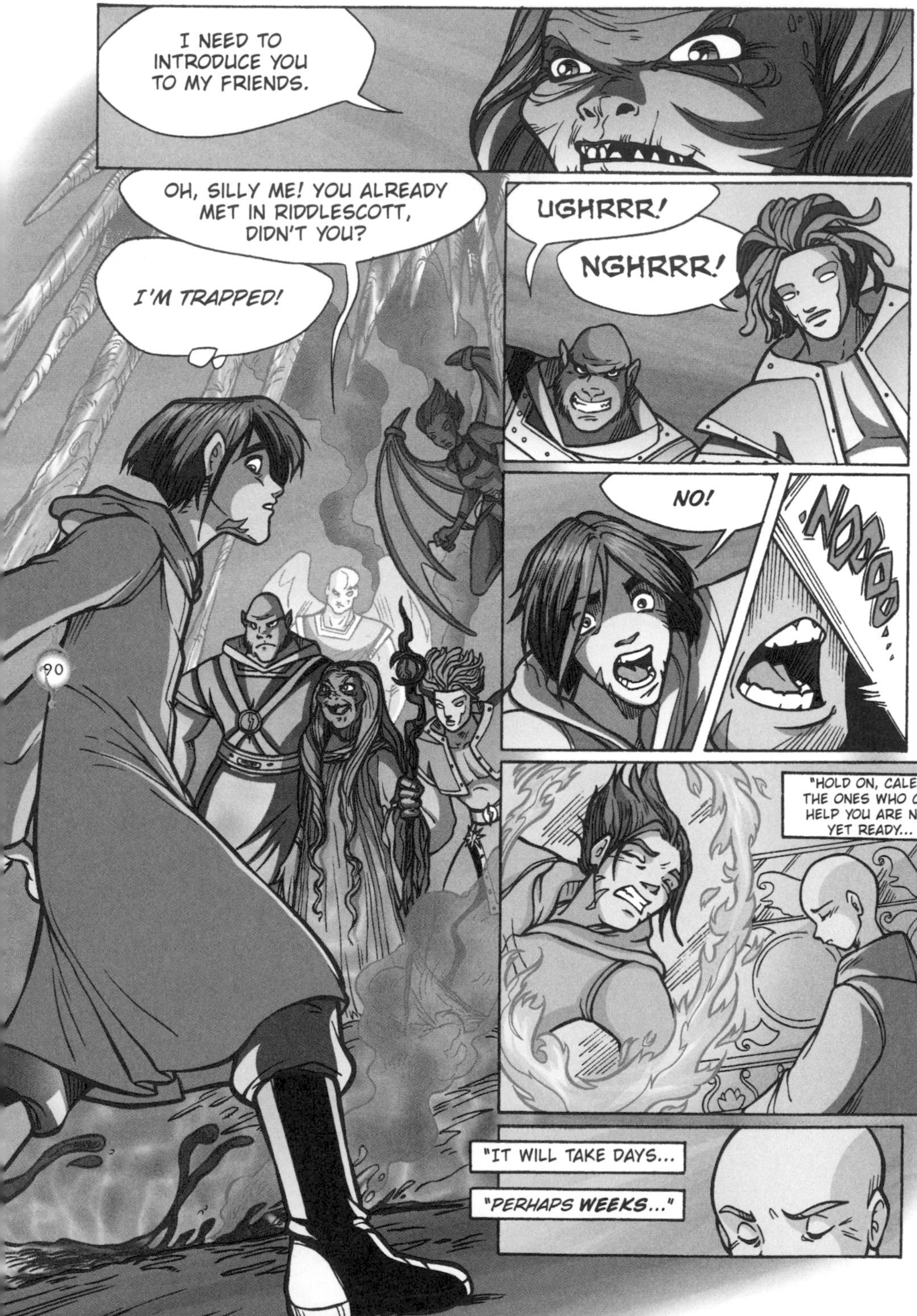
I NEED TO INTRODUCE YOU TO MY FRIENDS.
OH, SILLY ME! YOU ALREADY MET IN RIDDLESCOTT, DIDN'T YOU?
I'M TRAPPED!
UGHRRR!
NGHRRR!
NO!
NOOOO
"HOLD ON, CALEB. THE ONES WHO CAN HELP YOU ARE NOT YET READY...
"IT WILL TAKE DAYS...
"*PERHAPS* ***WEEKS***..."

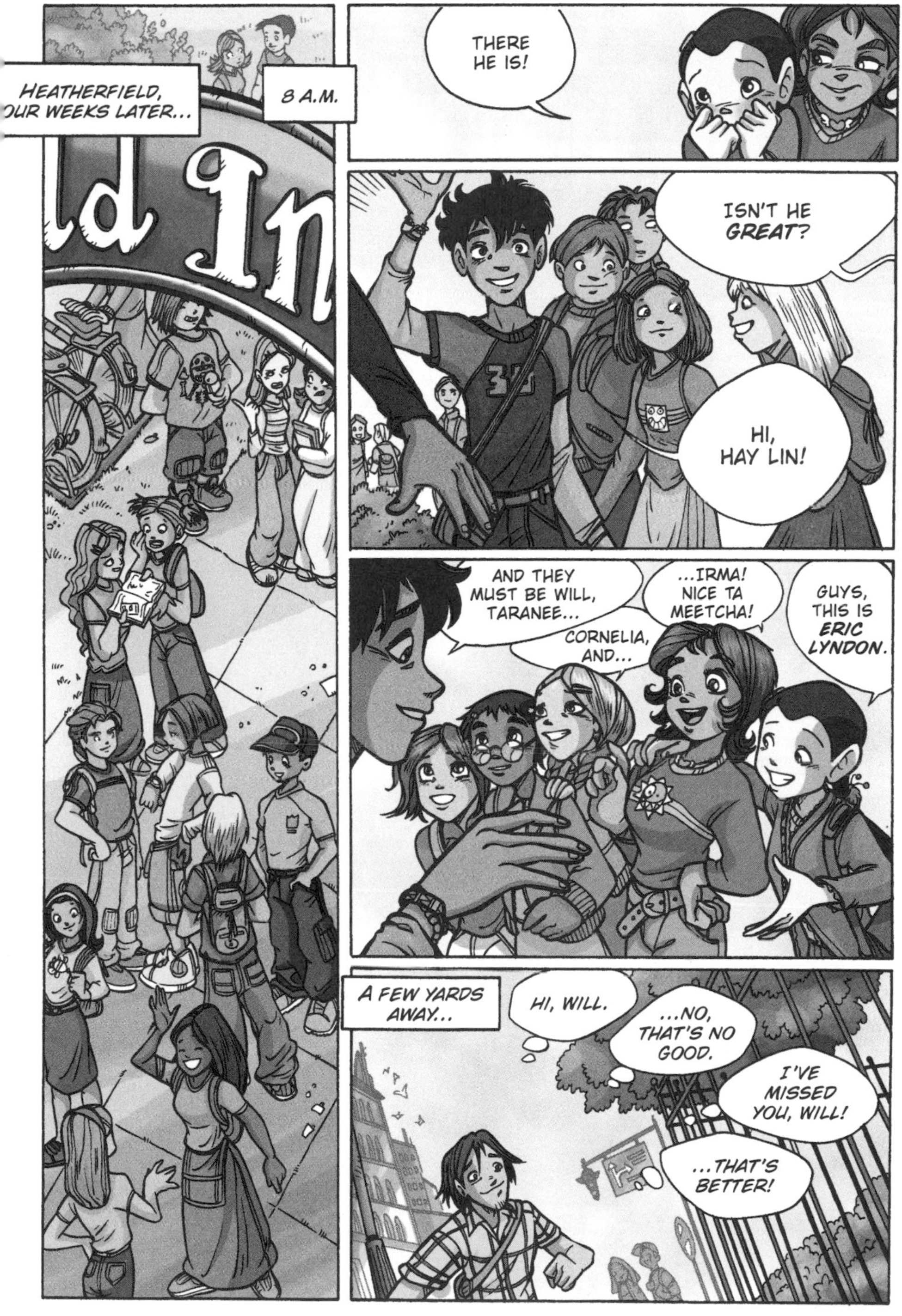
HEATHERFIELD, OUR WEEKS LATER...
8 A.M.
THERE HE IS!
ISN'T HE GREAT?
HI, HAY LIN!
AND THEY MUST BE WILL, TARANEE...
CORNELIA, AND...
...IRMA! NICE TA MEETCHA!
GUYS, THIS IS ERIC LYNDON.
A FEW YARDS AWAY...
HI, WILL.
...NO, THAT'S NO GOOD.
I'VE MISSED YOU, WILL!
...THAT'S BETTER!

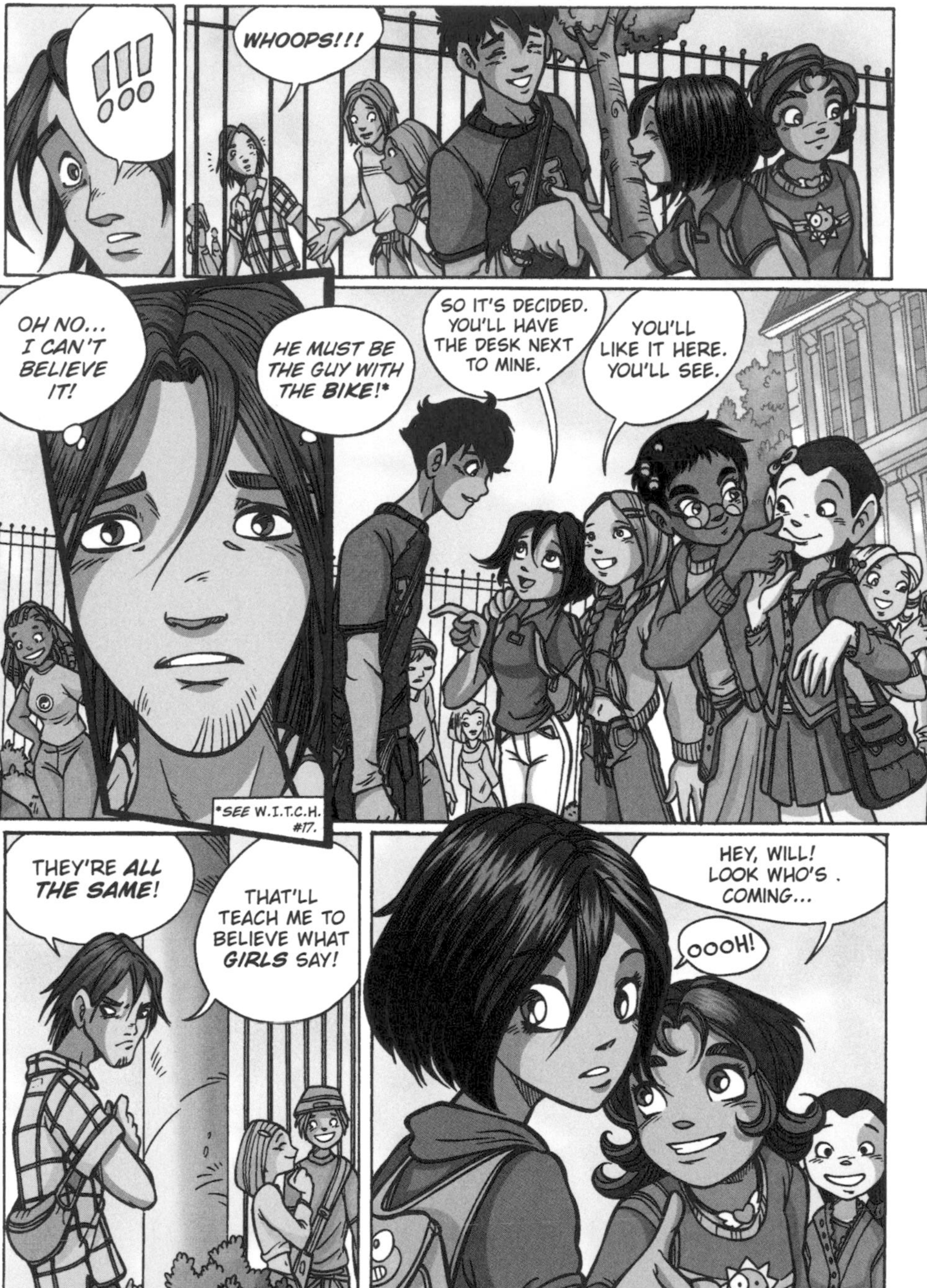
!!!
OOO
WHOOPS!!!
OH NO... I CAN'T BELIEVE IT!
HE MUST BE THE GUY WITH THE BIKE!*
SO IT'S DECIDED. YOU'LL HAVE THE DESK NEXT TO MINE.
YOU'LL LIKE IT HERE. YOU'LL SEE.
*SEE W.I.T.C.H. #17.
THEY'RE ALL THE SAME!
THAT'LL TEACH ME TO BELIEVE WHAT GIRLS SAY!
HEY, WILL! LOOK WHO'S . COMING...
OOOH!

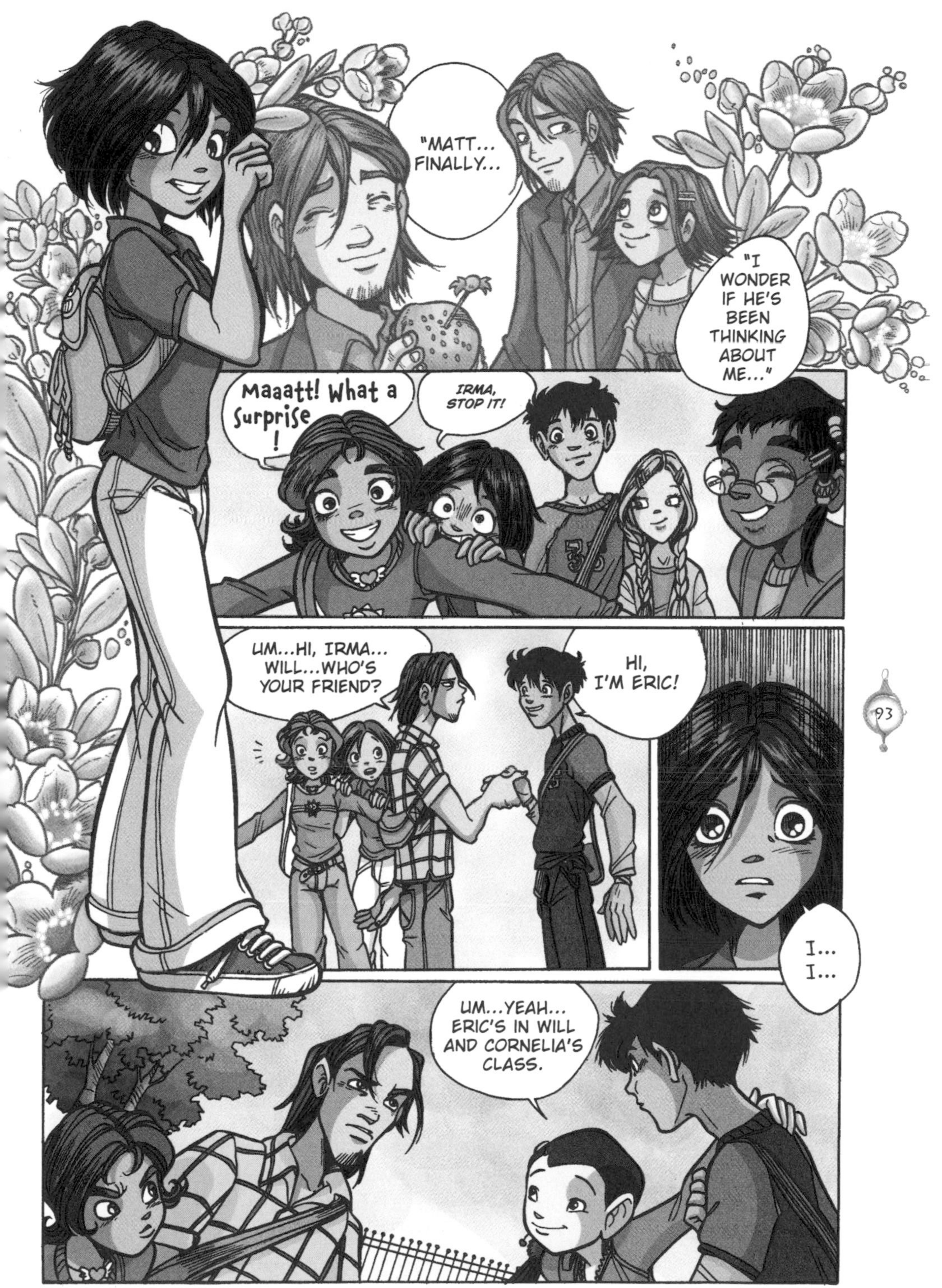
"MATT... FINALLY...
"I WONDER IF HE'S BEEN THINKING ABOUT ME..."
Maaatt! What a surprise!
IRMA, STOP IT!
UM...HI, IRMA... WILL...WHO'S YOUR FRIEND?
HI, I'M ERIC!
I... I...
UM...YEAH... ERIC'S IN WILL AND CORNELIA'S CLASS.

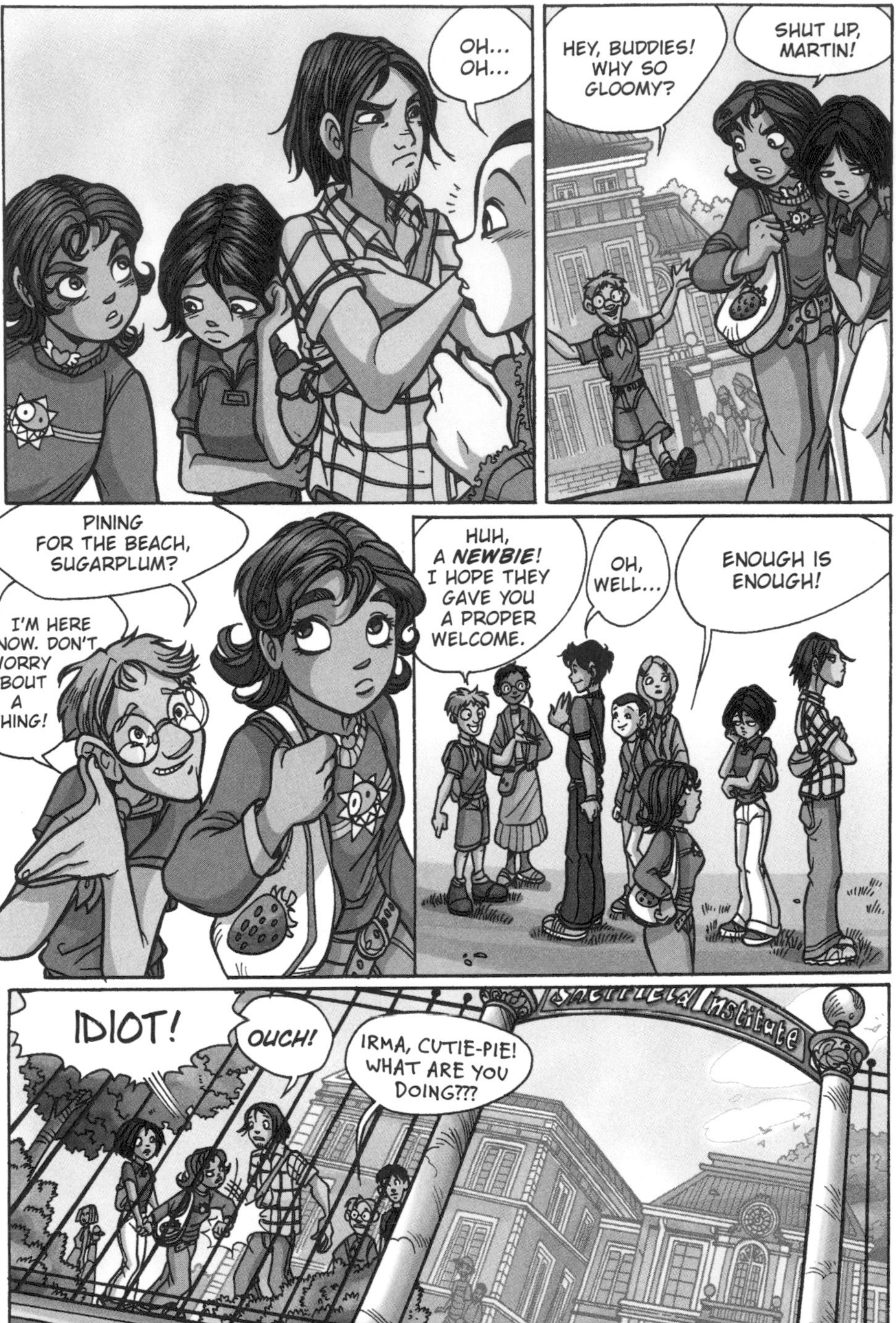
OH... OH...
HEY, BUDDIES! WHY SO GLOOMY?
SHUT UP, MARTIN!
PINING FOR THE BEACH, SUGARPLUM?
I'M HERE NOW. DON'T WORRY ABOUT A THING!
HUH, A NEWBIE! I HOPE THEY GAVE YOU A PROPER WELCOME.
OH, WELL...
ENOUGH IS ENOUGH!
IDIOT!
OUCH!
IRMA, CUTIE-PIE! WHAT ARE YOU DOING???

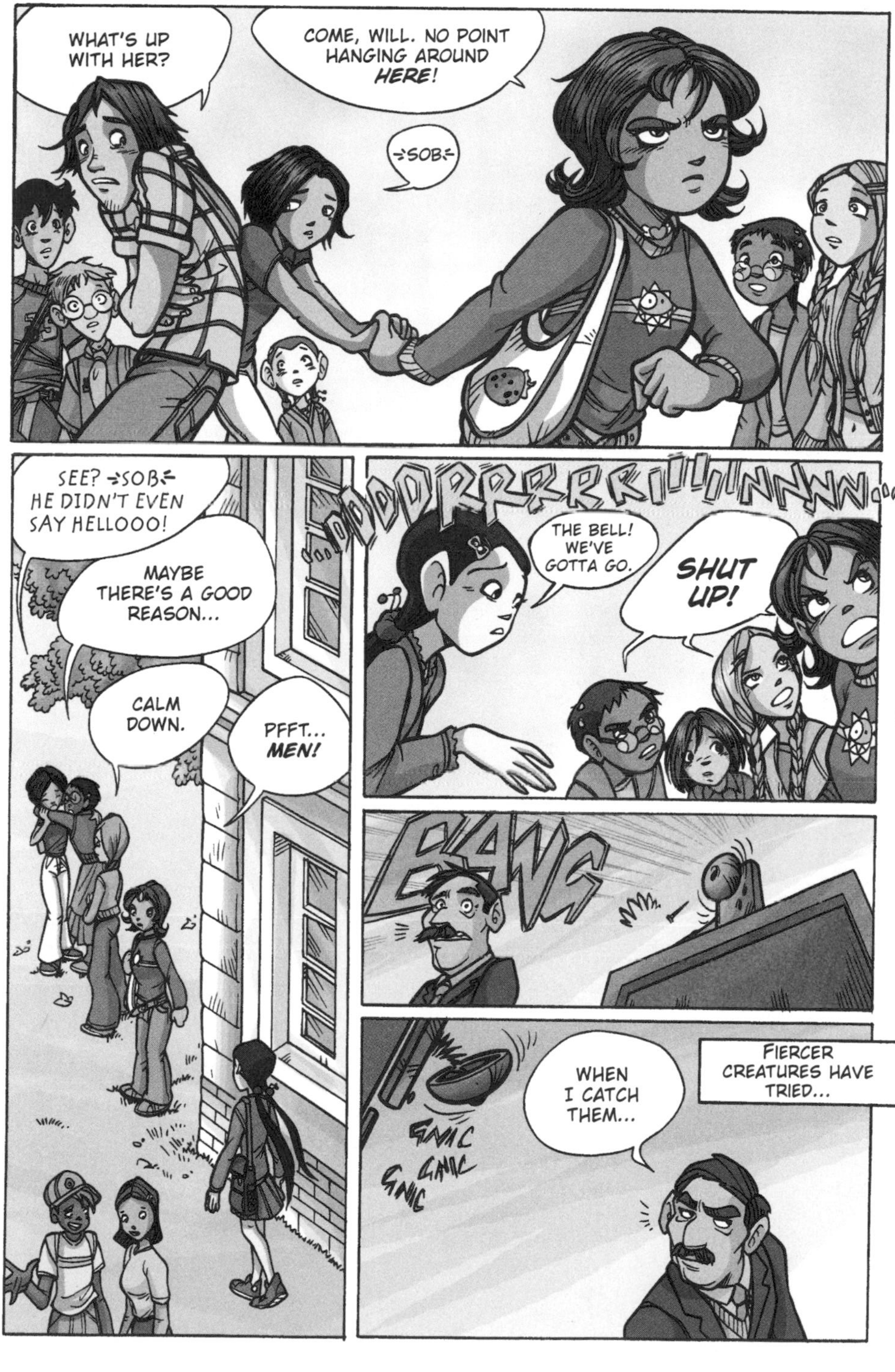
WHAT'S UP WITH HER?
COME, WILL. NO POINT HANGING AROUND *HERE*!
SOB
SEE? SOB HE DIDN'T EVEN SAY HELLOOO!
MAYBE THERE'S A GOOD REASON...
CALM DOWN.
PFFT... *MEN!*
DDDDRRRRRIIIIIINNNN...
THE BELL! WE'VE GOTTA GO.
SHUT UP!
BLANG
WHEN I CATCH THEM...
FIERCER CREATURES HAVE TRIED...

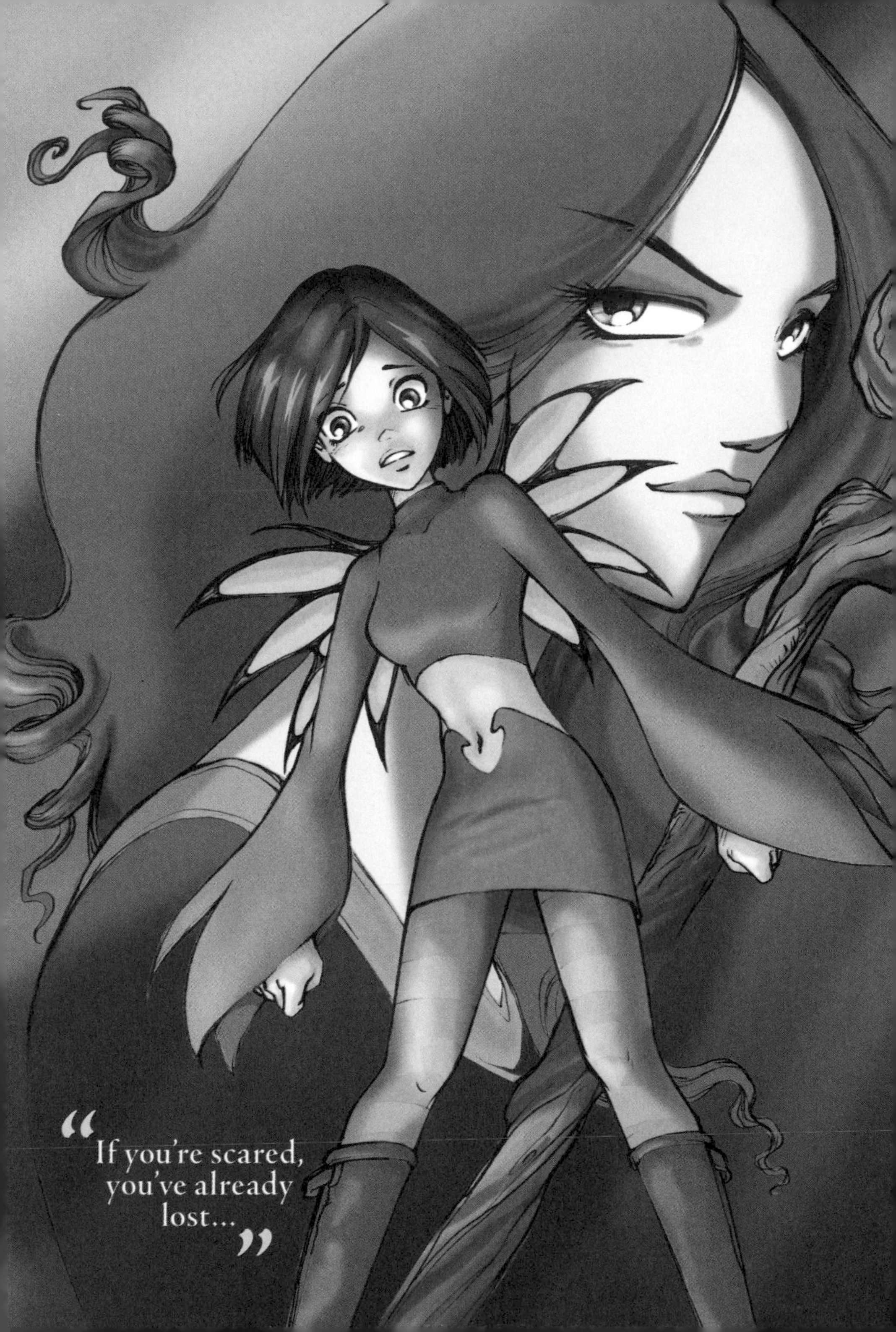
"If you're scared, you've already lost..."

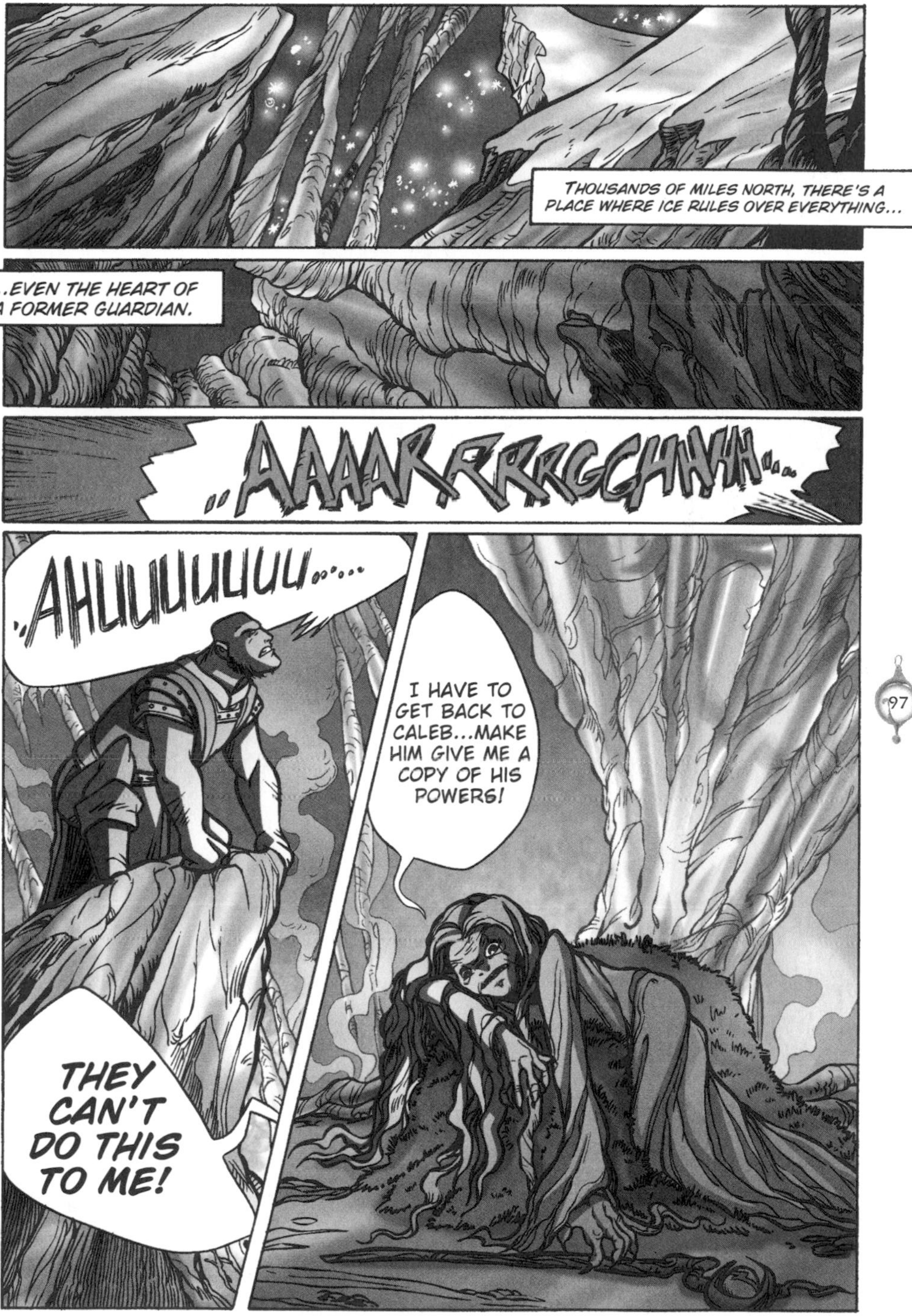
THOUSANDS OF MILES NORTH, THERE'S A PLACE WHERE ICE RULES OVER EVERYTHING...
...EVEN THE HEART OF A FORMER GUARDIAN.
..AAAARRRRGCHHHH...
..AHUUUUUUUU.....
I HAVE TO GET BACK TO CALEB...MAKE HIM GIVE ME A COPY OF HIS POWERS!
THEY CAN'T DO THIS TO ME!

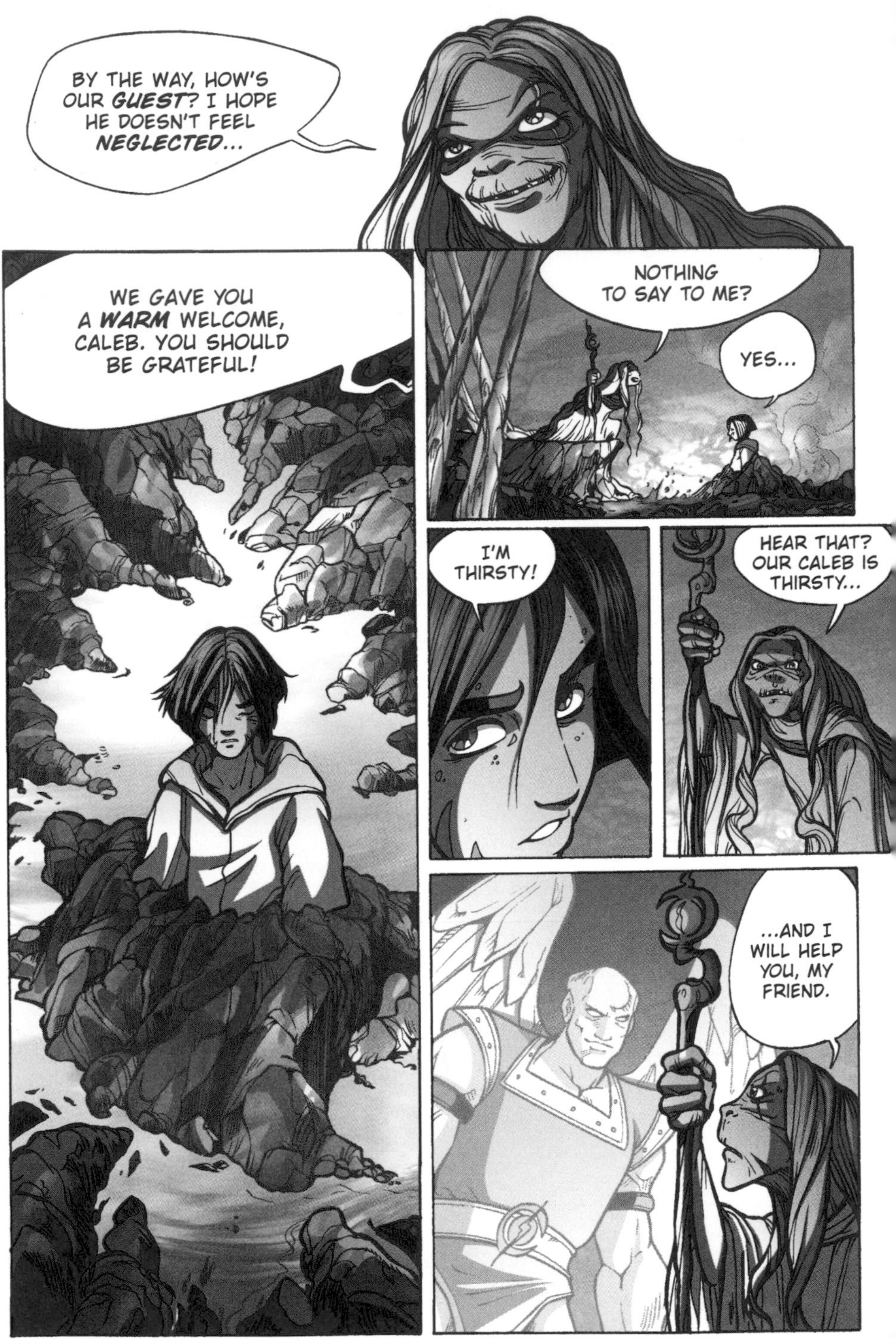
BY THE WAY, HOW'S OUR *GUEST*? I HOPE HE DOESN'T FEEL *NEGLECTED*...
WE GAVE YOU A *WARM* WELCOME, CALEB. YOU SHOULD BE GRATEFUL!
NOTHING TO SAY TO ME?
YES...
I'M THIRSTY!
HEAR THAT? OUR CALEB IS THIRSTY...
...AND I WILL HELP YOU, MY FRIEND.

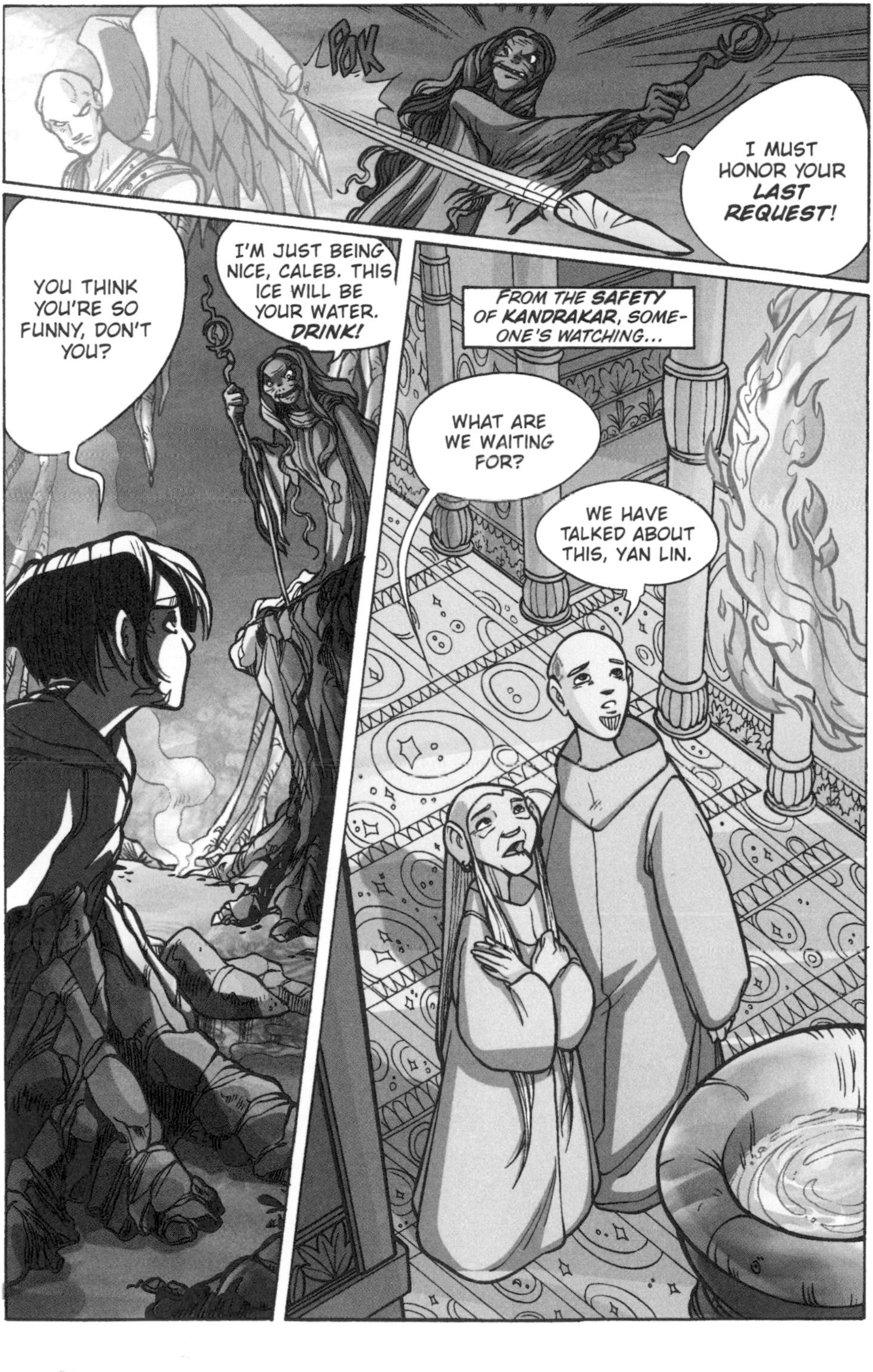
POK
I MUST HONOR YOUR LAST REQUEST!
YOU THINK YOU'RE SO FUNNY, DON'T YOU?
I'M JUST BEING NICE, CALEB. THIS ICE WILL BE YOUR WATER. DRINK!
FROM THE SAFETY OF KANDRAKAR, SOME-ONE'S WATCHING...
WHAT ARE WE WAITING FOR?
WE HAVE TALKED ABOUT THIS, YAN LIN.

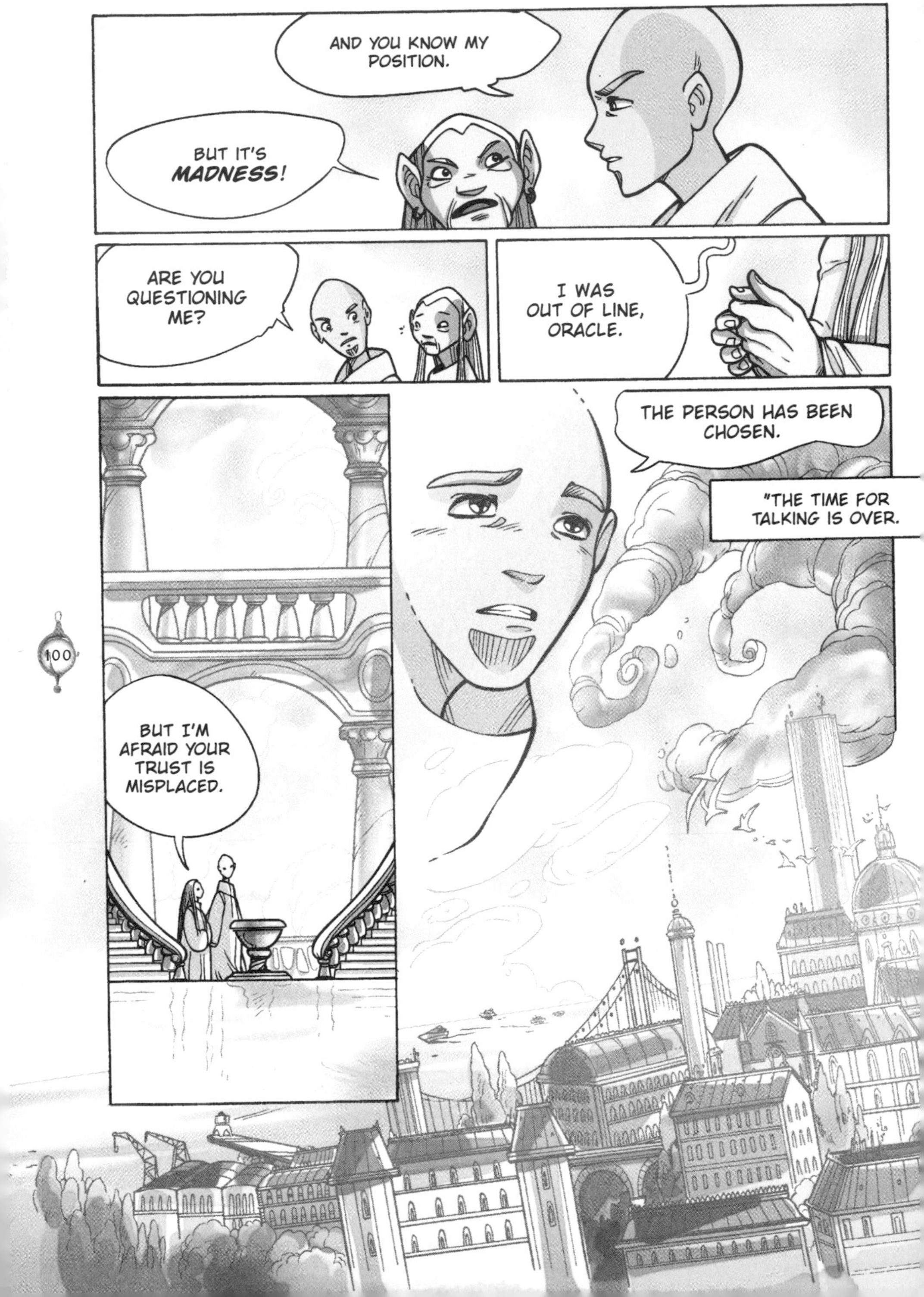
AND YOU KNOW MY POSITION.
BUT IT'S ***MADNESS!***
ARE YOU QUESTIONING ME?
I WAS OUT OF LINE, ORACLE.
THE PERSON HAS BEEN CHOSEN.
"THE TIME FOR TALKING IS OVER.
BUT I'M AFRAID YOUR TRUST IS MISPLACED.

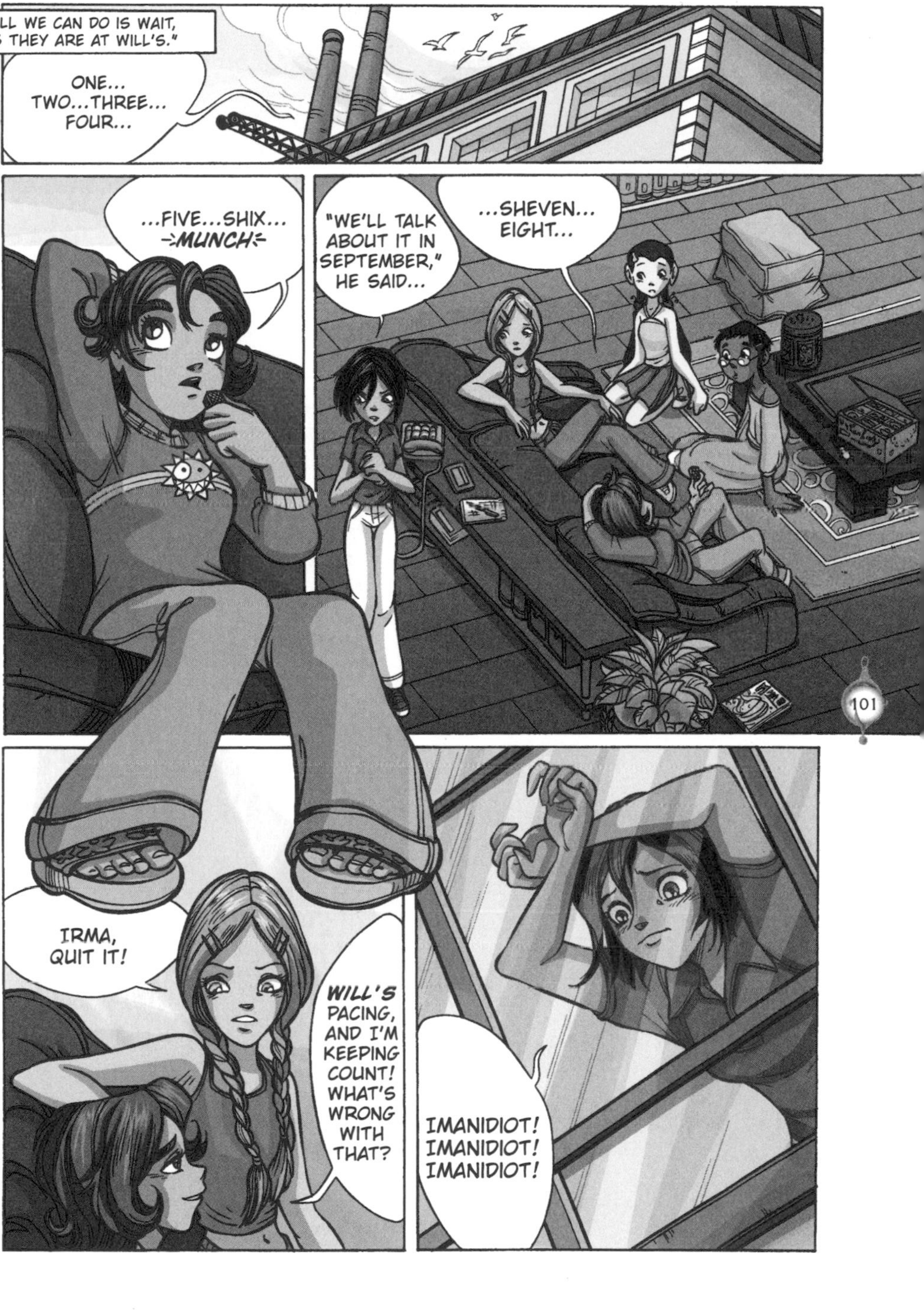
"ALL WE CAN DO IS WAIT, AS THEY ARE AT WILL'S."
ONE... TWO...THREE... FOUR...
...FIVE...SHIX... MUNCH
"WE'LL TALK ABOUT IT IN SEPTEMBER," HE SAID...
...SHEVEN... EIGHT...
IRMA, QUIT IT!
WILL'S PACING, AND I'M KEEPING COUNT! WHAT'S WRONG WITH THAT?
IMANIDIOT! IMANIDIOT! IMANIDIOT!

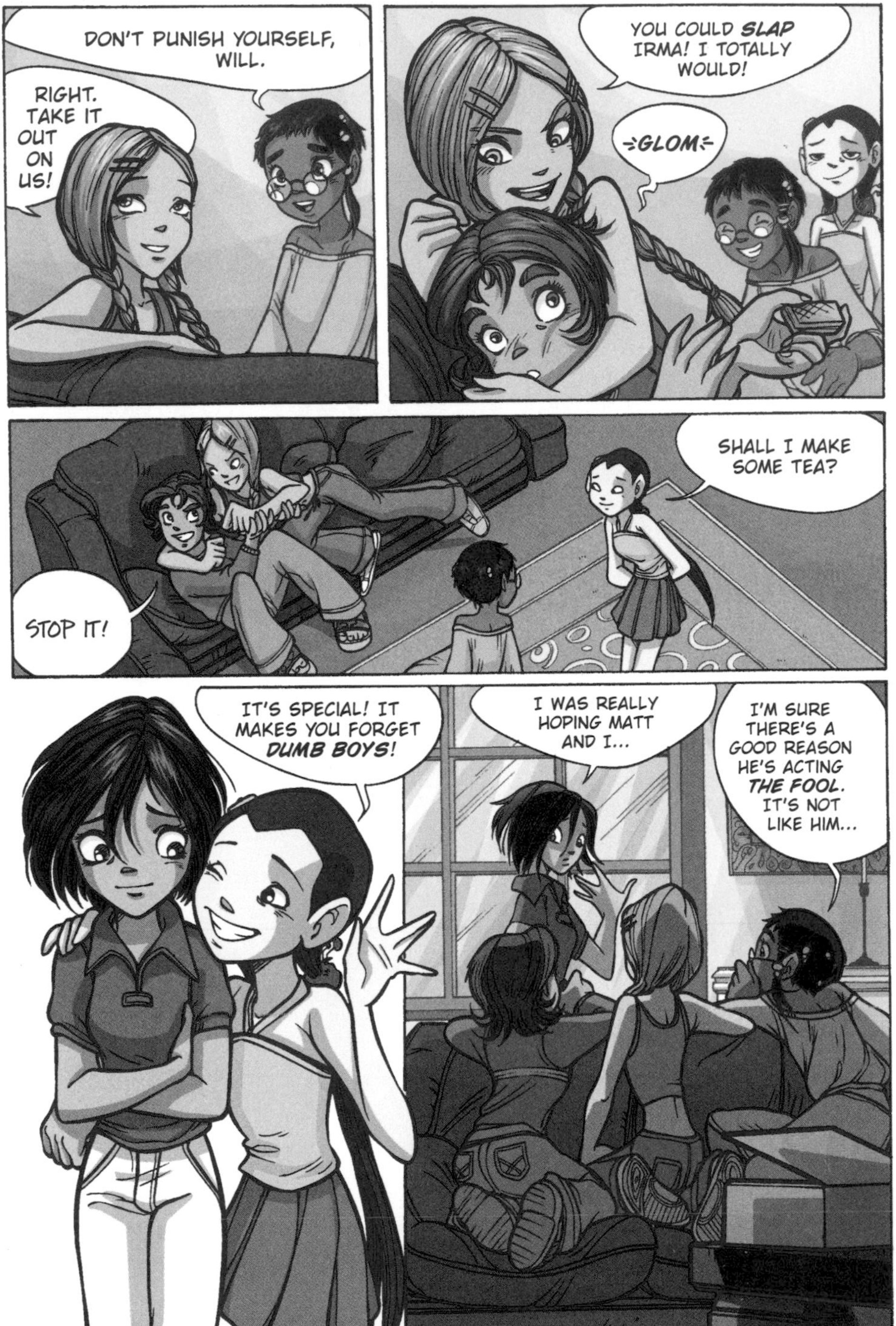
DON'T PUNISH YOURSELF, WILL.
RIGHT. TAKE IT OUT ON US!
YOU COULD SLAP IRMA! I TOTALLY WOULD!
GLOM
SHALL I MAKE SOME TEA?
STOP IT!
IT'S SPECIAL! IT MAKES YOU FORGET DUMB BOYS!
I WAS REALLY HOPING MATT AND I...
I'M SURE THERE'S A GOOD REASON HE'S ACTING THE FOOL. IT'S NOT LIKE HIM...

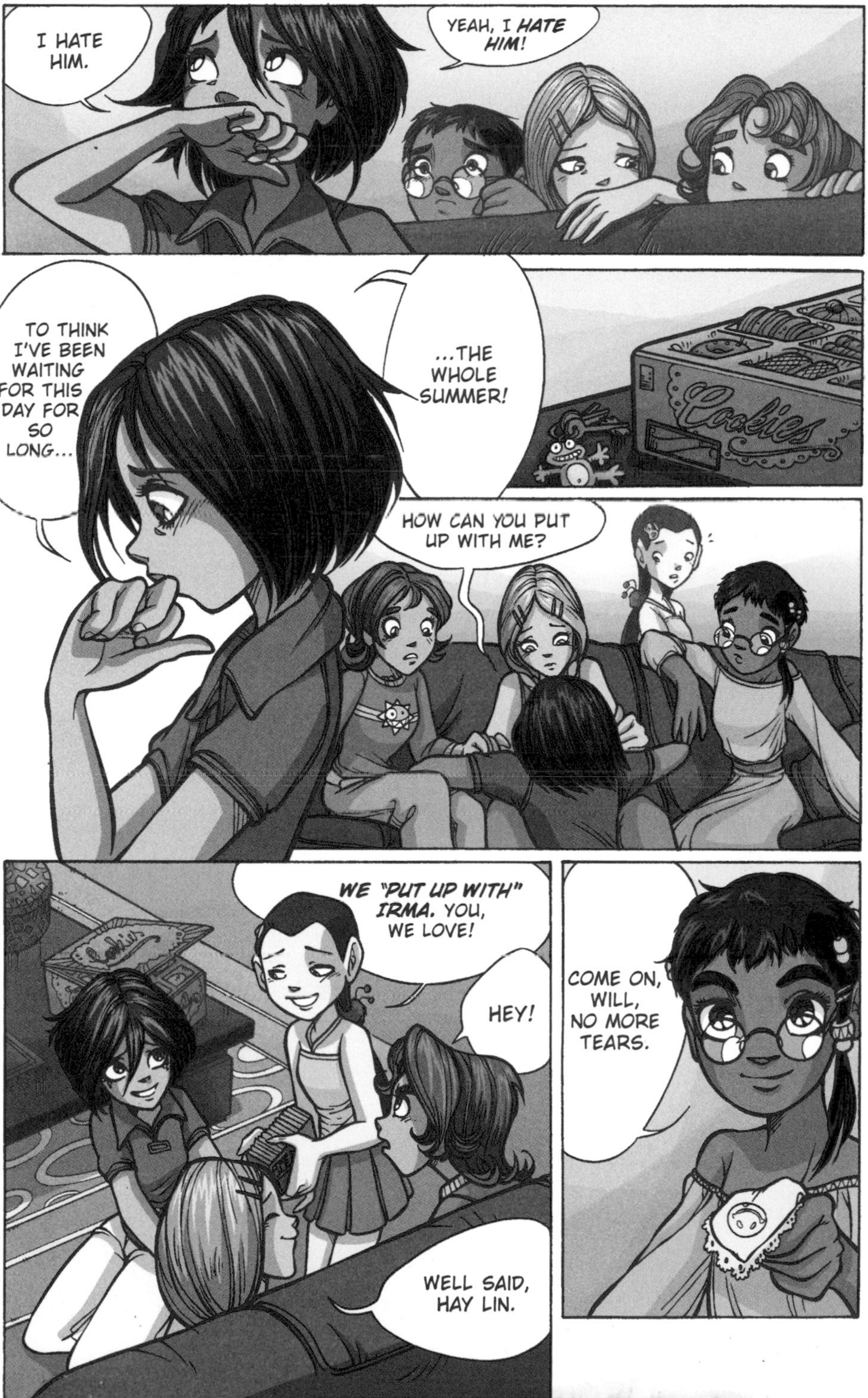

I HATE HIM.
YEAH, I *HATE HIM*!
TO THINK I'VE BEEN WAITING FOR THIS DAY FOR SO LONG...
...THE WHOLE SUMMER!
HOW CAN YOU PUT UP WITH ME?
WE "PUT UP WITH" IRMA. YOU, WE LOVE!
HEY!
WELL SAID, HAY LIN.
COME ON, WILL, NO MORE TEARS.

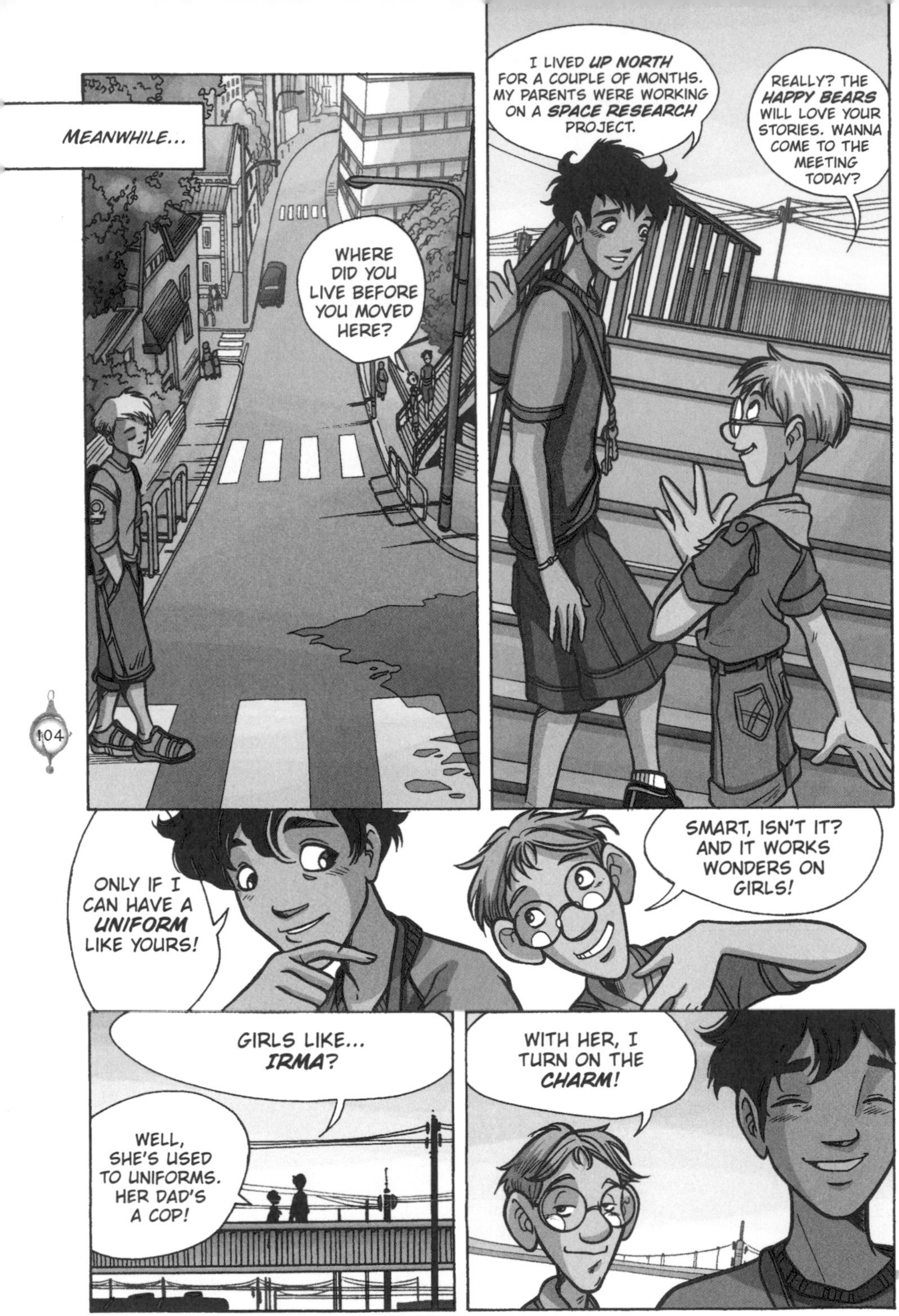
MEANWHILE...
WHERE DID YOU LIVE BEFORE YOU MOVED HERE?
I LIVED UP NORTH FOR A COUPLE OF MONTHS. MY PARENTS WERE WORKING ON A SPACE RESEARCH PROJECT.
REALLY? THE HAPPY BEARS WILL LOVE YOUR STORIES. WANNA COME TO THE MEETING TODAY?
ONLY IF I CAN HAVE A UNIFORM LIKE YOURS!
SMART, ISN'T IT? AND IT WORKS WONDERS ON GIRLS!
GIRLS LIKE... IRMA?
WELL, SHE'S USED TO UNIFORMS. HER DAD'S A COP!
WITH HER, I TURN ON THE CHARM!

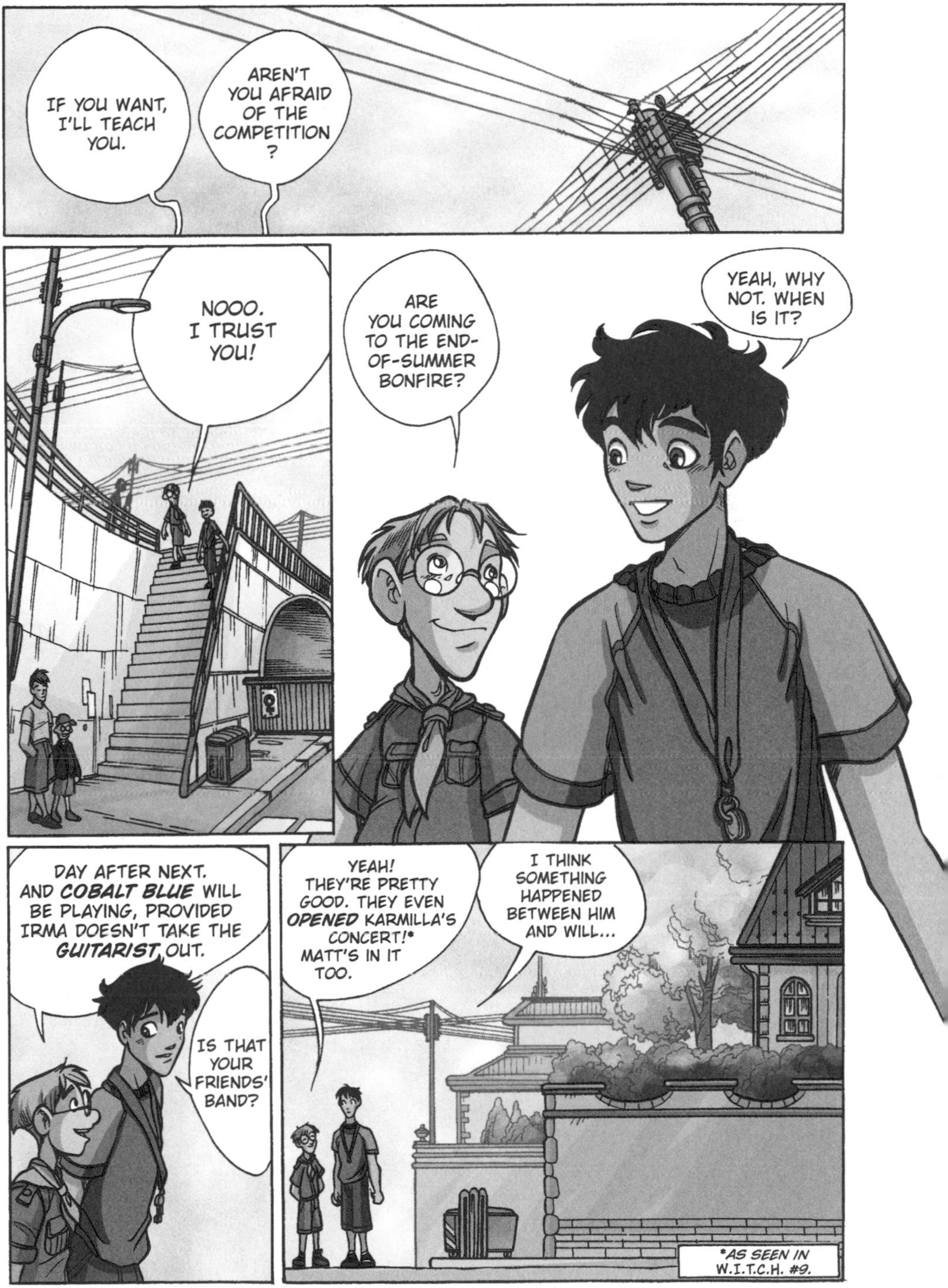
IF YOU WANT, I'LL TEACH YOU.
AREN'T YOU AFRAID OF THE COMPETITION?
NOOO. I TRUST YOU!
ARE YOU COMING TO THE END-OF-SUMMER BONFIRE?
YEAH, WHY NOT. WHEN IS IT?
DAY AFTER NEXT. AND COBALT BLUE WILL BE PLAYING, PROVIDED IRMA DOESN'T TAKE THE GUITARIST OUT.
IS THAT YOUR FRIENDS' BAND?
YEAH! THEY'RE PRETTY GOOD. THEY EVEN OPENED KARMILLA'S CONCERT!* MATT'S IN IT TOO.
I THINK SOMETHING HAPPENED BETWEEN HIM AND WILL...
*AS SEEN IN W.I.T.C.H. #9.

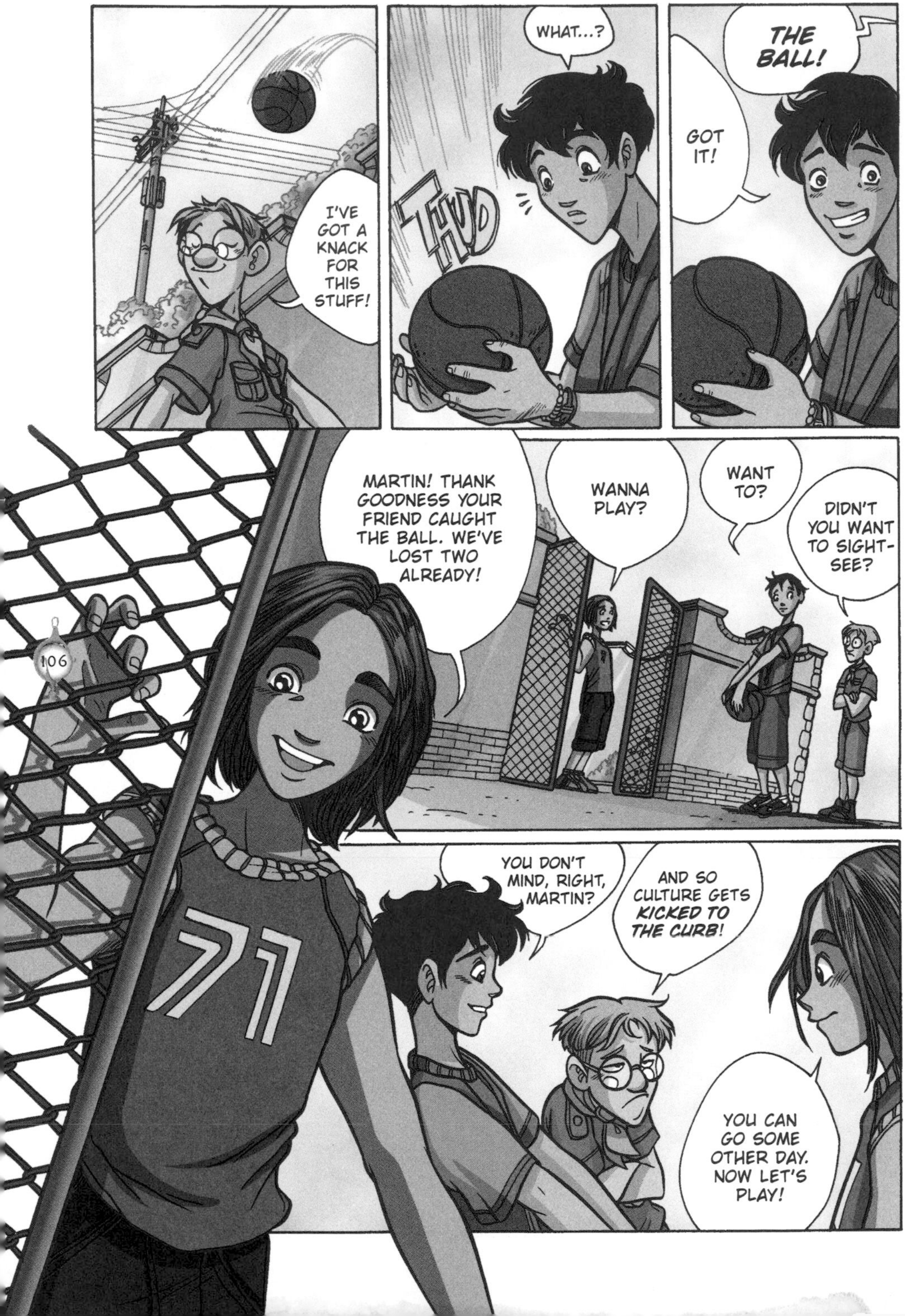
I'VE GOT A KNACK FOR THIS STUFF!
WHAT...?
THUD
THE BALL!
GOT IT!
MARTIN! THANK GOODNESS YOUR FRIEND CAUGHT THE BALL. WE'VE LOST TWO ALREADY!
WANNA PLAY?
WANT TO?
DIDN'T YOU WANT TO SIGHT-SEE?
YOU DON'T MIND, RIGHT, MARTIN?
AND SO CULTURE GETS KICKED TO THE CURB!
YOU CAN GO SOME OTHER DAY. NOW LET'S PLAY!

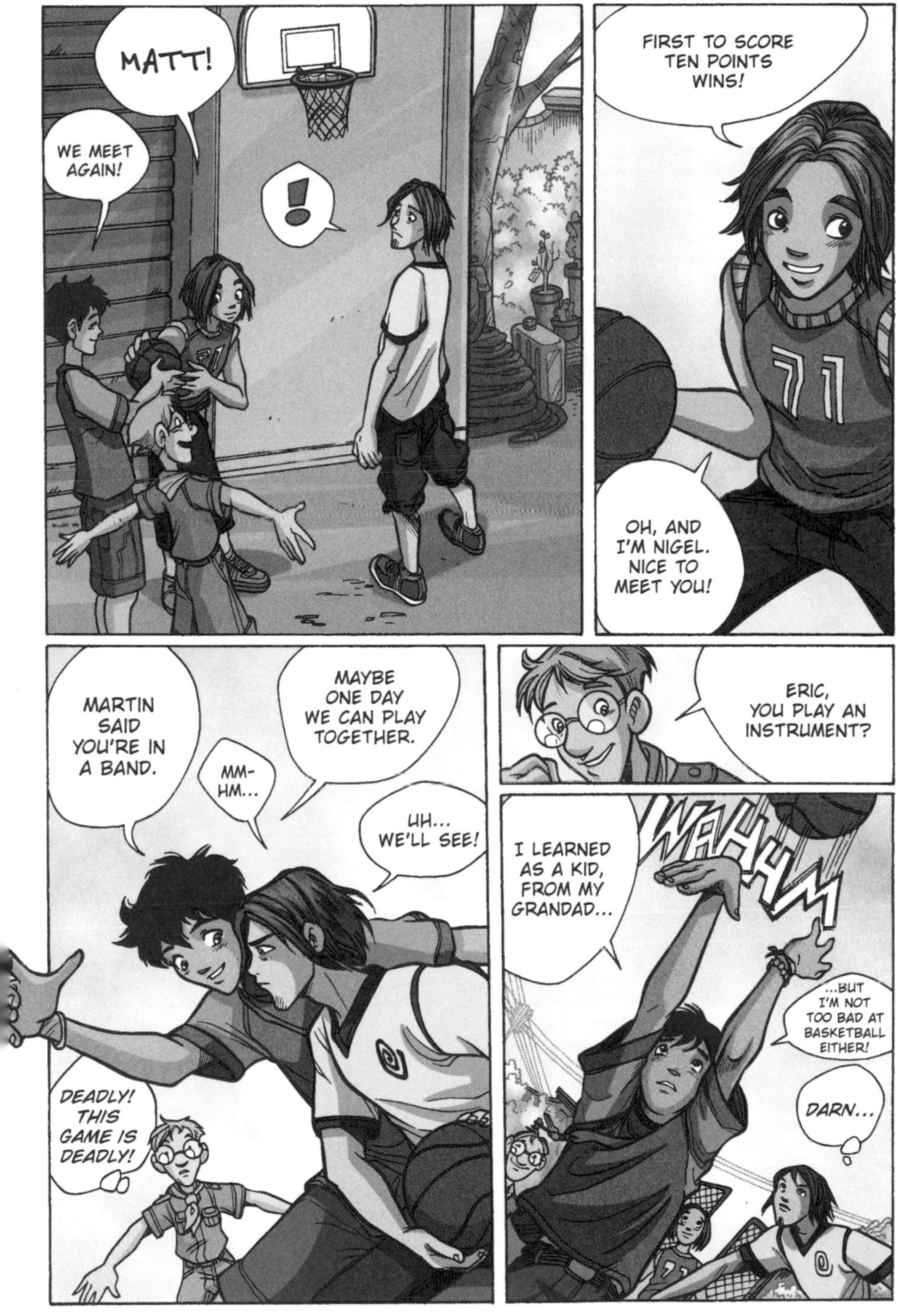
MATT!
WE MEET AGAIN!
!
FIRST TO SCORE TEN POINTS WINS!
OH, AND I'M NIGEL. NICE TO MEET YOU!
MARTIN SAID YOU'RE IN A BAND.
MM-HM...
MAYBE ONE DAY WE CAN PLAY TOGETHER.
UH... WE'LL SEE!
DEADLY! THIS GAME IS DEADLY!
ERIC, YOU PLAY AN INSTRUMENT?
I LEARNED AS A KID, FROM MY GRANDAD...
WAHUM
...BUT I'M NOT TOO BAD AT BASKETBALL EITHER!
DARN...

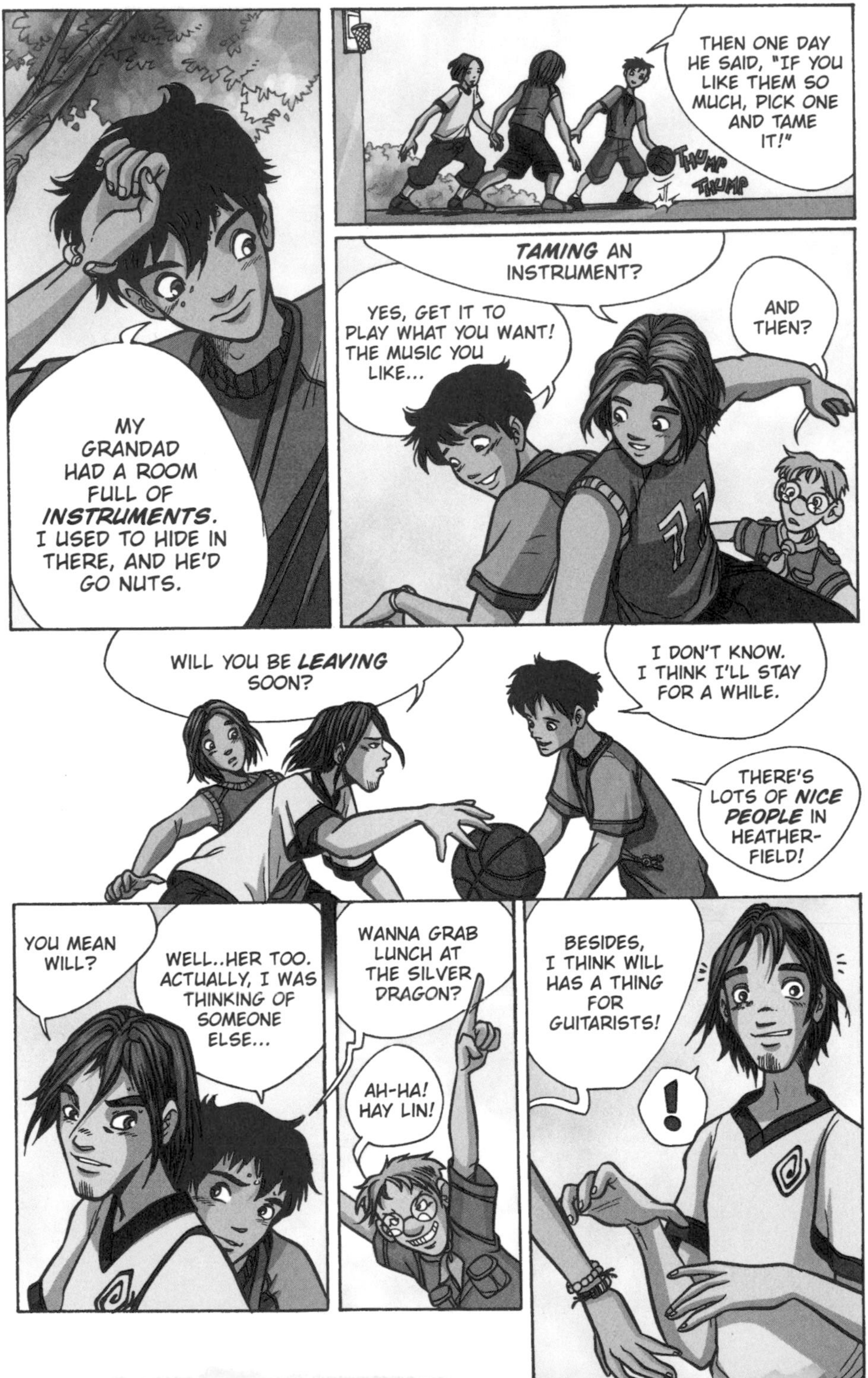
MY GRANDAD HAD A ROOM FULL OF INSTRUMENTS. I USED TO HIDE IN THERE, AND HE'D GO NUTS.
THEN ONE DAY HE SAID, "IF YOU LIKE THEM SO MUCH, PICK ONE AND TAME IT!"
THUMP
THUMP
TAMING AN INSTRUMENT?
YES, GET IT TO PLAY WHAT YOU WANT! THE MUSIC YOU LIKE...
AND THEN?
WILL YOU BE LEAVING SOON?
I DON'T KNOW. I THINK I'LL STAY FOR A WHILE.
THERE'S LOTS OF NICE PEOPLE IN HEATHER-FIELD!
YOU MEAN WILL?
WELL..HER TOO. ACTUALLY, I WAS THINKING OF SOMEONE ELSE...
WANNA GRAB LUNCH AT THE SILVER DRAGON?
AH-HA! HAY LIN!
BESIDES, I THINK WILL HAS A THING FOR GUITARISTS!
!

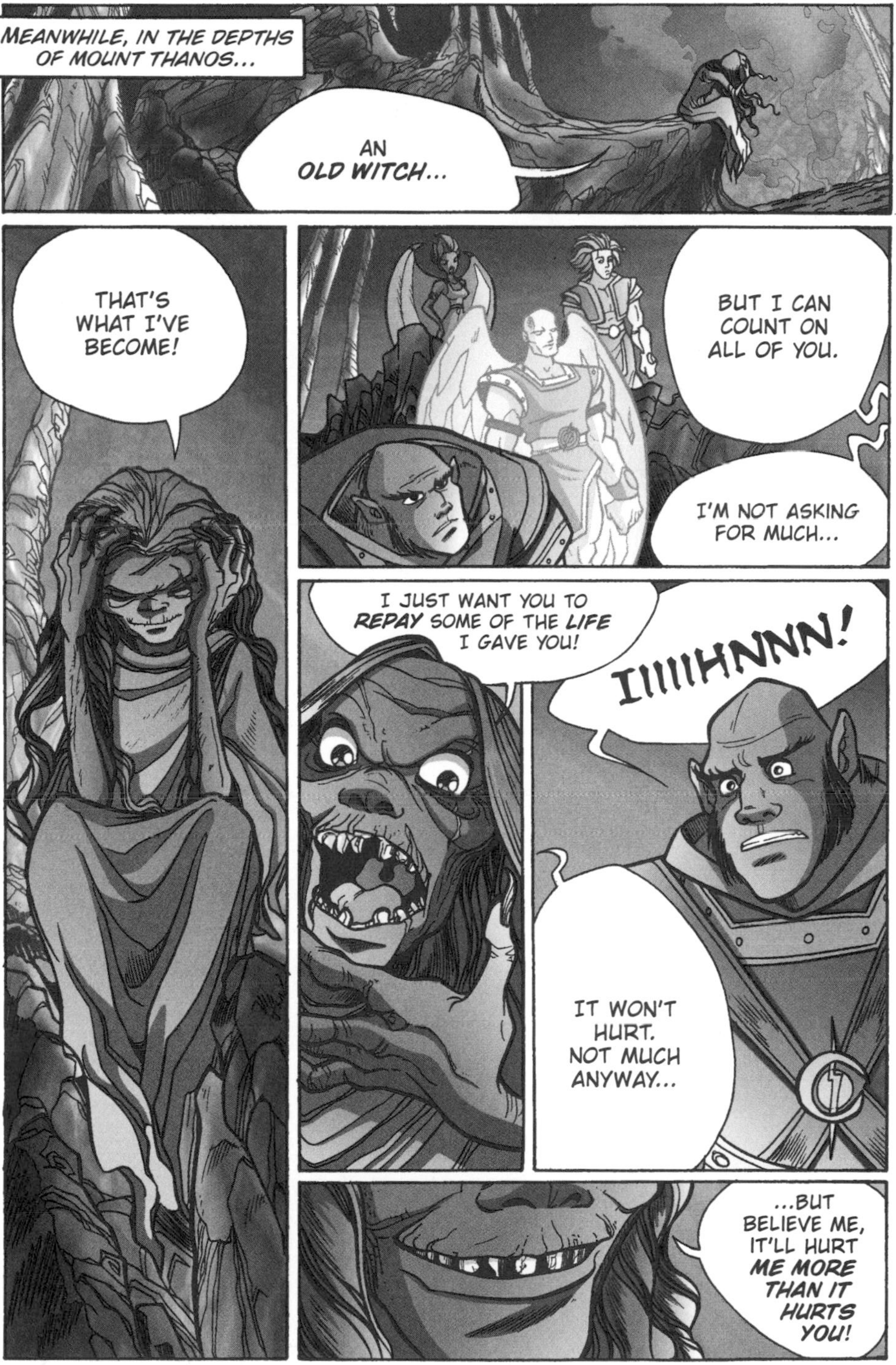

MEANWHILE, IN THE DEPTHS OF MOUNT THANOS...
AN OLD WITCH...
THAT'S WHAT I'VE BECOME!
BUT I CAN COUNT ON ALL OF YOU.
I'M NOT ASKING FOR MUCH...
I JUST WANT YOU TO REPAY SOME OF THE LIFE I GAVE YOU!
IIIIHNNN!
IT WON'T HURT. NOT MUCH ANYWAY...
...BUT BELIEVE ME, IT'LL HURT ME MORE THAN IT HURTS YOU!

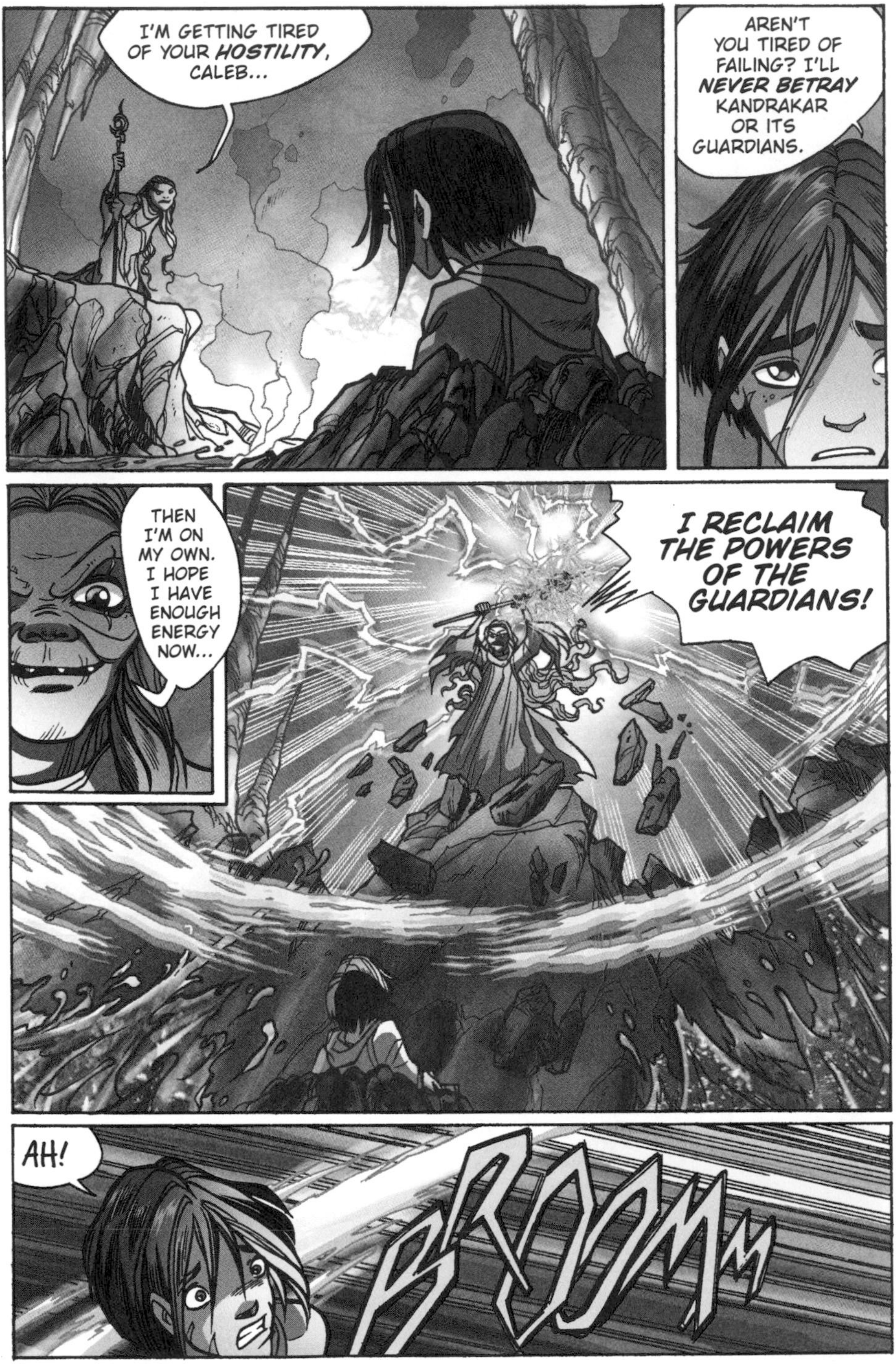
I'M GETTING TIRED OF YOUR HOSTILITY, CALEB...
AREN'T YOU TIRED OF FAILING? I'LL NEVER BETRAY KANDRAKAR OR ITS GUARDIANS.
THEN I'M ON MY OWN. I HOPE I HAVE ENOUGH ENERGY NOW...
I RECLAIM THE POWERS OF THE GUARDIANS!
AH!
BROOMM

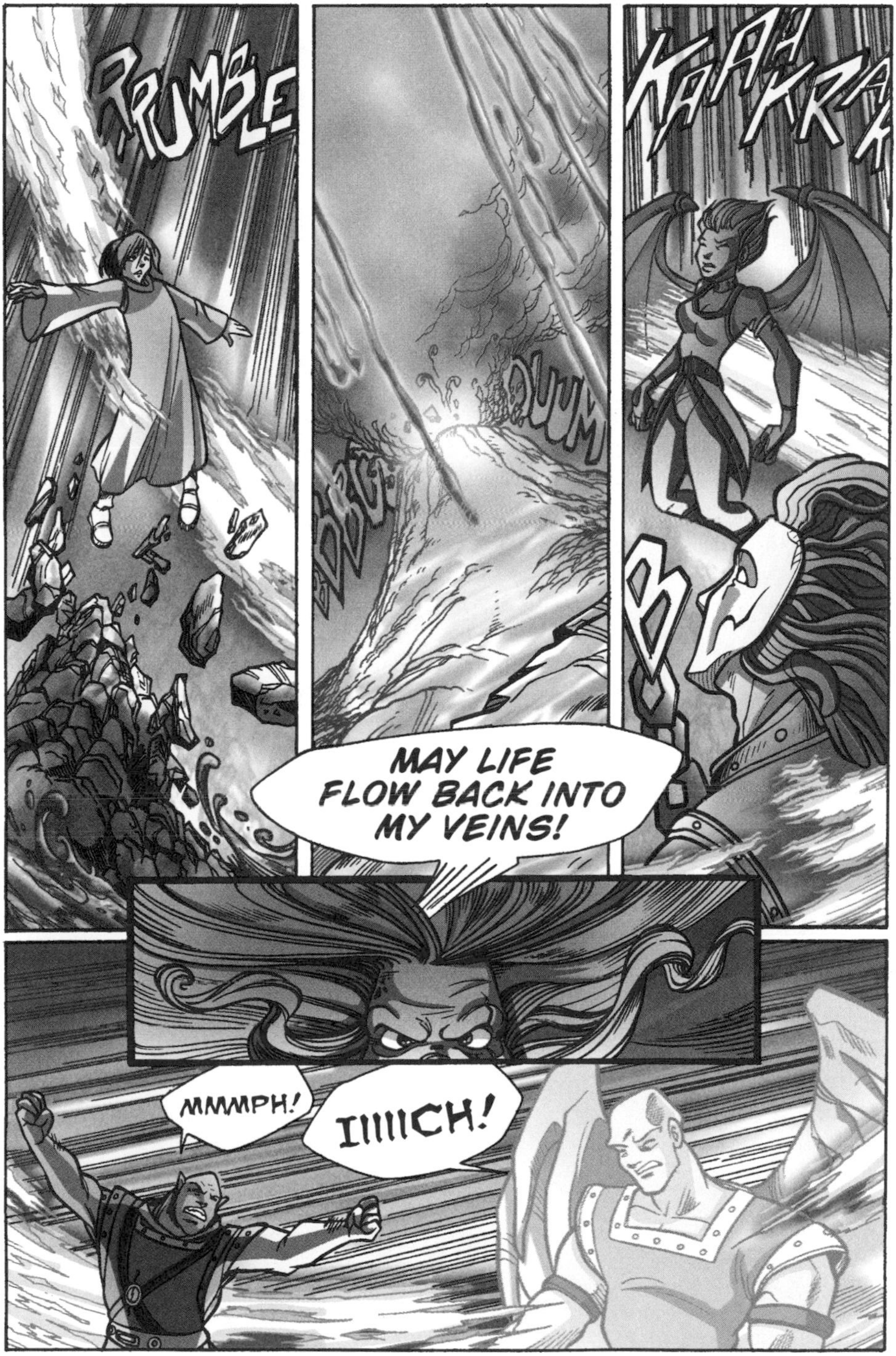
RRUMBLE
BBBG
DUUM
KAAHKRRK
B
MAY LIFE FLOW BACK INTO MY VEINS!
MMMPH!
IIIIICH!

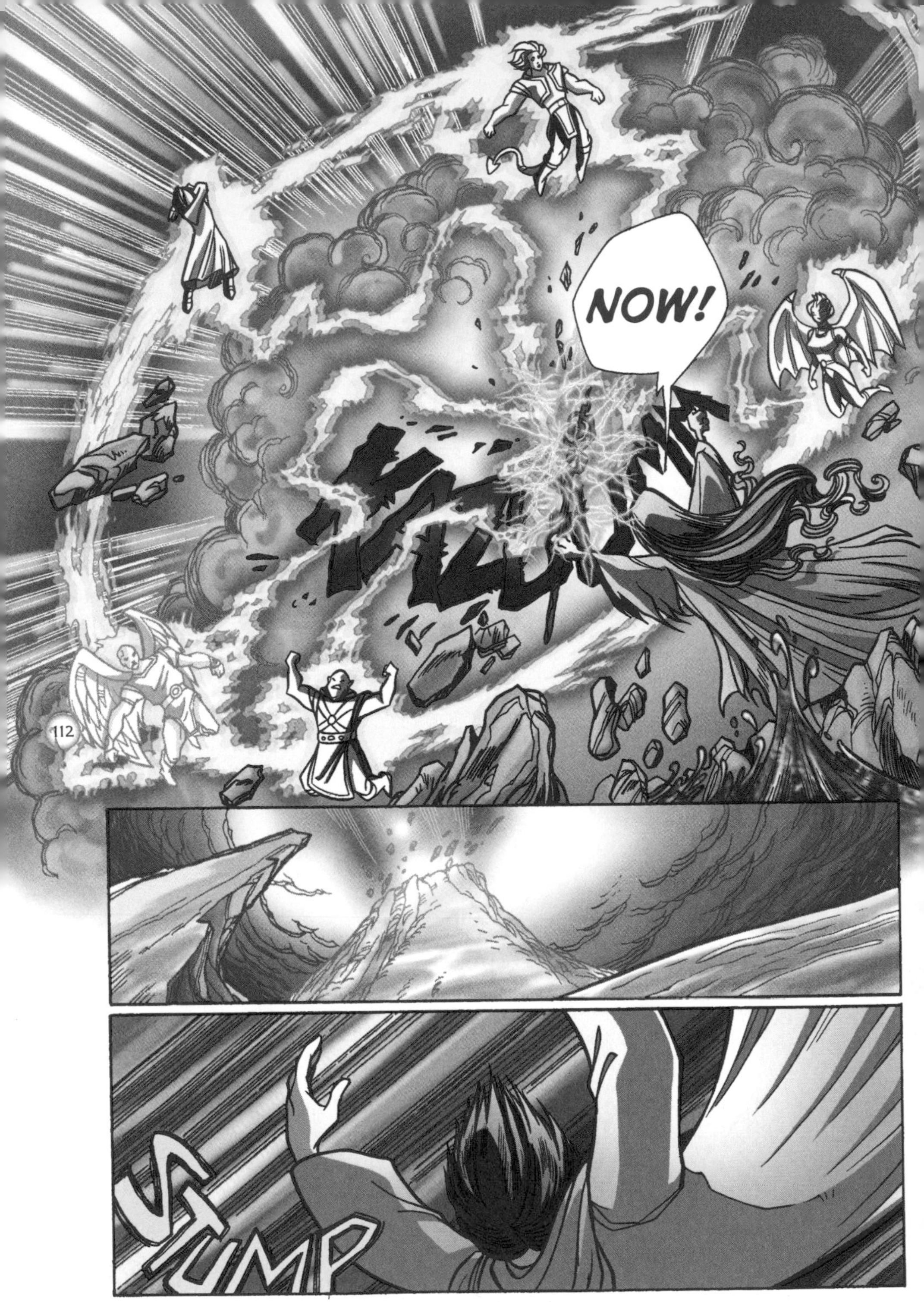
NOW!
STUMP

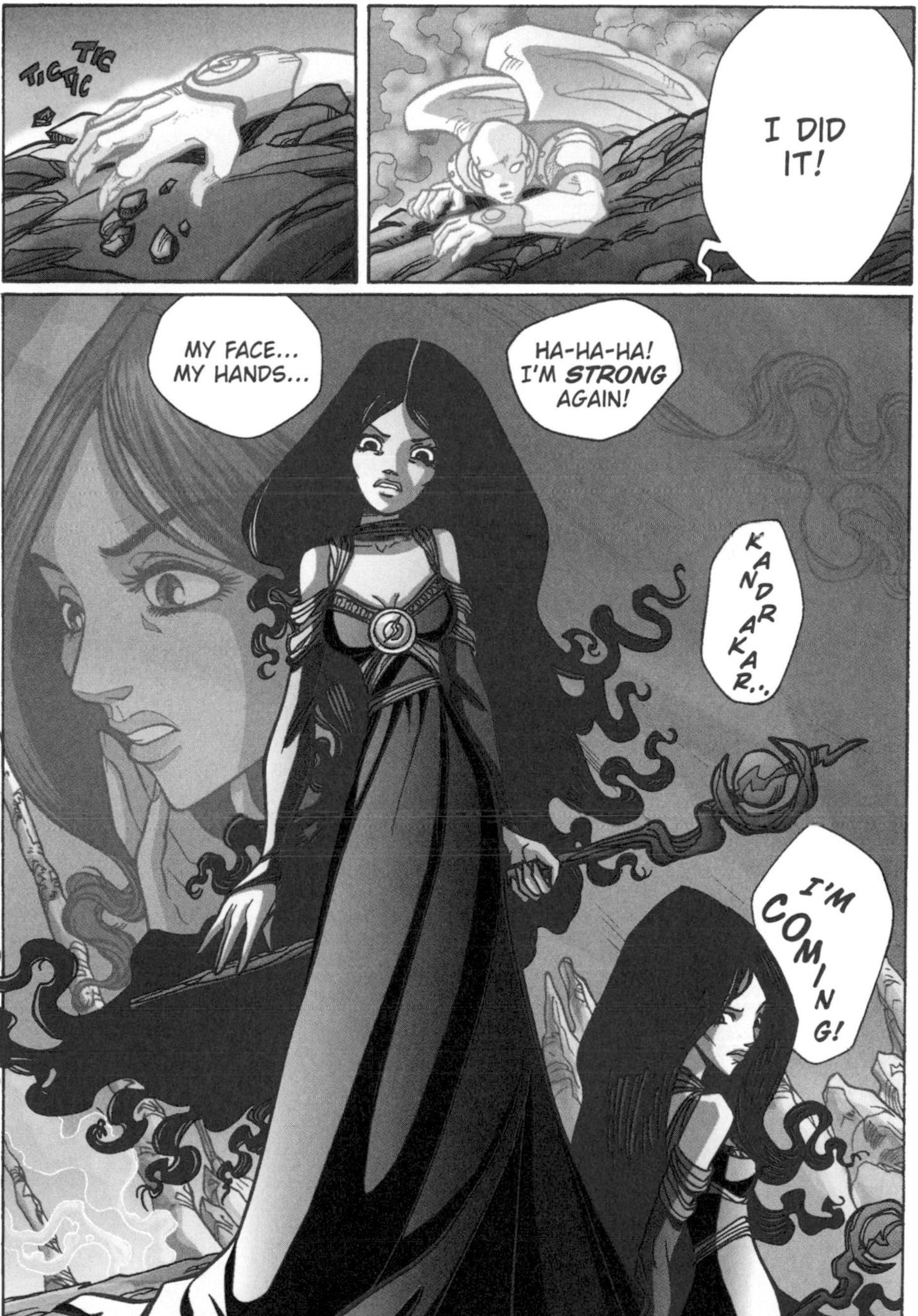
TIC TIC TIC
I DID IT!
MY FACE... MY HANDS...
HA-HA-HA! I'M **STRONG** AGAIN!
KANDRAKAR...
I'M COMING!

THE CLEAR SKY OF KANDRAKAR, IN THE MIDST OF INFINITY...

KA-KRAK

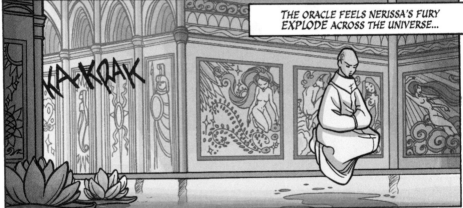

THE ORACLE FEELS NERISSA'S FURY EXPLODE ACROSS THE UNIVERSE...

KA-KRAK

NERISSA... YOU'VE GONE *TOO FAR!*

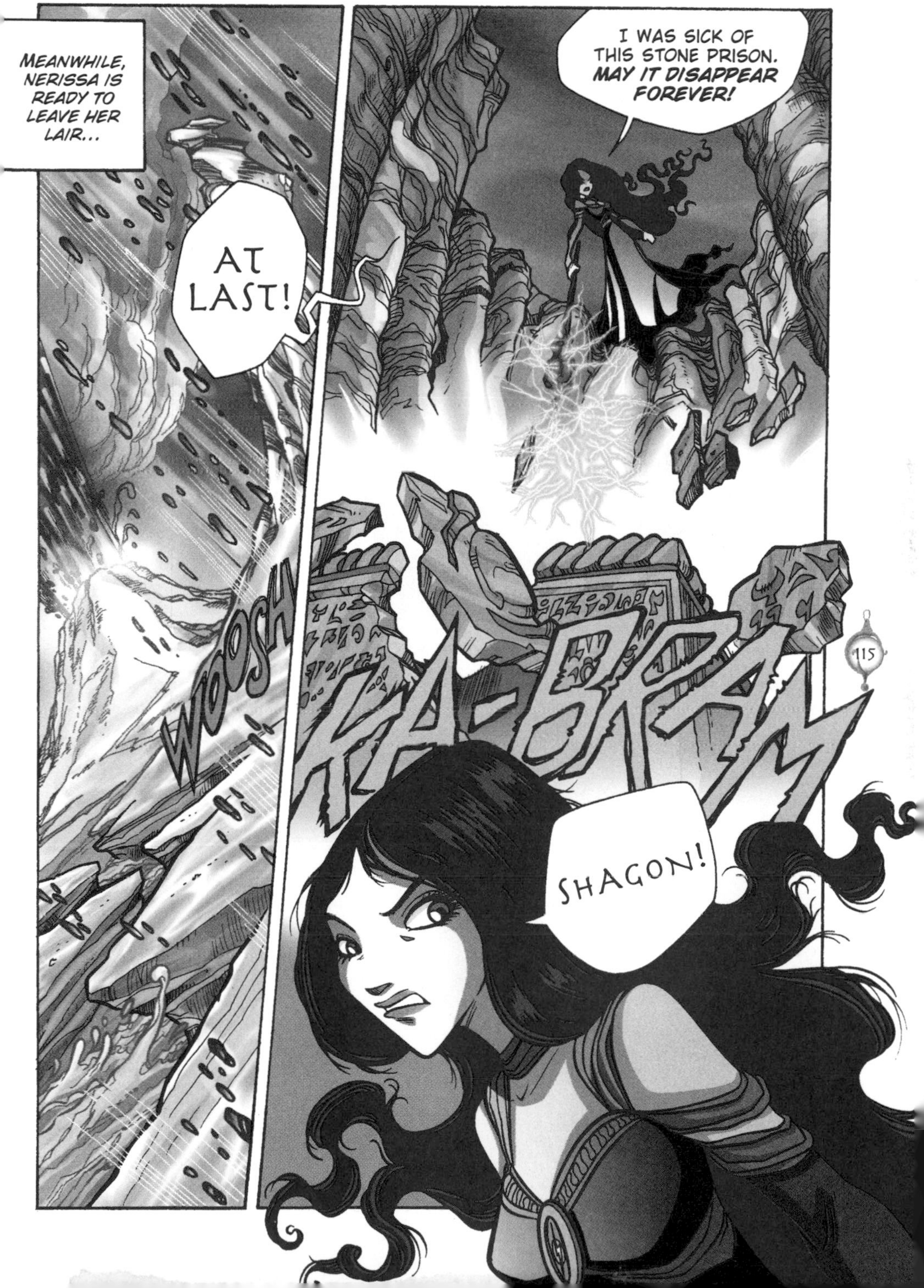

MEANWHILE, NERISSA IS READY TO LEAVE HER LAIR...
AT LAST!
I WAS SICK OF THIS STONE PRISON. MAY IT DISAPPEAR FOREVER!
WOOSH
KA-BRAM
SHAGON!

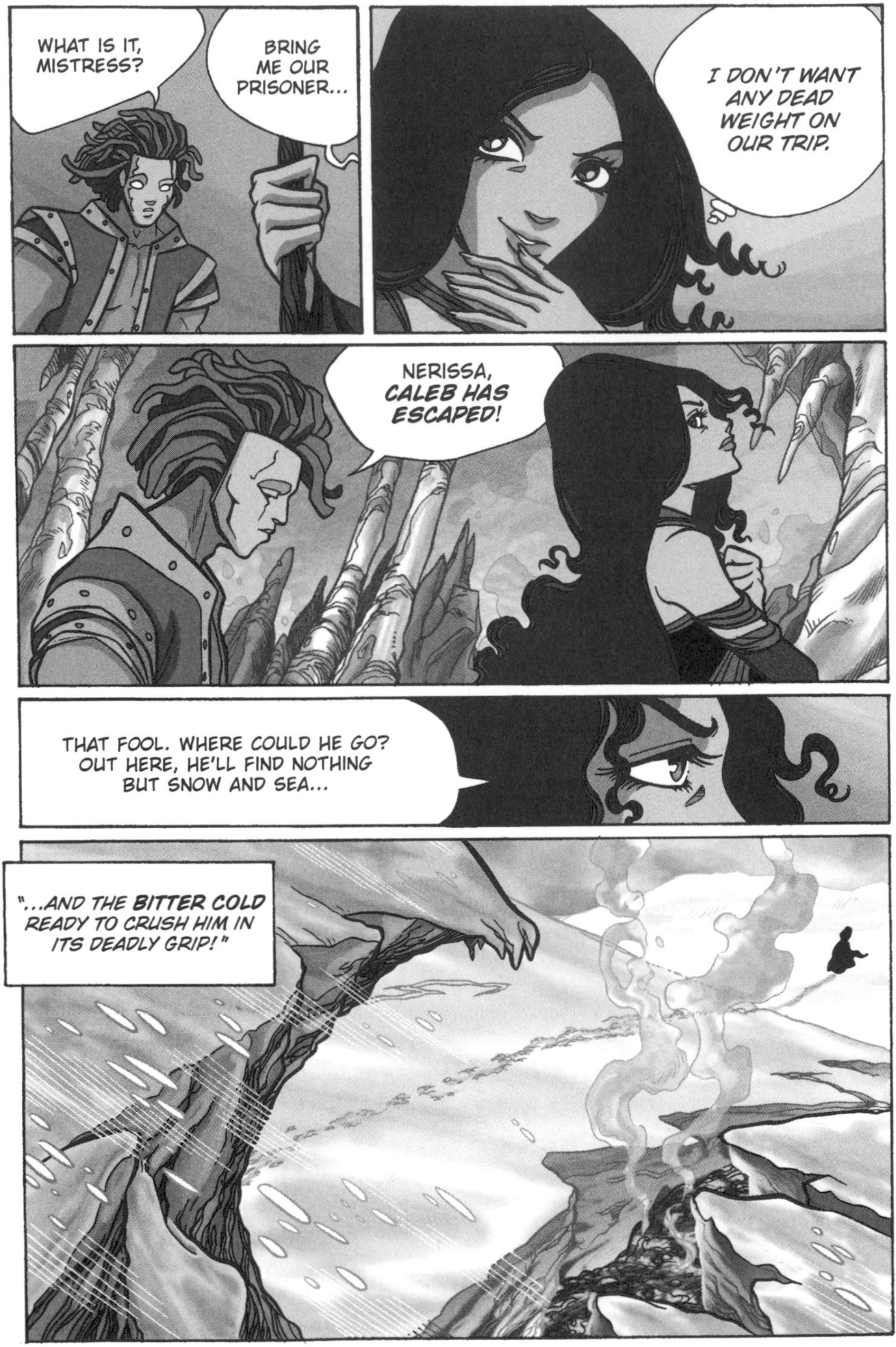
WHAT IS IT, MISTRESS?
BRING ME OUR PRISONER...
I DON'T WANT ANY DEAD WEIGHT ON OUR TRIP.
NERISSA, CALEB HAS ESCAPED!
THAT FOOL. WHERE COULD HE GO? OUT HERE, HE'LL FIND NOTHING BUT SNOW AND SEA...
"...AND THE BITTER COLD READY TO CRUSH HIM IN ITS DEADLY GRIP!"

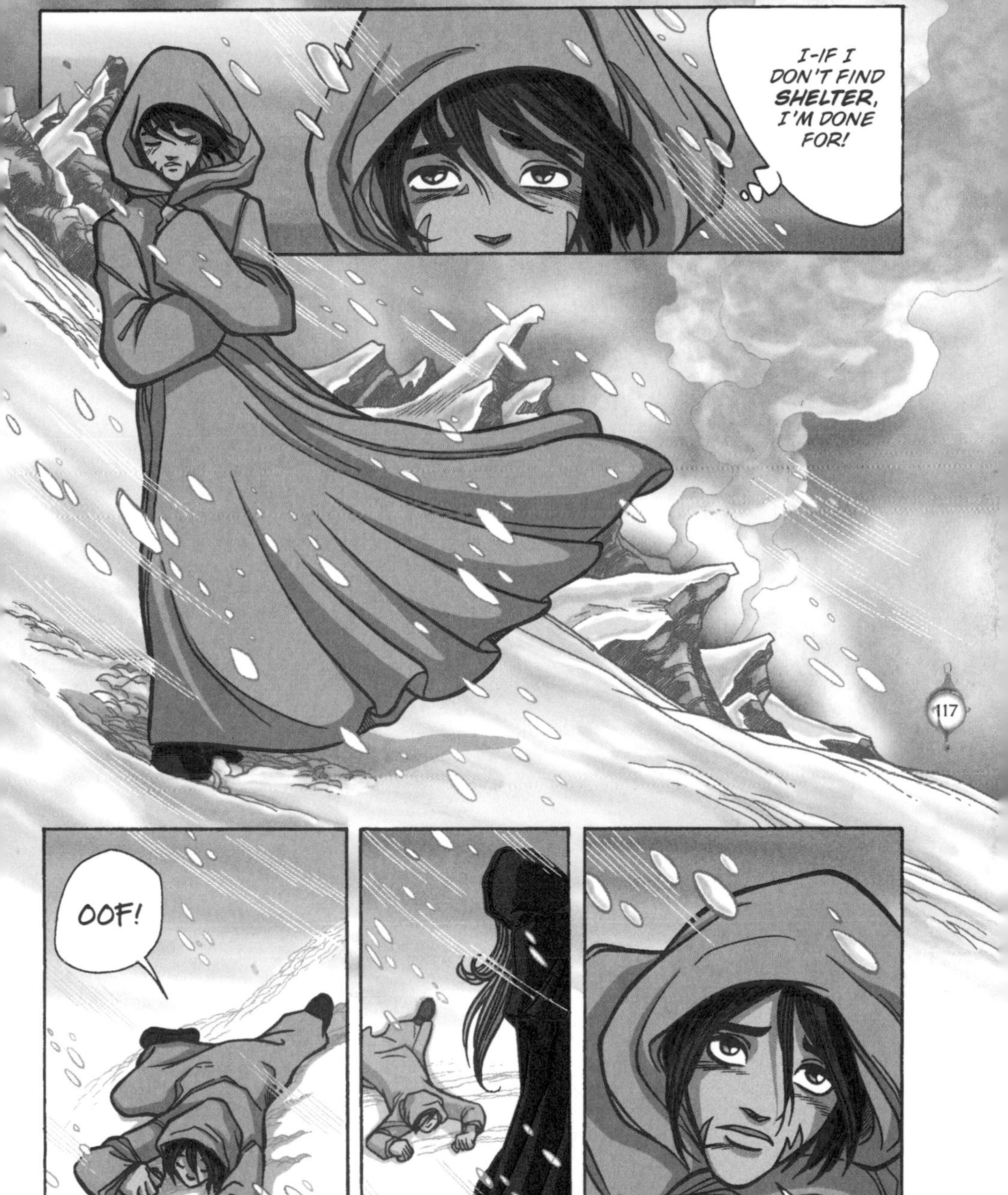
I-IF I DON'T FIND SHELTER, I'M DONE FOR!
OOF!
YOU!

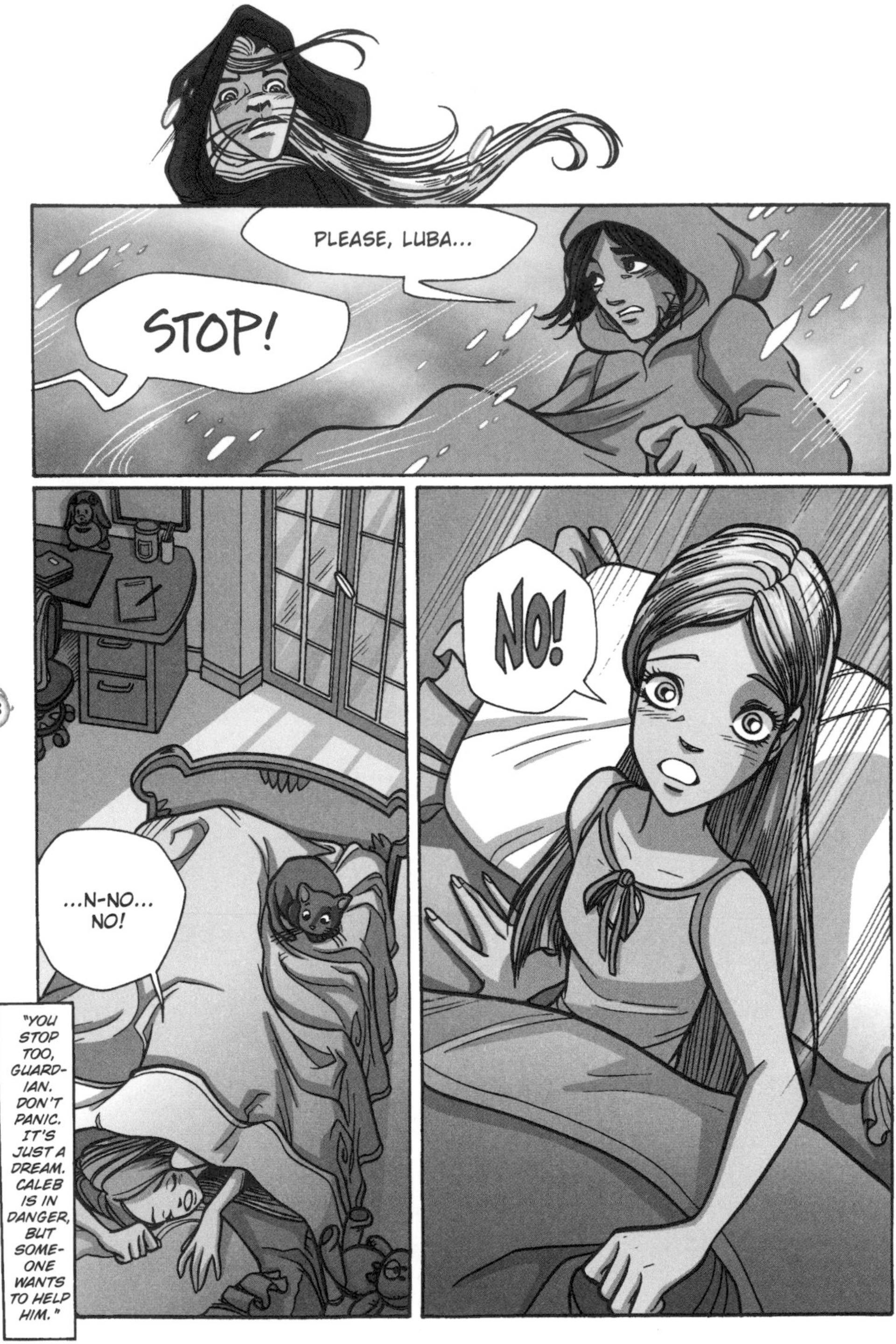
PLEASE, LUBA...
STOP!
NO!
...N-NO... NO!
"YOU STOP TOO, GUARD-IAN. DON'T PANIC. IT'S JUST A DREAM. CALEB IS IN DANGER, BUT SOME-ONE WANTS TO HELP HIM."

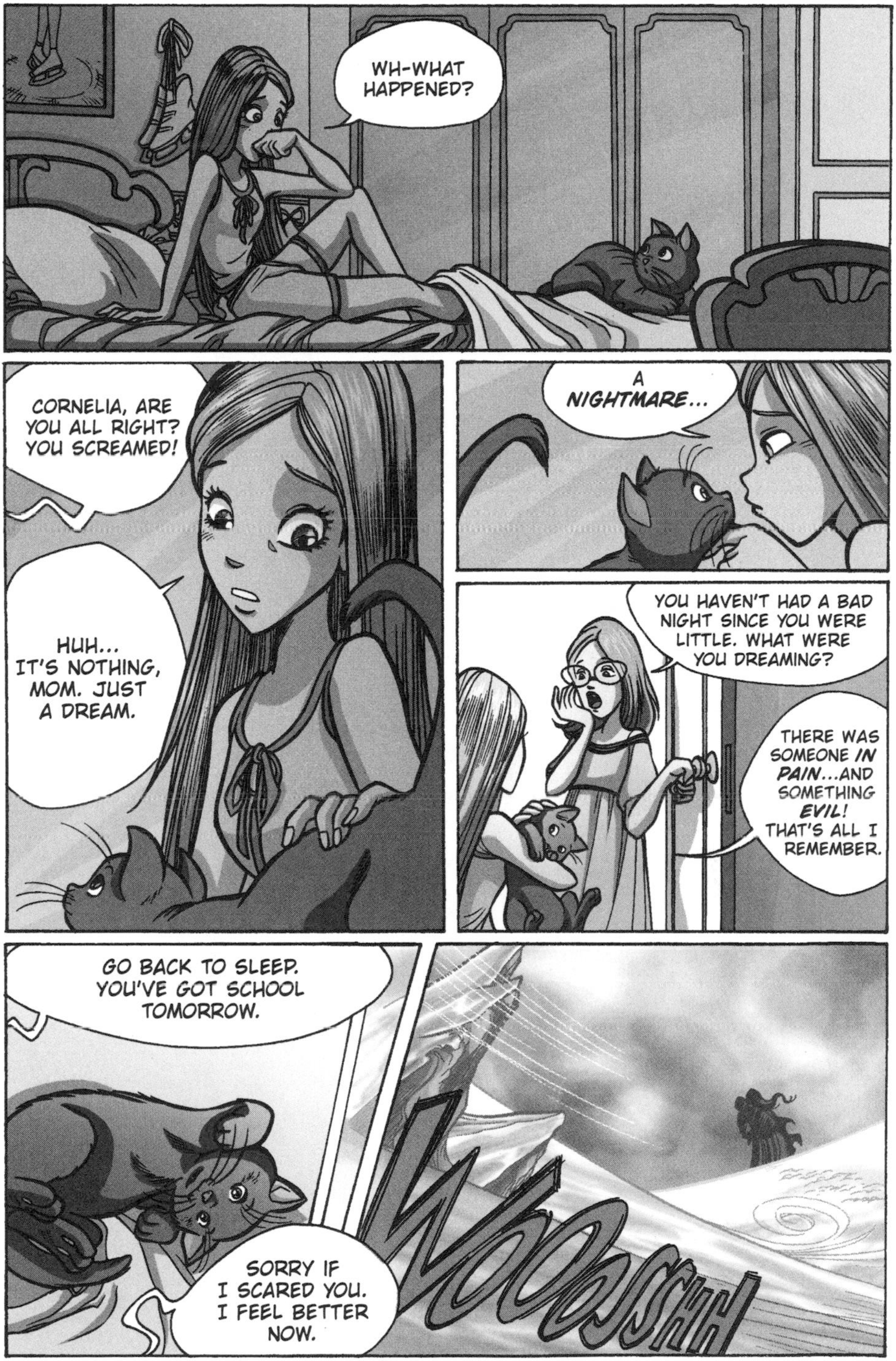
WH-WHAT HAPPENED?
CORNELIA, ARE YOU ALL RIGHT? YOU SCREAMED!
HUH... IT'S NOTHING, MOM. JUST A DREAM.
A *NIGHTMARE*...
YOU HAVEN'T HAD A BAD NIGHT SINCE YOU WERE LITTLE. WHAT WERE YOU DREAMING?
THERE WAS SOMEONE *IN PAIN*...AND SOMETHING *EVIL*! THAT'S ALL I REMEMBER.
GO BACK TO SLEEP. YOU'VE GOT SCHOOL TOMORROW.
SORRY IF I SCARED YOU. I FEEL BETTER NOW.
WOOOSSHH

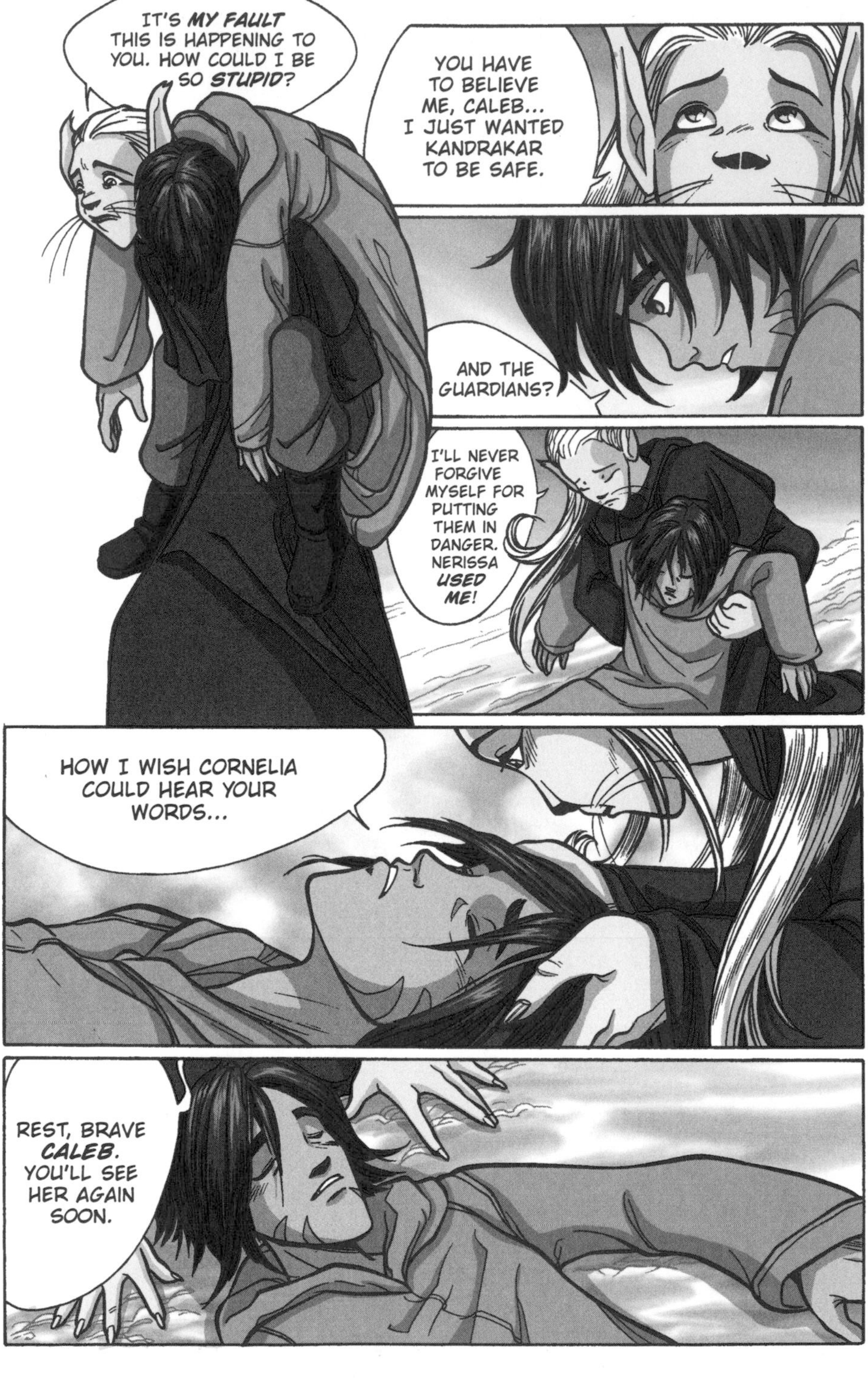
IT'S MY FAULT THIS IS HAPPENING TO YOU. HOW COULD I BE SO STUPID?
YOU HAVE TO BELIEVE ME, CALEB... I JUST WANTED KANDRAKAR TO BE SAFE.
AND THE GUARDIANS?
I'LL NEVER FORGIVE MYSELF FOR PUTTING THEM IN DANGER. NERISSA USED ME!
HOW I WISH CORNELIA COULD HEAR YOUR WORDS...
REST, BRAVE CALEB. YOU'LL SEE HER AGAIN SOON.

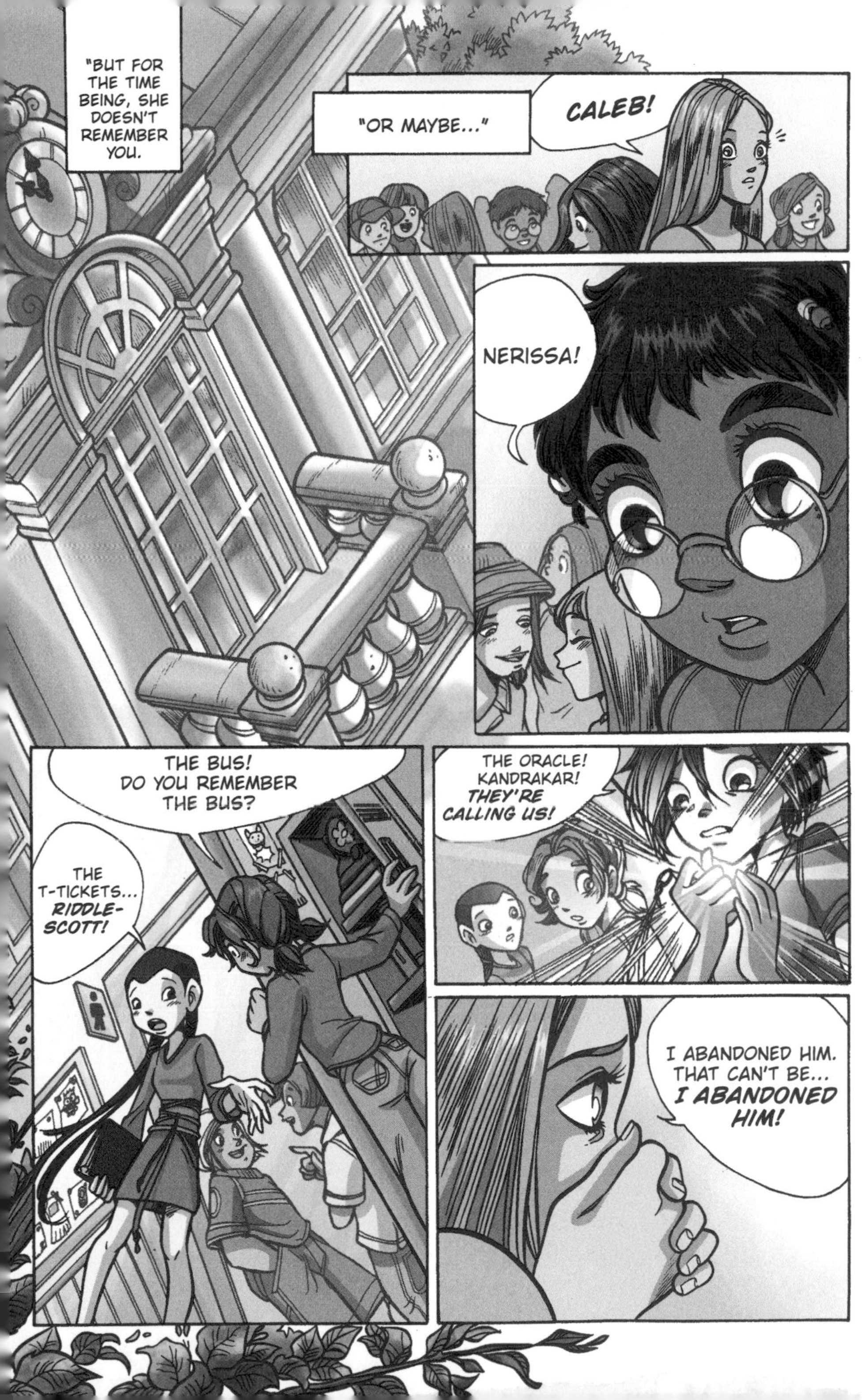
"BUT FOR THE TIME BEING, SHE DOESN'T REMEMBER YOU.
"OR MAYBE..."
CALEB!
NERISSA!
THE BUS! DO YOU REMEMBER THE BUS?
THE T-TICKETS... RIDDLE-SCOTT!
THE ORACLE! KANDRAKAR! THEY'RE CALLING US!
I ABANDONED HIM. THAT CAN'T BE... I ABANDONED HIM!

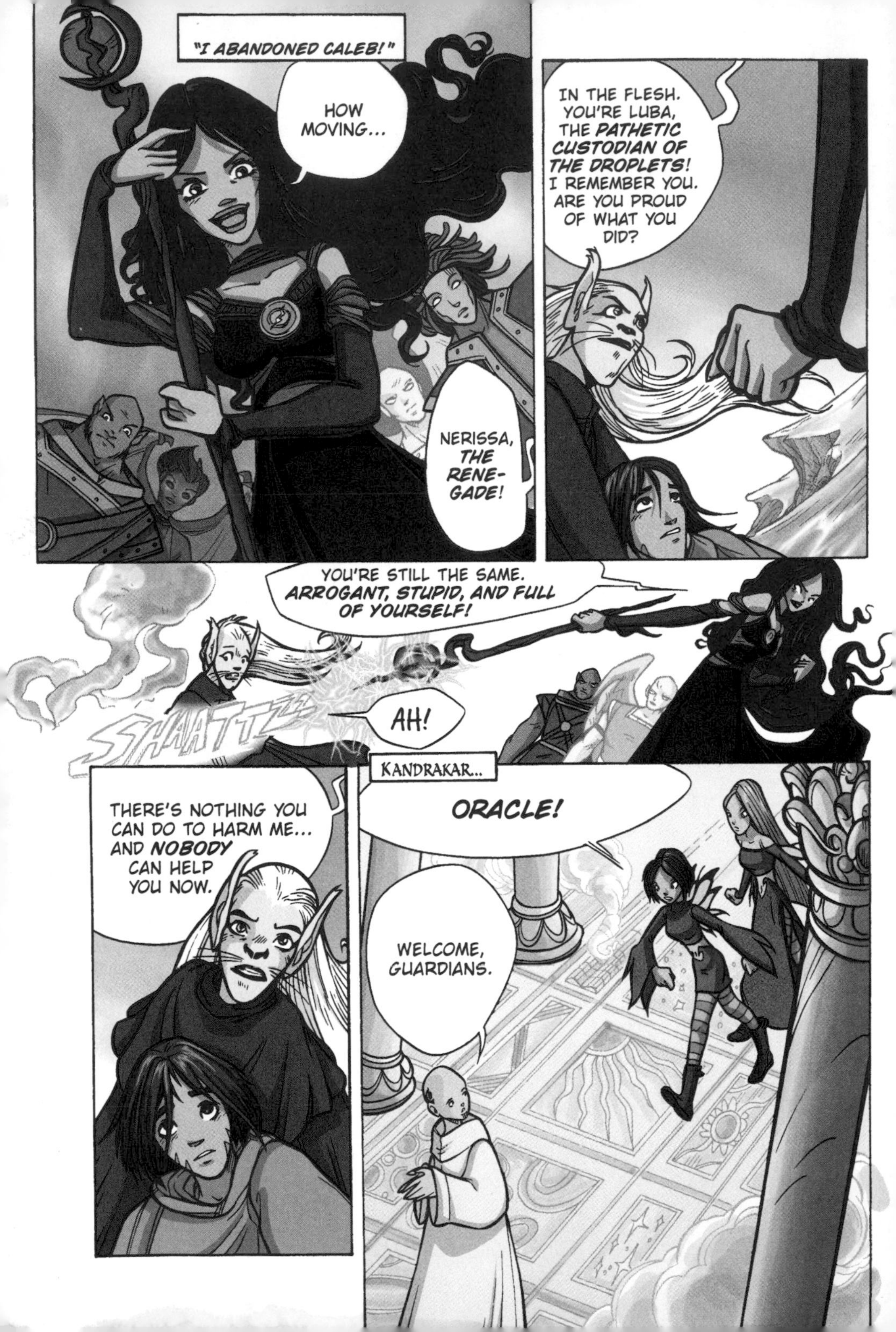
"I ABANDONED CALEB!"
HOW MOVING...
NERISSA, THE RENE-GADE!
IN THE FLESH. YOU'RE LUBA, THE PATHETIC CUSTODIAN OF THE DROPLETS! I REMEMBER YOU. ARE YOU PROUD OF WHAT YOU DID?
YOU'RE STILL THE SAME. ARROGANT, STUPID, AND FULL OF YOURSELF!
SHAATTZ
AH!
THERE'S NOTHING YOU CAN DO TO HARM ME... AND NOBODY CAN HELP YOU NOW.
KANDRAKAR...
ORACLE!
WELCOME, GUARDIANS.

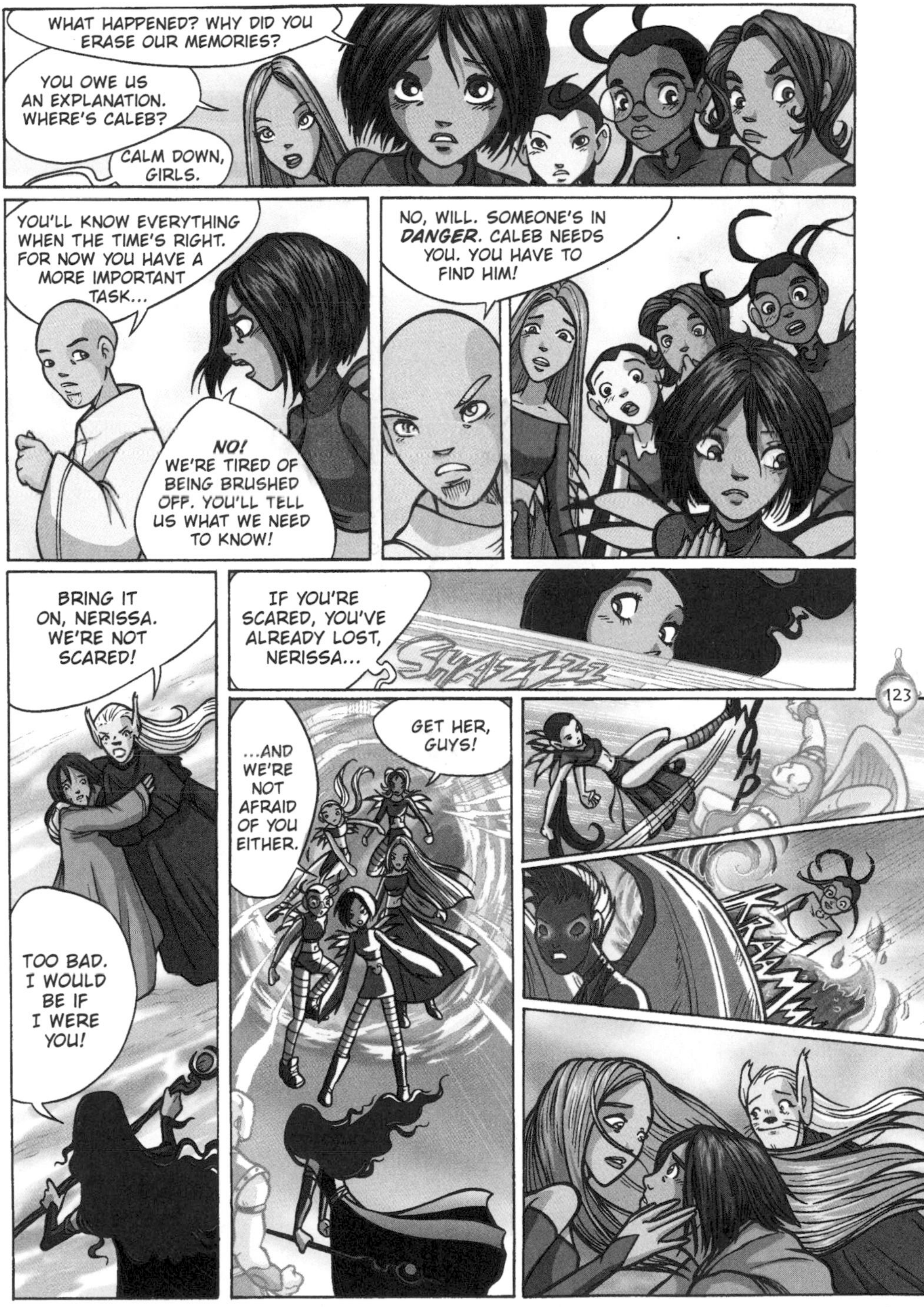

WHAT HAPPENED? WHY DID YOU ERASE OUR MEMORIES?
YOU OWE US AN EXPLANATION. WHERE'S CALEB?
CALM DOWN, GIRLS.
YOU'LL KNOW EVERYTHING WHEN THE TIME'S RIGHT. FOR NOW YOU HAVE A MORE IMPORTANT TASK...
NO! WE'RE TIRED OF BEING BRUSHED OFF. YOU'LL TELL US WHAT WE NEED TO KNOW!
NO, WILL. SOMEONE'S IN DANGER. CALEB NEEDS YOU. YOU HAVE TO FIND HIM!
BRING IT ON, NERISSA. WE'RE NOT SCARED!
TOO BAD. I WOULD BE IF I WERE YOU!
IF YOU'RE SCARED, YOU'VE ALREADY LOST, NERISSA...
SHAZAZZZ
...AND WE'RE NOT AFRAID OF YOU EITHER.
GET HER, GUYS!

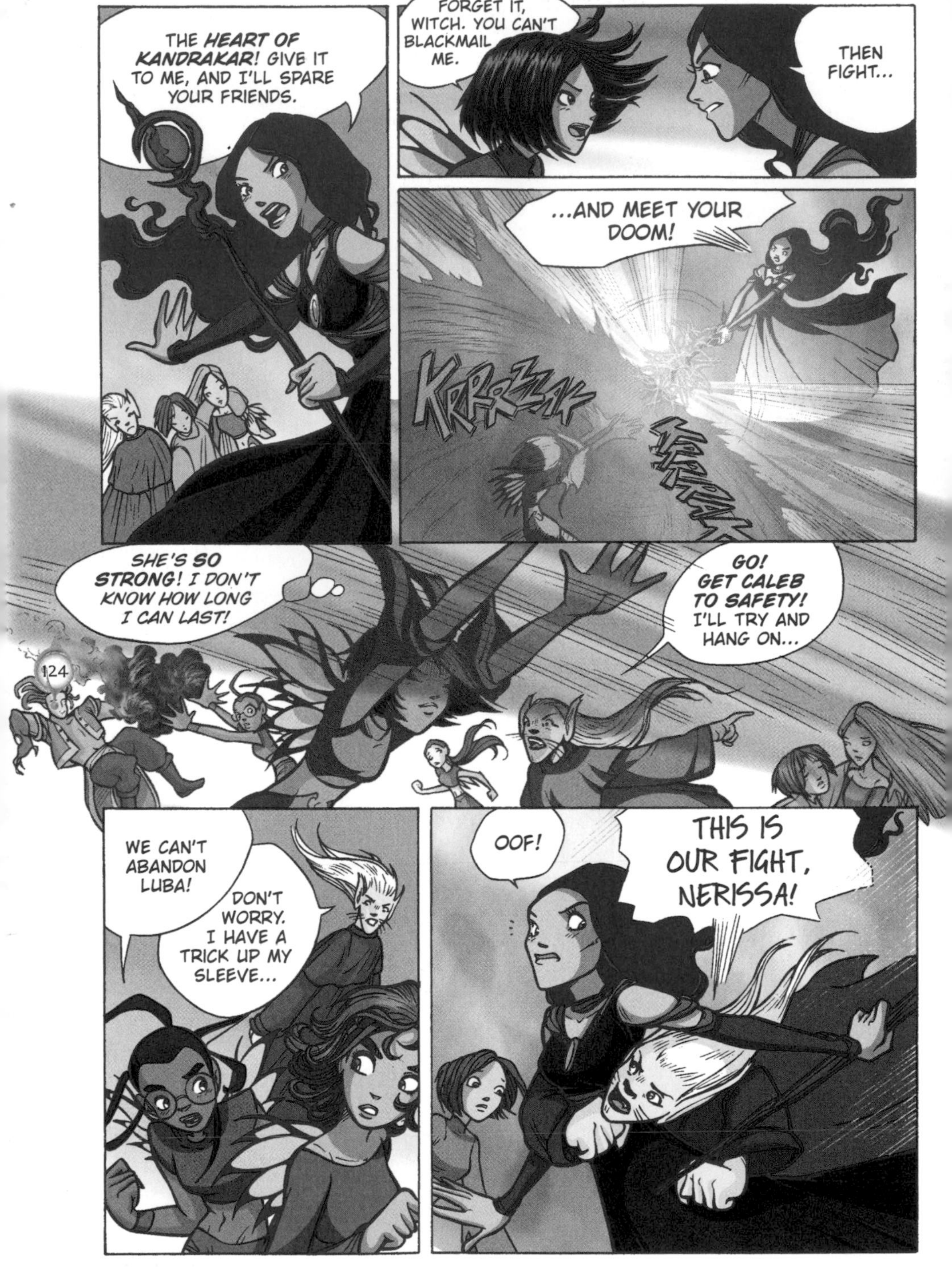
THE HEART OF KANDRAKAR! GIVE IT TO ME, AND I'LL SPARE YOUR FRIENDS.
FORGET IT, WITCH. YOU CAN'T BLACKMAIL ME.
THEN FIGHT...
...AND MEET YOUR DOOM!
KRRRZZZAK
SHE'S SO STRONG! I DON'T KNOW HOW LONG I CAN LAST!
GO! GET CALEB TO SAFETY! I'LL TRY AND HANG ON...
WE CAN'T ABANDON LUBA!
DON'T WORRY. I HAVE A TRICK UP MY SLEEVE...
OOF!
THIS IS OUR FIGHT, NERISSA!

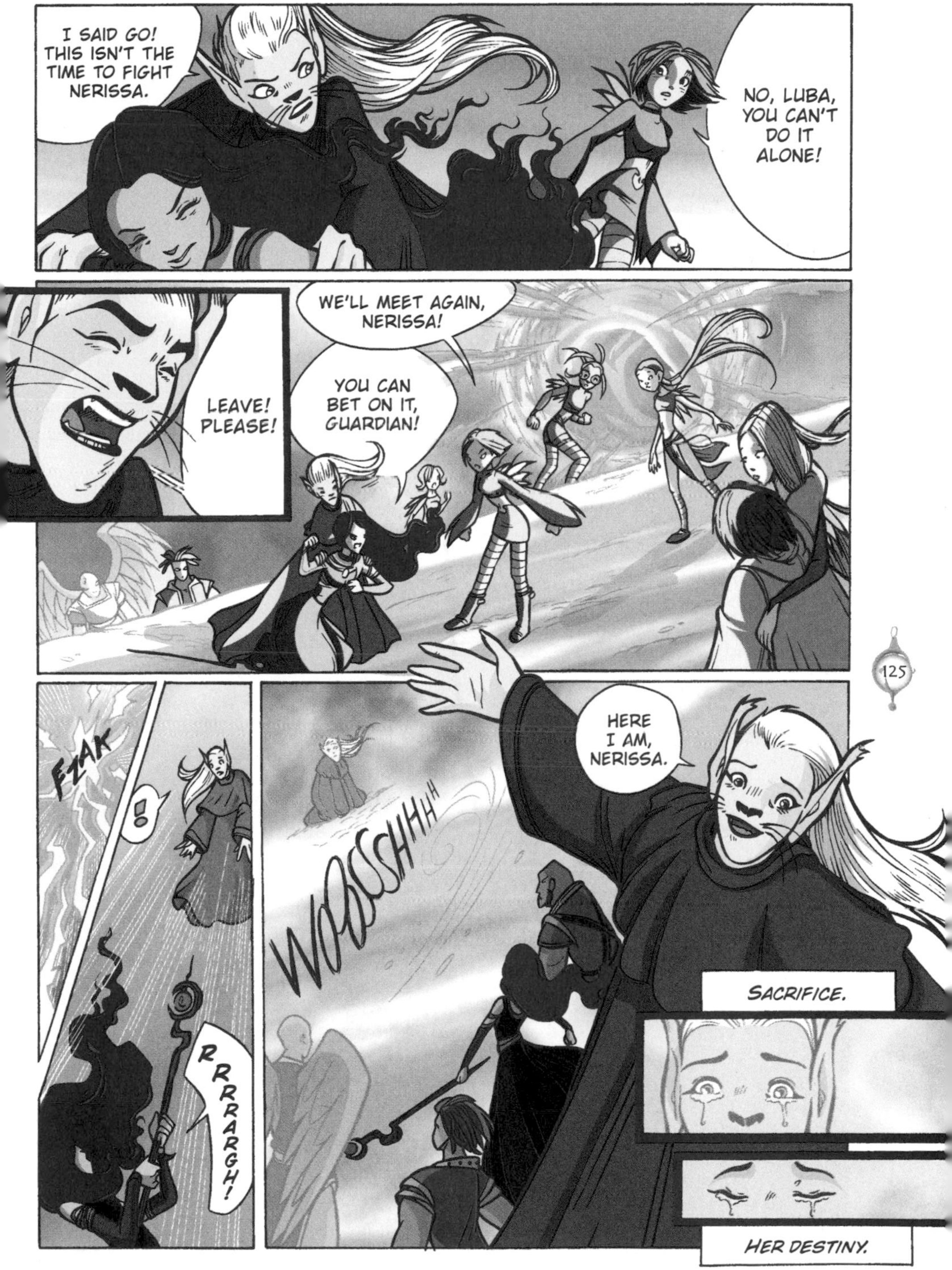
I SAID GO! THIS ISN'T THE TIME TO FIGHT NERISSA.
NO, LUBA, YOU CAN'T DO IT ALONE!
LEAVE! PLEASE!
WE'LL MEET AGAIN, NERISSA!
YOU CAN BET ON IT, GUARDIAN!
FZAK
!
RRRRARGH!
HERE I AM, NERISSA.
WOOSSHHHH
SACRIFICE.
HER DESTINY.

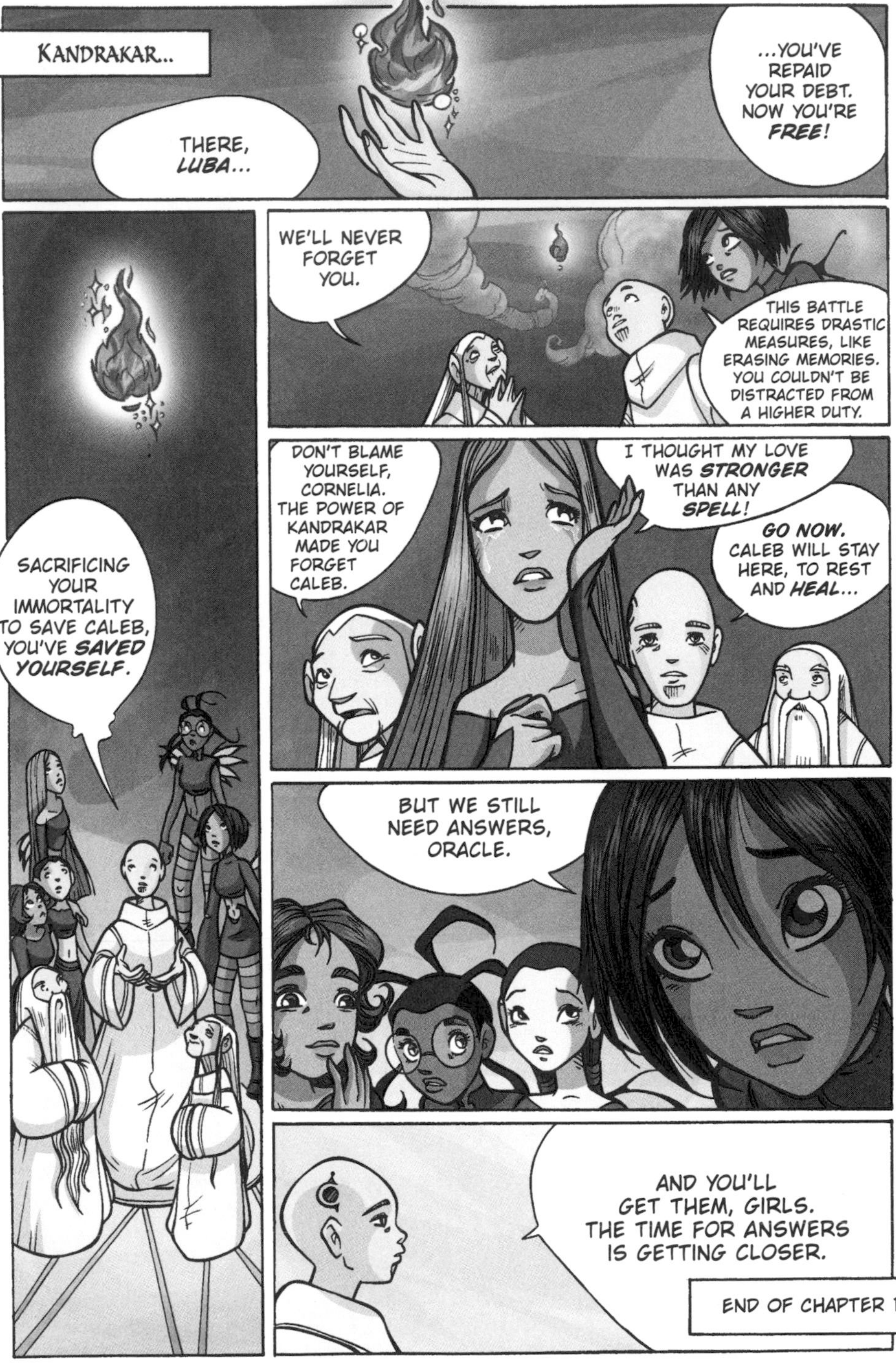
KANDRAKAR...
THERE, LUBA...
...YOU'VE REPAID YOUR DEBT. NOW YOU'RE FREE!
SACRIFICING YOUR IMMORTALITY TO SAVE CALEB, YOU'VE SAVED YOURSELF.
WE'LL NEVER FORGET YOU.
THIS BATTLE REQUIRES DRASTIC MEASURES, LIKE ERASING MEMORIES. YOU COULDN'T BE DISTRACTED FROM A HIGHER DUTY.
DON'T BLAME YOURSELF, CORNELIA. THE POWER OF KANDRAKAR MADE YOU FORGET CALEB.
I THOUGHT MY LOVE WAS STRONGER THAN ANY SPELL!
GO NOW. CALEB WILL STAY HERE, TO REST AND HEAL...
BUT WE STILL NEED ANSWERS, ORACLE.
AND YOU'LL GET THEM, GIRLS. THE TIME FOR ANSWERS IS GETTING CLOSER.
END OF CHAPTER 18

19

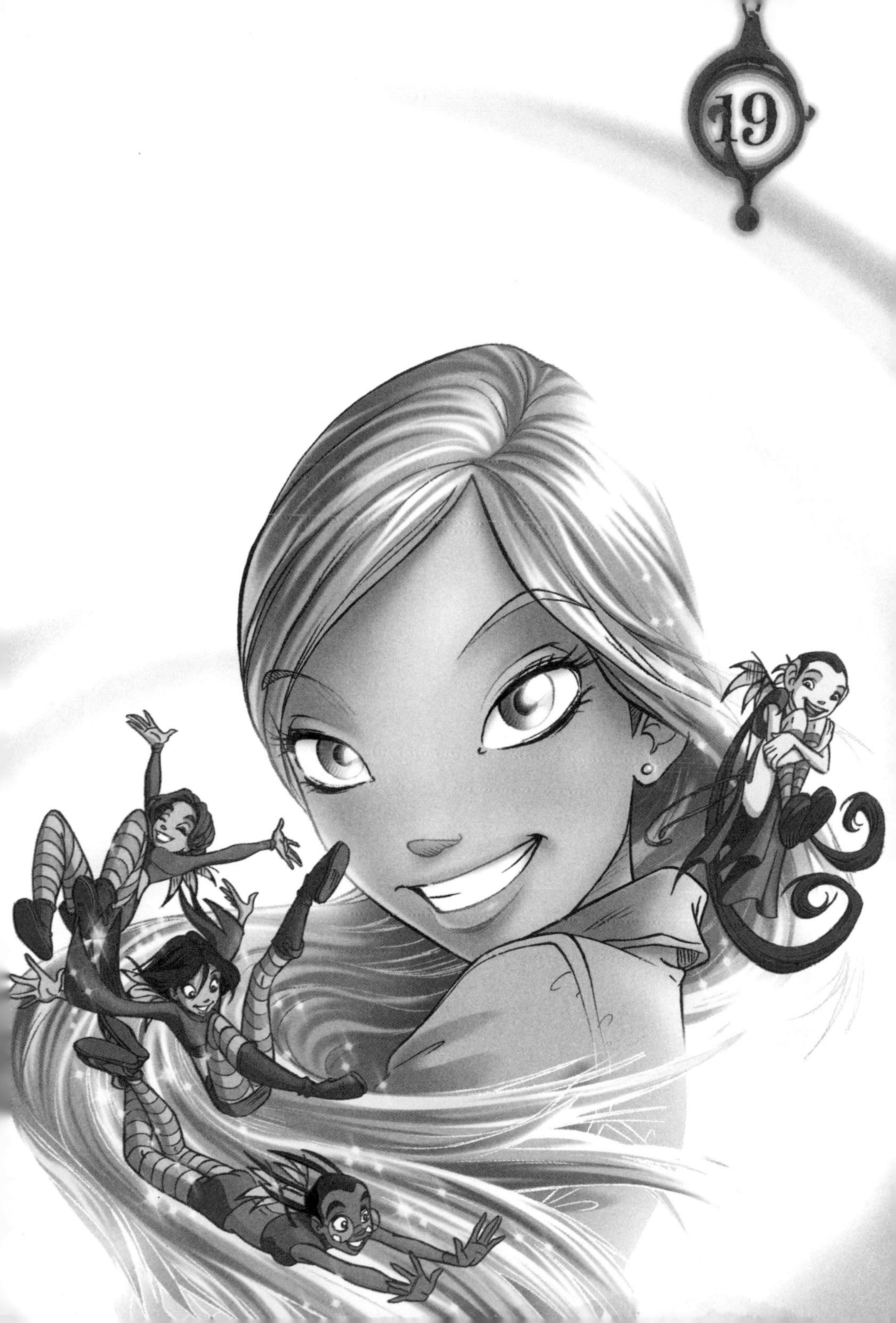

THE OTHER TRUTH

"Some questions have answers, and some answers don't need questions."

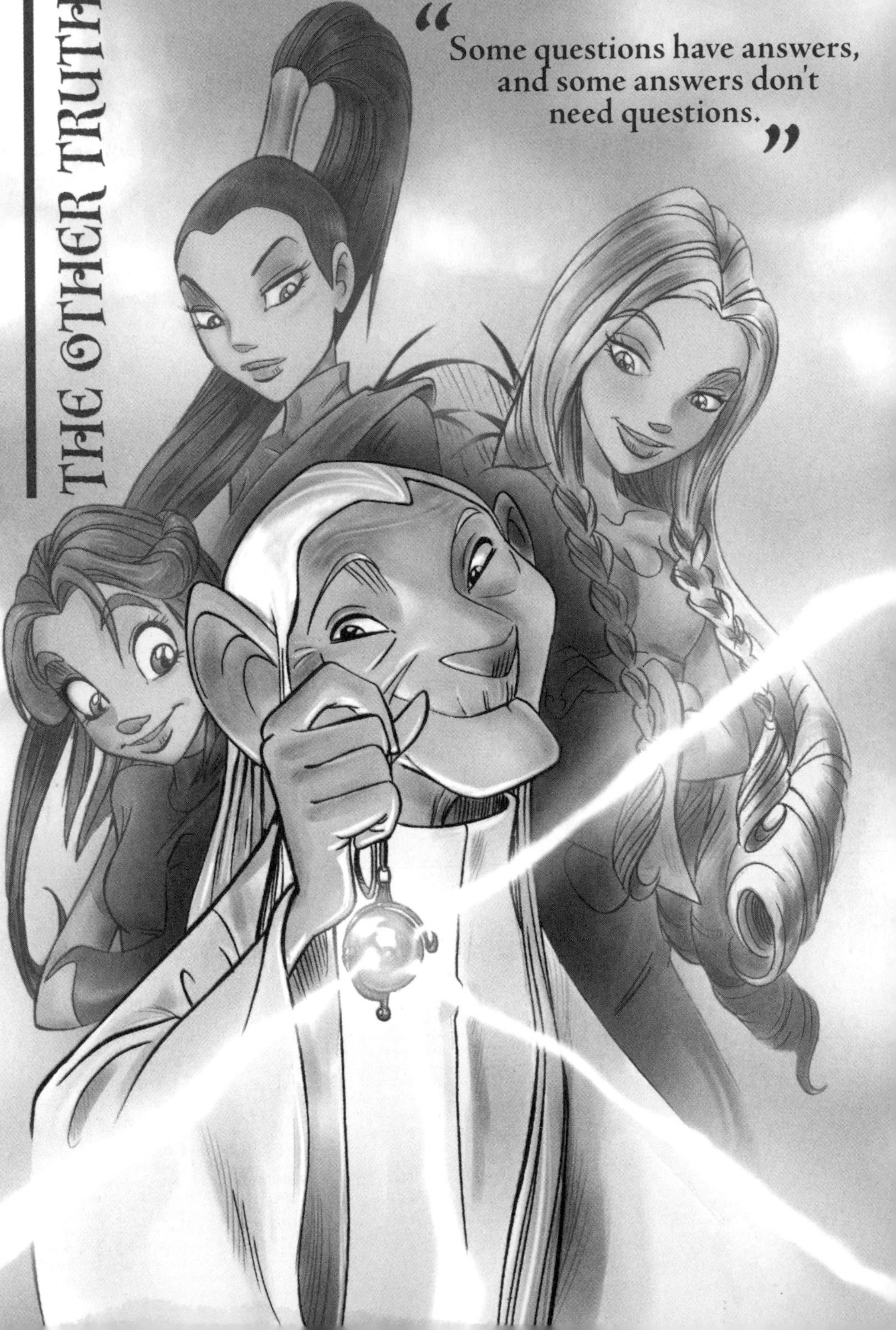

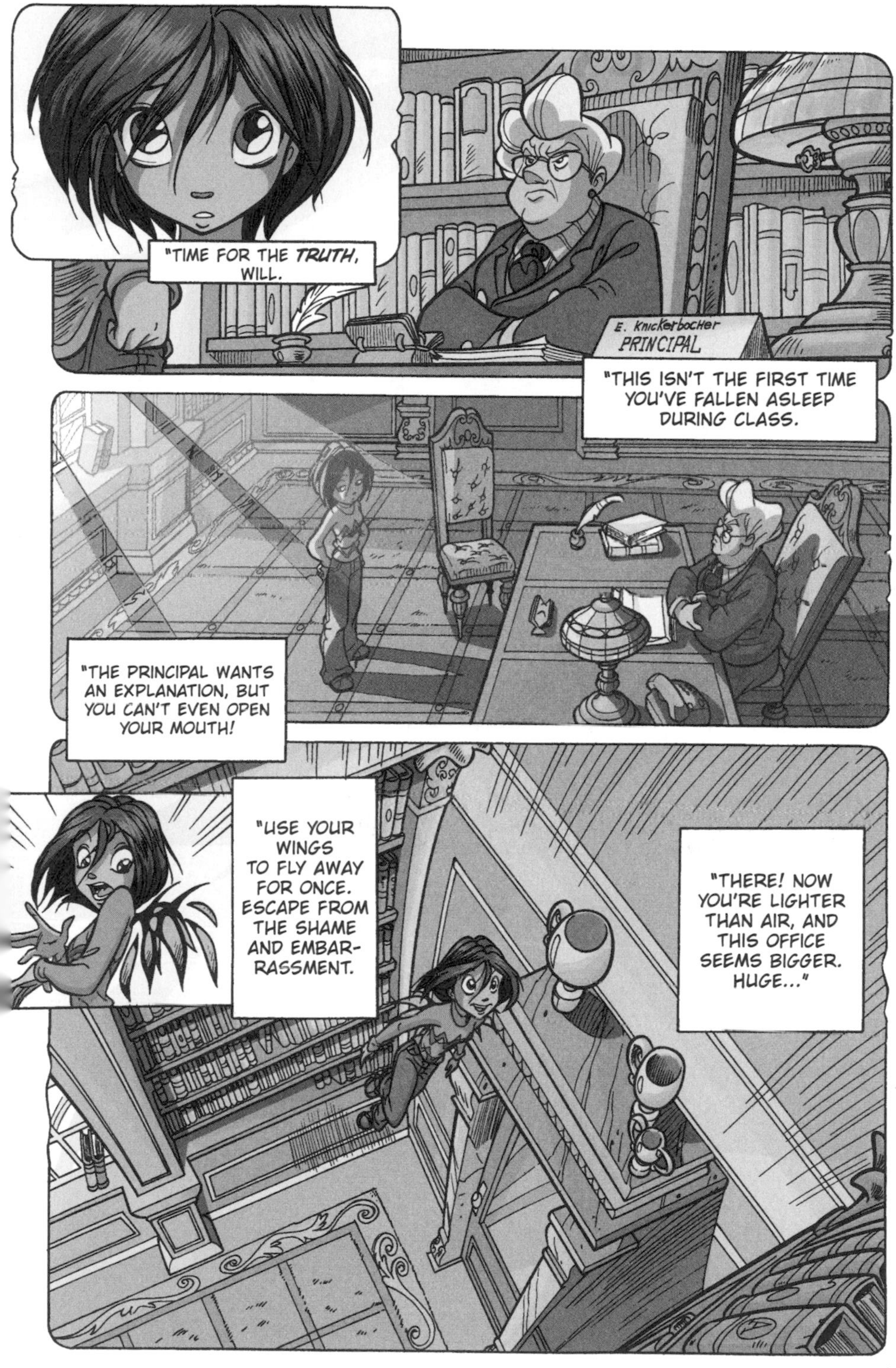
"TIME FOR THE TRUTH, WILL.
E. Knickerbocher
PRINCIPAL
"THIS ISN'T THE FIRST TIME YOU'VE FALLEN ASLEEP DURING CLASS.
"THE PRINCIPAL WANTS AN EXPLANATION, BUT YOU CAN'T EVEN OPEN YOUR MOUTH!
"USE YOUR WINGS TO FLY AWAY FOR ONCE. ESCAPE FROM THE SHAME AND EMBARRASSMENT.
"THERE! NOW YOU'RE LIGHTER THAN AIR, AND THIS OFFICE SEEMS BIGGER. HUGE..."

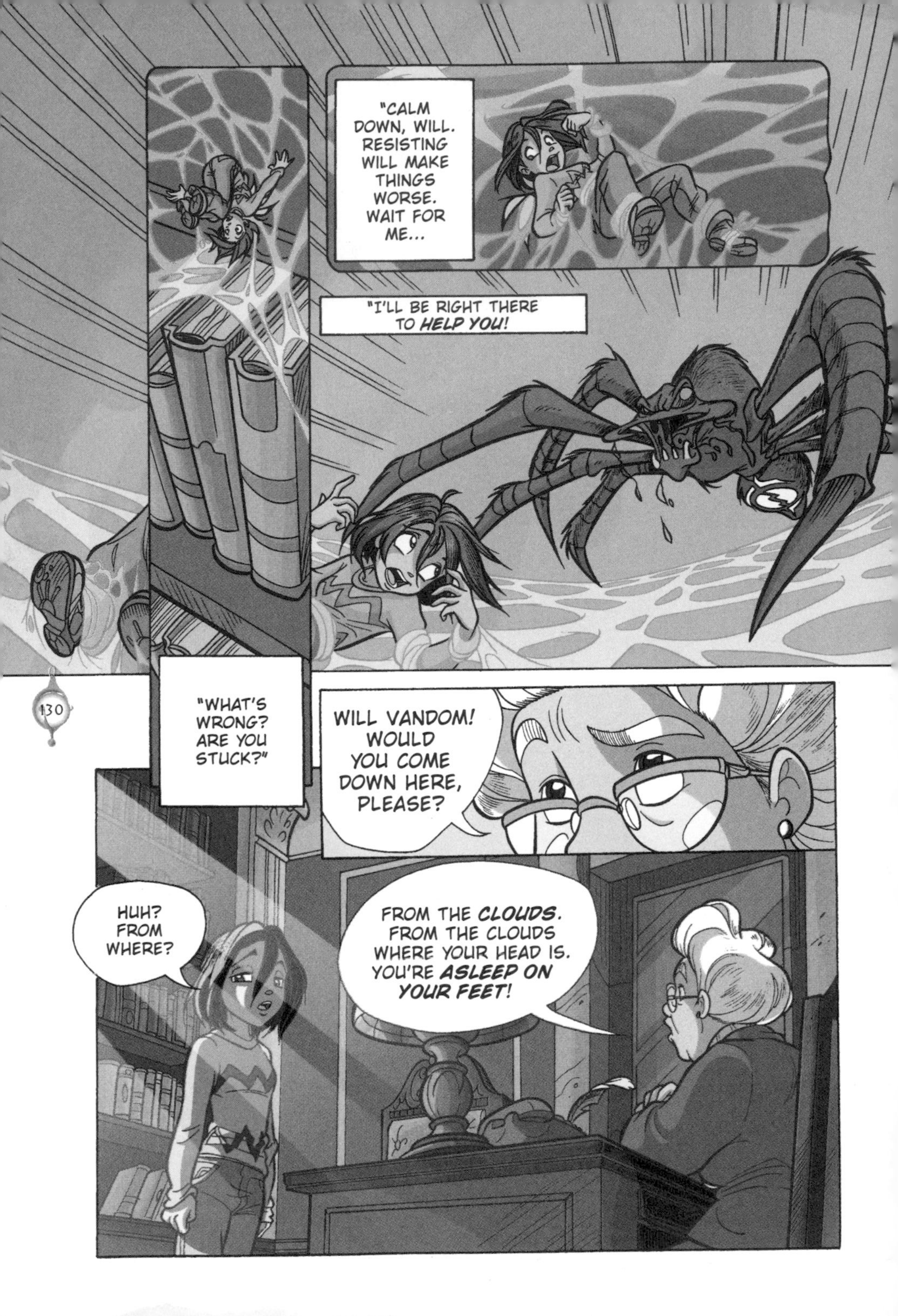

"CALM DOWN, WILL. RESISTING WILL MAKE THINGS WORSE. WAIT FOR ME...
"I'LL BE RIGHT THERE TO HELP YOU!
"WHAT'S WRONG? ARE YOU STUCK?"
WILL VANDOM! WOULD YOU COME DOWN HERE, PLEASE?
HUH? FROM WHERE?
FROM THE CLOUDS. FROM THE CLOUDS WHERE YOUR HEAD IS. YOU'RE ASLEEP ON YOUR FEET!

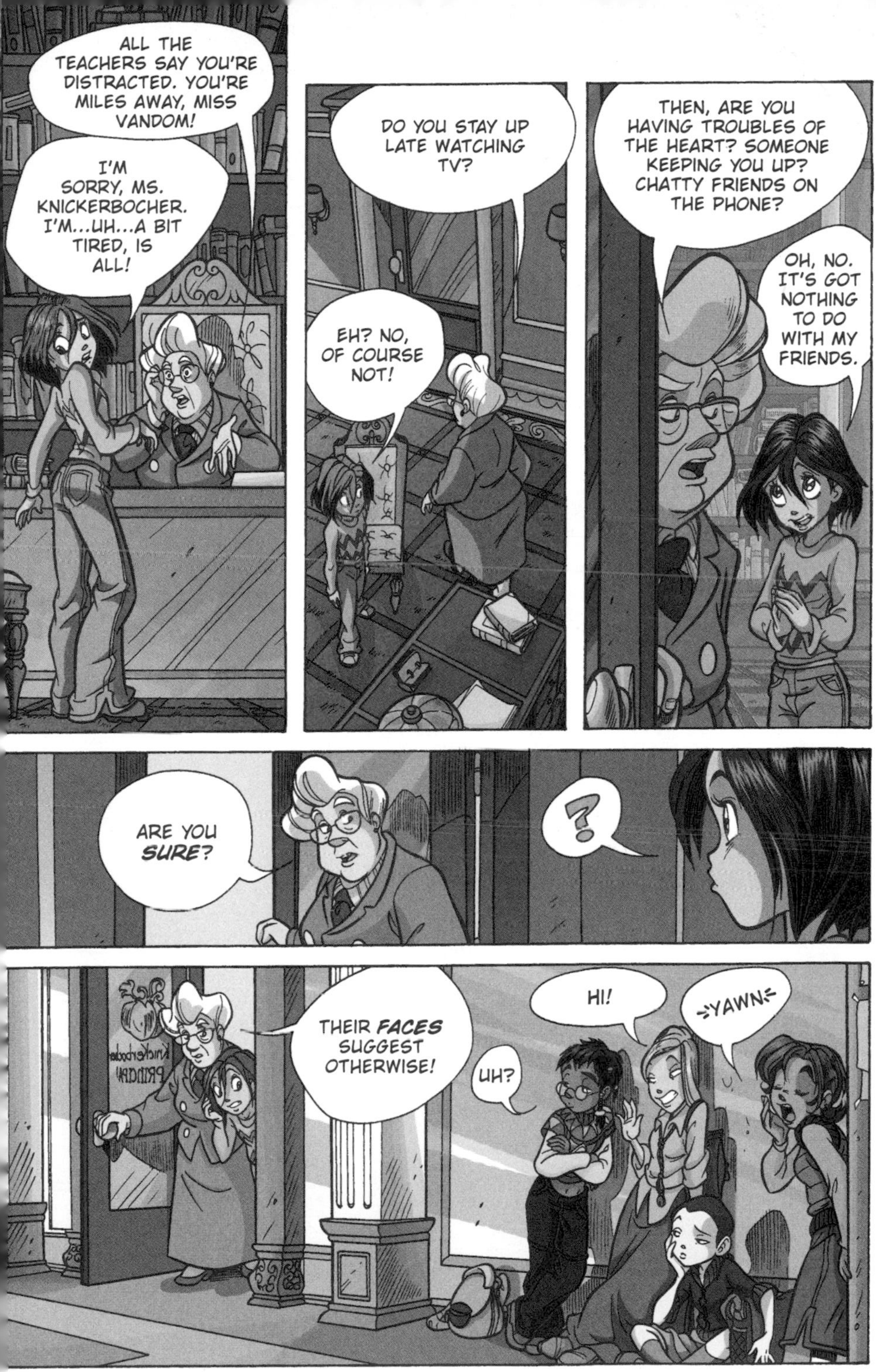
ALL THE TEACHERS SAY YOU'RE DISTRACTED. YOU'RE MILES AWAY, MISS VANDOM!
I'M SORRY, MS. KNICKERBOCHER. I'M...UH...A BIT TIRED, IS ALL!
DO YOU STAY UP LATE WATCHING TV?
EH? NO, OF COURSE NOT!
THEN, ARE YOU HAVING TROUBLES OF THE HEART? SOMEONE KEEPING YOU UP? CHATTY FRIENDS ON THE PHONE?
OH, NO. IT'S GOT NOTHING TO DO WITH MY FRIENDS.
ARE YOU SURE?
?
THEIR FACES SUGGEST OTHERWISE!
UH?
HI!
YAWN

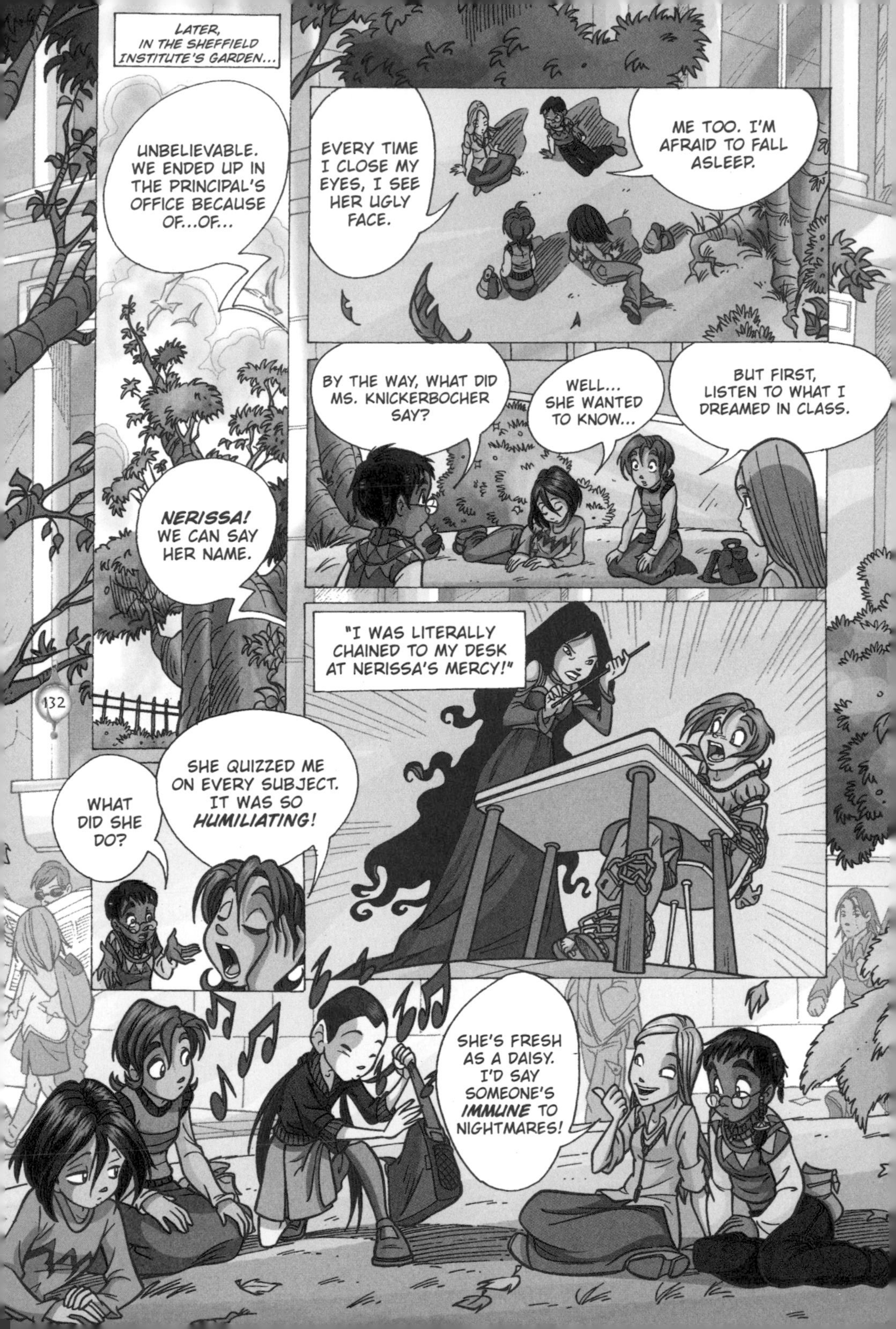

LATER, IN THE SHEFFIELD INSTITUTE'S GARDEN...
UNBELIEVABLE. WE ENDED UP IN THE PRINCIPAL'S OFFICE BECAUSE OF...OF...
EVERY TIME I CLOSE MY EYES, I SEE HER UGLY FACE.
ME TOO. I'M AFRAID TO FALL ASLEEP.
NERISSA! WE CAN SAY HER NAME.
BY THE WAY, WHAT DID MS. KNICKERBOCHER SAY?
WELL... SHE WANTED TO KNOW...
BUT FIRST, LISTEN TO WHAT I DREAMED IN CLASS.
"I WAS LITERALLY CHAINED TO MY DESK AT NERISSA'S MERCY!"
WHAT DID SHE DO?
SHE QUIZZED ME ON EVERY SUBJECT. IT WAS SO HUMILIATING!
SHE'S FRESH AS A DAISY. I'D SAY SOMEONE'S IMMUNE TO NIGHTMARES!

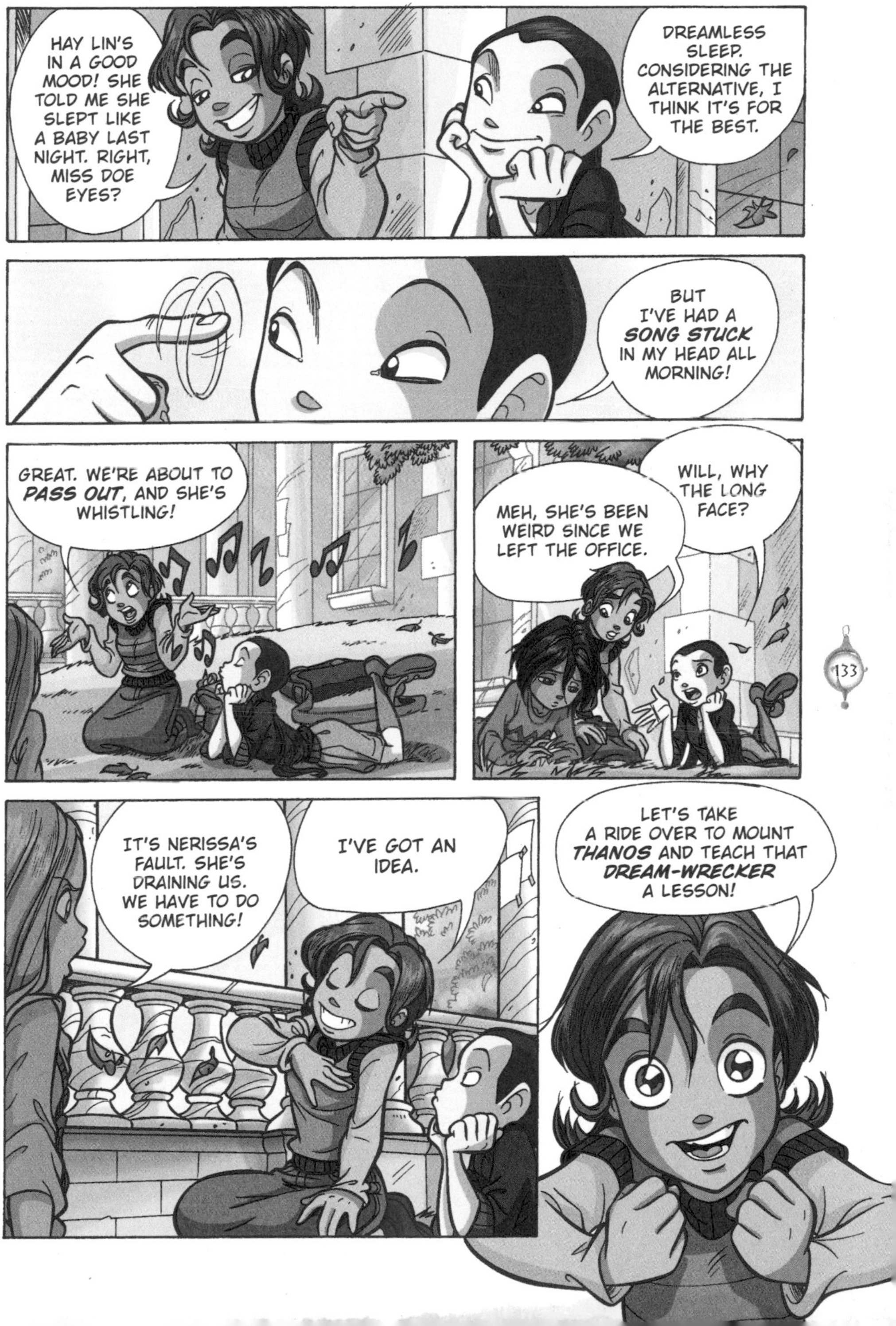
HAY LIN'S IN A GOOD MOOD! SHE TOLD ME SHE SLEPT LIKE A BABY LAST NIGHT. RIGHT, MISS DOE EYES?
DREAMLESS SLEEP. CONSIDERING THE ALTERNATIVE, I THINK IT'S FOR THE BEST.
BUT I'VE HAD A SONG STUCK IN MY HEAD ALL MORNING!
GREAT. WE'RE ABOUT TO PASS OUT, AND SHE'S WHISTLING!
WILL, WHY THE LONG FACE?
MEH, SHE'S BEEN WEIRD SINCE WE LEFT THE OFFICE.
IT'S NERISSA'S FAULT. SHE'S DRAINING US. WE HAVE TO DO SOMETHING!
I'VE GOT AN IDEA.
LET'S TAKE A RIDE OVER TO MOUNT THANOS AND TEACH THAT DREAM-WRECKER A LESSON!

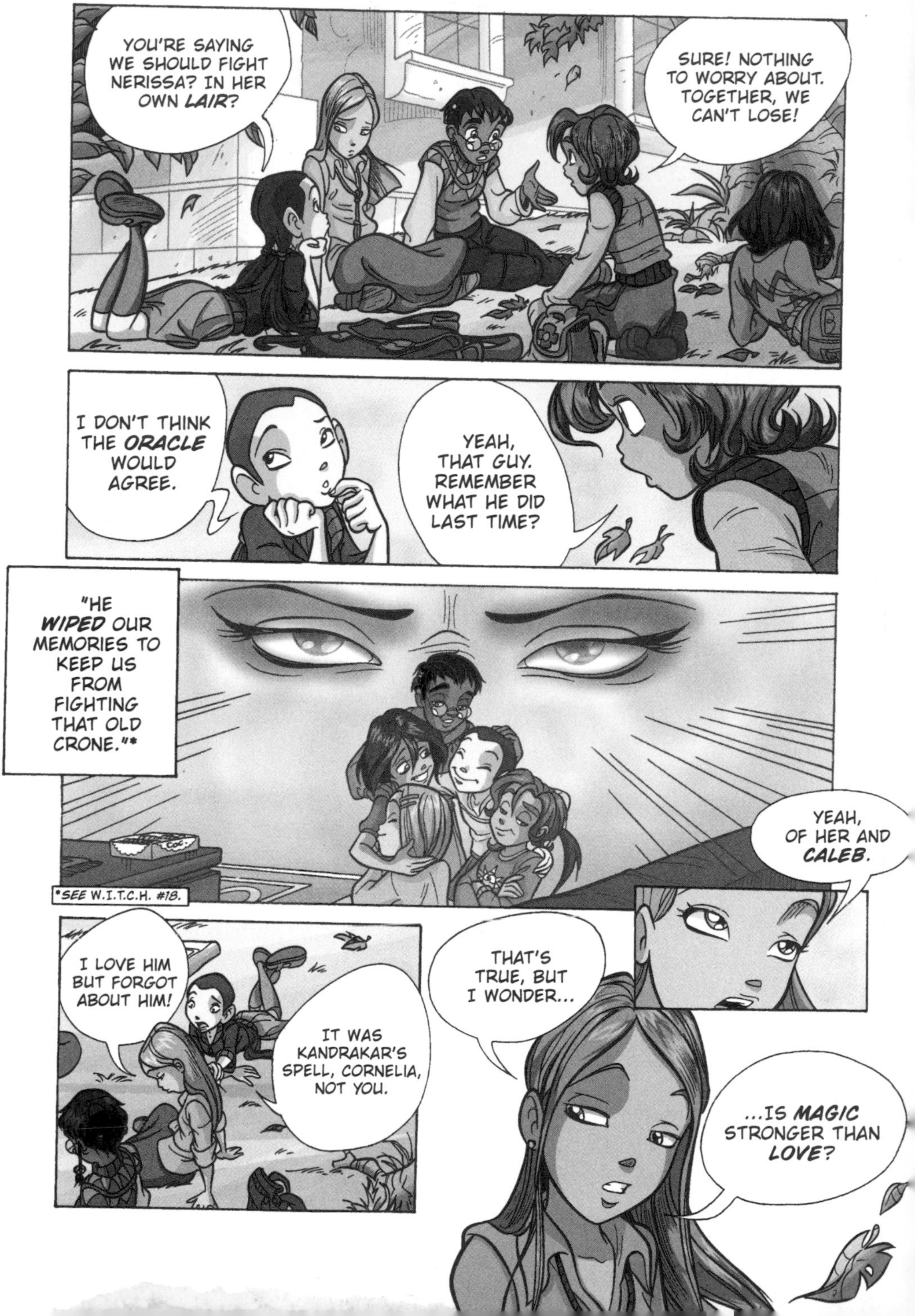
YOU'RE SAYING WE SHOULD FIGHT NERISSA? IN HER OWN *LAIR*?
SURE! NOTHING TO WORRY ABOUT. TOGETHER, WE CAN'T LOSE!
I DON'T THINK THE *ORACLE* WOULD AGREE.
YEAH, THAT GUY. REMEMBER WHAT HE DID LAST TIME?
"HE *WIPED* OUR MEMORIES TO KEEP US FROM FIGHTING THAT OLD CRONE."*
*SEE W.I.T.C.H. #18.
YEAH, OF HER AND *CALEB*.
I LOVE HIM BUT FORGOT ABOUT HIM!
IT WAS KANDRAKAR'S SPELL, CORNELIA, NOT YOU.
THAT'S TRUE, BUT I WONDER...
...IS *MAGIC* STRONGER THAN *LOVE*?

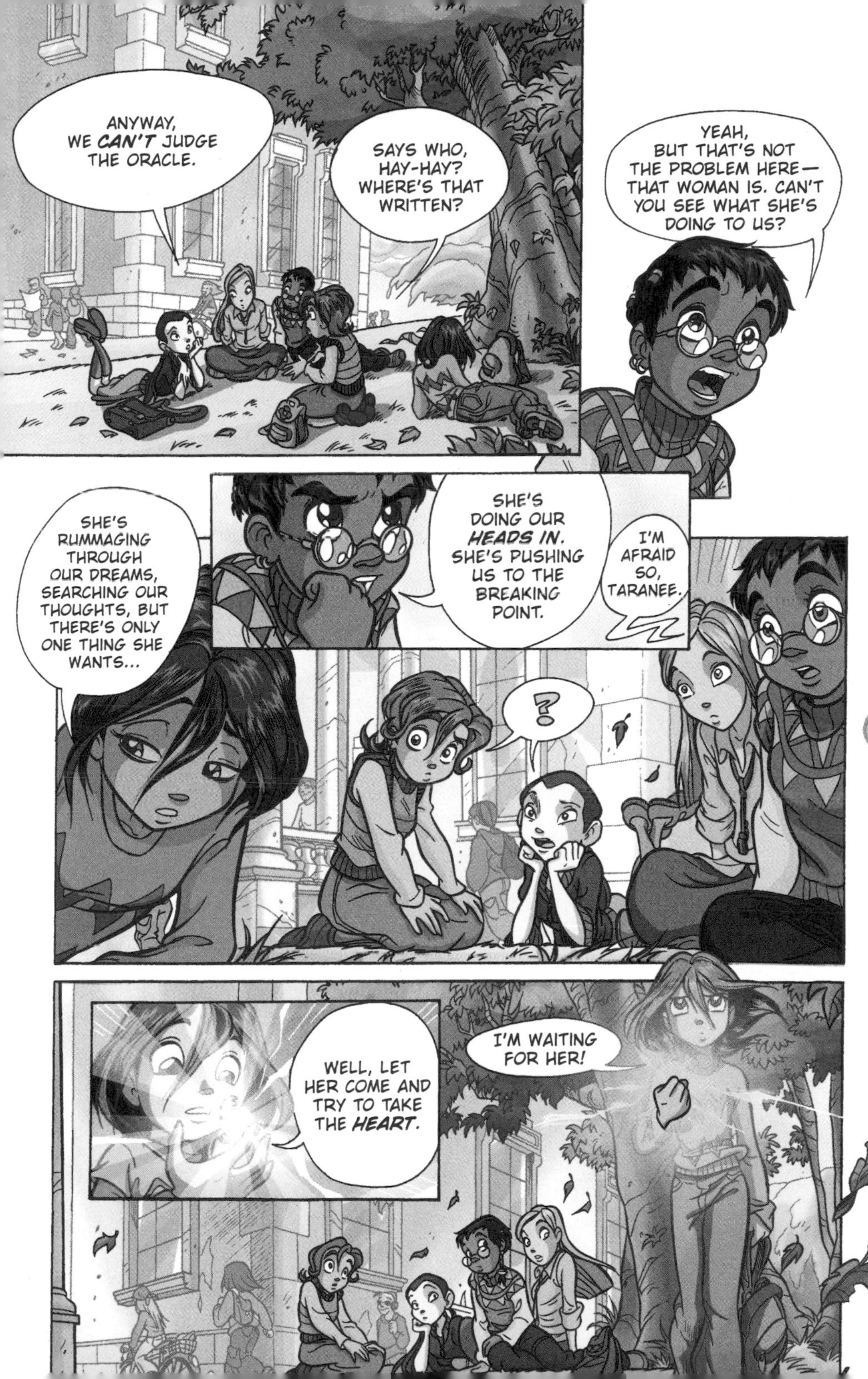

ANYWAY, WE CAN'T JUDGE THE ORACLE.
SAYS WHO, HAY-HAY? WHERE'S THAT WRITTEN?
YEAH, BUT THAT'S NOT THE PROBLEM HERE— THAT WOMAN IS. CAN'T YOU SEE WHAT SHE'S DOING TO US?
SHE'S DOING OUR HEADS IN. SHE'S PUSHING US TO THE BREAKING POINT.
I'M AFRAID SO, TARANEE.
SHE'S RUMMAGING THROUGH OUR DREAMS, SEARCHING OUR THOUGHTS, BUT THERE'S ONLY ONE THING SHE WANTS...
?
I'M WAITING FOR HER!
WELL, LET HER COME AND TRY TO TAKE THE HEART.

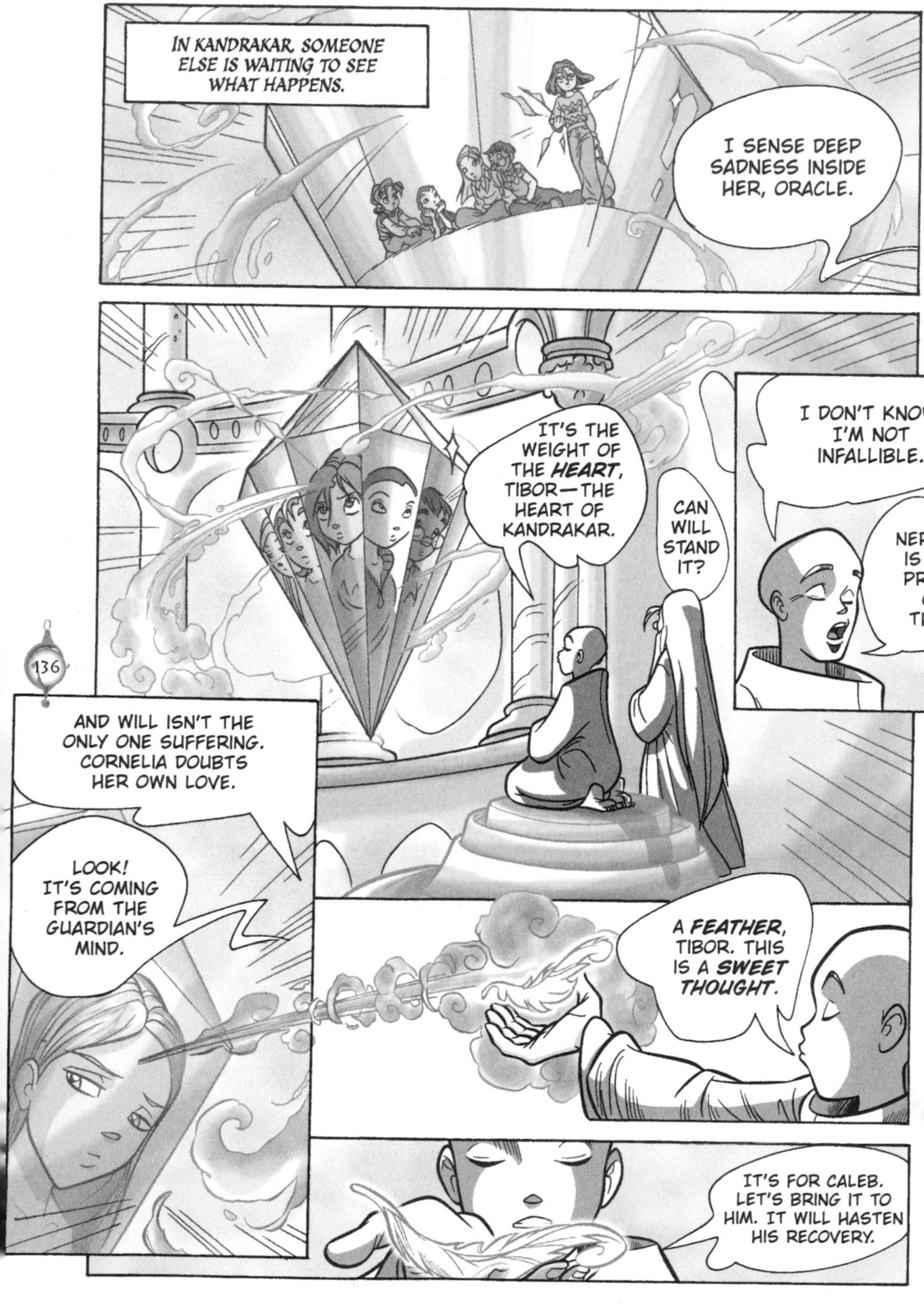
IN KANDRAKAR, SOMEONE ELSE IS WAITING TO SEE WHAT HAPPENS.
I SENSE DEEP SADNESS INSIDE HER, ORACLE.
IT'S THE WEIGHT OF THE *HEART*, TIBOR—THE HEART OF KANDRAKAR.
CAN WILL STAND IT?
I DON'T KNOW. I'M NOT INFALLIBLE.
NERISSA IS THE PROOF OF THAT.
AND WILL ISN'T THE ONLY ONE SUFFERING. CORNELIA DOUBTS HER OWN LOVE.
LOOK! IT'S COMING FROM THE GUARDIAN'S MIND.
A *FEATHER*, TIBOR. THIS IS A *SWEET THOUGHT*.
IT'S FOR CALEB. LET'S BRING IT TO HIM. IT WILL HASTEN HIS RECOVERY.

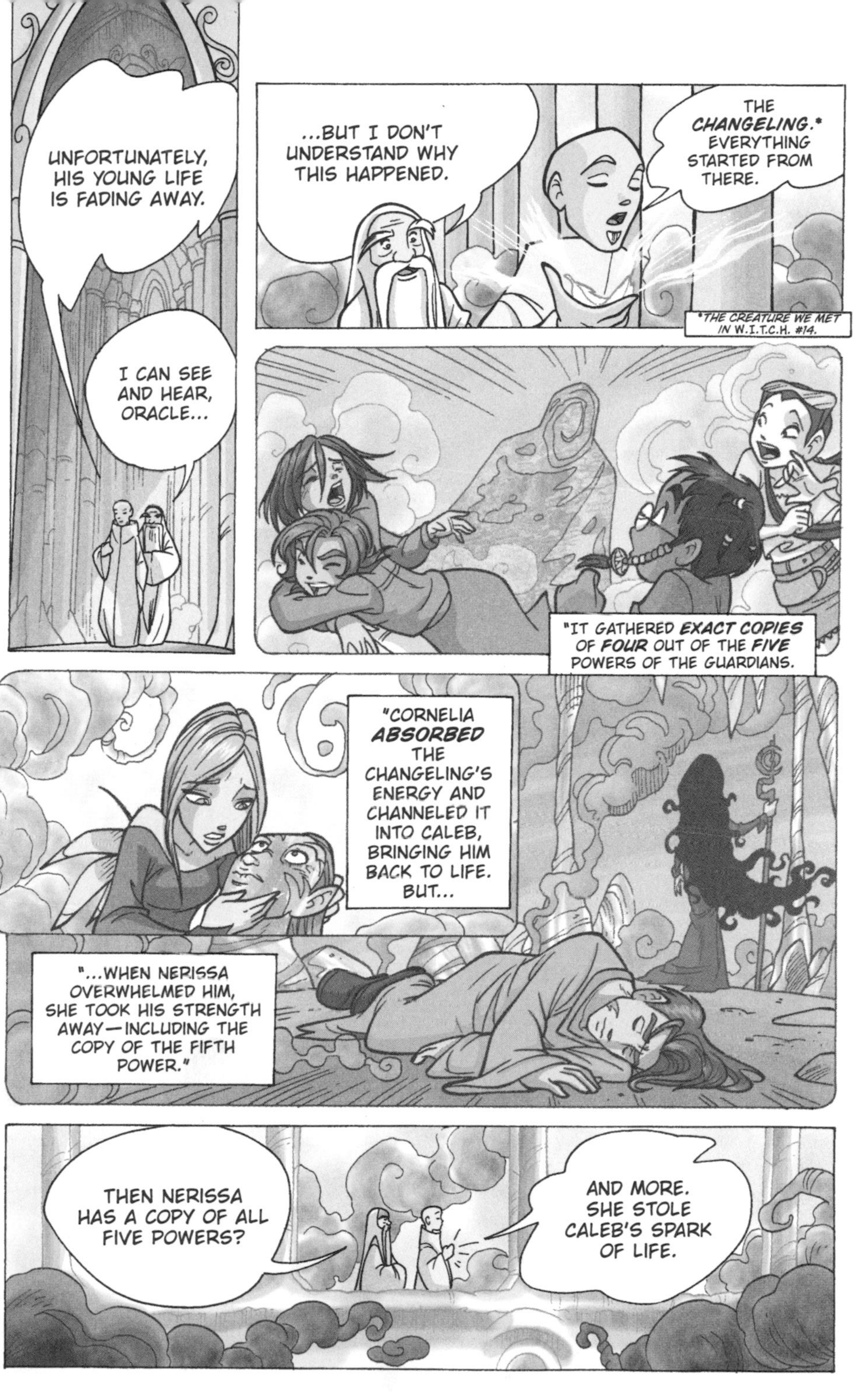
UNFORTUNATELY, HIS YOUNG LIFE IS FADING AWAY.
...BUT I DON'T UNDERSTAND WHY THIS HAPPENED.
THE CHANGELING.* EVERYTHING STARTED FROM THERE.
*THE CREATURE WE MET IN W.I.T.C.H. #14.
I CAN SEE AND HEAR, ORACLE...
"IT GATHERED EXACT COPIES OF FOUR OUT OF THE FIVE POWERS OF THE GUARDIANS.
"CORNELIA ABSORBED THE CHANGELING'S ENERGY AND CHANNELED IT INTO CALEB, BRINGING HIM BACK TO LIFE. BUT...
"...WHEN NERISSA OVERWHELMED HIM, SHE TOOK HIS STRENGTH AWAY—INCLUDING THE COPY OF THE FIFTH POWER."
THEN NERISSA HAS A COPY OF ALL FIVE POWERS?
AND MORE. SHE STOLE CALEB'S SPARK OF LIFE.

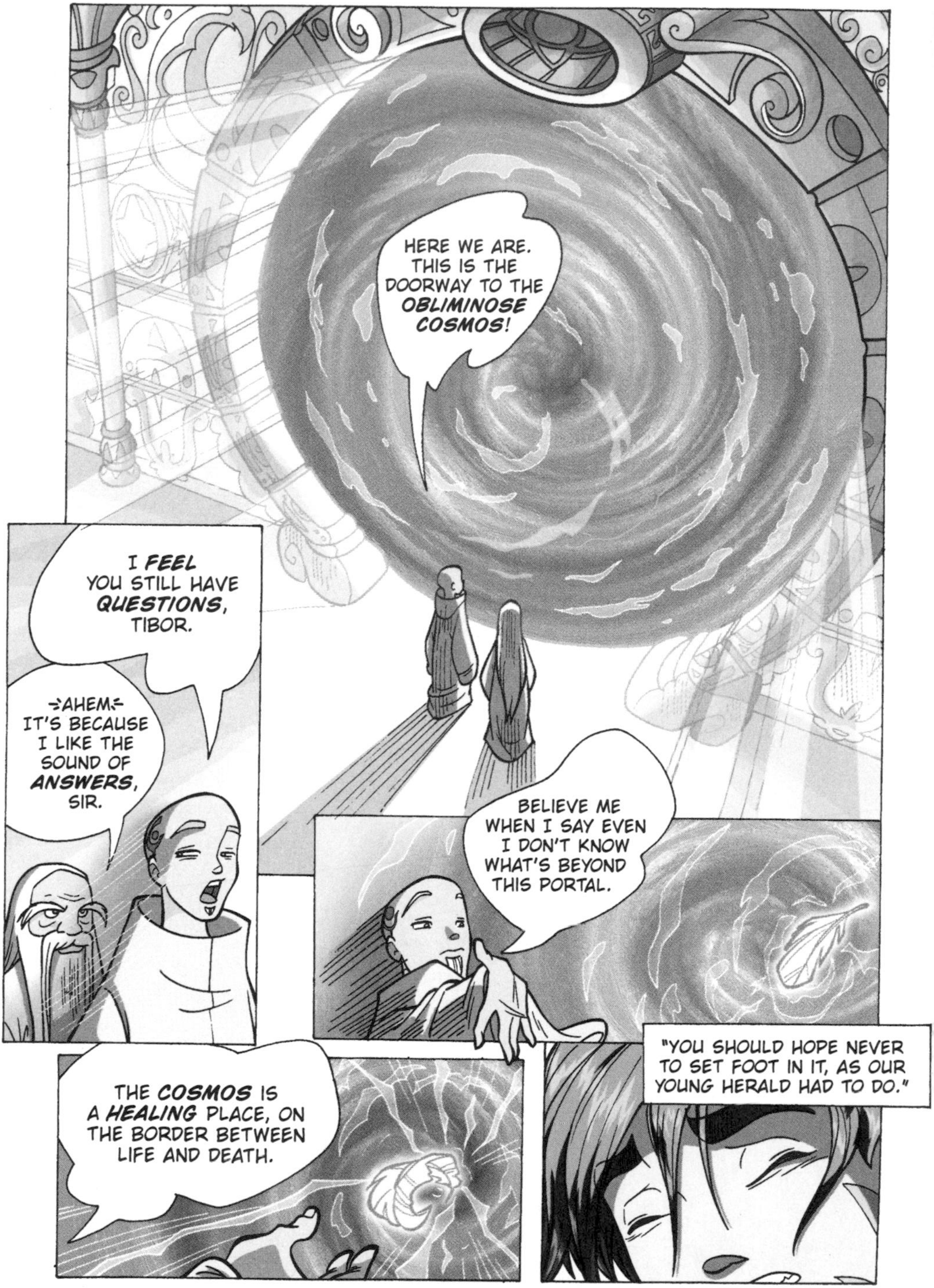

HERE WE ARE. THIS IS THE DOORWAY TO THE ***OBLIMINOSE COSMOS!***
I ***FEEL*** YOU STILL HAVE ***QUESTIONS***, TIBOR.
AHEM IT'S BECAUSE I LIKE THE SOUND OF ***ANSWERS***, SIR.
BELIEVE ME WHEN I SAY EVEN I DON'T KNOW WHAT'S BEYOND THIS PORTAL.
THE ***COSMOS*** IS A ***HEALING*** PLACE, ON THE BORDER BETWEEN LIFE AND DEATH.
"YOU SHOULD HOPE NEVER TO SET FOOT IN IT, AS OUR YOUNG HERALD HAD TO DO."

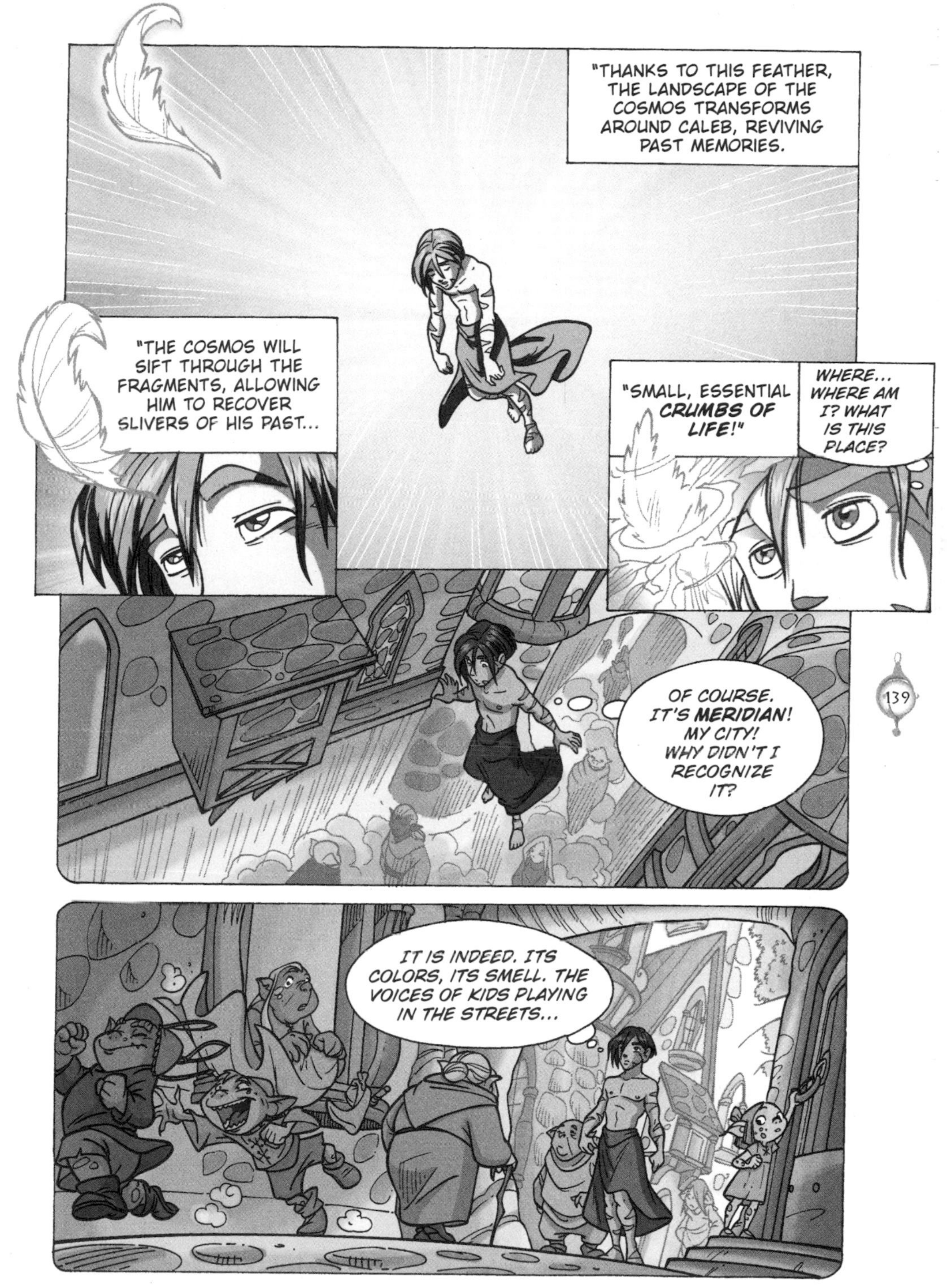
"THANKS TO THIS FEATHER, THE LANDSCAPE OF THE COSMOS TRANSFORMS AROUND CALEB, REVIVING PAST MEMORIES.
"THE COSMOS WILL SIFT THROUGH THE FRAGMENTS, ALLOWING HIM TO RECOVER SLIVERS OF HIS PAST...
"SMALL, ESSENTIAL CRUMBS OF LIFE!"
WHERE... WHERE AM I? WHAT IS THIS PLACE?
OF COURSE. IT'S MERIDIAN! MY CITY! WHY DIDN'T I RECOGNIZE IT?
IT IS INDEED. ITS COLORS, ITS SMELL. THE VOICES OF KIDS PLAYING IN THE STREETS...

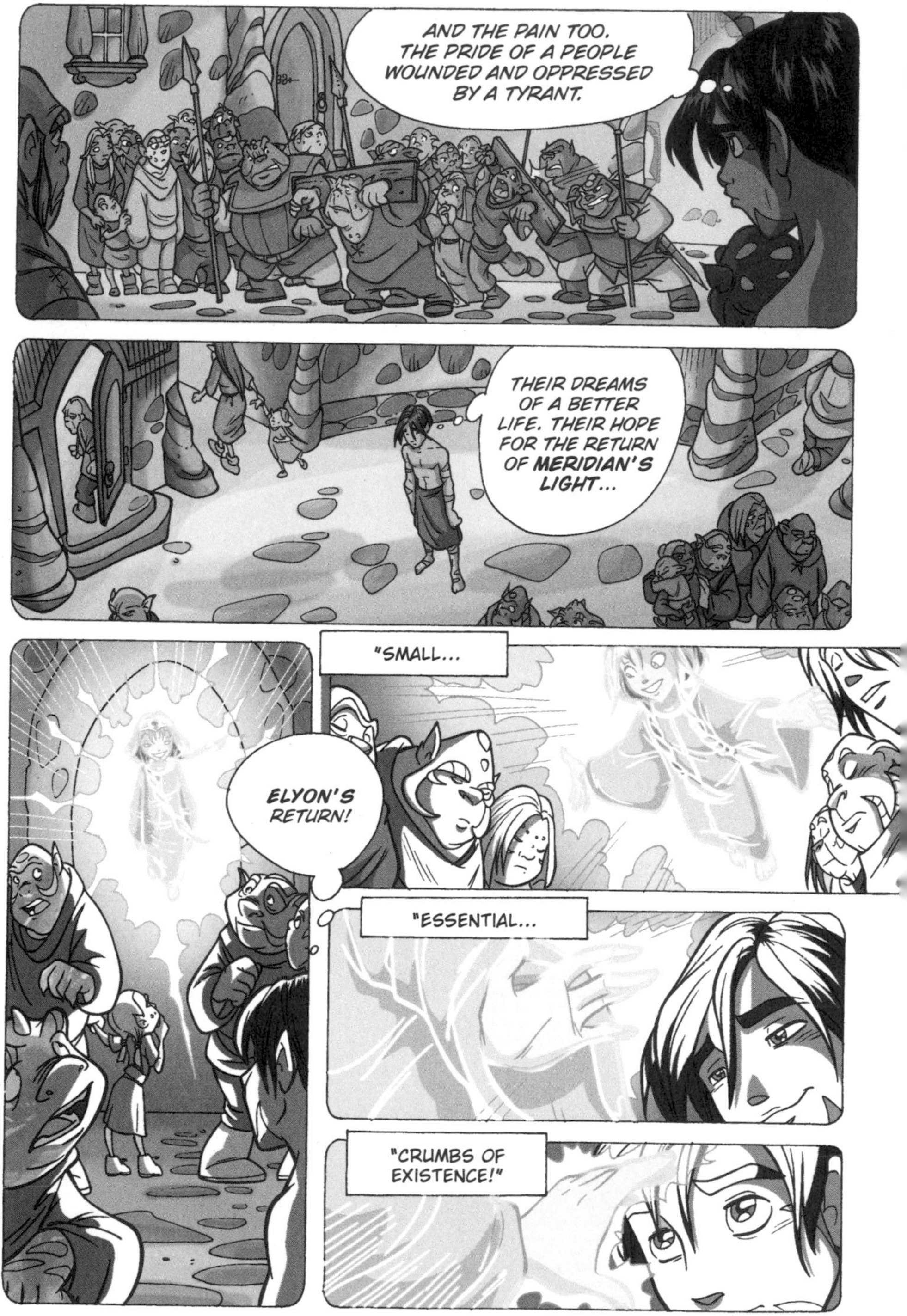
AND THE PAIN TOO. THE PRIDE OF A PEOPLE WOUNDED AND OPPRESSED BY A TYRANT.
THEIR DREAMS OF A BETTER LIFE. THEIR HOPE FOR THE RETURN OF MERIDIAN'S LIGHT...
"SMALL...
ELYON'S RETURN!
"ESSENTIAL...
"CRUMBS OF EXISTENCE!"

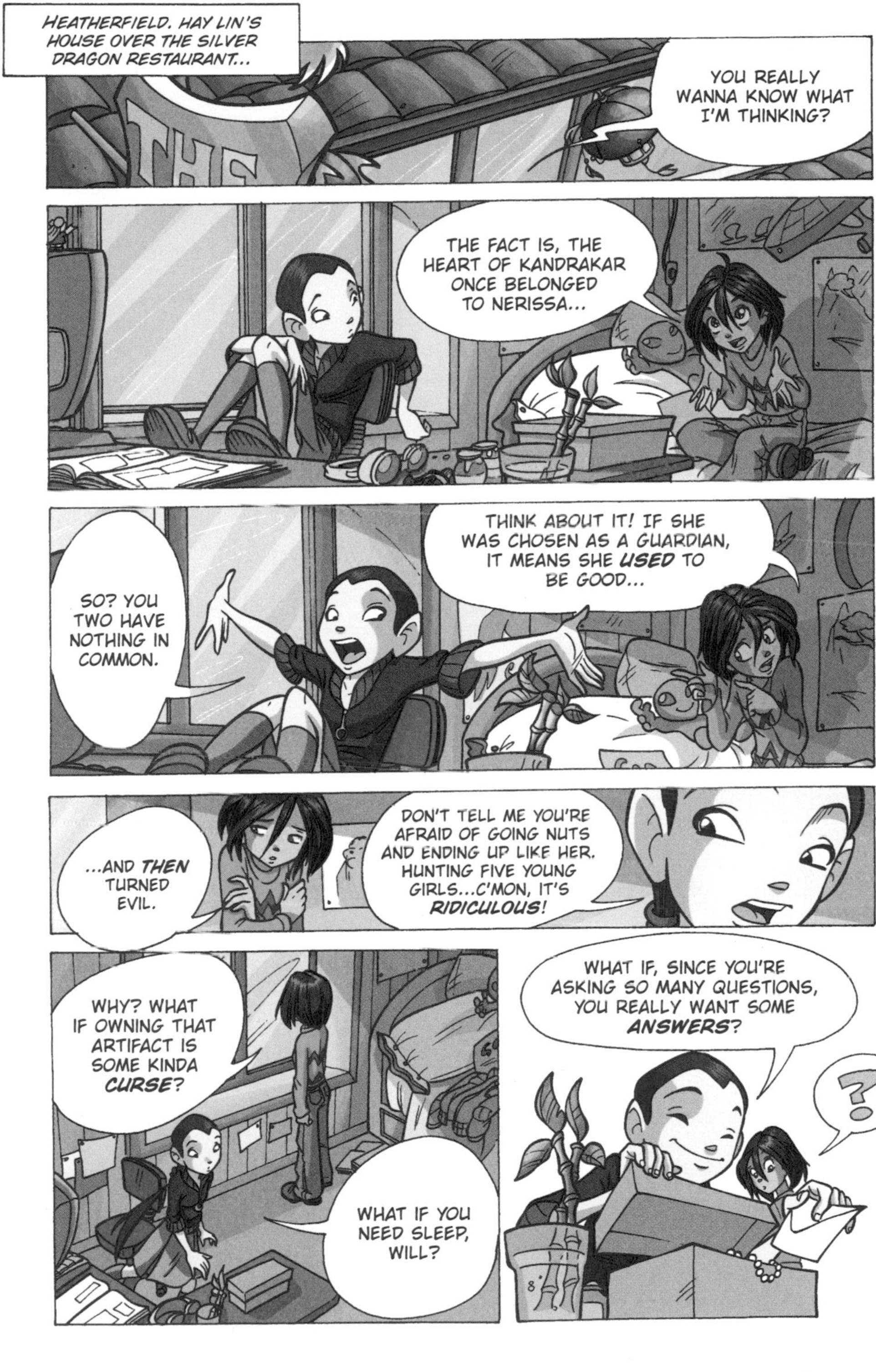
HEATHERFIELD. HAY LIN'S HOUSE OVER THE SILVER DRAGON RESTAURANT...
YOU REALLY WANNA KNOW WHAT I'M THINKING?
THE FACT IS, THE HEART OF KANDRAKAR ONCE BELONGED TO NERISSA...
SO? YOU TWO HAVE NOTHING IN COMMON.
THINK ABOUT IT! IF SHE WAS CHOSEN AS A GUARDIAN, IT MEANS SHE USED TO BE GOOD...
...AND THEN TURNED EVIL.
DON'T TELL ME YOU'RE AFRAID OF GOING NUTS AND ENDING UP LIKE HER. HUNTING FIVE YOUNG GIRLS...C'MON, IT'S RIDICULOUS!
WHY? WHAT IF OWNING THAT ARTIFACT IS SOME KINDA CURSE?
WHAT IF YOU NEED SLEEP, WILL?
WHAT IF, SINCE YOU'RE ASKING SO MANY QUESTIONS, YOU REALLY WANT SOME ANSWERS?
?

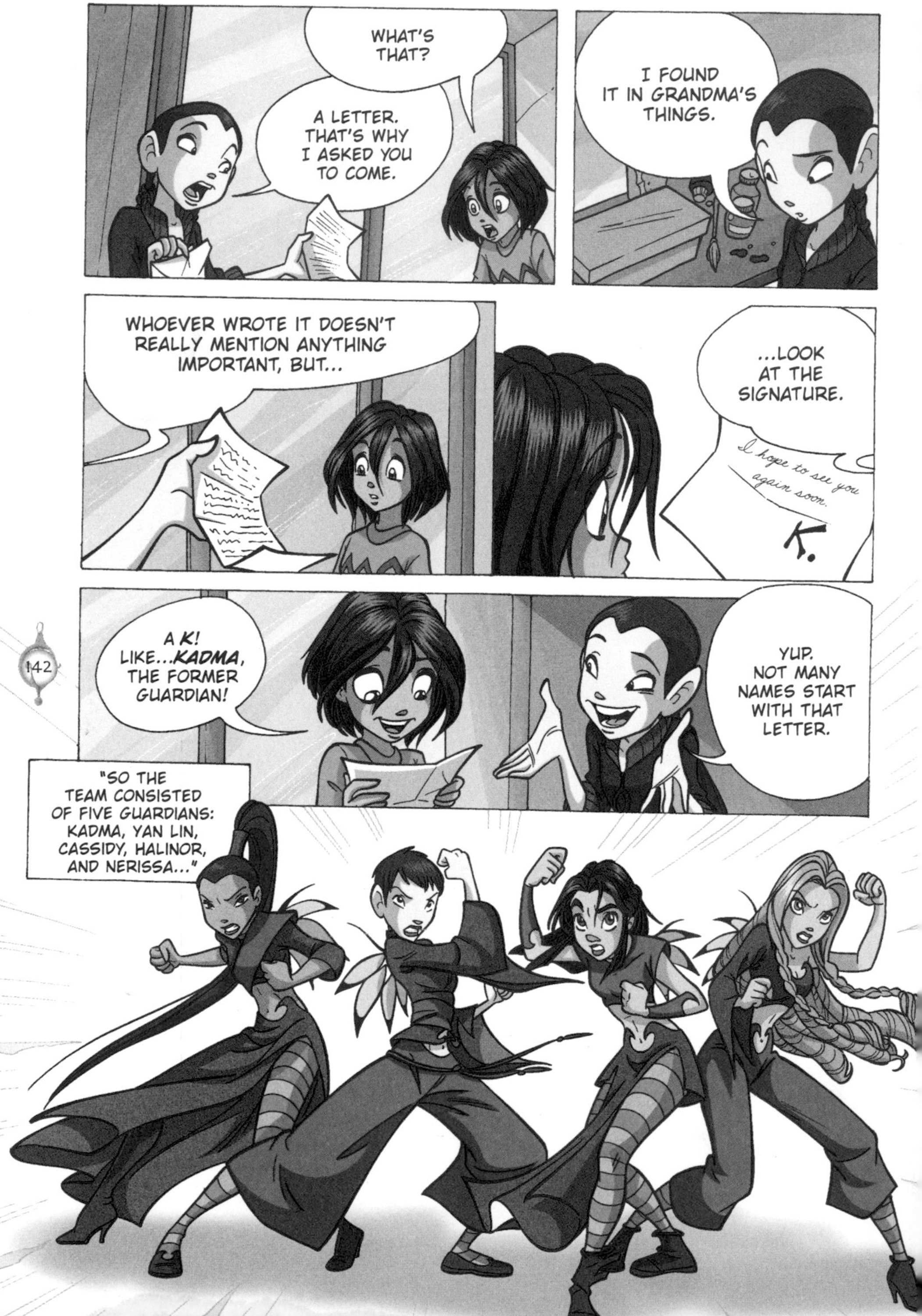
WHAT'S THAT?
A LETTER. THAT'S WHY I ASKED YOU TO COME.
I FOUND IT IN GRANDMA'S THINGS.
WHOEVER WROTE IT DOESN'T REALLY MENTION ANYTHING IMPORTANT, BUT...
...LOOK AT THE SIGNATURE.
I hope to see you again soon.
K.
A K! LIKE...KADMA, THE FORMER GUARDIAN!
YUP. NOT MANY NAMES START WITH THAT LETTER.
"SO THE TEAM CONSISTED OF FIVE GUARDIANS: KADMA, YAN LIN, CASSIDY, HALINOR, AND NERISSA..."

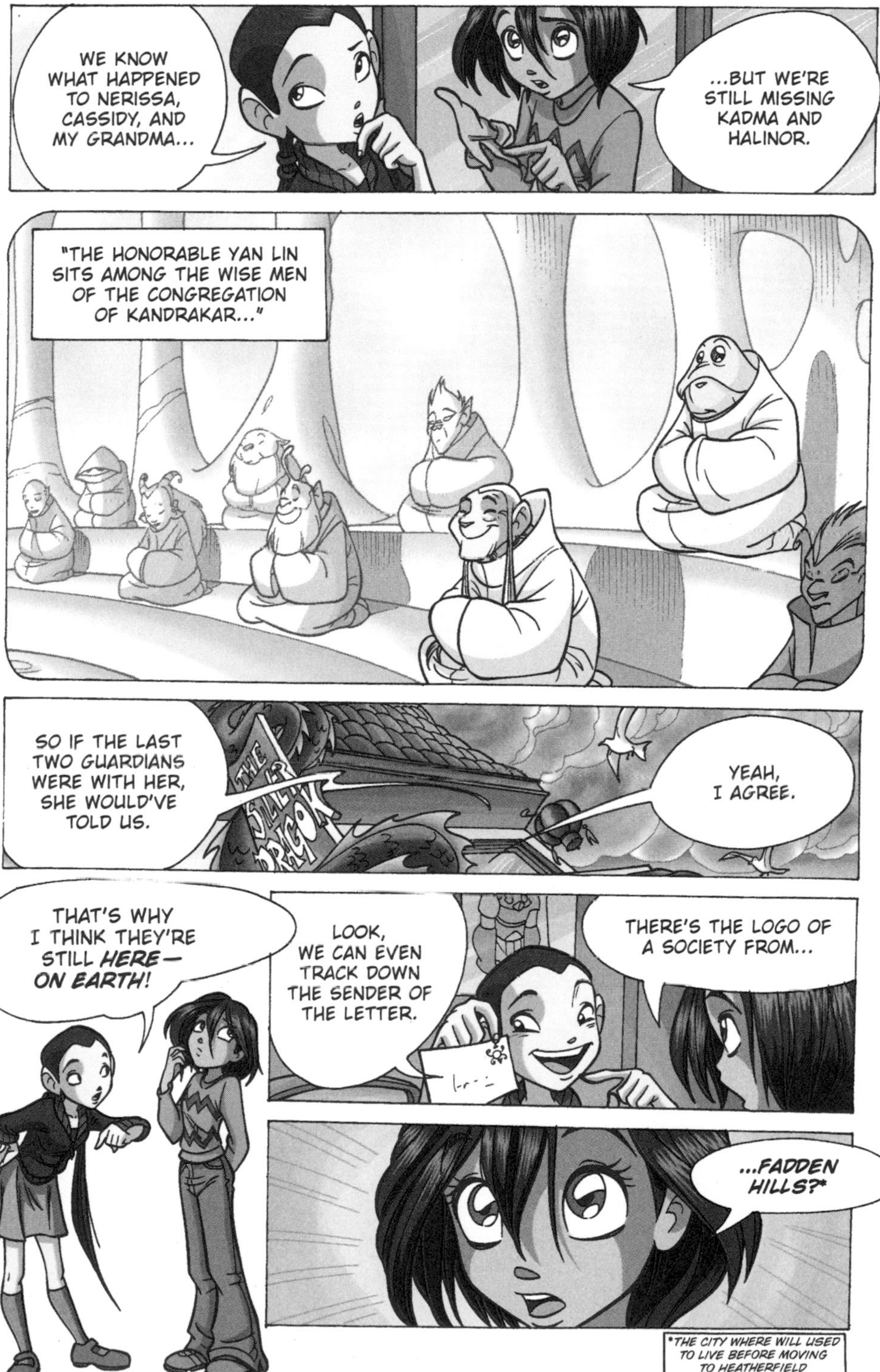

WE KNOW WHAT HAPPENED TO NERISSA, CASSIDY, AND MY GRANDMA...
...BUT WE'RE STILL MISSING KADMA AND HALINOR.
"THE HONORABLE YAN LIN SITS AMONG THE WISE MEN OF THE CONGREGATION OF KANDRAKAR..."
SO IF THE LAST TWO GUARDIANS WERE WITH HER, SHE WOULD'VE TOLD US.
YEAH, I AGREE.
THAT'S WHY I THINK THEY'RE STILL *HERE— ON EARTH*!
LOOK, WE CAN EVEN TRACK DOWN THE SENDER OF THE LETTER.
THERE'S THE LOGO OF A SOCIETY FROM...
*...FADDEN HILLS?**
*THE CITY WHERE WILL USED TO LIVE BEFORE MOVING TO HEATHERFIELD

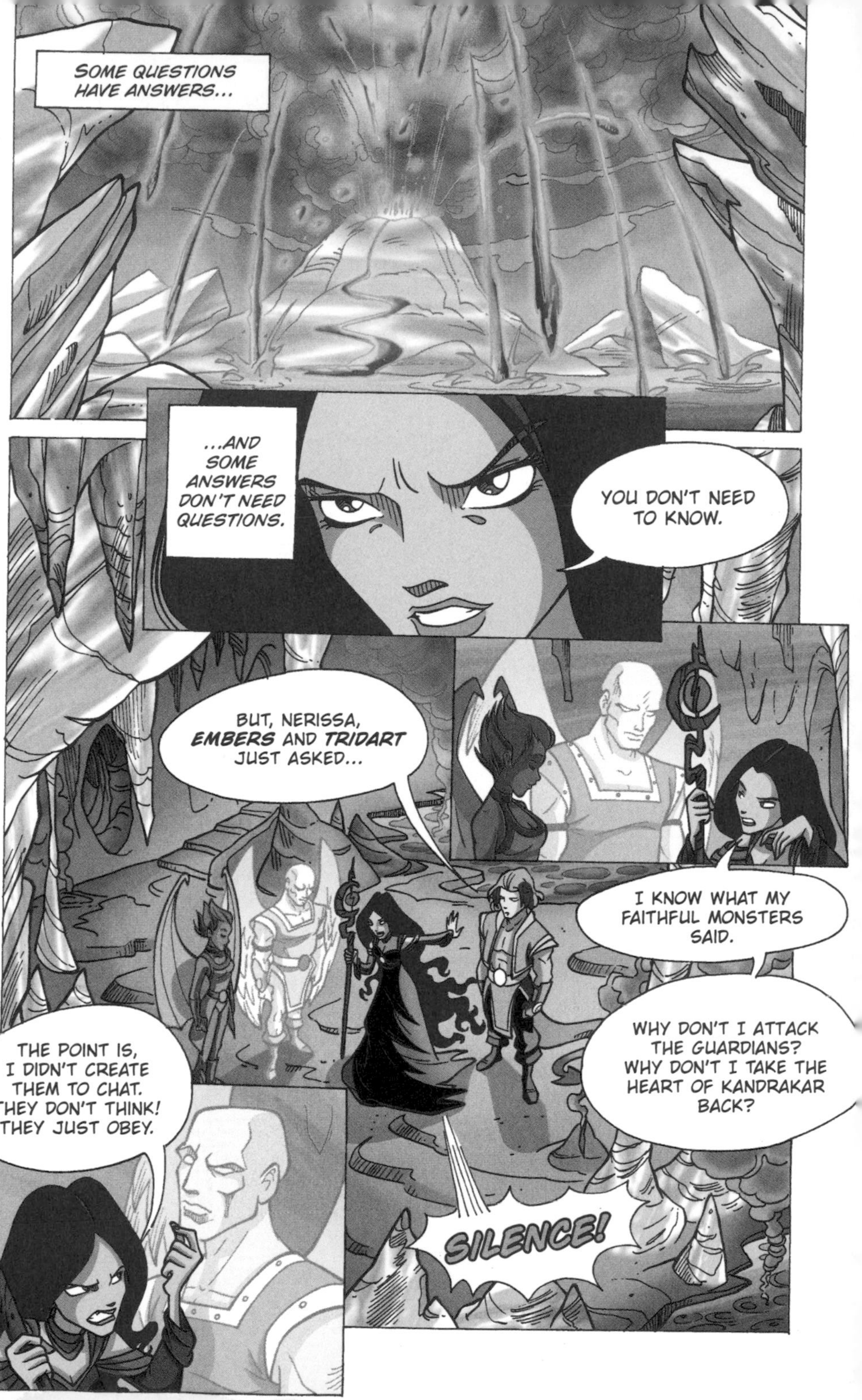
SOME QUESTIONS HAVE ANSWERS...
...AND SOME ANSWERS DON'T NEED QUESTIONS.
YOU DON'T NEED TO KNOW.
BUT, NERISSA, **EMBERS** AND **TRIDART** JUST ASKED...
I KNOW WHAT MY FAITHFUL MONSTERS SAID.
WHY DON'T I ATTACK THE GUARDIANS? WHY DON'T I TAKE THE HEART OF KANDRAKAR BACK?
THE POINT IS, I DIDN'T CREATE THEM TO CHAT. THEY DON'T THINK! THEY JUST OBEY.
SILENCE!

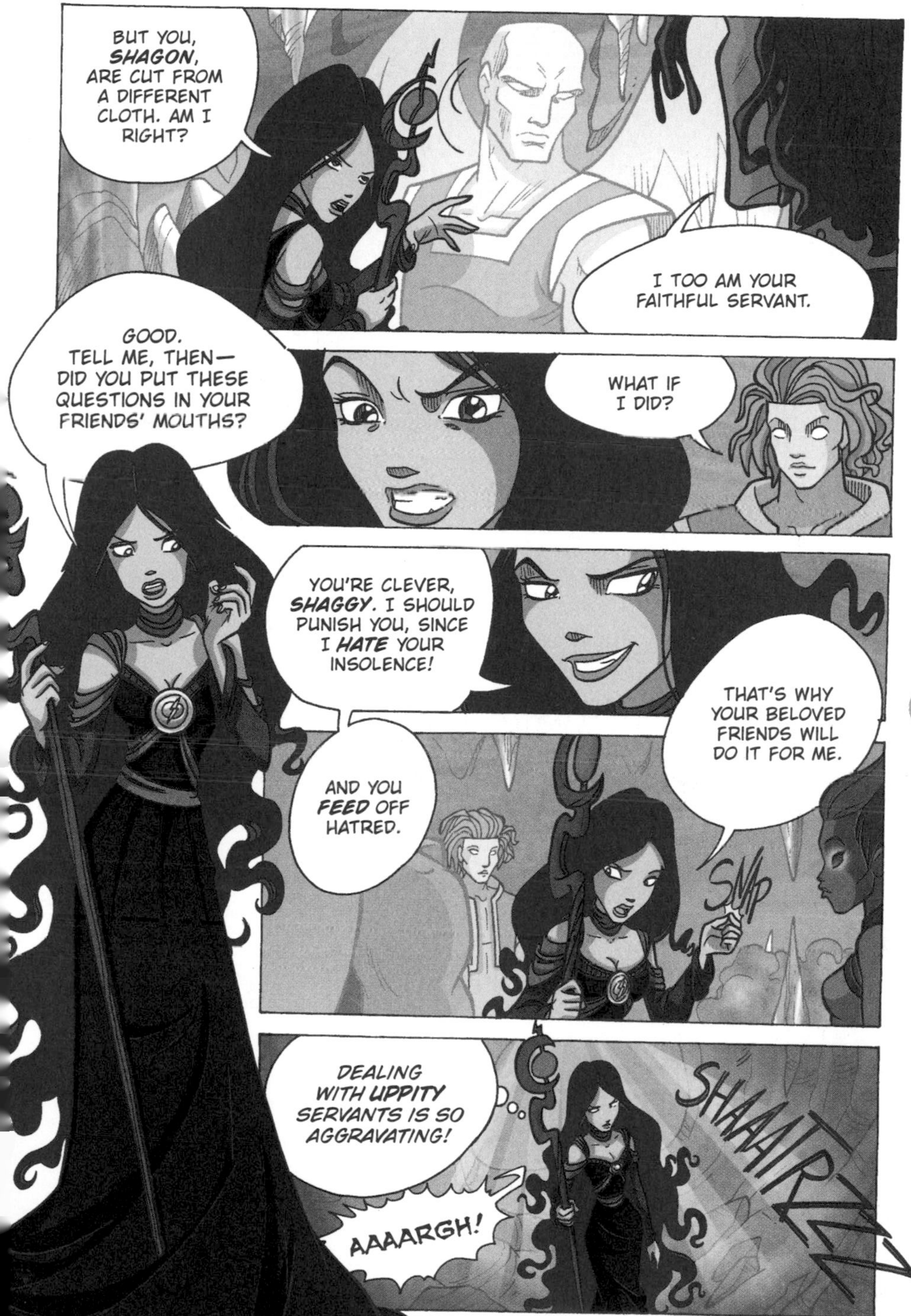

BUT YOU, SHAGON, ARE CUT FROM A DIFFERENT CLOTH. AM I RIGHT?
I TOO AM YOUR FAITHFUL SERVANT.
GOOD. TELL ME, THEN— DID YOU PUT THESE QUESTIONS IN YOUR FRIENDS' MOUTHS?
WHAT IF I DID?
YOU'RE CLEVER, SHAGGY. I SHOULD PUNISH YOU, SINCE I HATE YOUR INSOLENCE!
AND YOU FEED OFF HATRED.
THAT'S WHY YOUR BELOVED FRIENDS WILL DO IT FOR ME.
SNAP
DEALING WITH UPPITY SERVANTS IS SO AGGRAVATING!
SHAAATRZZZ
AAAARGH!

THE TRUTH IS, I **CAN'T** ATTACK THE GUARDIANS DIRECTLY.

I CAN ONLY BREAK INTO THEIR DREAMS. I HAVE TO **WEAR THEM DOWN**, MAKE THEM WEAK...

146

...BEFORE **I STRIKE!**

SNAP

BUT CREATING THESE **NIGHMARES** IS EXHAUSTING!

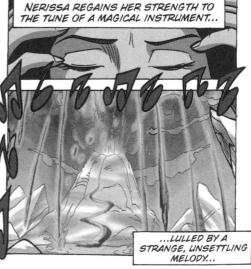

NERISSA REGAINS HER STRENGTH TO THE TUNE OF A MAGICAL INSTRUMENT...

...LULLED BY A STRANGE, UNSETTLING MELODY...

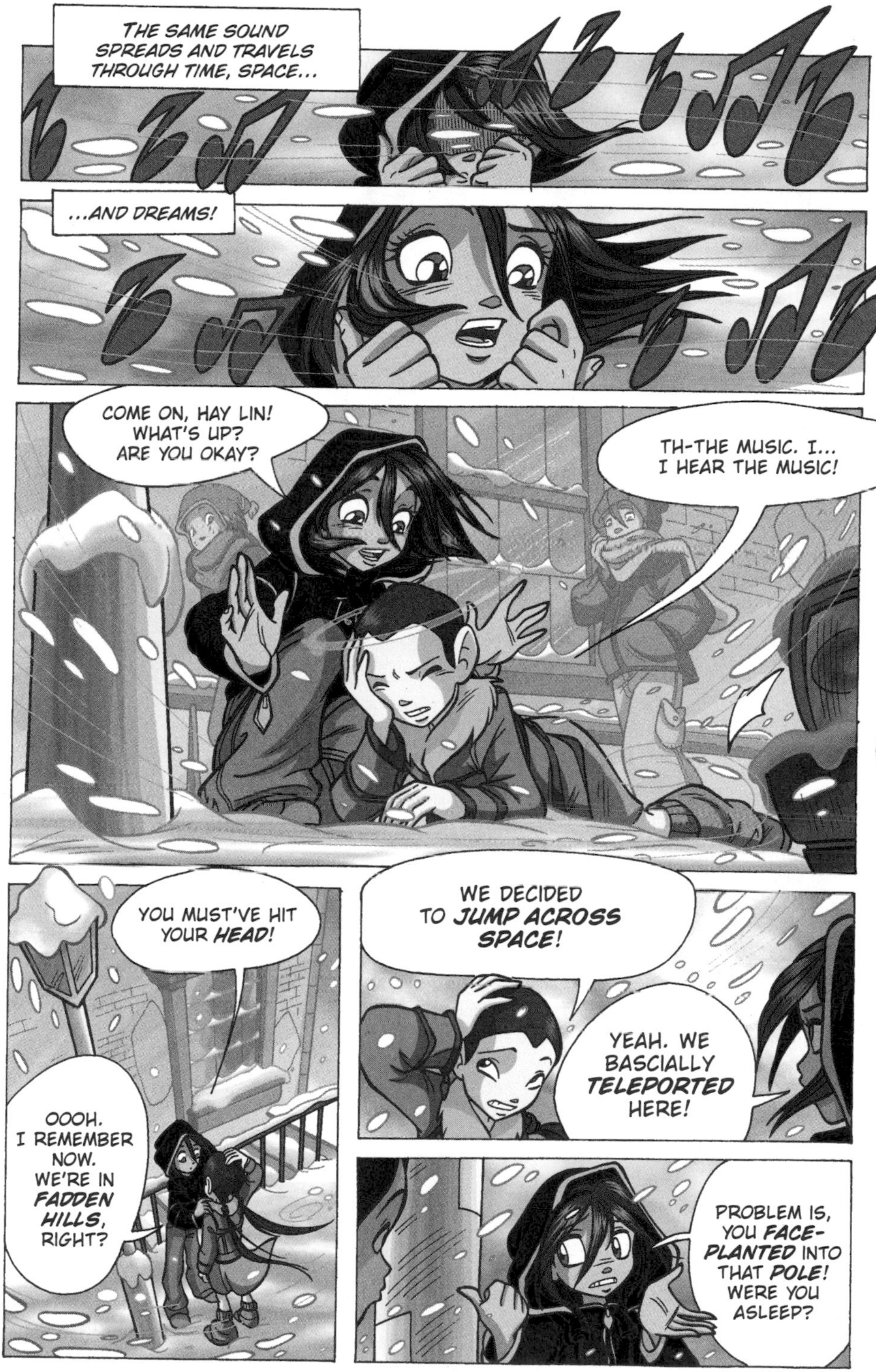

THE SAME SOUND SPREADS AND TRAVELS THROUGH TIME, SPACE...
...AND DREAMS!
COME ON, HAY LIN! WHAT'S UP? ARE YOU OKAY?
TH-THE MUSIC. I... I HEAR THE MUSIC!
YOU MUST'VE HIT YOUR HEAD!
OOOH. I REMEMBER NOW. WE'RE IN FADDEN HILLS, RIGHT?
WE DECIDED TO JUMP ACROSS SPACE!
YEAH. WE BASCIALLY TELEPORTED HERE!
PROBLEM IS, YOU FACE-PLANTED INTO THAT POLE! WERE YOU ASLEEP?

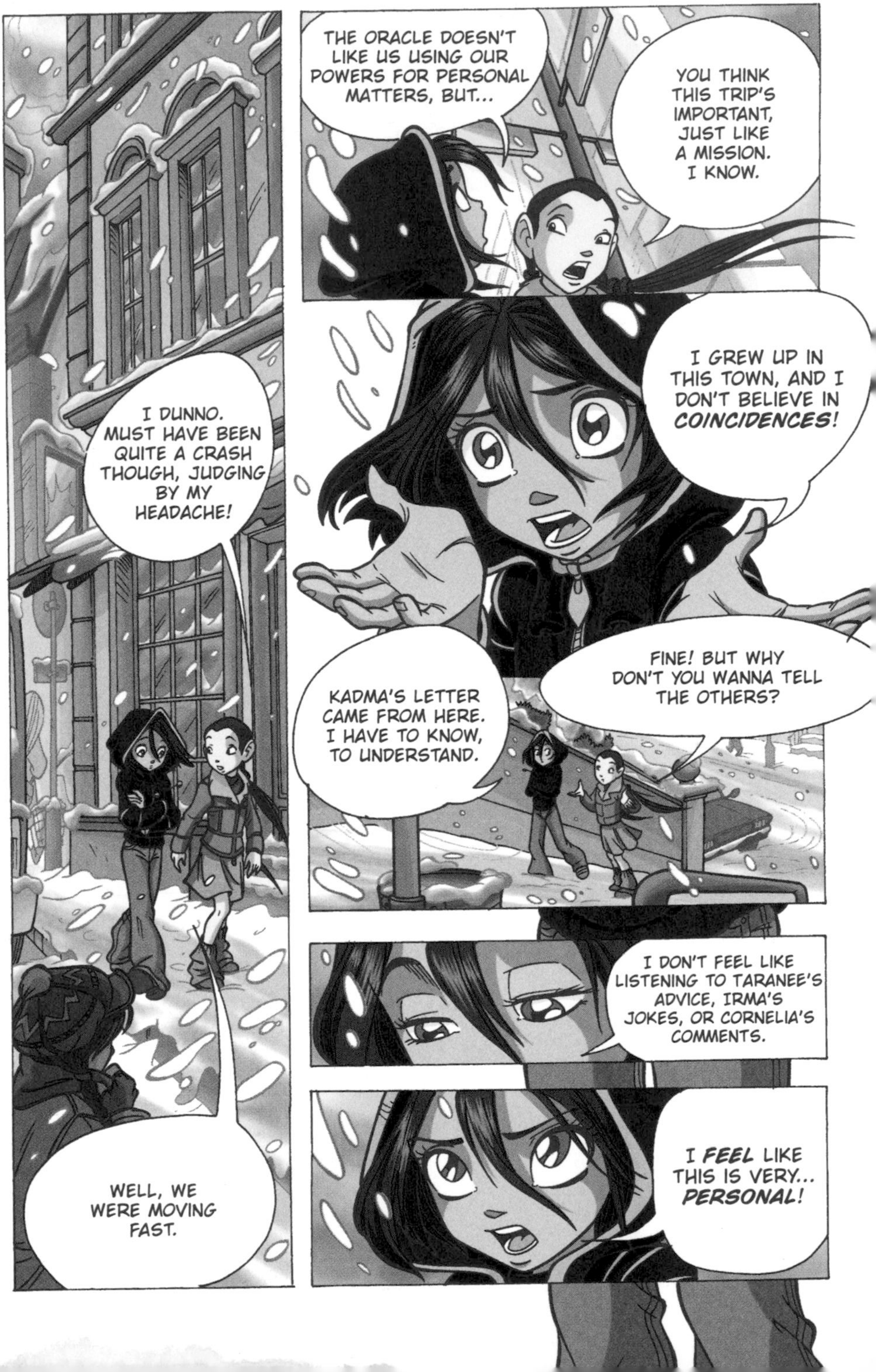
THE ORACLE DOESN'T LIKE US USING OUR POWERS FOR PERSONAL MATTERS, BUT...
YOU THINK THIS TRIP'S IMPORTANT, JUST LIKE A MISSION. I KNOW.
I DUNNO. MUST HAVE BEEN QUITE A CRASH THOUGH, JUDGING BY MY HEADACHE!
I GREW UP IN THIS TOWN, AND I DON'T BELIEVE IN COINCIDENCES!
FINE! BUT WHY DON'T YOU WANNA TELL THE OTHERS?
KADMA'S LETTER CAME FROM HERE. I HAVE TO KNOW, TO UNDERSTAND.
I DON'T FEEL LIKE LISTENING TO TARANEE'S ADVICE, IRMA'S JOKES, OR CORNELIA'S COMMENTS.
WELL, WE WERE MOVING FAST.
I FEEL LIKE THIS IS VERY... PERSONAL!

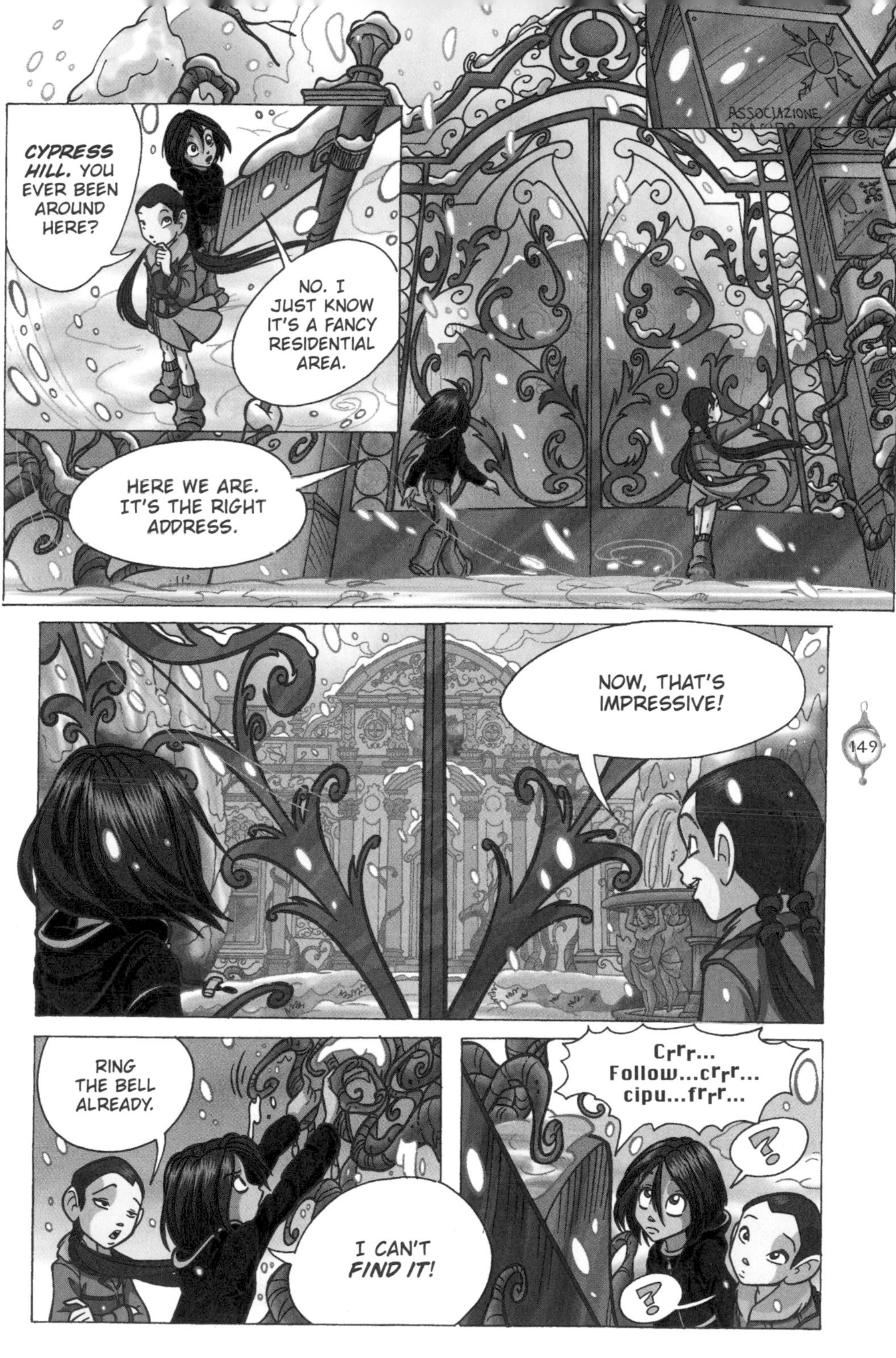
ASSOCIAZIONE
CYPRESS HILL. YOU EVER BEEN AROUND HERE?
NO. I JUST KNOW IT'S A FANCY RESIDENTIAL AREA.
HERE WE ARE. IT'S THE RIGHT ADDRESS.
NOW, THAT'S IMPRESSIVE!
RING THE BELL ALREADY.
I CAN'T FIND IT!
Crrr... Follow...crrr... cipu...frrr...
?
?

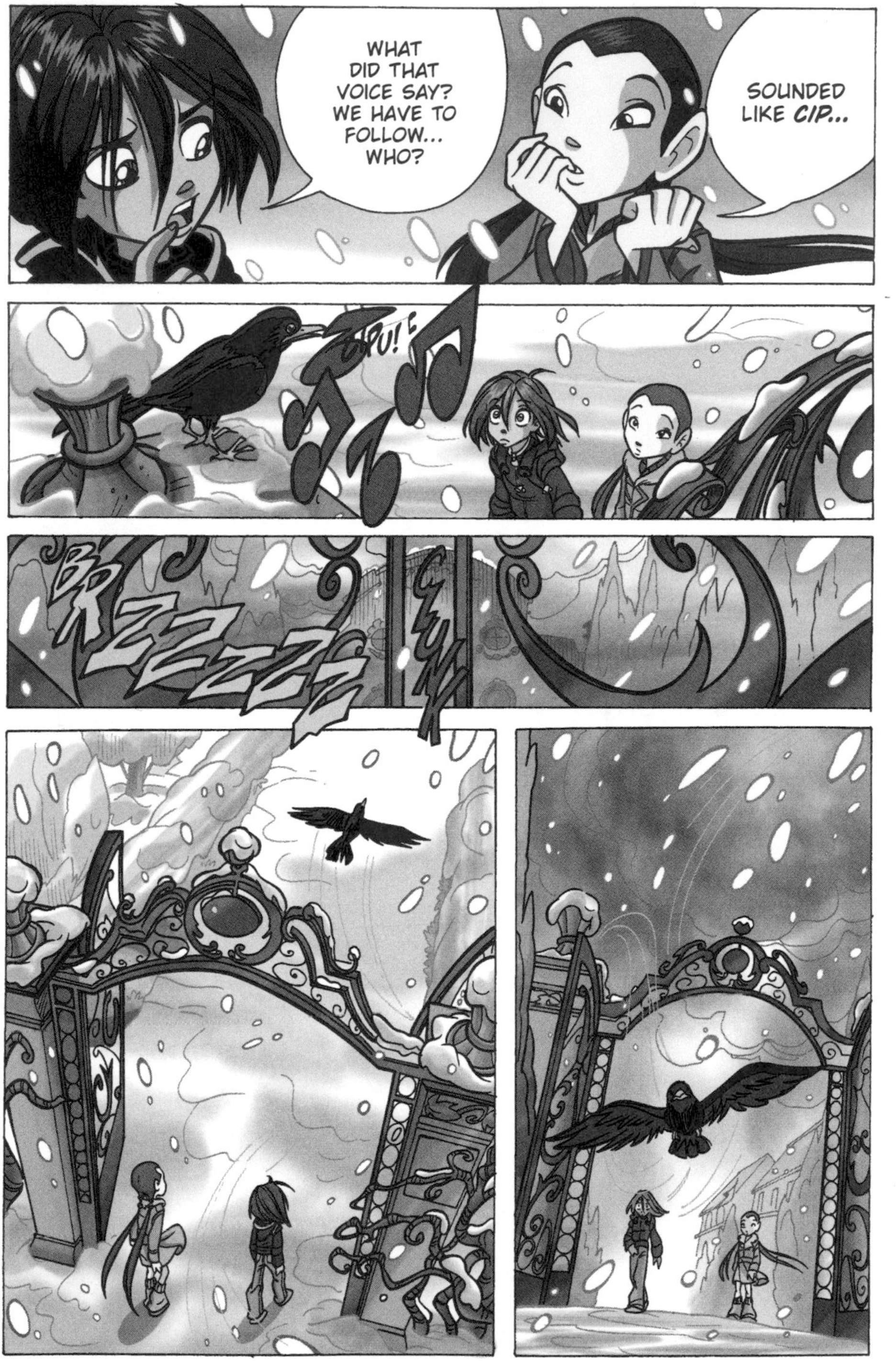
WHAT DID THAT VOICE SAY? WE HAVE TO FOLLOW... WHO?
SOUNDED LIKE *CIP*...
BRZZZZZZ

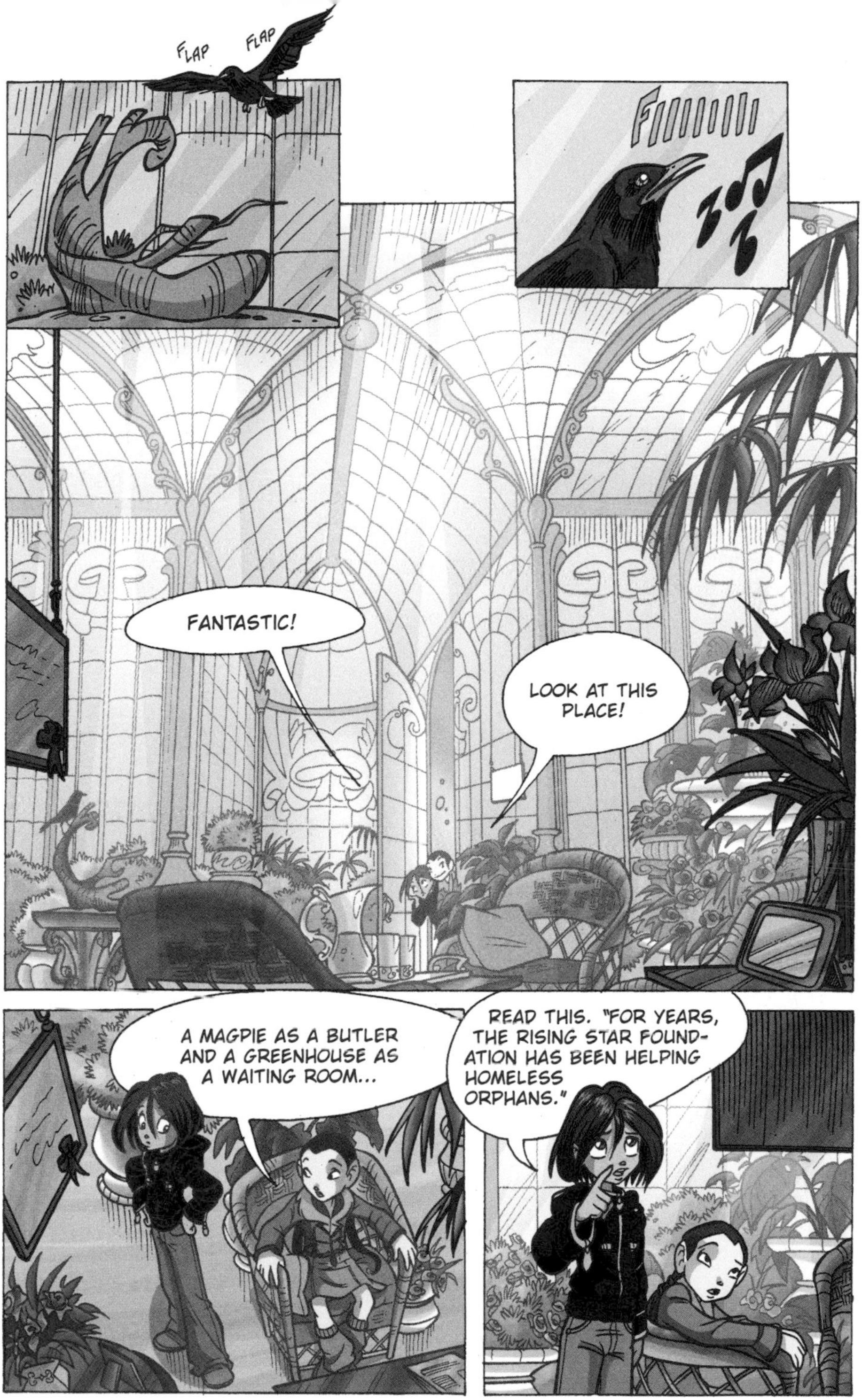
FLAP FLAP
FIIIIIIII
FANTASTIC!
LOOK AT THIS PLACE!
A MAGPIE AS A BUTLER AND A GREENHOUSE AS A WAITING ROOM...
READ THIS. "FOR YEARS, THE RISING STAR FOUNDATION HAS BEEN HELPING HOMELESS ORPHANS."

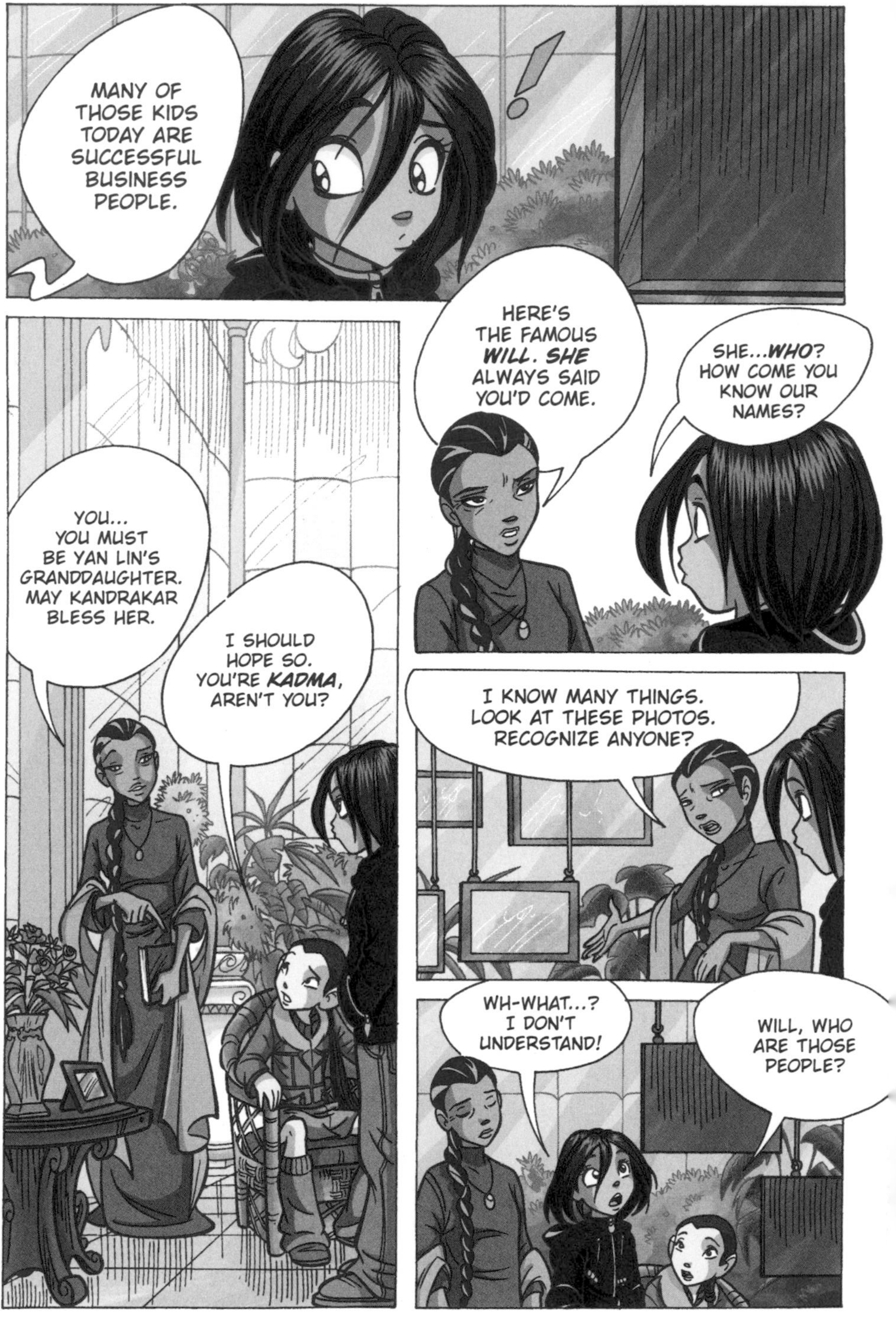
MANY OF THOSE KIDS TODAY ARE SUCCESSFUL BUSINESS PEOPLE.
YOU... YOU MUST BE YAN LIN'S GRANDDAUGHTER. MAY KANDRAKAR BLESS HER.
I SHOULD HOPE SO. YOU'RE KADMA, AREN'T YOU?
HERE'S THE FAMOUS WILL. SHE ALWAYS SAID YOU'D COME.
SHE...WHO? HOW COME YOU KNOW OUR NAMES?
I KNOW MANY THINGS. LOOK AT THESE PHOTOS. RECOGNIZE ANYONE?
WH-WHAT...? I DON'T UNDERSTAND!
WILL, WHO ARE THOSE PEOPLE?

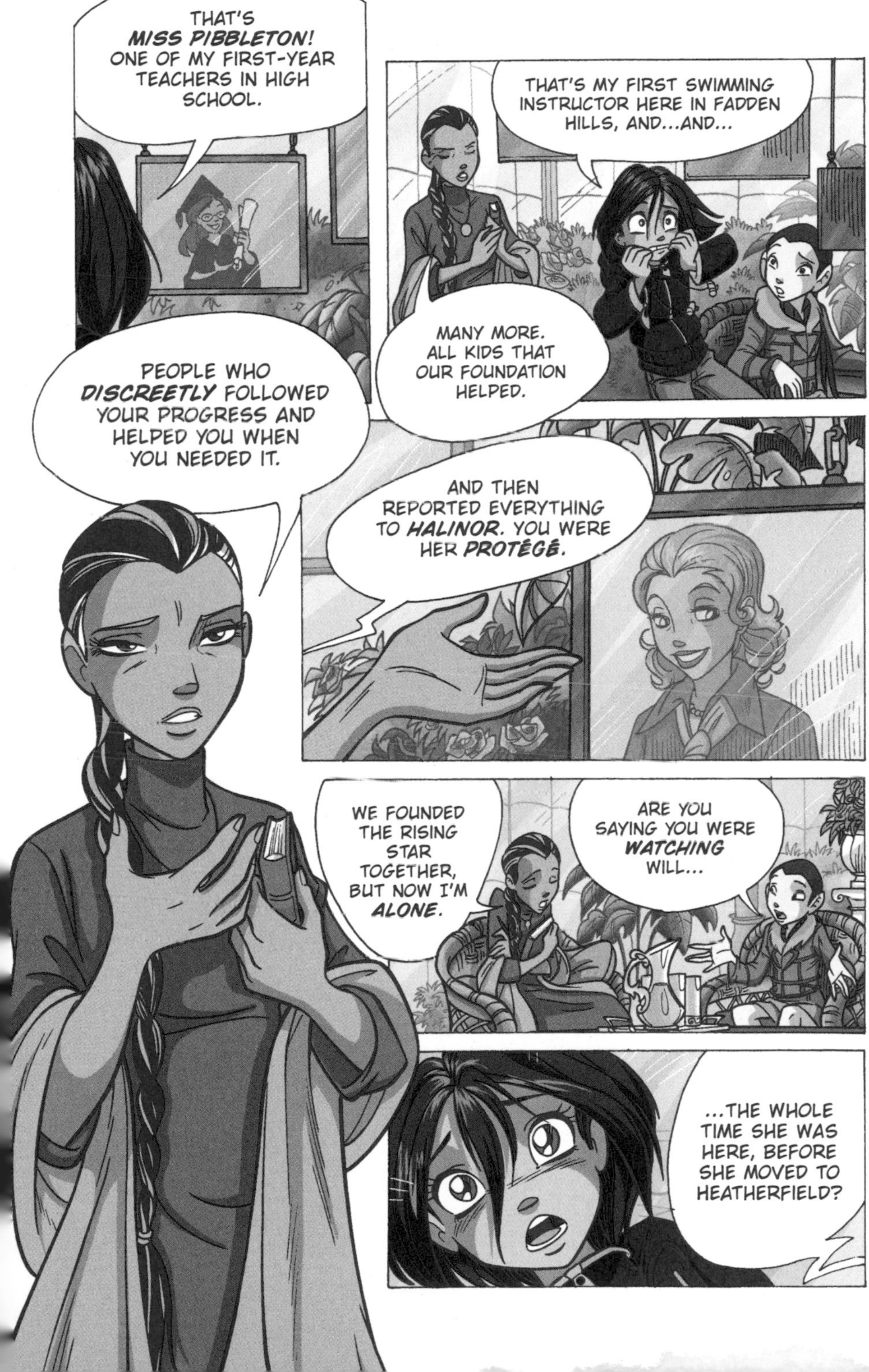
THAT'S MISS PIBBLETON! ONE OF MY FIRST-YEAR TEACHERS IN HIGH SCHOOL.
THAT'S MY FIRST SWIMMING INSTRUCTOR HERE IN FADDEN HILLS, AND...AND...
MANY MORE. ALL KIDS THAT OUR FOUNDATION HELPED.
PEOPLE WHO DISCREETLY FOLLOWED YOUR PROGRESS AND HELPED YOU WHEN YOU NEEDED IT.
AND THEN REPORTED EVERYTHING TO HALINOR. YOU WERE HER PROTÉGÉ.
WE FOUNDED THE RISING STAR TOGETHER, BUT NOW I'M ALONE.
ARE YOU SAYING YOU WERE WATCHING WILL...
...THE WHOLE TIME SHE WAS HERE, BEFORE SHE MOVED TO HEATHERFIELD?

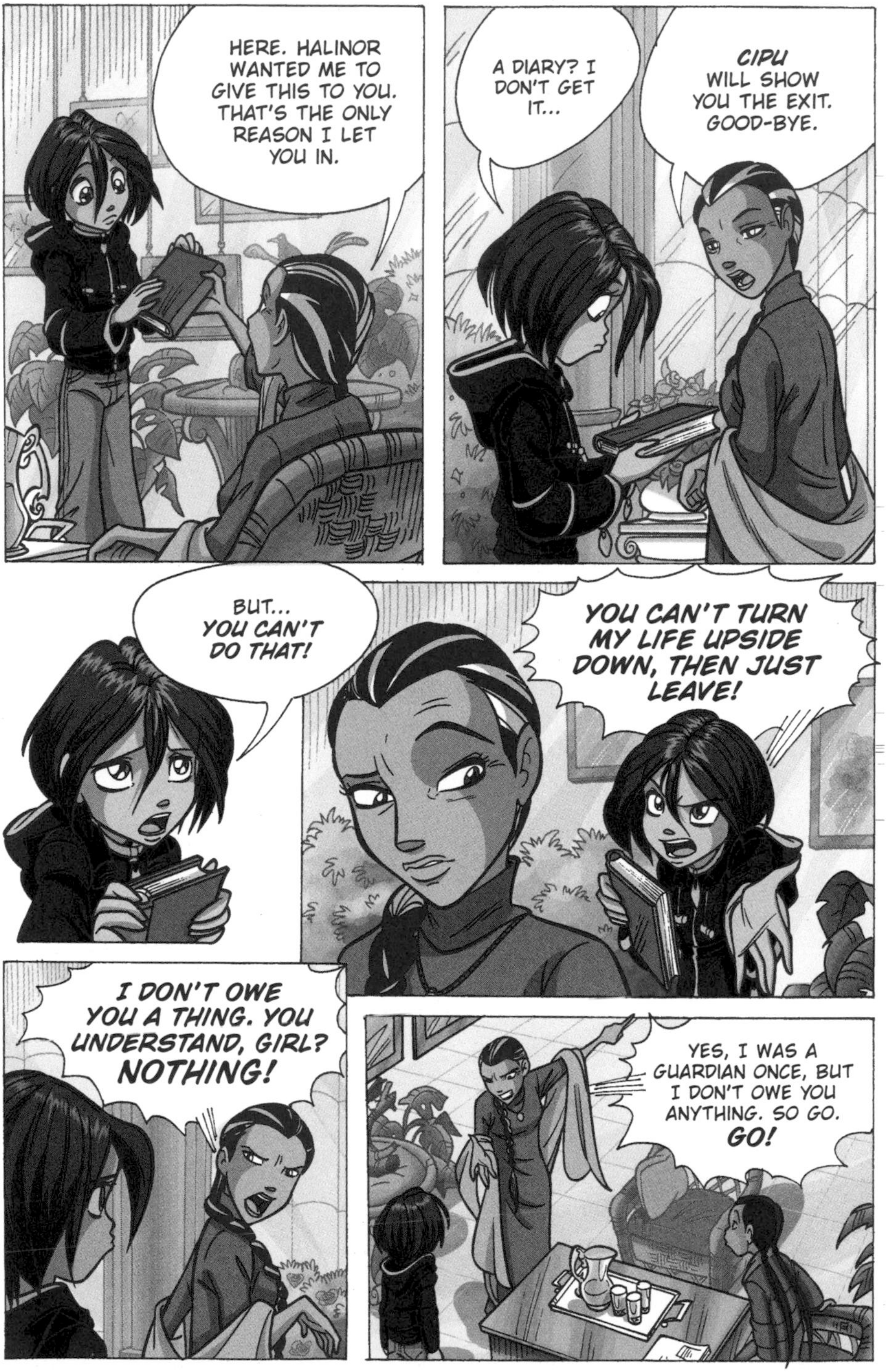

HERE. HALINOR WANTED ME TO GIVE THIS TO YOU. THAT'S THE ONLY REASON I LET YOU IN.
A DIARY? I DON'T GET IT...
CIPU WILL SHOW YOU THE EXIT. GOOD-BYE.
BUT... YOU CAN'T DO THAT!
YOU CAN'T TURN MY LIFE UPSIDE DOWN, THEN JUST LEAVE!
I DON'T OWE YOU A THING. YOU UNDERSTAND, GIRL? NOTHING!
YES, I WAS A GUARDIAN ONCE, BUT I DON'T OWE YOU ANYTHING. SO GO. GO!

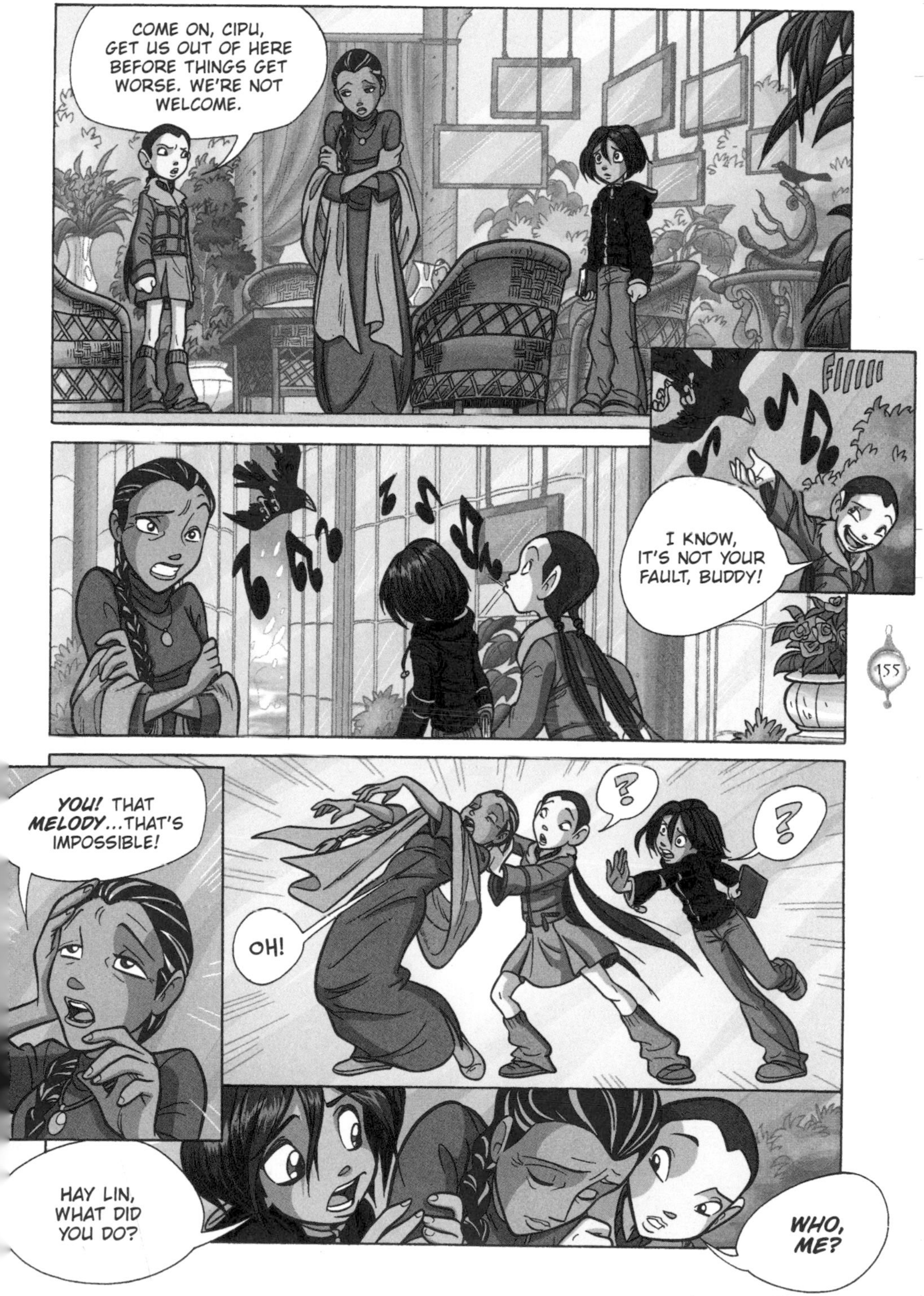
COME ON, CIPU, GET US OUT OF HERE BEFORE THINGS GET WORSE. WE'RE NOT WELCOME.
FIIIIII
I KNOW, IT'S NOT YOUR FAULT, BUDDY!
YOU! THAT MELODY...THAT'S IMPOSSIBLE!
OH!
?
?
HAY LIN, WHAT DID YOU DO?
WHO, ME?

"I WAS JUST *WHISTLING* THAT TUNE THAT'S BEEN IN MY HEAD FOR DAYS."

SO, *NERISSA'S* BACK! HAD I KNOWN, I...

YOU WOULDN'T HAVE BEEN SO *RUDE*?

THAT'S WHAT I DO... ONCE, I HELD THE *POWER OF THE EARTH.*

I SEE THE *CONNECTION.* OUR CORNELIA'S A *BUNDLE OF JOY* TOO...

A FORMER GUARDIAN COMPOSED THAT TUNE.

"SHE WAS A MUSICIAN. SHE NAMED THAT TUNE *NERISSA'S SONG.*"

BACK THEN, SHE AND YOUR GRANDMOTHER WERE REALLY *CLOSE.*

MAYBE THAT'S WHY HAY LIN'S *IMMUNE* TO HER NIGHTMARES.

MAYBE. BUT THAT TUNE'S AN *ALARM SIREN!*

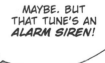

IT MEANS NERISSA'S ALIVE AND WANTS *REVENGE.*

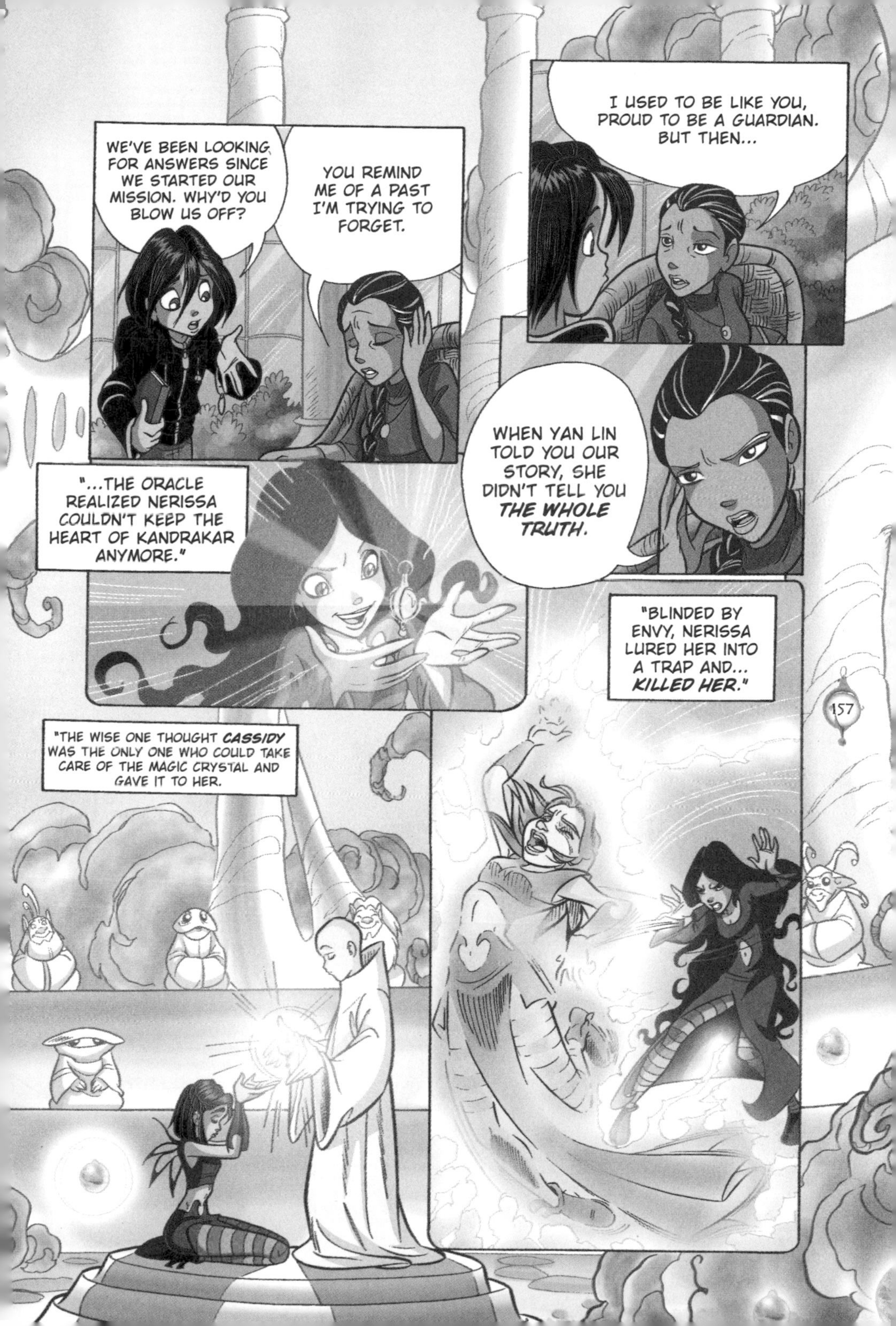
WE'VE BEEN LOOKING FOR ANSWERS SINCE WE STARTED OUR MISSION. WHY'D YOU BLOW US OFF?
YOU REMIND ME OF A PAST I'M TRYING TO FORGET.
I USED TO BE LIKE YOU, PROUD TO BE A GUARDIAN. BUT THEN...
WHEN YAN LIN TOLD YOU OUR STORY, SHE DIDN'T TELL YOU THE WHOLE TRUTH.
"...THE ORACLE REALIZED NERISSA COULDN'T KEEP THE HEART OF KANDRAKAR ANYMORE."
"BLINDED BY ENVY, NERISSA LURED HER INTO A TRAP AND... KILLED HER."
"THE WISE ONE THOUGHT CASSIDY WAS THE ONLY ONE WHO COULD TAKE CARE OF THE MAGIC CRYSTAL AND GAVE IT TO HER.

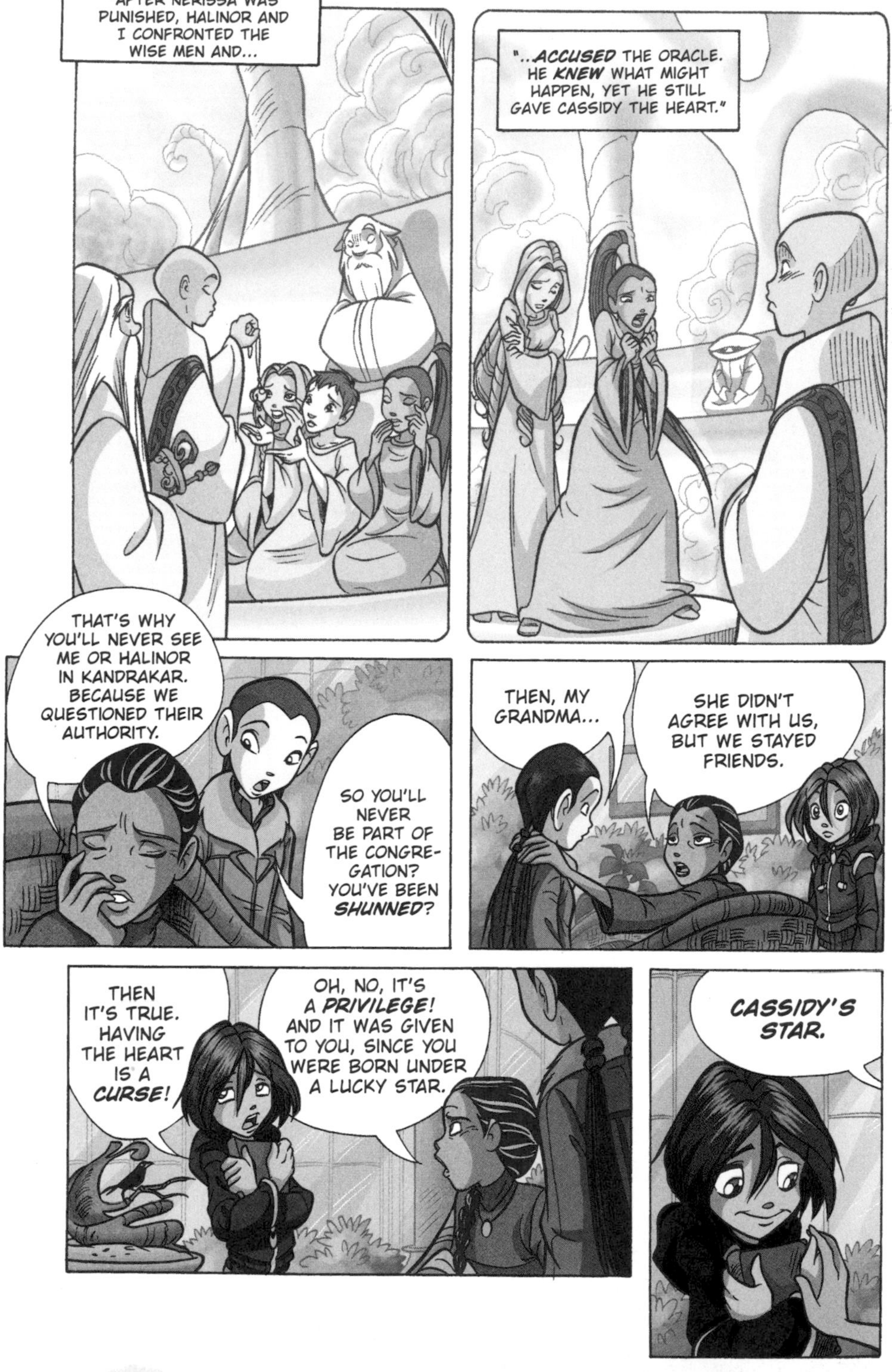
"AFTER NERISSA WAS PUNISHED, HALINOR AND I CONFRONTED THE WISE MEN AND...
"...ACCUSED THE ORACLE. HE KNEW WHAT MIGHT HAPPEN, YET HE STILL GAVE CASSIDY THE HEART."
THAT'S WHY YOU'LL NEVER SEE ME OR HALINOR IN KANDRAKAR. BECAUSE WE QUESTIONED THEIR AUTHORITY.
SO YOU'LL NEVER BE PART OF THE CONGRE-GATION? YOU'VE BEEN SHUNNED?
THEN, MY GRANDMA...
SHE DIDN'T AGREE WITH US, BUT WE STAYED FRIENDS.
THEN IT'S TRUE. HAVING THE HEART IS A CURSE!
OH, NO, IT'S A PRIVILEGE! AND IT WAS GIVEN TO YOU, SINCE YOU WERE BORN UNDER A LUCKY STAR.
CASSIDY'S STAR.

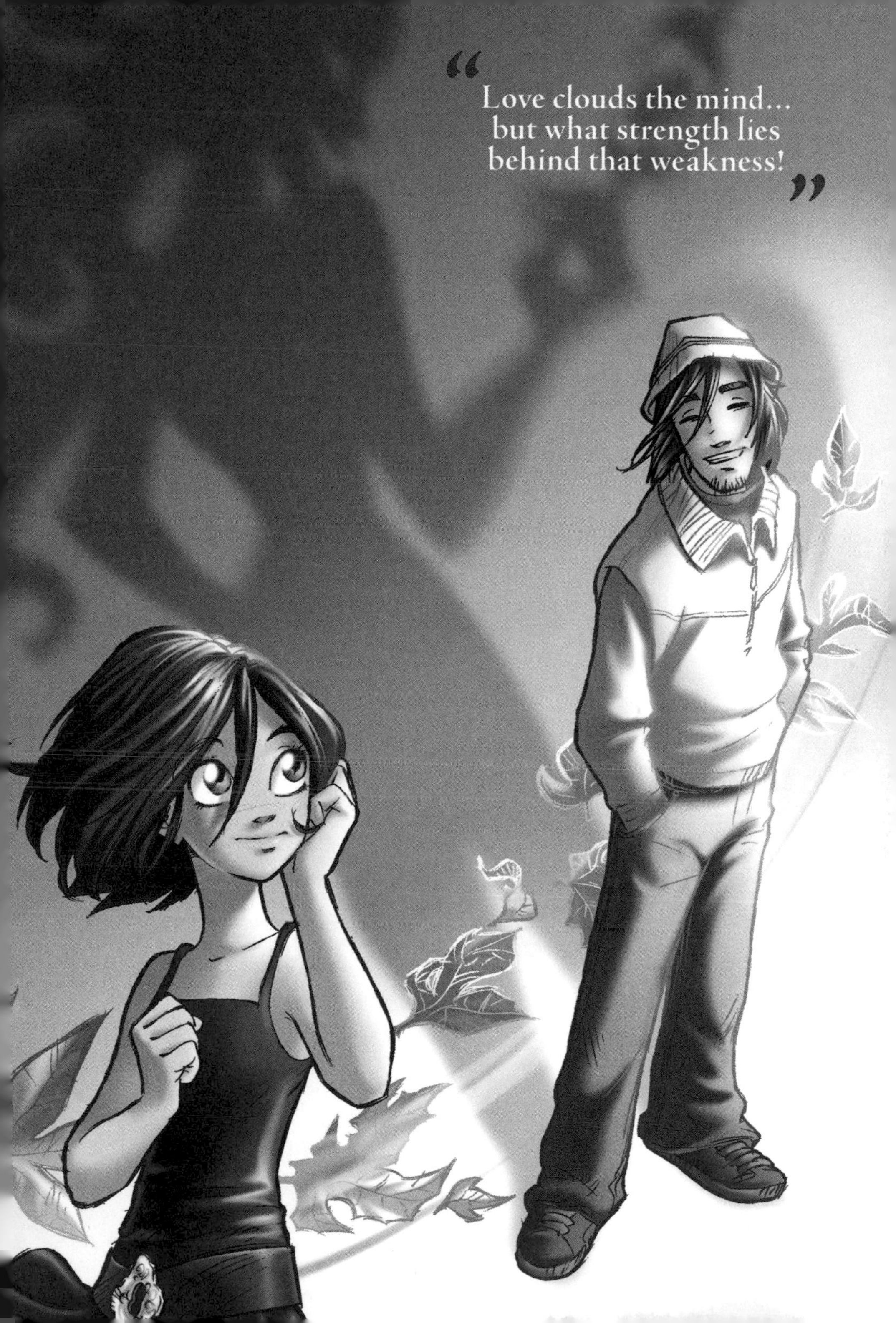
"Love clouds the mind...
but what strength lies
behind that weakness!"

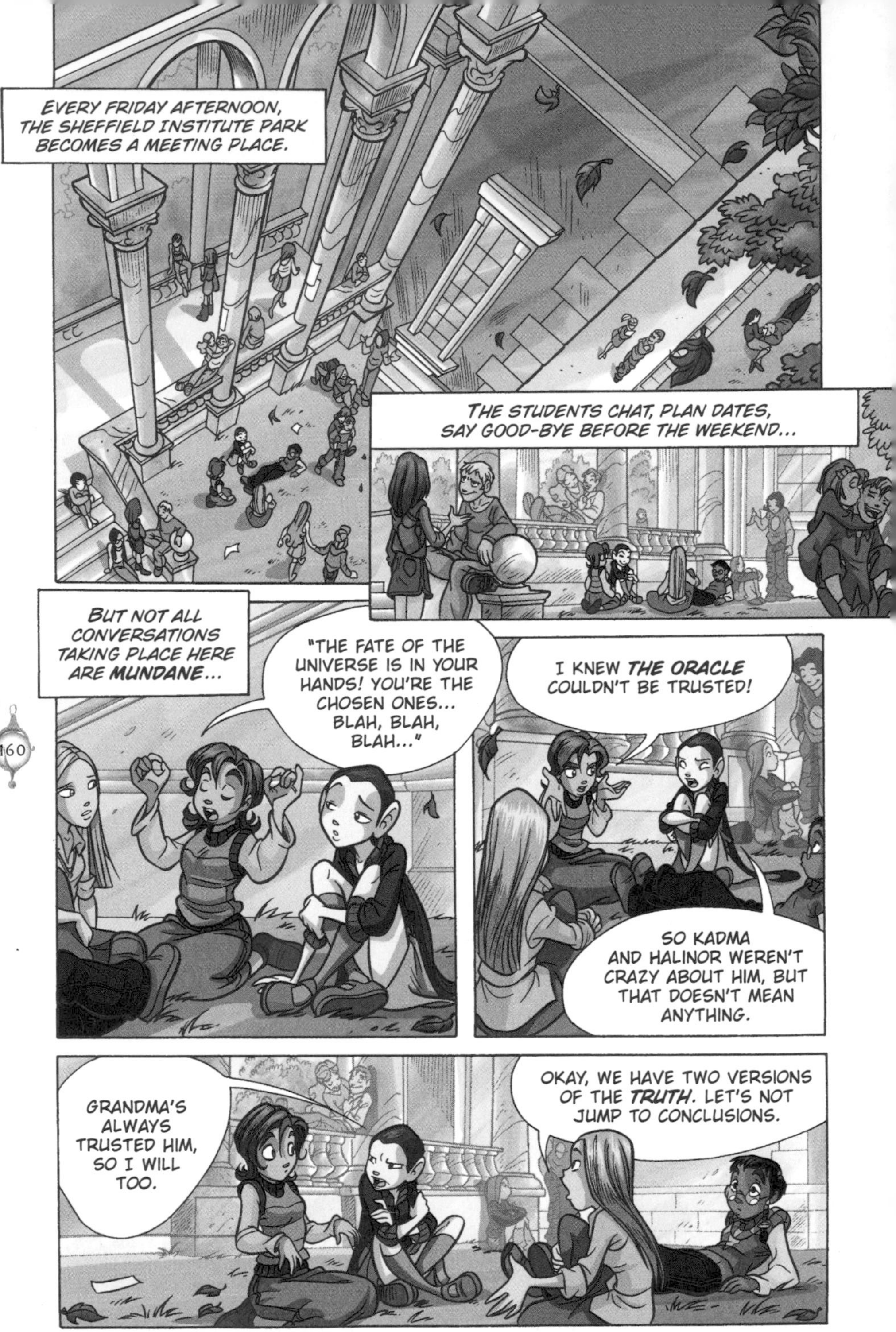
EVERY FRIDAY AFTERNOON, THE SHEFFIELD INSTITUTE PARK BECOMES A MEETING PLACE.
THE STUDENTS CHAT, PLAN DATES, SAY GOOD-BYE BEFORE THE WEEKEND...
BUT NOT ALL CONVERSATIONS TAKING PLACE HERE ARE MUNDANE...
"THE FATE OF THE UNIVERSE IS IN YOUR HANDS! YOU'RE THE CHOSEN ONES... BLAH, BLAH, BLAH..."
I KNEW THE ORACLE COULDN'T BE TRUSTED!
SO KADMA AND HALINOR WEREN'T CRAZY ABOUT HIM, BUT THAT DOESN'T MEAN ANYTHING.
GRANDMA'S ALWAYS TRUSTED HIM, SO I WILL TOO.
OKAY, WE HAVE TWO VERSIONS OF THE TRUTH. LET'S NOT JUMP TO CONCLUSIONS.

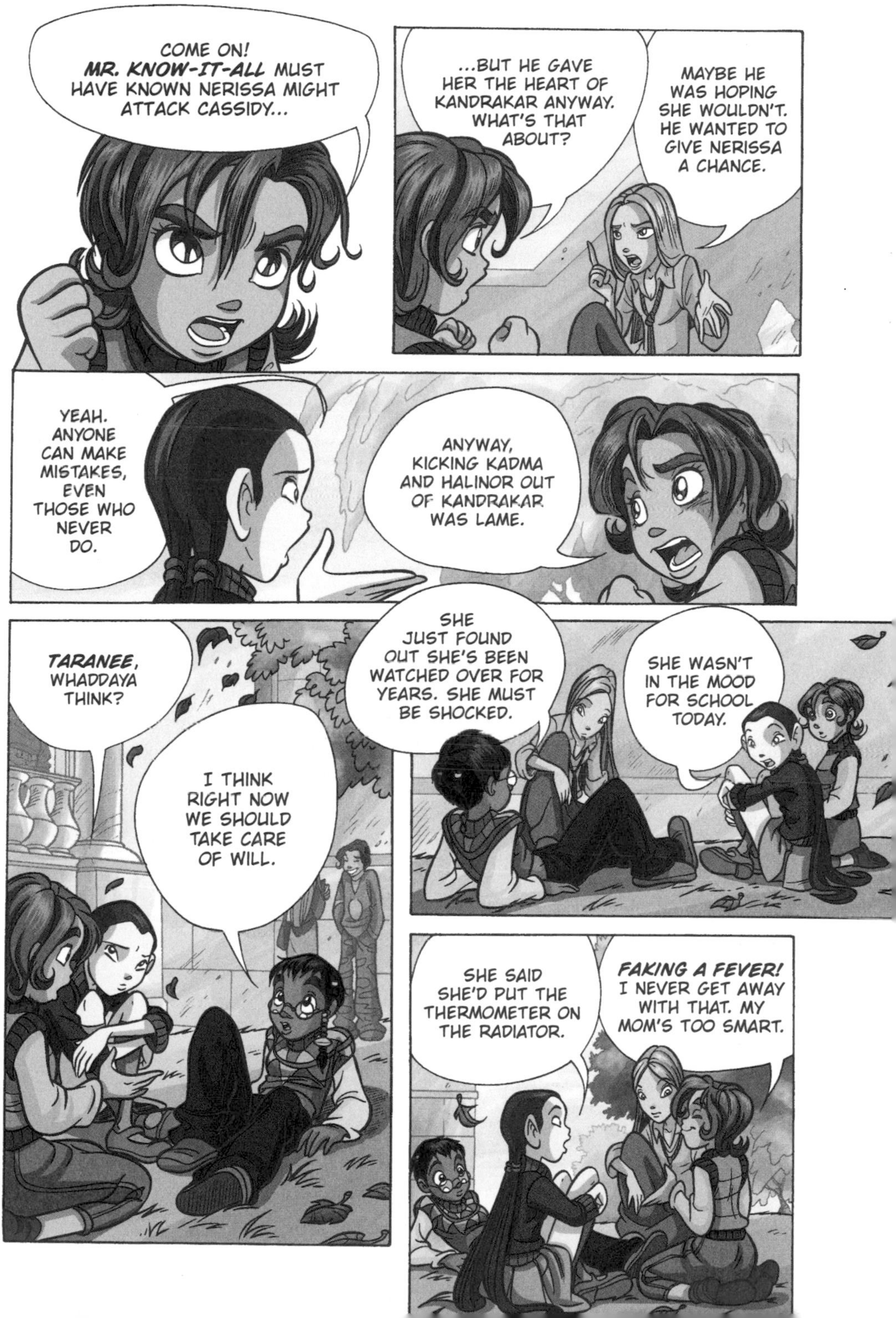
COME ON! MR. KNOW-IT-ALL MUST HAVE KNOWN NERISSA MIGHT ATTACK CASSIDY...
...BUT HE GAVE HER THE HEART OF KANDRAKAR ANYWAY. WHAT'S THAT ABOUT?
MAYBE HE WAS HOPING SHE WOULDN'T. HE WANTED TO GIVE NERISSA A CHANCE.
YEAH. ANYONE CAN MAKE MISTAKES, EVEN THOSE WHO NEVER DO.
ANYWAY, KICKING KADMA AND HALINOR OUT OF KANDRAKAR WAS LAME.
TARANEE, WHADDAYA THINK?
I THINK RIGHT NOW WE SHOULD TAKE CARE OF WILL.
SHE JUST FOUND OUT SHE'S BEEN WATCHED OVER FOR YEARS. SHE MUST BE SHOCKED.
SHE WASN'T IN THE MOOD FOR SCHOOL TODAY.
SHE SAID SHE'D PUT THE THERMOMETER ON THE RADIATOR.
FAKING A FEVER! I NEVER GET AWAY WITH THAT. MY MOM'S TOO SMART.

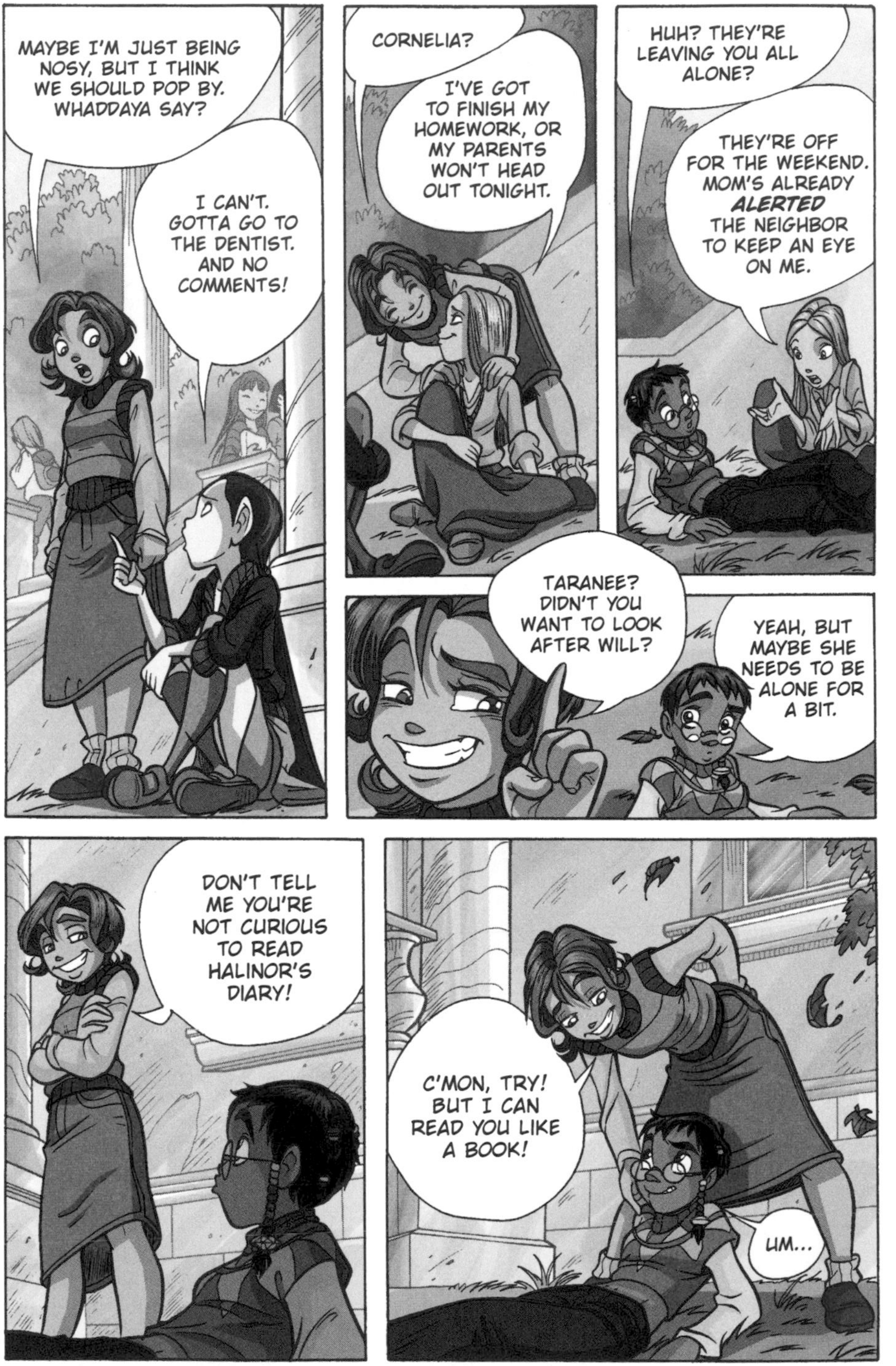

MAYBE I'M JUST BEING NOSY, BUT I THINK WE SHOULD POP BY. WHADDAYA SAY?
I CAN'T. GOTTA GO TO THE DENTIST. AND NO COMMENTS!
CORNELIA?
I'VE GOT TO FINISH MY HOMEWORK, OR MY PARENTS WON'T HEAD OUT TONIGHT.
HUH? THEY'RE LEAVING YOU ALL ALONE?
THEY'RE OFF FOR THE WEEKEND. MOM'S ALREADY ***ALERTED*** THE NEIGHBOR TO KEEP AN EYE ON ME.
TARANEE? DIDN'T YOU WANT TO LOOK AFTER WILL?
YEAH, BUT MAYBE SHE NEEDS TO BE ALONE FOR A BIT.
DON'T TELL ME YOU'RE NOT CURIOUS TO READ HALINOR'S DIARY!
C'MON, TRY! BUT I CAN READ YOU LIKE A BOOK!
UM...

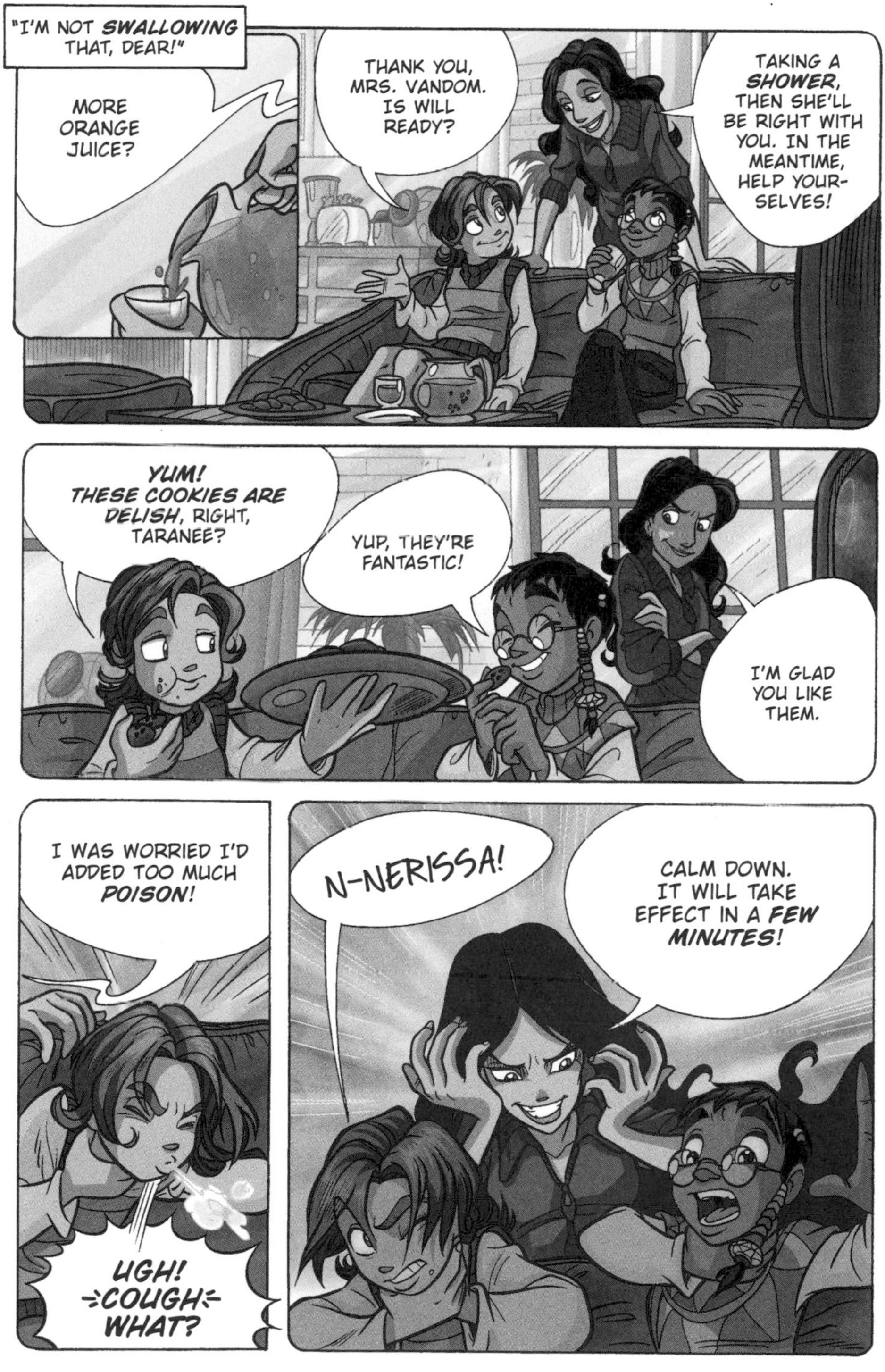
"I'M NOT SWALLOWING THAT, DEAR!"
MORE ORANGE JUICE?
THANK YOU, MRS. VANDOM. IS WILL READY?
TAKING A SHOWER, THEN SHE'LL BE RIGHT WITH YOU. IN THE MEANTIME, HELP YOURSELVES!
YUM! THESE COOKIES ARE DELISH, RIGHT, TARANEE?
YUP, THEY'RE FANTASTIC!
I'M GLAD YOU LIKE THEM.
I WAS WORRIED I'D ADDED TOO MUCH POISON!
UGH! COUGH WHAT?
N-NERISSA!
CALM DOWN. IT WILL TAKE EFFECT IN A FEW MINUTES!

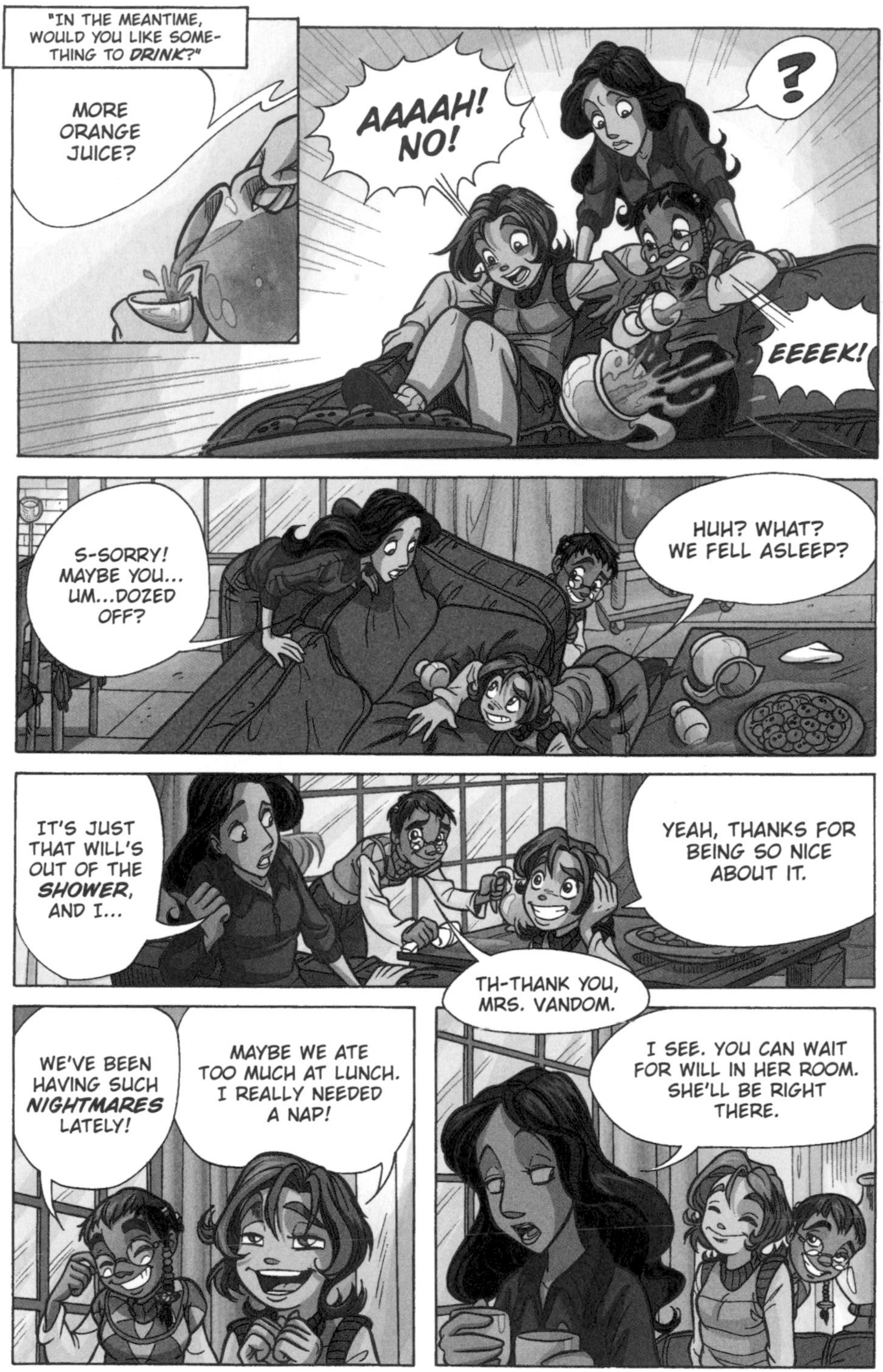
"IN THE MEANTIME, WOULD YOU LIKE SOMETHING TO DRINK?"
MORE ORANGE JUICE?
AAAAH! NO!
?
EEEEK!
S-SORRY! MAYBE YOU... UM...DOZED OFF?
HUH? WHAT? WE FELL ASLEEP?
IT'S JUST THAT WILL'S OUT OF THE SHOWER, AND I...
YEAH, THANKS FOR BEING SO NICE ABOUT IT.
TH-THANK YOU, MRS. VANDOM.
WE'VE BEEN HAVING SUCH NIGHTMARES LATELY!
MAYBE WE ATE TOO MUCH AT LUNCH. I REALLY NEEDED A NAP!
I SEE. YOU CAN WAIT FOR WILL IN HER ROOM. SHE'LL BE RIGHT THERE.

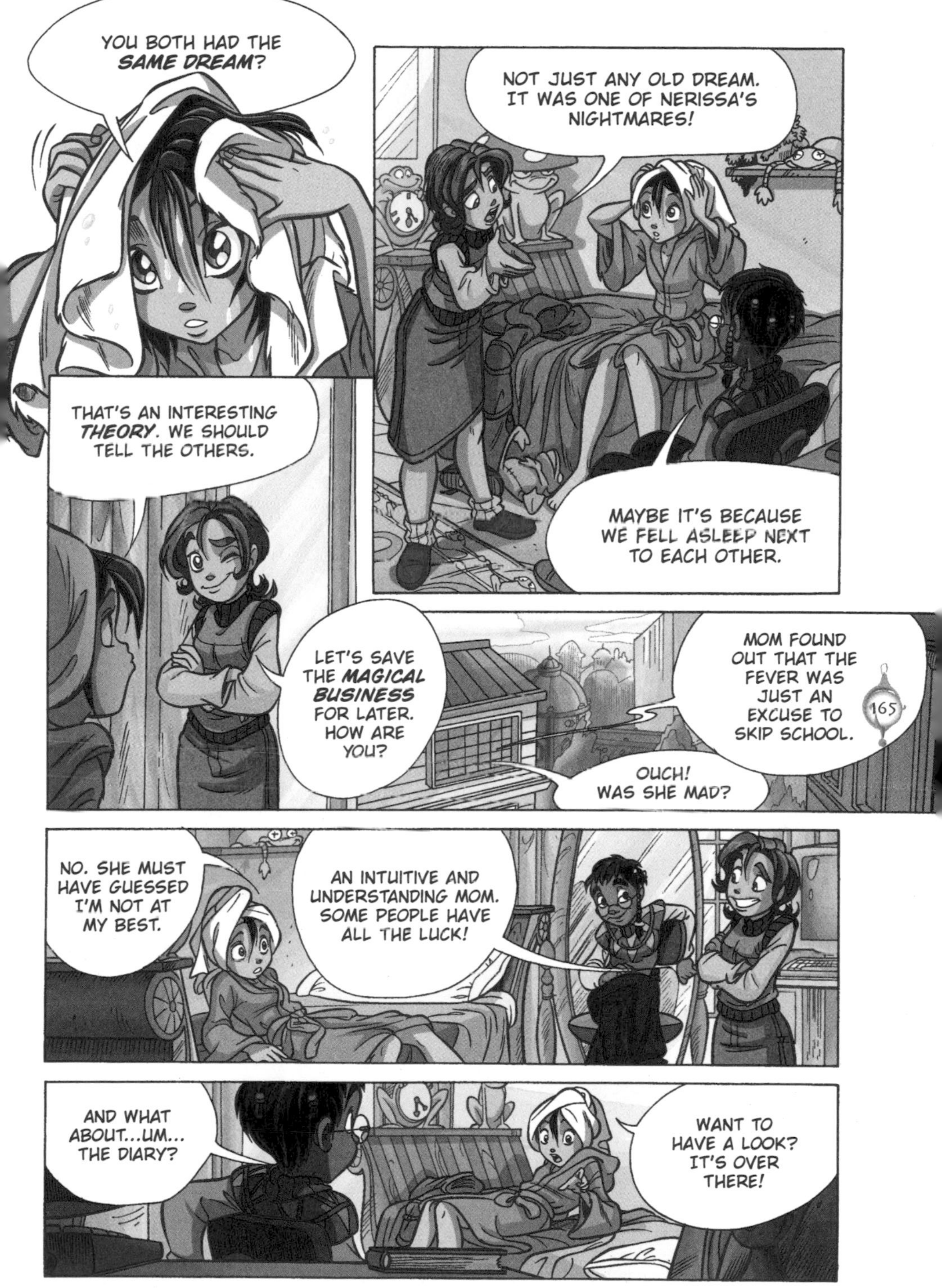
YOU BOTH HAD THE *SAME DREAM*?
NOT JUST ANY OLD DREAM. IT WAS ONE OF NERISSA'S NIGHTMARES!
MAYBE IT'S BECAUSE WE FELL ASLEEP NEXT TO EACH OTHER.
THAT'S AN INTERESTING *THEORY*. WE SHOULD TELL THE OTHERS.
LET'S SAVE THE *MAGICAL BUSINESS* FOR LATER. HOW ARE YOU?
MOM FOUND OUT THAT THE FEVER WAS JUST AN EXCUSE TO SKIP SCHOOL.
OUCH! WAS SHE MAD?
NO. SHE MUST HAVE GUESSED I'M NOT AT MY BEST.
AN INTUITIVE AND UNDERSTANDING MOM. SOME PEOPLE HAVE ALL THE LUCK!
AND WHAT ABOUT...UM... THE DIARY?
WANT TO HAVE A LOOK? IT'S OVER THERE!

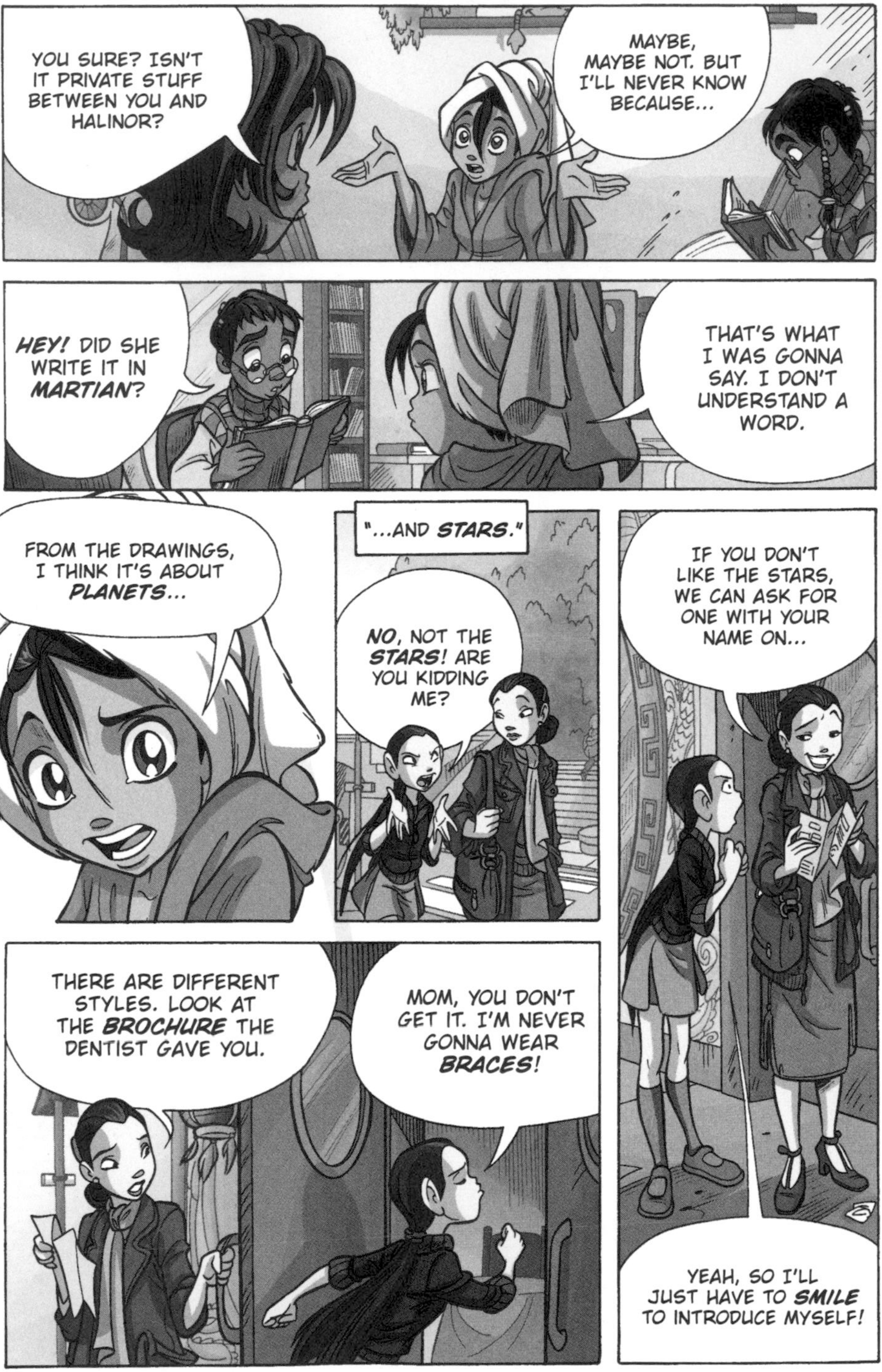
YOU SURE? ISN'T IT PRIVATE STUFF BETWEEN YOU AND HALINOR?
MAYBE, MAYBE NOT. BUT I'LL NEVER KNOW BECAUSE...
HEY! DID SHE WRITE IT IN MARTIAN?
THAT'S WHAT I WAS GONNA SAY. I DON'T UNDERSTAND A WORD.
FROM THE DRAWINGS, I THINK IT'S ABOUT PLANETS...
"...AND STARS."
NO, NOT THE STARS! ARE YOU KIDDING ME?
IF YOU DON'T LIKE THE STARS, WE CAN ASK FOR ONE WITH YOUR NAME ON...
THERE ARE DIFFERENT STYLES. LOOK AT THE BROCHURE THE DENTIST GAVE YOU.
MOM, YOU DON'T GET IT. I'M NEVER GONNA WEAR BRACES!
YEAH, SO I'LL JUST HAVE TO SMILE TO INTRODUCE MYSELF!

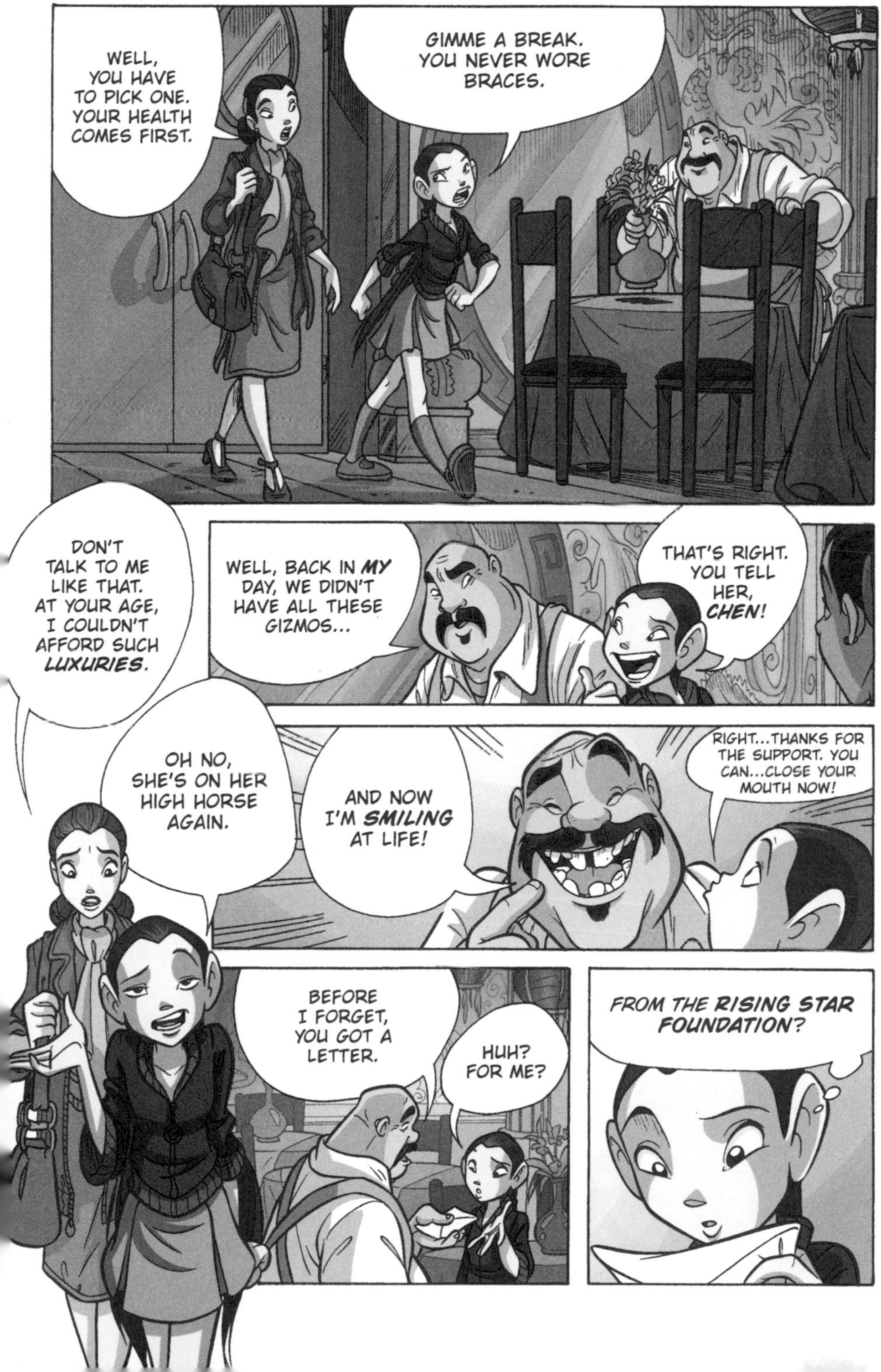

WELL, YOU HAVE TO PICK ONE. YOUR HEALTH COMES FIRST.
GIMME A BREAK. YOU NEVER WORE BRACES.
DON'T TALK TO ME LIKE THAT. AT YOUR AGE, I COULDN'T AFFORD SUCH *LUXURIES*.
WELL, BACK IN *MY* DAY, WE DIDN'T HAVE ALL THESE GIZMOS...
THAT'S RIGHT. YOU TELL HER, *CHEN*!
OH NO, SHE'S ON HER HIGH HORSE AGAIN.
AND NOW I'M *SMILING* AT LIFE!
RIGHT...THANKS FOR THE SUPPORT. YOU CAN...CLOSE YOUR MOUTH NOW!
BEFORE I FORGET, YOU GOT A LETTER.
HUH? FOR ME?
*FROM THE **RISING STAR FOUNDATION**?*

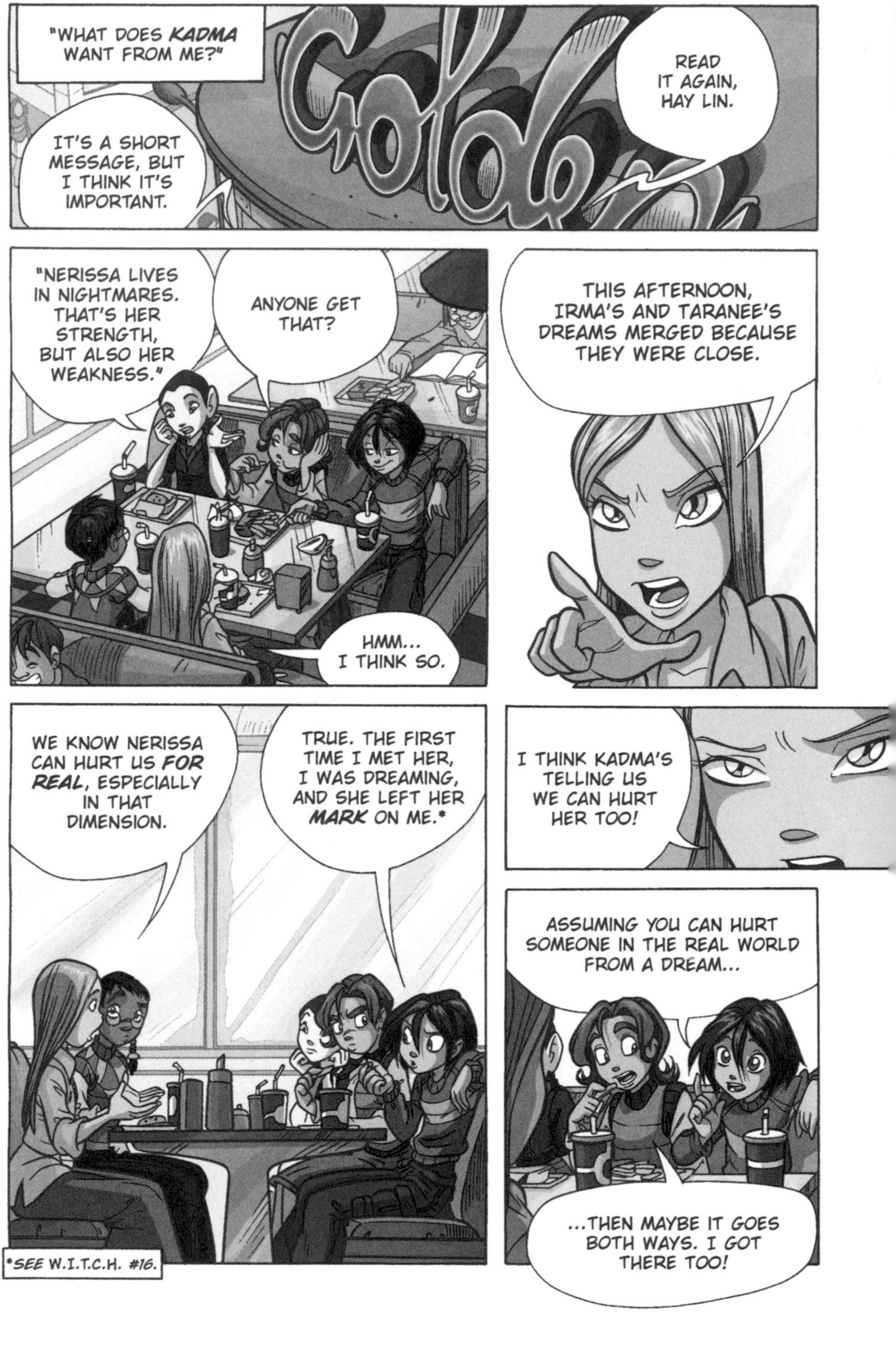
"WHAT DOES KADMA WANT FROM ME?"
READ IT AGAIN, HAY LIN.
IT'S A SHORT MESSAGE, BUT I THINK IT'S IMPORTANT.
"NERISSA LIVES IN NIGHTMARES. THAT'S HER STRENGTH, BUT ALSO HER WEAKNESS."
ANYONE GET THAT?
HMM... I THINK SO.
THIS AFTERNOON, IRMA'S AND TARANEE'S DREAMS MERGED BECAUSE THEY WERE CLOSE.
WE KNOW NERISSA CAN HURT US FOR REAL, ESPECIALLY IN THAT DIMENSION.
TRUE. THE FIRST TIME I MET HER, I WAS DREAMING, AND SHE LEFT HER MARK ON ME.*
I THINK KADMA'S TELLING US WE CAN HURT HER TOO!
ASSUMING YOU CAN HURT SOMEONE IN THE REAL WORLD FROM A DREAM...
...THEN MAYBE IT GOES BOTH WAYS. I GOT THERE TOO!

*SEE W.I.T.C.H. #16.

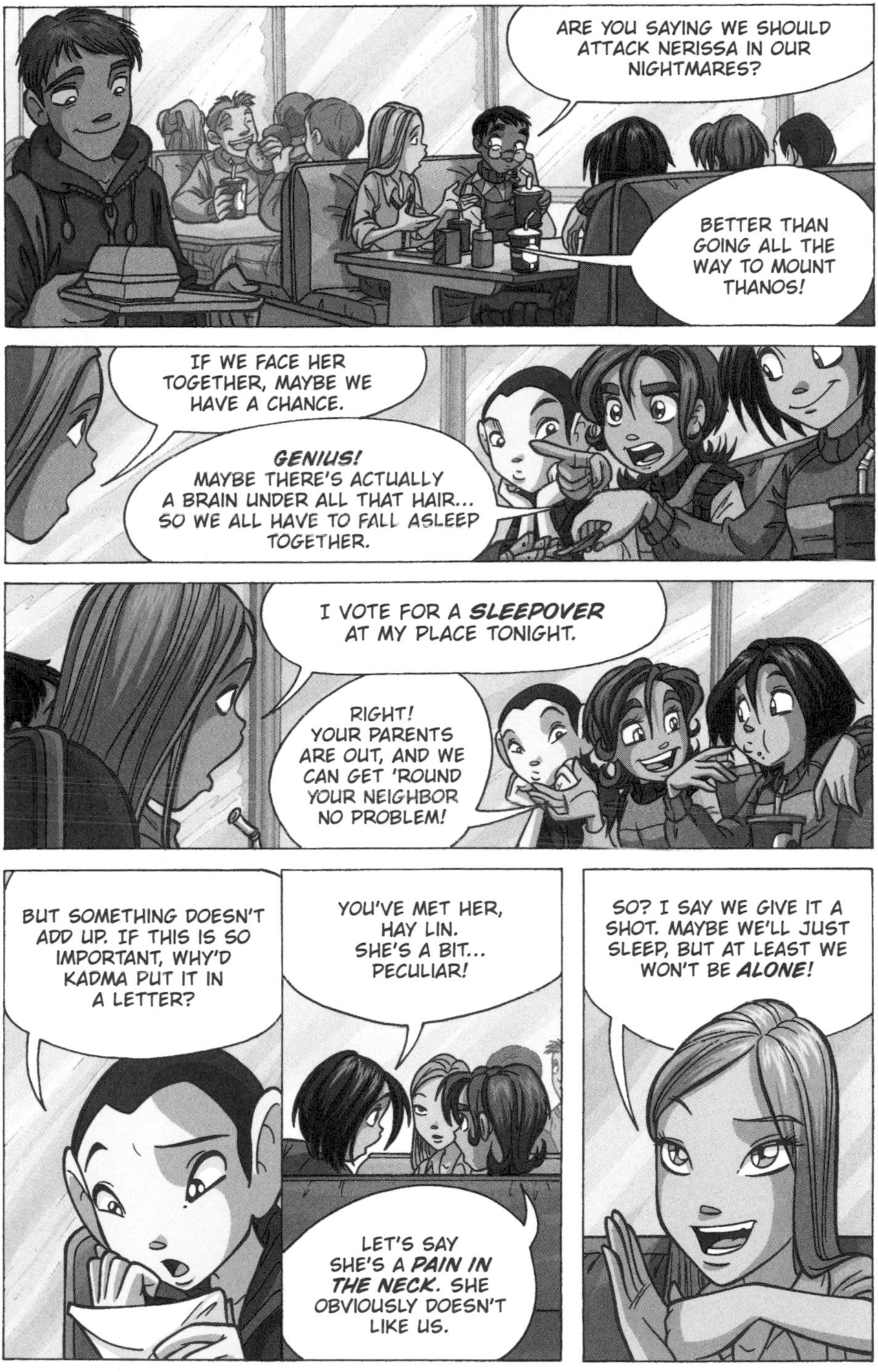
ARE YOU SAYING WE SHOULD ATTACK NERISSA IN OUR NIGHTMARES?
BETTER THAN GOING ALL THE WAY TO MOUNT THANOS!
IF WE FACE HER TOGETHER, MAYBE WE HAVE A CHANCE.
GENIUS! MAYBE THERE'S ACTUALLY A BRAIN UNDER ALL THAT HAIR... SO WE ALL HAVE TO FALL ASLEEP TOGETHER.
I VOTE FOR A SLEEPOVER AT MY PLACE TONIGHT.
RIGHT! YOUR PARENTS ARE OUT, AND WE CAN GET 'ROUND YOUR NEIGHBOR NO PROBLEM!
BUT SOMETHING DOESN'T ADD UP. IF THIS IS SO IMPORTANT, WHY'D KADMA PUT IT IN A LETTER?
YOU'VE MET HER, HAY LIN. SHE'S A BIT... PECULIAR!
LET'S SAY SHE'S A PAIN IN THE NECK. SHE OBVIOUSLY DOESN'T LIKE US.
SO? I SAY WE GIVE IT A SHOT. MAYBE WE'LL JUST SLEEP, BUT AT LEAST WE WON'T BE ALONE!

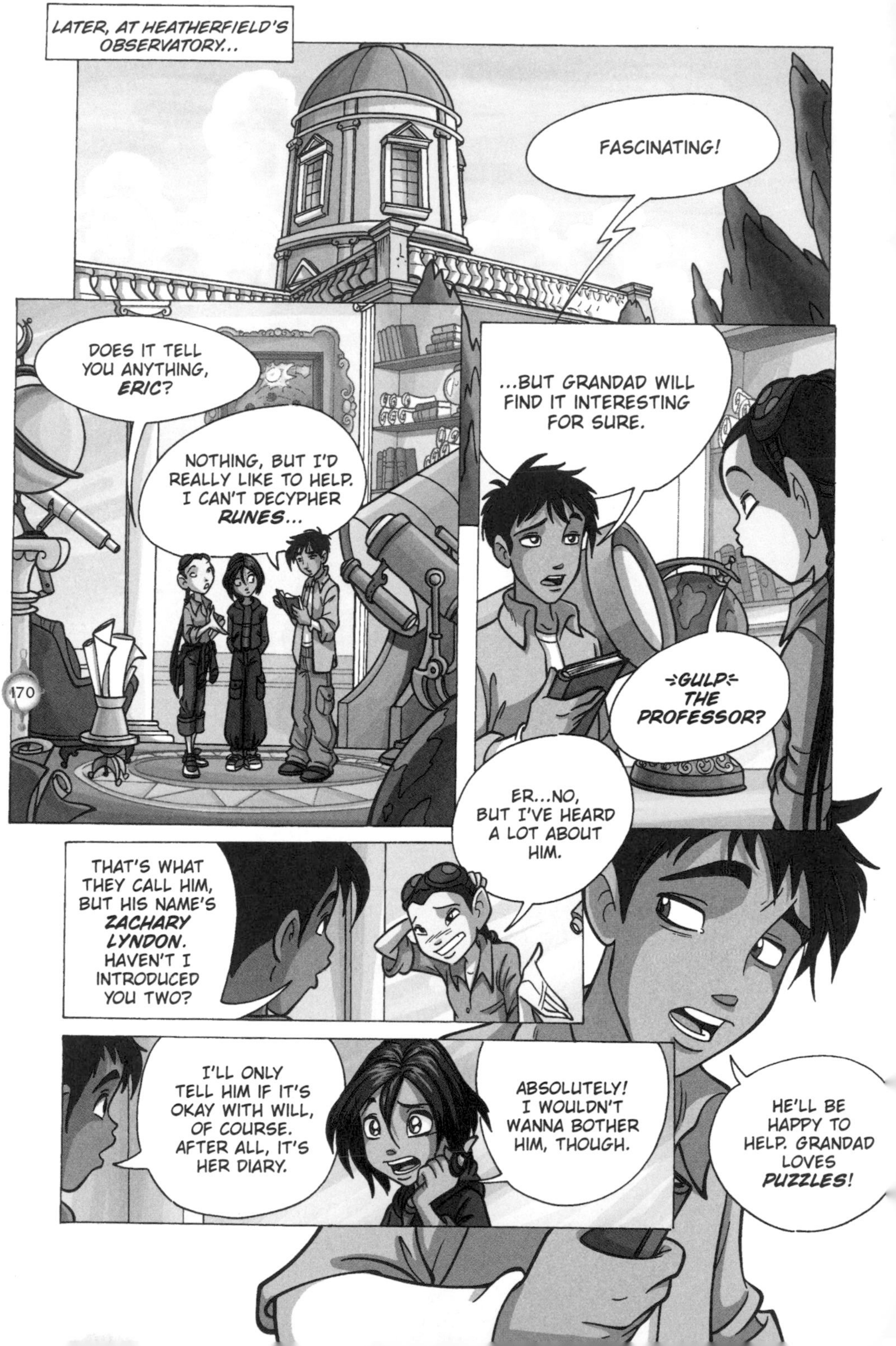
LATER, AT HEATHERFIELD'S OBSERVATORY...
FASCINATING!
DOES IT TELL YOU ANYTHING, ERIC?
NOTHING, BUT I'D REALLY LIKE TO HELP. I CAN'T DECYPHER RUNES...
...BUT GRANDAD WILL FIND IT INTERESTING FOR SURE.
=GULP= THE PROFESSOR?
ER...NO, BUT I'VE HEARD A LOT ABOUT HIM.
THAT'S WHAT THEY CALL HIM, BUT HIS NAME'S ZACHARY LYNDON. HAVEN'T I INTRODUCED YOU TWO?
HE'LL BE HAPPY TO HELP. GRANDAD LOVES PUZZLES!
ABSOLUTELY! I WOULDN'T WANNA BOTHER HIM, THOUGH.
I'LL ONLY TELL HIM IF IT'S OKAY WITH WILL, OF COURSE. AFTER ALL, IT'S HER DIARY.

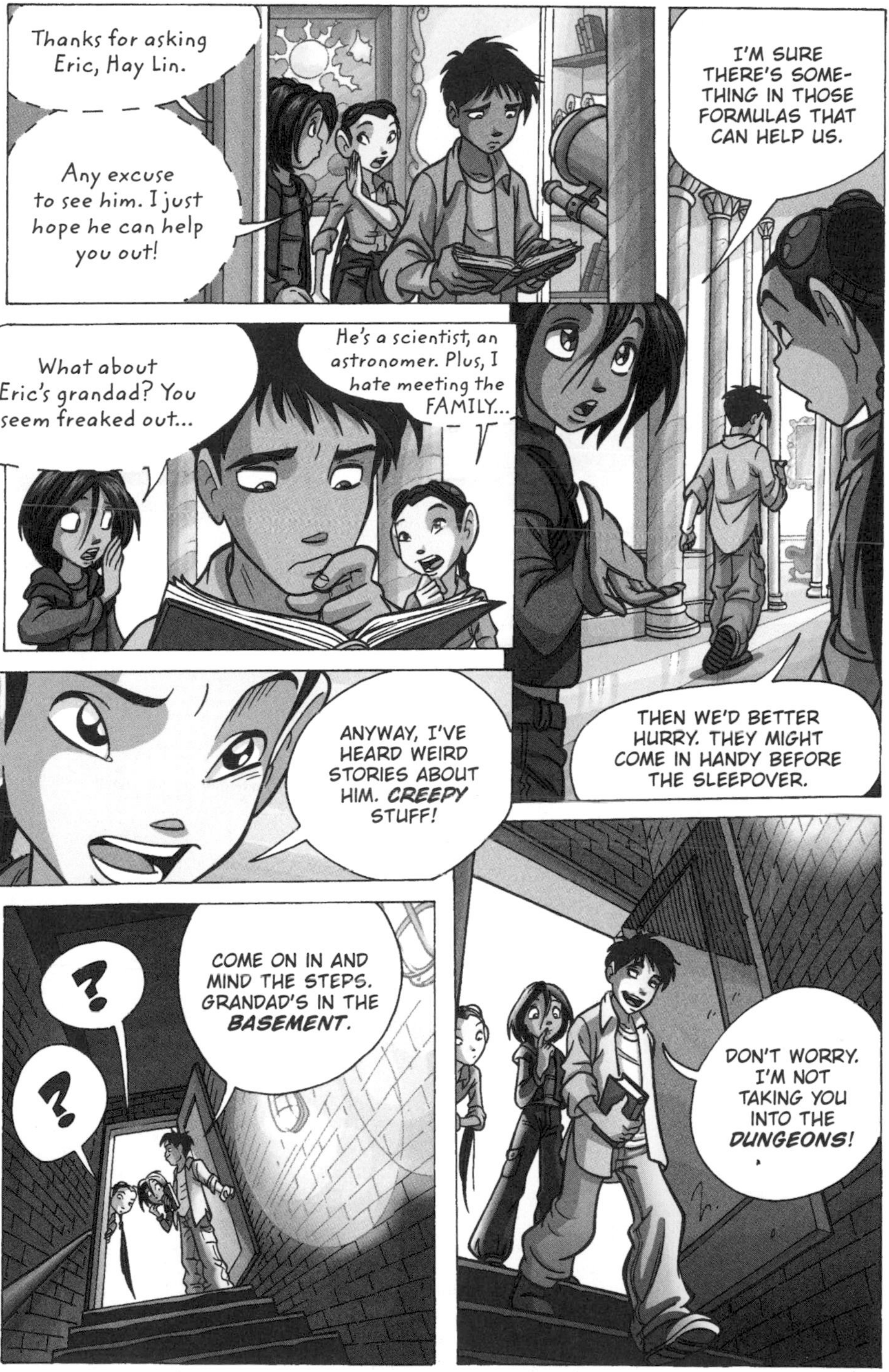
Thanks for asking Eric, Hay Lin.
Any excuse to see him. I just hope he can help you out!
I'M SURE THERE'S SOMETHING IN THOSE FORMULAS THAT CAN HELP US.
What about Eric's grandad? You seem freaked out...
He's a scientist, an astronomer. Plus, I hate meeting the FAMILY...
ANYWAY, I'VE HEARD WEIRD STORIES ABOUT HIM. *CREEPY* STUFF!
THEN WE'D BETTER HURRY. THEY MIGHT COME IN HANDY BEFORE THE SLEEPOVER.
COME ON IN AND MIND THE STEPS. GRANDAD'S IN THE *BASEMENT*.
?
?
DON'T WORRY. I'M NOT TAKING YOU INTO THE *DUNGEONS*!

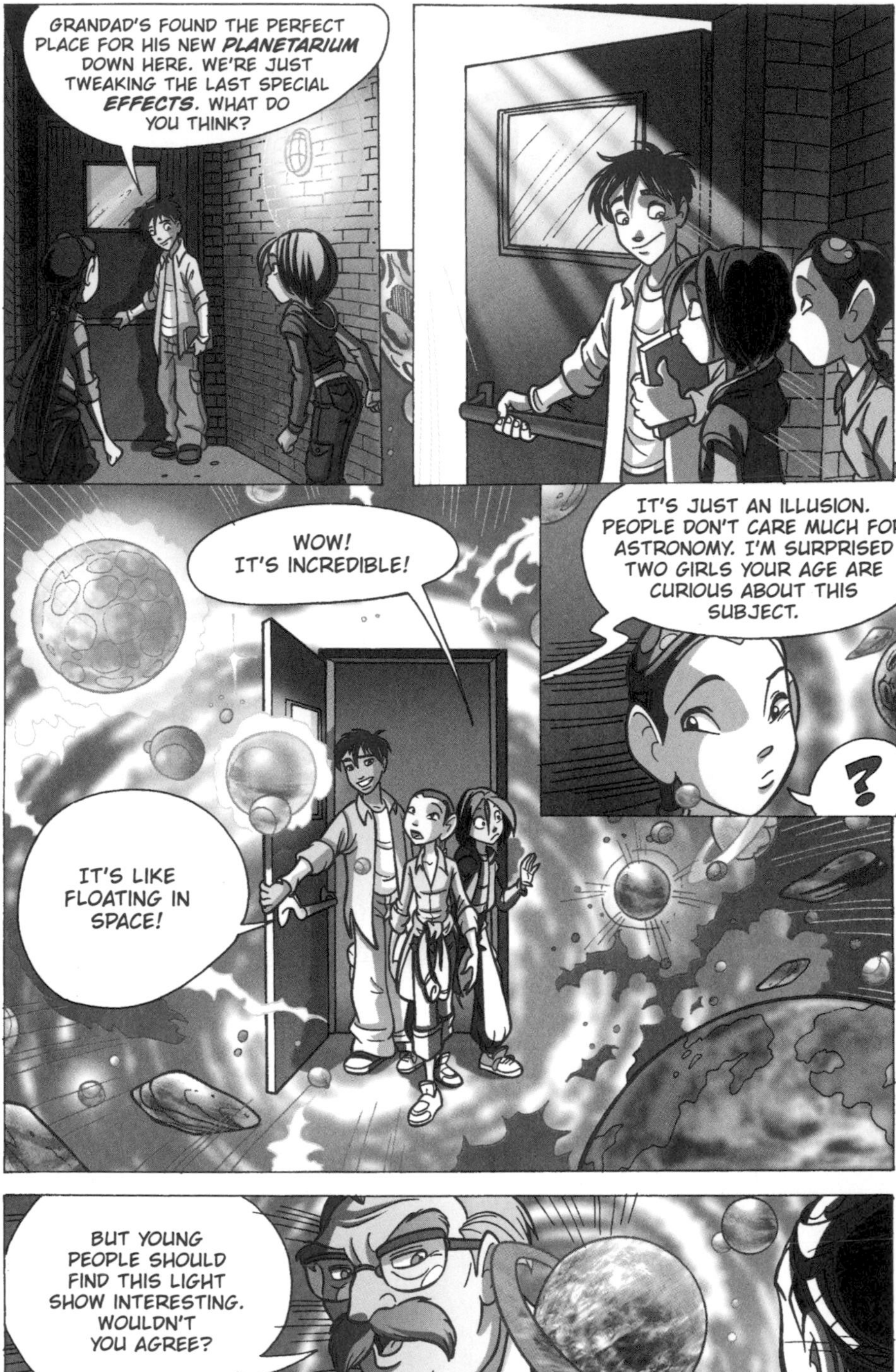
GRANDAD'S FOUND THE PERFECT PLACE FOR HIS NEW PLANETARIUM DOWN HERE. WE'RE JUST TWEAKING THE LAST SPECIAL EFFECTS. WHAT DO YOU THINK?
WOW! IT'S INCREDIBLE!
IT'S JUST AN ILLUSION. PEOPLE DON'T CARE MUCH FOR ASTRONOMY. I'M SURPRISED TWO GIRLS YOUR AGE ARE CURIOUS ABOUT THIS SUBJECT.
?
IT'S LIKE FLOATING IN SPACE!
BUT YOUNG PEOPLE SHOULD FIND THIS LIGHT SHOW INTERESTING. WOULDN'T YOU AGREE?

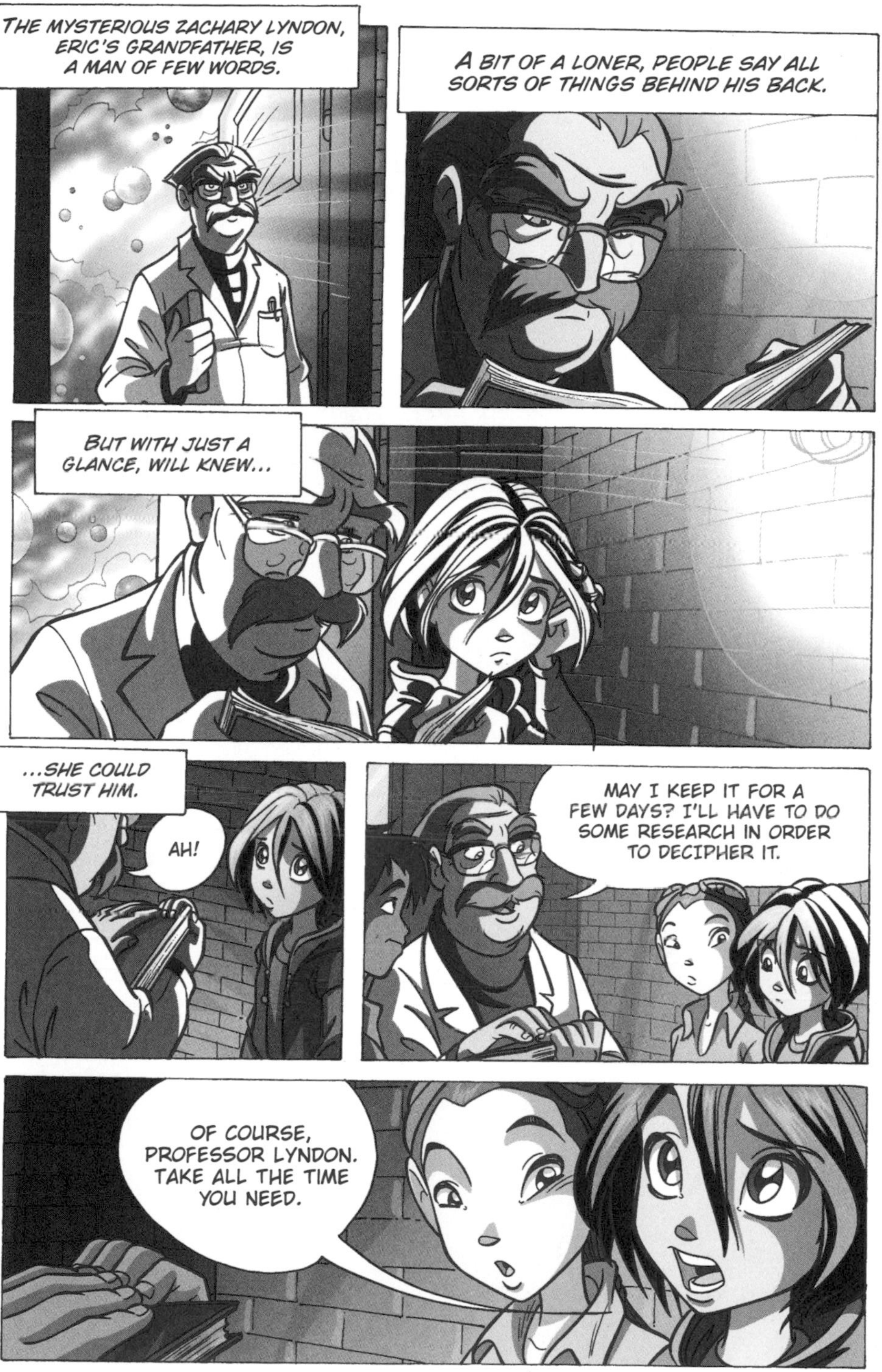
THE MYSTERIOUS ZACHARY LYNDON, ERIC'S GRANDFATHER, IS A MAN OF FEW WORDS.
A BIT OF A LONER, PEOPLE SAY ALL SORTS OF THINGS BEHIND HIS BACK.
BUT WITH JUST A GLANCE, WILL KNEW...
...SHE COULD TRUST HIM.
AH!
MAY I KEEP IT FOR A FEW DAYS? I'LL HAVE TO DO SOME RESEARCH IN ORDER TO DECIPHER IT.
OF COURSE, PROFESSOR LYNDON. TAKE ALL THE TIME YOU NEED.

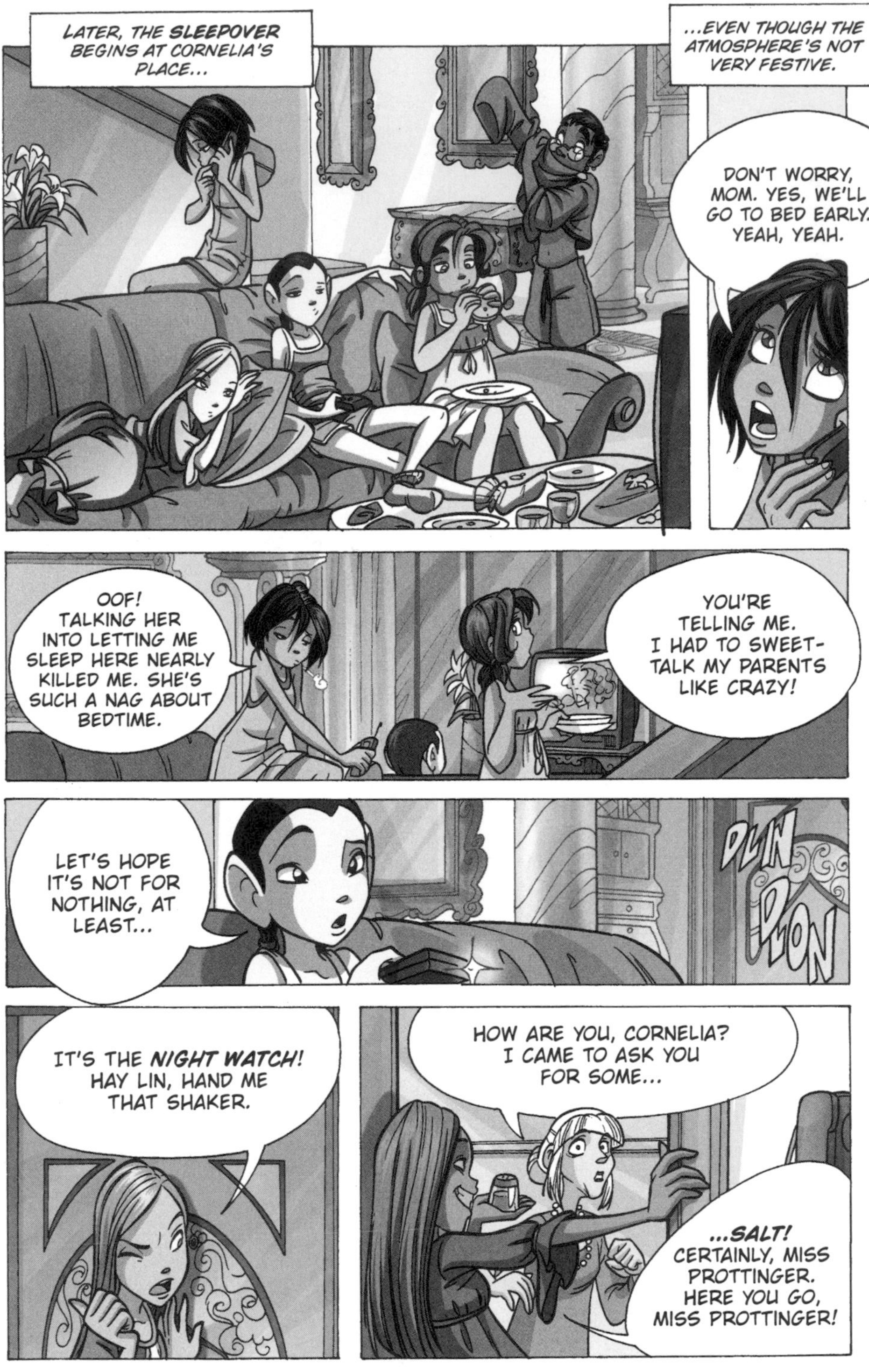
LATER, THE **SLEEPOVER** BEGINS AT CORNELIA'S PLACE...
...EVEN THOUGH THE ATMOSPHERE'S NOT VERY FESTIVE.
DON'T WORRY, MOM. YES, WE'LL GO TO BED EARLY. YEAH, YEAH.
OOF! TALKING HER INTO LETTING ME SLEEP HERE NEARLY KILLED ME. SHE'S SUCH A NAG ABOUT BEDTIME.
YOU'RE TELLING ME. I HAD TO SWEET-TALK MY PARENTS LIKE CRAZY!
LET'S HOPE IT'S NOT FOR NOTHING, AT LEAST...
DLIN DLON
IT'S THE ***NIGHT WATCH***! HAY LIN, HAND ME THAT SHAKER.
HOW ARE YOU, CORNELIA? I CAME TO ASK YOU FOR SOME...
...SALT! CERTAINLY, MISS PROTTINGER. HERE YOU GO, MISS PROTTINGER!

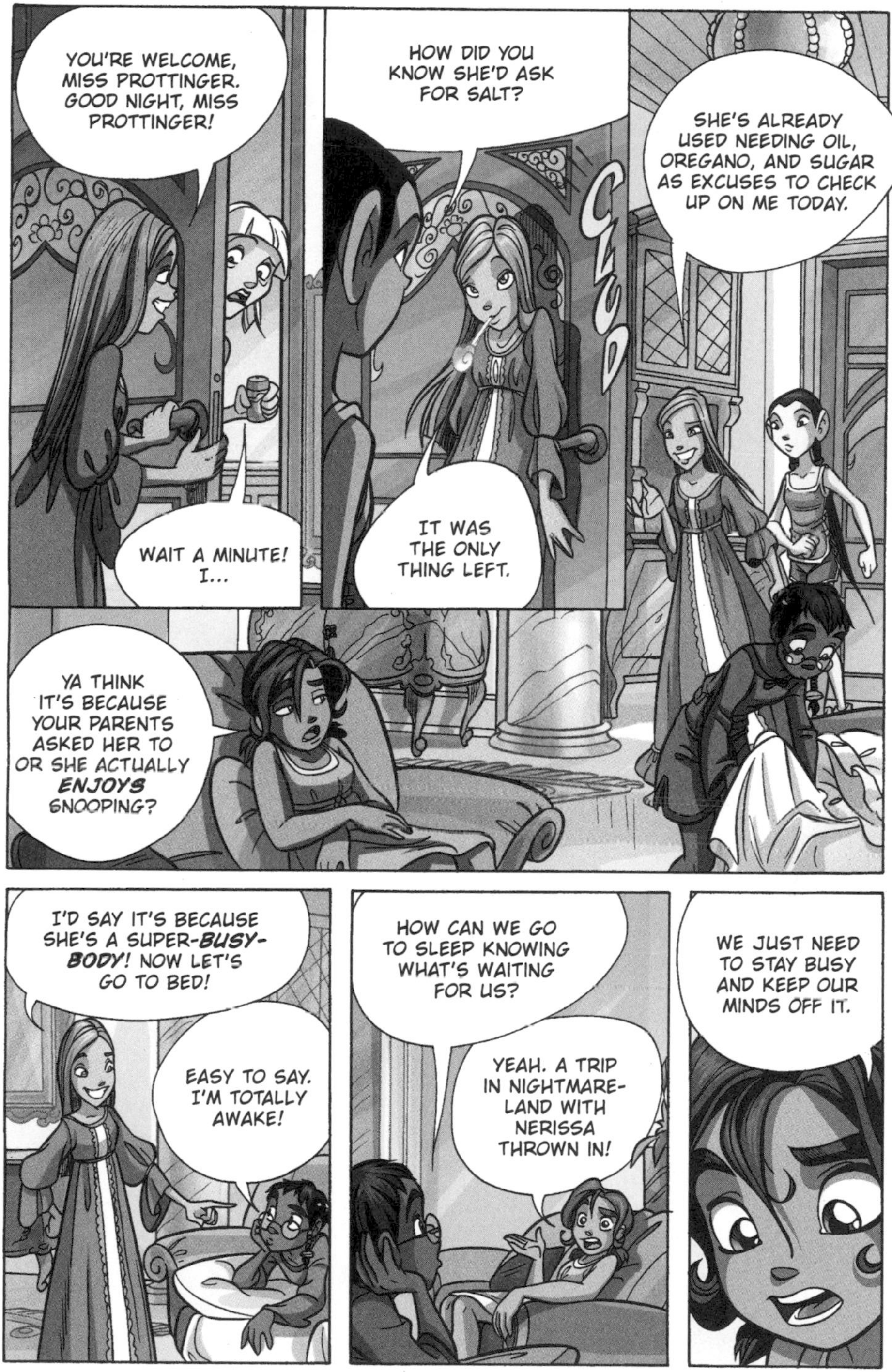
YOU'RE WELCOME, MISS PROTTINGER. GOOD NIGHT, MISS PROTTINGER!
WAIT A MINUTE! I...
HOW DID YOU KNOW SHE'D ASK FOR SALT?
IT WAS THE ONLY THING LEFT.
CLUD
SHE'S ALREADY USED NEEDING OIL, OREGANO, AND SUGAR AS EXCUSES TO CHECK UP ON ME TODAY.
YA THINK IT'S BECAUSE YOUR PARENTS ASKED HER TO OR SHE ACTUALLY ***ENJOYS*** SNOOPING?
I'D SAY IT'S BECAUSE SHE'S A SUPER-***BUSY-BODY***! NOW LET'S GO TO BED!
EASY TO SAY. I'M TOTALLY AWAKE!
HOW CAN WE GO TO SLEEP KNOWING WHAT'S WAITING FOR US?
YEAH. A TRIP IN NIGHTMARE-LAND WITH NERISSA THROWN IN!
WE JUST NEED TO STAY BUSY AND KEEP OUR MINDS OFF IT.

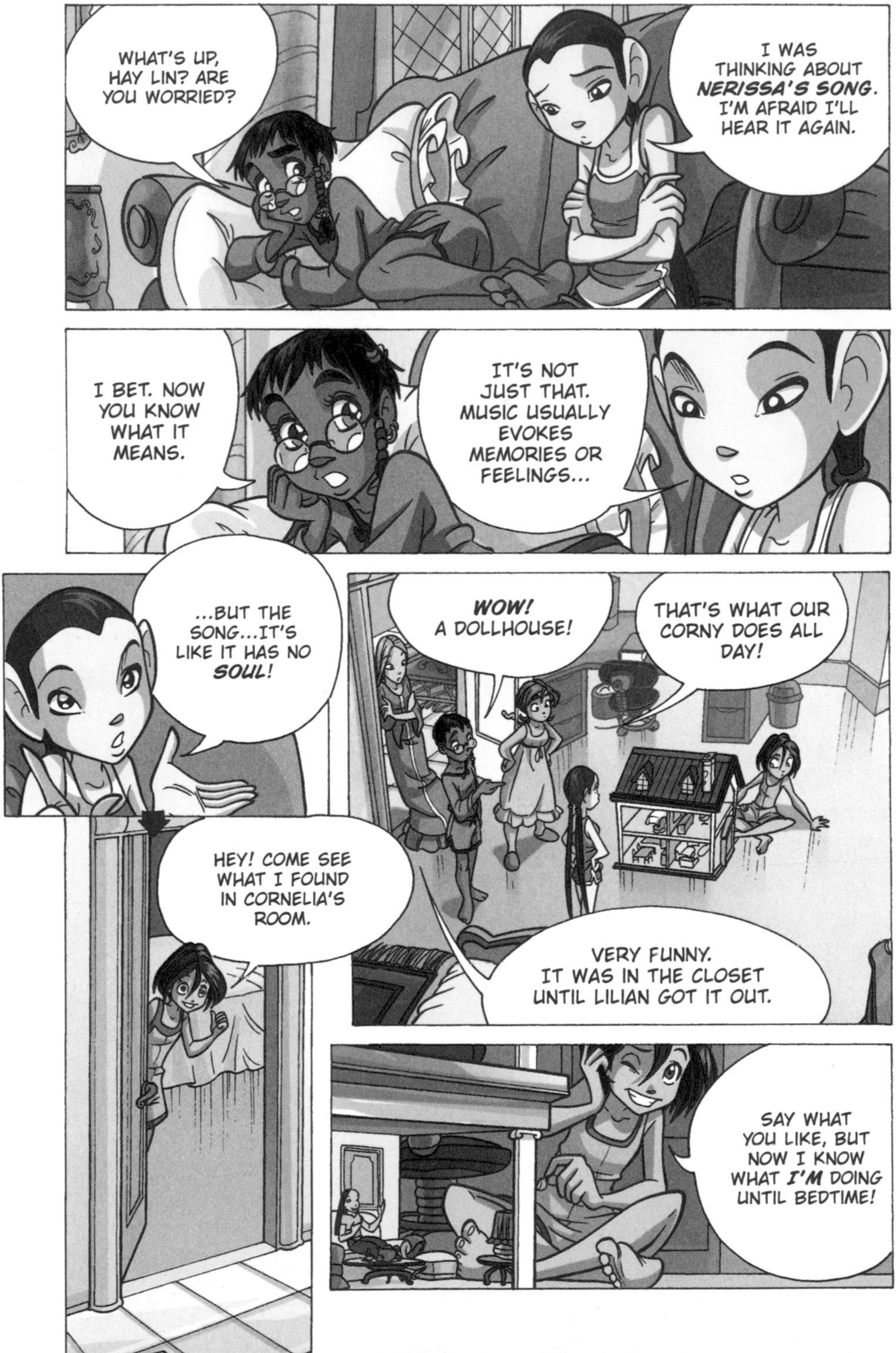
WHAT'S UP, HAY LIN? ARE YOU WORRIED?
I WAS THINKING ABOUT NERISSA'S SONG. I'M AFRAID I'LL HEAR IT AGAIN.
I BET. NOW YOU KNOW WHAT IT MEANS.
IT'S NOT JUST THAT. MUSIC USUALLY EVOKES MEMORIES OR FEELINGS...
...BUT THE SONG...IT'S LIKE IT HAS NO SOUL!
HEY! COME SEE WHAT I FOUND IN CORNELIA'S ROOM.
WOW! A DOLLHOUSE!
THAT'S WHAT OUR CORNY DOES ALL DAY!
VERY FUNNY. IT WAS IN THE CLOSET UNTIL LILIAN GOT IT OUT.
SAY WHAT YOU LIKE, BUT NOW I KNOW WHAT I'M DOING UNTIL BEDTIME!

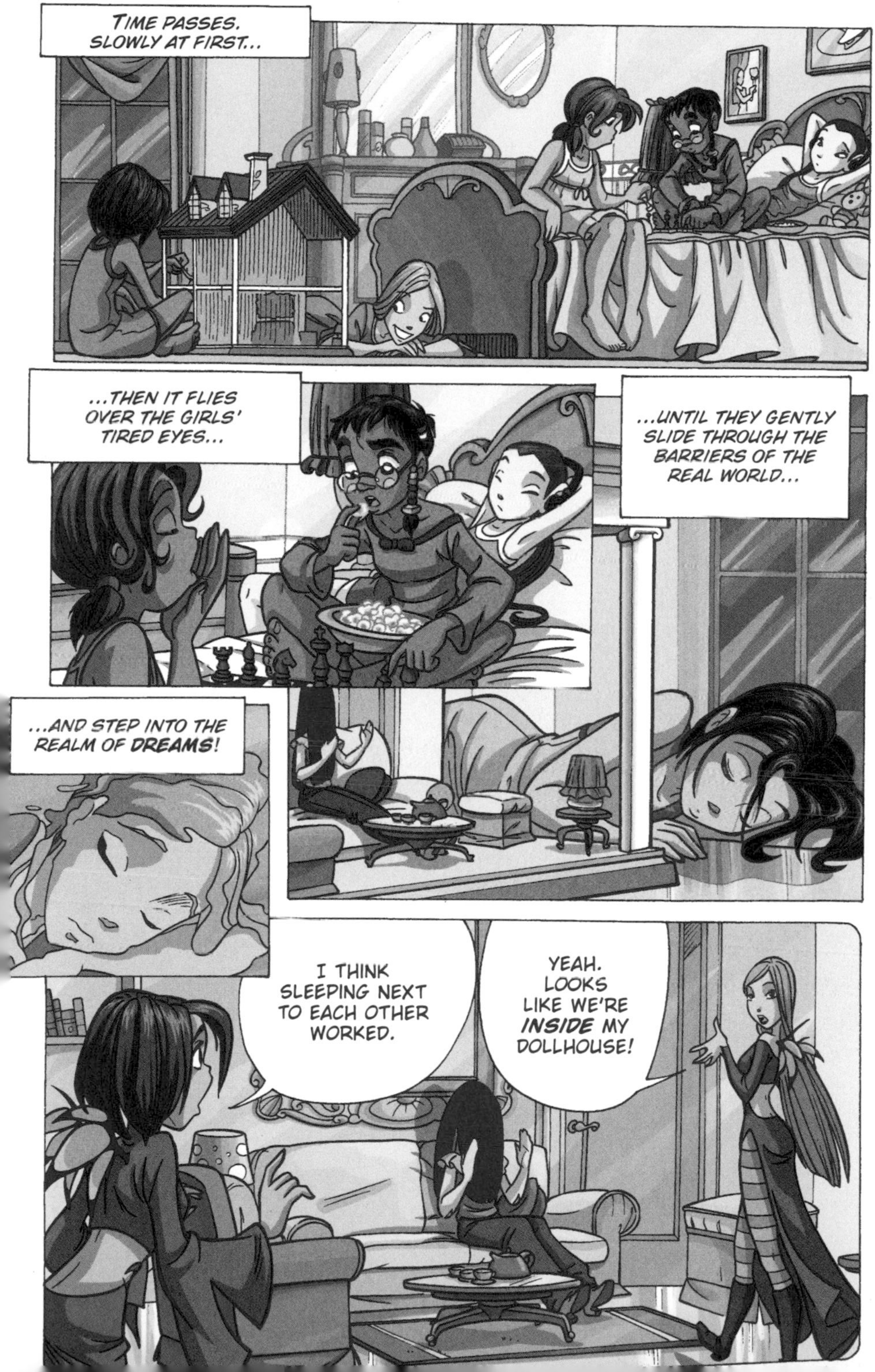
TIME PASSES. SLOWLY AT FIRST...
...THEN IT FLIES OVER THE GIRLS' TIRED EYES...
...UNTIL THEY GENTLY SLIDE THROUGH THE BARRIERS OF THE REAL WORLD...
...AND STEP INTO THE REALM OF DREAMS!
I THINK SLEEPING NEXT TO EACH OTHER WORKED.
YEAH. LOOKS LIKE WE'RE INSIDE MY DOLLHOUSE!

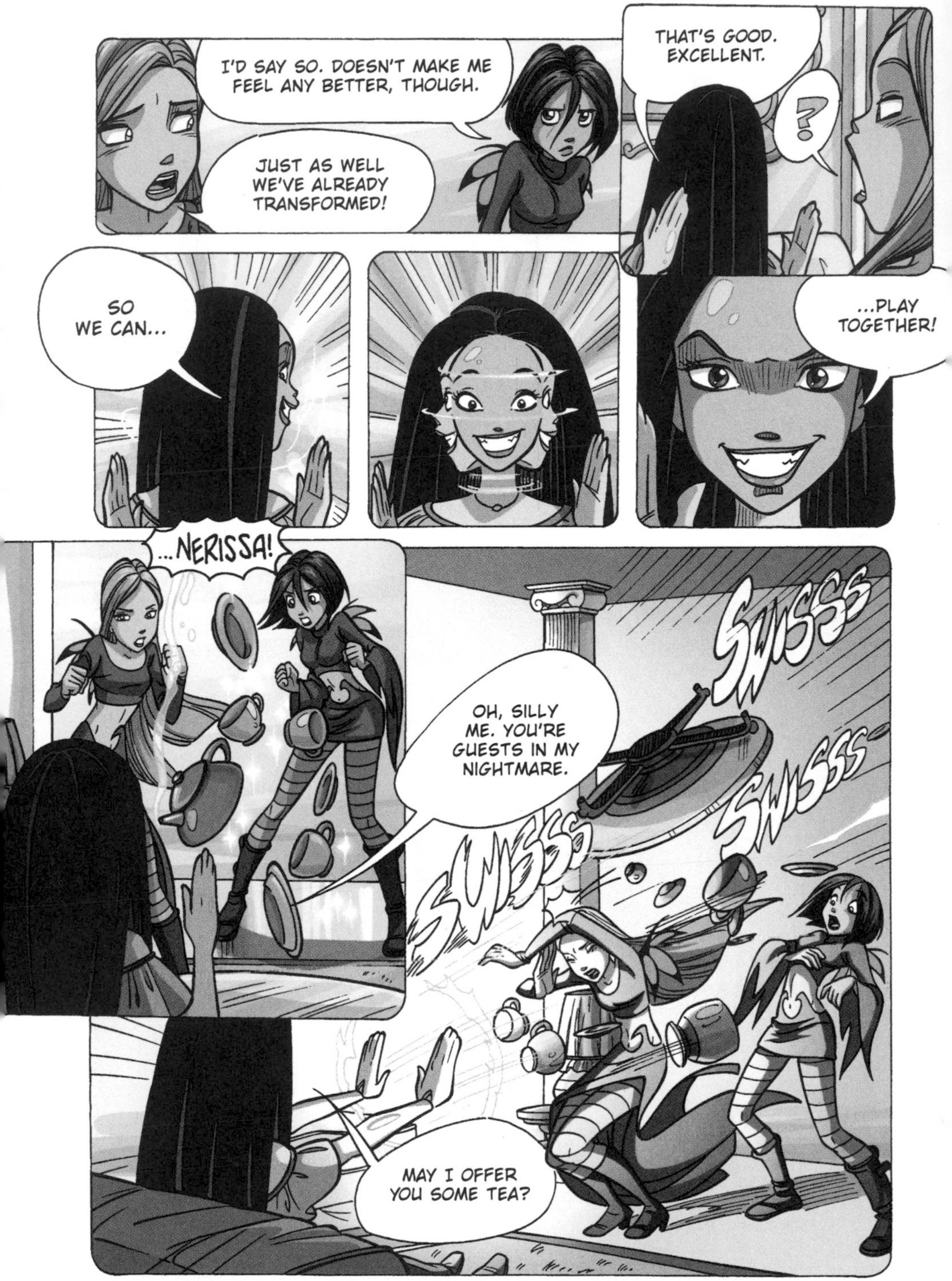
I'D SAY SO. DOESN'T MAKE ME FEEL ANY BETTER, THOUGH.
JUST AS WELL WE'VE ALREADY TRANSFORMED!
THAT'S GOOD. EXCELLENT.
?
SO WE CAN...
...PLAY TOGETHER!
...NERISSA!
OH, SILLY ME. YOU'RE GUESTS IN MY NIGHTMARE.
SWISSS
SWISSSS-
SWISSS
MAY I OFFER YOU SOME TEA?

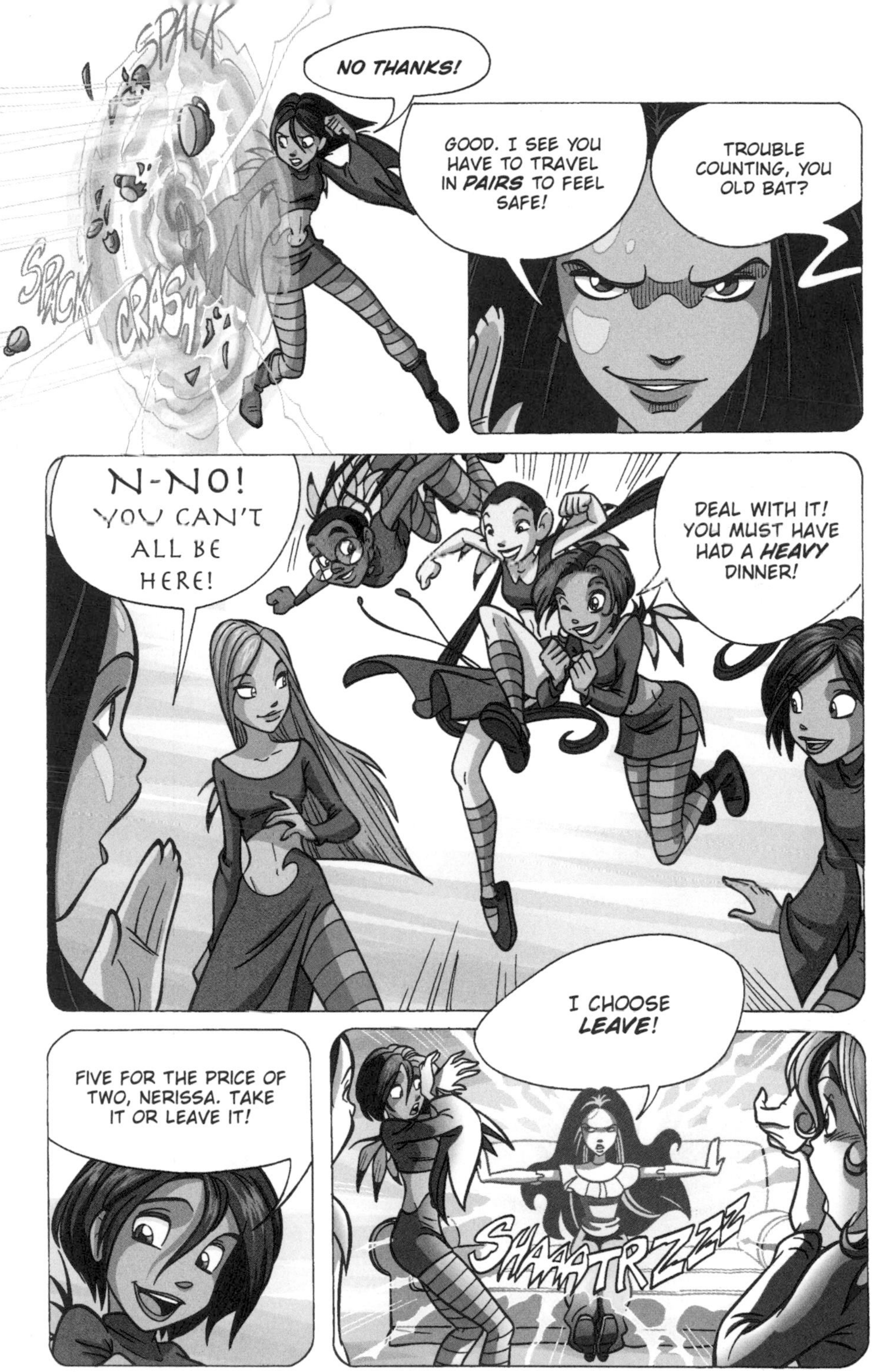
SPACK
NO THANKS!
SPACK
CRASH
GOOD. I SEE YOU HAVE TO TRAVEL IN **PAIRS** TO FEEL SAFE!
TROUBLE COUNTING, YOU OLD BAT?
N-NO! YOU CAN'T ALL BE HERE!
DEAL WITH IT! YOU MUST HAVE HAD A **HEAVY** DINNER!
FIVE FOR THE PRICE OF TWO, NERISSA. TAKE IT OR LEAVE IT!
I CHOOSE **LEAVE**!
SHAAATRZZZ

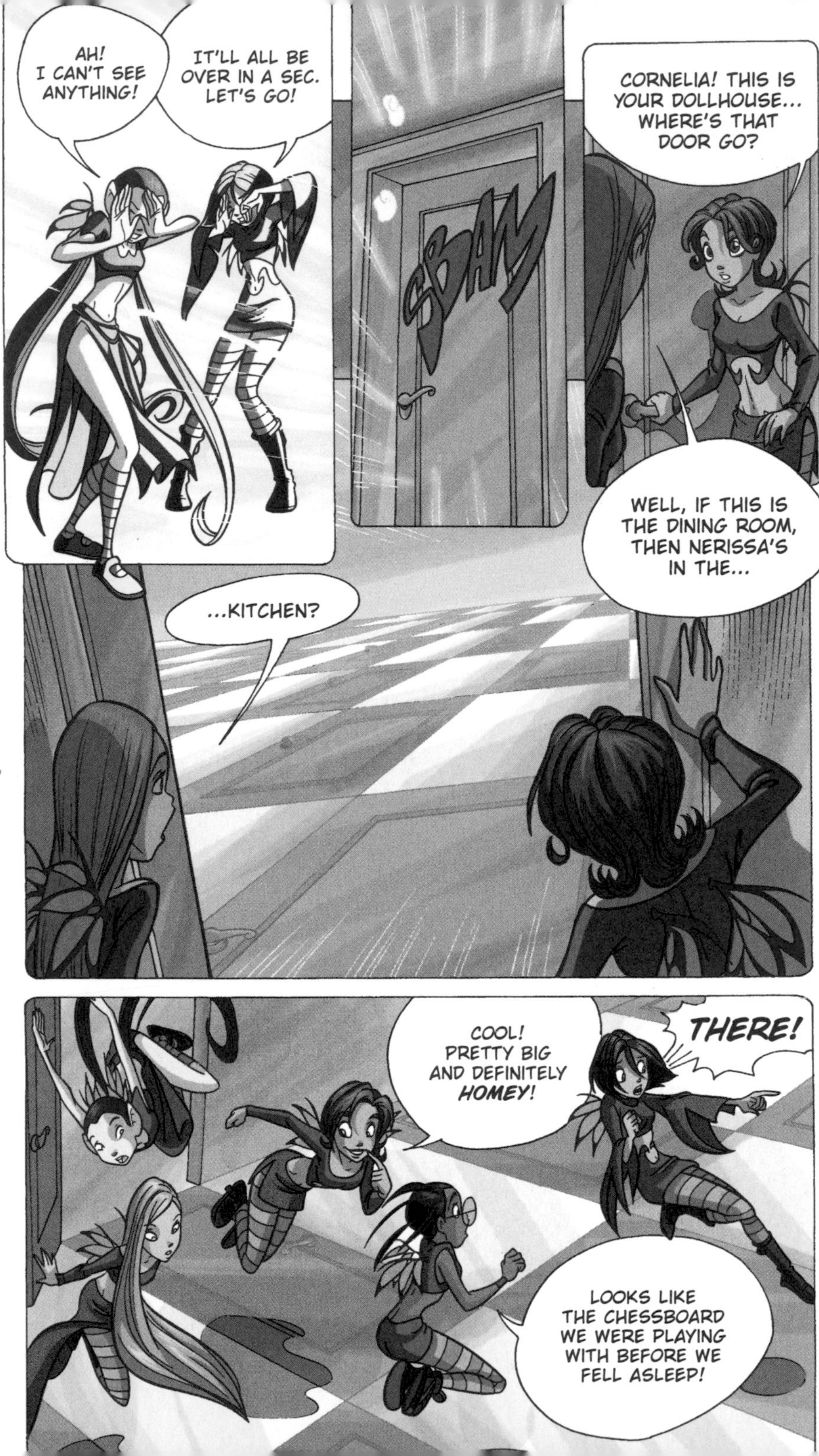
AH! I CAN'T SEE ANYTHING!
IT'LL ALL BE OVER IN A SEC. LET'S GO!
SBAM
CORNELIA! THIS IS YOUR DOLLHOUSE... WHERE'S THAT DOOR GO?
WELL, IF THIS IS THE DINING ROOM, THEN NERISSA'S IN THE...
...KITCHEN?
THERE!
COOL! PRETTY BIG AND DEFINITELY *HOMEY*!
LOOKS LIKE THE CHESSBOARD WE WERE PLAYING WITH BEFORE WE FELL ASLEEP!

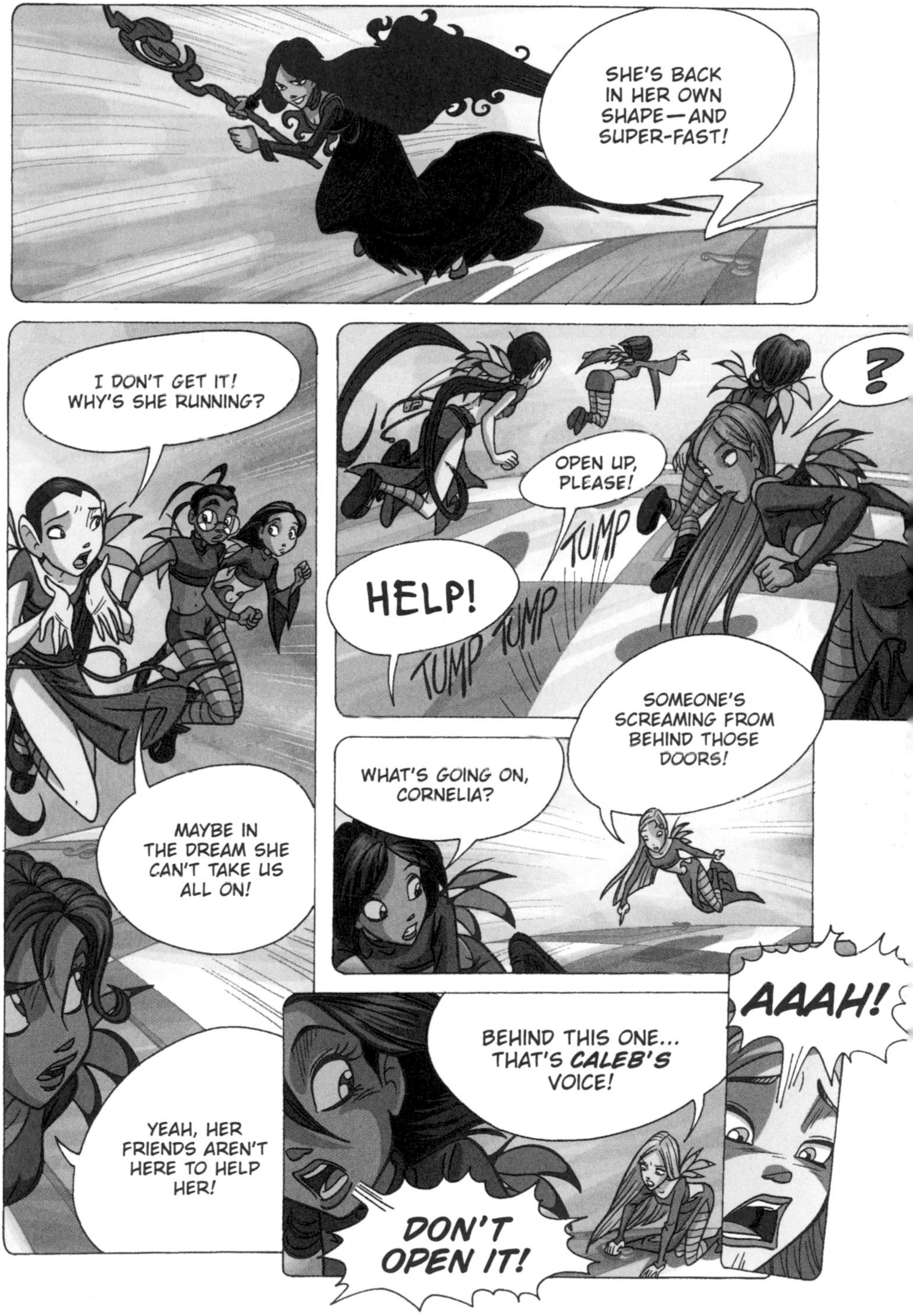
SHE'S BACK IN HER OWN SHAPE—AND SUPER-FAST!
I DON'T GET IT! WHY'S SHE RUNNING?
OPEN UP, PLEASE!
?
HELP!
TUMP TUMP TUMP TUMP
SOMEONE'S SCREAMING FROM BEHIND THOSE DOORS!
WHAT'S GOING ON, CORNELIA?
MAYBE IN THE DREAM SHE CAN'T TAKE US ALL ON!
YEAH, HER FRIENDS AREN'T HERE TO HELP HER!
BEHIND THIS ONE... THAT'S CALEB'S VOICE!
AAAH!
DON'T OPEN IT!

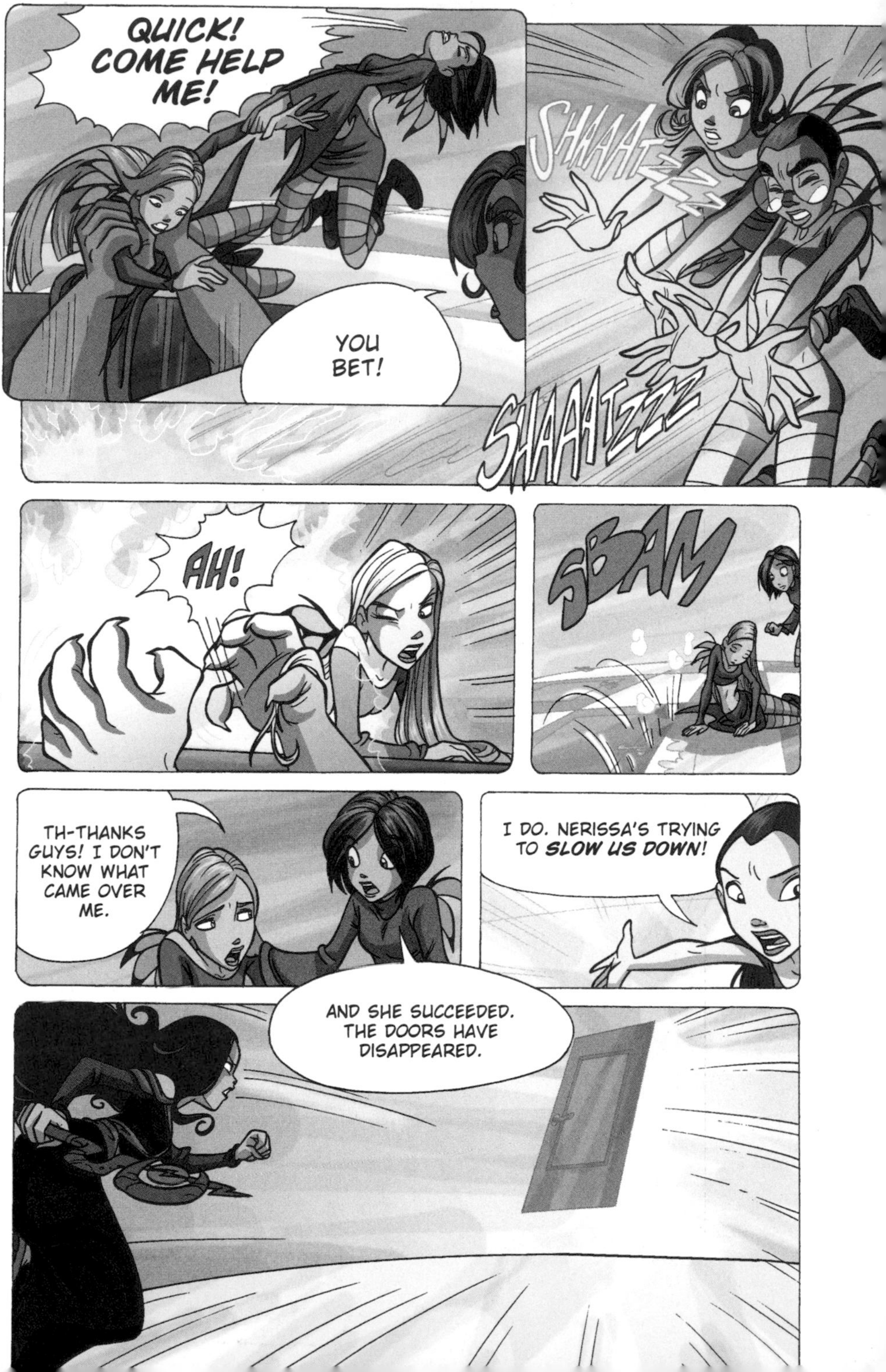
QUICK! COME HELP ME!
YOU BET!
SHAAAIZZZ
SHAAAIZZZ
AH!
SBAM
TH-THANKS GUYS! I DON'T KNOW WHAT CAME OVER ME.
I DO. NERISSA'S TRYING TO SLOW US DOWN!
AND SHE SUCCEEDED. THE DOORS HAVE DISAPPEARED.

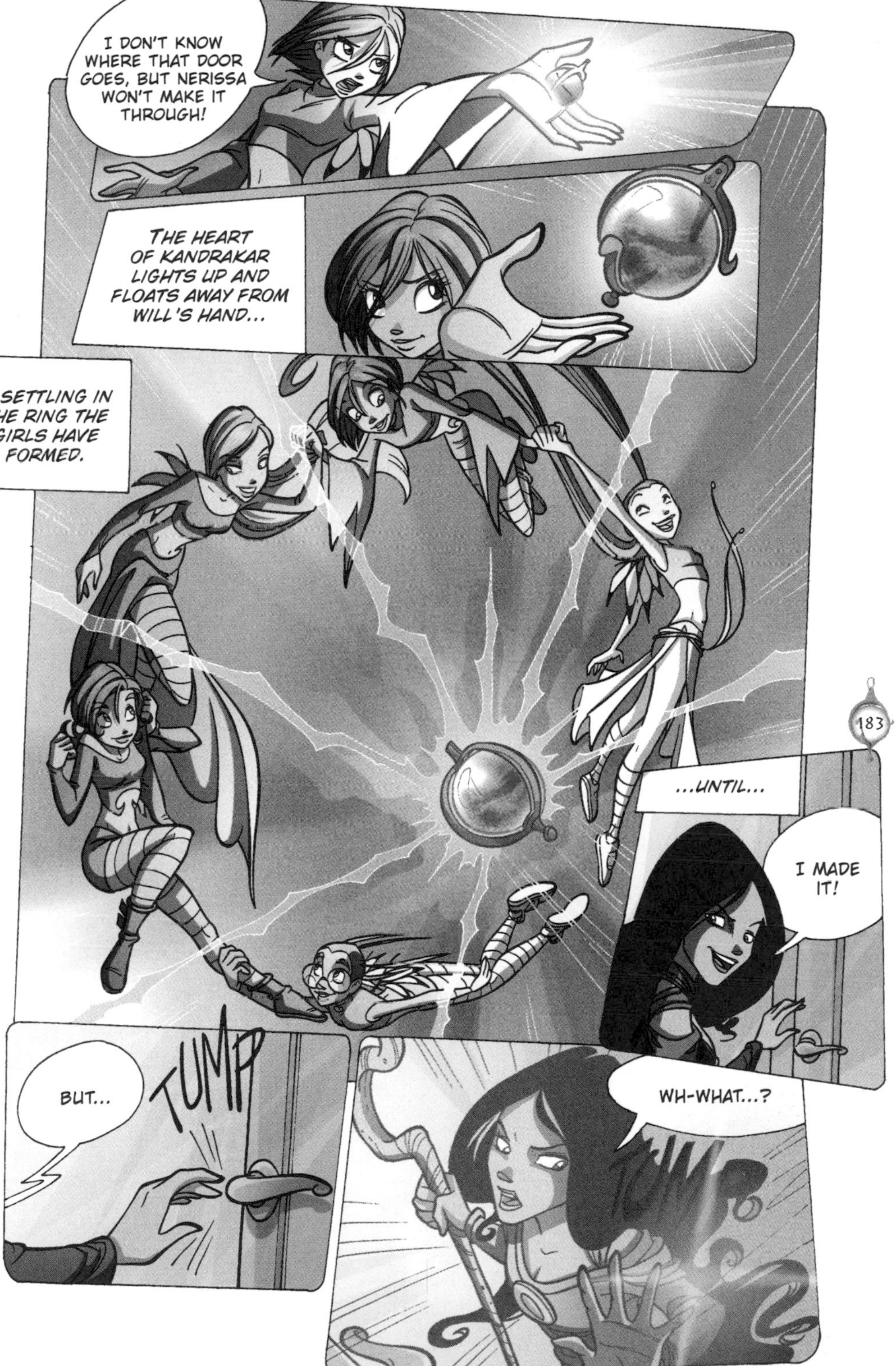
I DON'T KNOW WHERE THAT DOOR GOES, BUT NERISSA WON'T MAKE IT THROUGH!
THE HEART OF KANDRAKAR LIGHTS UP AND FLOATS AWAY FROM WILL'S HAND...
...SETTLING IN THE RING THE GIRLS HAVE FORMED.
...UNTIL...
I MADE IT!
BUT...
TUMP
WH-WHAT...?

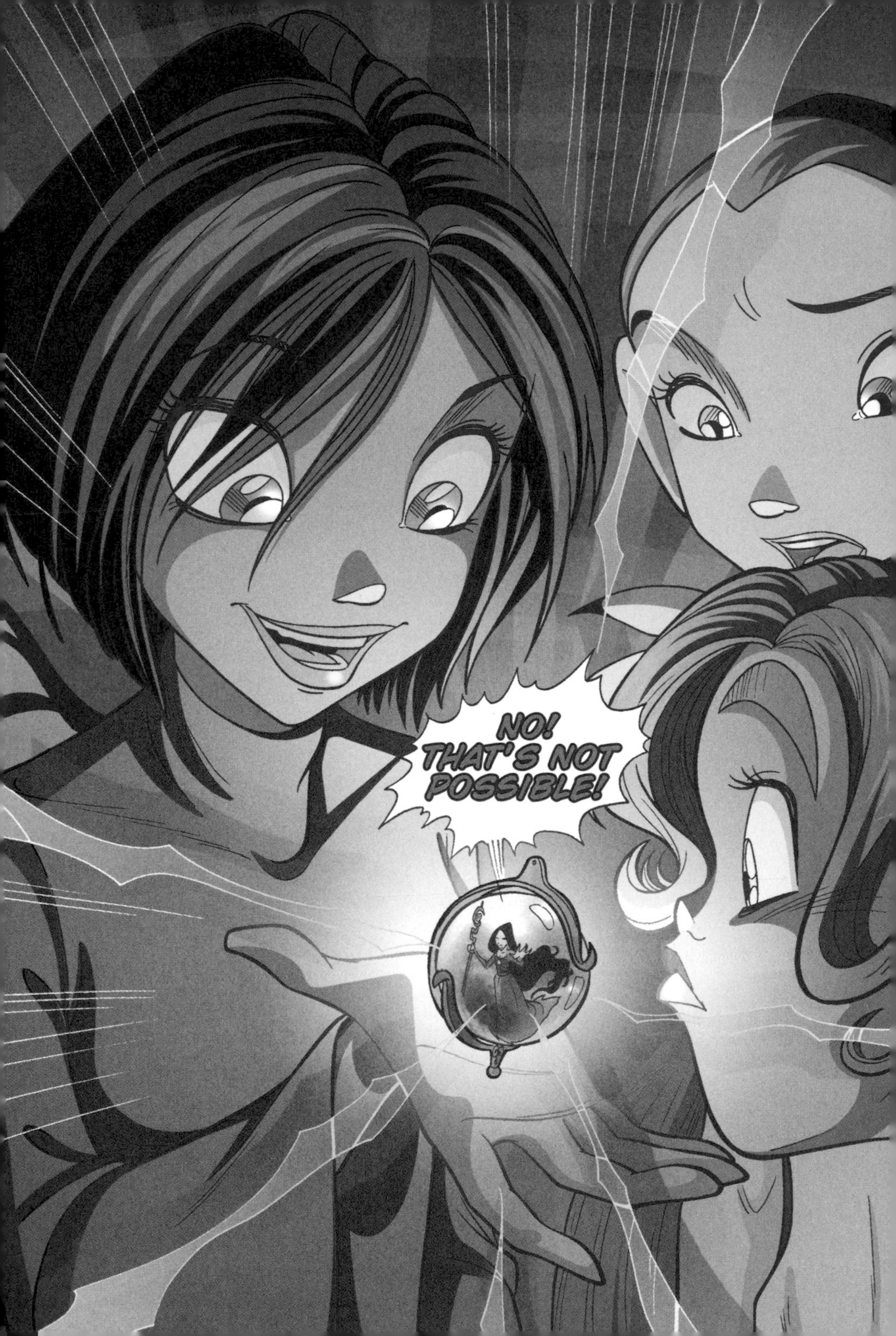
NO! THAT'S NOT POSSIBLE!

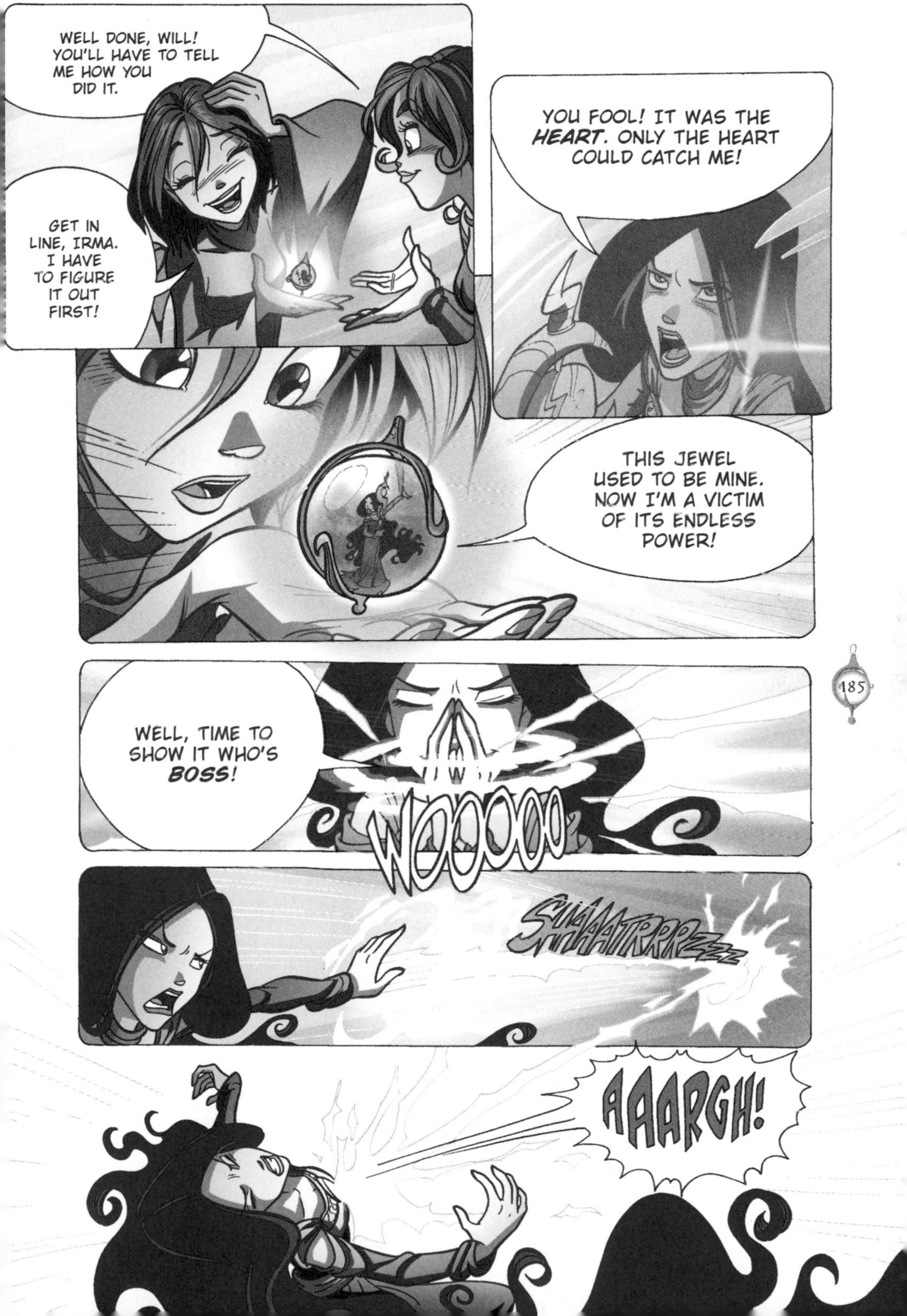
WELL DONE, WILL! YOU'LL HAVE TO TELL ME HOW YOU DID IT.
GET IN LINE, IRMA. I HAVE TO FIGURE IT OUT FIRST!
YOU FOOL! IT WAS THE HEART. ONLY THE HEART COULD CATCH ME!
THIS JEWEL USED TO BE MINE. NOW I'M A VICTIM OF ITS ENDLESS POWER!
WELL, TIME TO SHOW IT WHO'S BOSS!
WOOOOO
SHAAATRRRZZZZ
AAARGH!

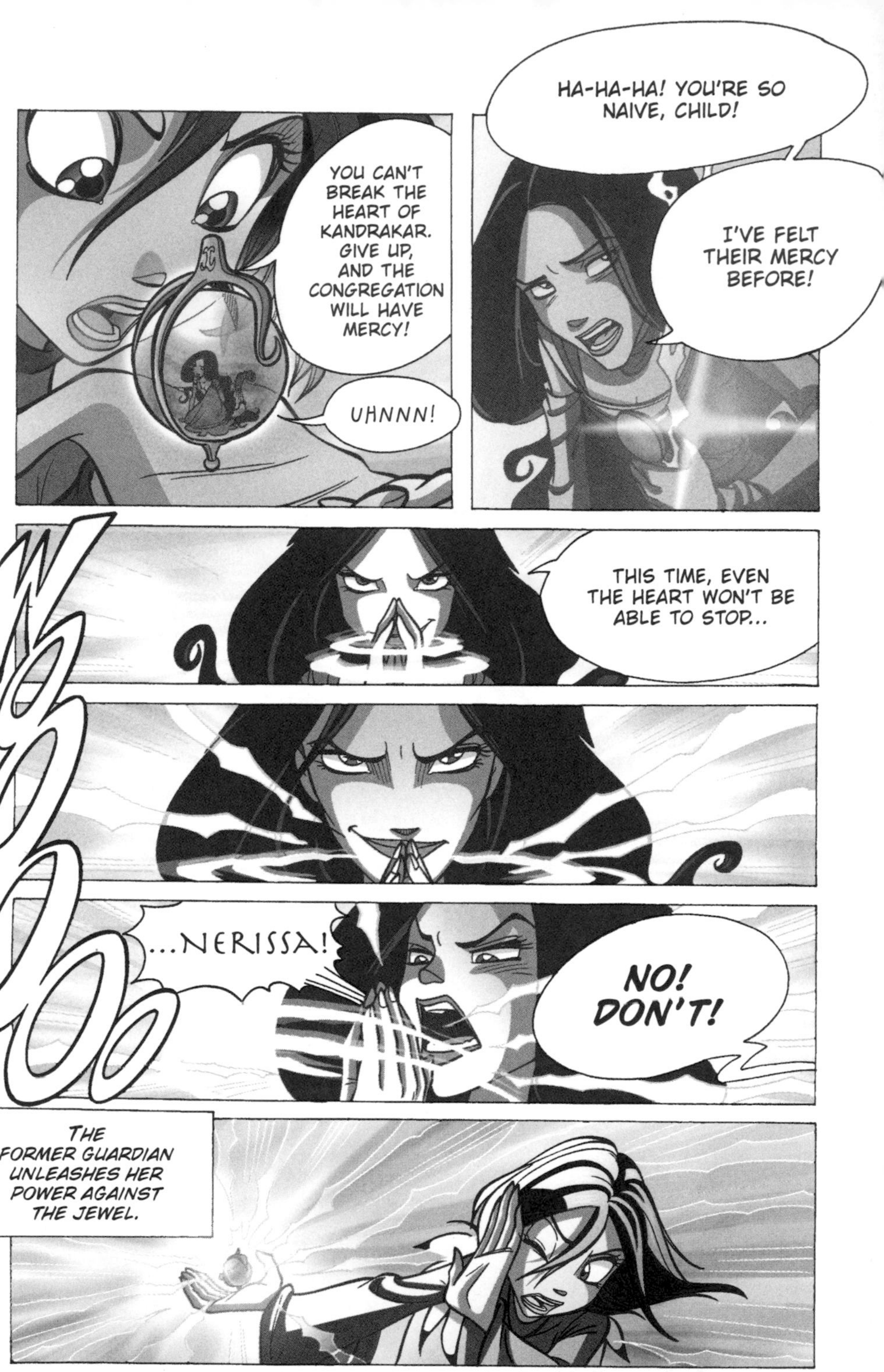
YOU CAN'T BREAK THE HEART OF KANDRAKAR. GIVE UP, AND THE CONGREGATION WILL HAVE MERCY!
UHNNN!
HA-HA-HA! YOU'RE SO NAIVE, CHILD!
I'VE FELT THEIR MERCY BEFORE!
WOOOOOO
THIS TIME, EVEN THE HEART WON'T BE ABLE TO STOP...
...NERISSA!
NO! DON'T!
THE FORMER GUARDIAN UNLEASHES HER POWER AGAINST THE JEWEL.

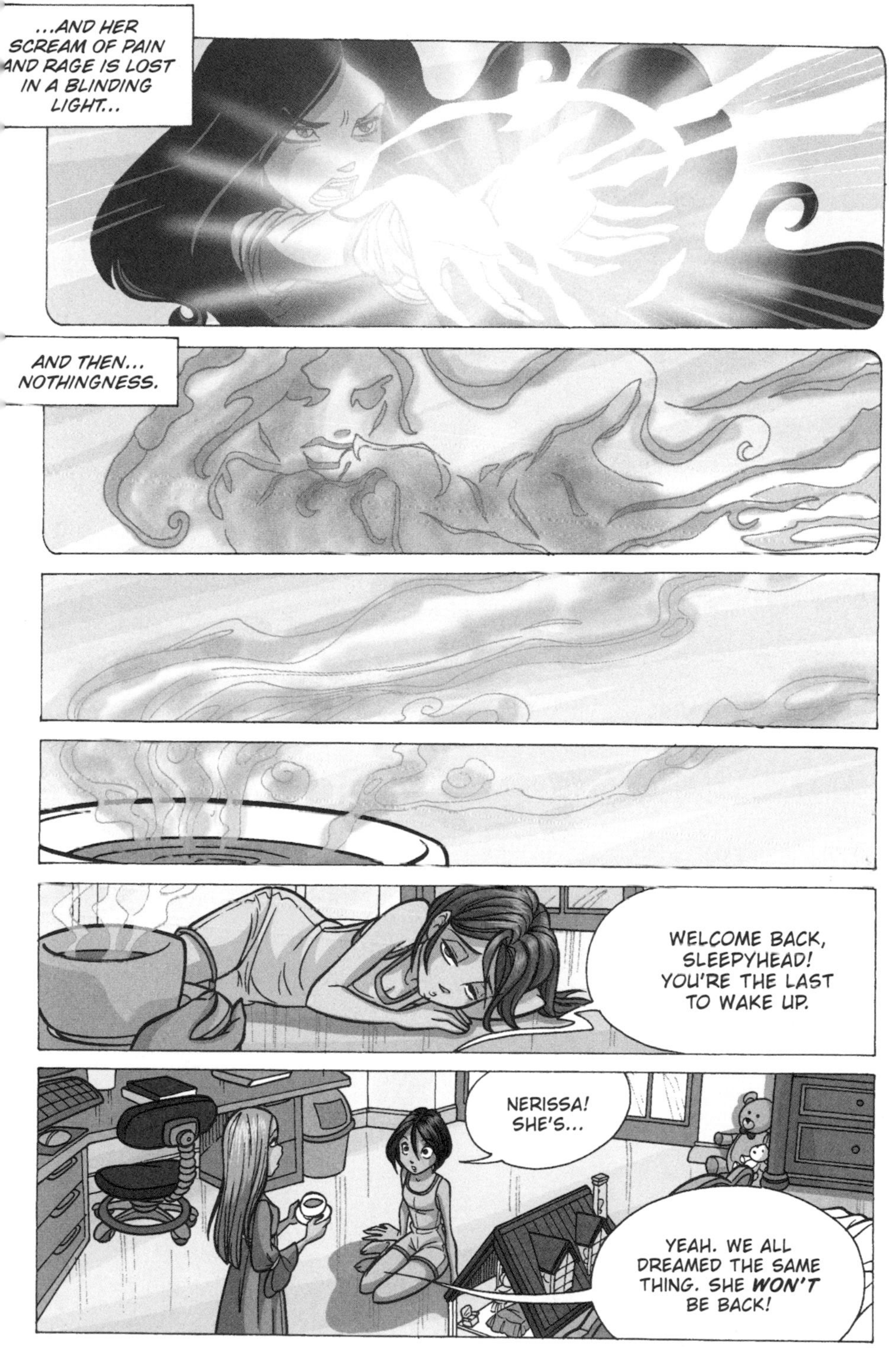
...AND HER SCREAM OF PAIN AND RAGE IS LOST IN A BLINDING LIGHT...
AND THEN... NOTHINGNESS.
WELCOME BACK, SLEEPYHEAD! YOU'RE THE LAST TO WAKE UP.
NERISSA! SHE'S...
YEAH. WE ALL DREAMED THE SAME THING. SHE WON'T BE BACK!

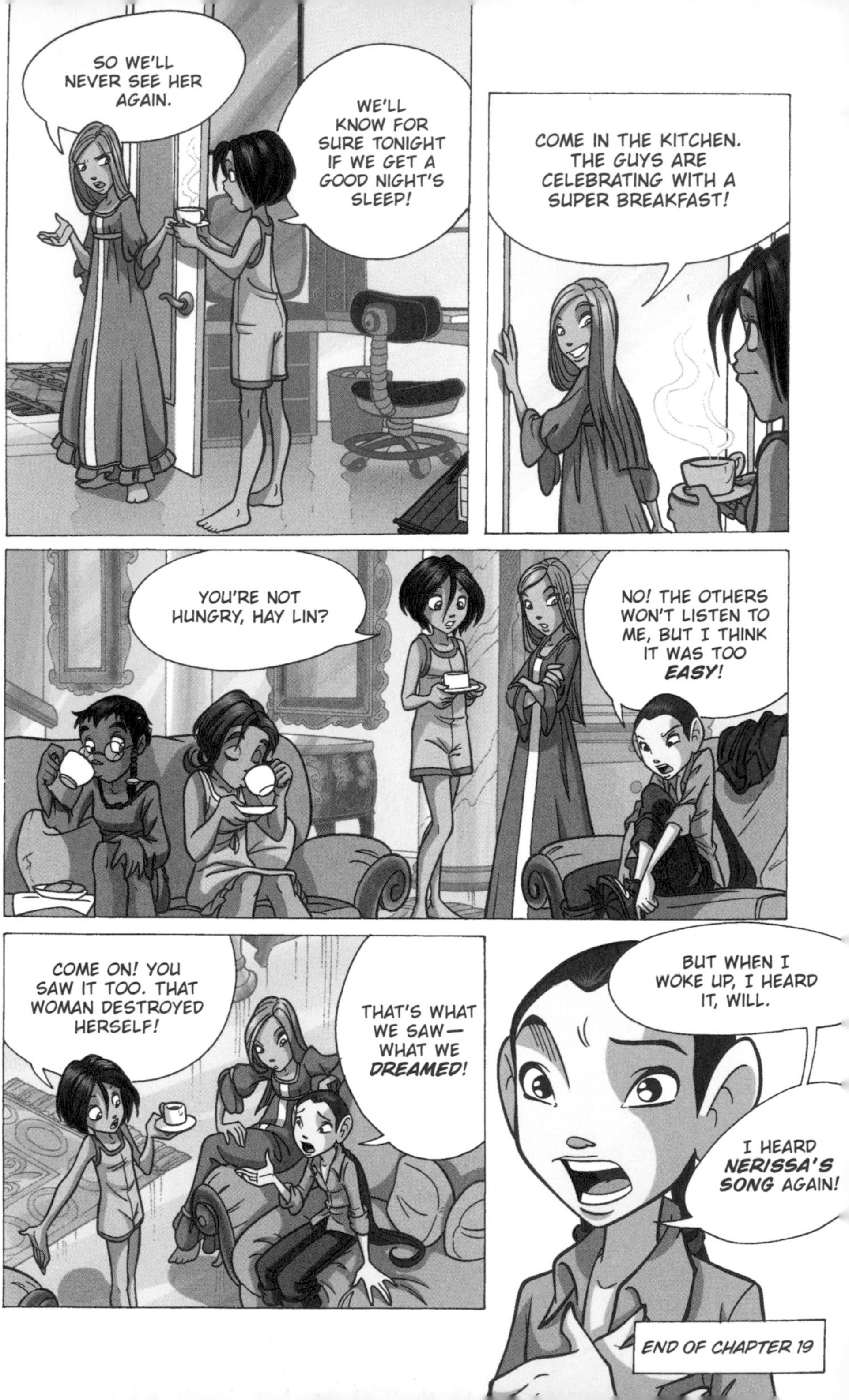

SO WE'LL NEVER SEE HER AGAIN.
WE'LL KNOW FOR SURE TONIGHT IF WE GET A GOOD NIGHT'S SLEEP!
COME IN THE KITCHEN. THE GUYS ARE CELEBRATING WITH A SUPER BREAKFAST!
YOU'RE NOT HUNGRY, HAY LIN?
NO! THE OTHERS WON'T LISTEN TO ME, BUT I THINK IT WAS TOO *EASY*!
COME ON! YOU SAW IT TOO. THAT WOMAN DESTROYED HERSELF!
THAT'S WHAT WE SAW—WHAT WE *DREAMED*!
BUT WHEN I WOKE UP, I HEARD IT, WILL.
I HEARD *NERISSA'S SONG* AGAIN!
END OF CHAPTER 19

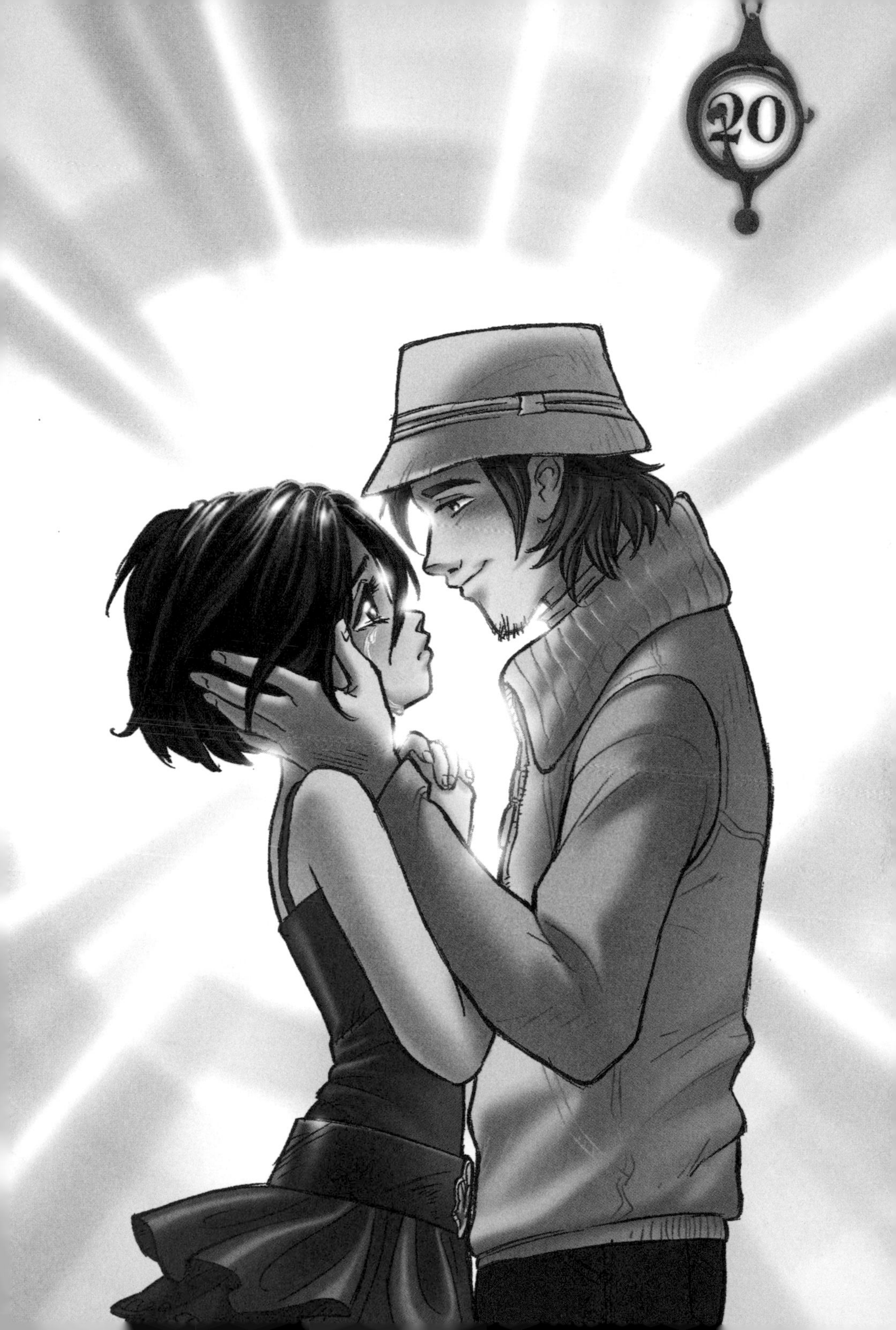
20

WHISPERS OF HATRED

"On a stormy day,
who's stronger?
The oak or the rush?"

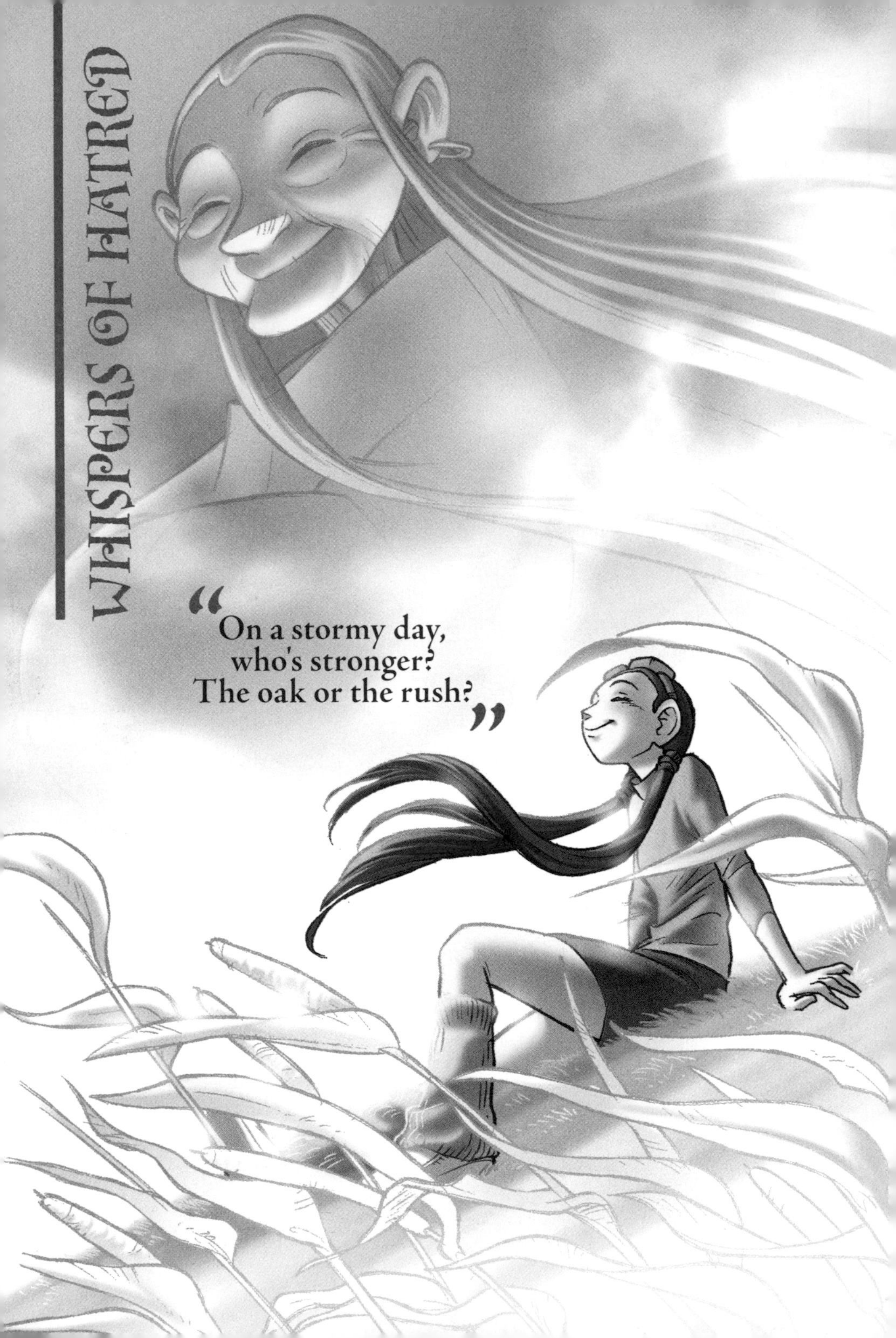

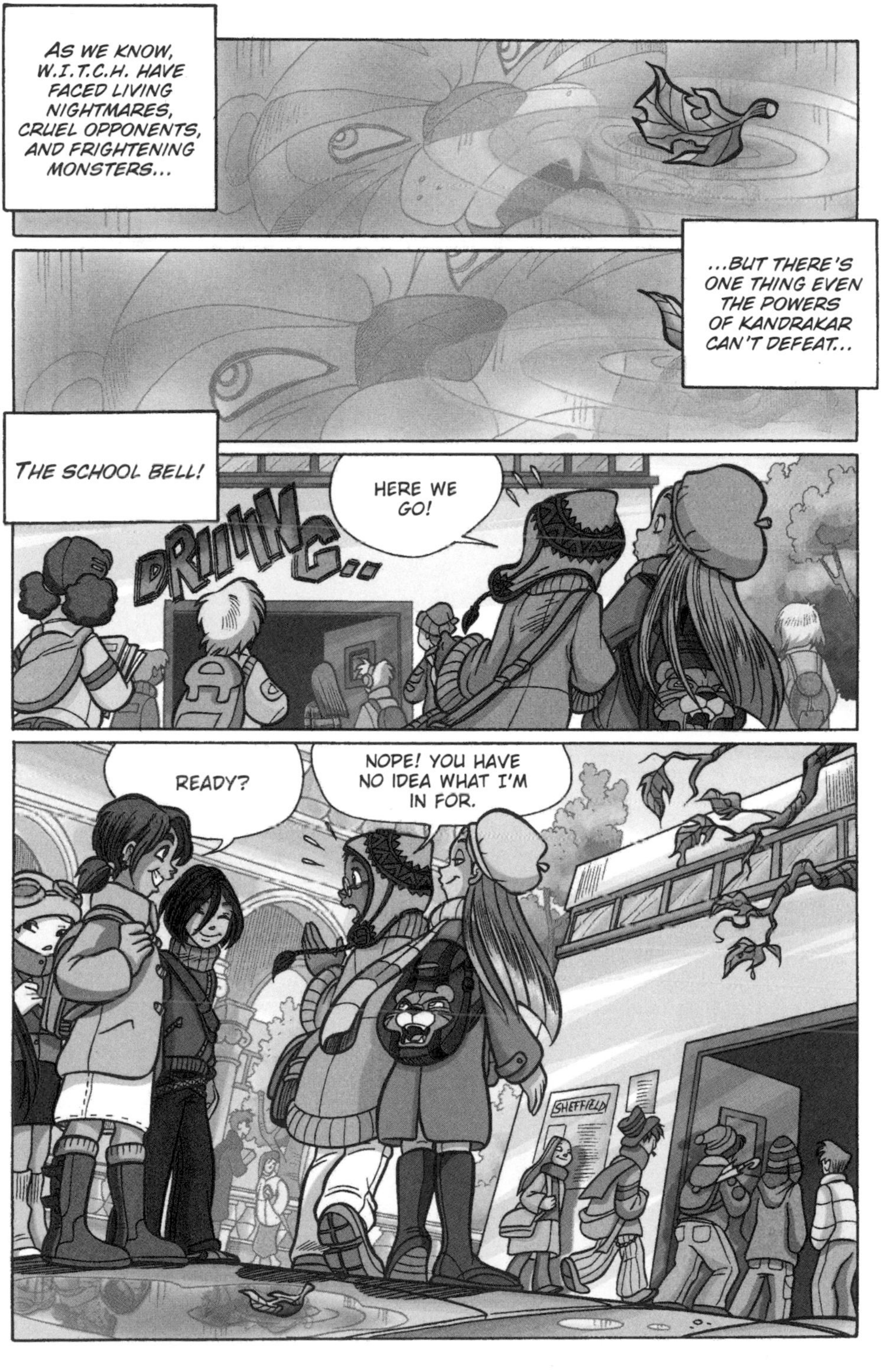
AS WE KNOW, W.I.T.C.H. HAVE FACED LIVING NIGHTMARES, CRUEL OPPONENTS, AND FRIGHTENING MONSTERS...
...BUT THERE'S ONE THING EVEN THE POWERS OF KANDRAKAR CAN'T DEFEAT...
THE SCHOOL BELL!
DRIIIING...
HERE WE GO!
READY?
NOPE! YOU HAVE NO IDEA WHAT I'M IN FOR.
SHEFFIELD

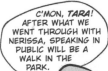

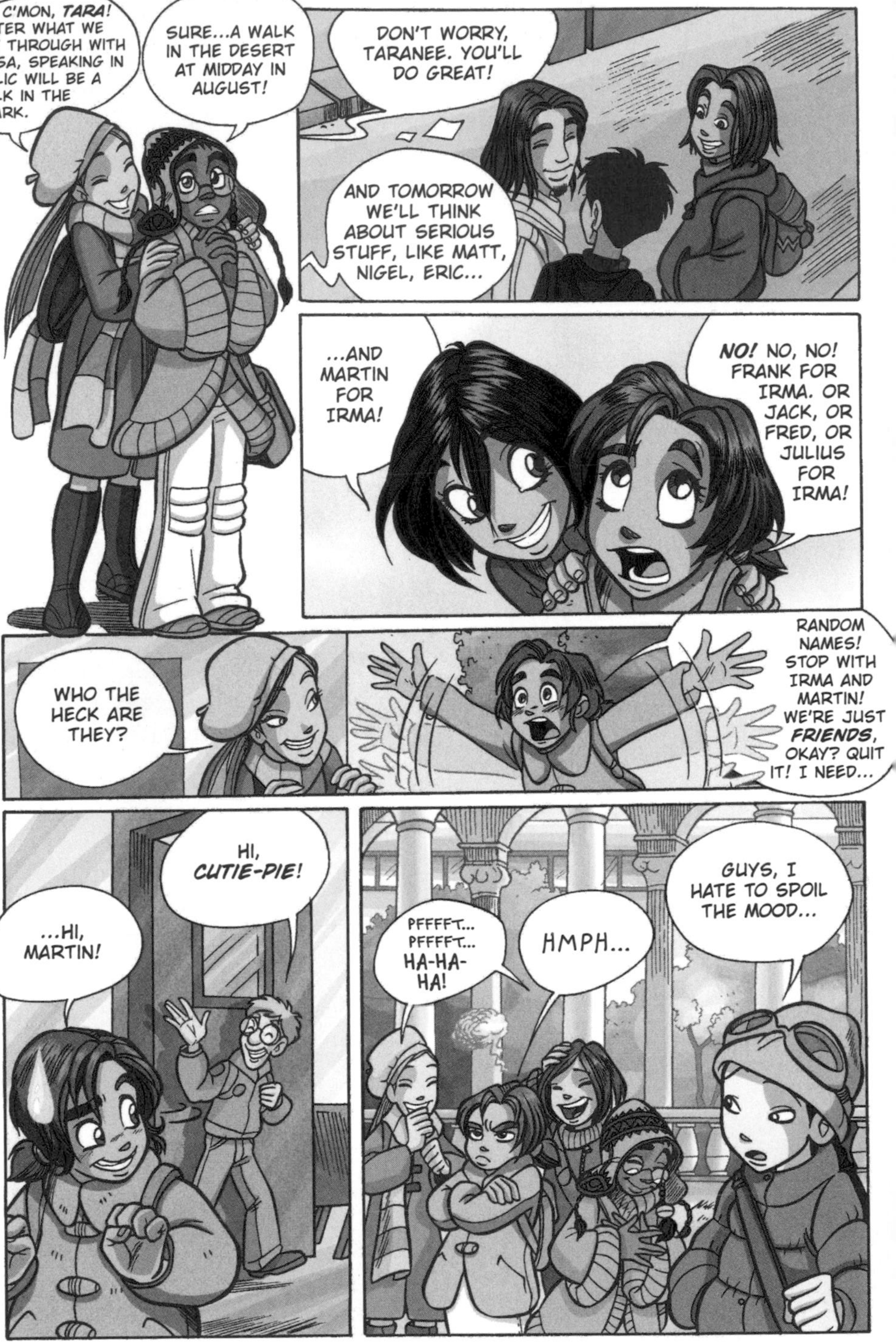
C'MON, TARA! AFTER WHAT WE WENT THROUGH WITH NERISSA, SPEAKING IN PUBLIC WILL BE A WALK IN THE PARK.
SURE...A WALK IN THE DESERT AT MIDDAY IN AUGUST!
DON'T WORRY, TARANEE. YOU'LL DO GREAT!
AND TOMORROW WE'LL THINK ABOUT SERIOUS STUFF, LIKE MATT, NIGEL, ERIC...
...AND MARTIN FOR IRMA!
NO! NO, NO! FRANK FOR IRMA. OR JACK, OR FRED, OR JULIUS FOR IRMA!
WHO THE HECK ARE THEY?
RANDOM NAMES! STOP WITH IRMA AND MARTIN! WE'RE JUST FRIENDS, OKAY? QUIT IT! I NEED...
HI, CUTIE-PIE!
...HI, MARTIN!
PFFFFT... PFFFFT... HA-HA-HA!
HMPH...
GUYS, I HATE TO SPOIL THE MOOD...

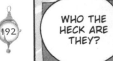

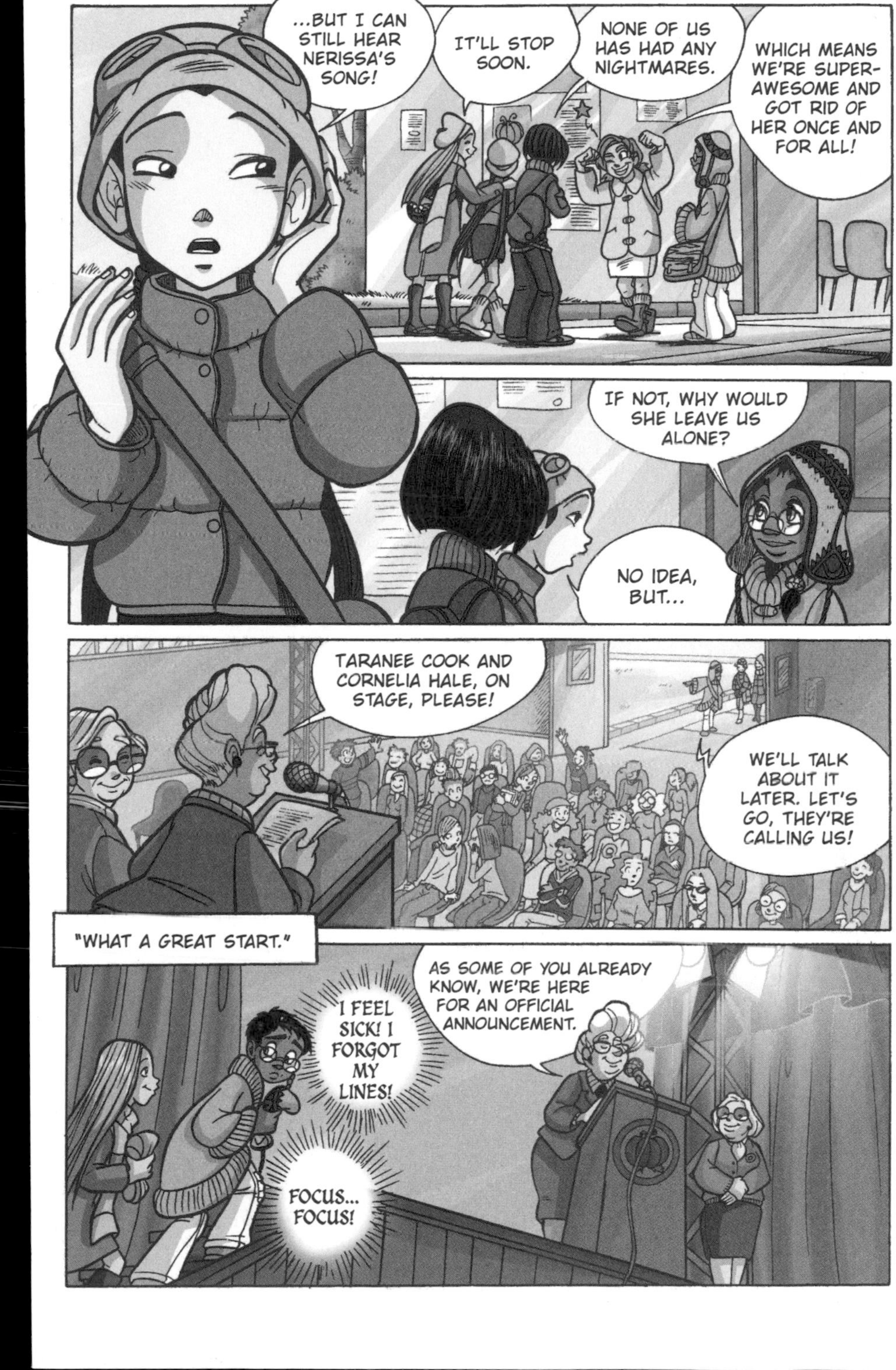
...BUT I CAN STILL HEAR NERISSA'S SONG!
IT'LL STOP SOON.
NONE OF US HAS HAD ANY NIGHTMARES.
WHICH MEANS WE'RE SUPER-AWESOME AND GOT RID OF HER ONCE AND FOR ALL!
IF NOT, WHY WOULD SHE LEAVE US ALONE?
NO IDEA, BUT...
TARANEE COOK AND CORNELIA HALE, ON STAGE, PLEASE!
WE'LL TALK ABOUT IT LATER. LET'S GO, THEY'RE CALLING US!
"WHAT A GREAT START."
AS SOME OF YOU ALREADY KNOW, WE'RE HERE FOR AN OFFICIAL ANNOUNCEMENT.
I FEEL SICK! I FORGOT MY LINES!
FOCUS... FOCUS!

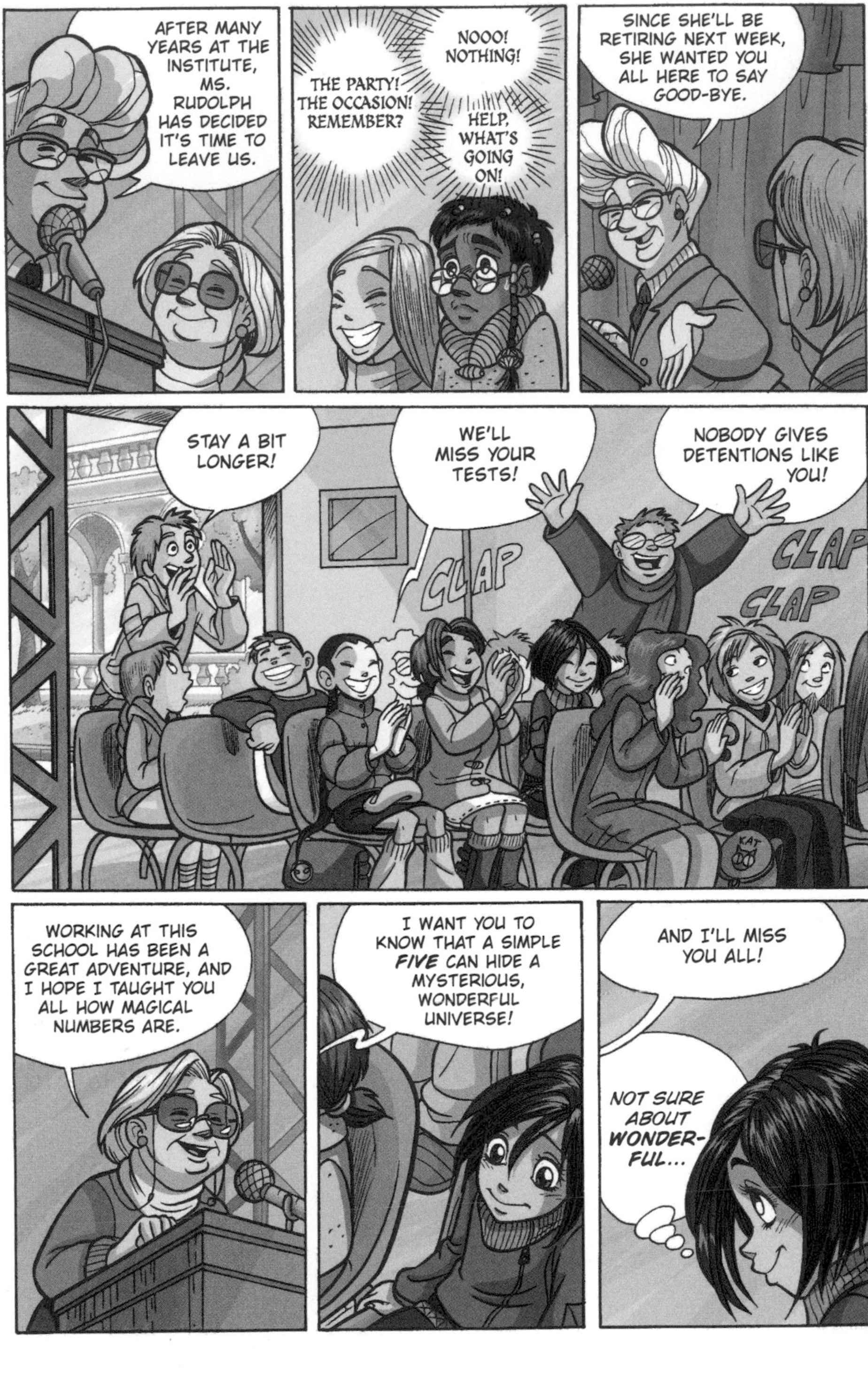
AFTER MANY YEARS AT THE INSTITUTE, MS. RUDOLPH HAS DECIDED IT'S TIME TO LEAVE US.
THE PARTY! THE OCCASION! REMEMBER?
NOOO! NOTHING!
HELP, WHAT'S GOING ON!
SINCE SHE'LL BE RETIRING NEXT WEEK, SHE WANTED YOU ALL HERE TO SAY GOOD-BYE.
STAY A BIT LONGER!
WE'LL MISS YOUR TESTS!
NOBODY GIVES DETENTIONS LIKE YOU!
CLAP
CLAP
CLAP
WORKING AT THIS SCHOOL HAS BEEN A GREAT ADVENTURE, AND I HOPE I TAUGHT YOU ALL HOW MAGICAL NUMBERS ARE.
I WANT YOU TO KNOW THAT A SIMPLE *FIVE* CAN HIDE A MYSTERIOUS, WONDERFUL UNIVERSE!
AND I'LL MISS YOU ALL!
*NOT SURE ABOUT **WONDER-FUL**...*

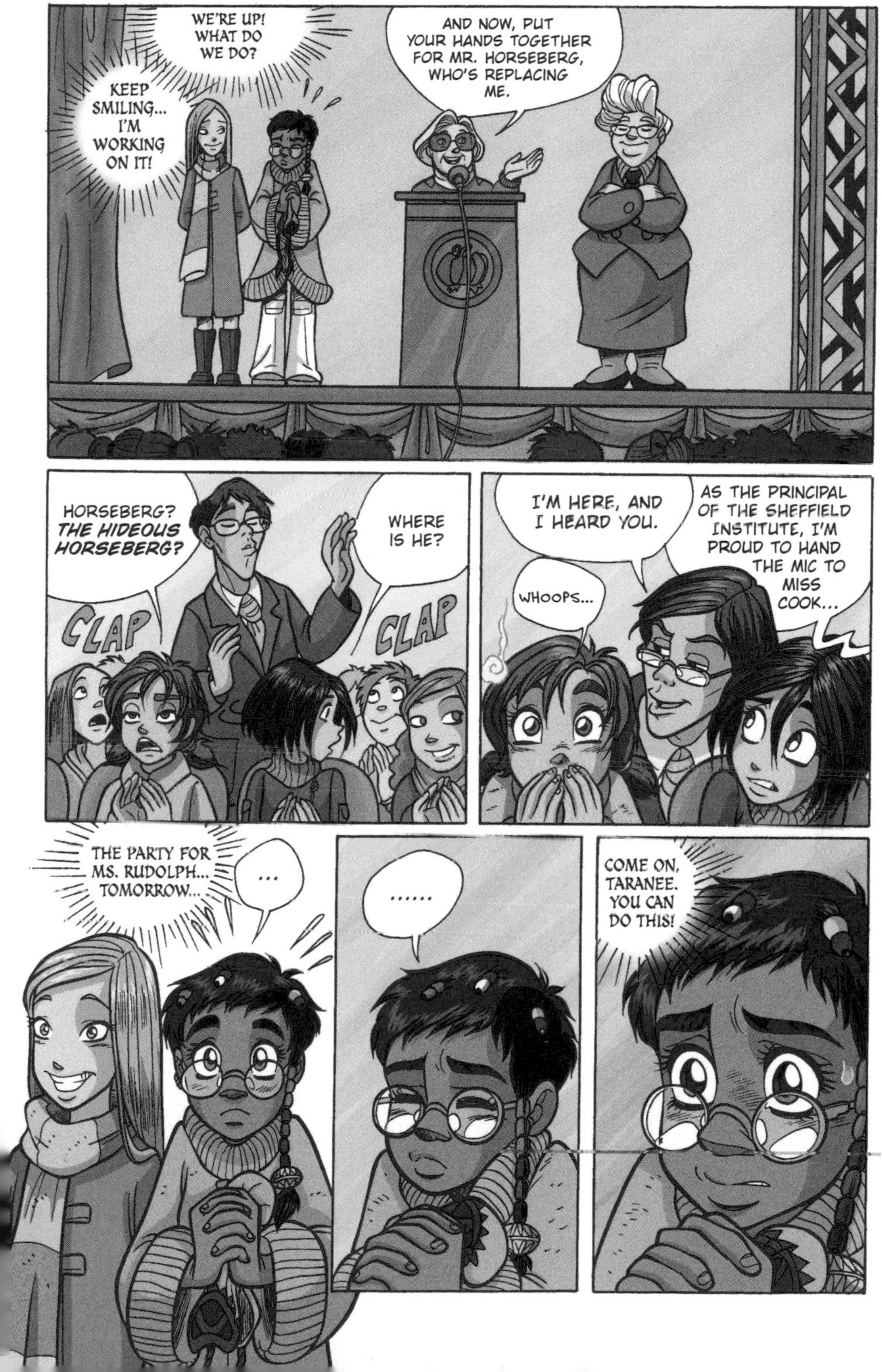

WE'RE UP! WHAT DO WE DO?
KEEP SMILING... I'M WORKING ON IT!
AND NOW, PUT YOUR HANDS TOGETHER FOR MR. HORSEBERG, WHO'S REPLACING ME.
HORSEBERG? THE HIDEOUS HORSEBERG?
WHERE IS HE?
CLAP
CLAP
I'M HERE, AND I HEARD YOU.
AS THE PRINCIPAL OF THE SHEFFIELD INSTITUTE, I'M PROUD TO HAND THE MIC TO MISS COOK...
WHOOPS...
THE PARTY FOR MS. RUDOLPH... TOMORROW...
...
......
COME ON, TARANEE. YOU CAN DO THIS!

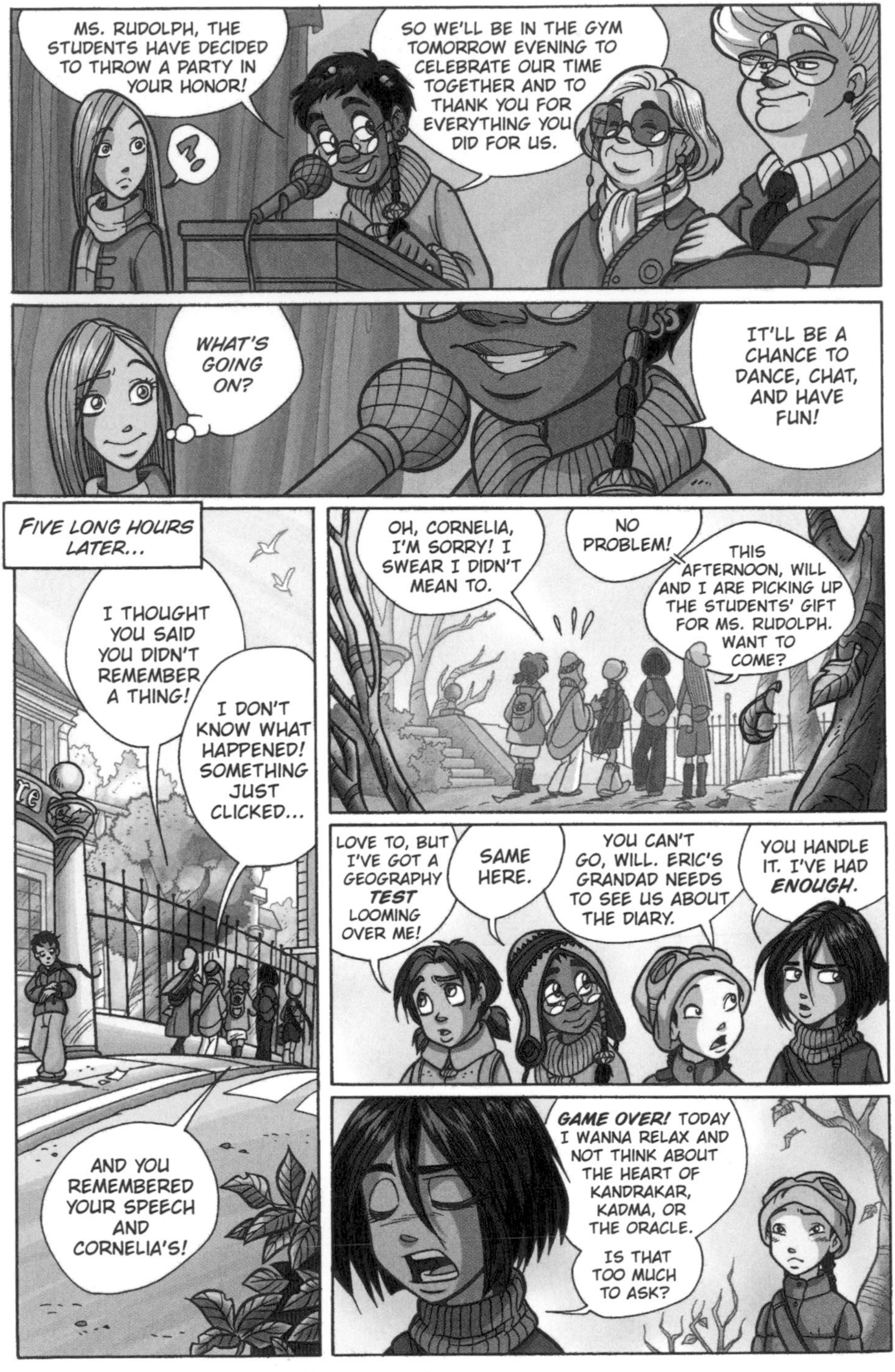
MS. RUDOLPH, THE STUDENTS HAVE DECIDED TO THROW A PARTY IN YOUR HONOR!
?
SO WE'LL BE IN THE GYM TOMORROW EVENING TO CELEBRATE OUR TIME TOGETHER AND TO THANK YOU FOR EVERYTHING YOU DID FOR US.
WHAT'S GOING ON?
IT'LL BE A CHANCE TO DANCE, CHAT, AND HAVE FUN!
FIVE LONG HOURS LATER...
I THOUGHT YOU SAID YOU DIDN'T REMEMBER A THING!
I DON'T KNOW WHAT HAPPENED! SOMETHING JUST CLICKED...
AND YOU REMEMBERED YOUR SPEECH AND CORNELIA'S!
OH, CORNELIA, I'M SORRY! I SWEAR I DIDN'T MEAN TO.
NO PROBLEM!
THIS AFTERNOON, WILL AND I ARE PICKING UP THE STUDENTS' GIFT FOR MS. RUDOLPH. WANT TO COME?
LOVE TO, BUT I'VE GOT A GEOGRAPHY TEST LOOMING OVER ME!
SAME HERE.
YOU CAN'T GO, WILL. ERIC'S GRANDAD NEEDS TO SEE US ABOUT THE DIARY.
YOU HANDLE IT. I'VE HAD ENOUGH.
GAME OVER! TODAY I WANNA RELAX AND NOT THINK ABOUT THE HEART OF KANDRAKAR, KADMA, OR THE ORACLE.
IS THAT TOO MUCH TO ASK?

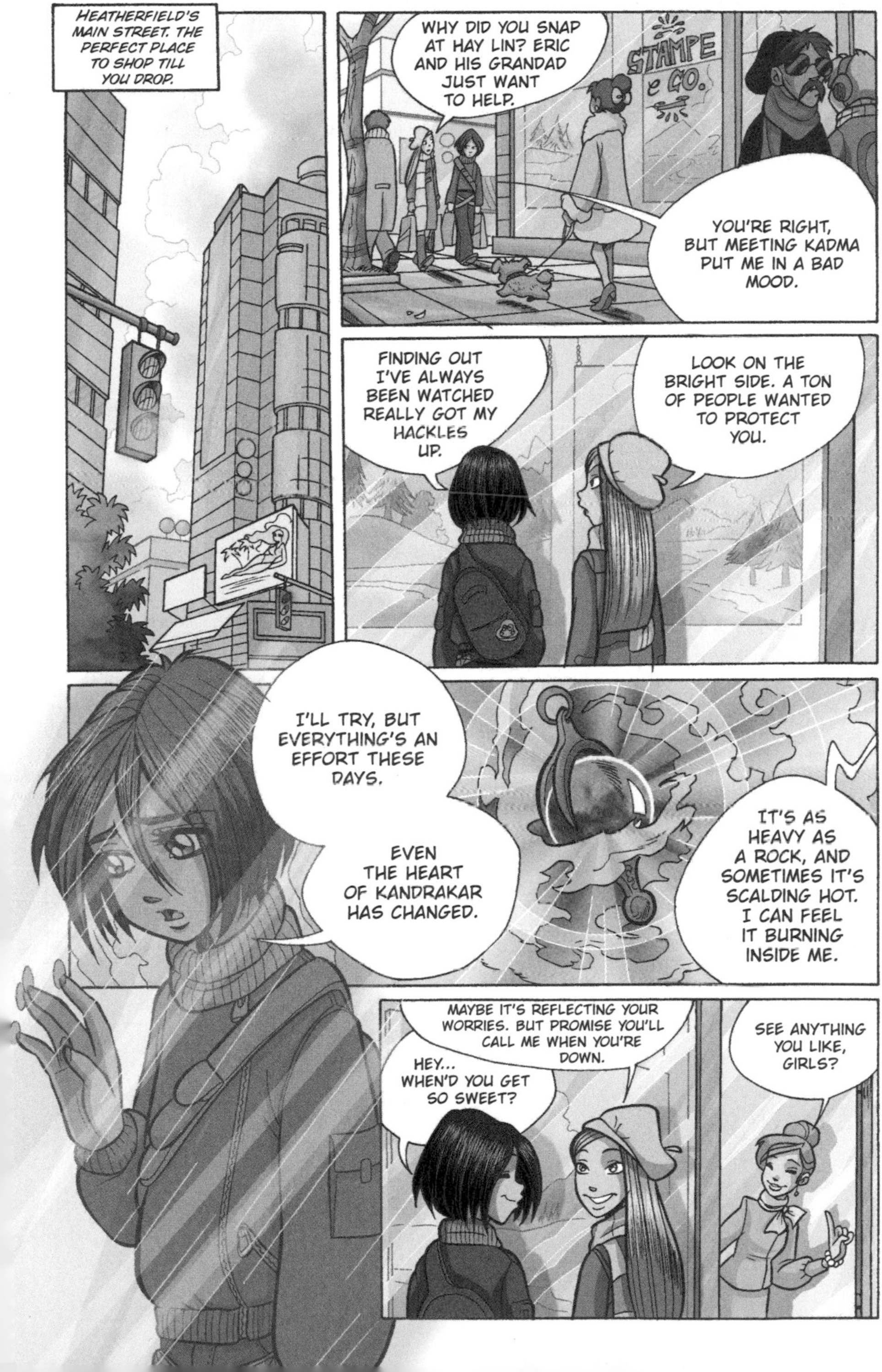
HEATHERFIELD'S MAIN STREET. THE PERFECT PLACE TO SHOP TILL YOU DROP.
WHY DID YOU SNAP AT HAY LIN? ERIC AND HIS GRANDAD JUST WANT TO HELP.
STAMPE e GO.
YOU'RE RIGHT, BUT MEETING KADMA PUT ME IN A BAD MOOD.
FINDING OUT I'VE ALWAYS BEEN WATCHED REALLY GOT MY HACKLES UP.
LOOK ON THE BRIGHT SIDE. A TON OF PEOPLE WANTED TO PROTECT YOU.
I'LL TRY, BUT EVERYTHING'S AN EFFORT THESE DAYS.
EVEN THE HEART OF KANDRAKAR HAS CHANGED.
IT'S AS HEAVY AS A ROCK, AND SOMETIMES IT'S SCALDING HOT. I CAN FEEL IT BURNING INSIDE ME.
MAYBE IT'S REFLECTING YOUR WORRIES. BUT PROMISE YOU'LL CALL ME WHEN YOU'RE DOWN.
HEY... WHEN'D YOU GET SO SWEET?
SEE ANYTHING YOU LIKE, GIRLS?

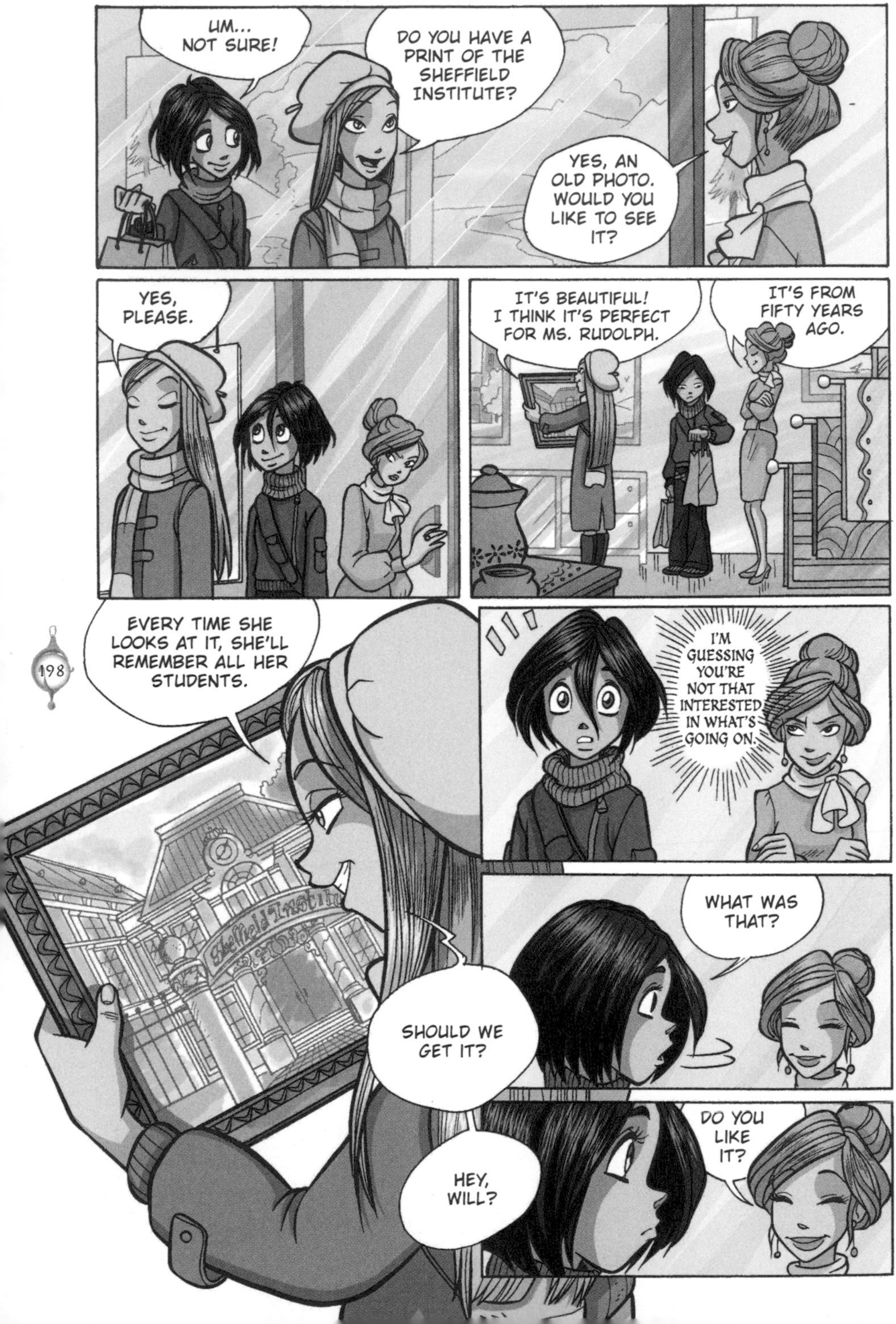
UM...
NOT SURE!
DO YOU HAVE A PRINT OF THE SHEFFIELD INSTITUTE?
YES, AN OLD PHOTO. WOULD YOU LIKE TO SEE IT?
YES, PLEASE.
IT'S BEAUTIFUL! I THINK IT'S PERFECT FOR MS. RUDOLPH.
IT'S FROM FIFTY YEARS AGO.
EVERY TIME SHE LOOKS AT IT, SHE'LL REMEMBER ALL HER STUDENTS.
I'M GUESSING YOU'RE NOT THAT INTERESTED IN WHAT'S GOING ON.
WHAT WAS THAT?
SHOULD WE GET IT?
DO YOU LIKE IT?
HEY, WILL?

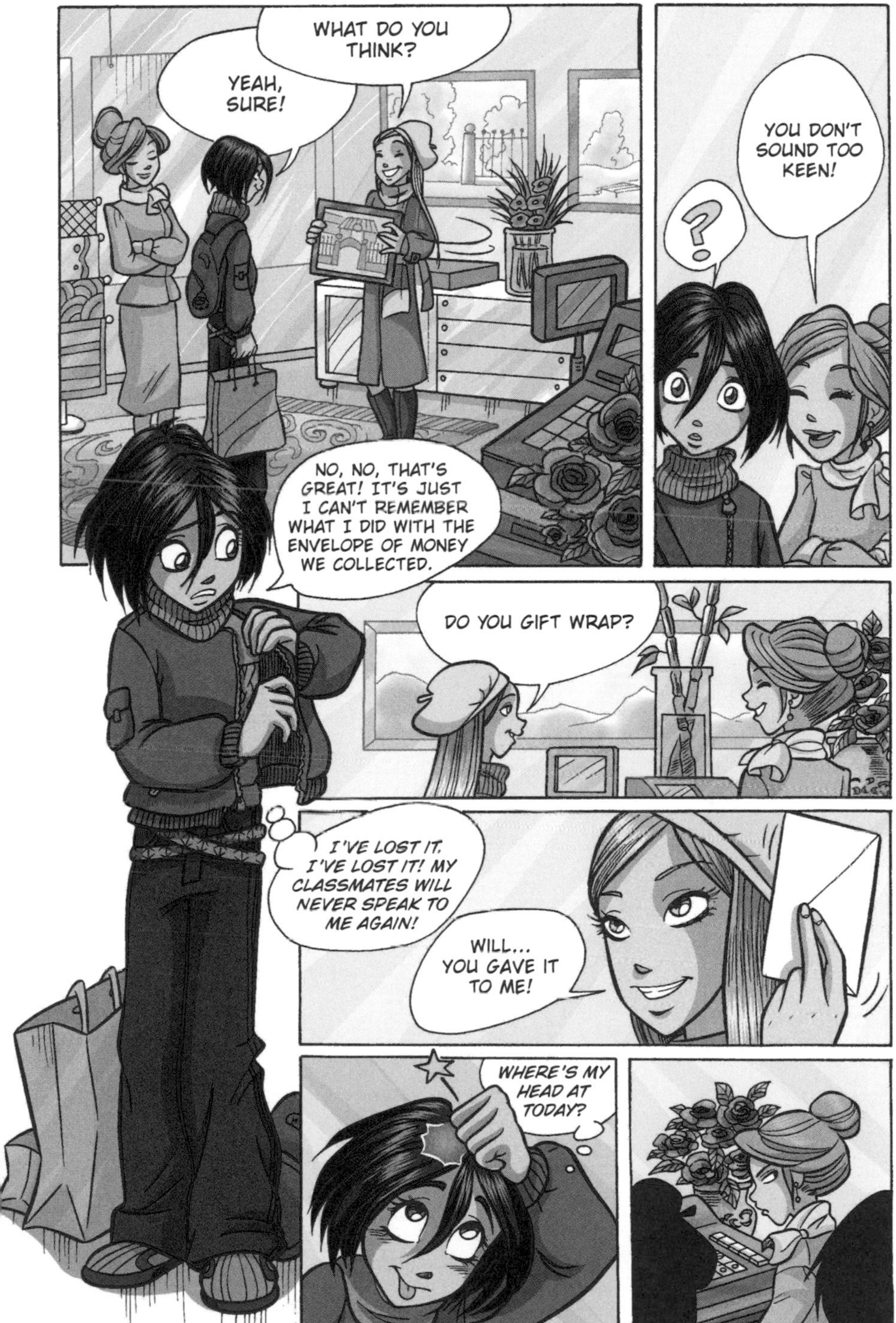
WHAT DO YOU THINK?
YEAH, SURE!
YOU DON'T SOUND TOO KEEN!
?
NO, NO, THAT'S GREAT! IT'S JUST I CAN'T REMEMBER WHAT I DID WITH THE ENVELOPE OF MONEY WE COLLECTED.
DO YOU GIFT WRAP?
I'VE LOST IT. I'VE LOST IT! MY CLASSMATES WILL NEVER SPEAK TO ME AGAIN!
WILL... YOU GAVE IT TO ME!
WHERE'S MY HEAD AT TODAY?

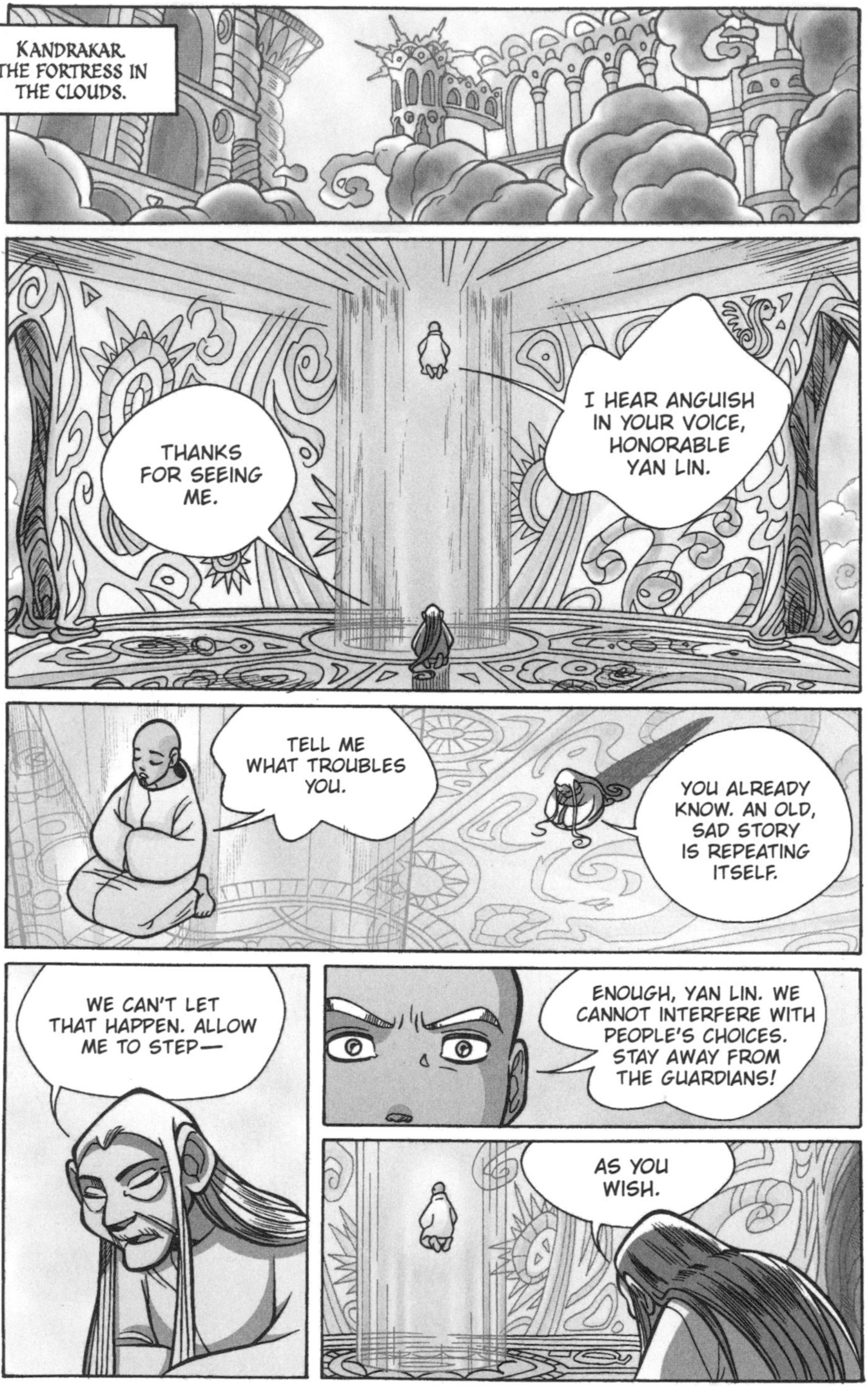
KANDRAKAR. THE FORTRESS IN THE CLOUDS.
THANKS FOR SEEING ME.
I HEAR ANGUISH IN YOUR VOICE, HONORABLE YAN LIN.
TELL ME WHAT TROUBLES YOU.
YOU ALREADY KNOW. AN OLD, SAD STORY IS REPEATING ITSELF.
WE CAN'T LET THAT HAPPEN. ALLOW ME TO STEP—
ENOUGH, YAN LIN. WE CANNOT INTERFERE WITH PEOPLE'S CHOICES. STAY AWAY FROM THE GUARDIANS!
AS YOU WISH.

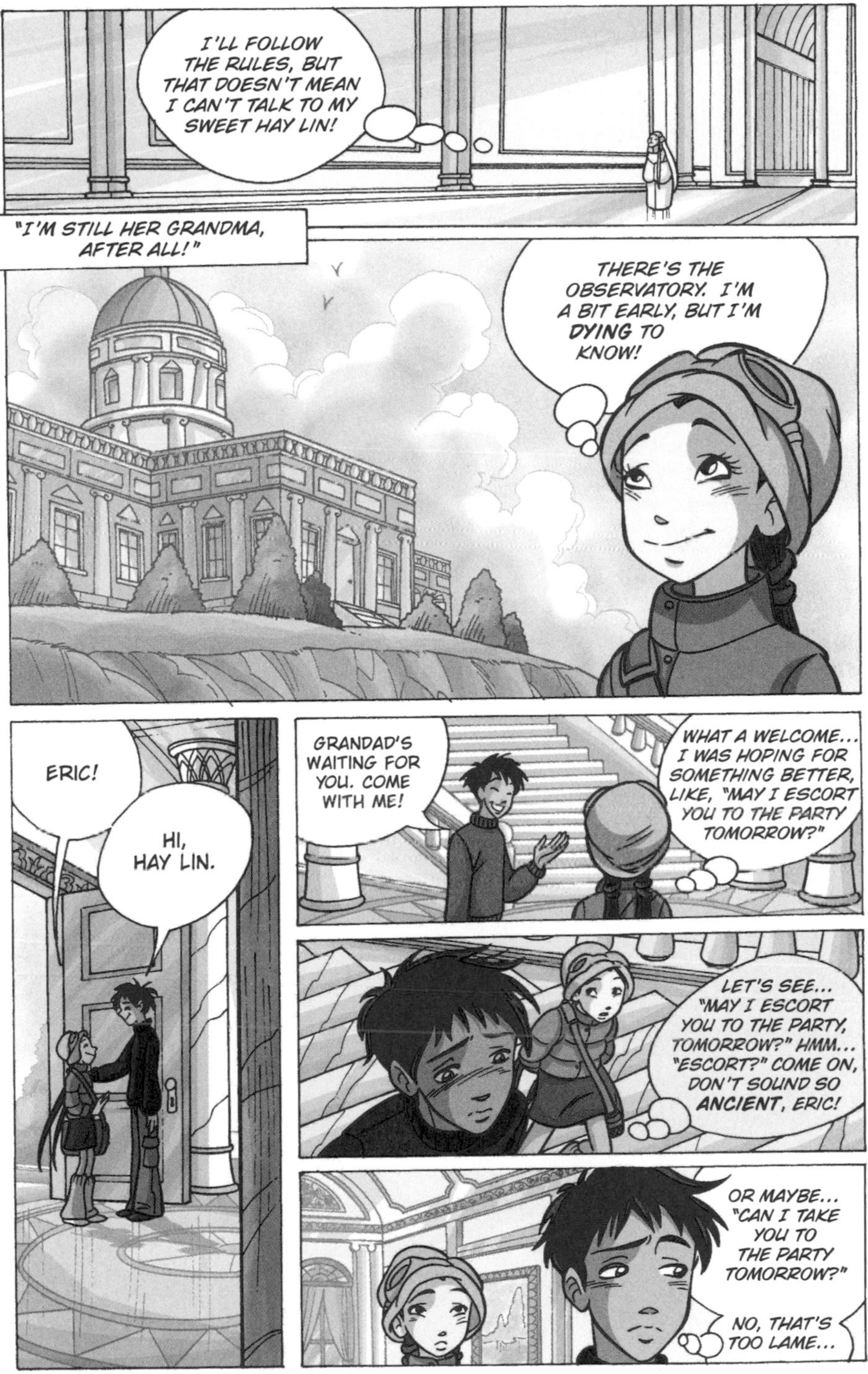
I'LL FOLLOW THE RULES, BUT THAT DOESN'T MEAN I CAN'T TALK TO MY SWEET HAY LIN!
"I'M STILL HER GRANDMA, AFTER ALL!"
THERE'S THE OBSERVATORY. I'M A BIT EARLY, BUT I'M **DYING** TO KNOW!
ERIC!
HI, HAY LIN.
GRANDAD'S WAITING FOR YOU. COME WITH ME!
WHAT A WELCOME... I WAS HOPING FOR SOMETHING BETTER, LIKE, "MAY I ESCORT YOU TO THE PARTY TOMORROW?"
LET'S SEE... "MAY I ESCORT YOU TO THE PARTY, TOMORROW?" HMM... "ESCORT?" COME ON, DON'T SOUND SO **ANCIENT**, ERIC!
OR MAYBE... "CAN I TAKE YOU TO THE PARTY TOMORROW?"
NO, THAT'S TOO LAME...

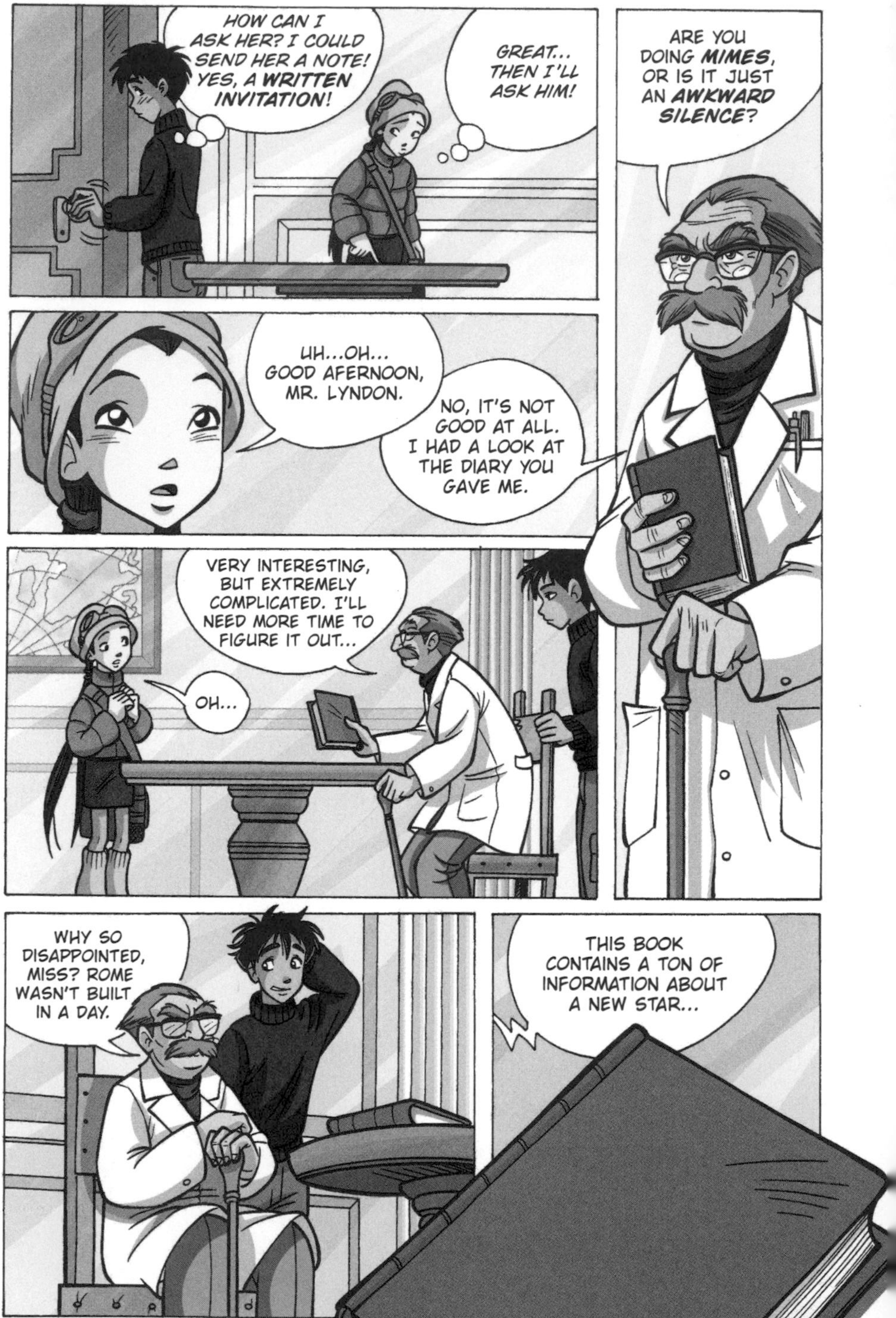
HOW CAN I ASK HER? I COULD SEND HER A NOTE! YES, A WRITTEN INVITATION!
GREAT... THEN I'LL ASK HIM!
ARE YOU DOING MIMES, OR IS IT JUST AN AWKWARD SILENCE?
UH...OH... GOOD AFERNOON, MR. LYNDON.
NO, IT'S NOT GOOD AT ALL. I HAD A LOOK AT THE DIARY YOU GAVE ME.
VERY INTERESTING, BUT EXTREMELY COMPLICATED. I'LL NEED MORE TIME TO FIGURE IT OUT...
OH...
WHY SO DISAPPOINTED, MISS? ROME WASN'T BUILT IN A DAY.
THIS BOOK CONTAINS A TON OF INFORMATION ABOUT A NEW STAR...

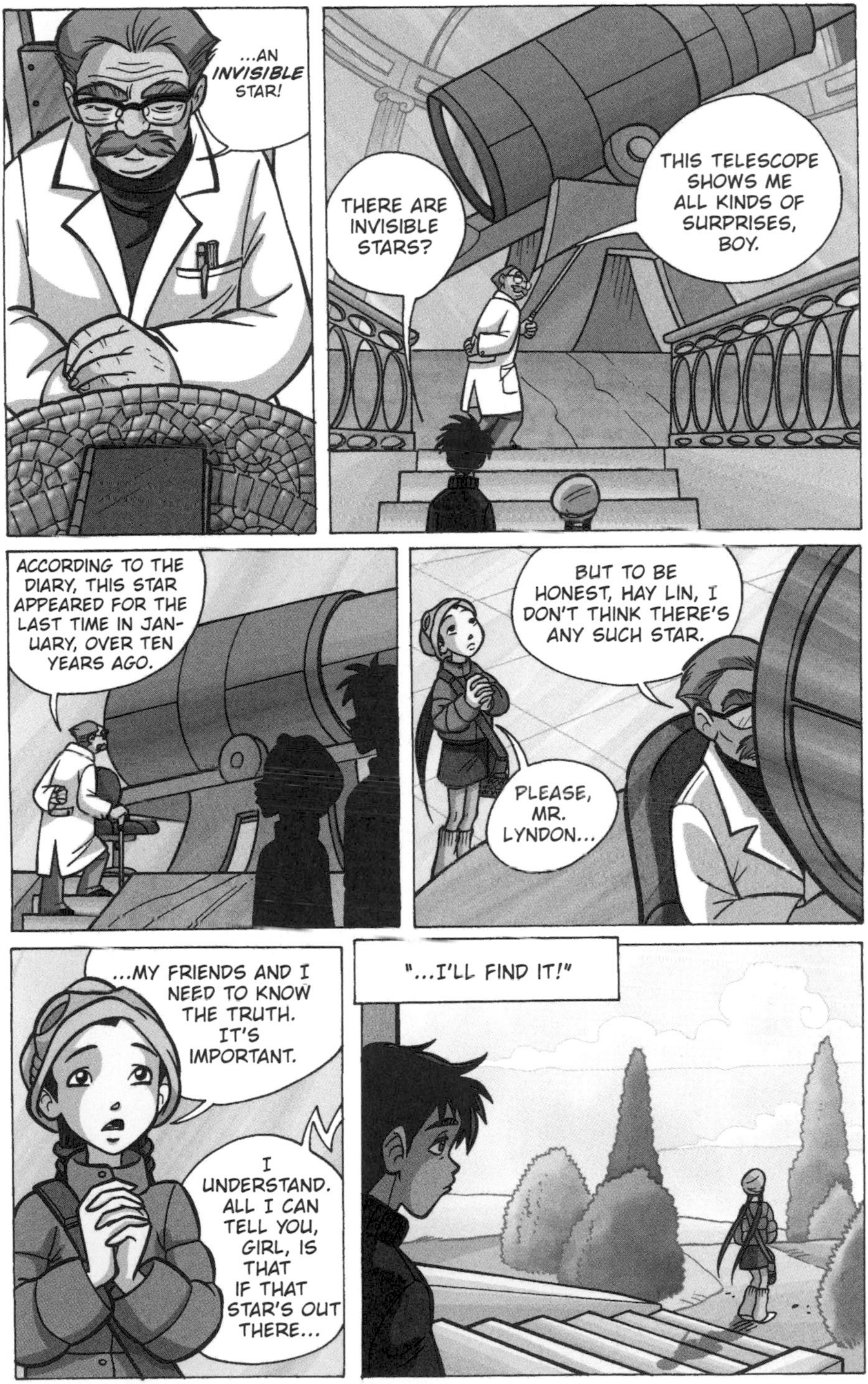

...AN *INVISIBLE* STAR!
THERE ARE INVISIBLE STARS?
THIS TELESCOPE SHOWS ME ALL KINDS OF SURPRISES, BOY.
ACCORDING TO THE DIARY, THIS STAR APPEARED FOR THE LAST TIME IN JANUARY, OVER TEN YEARS AGO.
BUT TO BE HONEST, HAY LIN, I DON'T THINK THERE'S ANY SUCH STAR.
PLEASE, MR. LYNDON...
...MY FRIENDS AND I NEED TO KNOW THE TRUTH. IT'S IMPORTANT.
I UNDERSTAND. ALL I CAN TELL YOU, GIRL, IS THAT IF THAT STAR'S OUT THERE...
"...I'LL FIND IT!"

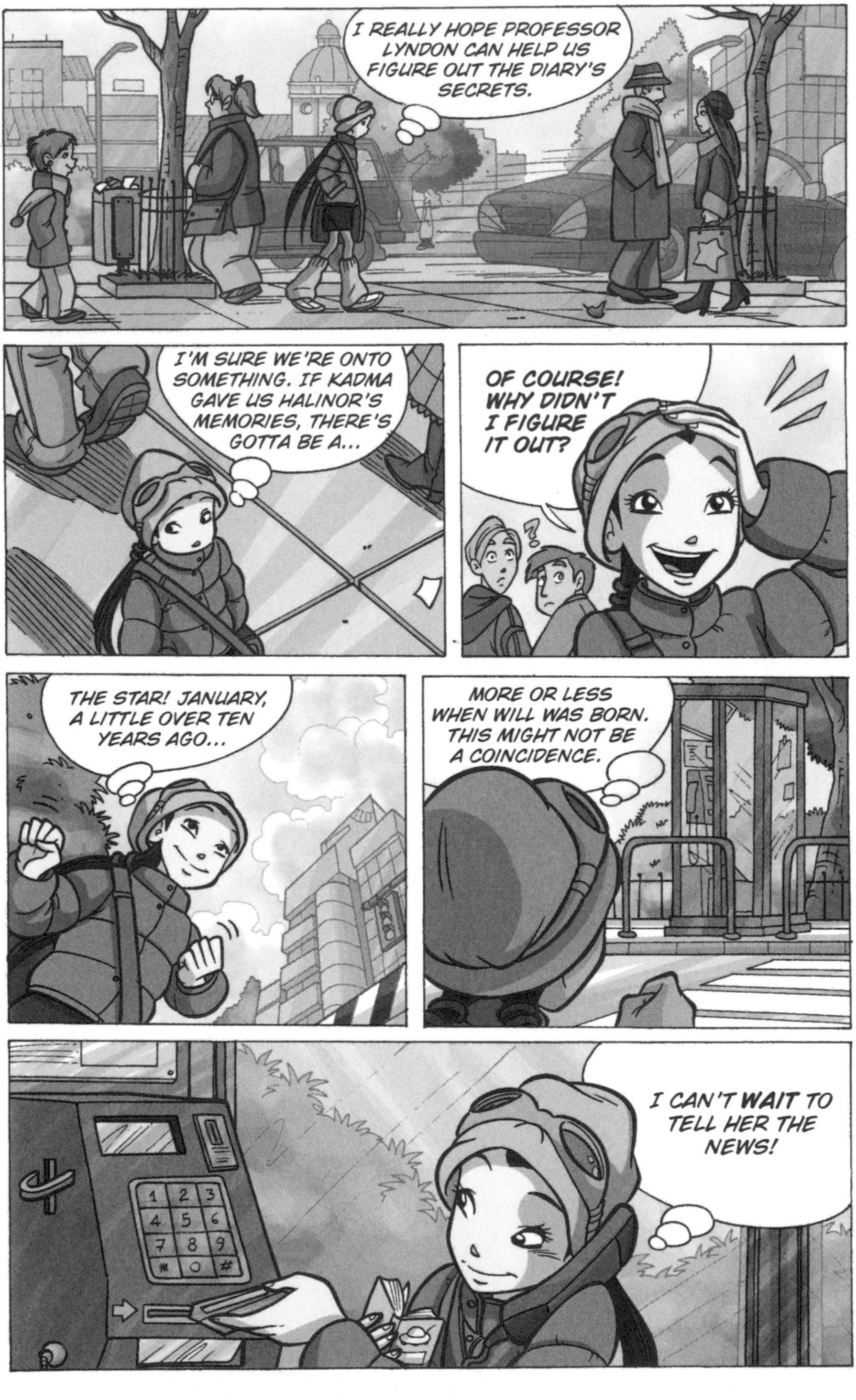
I REALLY HOPE PROFESSOR LYNDON CAN HELP US FIGURE OUT THE DIARY'S SECRETS.
I'M SURE WE'RE ONTO SOMETHING. IF KADMA GAVE US HALINOR'S MEMORIES, THERE'S GOTTA BE A...
OF COURSE! WHY DIDN'T I FIGURE IT OUT?
?
THE STAR! JANUARY, A LITTLE OVER TEN YEARS AGO...
MORE OR LESS WHEN WILL WAS BORN. THIS MIGHT NOT BE A COINCIDENCE.
I CAN'T WAIT TO TELL HER THE NEWS!

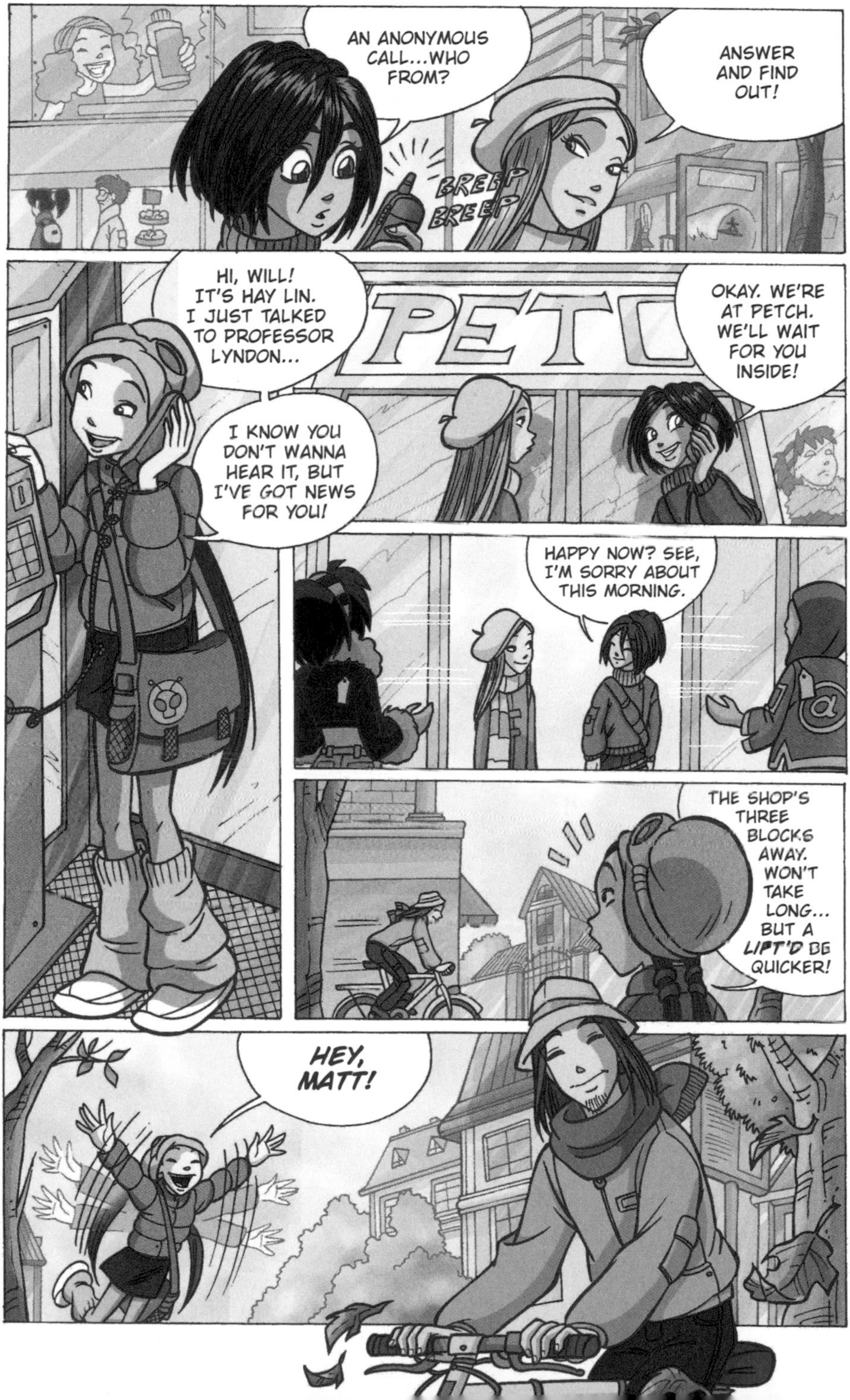
AN ANONYMOUS CALL...WHO FROM?
BREEP BREEP
ANSWER AND FIND OUT!
HI, WILL! IT'S HAY LIN. I JUST TALKED TO PROFESSOR LYNDON...
I KNOW YOU DON'T WANNA HEAR IT, BUT I'VE GOT NEWS FOR YOU!
PETC
OKAY. WE'RE AT PETCH. WE'LL WAIT FOR YOU INSIDE!
HAPPY NOW? SEE, I'M SORRY ABOUT THIS MORNING.
THE SHOP'S THREE BLOCKS AWAY. WON'T TAKE LONG... BUT A LIFT'D BE QUICKER!
HEY, MATT!

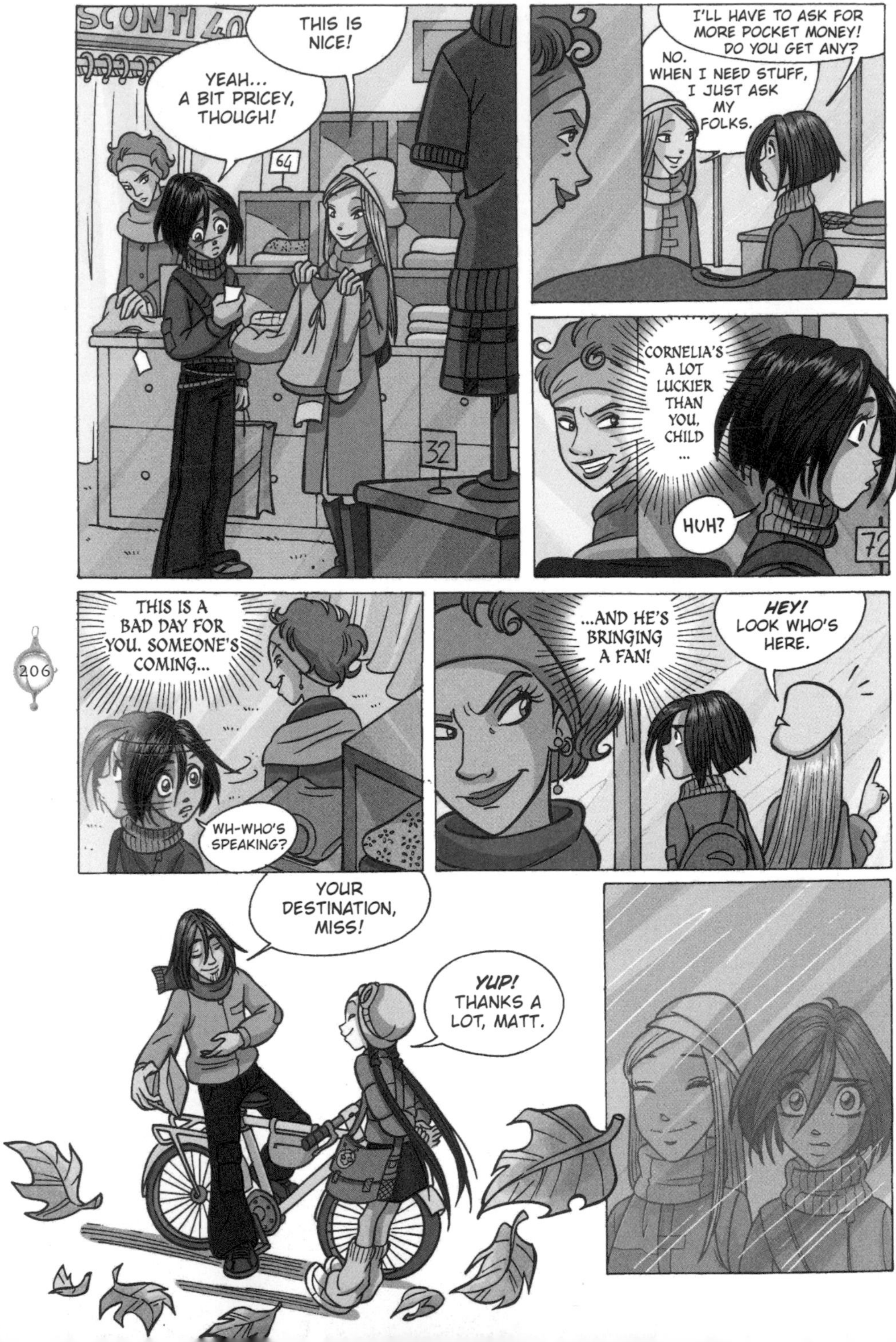
SCONTI 40
THIS IS NICE!
YEAH... A BIT PRICEY, THOUGH!
I'LL HAVE TO ASK FOR MORE POCKET MONEY! DO YOU GET ANY?
NO. WHEN I NEED STUFF, I JUST ASK MY FOLKS.
CORNELIA'S A LOT LUCKIER THAN YOU, CHILD ...
HUH?
THIS IS A BAD DAY FOR YOU. SOMEONE'S COMING...
WH-WHO'S SPEAKING?
...AND HE'S BRINGING A FAN!
HEY! LOOK WHO'S HERE.
YOUR DESTINATION, MISS!
YUP! THANKS A LOT, MATT.

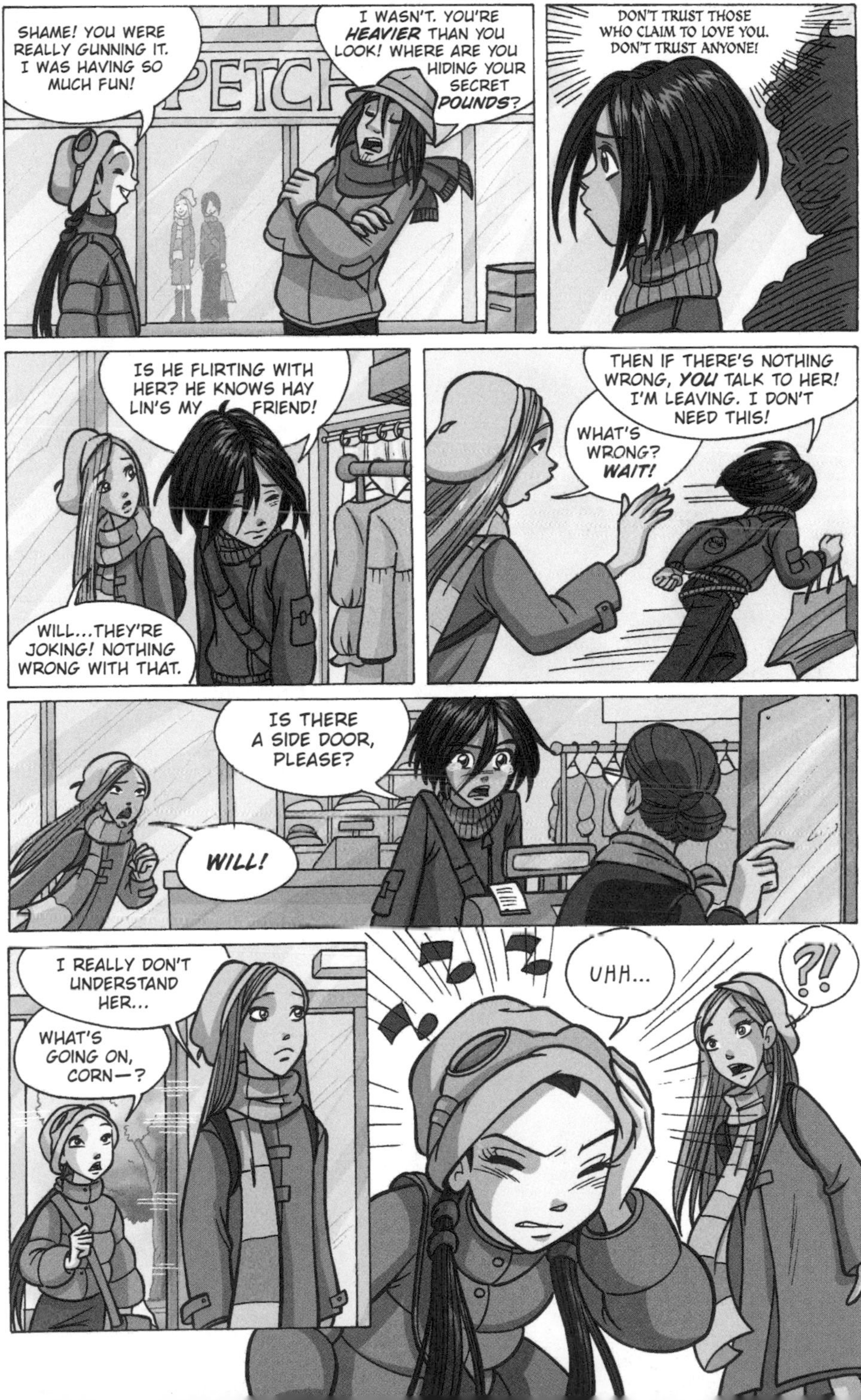
SHAME! YOU WERE REALLY GUNNING IT. I WAS HAVING SO MUCH FUN!
PETCH
I WASN'T. YOU'RE HEAVIER THAN YOU LOOK! WHERE ARE YOU HIDING YOUR SECRET POUNDS?
DON'T TRUST THOSE WHO CLAIM TO LOVE YOU. DON'T TRUST ANYONE!
IS HE FLIRTING WITH HER? HE KNOWS HAY LIN'S MY FRIEND!
WILL...THEY'RE JOKING! NOTHING WRONG WITH THAT.
WHAT'S WRONG? WAIT!
THEN IF THERE'S NOTHING WRONG, YOU TALK TO HER! I'M LEAVING. I DON'T NEED THIS!
WILL!
IS THERE A SIDE DOOR, PLEASE?
I REALLY DON'T UNDERSTAND HER...
WHAT'S GOING ON, CORN—?
UHH...
?!

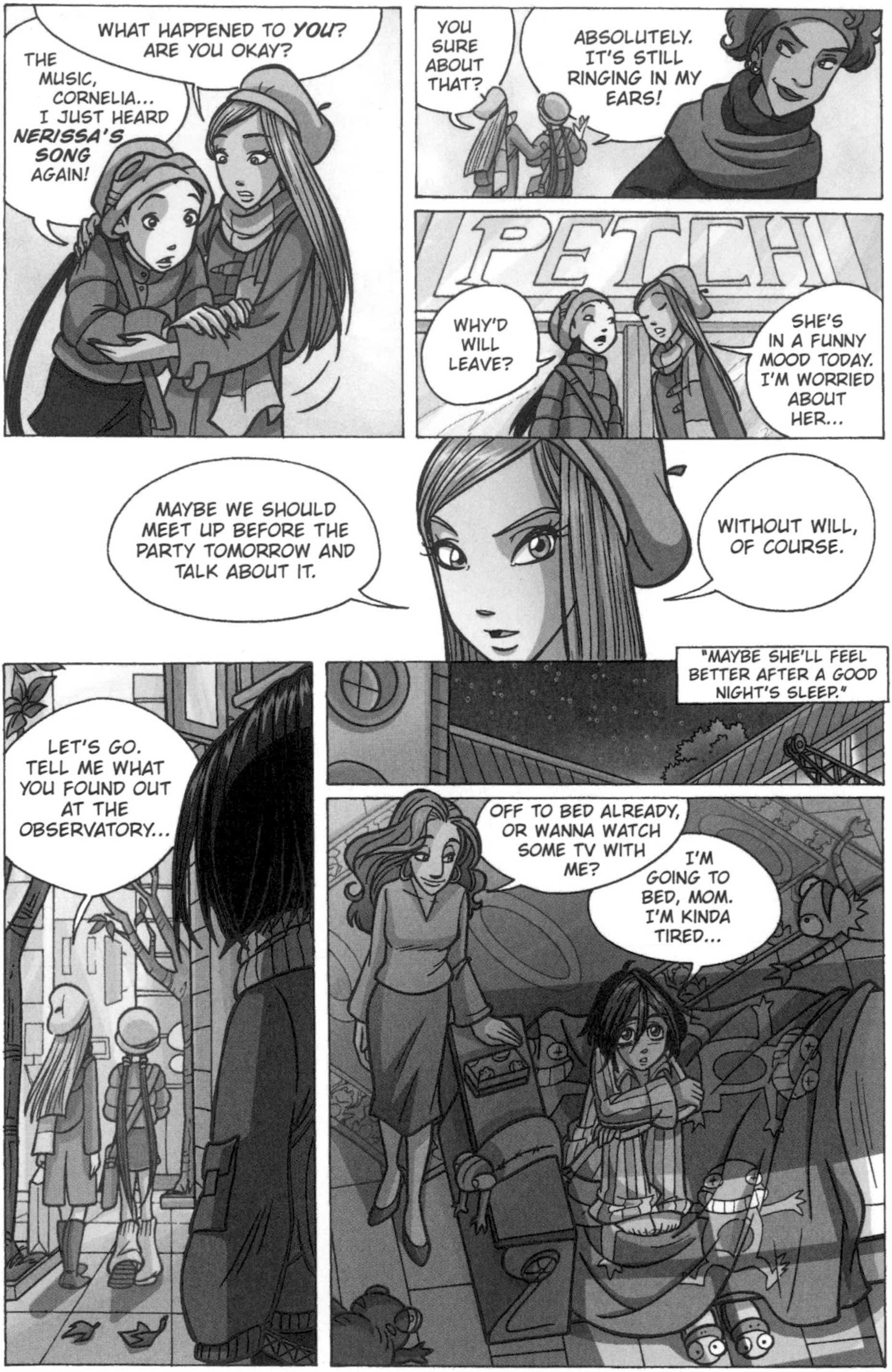
WHAT HAPPENED TO YOU? ARE YOU OKAY?
THE MUSIC, CORNELIA... I JUST HEARD NERISSA'S SONG AGAIN!
YOU SURE ABOUT THAT?
ABSOLUTELY. IT'S STILL RINGING IN MY EARS!
PETCH
WHY'D WILL LEAVE?
SHE'S IN A FUNNY MOOD TODAY. I'M WORRIED ABOUT HER...
MAYBE WE SHOULD MEET UP BEFORE THE PARTY TOMORROW AND TALK ABOUT IT.
WITHOUT WILL, OF COURSE.
LET'S GO. TELL ME WHAT YOU FOUND OUT AT THE OBSERVATORY...
"MAYBE SHE'LL FEEL BETTER AFTER A GOOD NIGHT'S SLEEP."
OFF TO BED ALREADY, OR WANNA WATCH SOME TV WITH ME?
I'M GOING TO BED, MOM. I'M KINDA TIRED...

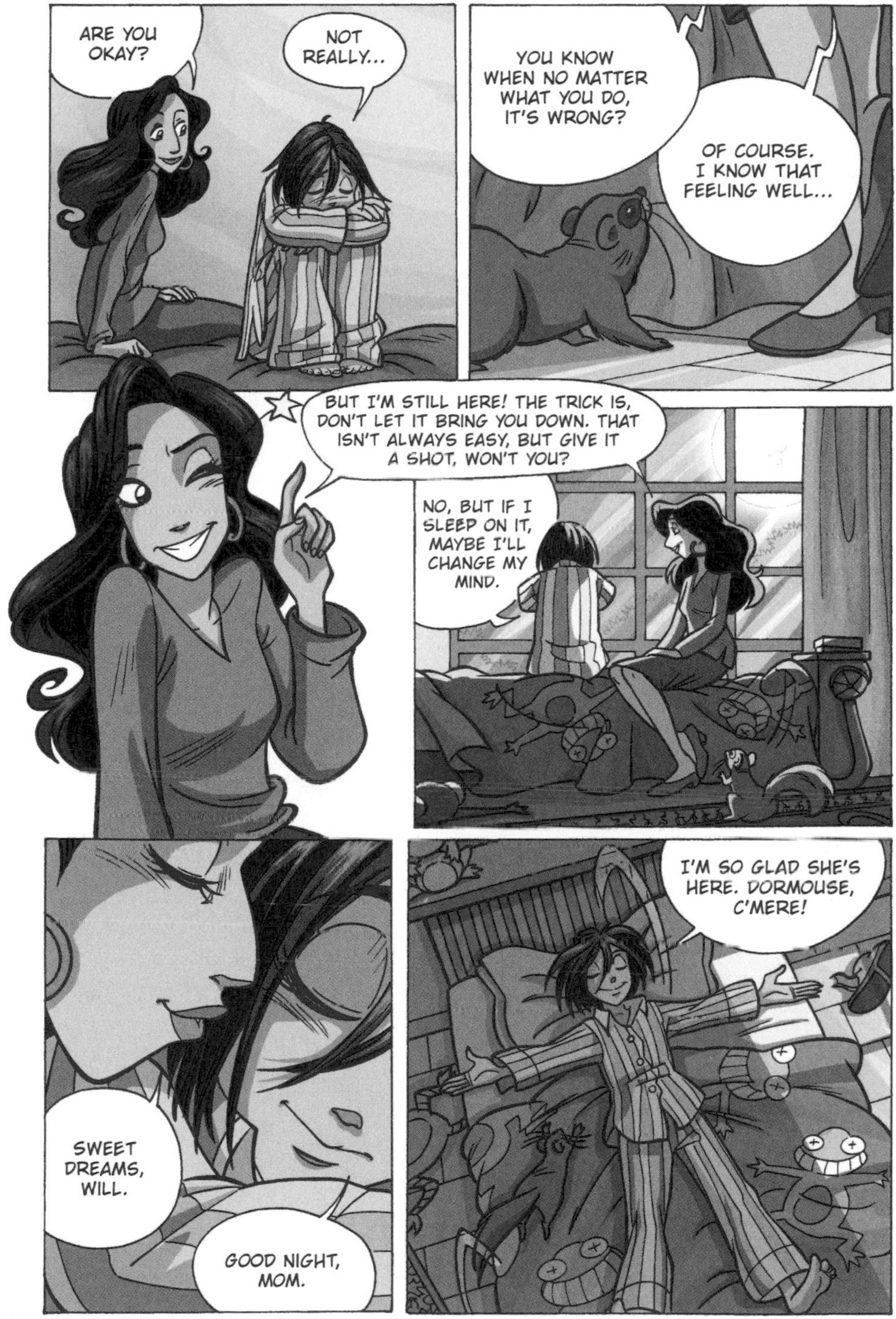

ARE YOU OKAY?
NOT REALLY...
YOU KNOW WHEN NO MATTER WHAT YOU DO, IT'S WRONG?
OF COURSE. I KNOW THAT FEELING WELL...
BUT I'M STILL HERE! THE TRICK IS, DON'T LET IT BRING YOU DOWN. THAT ISN'T ALWAYS EASY, BUT GIVE IT A SHOT, WON'T YOU?
NO, BUT IF I SLEEP ON IT, MAYBE I'LL CHANGE MY MIND.
SWEET DREAMS, WILL.
GOOD NIGHT, MOM.
I'M SO GLAD SHE'S HERE. DORMOUSE, C'MERE!

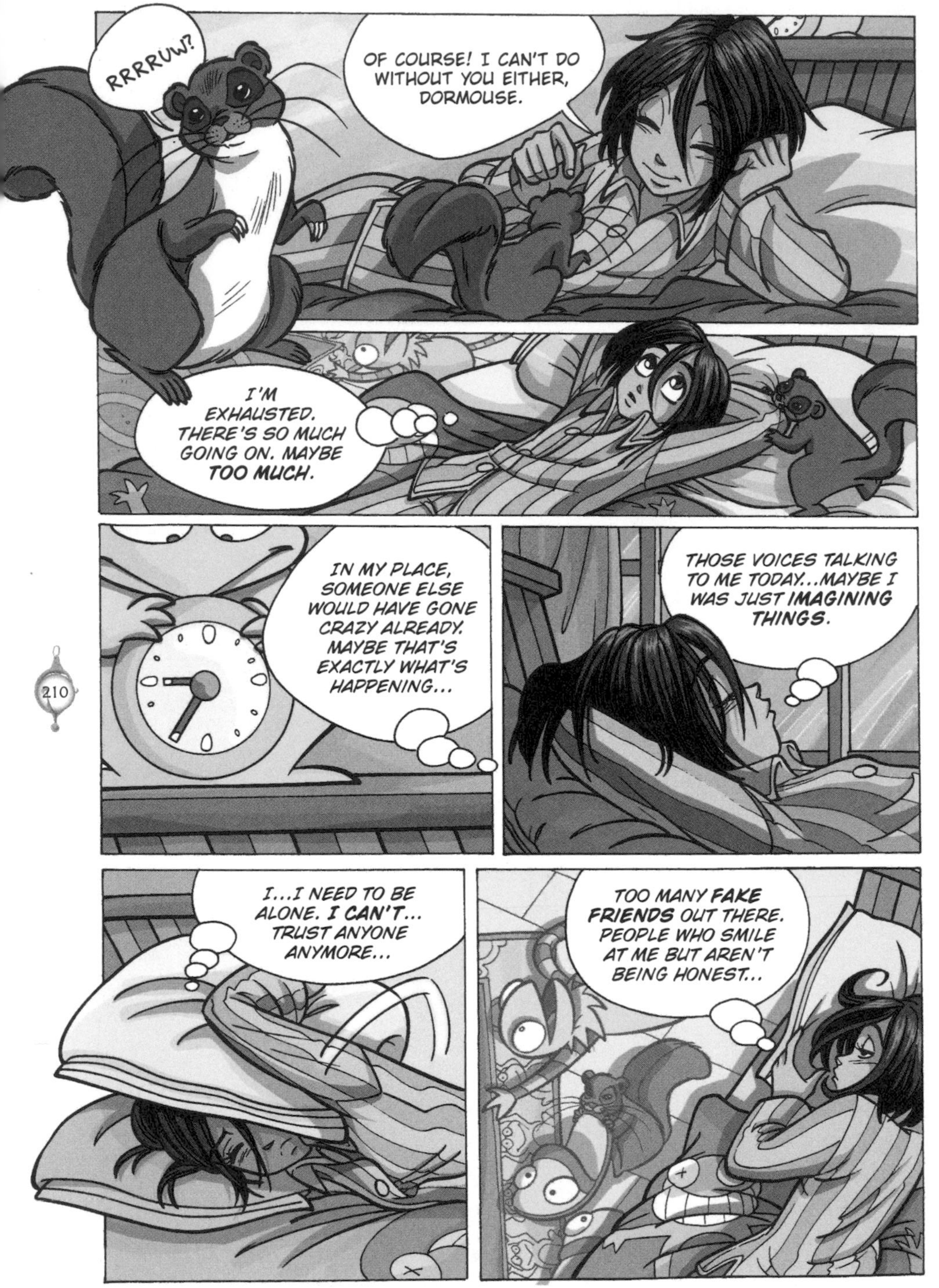
RRRRUW?
OF COURSE! I CAN'T DO WITHOUT YOU EITHER, DORMOUSE.
I'M EXHAUSTED. THERE'S SO MUCH GOING ON. MAYBE TOO MUCH.
IN MY PLACE, SOMEONE ELSE WOULD HAVE GONE CRAZY ALREADY. MAYBE THAT'S EXACTLY WHAT'S HAPPENING...
THOSE VOICES TALKING TO ME TODAY...MAYBE I WAS JUST IMAGINING THINGS.
I...I NEED TO BE ALONE. I CAN'T... TRUST ANYONE ANYMORE...
TOO MANY FAKE FRIENDS OUT THERE. PEOPLE WHO SMILE AT ME BUT AREN'T BEING HONEST...

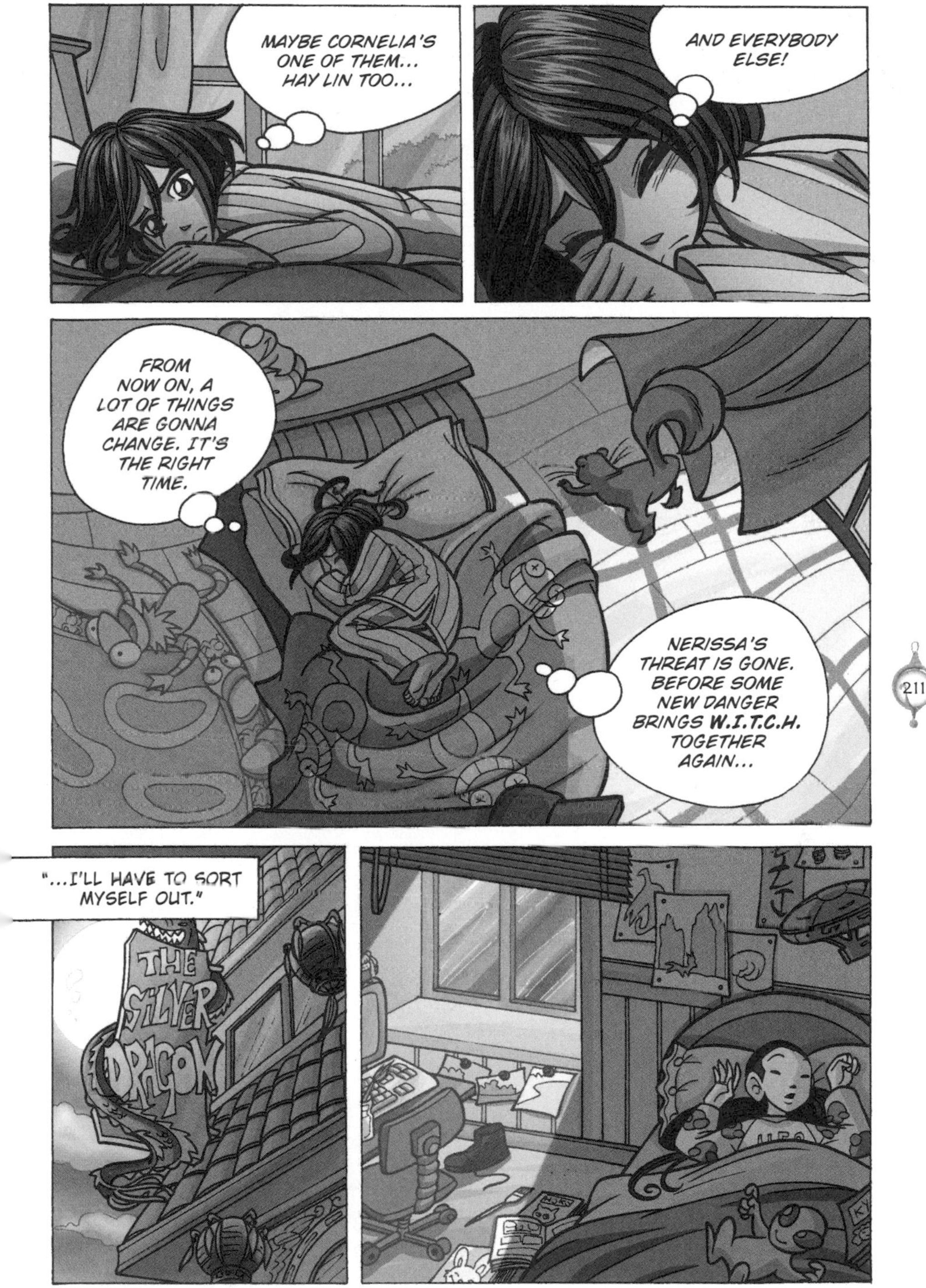
MAYBE CORNELIA'S ONE OF THEM... HAY LIN TOO...
AND EVERYBODY ELSE!
FROM NOW ON, A LOT OF THINGS ARE GONNA CHANGE. IT'S THE RIGHT TIME.
NERISSA'S THREAT IS GONE. BEFORE SOME NEW DANGER BRINGS W.I.T.C.H. TOGETHER AGAIN...
"...I'LL HAVE TO SORT MYSELF OUT."
THE SILVER DRAGON

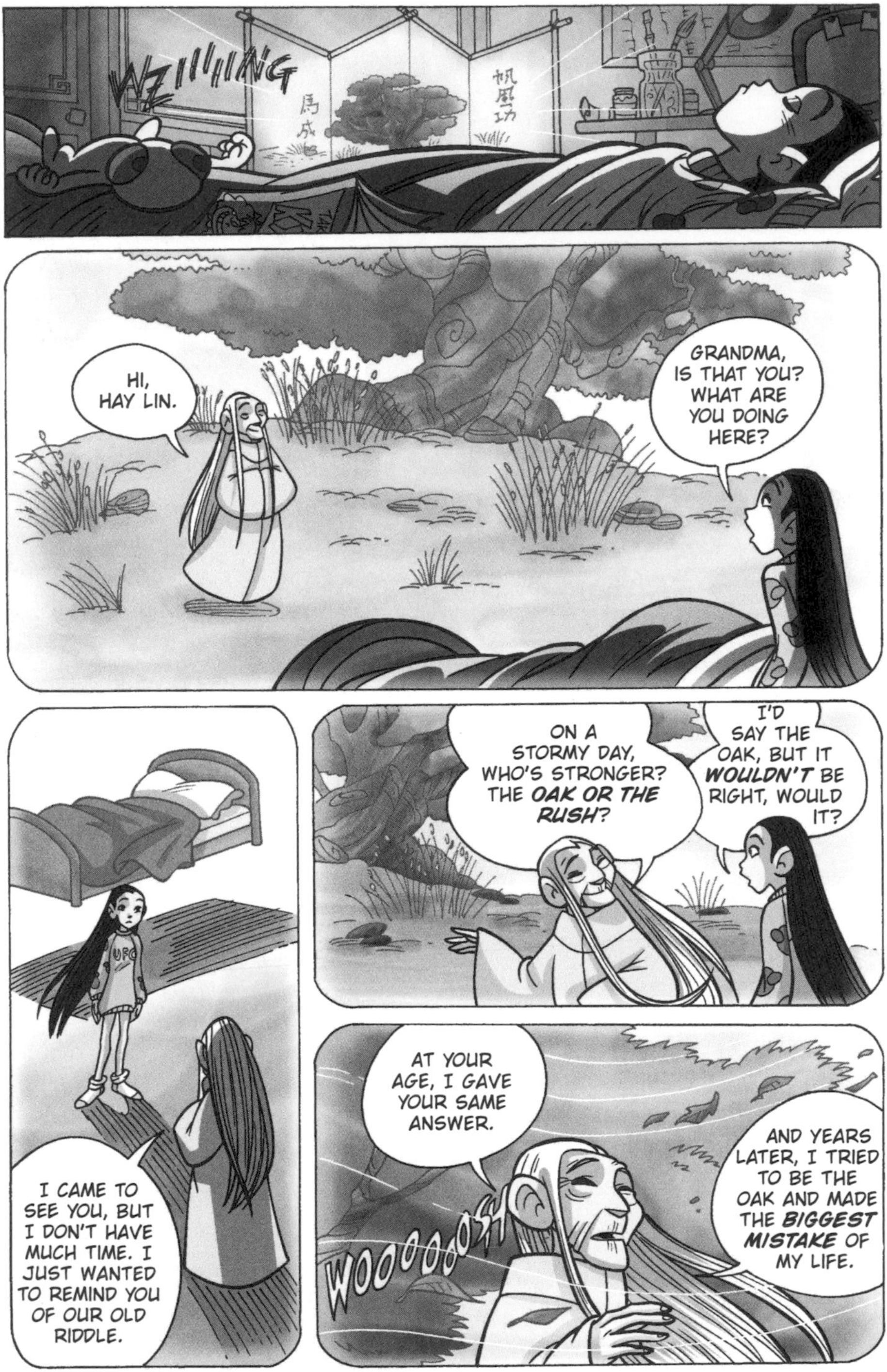
WZIIIIING
HI, HAY LIN.
GRANDMA, IS THAT YOU? WHAT ARE YOU DOING HERE?
I CAME TO SEE YOU, BUT I DON'T HAVE MUCH TIME. I JUST WANTED TO REMIND YOU OF OUR OLD RIDDLE.
ON A STORMY DAY, WHO'S STRONGER? THE OAK OR THE RUSH?
I'D SAY THE OAK, BUT IT WOULDN'T BE RIGHT, WOULD IT?
AT YOUR AGE, I GAVE YOUR SAME ANSWER.
AND YEARS LATER, I TRIED TO BE THE OAK AND MADE THE BIGGEST MISTAKE OF MY LIFE.
WOOOOOOOSH

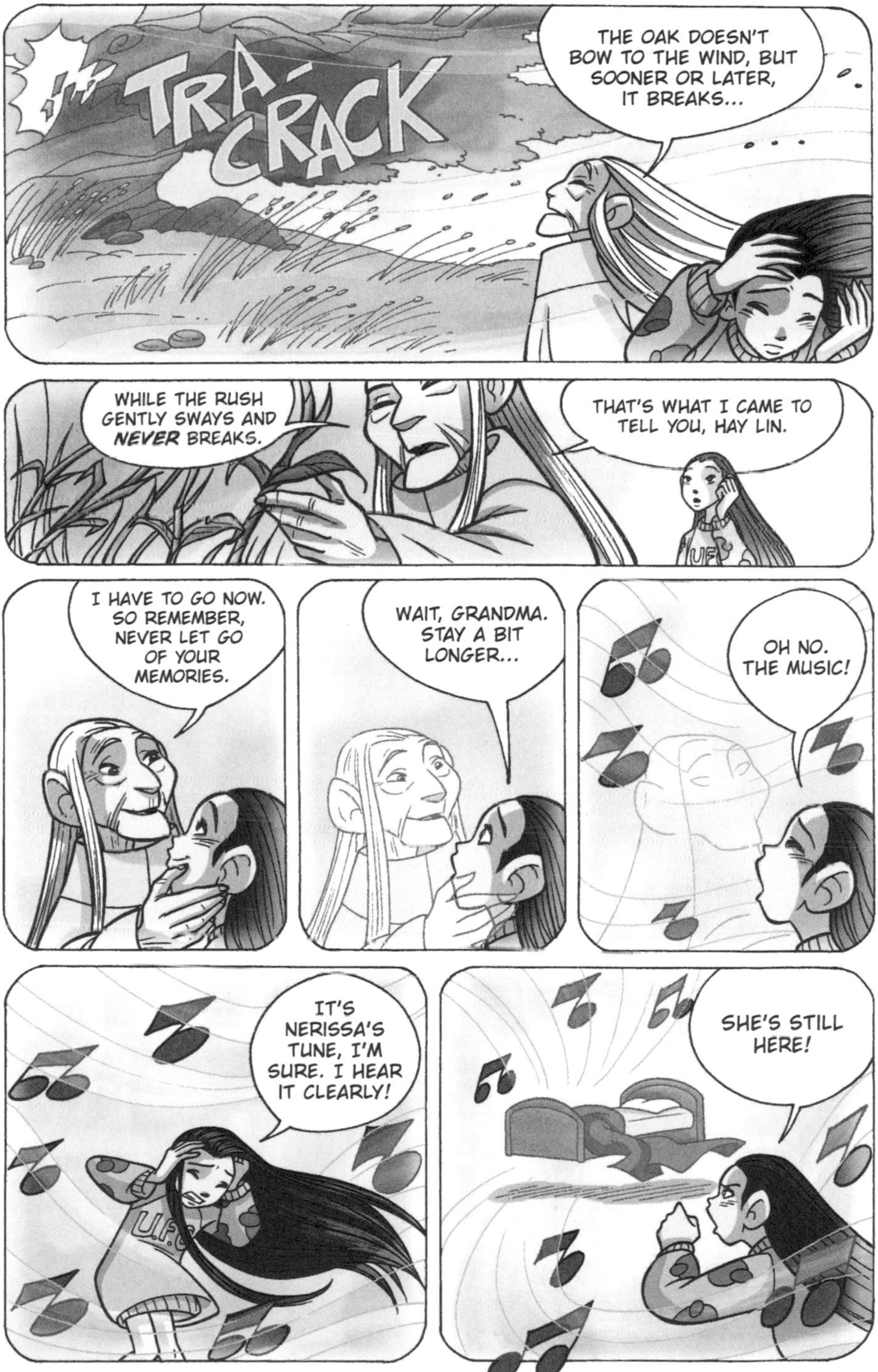
TRA-CRACK
THE OAK DOESN'T BOW TO THE WIND, BUT SOONER OR LATER, IT BREAKS...
WHILE THE RUSH GENTLY SWAYS AND NEVER BREAKS.
THAT'S WHAT I CAME TO TELL YOU, HAY LIN.
I HAVE TO GO NOW. SO REMEMBER, NEVER LET GO OF YOUR MEMORIES.
WAIT, GRANDMA. STAY A BIT LONGER...
OH NO. THE MUSIC!
IT'S NERISSA'S TUNE, I'M SURE. I HEAR IT CLEARLY!
SHE'S STILL HERE!

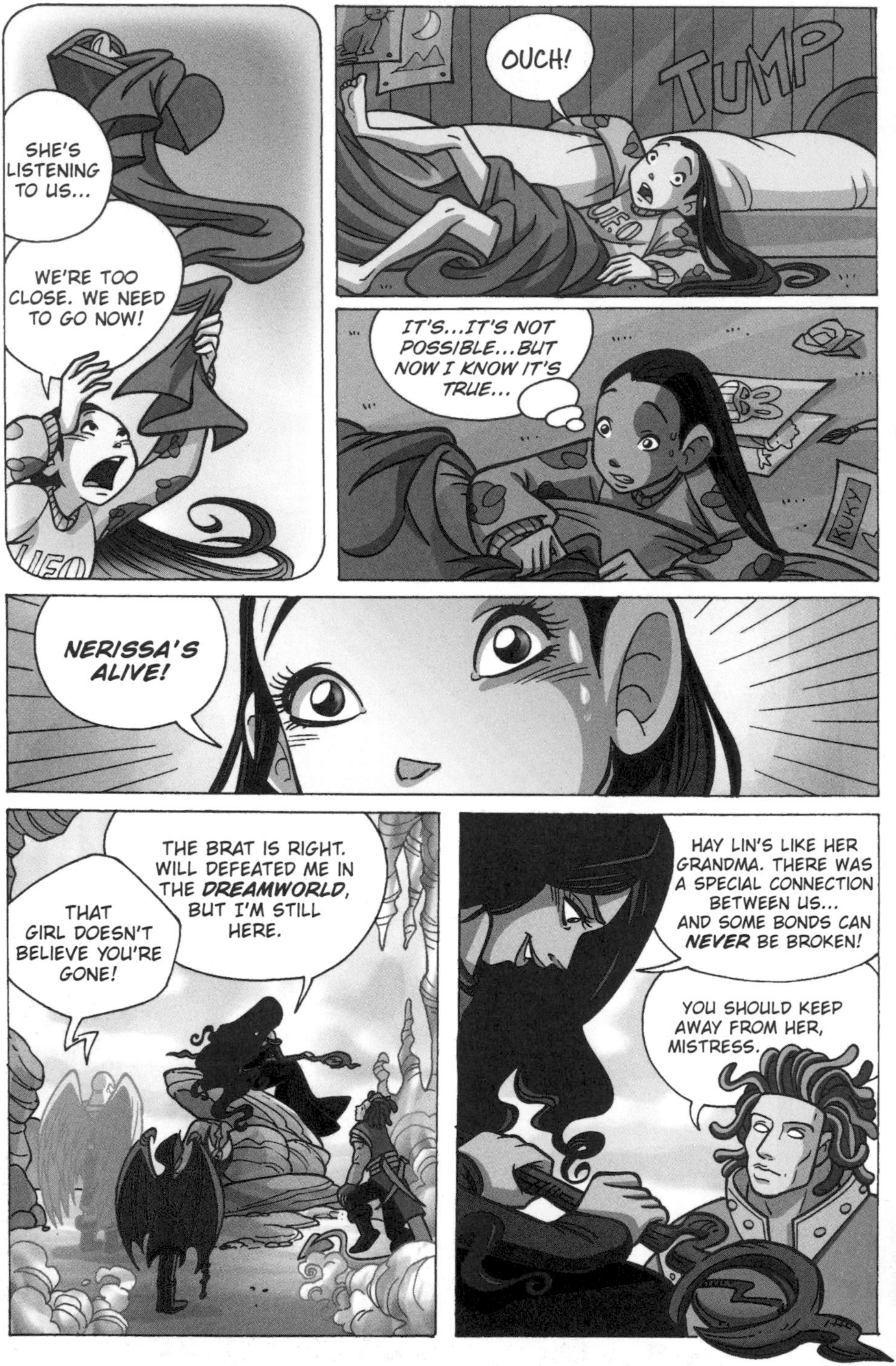
SHE'S LISTENING TO US...
WE'RE TOO CLOSE. WE NEED TO GO NOW!
UFO
OUCH!
TUMP
U.F.O
IT'S...IT'S NOT POSSIBLE...BUT NOW I KNOW IT'S TRUE...
KUKY
NERISSA'S ALIVE!
THAT GIRL DOESN'T BELIEVE YOU'RE GONE!
THE BRAT IS RIGHT. WILL DEFEATED ME IN THE DREAMWORLD, BUT I'M STILL HERE.
HAY LIN'S LIKE HER GRANDMA. THERE WAS A SPECIAL CONNECTION BETWEEN US... AND SOME BONDS CAN NEVER BE BROKEN!
YOU SHOULD KEEP AWAY FROM HER, MISTRESS.

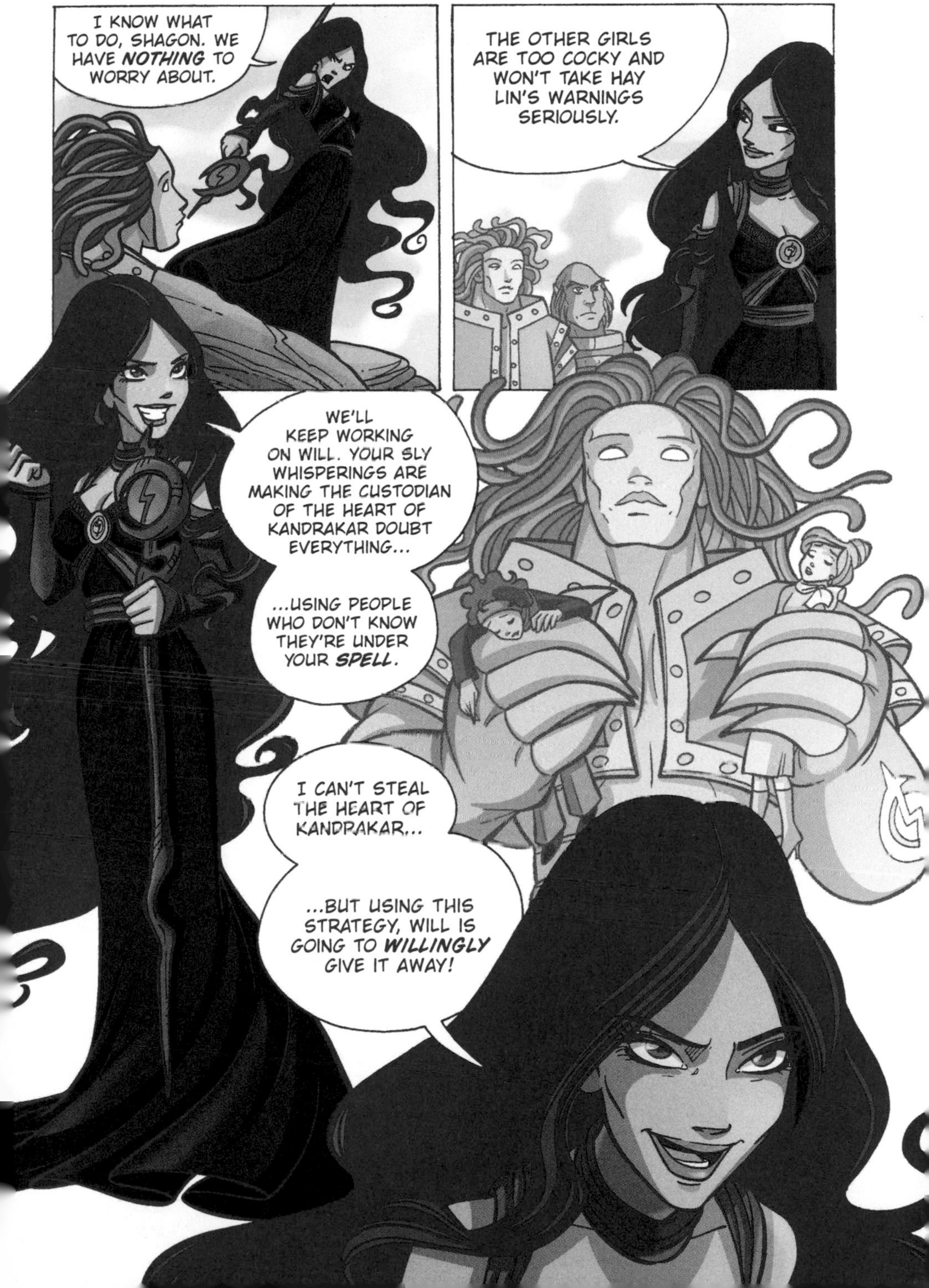
I KNOW WHAT TO DO, SHAGON. WE HAVE NOTHING TO WORRY ABOUT.
THE OTHER GIRLS ARE TOO COCKY AND WON'T TAKE HAY LIN'S WARNINGS SERIOUSLY.
WE'LL KEEP WORKING ON WILL. YOUR SLY WHISPERINGS ARE MAKING THE CUSTODIAN OF THE HEART OF KANDRAKAR DOUBT EVERYTHING...
...USING PEOPLE WHO DON'T KNOW THEY'RE UNDER YOUR SPELL.
I CAN'T STEAL THE HEART OF KANDRAKAR...
...BUT USING THIS STRATEGY, WILL IS GOING TO WILLINGLY GIVE IT AWAY!

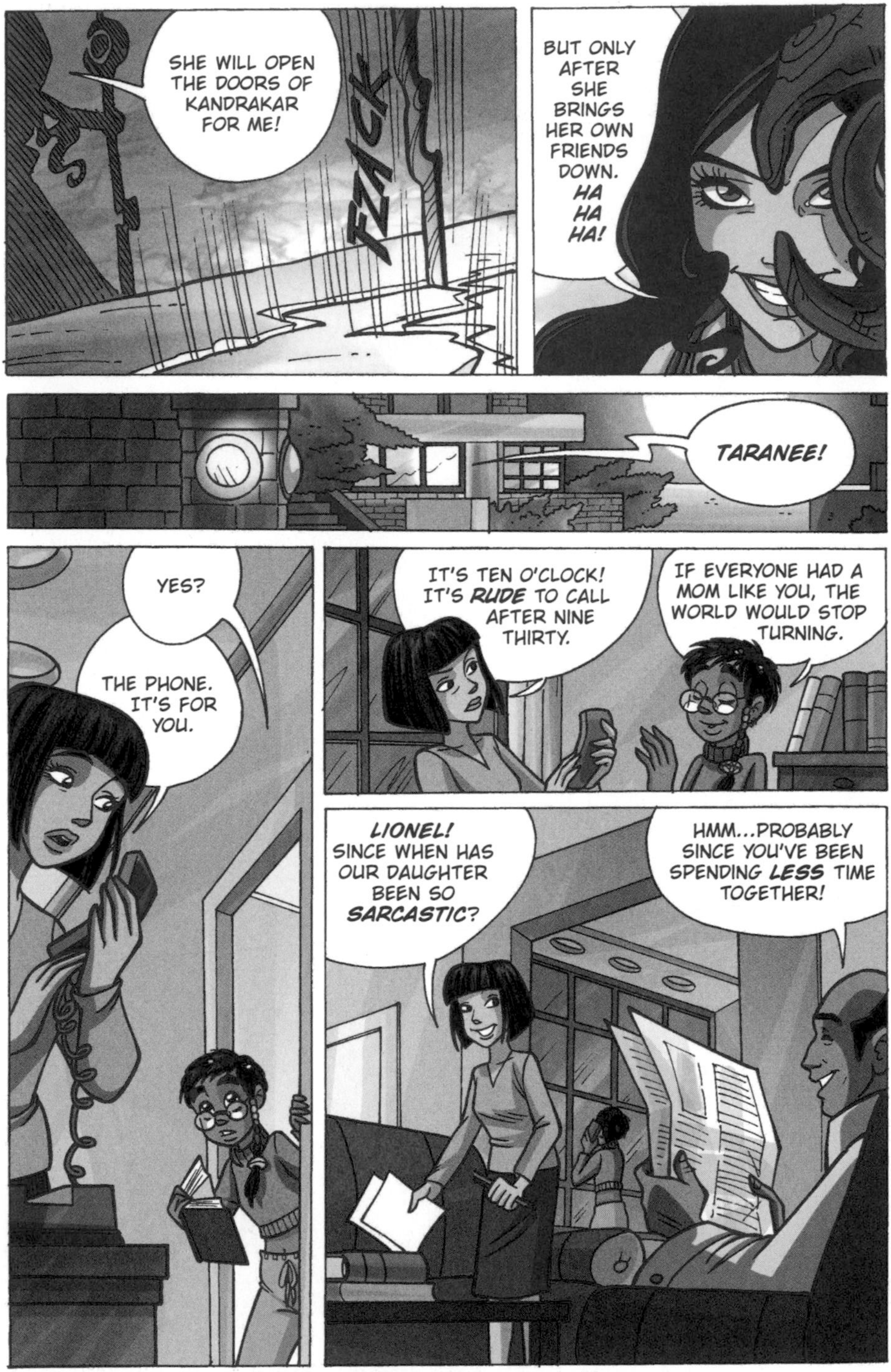
SHE WILL OPEN THE DOORS OF KANDRAKAR FOR ME!
FZACK
BUT ONLY AFTER SHE BRINGS HER OWN FRIENDS DOWN. HA HA HA!
TARANEE!
YES?
THE PHONE. IT'S FOR YOU.
IT'S TEN O'CLOCK! IT'S RUDE TO CALL AFTER NINE THIRTY.
IF EVERYONE HAD A MOM LIKE YOU, THE WORLD WOULD STOP TURNING.
LIONEL! SINCE WHEN HAS OUR DAUGHTER BEEN SO SARCASTIC?
HMM...PROBABLY SINCE YOU'VE BEEN SPENDING LESS TIME TOGETHER!

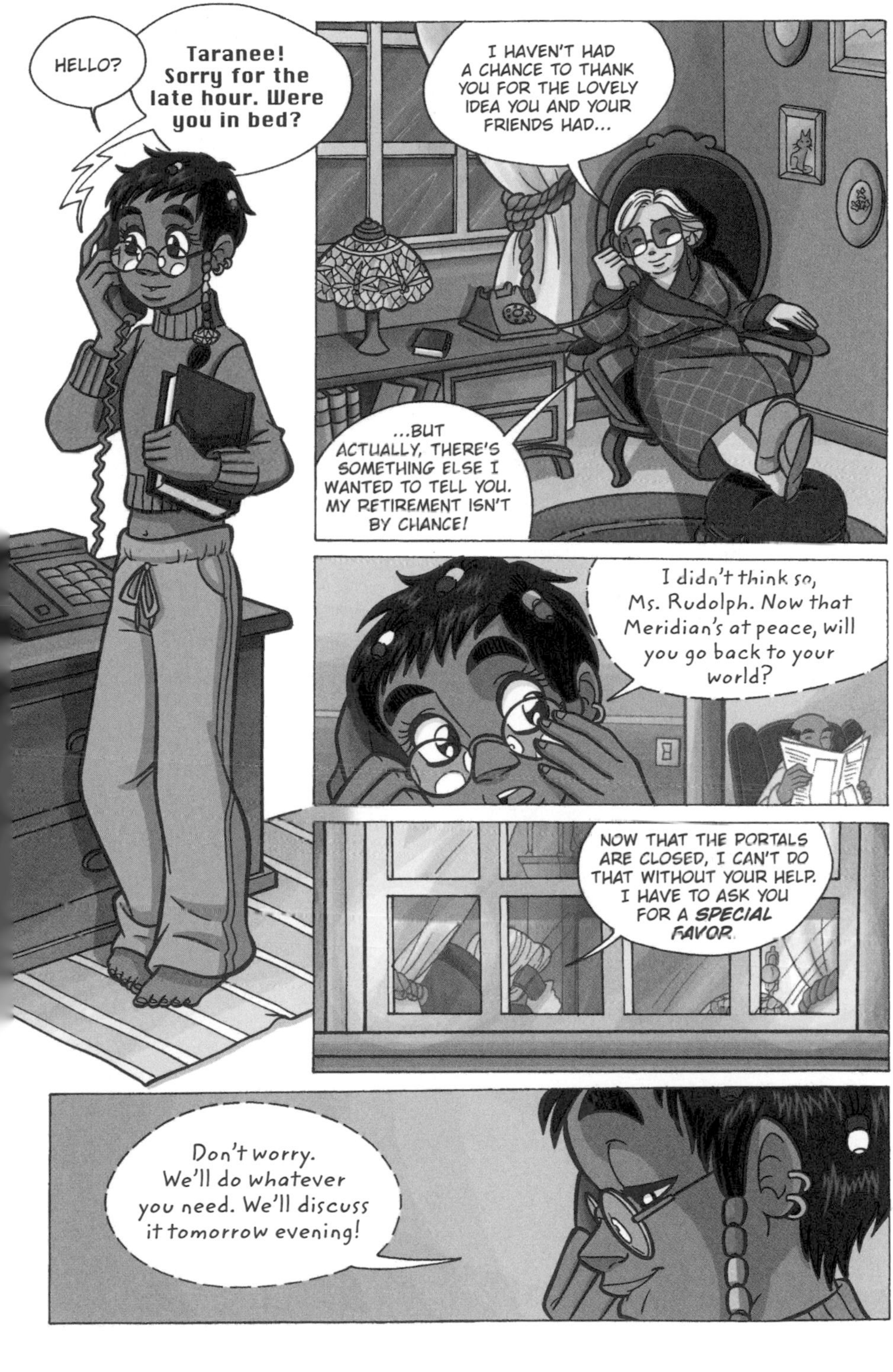
HELLO?
Taranee! Sorry for the late hour. Were you in bed?
I HAVEN'T HAD A CHANCE TO THANK YOU FOR THE LOVELY IDEA YOU AND YOUR FRIENDS HAD...
...BUT ACTUALLY, THERE'S SOMETHING ELSE I WANTED TO TELL YOU. MY RETIREMENT ISN'T BY CHANCE!
I didn't think so, Ms. Rudolph. Now that Meridian's at peace, will you go back to your world?
NOW THAT THE PORTALS ARE CLOSED, I CAN'T DO THAT WITHOUT YOUR HELP. I HAVE TO ASK YOU FOR A SPECIAL FAVOR.
Don't worry. We'll do whatever you need. We'll discuss it tomorrow evening!

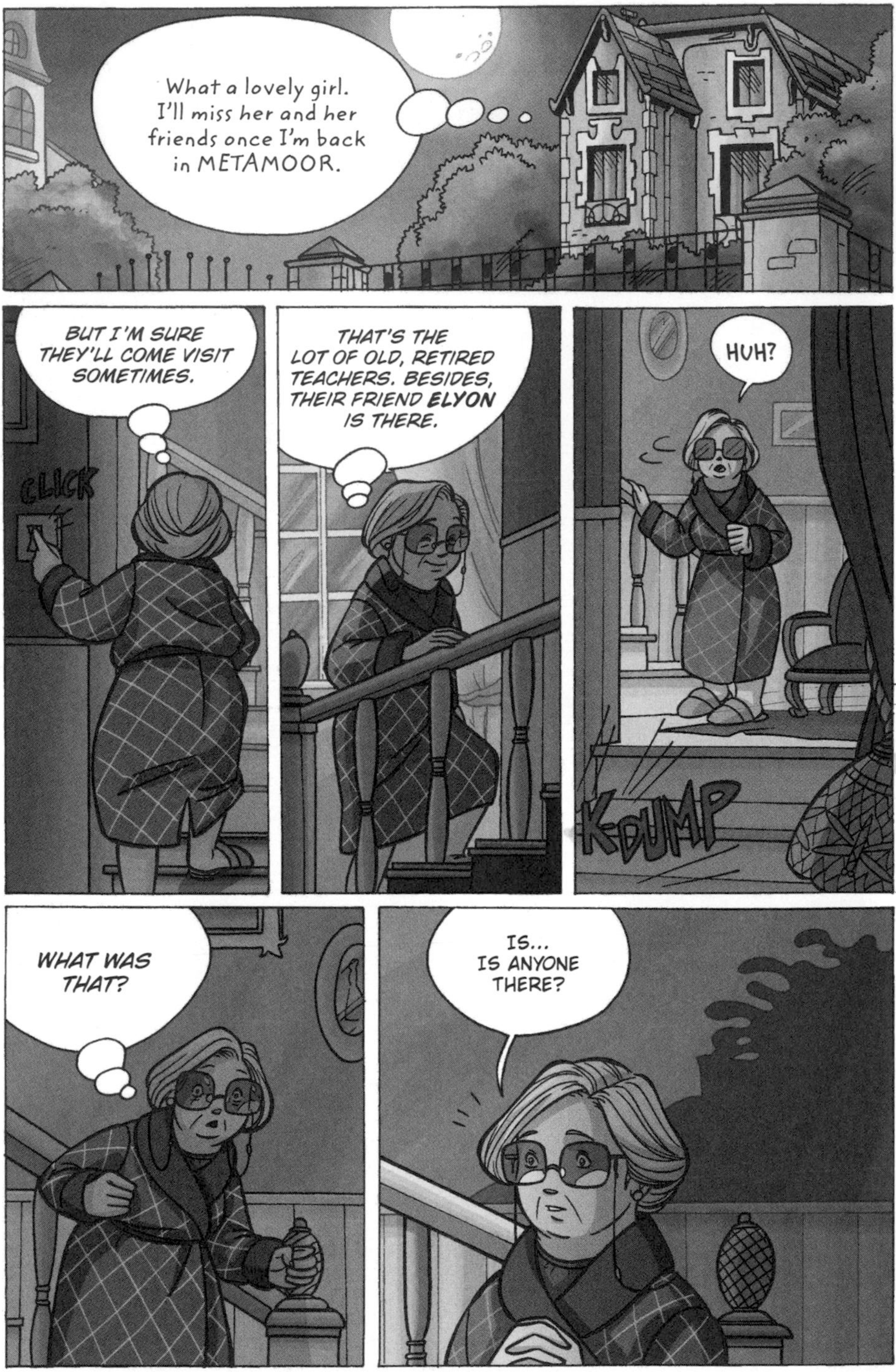

What a lovely girl. I'll miss her and her friends once I'm back in METAMOOR.
BUT I'M SURE THEY'LL COME VISIT SOMETIMES.
CLICK
THAT'S THE LOT OF OLD, RETIRED TEACHERS. BESIDES, THEIR FRIEND ELYON IS THERE.
HUH?
K-DUMP
WHAT WAS THAT?
IS... IS ANYONE THERE?

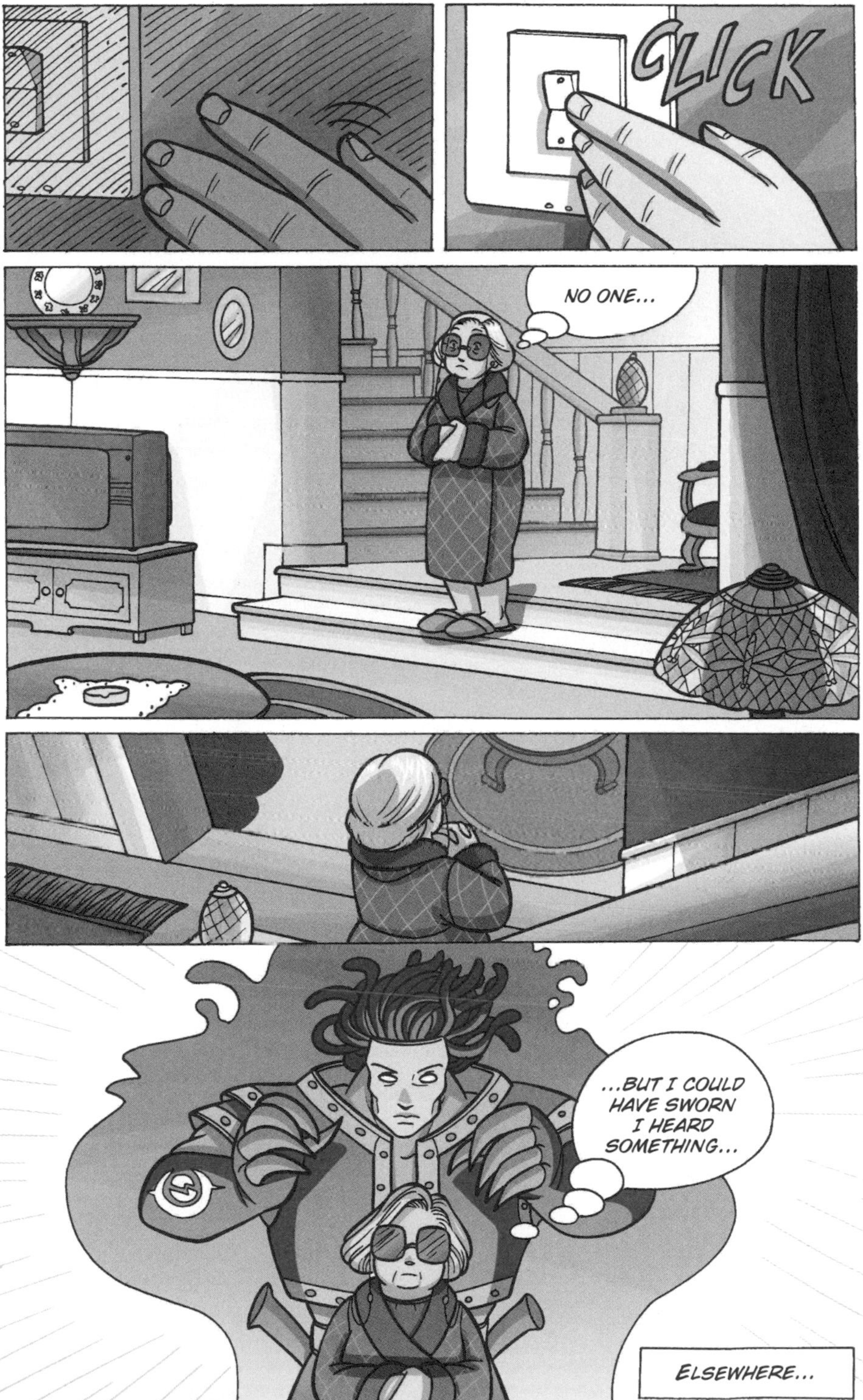
CLICK
NO ONE...
...BUT I COULD HAVE SWORN I HEARD SOMETHING...
ELSEWHERE...

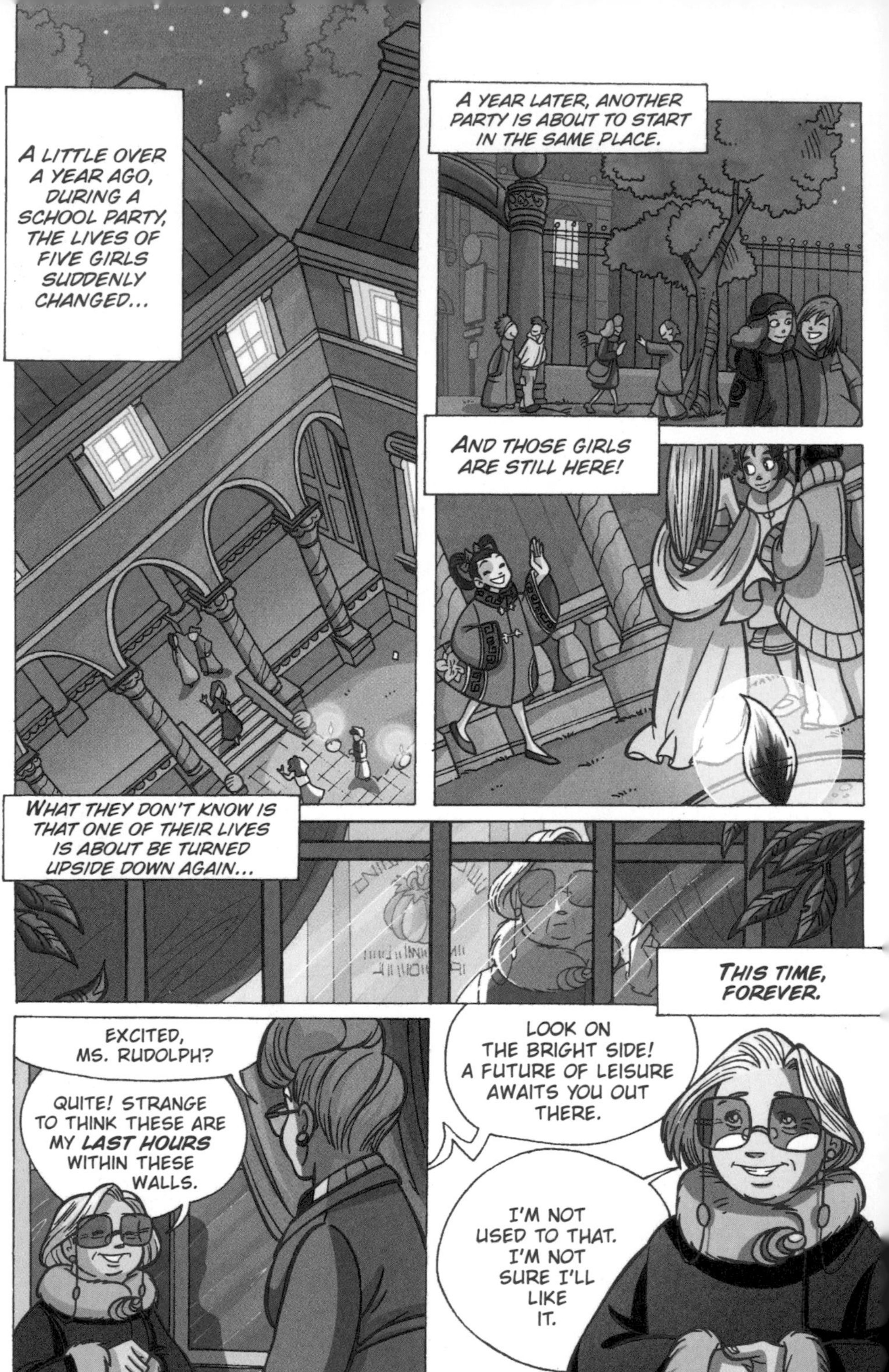
A LITTLE OVER A YEAR AGO, DURING A SCHOOL PARTY, THE LIVES OF FIVE GIRLS SUDDENLY CHANGED...
A YEAR LATER, ANOTHER PARTY IS ABOUT TO START IN THE SAME PLACE.
AND THOSE GIRLS ARE STILL HERE!
WHAT THEY DON'T KNOW IS THAT ONE OF THEIR LIVES IS ABOUT BE TURNED UPSIDE DOWN AGAIN...
THIS TIME, FOREVER.
EXCITED, MS. RUDOLPH?
QUITE! STRANGE TO THINK THESE ARE MY LAST HOURS WITHIN THESE WALLS.
LOOK ON THE BRIGHT SIDE! A FUTURE OF LEISURE AWAITS YOU OUT THERE.
I'M NOT USED TO THAT. I'M NOT SURE I'LL LIKE IT.

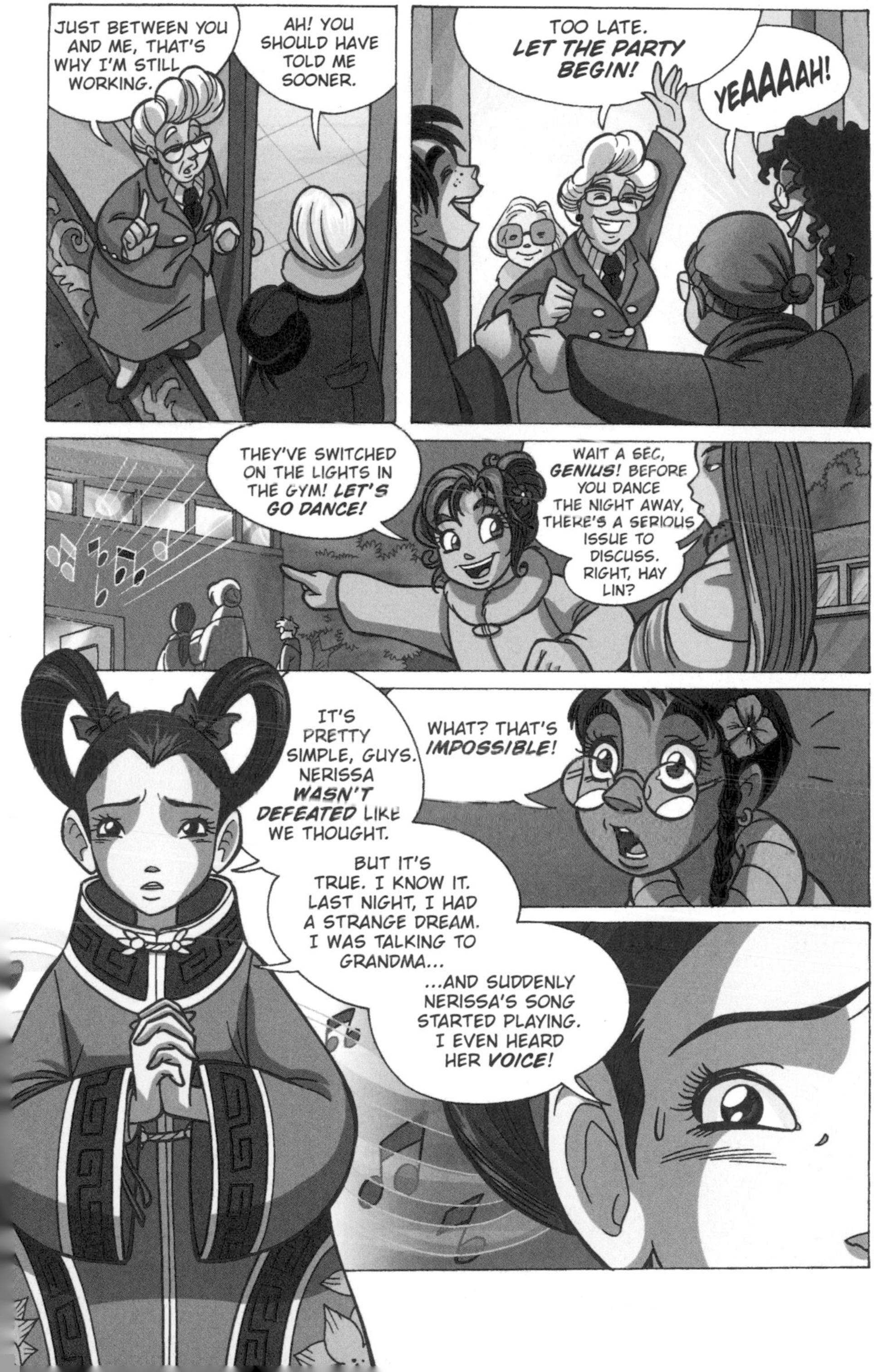
JUST BETWEEN YOU AND ME, THAT'S WHY I'M STILL WORKING.
AH! YOU SHOULD HAVE TOLD ME SOONER.
TOO LATE. LET THE PARTY BEGIN!
YEAAAAH!
THEY'VE SWITCHED ON THE LIGHTS IN THE GYM! LET'S GO DANCE!
WAIT A SEC, GENIUS! BEFORE YOU DANCE THE NIGHT AWAY, THERE'S A SERIOUS ISSUE TO DISCUSS. RIGHT, HAY LIN?
IT'S PRETTY SIMPLE, GUYS. NERISSA WASN'T DEFEATED LIKE WE THOUGHT.
WHAT? THAT'S IMPOSSIBLE!
BUT IT'S TRUE. I KNOW IT. LAST NIGHT, I HAD A STRANGE DREAM. I WAS TALKING TO GRANDMA...
...AND SUDDENLY NERISSA'S SONG STARTED PLAYING. I EVEN HEARD HER VOICE!

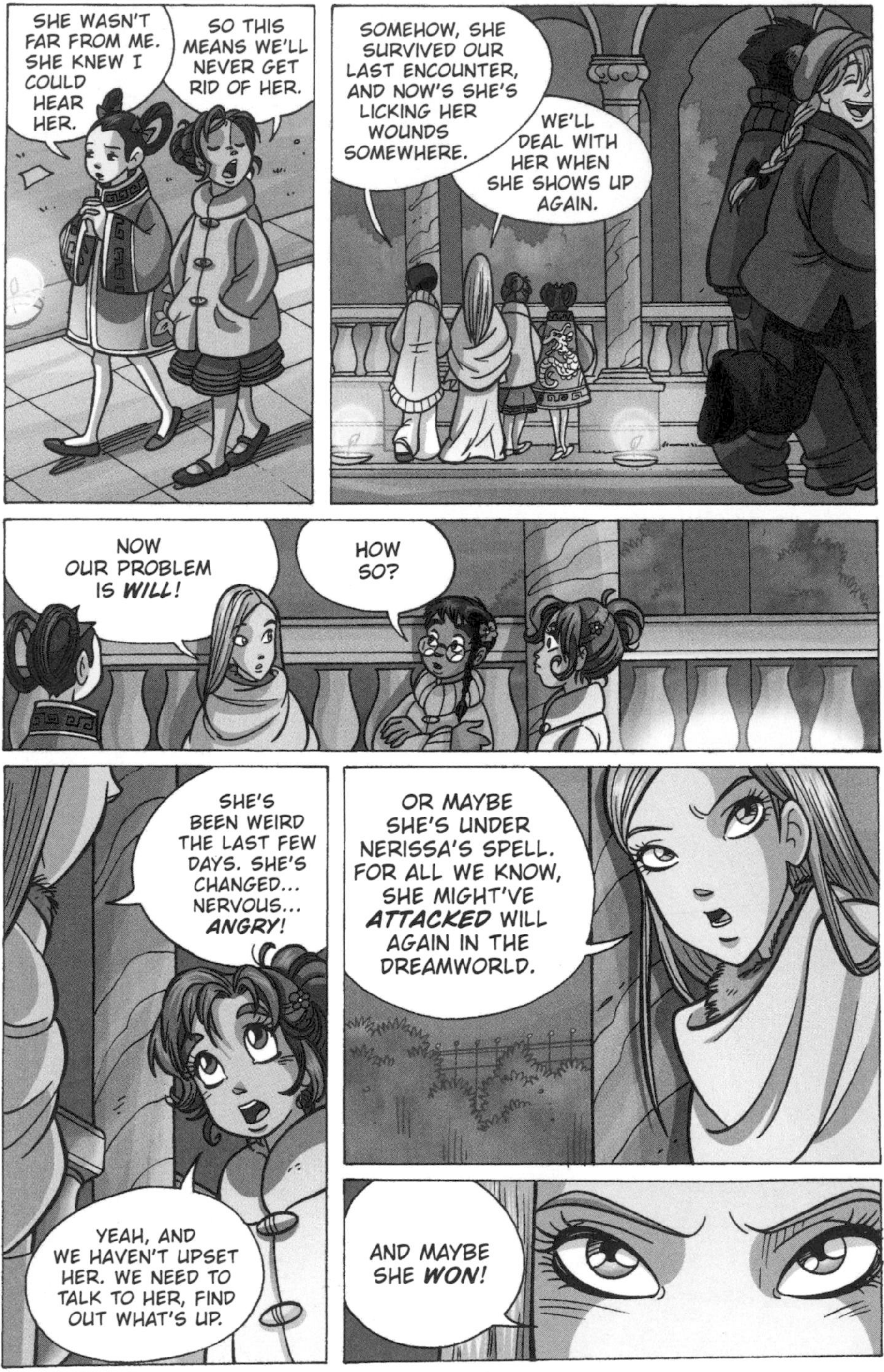
SHE WASN'T FAR FROM ME. SHE KNEW I COULD HEAR HER.
SO THIS MEANS WE'LL NEVER GET RID OF HER.
SOMEHOW, SHE SURVIVED OUR LAST ENCOUNTER, AND NOW'S SHE'S LICKING HER WOUNDS SOMEWHERE.
WE'LL DEAL WITH HER WHEN SHE SHOWS UP AGAIN.
NOW OUR PROBLEM IS *WILL*!
HOW SO?
SHE'S BEEN WEIRD THE LAST FEW DAYS. SHE'S CHANGED... NERVOUS... *ANGRY*!
YEAH, AND WE HAVEN'T UPSET HER. WE NEED TO TALK TO HER, FIND OUT WHAT'S UP.
OR MAYBE SHE'S UNDER NERISSA'S SPELL. FOR ALL WE KNOW, SHE MIGHT'VE *ATTACKED* WILL AGAIN IN THE DREAMWORLD.
AND MAYBE SHE *WON*!

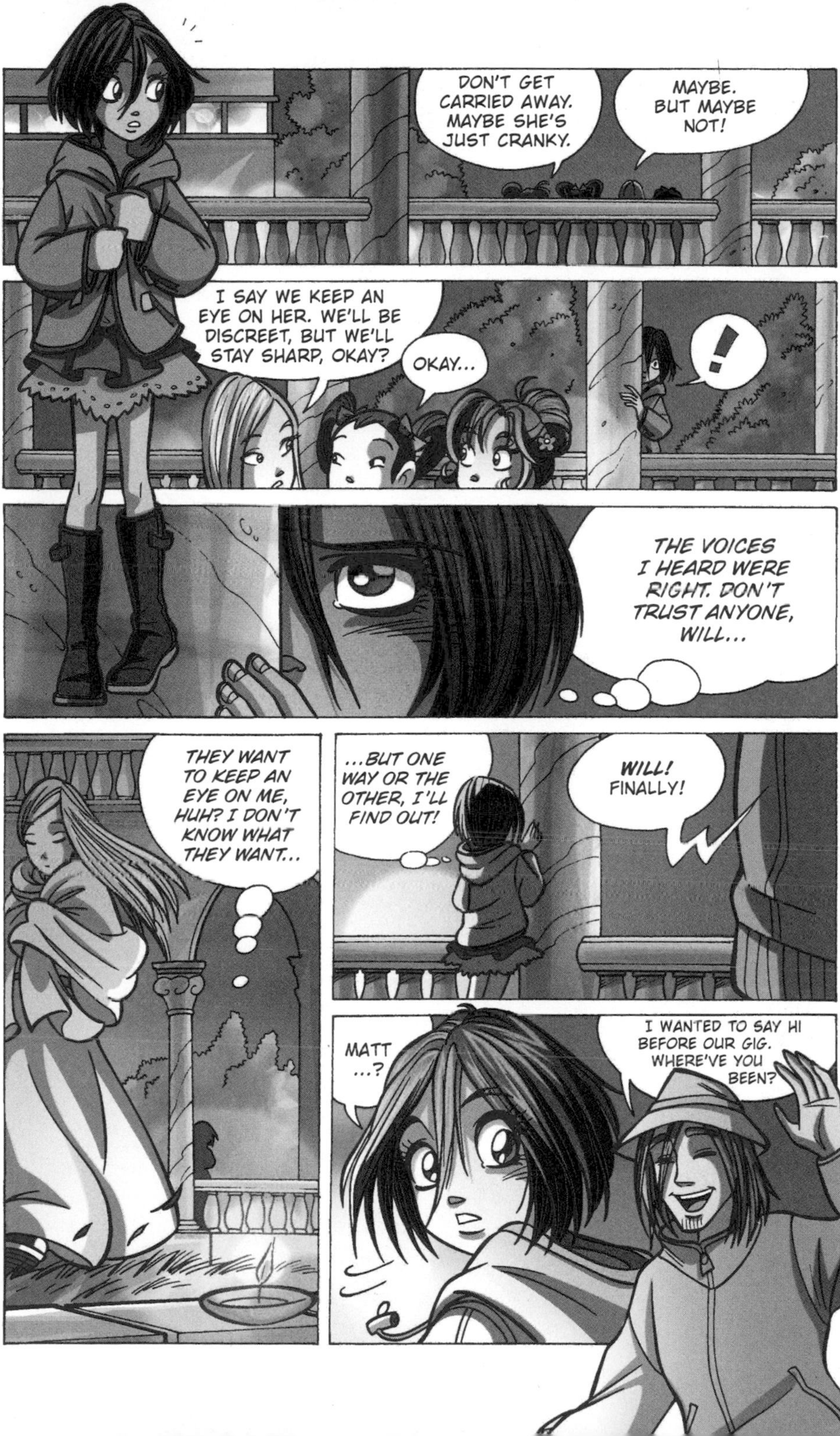
DON'T GET CARRIED AWAY. MAYBE SHE'S JUST CRANKY.
MAYBE. BUT MAYBE NOT!
I SAY WE KEEP AN EYE ON HER. WE'LL BE DISCREET, BUT WE'LL STAY SHARP, OKAY?
OKAY...
!
THE VOICES I HEARD WERE RIGHT. DON'T TRUST ANYONE, WILL...
THEY WANT TO KEEP AN EYE ON ME, HUH? I DON'T KNOW WHAT THEY WANT...
...BUT ONE WAY OR THE OTHER, I'LL FIND OUT!
WILL! FINALLY!
MATT ...?
I WANTED TO SAY HI BEFORE OUR GIG. WHERE'VE YOU BEEN?

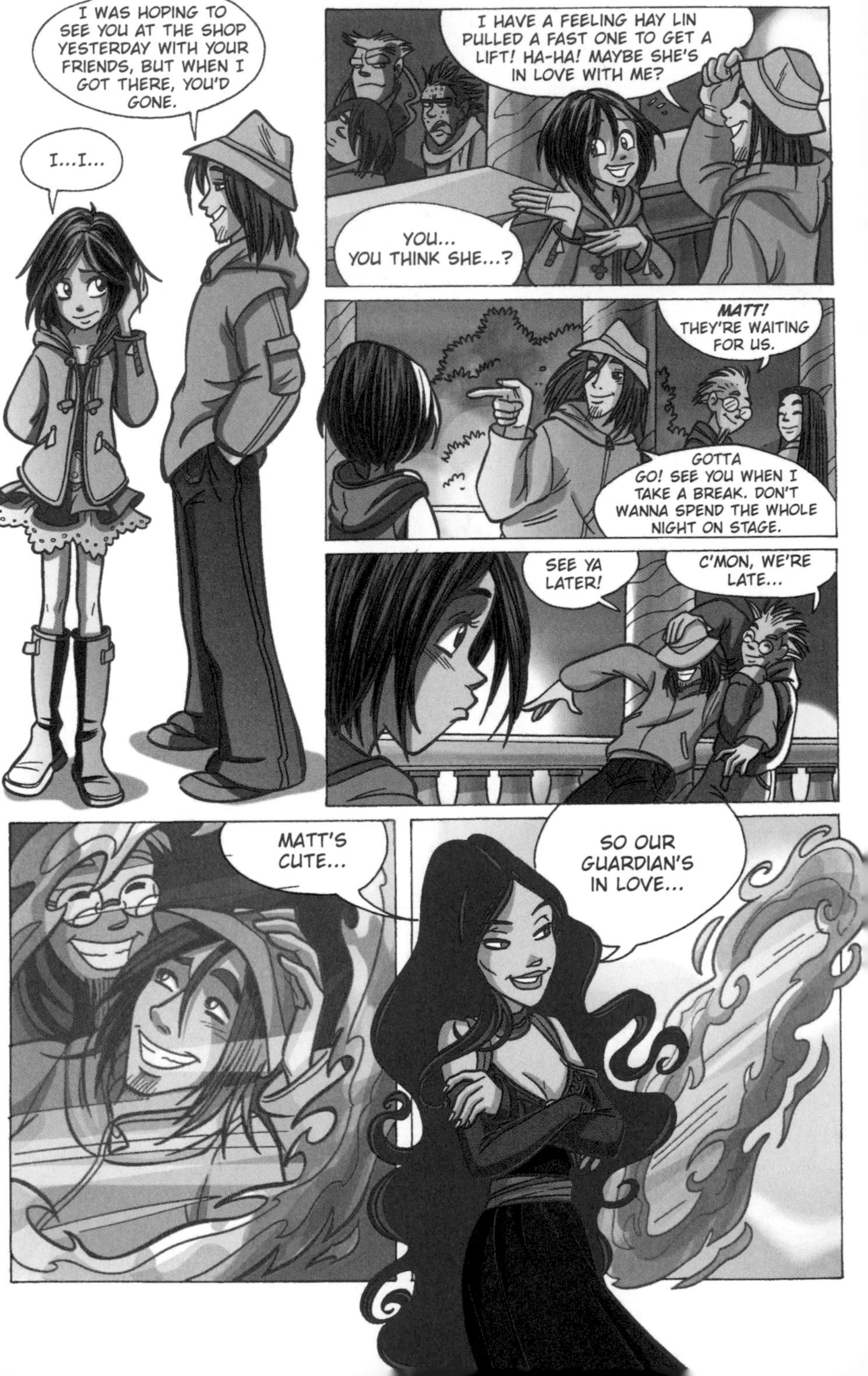
I WAS HOPING TO SEE YOU AT THE SHOP YESTERDAY WITH YOUR FRIENDS, BUT WHEN I GOT THERE, YOU'D GONE.
I...I...
I HAVE A FEELING HAY LIN PULLED A FAST ONE TO GET A LIFT! HA-HA! MAYBE SHE'S IN LOVE WITH ME?
YOU... YOU THINK SHE...?
MATT! THEY'RE WAITING FOR US.
GOTTA GO! SEE YOU WHEN I TAKE A BREAK. DON'T WANNA SPEND THE WHOLE NIGHT ON STAGE.
SEE YA LATER!
C'MON, WE'RE LATE...
MATT'S CUTE...
SO OUR GUARDIAN'S IN LOVE...

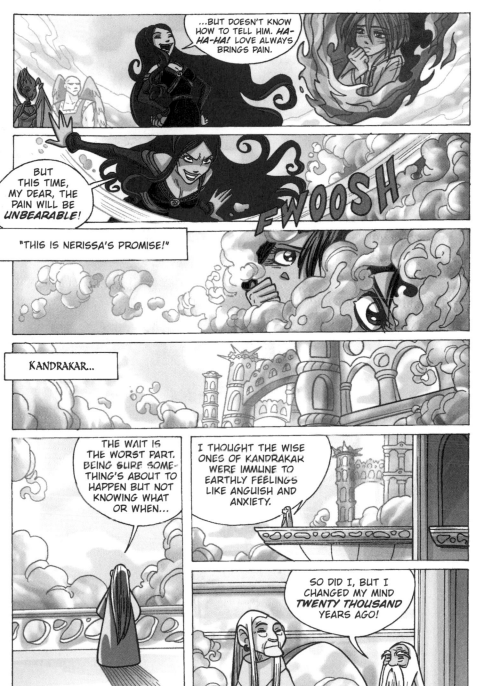

...BUT DOESN'T KNOW HOW TO TELL HIM. *HA-HA-HA!* LOVE ALWAYS BRINGS PAIN.

BUT THIS TIME, MY DEAR, THE PAIN WILL BE **UNBEARABLE!**

FWOOSH

"THIS IS NERISSA'S PROMISE!"

KANDRAKAR...

THE WAIT IS THE WORST PART. BEING SURE SOMETHING'S ABOUT TO HAPPEN BUT NOT KNOWING WHAT OR WHEN...

I THOUGHT THE WISE ONES OF KANDRAKAR WERE IMMUNE TO EARTHLY FEELINGS LIKE ANGUISH AND ANXIETY.

SO DID I, BUT I CHANGED MY MIND *TWENTY THOUSAND* YEARS AGO!

NERISSA...
I STILL REMEMBER
THE DAY I MET
HER. I KNEW RIGHT
AWAY SHE WAS
SPECIAL.

SHE WAS—
BEFORE
THE HEART
CORRUPTED
HER.

I DON'T
UNDERSTAND HOW
IT COULD HAPPEN.
WHY DID NO ONE
STOP IT?

WHY DIDN'T THE ORACLE
STOP NERISSA? WHY DID
HE LET HER DESTROY
CASSIDY'S LIFE?

WATCH
WHAT YOU SAY,
YAN LIN.

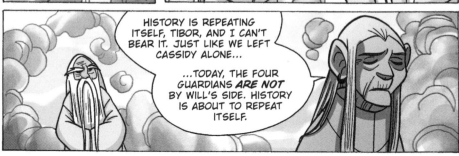

HISTORY IS REPEATING
ITSELF, TIBOR, AND I CAN'T
BEAR IT. JUST LIKE WE LEFT
CASSIDY ALONE...

...TODAY, THE FOUR
GUARDIANS **ARE NOT**
BY WILL'S SIDE. HISTORY
IS ABOUT TO REPEAT
ITSELF.

!

AND
ONCE AGAIN,
THE ORACLE
ISN'T HERE.

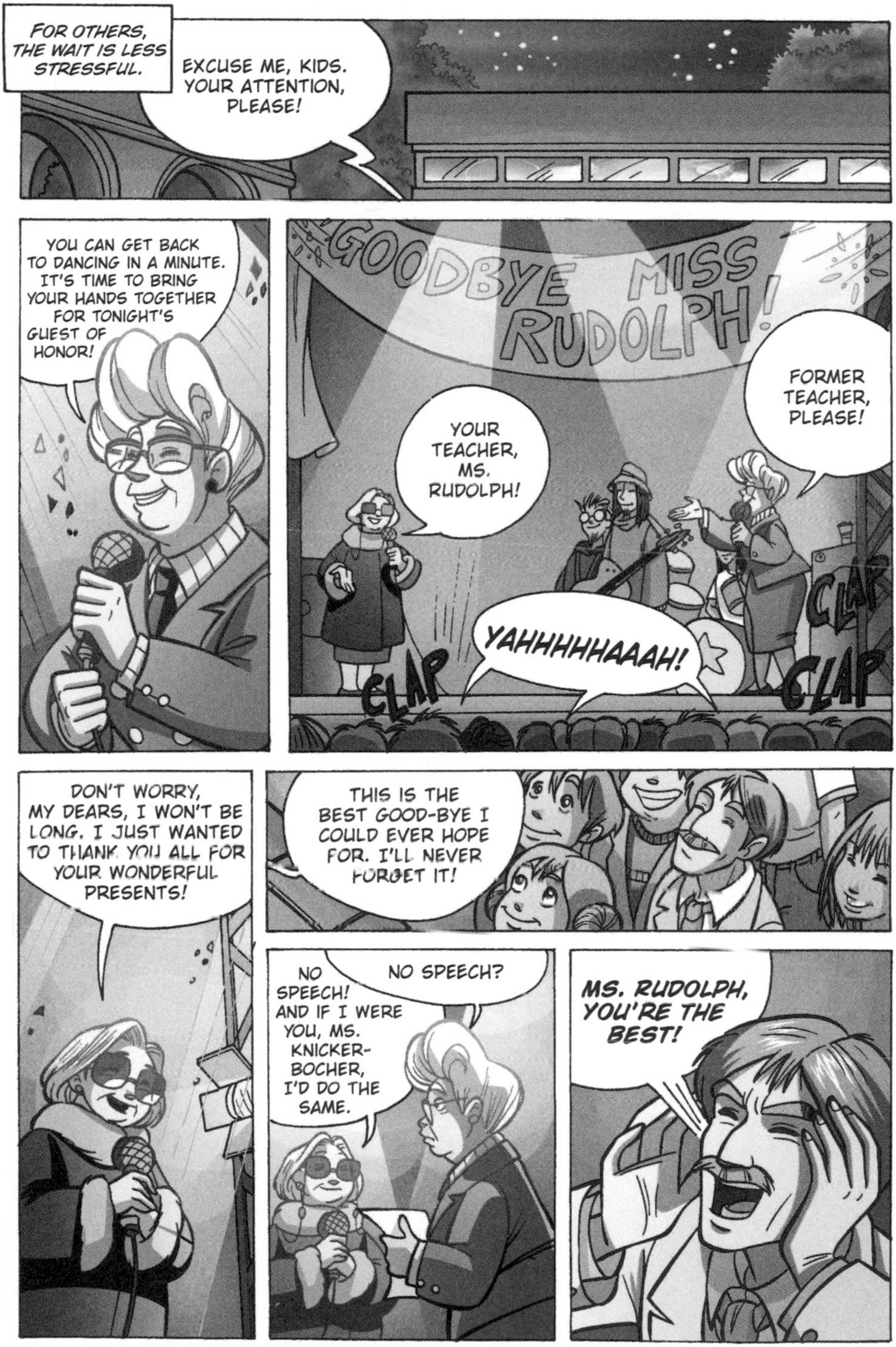
FOR OTHERS, THE WAIT IS LESS STRESSFUL.
EXCUSE ME, KIDS. YOUR ATTENTION, PLEASE!
YOU CAN GET BACK TO DANCING IN A MINUTE. IT'S TIME TO BRING YOUR HANDS TOGETHER FOR TONIGHT'S GUEST OF HONOR!
GOODBYE MISS RUDOLPH!
FORMER TEACHER, PLEASE!
YOUR TEACHER, MS. RUDOLPH!
YAHHHHHAAAH!
CLAP
CLAP
CLAP
DON'T WORRY, MY DEARS, I WON'T BE LONG. I JUST WANTED TO THANK YOU ALL FOR YOUR WONDERFUL PRESENTS!
THIS IS THE BEST GOOD-BYE I COULD EVER HOPE FOR. I'LL NEVER FORGET IT!
NO SPEECH?
NO SPEECH! AND IF I WERE YOU, MS. KNICKER-BOCHER, I'D DO THE SAME.
MS. RUDOLPH, YOU'RE THE BEST!

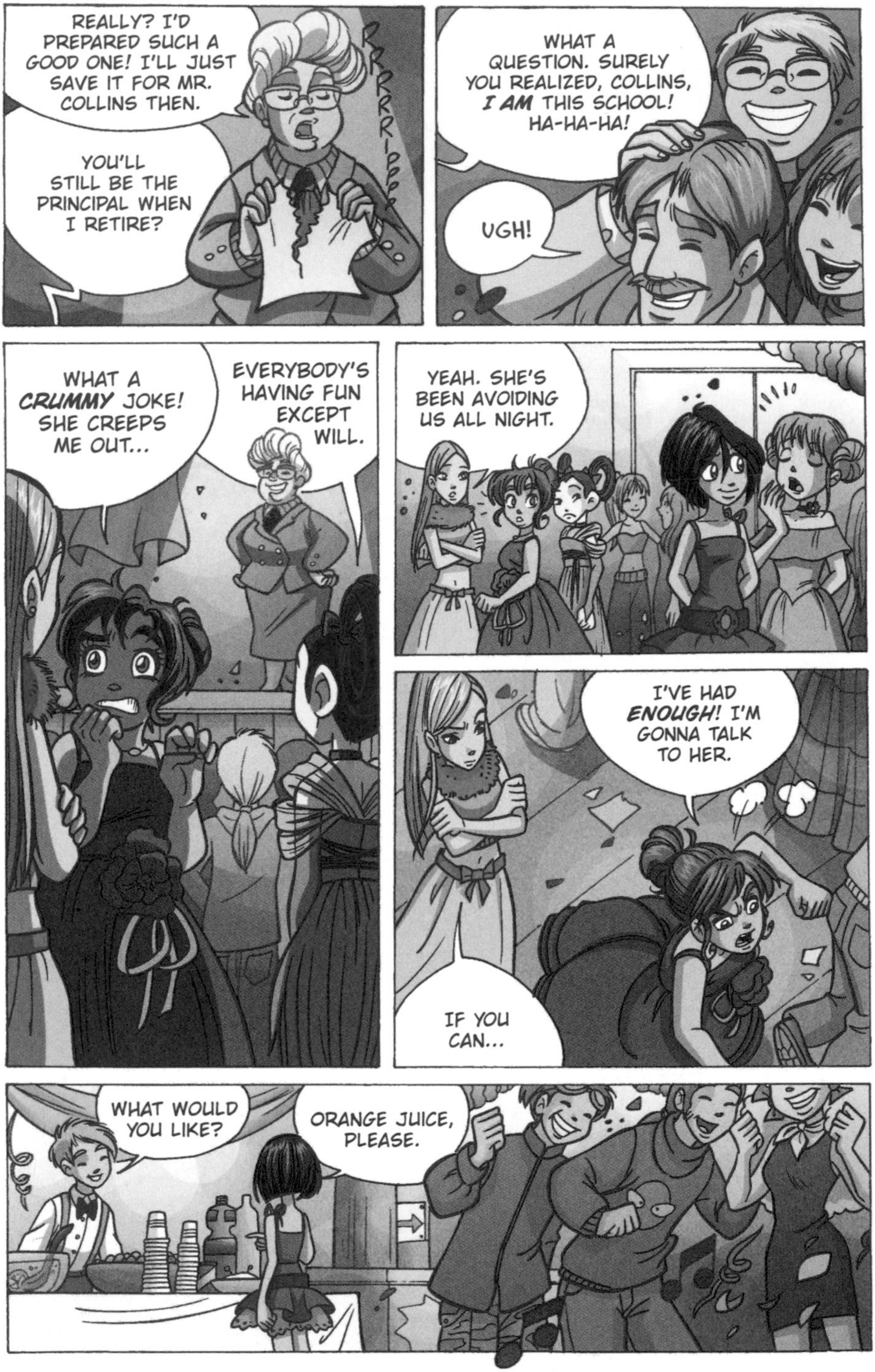
RRRRRRIPPPP
REALLY? I'D PREPARED SUCH A GOOD ONE! I'LL JUST SAVE IT FOR MR. COLLINS THEN.
YOU'LL STILL BE THE PRINCIPAL WHEN I RETIRE?
WHAT A QUESTION. SURELY YOU REALIZED, COLLINS, I AM THIS SCHOOL! HA-HA-HA!
UGH!
WHAT A CRUMMY JOKE! SHE CREEPS ME OUT...
EVERYBODY'S HAVING FUN EXCEPT WILL.
YEAH. SHE'S BEEN AVOIDING US ALL NIGHT.
I'VE HAD ENOUGH! I'M GONNA TALK TO HER.
IF YOU CAN...
WHAT WOULD YOU LIKE?
ORANGE JUICE, PLEASE.

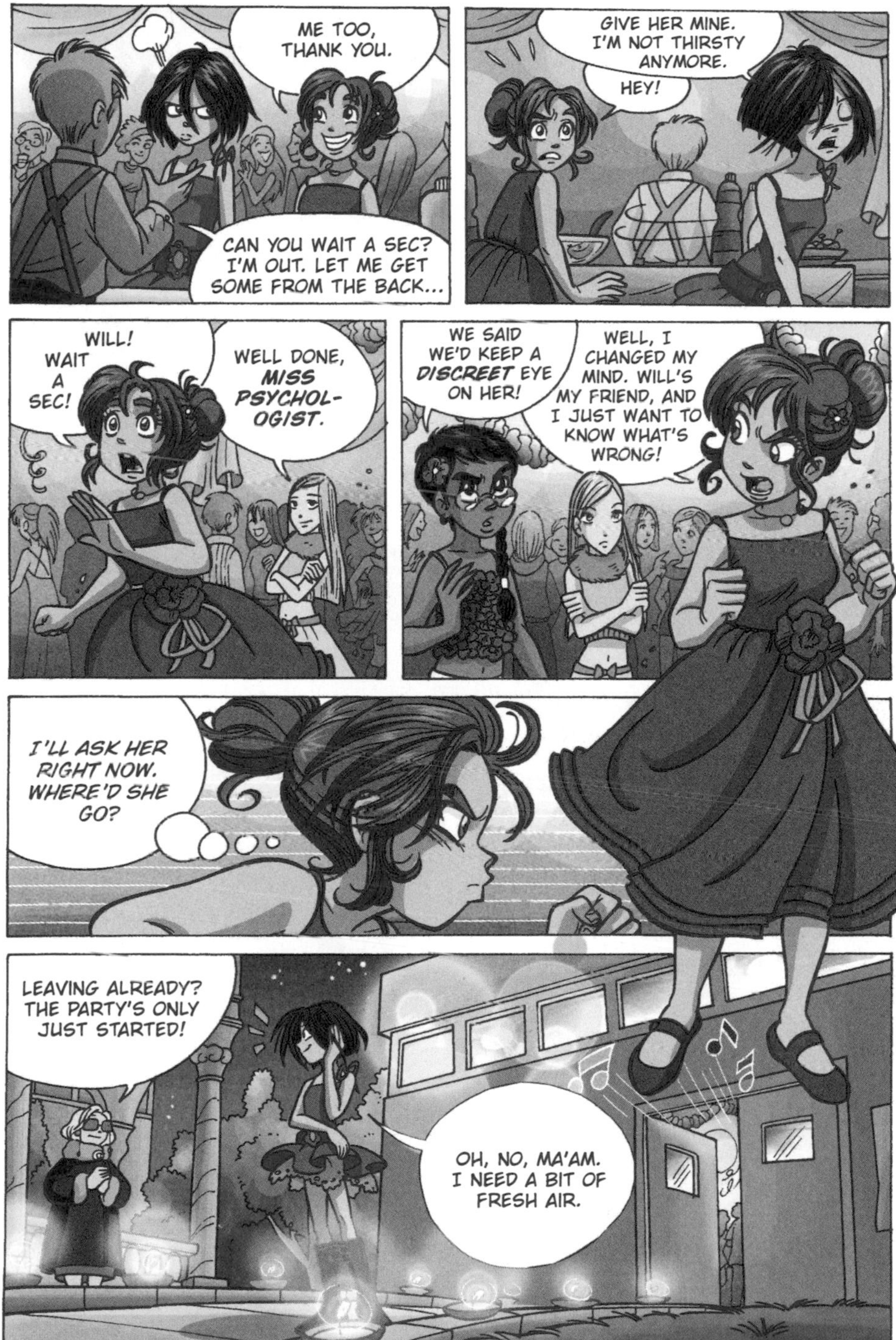

ME TOO, THANK YOU.
CAN YOU WAIT A SEC? I'M OUT. LET ME GET SOME FROM THE BACK...
GIVE HER MINE. I'M NOT THIRSTY ANYMORE.
HEY!
WILL! WAIT A SEC!
WELL DONE, MISS PSYCHOLOGIST.
WE SAID WE'D KEEP A DISCREET EYE ON HER!
WELL, I CHANGED MY MIND. WILL'S MY FRIEND, AND I JUST WANT TO KNOW WHAT'S WRONG!
I'LL ASK HER RIGHT NOW. WHERE'D SHE GO?
LEAVING ALREADY? THE PARTY'S ONLY JUST STARTED!
OH, NO, MA'AM. I NEED A BIT OF FRESH AIR.

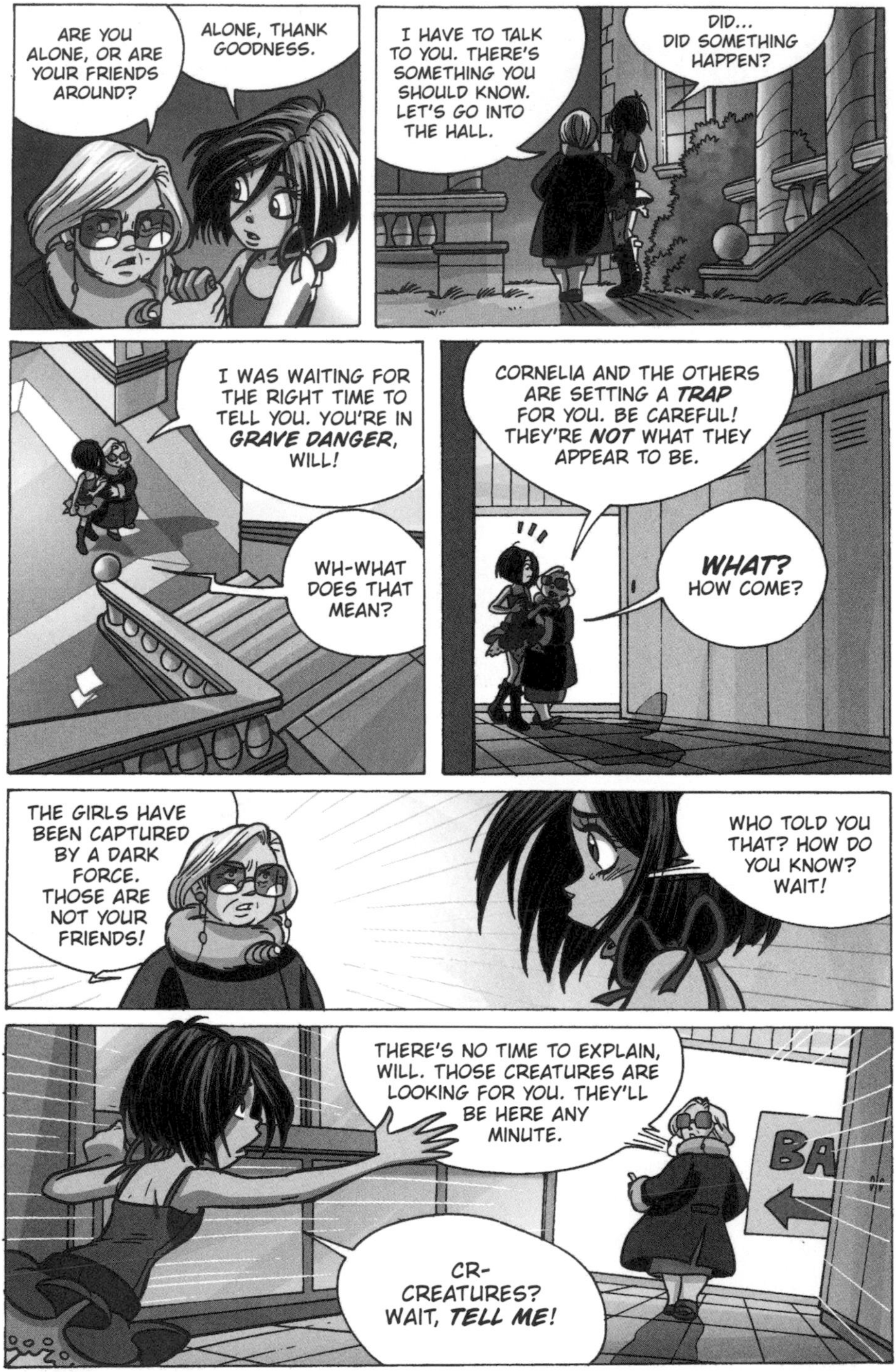
ARE YOU ALONE, OR ARE YOUR FRIENDS AROUND?
ALONE, THANK GOODNESS.
I HAVE TO TALK TO YOU. THERE'S SOMETHING YOU SHOULD KNOW. LET'S GO INTO THE HALL.
DID... DID SOMETHING HAPPEN?
I WAS WAITING FOR THE RIGHT TIME TO TELL YOU. YOU'RE IN GRAVE DANGER, WILL!
WH-WHAT DOES THAT MEAN?
CORNELIA AND THE OTHERS ARE SETTING A TRAP FOR YOU. BE CAREFUL! THEY'RE NOT WHAT THEY APPEAR TO BE.
WHAT? HOW COME?
THE GIRLS HAVE BEEN CAPTURED BY A DARK FORCE. THOSE ARE NOT YOUR FRIENDS!
WHO TOLD YOU THAT? HOW DO YOU KNOW? WAIT!
THERE'S NO TIME TO EXPLAIN, WILL. THOSE CREATURES ARE LOOKING FOR YOU. THEY'LL BE HERE ANY MINUTE.
CR- CREATURES? WAIT, TELL ME!

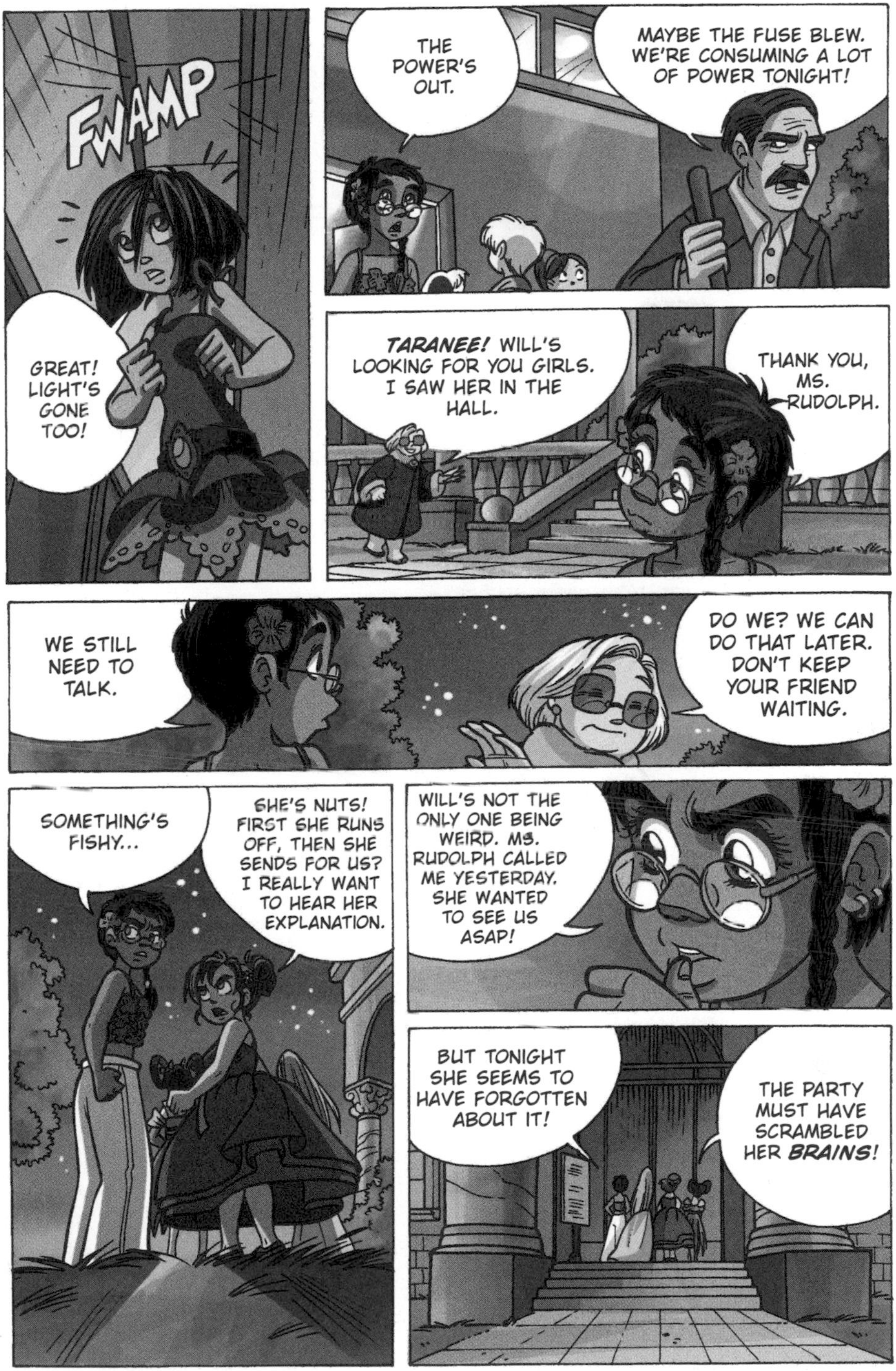
FWAMP
GREAT! LIGHT'S GONE TOO!
THE POWER'S OUT.
MAYBE THE FUSE BLEW. WE'RE CONSUMING A LOT OF POWER TONIGHT!
TARANEE! WILL'S LOOKING FOR YOU GIRLS. I SAW HER IN THE HALL.
THANK YOU, MS. RUDOLPH.
WE STILL NEED TO TALK.
DO WE? WE CAN DO THAT LATER. DON'T KEEP YOUR FRIEND WAITING.
SOMETHING'S FISHY...
SHE'S NUTS! FIRST SHE RUNS OFF, THEN SHE SENDS FOR US? I REALLY WANT TO HEAR HER EXPLANATION.
WILL'S NOT THE ONLY ONE BEING WEIRD. MS. RUDOLPH CALLED ME YESTERDAY. SHE WANTED TO SEE US ASAP!
BUT TONIGHT SHE SEEMS TO HAVE FORGOTTEN ABOUT IT!
THE PARTY MUST HAVE SCRAMBLED HER BRAINS!

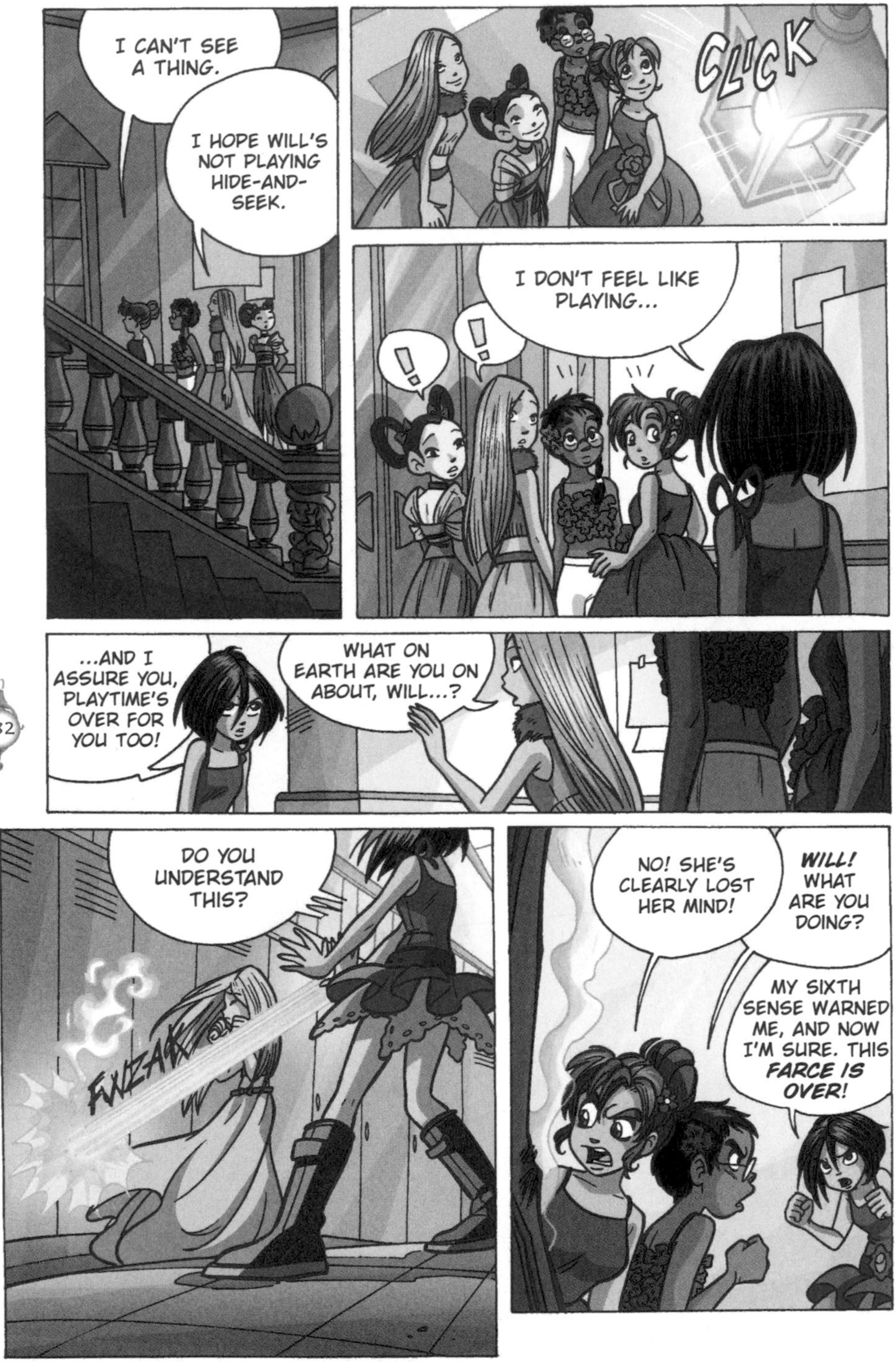
I CAN'T SEE A THING.
I HOPE WILL'S NOT PLAYING HIDE-AND-SEEK.
CLICK
I DON'T FEEL LIKE PLAYING...
!
!
...AND I ASSURE YOU, PLAYTIME'S OVER FOR YOU TOO!
WHAT ON EARTH ARE YOU ON ABOUT, WILL...?
DO YOU UNDERSTAND THIS?
FWZAK
NO! SHE'S CLEARLY LOST HER MIND!
WILL! WHAT ARE YOU DOING?
MY SIXTH SENSE WARNED ME, AND NOW I'M SURE. THIS FARCE IS OVER!

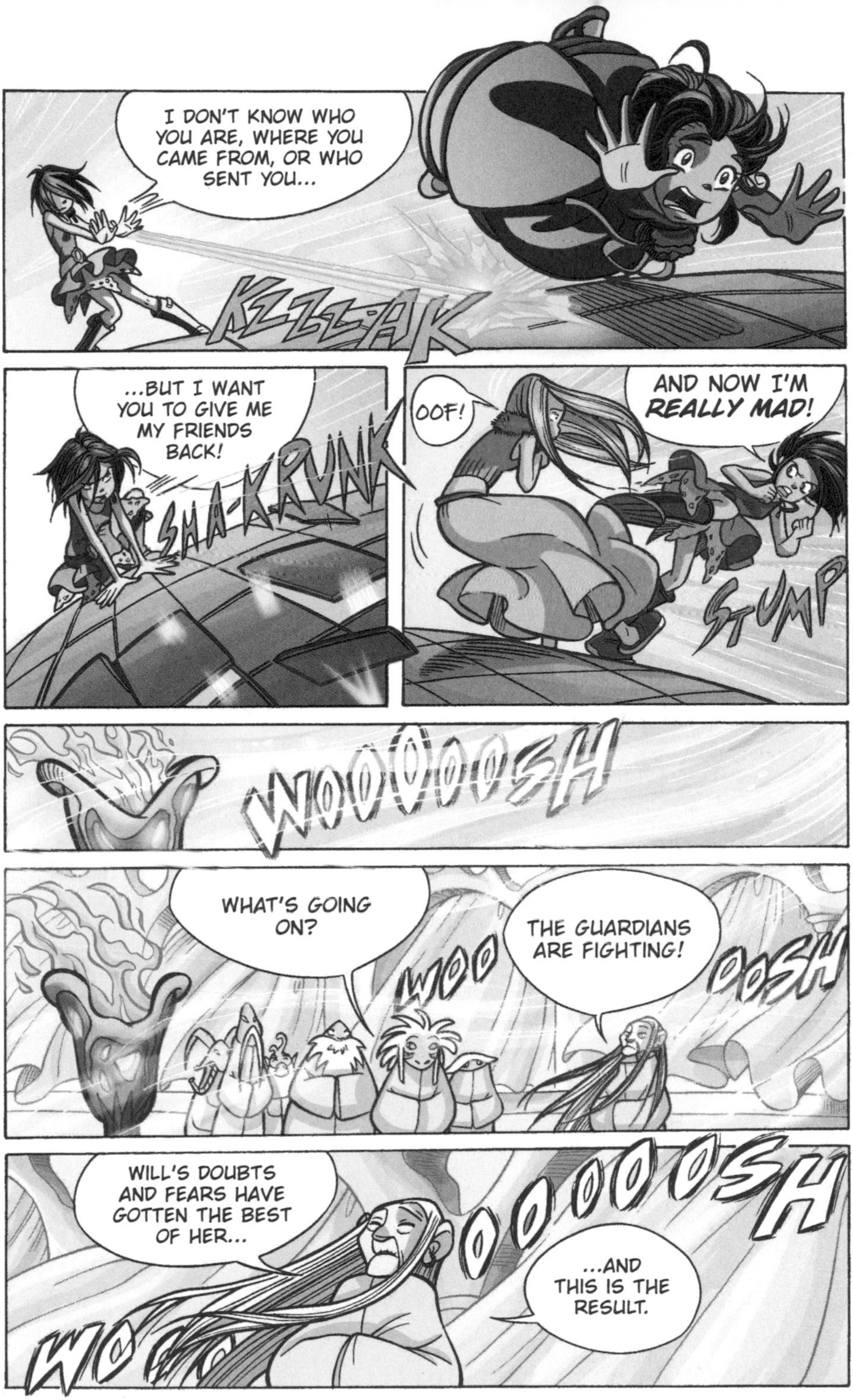
I DON'T KNOW WHO YOU ARE, WHERE YOU CAME FROM, OR WHO SENT YOU...
KZZZ-AK
...BUT I WANT YOU TO GIVE ME MY FRIENDS BACK!
SHA-KRUNK
OOF!
AND NOW I'M *REALLY MAD!*
STUMP
WOOOOOOSH
WHAT'S GOING ON?
THE GUARDIANS ARE FIGHTING!
WOO
OOSH
WILL'S DOUBTS AND FEARS HAVE GOTTEN THE BEST OF HER...
...AND THIS IS THE RESULT.
OOOOOOOSH
WOO

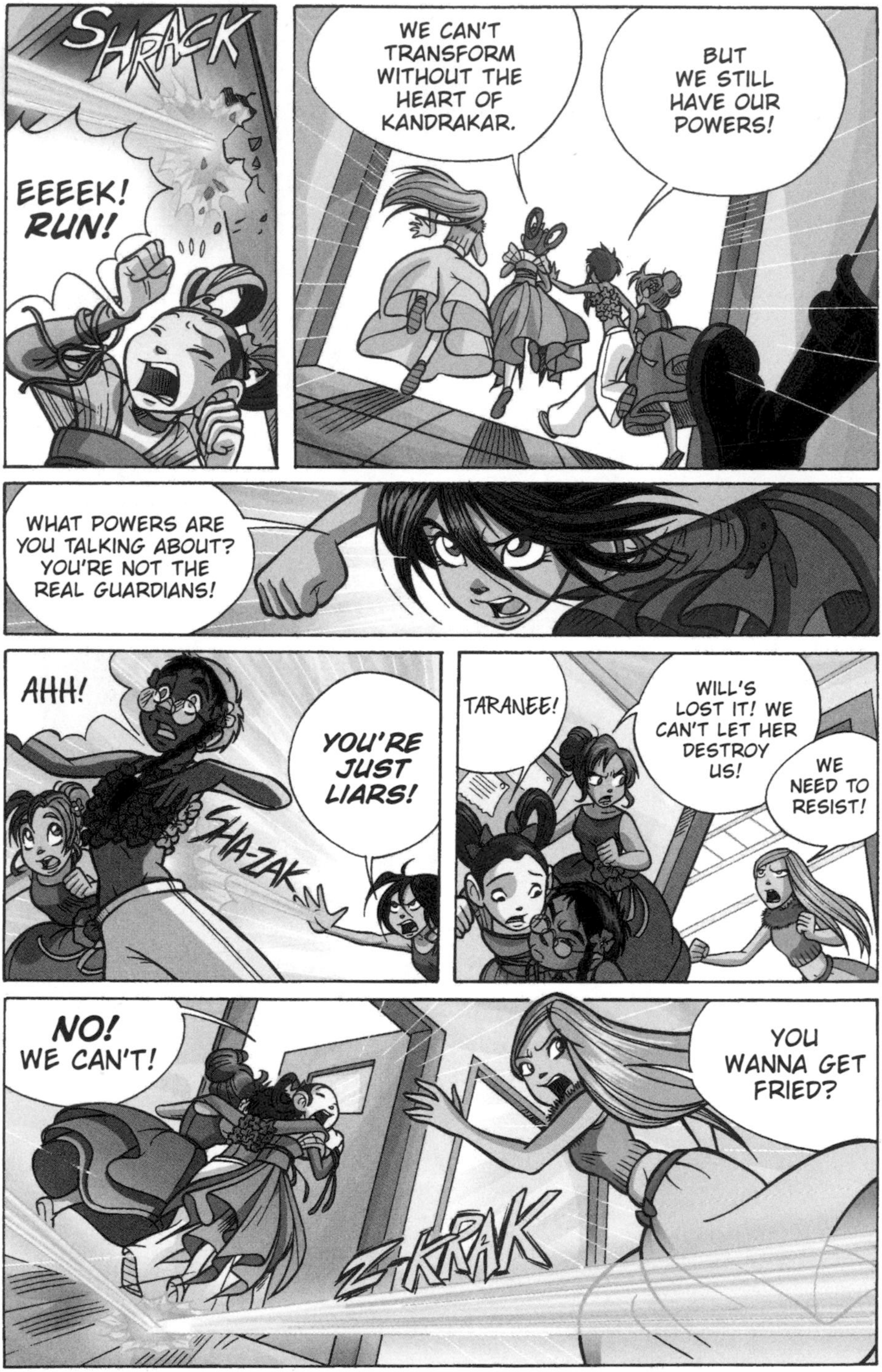
SHRACK
EEEEK! RUN!
WE CAN'T TRANSFORM WITHOUT THE HEART OF KANDRAKAR.
BUT WE STILL HAVE OUR POWERS!
WHAT POWERS ARE YOU TALKING ABOUT? YOU'RE NOT THE REAL GUARDIANS!
AHH!
YOU'RE JUST LIARS!
SHA-ZAK
TARANEE!
WILL'S LOST IT! WE CAN'T LET HER DESTROY US!
WE NEED TO RESIST!
NO! WE CAN'T!
YOU WANNA GET FRIED?
Z-KRAK

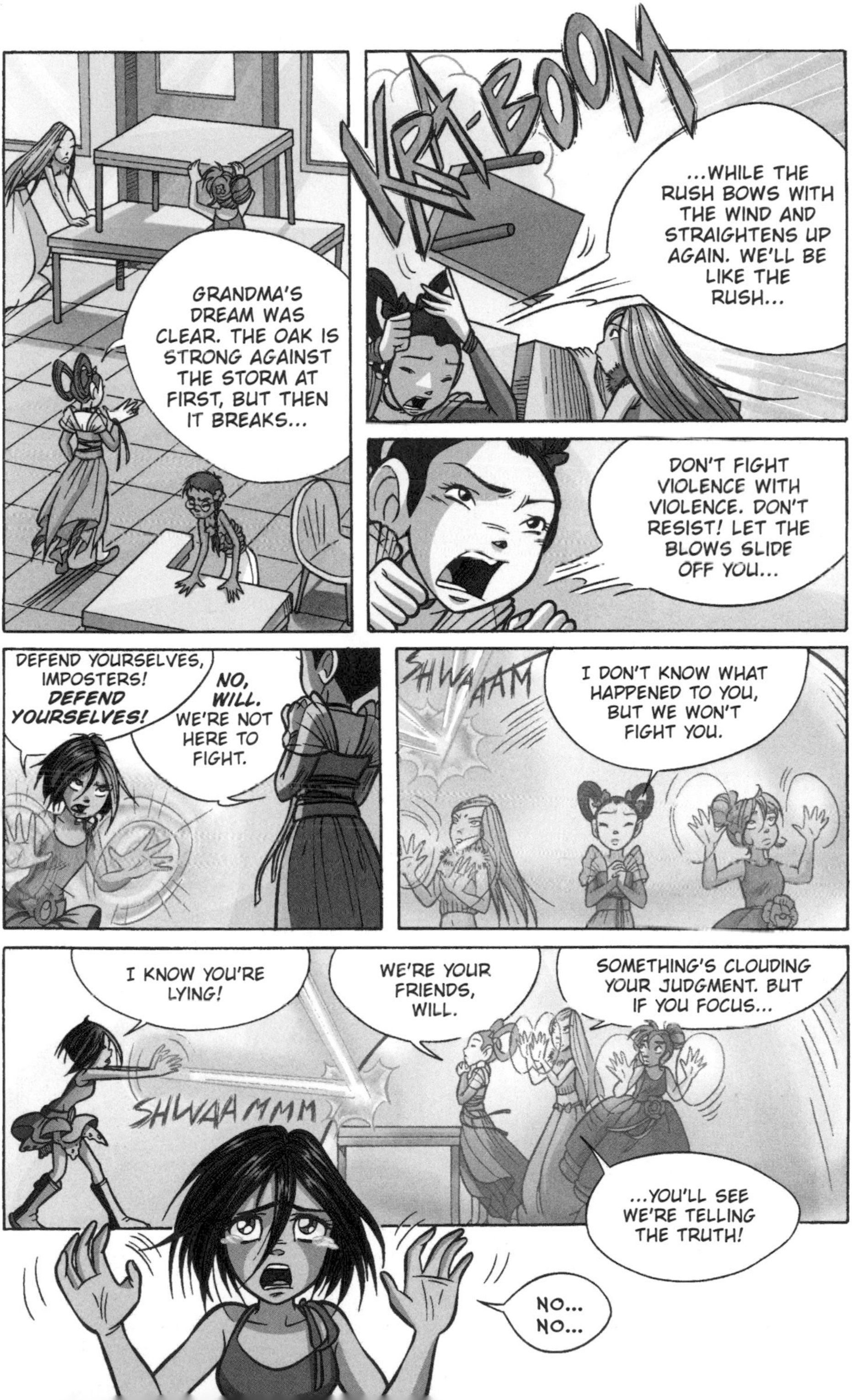
GRANDMA'S DREAM WAS CLEAR. THE OAK IS STRONG AGAINST THE STORM AT FIRST, BUT THEN IT BREAKS...
KRA-BOOM
...WHILE THE RUSH BOWS WITH THE WIND AND STRAIGHTENS UP AGAIN. WE'LL BE LIKE THE RUSH...
DON'T FIGHT VIOLENCE WITH VIOLENCE. DON'T RESIST! LET THE BLOWS SLIDE OFF YOU...
DEFEND YOURSELVES, IMPOSTERS! ***DEFEND YOURSELVES!***
NO, WILL. WE'RE NOT HERE TO FIGHT.
SHWAAAM
I DON'T KNOW WHAT HAPPENED TO YOU, BUT WE WON'T FIGHT YOU.
I KNOW YOU'RE LYING!
SHWAAMMM
WE'RE YOUR FRIENDS, WILL.
SOMETHING'S CLOUDING YOUR JUDGMENT. BUT IF YOU FOCUS...
...YOU'LL SEE WE'RE TELLING THE TRUTH!
NO... NO...

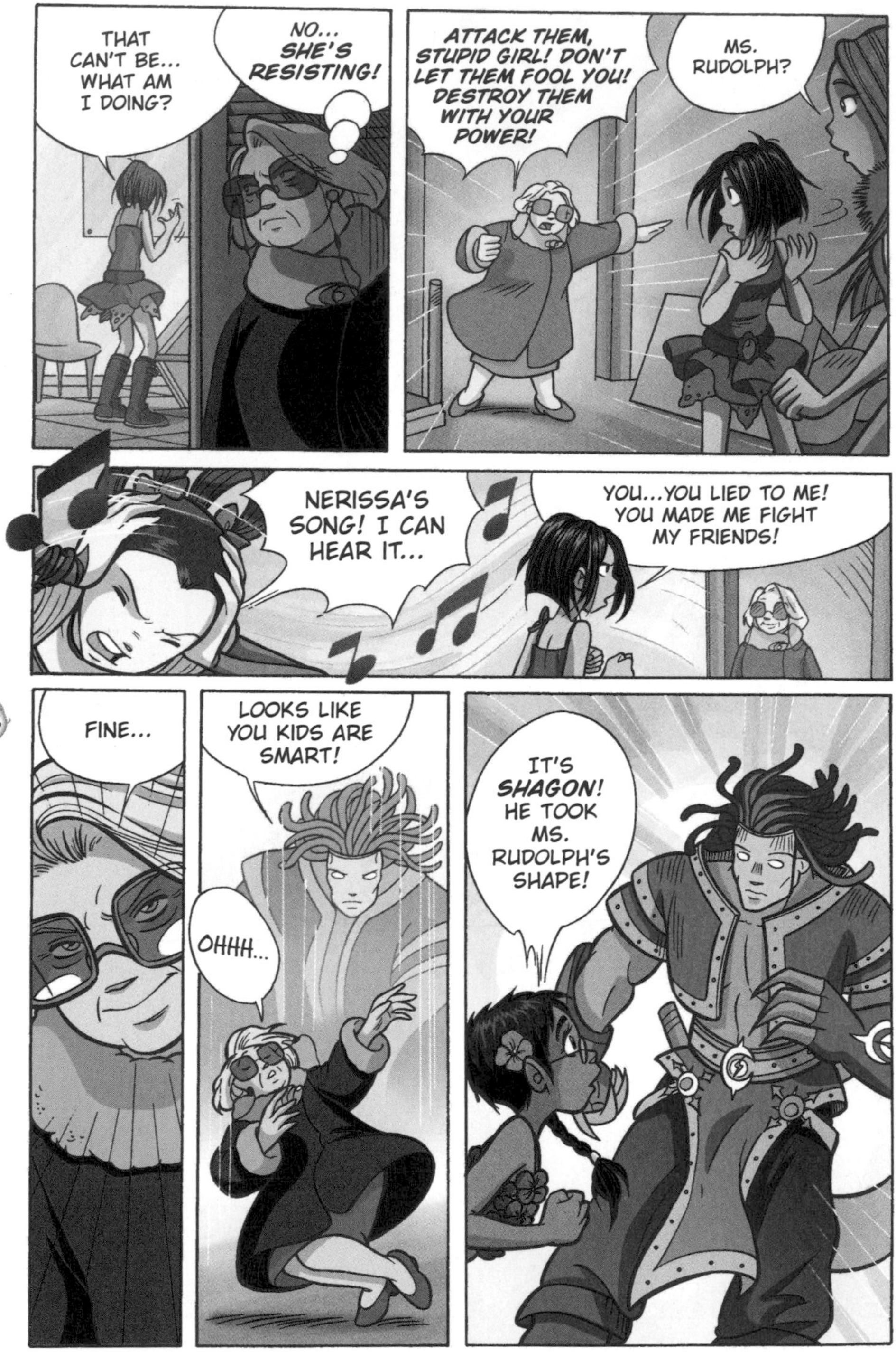
THAT CAN'T BE... WHAT AM I DOING?
NO... SHE'S RESISTING!
ATTACK THEM, STUPID GIRL! DON'T LET THEM FOOL YOU! DESTROY THEM WITH YOUR POWER!
MS. RUDOLPH?
NERISSA'S SONG! I CAN HEAR IT...
YOU...YOU LIED TO ME! YOU MADE ME FIGHT MY FRIENDS!
FINE...
LOOKS LIKE YOU KIDS ARE SMART!
OHHH...
IT'S SHAGON! HE TOOK MS. RUDOLPH'S SHAPE!

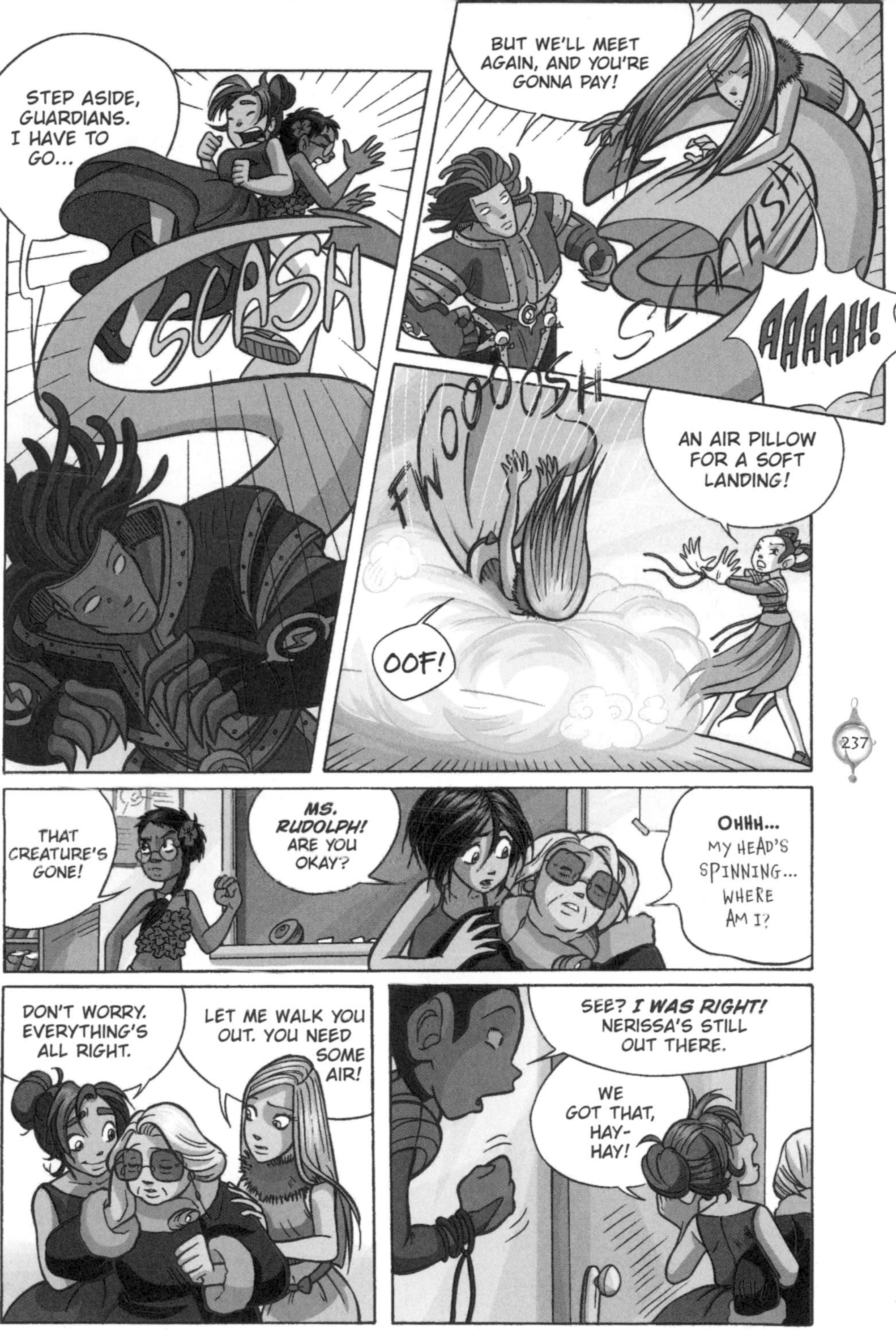
STEP ASIDE, GUARDIANS. I HAVE TO GO...
SLASH
BUT WE'LL MEET AGAIN, AND YOU'RE GONNA PAY!
SLAAASH
AAAAH!
FWOOOOSH
AN AIR PILLOW FOR A SOFT LANDING!
OOF!
THAT CREATURE'S GONE!
MS. RUDOLPH! ARE YOU OKAY?
OHHH... MY HEAD'S SPINNING... WHERE AM I?
DON'T WORRY. EVERYTHING'S ALL RIGHT.
LET ME WALK YOU OUT. YOU NEED SOME AIR!
SEE? I WAS RIGHT! NERISSA'S STILL OUT THERE.
WE GOT THAT, HAY-HAY!

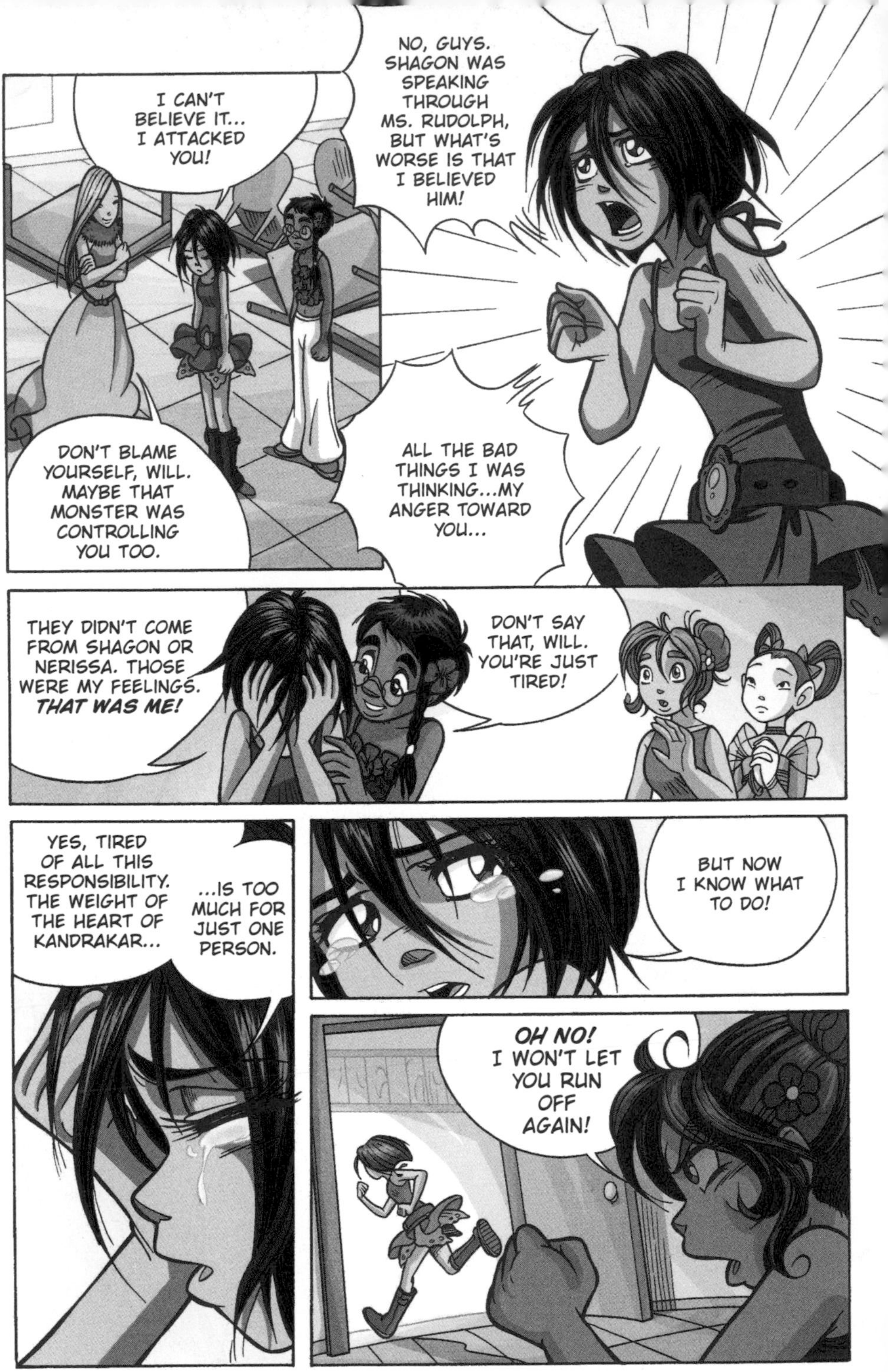

I CAN'T BELIEVE IT... I ATTACKED YOU!
DON'T BLAME YOURSELF, WILL. MAYBE THAT MONSTER WAS CONTROLLING YOU TOO.
NO, GUYS. SHAGON WAS SPEAKING THROUGH MS. RUDOLPH, BUT WHAT'S WORSE IS THAT I BELIEVED HIM!
ALL THE BAD THINGS I WAS THINKING...MY ANGER TOWARD YOU...
THEY DIDN'T COME FROM SHAGON OR NERISSA. THOSE WERE MY FEELINGS. ***THAT WAS ME!***
DON'T SAY THAT, WILL. YOU'RE JUST TIRED!
YES, TIRED OF ALL THIS RESPONSIBILITY. THE WEIGHT OF THE HEART OF KANDRAKAR...
...IS TOO MUCH FOR JUST ONE PERSON.
BUT NOW I KNOW WHAT TO DO!
OH NO! I WON'T LET YOU RUN OFF AGAIN!

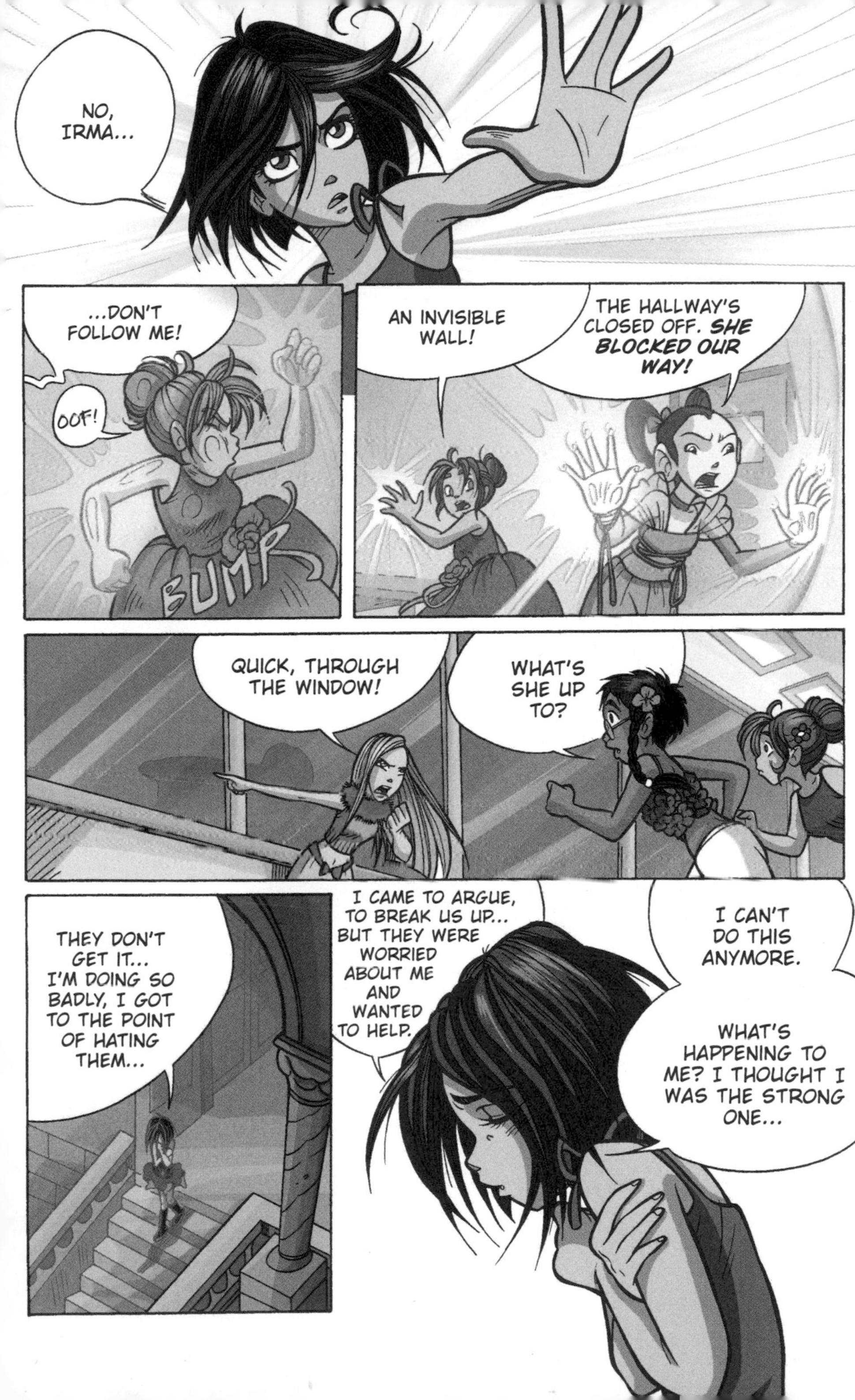
NO, IRMA...
...DON'T FOLLOW ME!
OOF!
BUMP
AN INVISIBLE WALL!
THE HALLWAY'S CLOSED OFF. SHE BLOCKED OUR WAY!
QUICK, THROUGH THE WINDOW!
WHAT'S SHE UP TO?
THEY DON'T GET IT... I'M DOING SO BADLY, I GOT TO THE POINT OF HATING THEM...
I CAME TO ARGUE, TO BREAK US UP... BUT THEY WERE WORRIED ABOUT ME AND WANTED TO HELP.
I CAN'T DO THIS ANYMORE.
WHAT'S HAPPENING TO ME? I THOUGHT I WAS THE STRONG ONE...

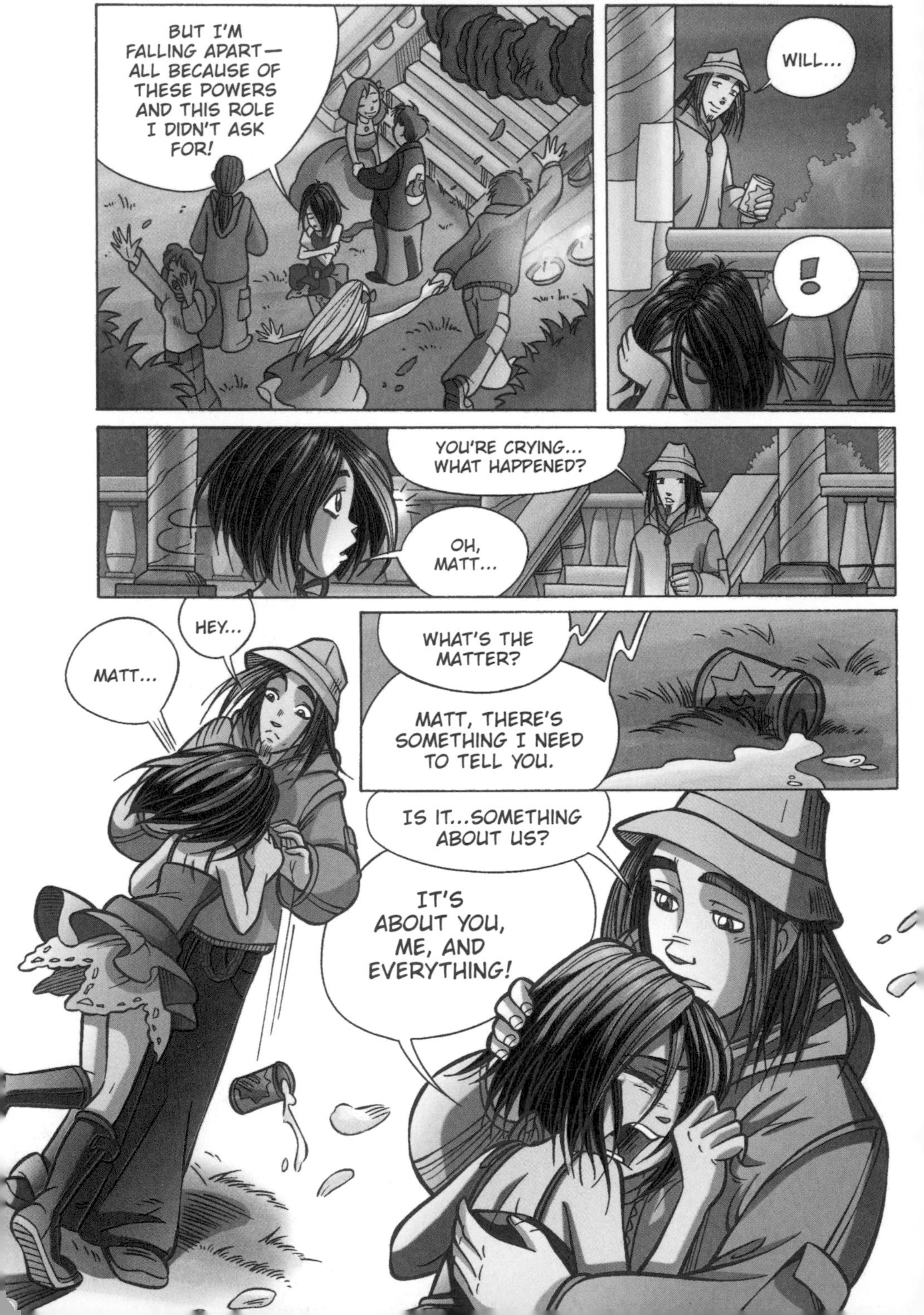
BUT I'M FALLING APART— ALL BECAUSE OF THESE POWERS AND THIS ROLE I DIDN'T ASK FOR!
WILL...
!
YOU'RE CRYING... WHAT HAPPENED?
OH, MATT...
HEY...
MATT...
WHAT'S THE MATTER?
MATT, THERE'S SOMETHING I NEED TO TELL YOU.
IS IT...SOMETHING ABOUT US?
IT'S ABOUT YOU, ME, AND EVERYTHING!

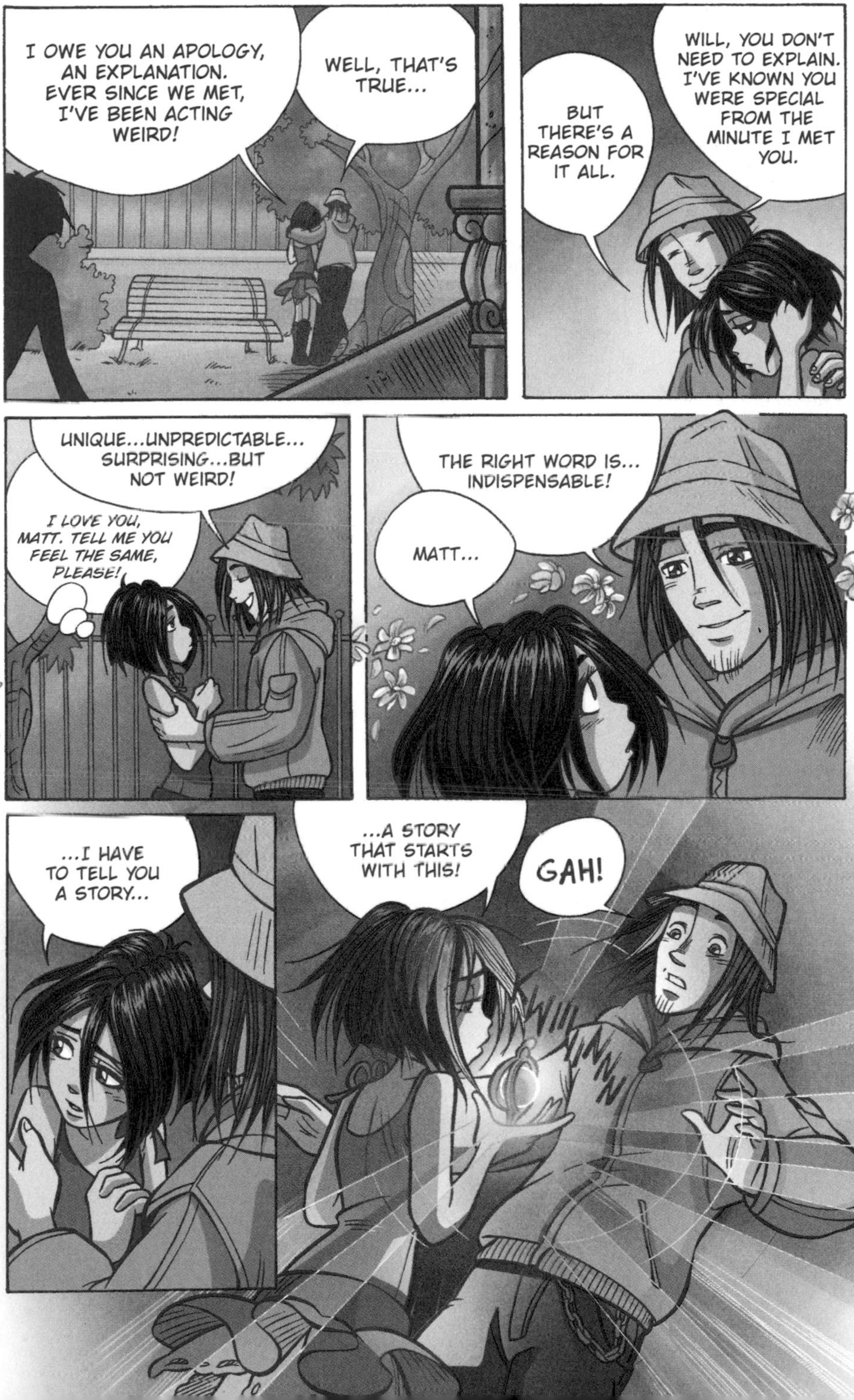
I OWE YOU AN APOLOGY, AN EXPLANATION. EVER SINCE WE MET, I'VE BEEN ACTING WEIRD!
WELL, THAT'S TRUE...
WILL, YOU DON'T NEED TO EXPLAIN. I'VE KNOWN YOU WERE SPECIAL FROM THE MINUTE I MET YOU.
BUT THERE'S A REASON FOR IT ALL.
UNIQUE...UNPREDICTABLE... SURPRISING...BUT NOT WEIRD!
I LOVE YOU, MATT. TELL ME YOU FEEL THE SAME, PLEASE!
THE RIGHT WORD IS... INDISPENSABLE!
MATT...
...I HAVE TO TELL YOU A STORY...
...A STORY THAT STARTS WITH THIS!
GAH!

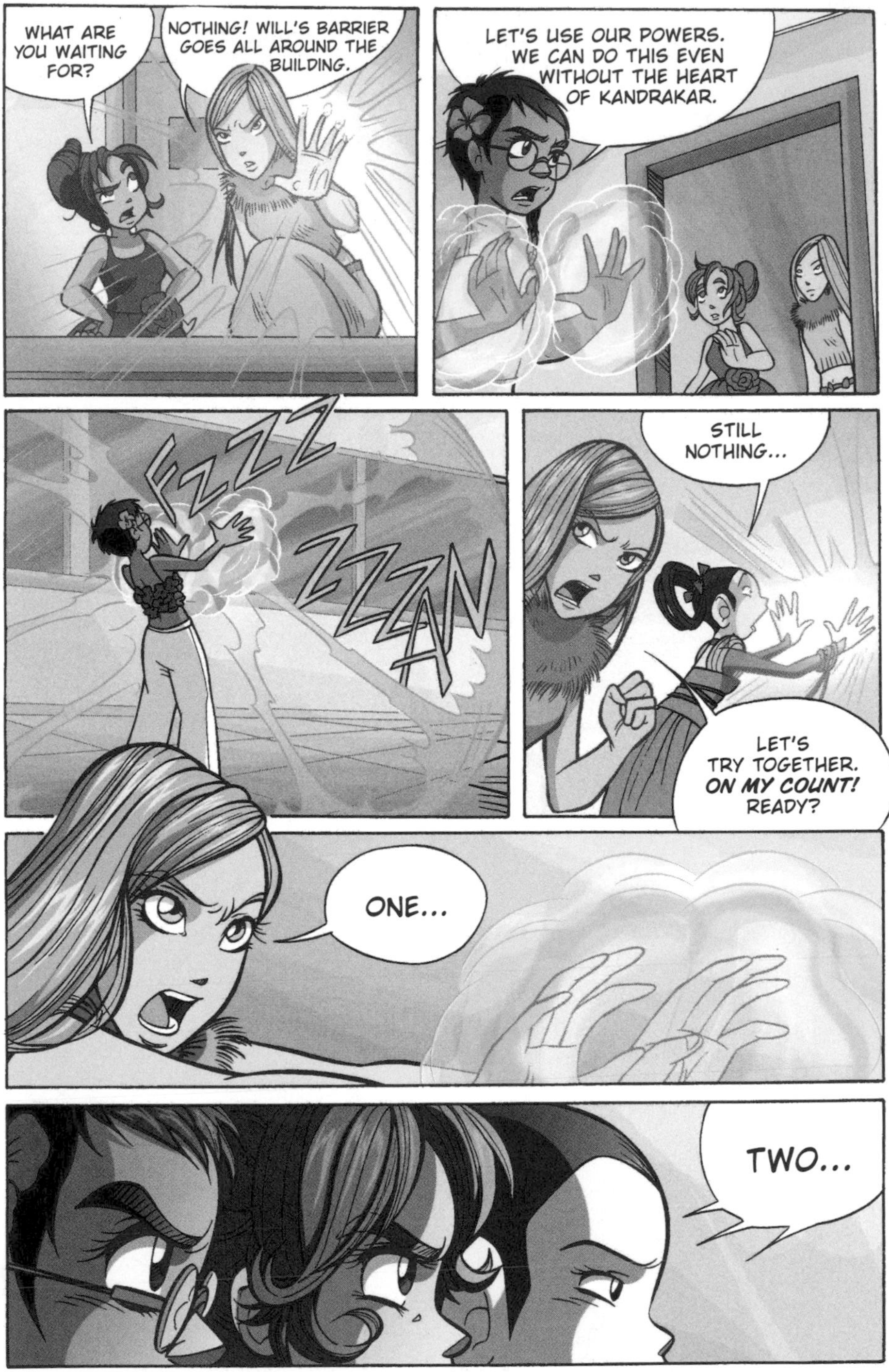
WHAT ARE YOU WAITING FOR?
NOTHING! WILL'S BARRIER GOES ALL AROUND THE BUILDING.
LET'S USE OUR POWERS. WE CAN DO THIS EVEN WITHOUT THE HEART OF KANDRAKAR.
FZZZZ
ZZZAN
STILL NOTHING...
LET'S TRY TOGETHER. ON MY COUNT! READY?
ONE...
TWO...

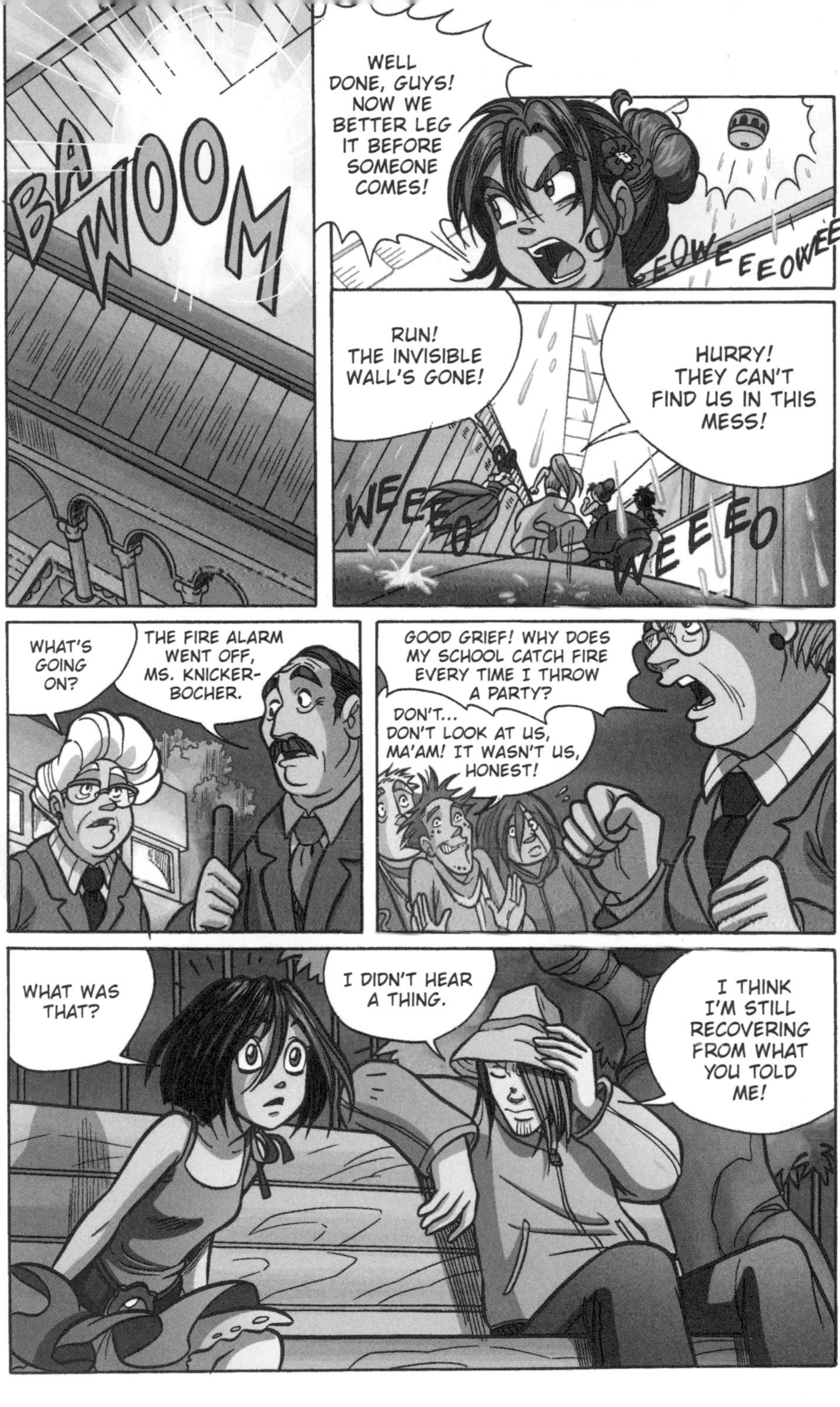
BA WOOM
WELL DONE, GUYS! NOW WE BETTER LEG IT BEFORE SOMEONE COMES!
EEOWEEEOWEEO
RUN! THE INVISIBLE WALL'S GONE!
HURRY! THEY CAN'T FIND US IN THIS MESS!
WEEEO
WEEEO
WHAT'S GOING ON?
THE FIRE ALARM WENT OFF, MS. KNICKER-BOCHER.
GOOD GRIEF! WHY DOES MY SCHOOL CATCH FIRE EVERY TIME I THROW A PARTY?
DON'T... DON'T LOOK AT US, MA'AM! IT WASN'T US, HONEST!
WHAT WAS THAT?
I DIDN'T HEAR A THING.
I THINK I'M STILL RECOVERING FROM WHAT YOU TOLD ME!

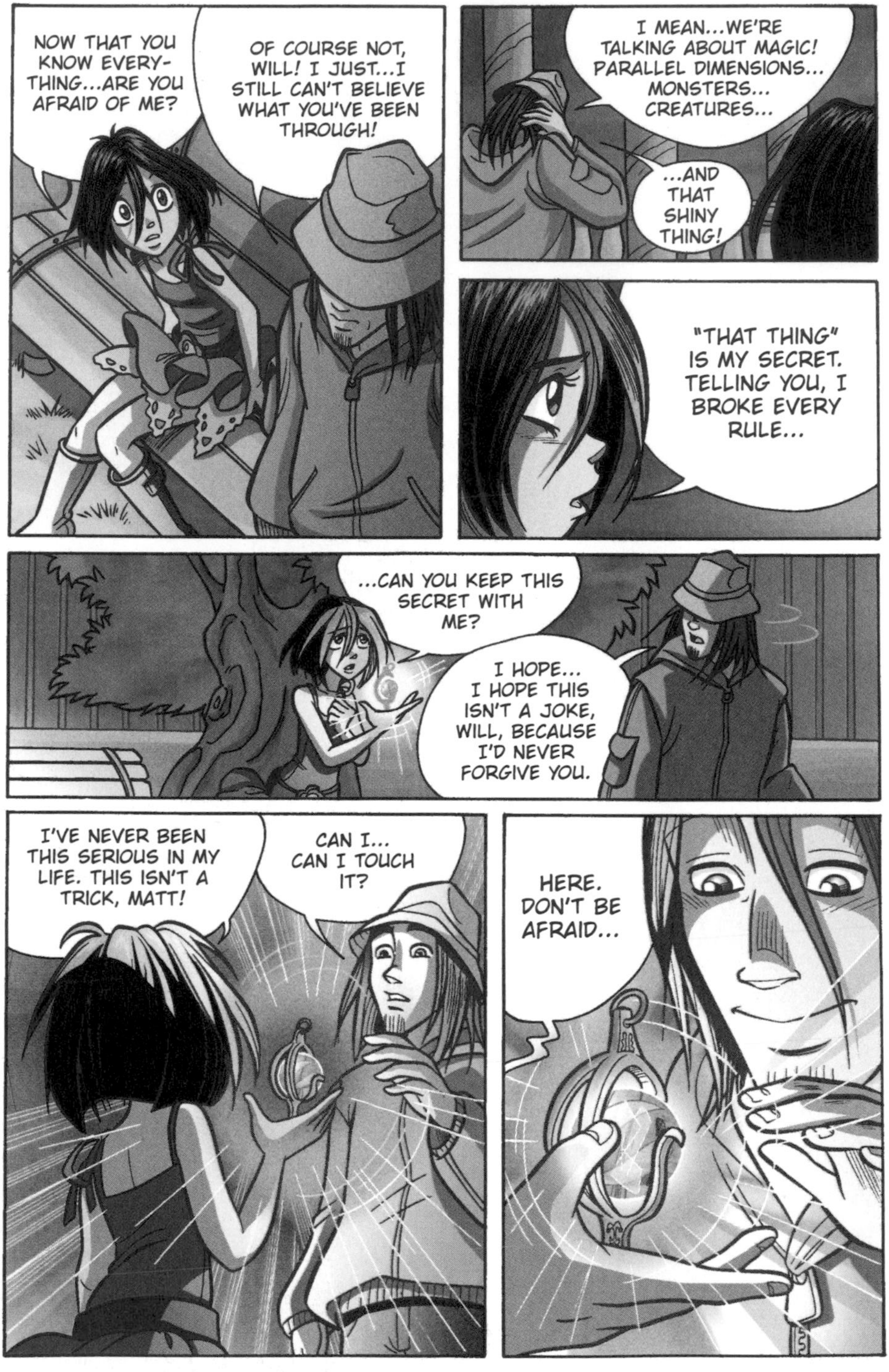
NOW THAT YOU KNOW EVERY-THING...ARE YOU AFRAID OF ME?
OF COURSE NOT, WILL! I JUST...I STILL CAN'T BELIEVE WHAT YOU'VE BEEN THROUGH!
I MEAN...WE'RE TALKING ABOUT MAGIC! PARALLEL DIMENSIONS... MONSTERS... CREATURES...
...AND THAT SHINY THING!
"THAT THING" IS MY SECRET. TELLING YOU, I BROKE EVERY RULE...
...CAN YOU KEEP THIS SECRET WITH ME?
I HOPE... I HOPE THIS ISN'T A JOKE, WILL, BECAUSE I'D NEVER FORGIVE YOU.
I'VE NEVER BEEN THIS SERIOUS IN MY LIFE. THIS ISN'T A TRICK, MATT!
CAN I... CAN I TOUCH IT?
HERE. DON'T BE AFRAID...

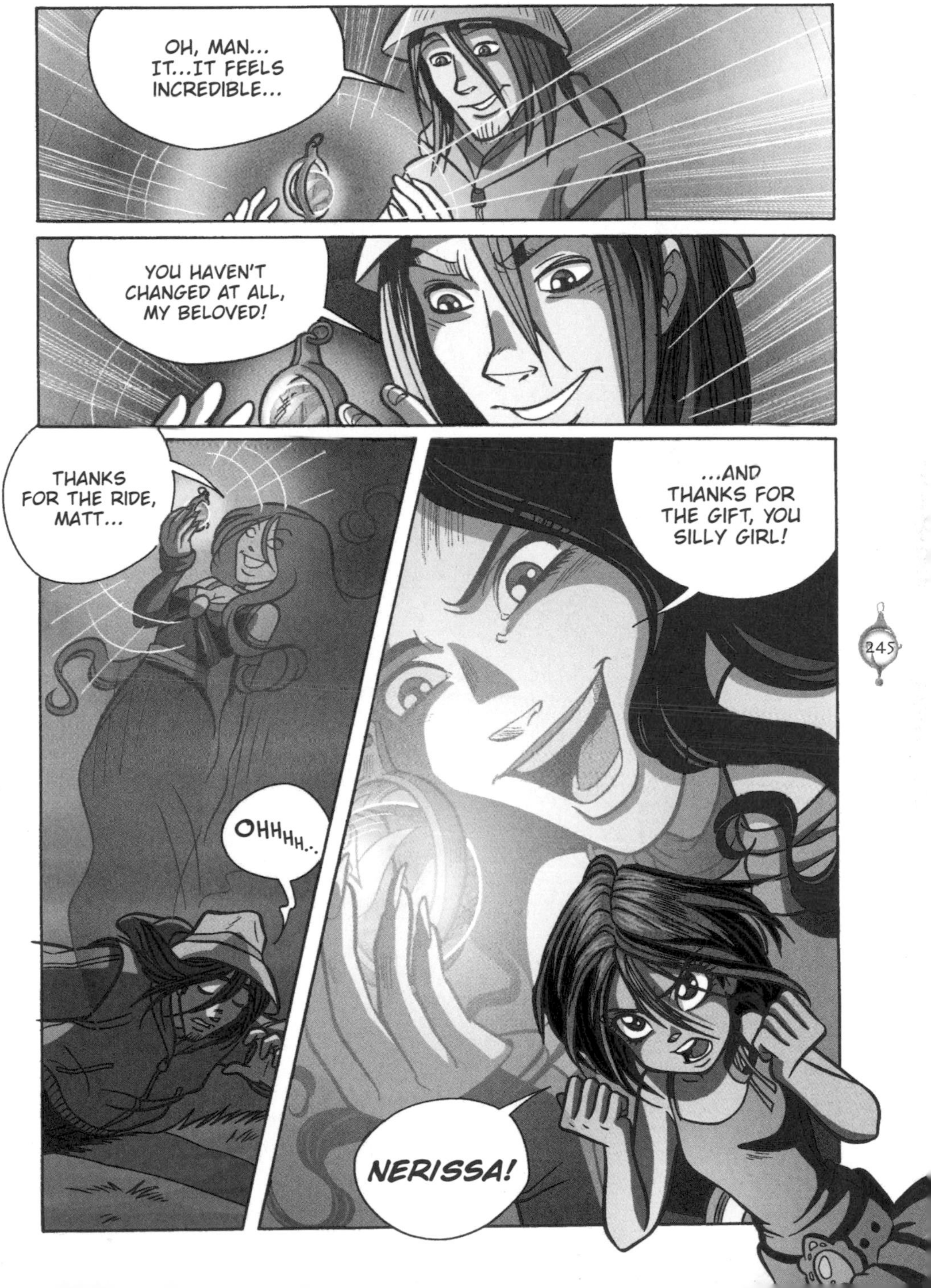
OH, MAN... IT...IT FEELS INCREDIBLE...
YOU HAVEN'T CHANGED AT ALL, MY BELOVED!
THANKS FOR THE RIDE, MATT...
...AND THANKS FOR THE GIFT, YOU SILLY GIRL!
OHHHH...
NERISSA!

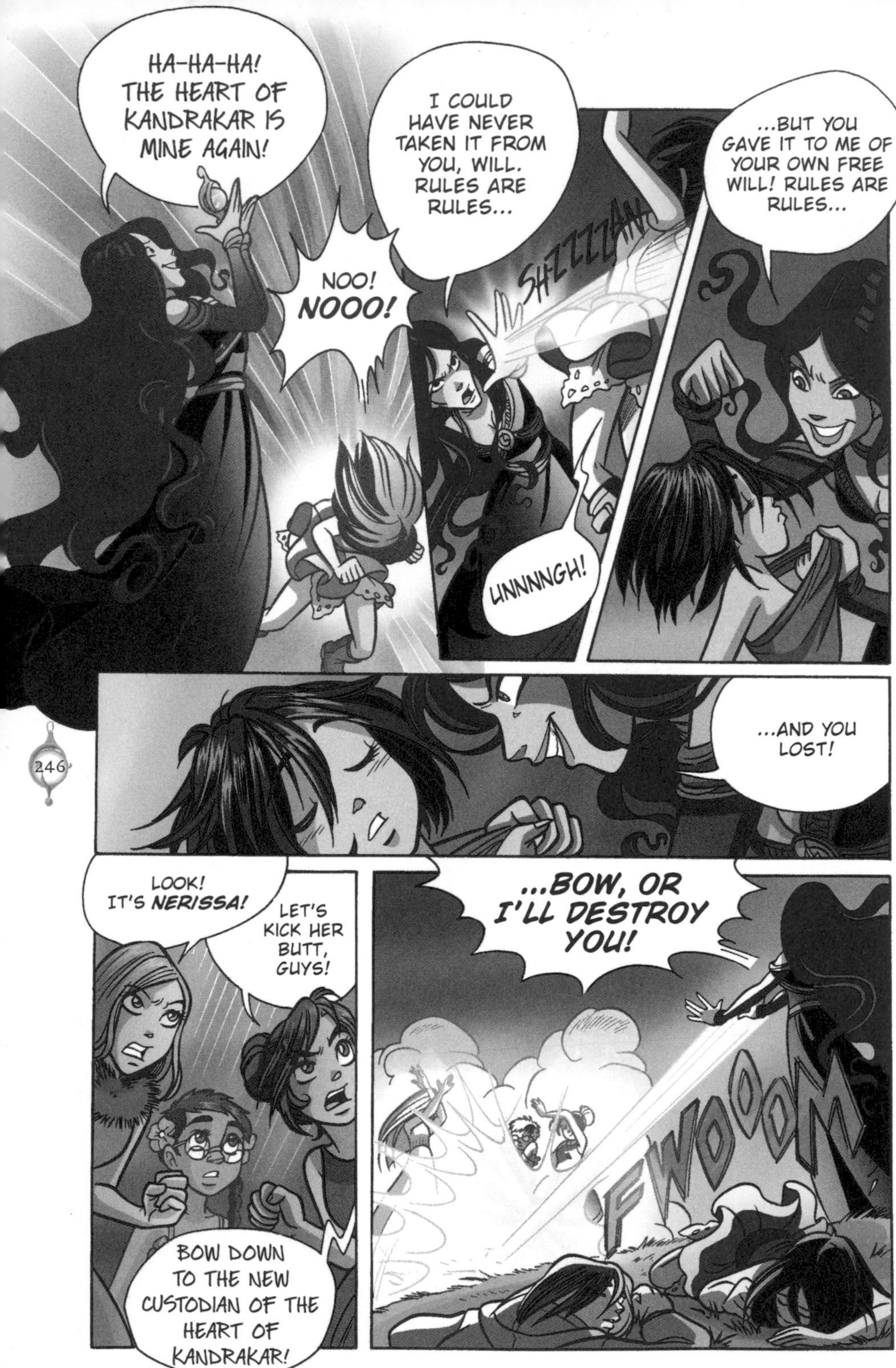
HA-HA-HA! THE HEART OF KANDRAKAR IS MINE AGAIN!
NOO! NOOO!
I COULD HAVE NEVER TAKEN IT FROM YOU, WILL. RULES ARE RULES...
SHZZZZAN
UNNNNGH!
...BUT YOU GAVE IT TO ME OF YOUR OWN FREE WILL! RULES ARE RULES...
...AND YOU LOST!
LOOK! IT'S NERISSA!
LET'S KICK HER BUTT, GUYS!
BOW DOWN TO THE NEW CUSTODIAN OF THE HEART OF KANDRAKAR!
...BOW, OR I'LL DESTROY YOU!
FWOOOM

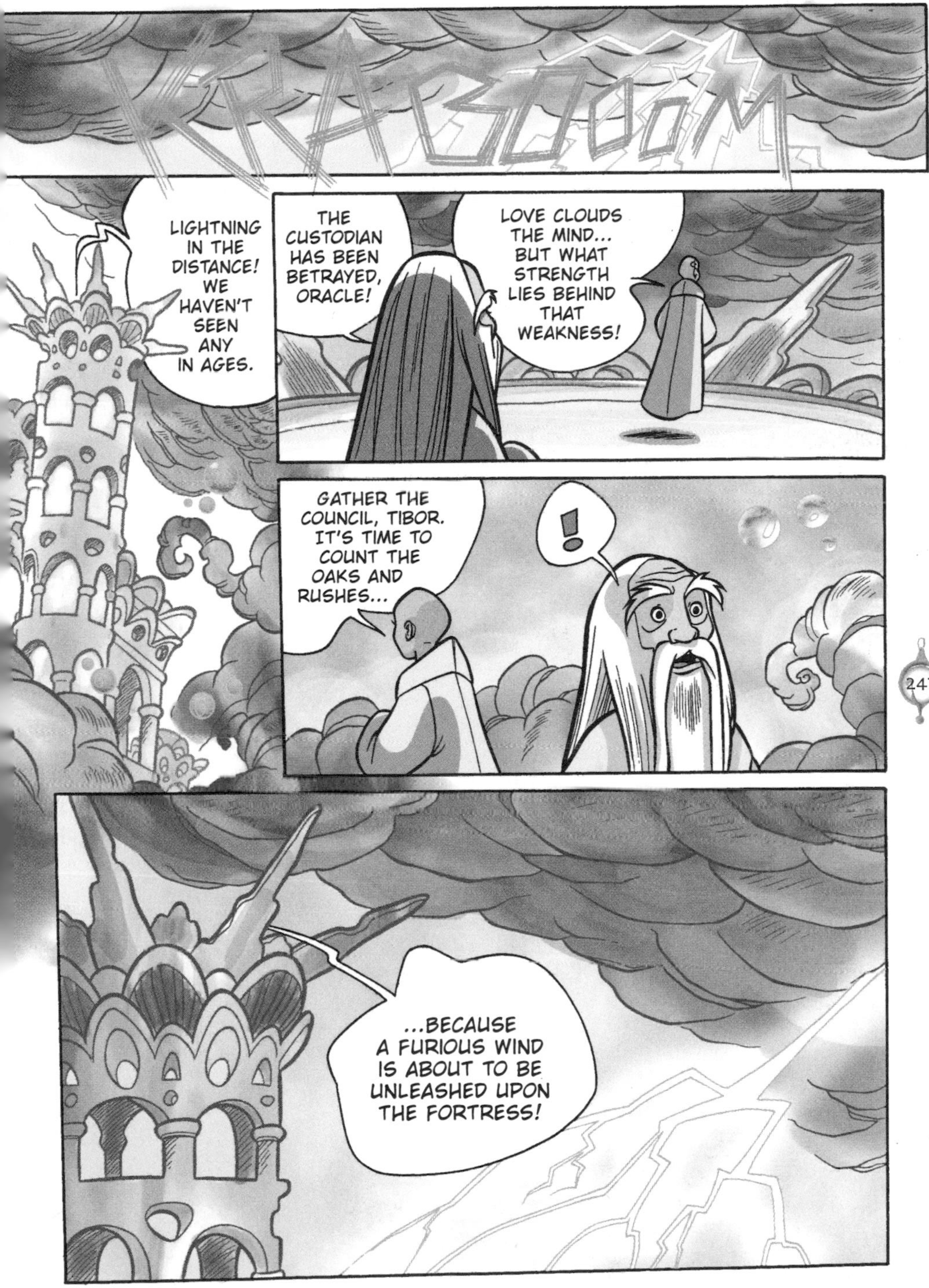
KRABOOOM
LIGHTNING IN THE DISTANCE! WE HAVEN'T SEEN ANY IN AGES.
THE CUSTODIAN HAS BEEN BETRAYED, ORACLE!
LOVE CLOUDS THE MIND... BUT WHAT STRENGTH LIES BEHIND THAT WEAKNESS!
GATHER THE COUNCIL, TIBOR. IT'S TIME TO COUNT THE OAKS AND RUSHES...
!
...BECAUSE A FURIOUS WIND IS ABOUT TO BE UNLEASHED UPON THE FORTRESS!

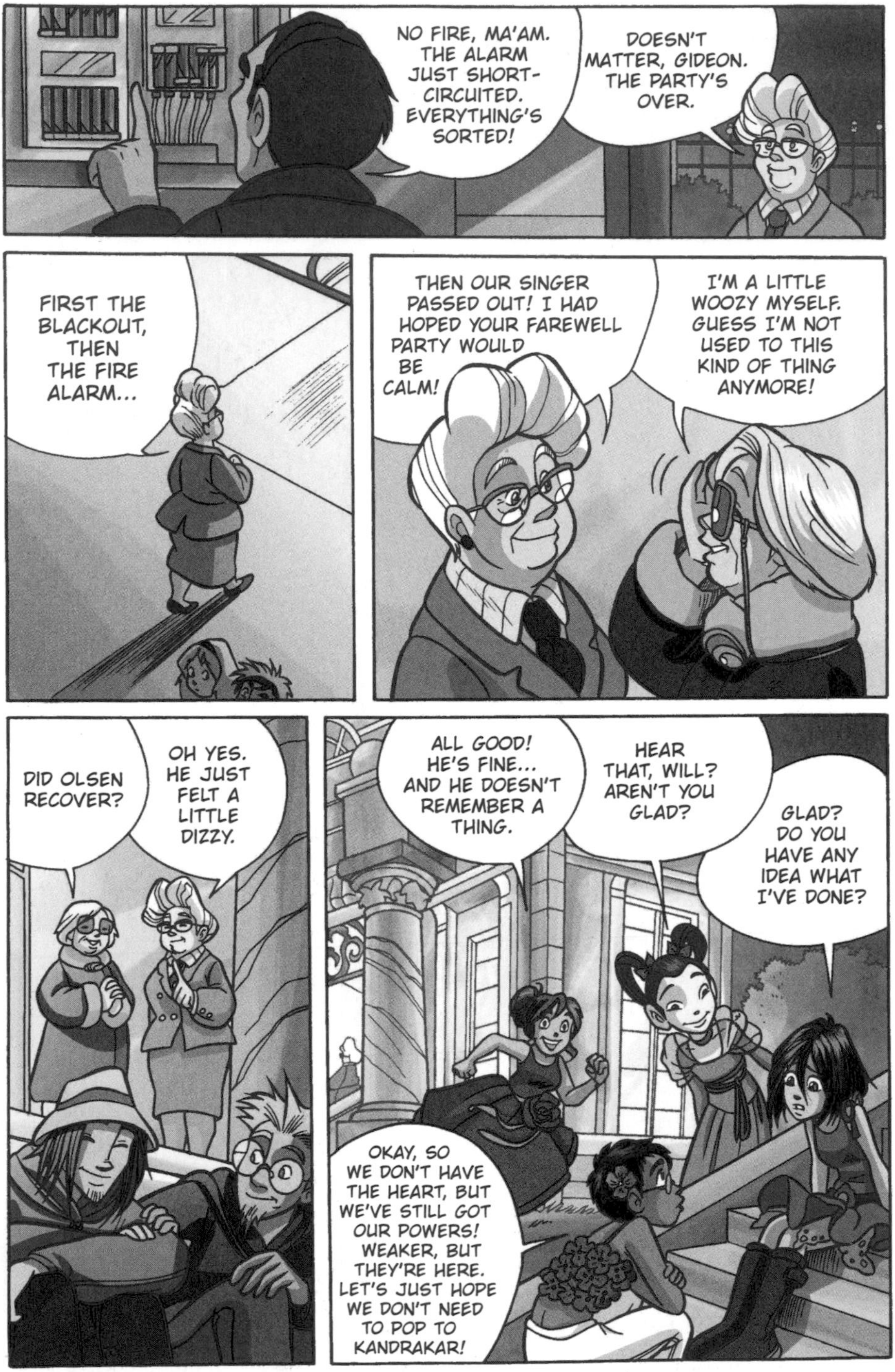
NO FIRE, MA'AM. THE ALARM JUST SHORT-CIRCUITED. EVERYTHING'S SORTED!
DOESN'T MATTER, GIDEON. THE PARTY'S OVER.
FIRST THE BLACKOUT, THEN THE FIRE ALARM...
THEN OUR SINGER PASSED OUT! I HAD HOPED YOUR FAREWELL PARTY WOULD BE CALM!
I'M A LITTLE WOOZY MYSELF. GUESS I'M NOT USED TO THIS KIND OF THING ANYMORE!
DID OLSEN RECOVER?
OH YES. HE JUST FELT A LITTLE DIZZY.
ALL GOOD! HE'S FINE... AND HE DOESN'T REMEMBER A THING.
HEAR THAT, WILL? AREN'T YOU GLAD?
GLAD? DO YOU HAVE ANY IDEA WHAT I'VE DONE?
OKAY, SO WE DON'T HAVE THE HEART, BUT WE'VE STILL GOT OUR POWERS! WEAKER, BUT THEY'RE HERE. LET'S JUST HOPE WE DON'T NEED TO POP TO KANDRAKAR!

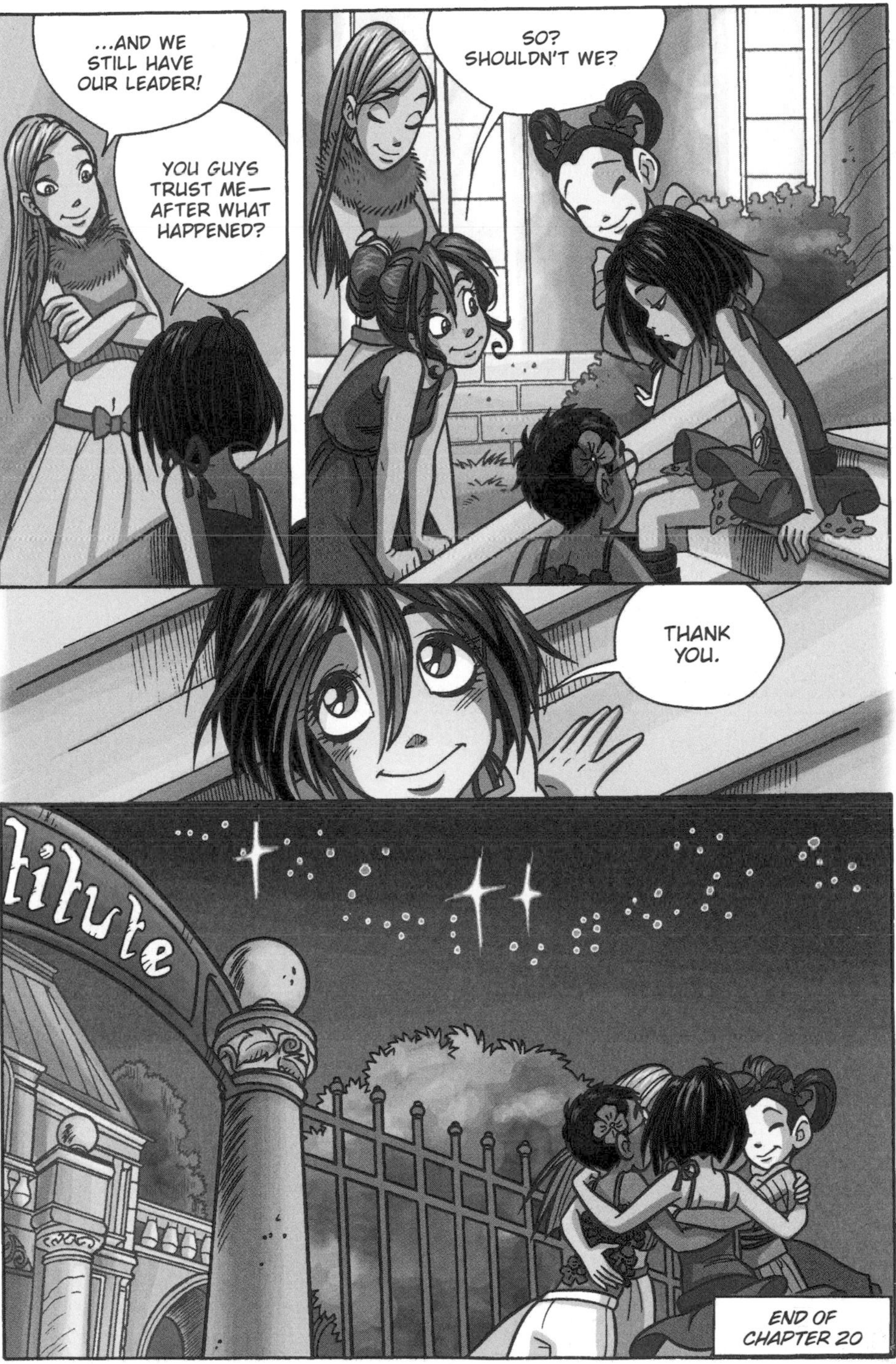
...AND WE STILL HAVE OUR LEADER!
YOU GUYS TRUST ME— AFTER WHAT HAPPENED?
SO? SHOULDN'T WE?
THANK YOU.
tilute
END OF CHAPTER 20

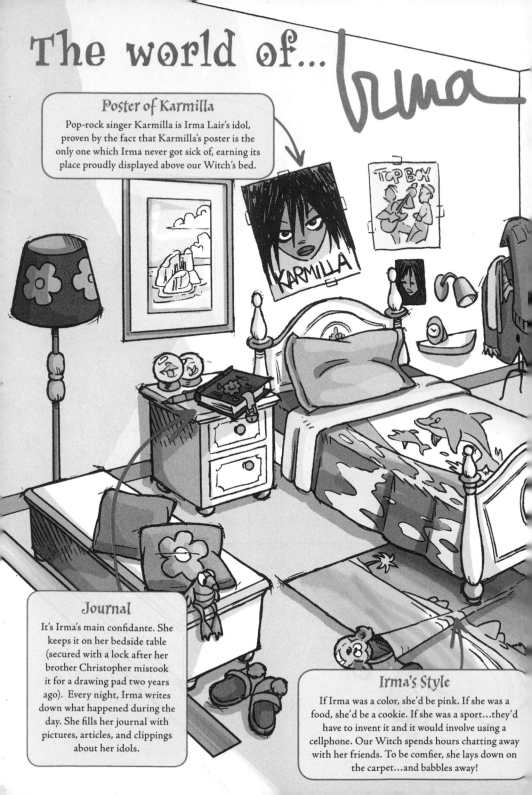

The world of... *Irma*

Poster of Karmilla

Pop-rock singer Karmilla is Irma Lair's idol, proven by the fact that Karmilla's poster is the only one which Irma never got sick of, earning its place proudly displayed above our Witch's bed.

Journal

It's Irma's main confidante. She keeps it on her bedside table (secured with a lock after her brother Christopher mistook it for a drawing pad two years ago). Every night, Irma writes down what happened during the day. She fills her journal with pictures, articles, and clippings about her idols.

Irma's Style

If Irma was a color, she'd be pink. If she was a food, she'd be a cookie. If she was a sport...they'd have to invent it and it would involve using a cellphone. Our Witch spends hours chatting away with her friends. To be comfier, she lays down on the carpet...and babbles away!

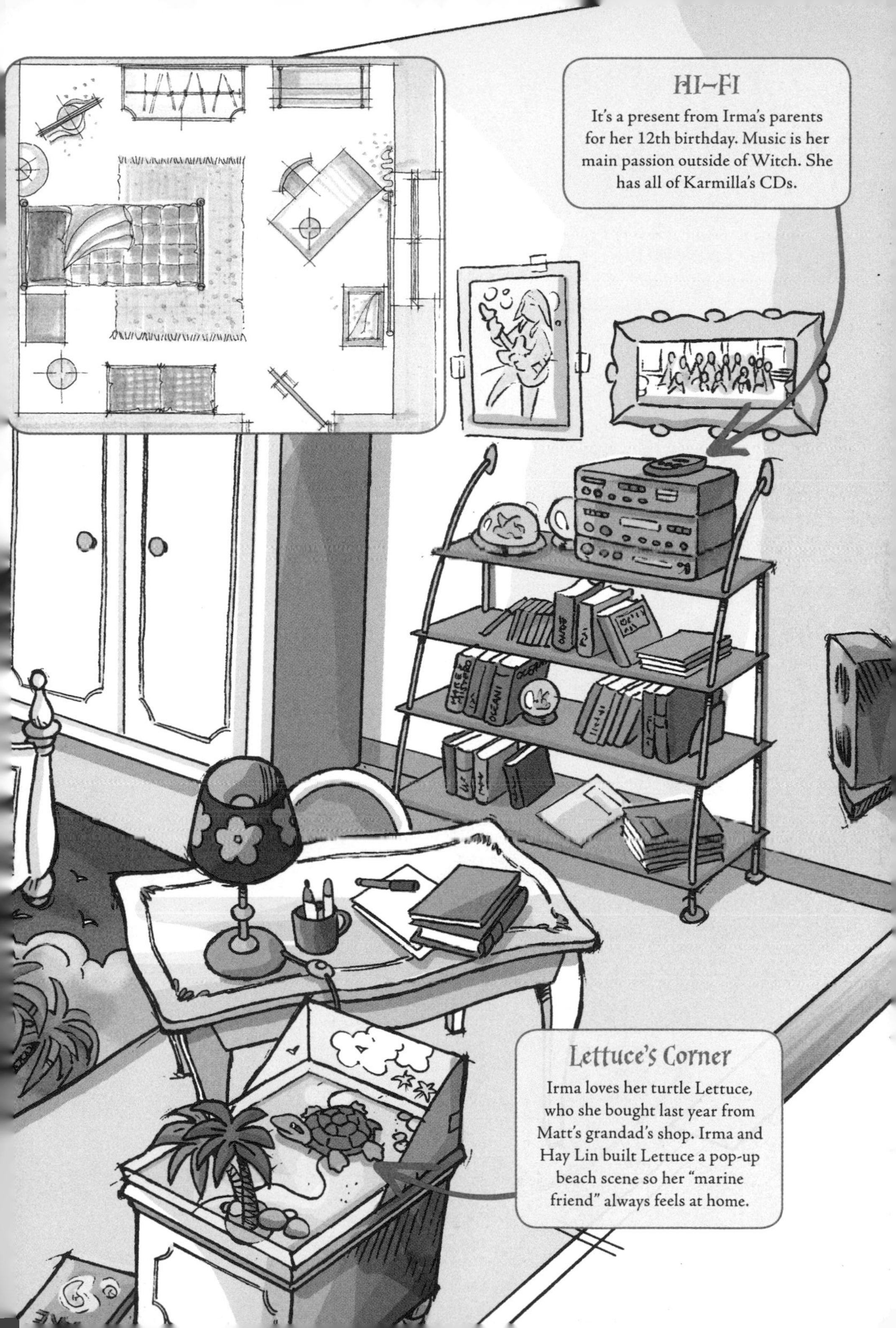
HI-FI
It's a present from Irma's parents for her 12th birthday. Music is her main passion outside of Witch. She has all of Karmilla's CDs.
Lettuce's Corner
Irma loves her turtle Lettuce, who she bought last year from Matt's grandad's shop. Irma and Hay Lin built Lettuce a pop-up beach scene so her "marine friend" always feels at home.

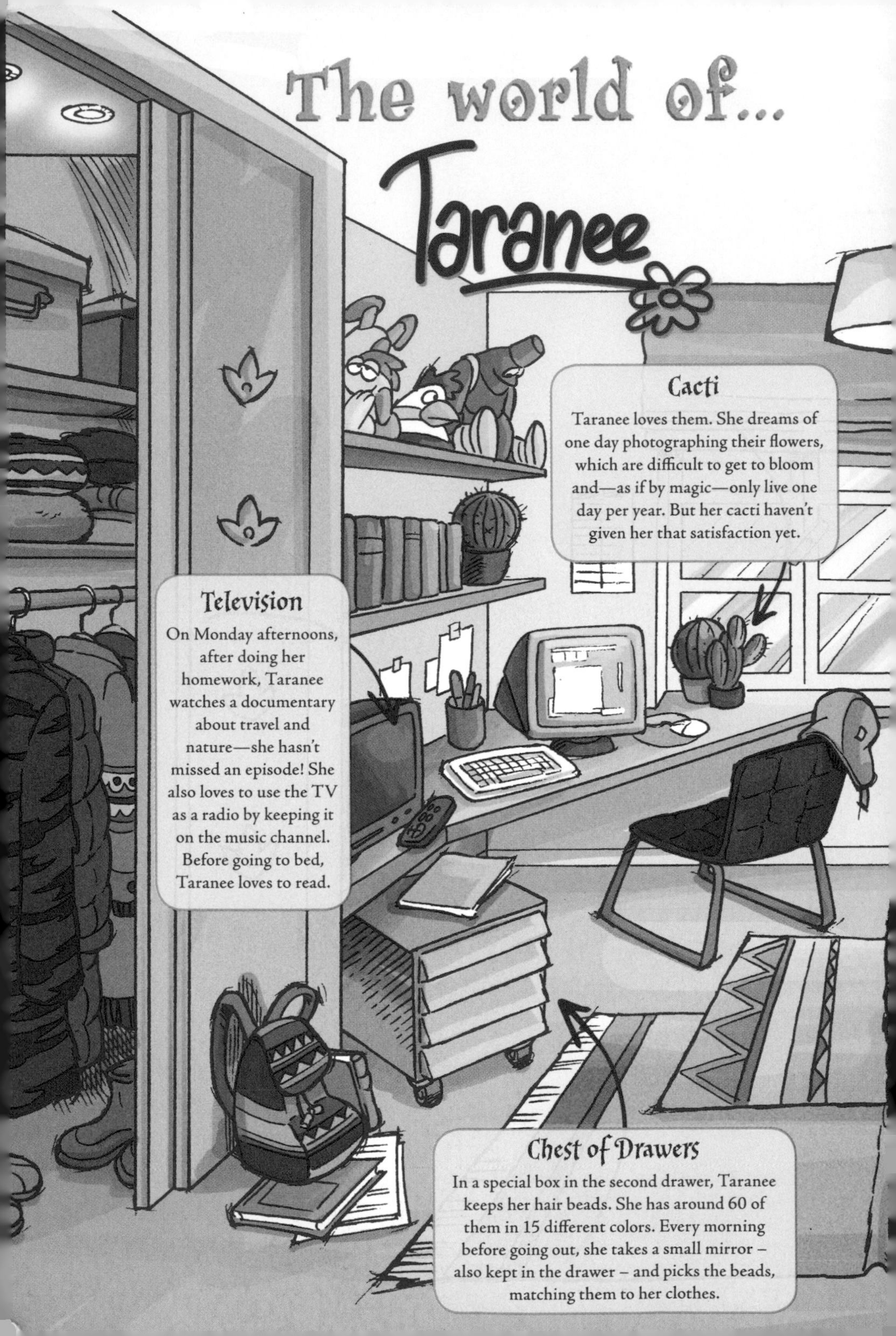
The world of...
Taranee
Cacti
Taranee loves them. She dreams of one day photographing their flowers, which are difficult to get to bloom and—as if by magic—only live one day per year. But her cacti haven't given her that satisfaction yet.
Television
On Monday afternoons, after doing her homework, Taranee watches a documentary about travel and nature—she hasn't missed an episode! She also loves to use the TV as a radio by keeping it on the music channel. Before going to bed, Taranee loves to read.
Chest of Drawers
In a special box in the second drawer, Taranee keeps her hair beads. She has around 60 of them in 15 different colors. Every morning before going out, she takes a small mirror – also kept in the drawer – and picks the beads, matching them to her clothes.

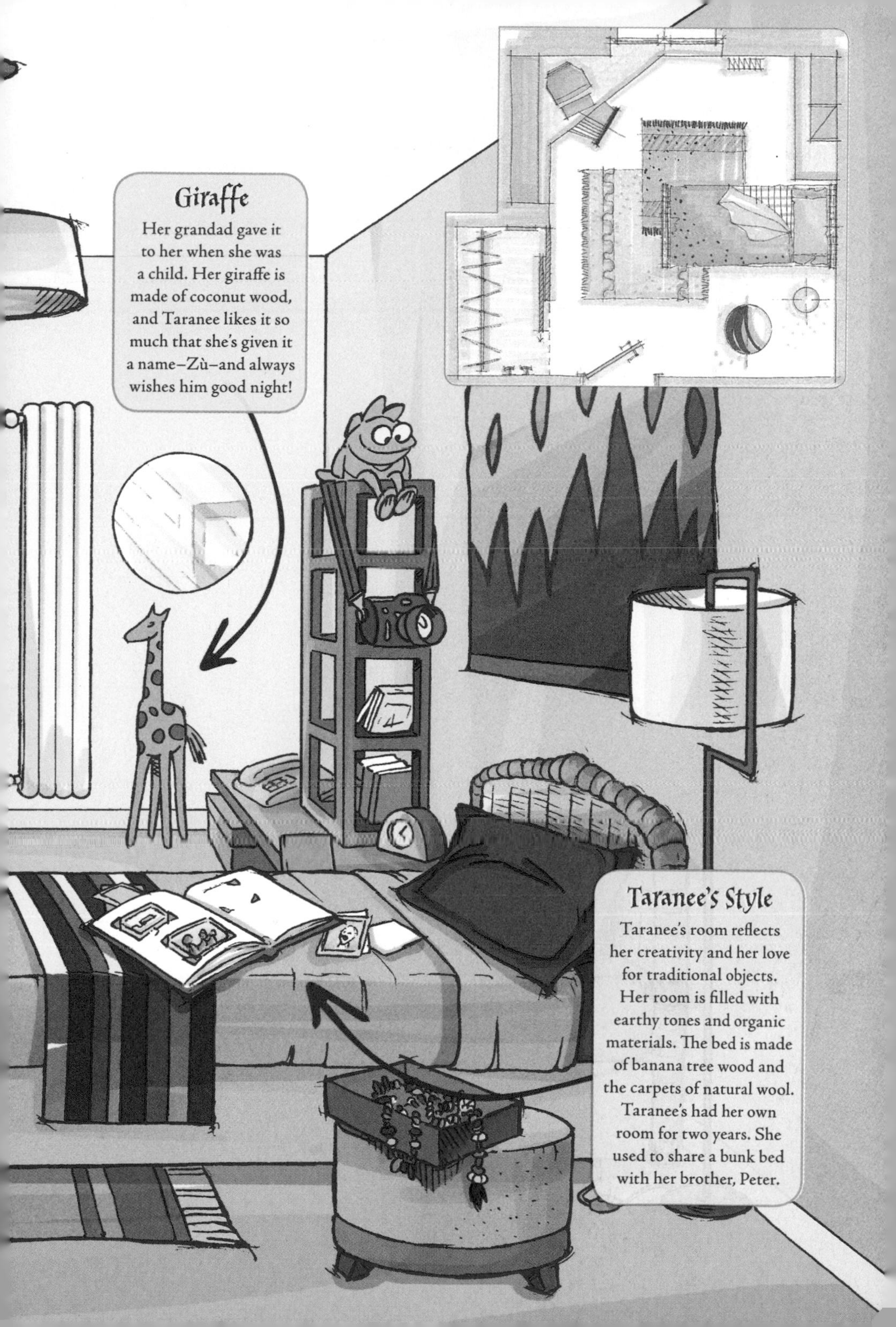
Giraffe
Her grandad gave it to her when she was a child. Her giraffe is made of coconut wood, and Taranee likes it so much that she's given it a name–Zù–and always wishes him good night!
Taranee's Style
Taranee's room reflects her creativity and her love for traditional objects. Her room is filled with earthy tones and organic materials. The bed is made of banana tree wood and the carpets of natural wool. Taranee's had her own room for two years. She used to share a bunk bed with her brother, Peter.

Read on in Volume 6!

W.I.T.C.H.

Will Irma Taranee Cornelia Hay Lin

Part II. Nerissa's Revenge • Volume 2

5

Series Created by Elisabetta Gnone
Comic Art Direction: Alessandro Barbucci, Barbara Canepa

This book is a work of fiction. Names, characters, places, and incidents are the product of the author's imagination or are used fictitiously. Any resemblance to actual events, locales, or persons, living or dead, is coincidental.

JY
1290 Avenue of the Americas
New York, NY 10104

Visit us at yenpress.com
facebook.com/yenpress
twitter.com/yenpress
yenpress.tumblr.com
instagram.com/yenpress

First JY Edition: January 2018

JY is an imprint of Yen Press, LLC.
The JY name and logo are trademarks of Yen Press, LLC.

The publisher is not responsible for websites (or their content) that are not owned by the publisher.

Library of Congress Control Number: 2017950917

ISBNs:
978-0-316-47705-5 (paperback)
978-0-316-41512-5 (ebook)

10 9 8 7 6 5 4 3 2

LSC-C

Printed in the United States of America

Cover Art by Manuela Razzi
Colors by Andrea Cagol

Translation by Linda Ghio and
Stephanie Dagg at Editing Zone
Lettering by Katie Blakeslee

DON'T CLOSE YOUR EYES

Concept and Script by Bruno Enna
Layout by Gianluca Panniello
Pencils by Giada Perissinotto
Inks by Marina Baggio and Roberta Zanotta
Color and Light Direction by Francesco Legramandi
Title Page Art by Giada Perissinotto
with Colors by Marco Colletti

FRAGMENTS OF SUMMER

Concept and Script by Giulia Conti
Layout and Pencils by Paolo Campinoti
Inks by Marina Baggio and Roberta Zanotta
Color and Light Direction by Francesco Legramandi
Title Page Art by Paolo Campinoti

THE OTHER TRUTH

Concept and Script by Bruno Enna
Layout and Pencils by Manuela Razzi
Inks by Marina Baggio and Roberta Zanotta
Color and Light Direction by Francesco Legramandi
Title Page Art by Manuela Razzi with
Colors by Federico Bertolucci

WHISPERS OF HATRED

Concept by Paola Mulazzi
Script by Francesco Artibani and Paola Mulazzi
Layout by Daniela Vetro
Pencils by Giada Perissinotto
Inks by Marina Baggio, Roberta Zanotta, and Santa Zangari
Color and Light Direction by Francesco Legramandi
Title Page Art by Daniela Vetro with
Colors by Andrea Cagol